PROLOGUE – 1954

HER goodbyes and moments of sheer panic had all happened the day before when she sailed on the overnight ferry from Devonport and watched the coast of Tasmania recede in the failing light. Common sense had made her insist that it was totally absurd for anyone, let alone the whole family, to spend two nights on the Bass Strait just to farewell her from Melbourne.

Now she felt very much alone as everyone else waved tearfully to their equally tearful family members on the quay. The paper streamers, symbolic of emotional ties, snapped one by one as the great ship left the harbour. In spite of her enthusiasm to come here in the first place, Sue felt that any ties she had formed in the last eight years could snap as easily as the paper streamers. As the last paper tore she turned her back firmly on a receding Australia. She had, without a doubt, reached the point of no return now and to wallow in nostalgia was mere self-indulgence.

Sue shivered slightly. A cool sea breeze was blowing across the unlimited expanse of ocean which now faced her. Reflecting that the next few weeks would provide plenty of opportunity to look at the sea, she turned and went down below to her cabin.

The other three occupants had taken advantage of her long sojourn on deck to select their bunks and start unpacking. Two of them were chatting like old friends, but the third was sitting on her bunk weeping noisily and twisting a handkerchief round in her fingers in between rather futile attempts to mop up her tears.

'Cheer up – it can't be that bad!' Sue said briskly. Her first reaction had been irritation, but her innate good nature came to the fore.

'I've never been away from home before – I didn't think it would be like this,' the girl sniffed.

Sue looked at the other two. They were all, including herself, around the same age, she guessed, anywhere between eighteen and twenty-two, so it was a pretty safe bet that this was the first major sortie into the Big Wide World for all of them. One of the girls, an impish raven-haired sprite who barely topped five feet, grinned at her and shrugged. 'It's my first time too,' she admitted, 'and I think it's great!'

The fourth girl was tall and blonde with a languid air that Sue guessed was more assumed than natural. She frowned slightly as she contemplated their snivelling companion. 'You don't intend to keep this up for the whole voyage, do you?'

This brought on a renewed burst of noisy weeping. 'Of course she isn't!' Sue snapped. 'Are you?' she demanded. The sternness of her tone had the desired effect – the snivelling stopped abruptly and the girl looked at Sue with surprise and respect, as, she noticed, did the other two.

'You a school teacher or something?' the blonde drawled.

'No, just an older sister,' Sue retorted.

'I'm the baby,' the weeper, with a final sniff and a gulp, volunteered.

'We can see that,' the blonde said, almost precipitating a fresh outburst.

'What about you?' Sue asked, more to stop her saying anything else derogatory than because she really wanted to know.

'Oh, I'm an only child.'

Sue managed not to throw the girl's own remark back in her face. Instead she just looked inquiringly at the one she already thought of as 'the bubbly one'.

Change of Skies

Change of Skies

LOUISE PAKEMAN

ROBERT HALE · LONDON

ISBN 0 7090 7674 6

Robert Hale Limited
Clerkenwell House
Clerkenwell Green
London EC1R 0HT

2 4 6 8 10 9 7 5 3 1

Typeset in 11/15pt Plantin
by Derek Doyle & Associates, Liverpool.
Printed in Great Britain by
St Edmundsbury Press, Bury St Edmunds, Suffolk.
Bound by Woolnough Bookbinding Ltd.

'I come right in the middle of a big family, seven of us all told.' She beamed cheerfully round at the others, her eyes finally resting on Sue. 'What about you?' she asked.

'I have the distinction of being the only girl,' Sue replied. 'I have one full brother, two half-brothers and three stepbrothers.'

There was a short silence while the others digested this information then, rather to Sue's surprise, the weeper, who was now almost dry-eyed, smiled up at her.

'I guess you also have a stepfather?'

Sue smiled back, suddenly deciding she rather liked her after all. 'I do,' she agreed, 'and he is the second one I've had. I'm Sue. I've lived in Tasmania for the last eight years but I was born and brought up in England.' She threw an inquiring glance at the others. 'What about the rest of you?'

'Angela,' the blonde girl drawled. 'Born and bred in Melbourne. Toorak, actually.'

'Gina,' the small dark one told them. 'My parents came out from Italy but I was born in Melbourne. My parents have a milk bar.' The three of them turned to look at the red-eyed girl on the bottom bunk.

'Priscilla,' she muttered, 'but my family call me Pixie.' At the mention of her family she began to look watery again.

'How did you scrape up the fare?' Gina asked, looking round at the others. 'I was lucky – Dad employed me evenings and weekends in the milk bar.'

'Oh, you Italians always have milk bars, or fish and chip shops or something.' Angela sounded supercilious but Gina was quick to retort.

'Yes – and we help one another out too.'

'How did you rake up the money, Angela?' Sue cut in quickly, fearing a fight before they were even one day out to sea.

The blonde girl looked smug. 'My parents gave me the ticket for my twenty-first birthday.'

Gina's lip curled scornfully and Sue was afraid the row had only been postponed when Pixie commented in a tone of real, or simulated, astonishment, 'Good heavens, are you twenty-one?' Without waiting for an answer she continued, 'I did the same as Gina – worked weekends, evenings, anything, shops, baby-sitting, you name it I've done it.'

Sue looked at her with new respect. 'I worked – but mostly at home – helping Mum with my twin brothers or my stepfather on the farm. They didn't pay my fare directly but I guess they helped no end by finding plenty for me to do.' She looked round the little group. Sharing this small space was already forming them into a surrogate family, no doubt with all the benefits and pitfalls of family life.

'Come on, let's go and explore and find out what this ship has to offer,' she suggested.

'You mean . . . boys?' Angela forgot to drawl at the prospect.

'Well, no,' Sue admitted, 'I was really meaning facilities, shops, things to do. We're on it for a month so we might as well make the most of what there is. I intend to enjoy the trip.'

'You do mean boys.' Angela confirmed, this time with a grin. They were all laughing as they left the cabin.

CHAPTER ONE

THEY found boys, Angela saw to that. Sue made friends with a New Zealander who also came from a farming background and as she and Nick compared notes they found there were many similarities between New Zealand and Tasmania. Sue was determined not to arrive in England with the added baggage of a broken heart. She knew how notorious shipboard romances were, so she kept their relationship on a light and friendly level.

Sue sat down hard on the lid of her case as they packed on the last day on board. She looked round at the others and knew she didn't want to lose touch with any of them.

Gina, always the warm impulsive one, voiced her thoughts as if she had read her mind.

'Let's make a pact . . .' she said, looking at each of them in turn as she spoke. 'We'll keep in touch for ever and we'll always be there for one another.'

Three gloomy faces lightened and three heads nodded eagerly.

'Super!' said Angela.

'Let's shake on it.' Sue held out her hands to the others and automatically they clasped hands in a tight circle.

'We'd better exchange addresses.' The ever-practical Pixie searched for biro and paper as they moved apart. 'I suppose we all know where we are going?' They had been too busy enjoying themselves since they sailed from Australia, wrapped in the illusion that this holiday lifestyle would last for ever, to talk about their individual plans when they reached England.

'I have a place booked at a Catholic girls' hostel – arranged by our parish priest – at Mum's prodding.' Gina's expression was so glum that the others laughed. Even Pixie managed a wan wavering of her lips as she admitted her mother had done much the same for her, the only difference being that she was to go to a Church of England Hostel.

'And she managed to organize a job for me too. I start on Monday.' She pulled a wry face, her mouth turned down at the corners.

'I have to go to my grandmother . . .' Angela admitted. 'For some absurd reason Mum doesn't think I am safe on my own.' She tossed her hair back and pouted. Sue was inclined to agree with her mother. The close proximity of life aboard ship meant that they knew one another pretty well and Sue knew that Angela's sophistication was only a thin veneer.

'What about you, Sue? Where are you going?'

'Oh, I have an old school friend in London. I told my mother I was staying with her.'

'And are you?' Pixie asked sharply.

Sue smiled. Once she had 'dried out', Pixie had surprised them all with her perspicacity and practicality. 'My mother thinks I am – that's what matters.'

'I would say it matters much more to you where you stay.' Pixie peered at her myopically. She only wore her glasses when absolutely essential since Angela had trotted out the old chestnut that men never made passes at girls who wore glasses. 'Does your friend know you are staying with her?' The tone of her voice made it clear she doubted whether the friend was a reality.

Sue felt herself colour slightly as she admitted, with a shrug, 'I don't know. Don't worry, I'll find somewhere.'

'Come with me – for one night at least,' Pixie begged. 'It would be great to have you along . . .' She trailed off, trying to sound casual even as her eyes pleaded with Sue to agree.

'OK, just for one night – if I can get in,' Sue said, and wondered which of them was the most relieved. She had been a little disappointed at the time at her mother's easy acceptance of her lie that she was staying with her friend from her English boarding school days. Though she would never admit it, she was envious of the other three girls whose mothers had obviously worried about what would happen to them when they landed in England. Her mother's life was so full and busy these days that Sue sometimes felt extraneous to it.

There was no problem about a place at the hostel when she and Pixie finally arrived after an emotional farewell with the other two and promises to meet up again. As she followed the warden and Pixie up the stairs, their footsteps echoing on the stone steps bare of carpet, Sue felt just as she had on her first day at boarding school, and vowed that her stay in this dreary place would be short-lived.

As she and Pixie sat down opposite each other on the institutional iron bedsteads in the small room they had been allocated, she expressed her feelings aloud.

Her companion shrugged in the helpless 'but what can I do' accepting manner that Sue sometimes found so irritating, she could see that the tears which always seemed so near the surface were threatening to spill from her eyes.

'Well!' Sue exclaimed, rather heartily and a good deal more optimistically than she felt. 'This will do for tonight, a week, two at the outside, but first thing tomorrow I am going out to look for something else. How about you?'

'Oh, I don't know. I don't think Mum . . .' She trailed off, her bottom lip trembling ominously.

'What made you leave home?' Sue asked impulsively. Pixie Shelton seemed such a timid traveller she must have had a powerful incentive to motivate her to leave the shelter of her home and family and travel to the other side of the world.

'I was so sick of being treated like a helpless baby,' Pixie retorted with a flash of spirit. 'I began to think I would never be allowed to make a decision for myself – so I made one. I decided to come to England and work here for at least a year.'

'Phew – some decision!' Sue began to revise her opinion of Pixie. It seemed there might be a core of steel beneath the quiet exterior. 'How did you stick to it?'

'With great difficulty,' Pixie admitted wryly, 'but I knew that if I didn't stick to my guns I was lost for ever – I would spend the whole of my life doing what my family felt was best for me.'

Sue nodded. 'All the same, it must have been difficult?'

'What made it hard was knowing that they really all loved me, but I was beginning to feel as if I was suffocating in a sea of marshmallow!'

Sue laughed at the picture this conjured up. All the same she felt a twinge of envy. 'I felt just the opposite,' she admitted. 'Not unloved exactly but just rather extraneous. When Mum married again and we all went out to Tasmania I was really excited, then she got pregnant – and had twins – and she was always so busy. She painted, bred horses, and Tom, my stepfather, always seemed to want her to do something on the farm.'

'Your mother painted?'

'Yeah, she used to, but that's another thing she doesn't seem to have time for these days.'

'Well, twins must be a lot of work, but I bet you were a help?'

'You can say that again!' Sue spoke with such feeling that Pixie thought they may have been one of the incentives for her to leave home. 'When I brought up the idea of coming back to England for a year or so Mum agreed quicker than I thought – on condition I enrolled in art school. She never had any formal art training and always wanted me to.'

'So that's what you're going to do?'

'Mmm,' Sue murmured, as the thought crossed her mind that she was not so unlike Pixie. Wasn't she allowing her family to arrange her life for her too?

Repressing the unwelcome thought, she leaned across the narrow gap between the two beds and touched Pixie on the knee. 'We could find a flat somewhere, just a tiny one, and share it. Think of it – no rules and regulations, no curfew, only ourselves to please. Come on, Pixie, be a devil for once. We'll start looking tomorrow – it's a Saturday, a good day for flat-hunting.'

Pixie looked up and her eyes studied Sue's face as if seeking reassurance, then suddenly she smiled and sat up a tad straighter and Sue caught a glimpse of the inner strength that had enabled her to leave her home and family.

'Yes – let's! I don't start work till Monday, so we can spend the whole weekend searching if we have to.'

They didn't need the whole weekend, or even a whole day. By lunchtime they had located a flat, or rather two rooms, one with a gas ring, and use of the bathroom at the top of an old Victorian house not far from Baker Street. They couldn't move in for another week so Sue decided to spend a couple of days visiting one of the few contacts she had in England.

'You don't mind, do you,' she asked Pixie, 'if I go off for a couple of days and look up my old nanny?'

'I thought you had no relatives in England?'

'I haven't – only some step-relations I'm not terribly enthused about. My nanny is the person who looked after me when I was a baby, not my grandmother.'

'You mean she was *paid* to look after you?' Such things were quite out of the realm of Pixie's experience. 'Did you . . . like her?' she asked curiously.

'I loved her,' Sue answered. 'She was with us years. She brought up my younger brother Michael as well as me and when she finally retired and went to live in Wales we used to go for a holiday there every year. I guess,' she added thoughtfully, 'she was almost more than a grandmother to me.' She sat quiet for a few moments, remembering. Nanny had been the one constant in her life throughout her childhood until she left England for Australia. 'I'll send her a postcard now and tell her I'll be there the day after tomorrow.'

As the local train chugged through the splendid scenery of North Wales to her final destination, Portmadoc, Sue thought that if anyone had told her when she first boarded the ship in Melbourne that she would choose to share a flat with Pixie she would have laughed. Gina, or even Angela maybe, but not Pixie, who she had first seen almost drowning in her own tears.

She was looking forward to visiting Nanny. She had been there for her ever since she could remember, not only in the bright days of her early childhood but through the less happy ones of her father's death and the unsettling wartime years. After she retired, summer holidays spent here with her on the Welsh coast had offered welcome relief from life at home with her first stepfather.

Sue felt the same thrill she had known as a child when she caught her first glimpse of the familiar coastline. Just as she had always done as a child, she took a deep breath and revelled in the smell of seaweed. The 'almost mist' folded round her like an embrace as she stepped down from the bus and began the short walk through the village.

It was just the same as she remembered, even down to the man on the far side of the road who seemed to have a vaguely familiar air. She would have been surprised to learn that he was wondering where he had seen her as he turned and strode off in the opposite direction.

If nothing else in the little village of Borth-y-Gest had changed, Nanny certainly had. She was no longer an elderly lady but an old woman. Sue hugged her tight to hide the distress and emotion she felt. Somehow she had always thought of her as immutable in an ever-changing world, but in spite of that she felt as secure in the older woman's embrace as she had as a small child.

'My, you're a young lady now!' Nanny stood back to look at her. 'I reckon life "down under" suits you.'

Nanny had changed but the sister she had lived with since her retirement was almost unrecognizable. In place of the round, jovial person she remembered Sue found a frail, bent old woman, barely able to move without her zimmer frame. Her voice was tremulous and petulant when she asked who Sue was and she peered at her through thick lenses with no sign of recognition. In response to Nanny's, 'Look who has come specially to see us, all the way from Australia!'

'I'm Sue – don't you remember me?' The old woman merely grunted before turning her attention to the afternoon tea. The scones were still as light as ever, the jam still homemade and the fruit cake rich and moist. Big afternoon teas were no longer what she and her stomach expected after eight years in Australia, but, being young and healthy, she managed to do justice to it and was rewarded by Nanny's beam of satisfaction.

'So, young Michael is going to be a veterinary surgeon? Now you're the one I would have expected to do that – always mad about animals you were, even that old rocking horse. What did you call him?'

'Prince,' Sue automatically supplied with a smile. Yes, she had loved that old wooden horse and had taken some great rides on him, whispering her secrets into his battered ears. 'Loving animals isn't enough, Nanny. You have to have a lot of brains and work hard too.'

'And has Michael, and does he?' Remembering the mischievous, carefree boy she had known, Nanny sounded doubtful.

'Oh, yes, he's very focused when he wants something, and he is quite set on a career as a vet.'

'And your mother? Tell me about her. Is she happy – really happy?' she asked intently, her eyes on Sue's face. She had first met Sue's mother when she arrived to take care of her new baby – now the lovely twenty-two-year-old sitting opposite her.

Nanny's relationship with the baby's mother had slowly evolved from that of employer and employee to a bond with ties as

15

close as any blood relationship. She sat back now, her eyes reflecting the memories that crowded her mind. 'You were just a couple of weeks old when I came, and I was still there caring for you when Michael was born.' She shook her head, tutting sadly. 'Then your father died and the war came and your mother ran the farm and took in evacuees. There was plenty for me to do so I just stayed.'

It must be hard, Sue thought, after a lifetime of looking after other people's children to find you were no longer needed.

'When your mother married again and you and Michael went to boarding school I came and lived here.' Nanny sighed and glanced across at her sister, who was nodding in her chair. 'But I still saw plenty of you. Do you remember the holidays you spent here, sometimes with your mother, sometimes on your own?'

'Michael and I just loved coming. We all did. Mum was ... different here.' She paused, remembering the heavy, repressive atmosphere that her first stepfather created.

Nanny shook her head. 'She made a big mistake in that marriage, but I think she wanted a father for you and Michael.'

'Mmmm,' Sue murmured, feeling a stab of guilt. It had never occurred to her before that she and Michael could possibly have had anything to do with her mother's second marriage. 'Such a pity she and your present stepfather lost touch in the war – she should have married him years ago,' the old woman reminisced, 'but if she is happy now it worked out in the end. A pity she couldn't have married that nice painter she got to know here. But then she was married to the doctor when she met him.'

'David Jones was married too,' Sue reminded her, adding thoughtfully, 'It was him who started her painting seriously. I don't suppose you ever hear anything of him these days? Mum asked me to give him her regards if I happened across him.'

'Oh yes, I see him now and then. He usually pops in and has a cuppa when he comes to his cottage. In fact he was here only yesterday.'

'You mean he's here in Borth-y-Gest now?' Sue asked in astonishment.

'No, dear, I don't think so.' Nanny shook her head. 'I think he was on his way back when he called.'

'Back to Wolverhampton? That was where he taught, wasn't it?'

'Oh, no, dear, he doesn't teach anymore. After his wife died he came and lived here in his old cottage for a year or so, painting and doing up the cottage. Now he lets it out to summer visitors—'

'Then surely he will be here, if he lives here for the winter?'

'You interrupted me.' Nanny spoke in the firm reproving voice Sue remembered from her childhood, and just as then, when she had been rude or misbehaved, she apologized. Nanny nodded in acknowledgment before continuing. 'As I was about to tell you, he has let it this year for the winter.'

'Do you know where he is?'

'He told me he was going to France to paint. He didn't say whereabouts but I think he intends to be away quite a while.'

'Oh well, I guess Mum's regards will just have to wait.'

'You could go to his cottage. Maybe the tenants will have an address for him,' Nanny suggested helpfully. 'If they don't, maybe Betty Pritchard at The Bobbing Boats will. She still sells some of his paintings, though I gather from what she says he is quite well known now.'

'I'll go in the morning,' Sue promised herself out loud. Never one to delay when any course of action had been decided upon, she would have gone straight away but at that moment a squally shower dimmed the light in the room and a few sharp bursts of rain hit the window. Just as well – after all, it was Nanny she had come to see, and she could hardly run out on her so soon.

Sue was quite glad when Nanny told her she looked tired and an early night would do no harm. Sentimental journeys into the past could be quite exhausting, she thought, after she had wandered back through the years with Nanny's photograph albums. In turn she had shown photos of her mother, the twins and the Tasmanian farm.

'Is she happy – really happy?' Nanny asked yet again.

'Oh, yes, I think so. Yes, I believe she is.' Sue had never stopped till now to wonder whether or not her mother was happy. 'She is very busy.'

'When I heard she had twins I just wished I could be there to help her.' Nanny looked wistfully somewhere into the middle distance. 'But I expect you were a big help. How old were you when they were born?'

'Sixteen.' Sue remembered those hectic days with mixed feelings. It was true she had been a big help to her mother, but not always a willing one. The arrival of two babies in the household had been a major eruption, and she too had often wished Nanny was there to help. 'They are six years old now, in their first year at school.'

'Your mother must miss them, especially as you and Michael have left home.'

It hadn't really occurred to Sue that her mother might miss any of them; she was always so busy with the farm and her horses. 'One of my stepbrothers is still at home,' she told Nanny, 'and Mum and Tom are always so busy with the farm and the Arab horse stud they started a few years back I don't think she has time to miss anyone.'

When they parted for bed, Nanny kissed her goodnight as tenderly as if she were indeed her grandmother. Sue hugged her back warmly, a sudden lump in her throat as she remembered the many times Nanny had been there for her when her mother had been too busy or too preoccupied with something or someone else to really care.

Up in her bedroom she leaned on the windowsill and looked out at the night sky, now clear and bright with stars. In the distance she could hear the lap of the waves, and the smell of salt and sea took her back in time to the happy holidays spent here and the winter they had spent in David's cottage when her mother was widowed for the second time. Yes, she should try and contact him.

With an old raincoat of Nanny's slung over her arm as insurance against the fickle Welsh weather, Sue set off next morning for David's cottage. Titivated up and painted, it was not quite as she remembered it, but was familiar enough to bring back nostalgic memories. The wooden bench was still there where she had sat with her mother and David looking out to sea and drinking lemonade while they drank red wine. She knocked on the door and waited.

After a few minutes, a youngish woman answered the door. She shook her head when Sue asked if she had an address for David. 'I'm sorry – no. You see, we deal through the agent.'

'But I thought he was here yesterday?'

'Oh, he was, but we still don't have an address. Like I said, we deal with the agent.'

'Do you have the agent's name and address?' she asked quickly before the woman retreated and closed the door in her face.

As she walked back down the hill she glanced at the slip of paper in her hand, and saw it was a Wolverhampton address. She shoved it in her pocket and headed for The Bobbing Boats.

The café was almost unchanged: both it and the smiling proprietress could have been caught in a time warp. Surprised and delighted to find it just as she remembered it, Sue forgot that she herself had changed. Betty Pritchard did not recognize her immediately, a puzzled frown almost chasing the smile from her round face when Sue ordered coffee. Sue looked round: paintings of local scenes still covered the walls, the work of artists who lived in the area. She walked across to look more closely at a picture of the cottage she had just left and knew why it had looked different. The rambling rose she remembered had been tamed and subdued into some sort of order, but here in the painting it was still a glorious riot. She recognized the three figures sitting on the bench outside as her younger brother Michael, her mother and herself.

Betty Pritchard's sudden joyful exclamation made Sue turn, and her homely face was now wreathed in smiles. 'Sue! It is you, isn't it, come back, have you? You came most summers and then you and your mother and brother, Michael, isn't it, spent a whole winter in Davey's cottage—'

'That's right . . .' Sue interrupted the flow, but Betty didn't seem to hear.

'It's a long time since I've seen you, and my word, you've grown up since you went off somewhere abroad – where was it now? Davey did tell me but I've forgotten. Has your mother come back with you?'

Sue shook her head. 'No, just me, and it was Tasmania we went to.'

'Tasmania, yes. Would that be part of Africa now?'

'Australia. It's that little island, which really isn't so little when you live there, about the size of Scotland so it is bigger than Wales . . .'

'Now don't you go comparing us with that other place!'

Sue laughed. 'Well, as I said it's the island at the bottom of Australia, you may not have noticed it, it sometimes gets left off the map, but that is where we all went. Mum married again,' she added, turning back to the painting that had captured her attention. Betty's eyes followed hers, and after studying the picture for a few moments she turned back to Sue.

'That would be you, with your mother and brother?'

Sue nodded. 'Yes – it's the first time I've actually seen it finished. He had only done a few preliminary sketches last time I saw it.' The painting took Sue back, she was once more the child teetering on the brink of womanhood sitting there in the sun beside her mother, who was between her and her brother Michael. She was startled to see how very beautiful her mother had been then, or was it, she wondered, David's portrayal of her? Impulsively she turned back to Betty. 'How much is it?' she asked, knowing even as she spoke that whatever the price she had to have it.

Betty Pritchard unhooked it from the wall and turned it round. 'Twenty-five pounds.'

Twenty-five pounds – a fortune! She would have to live on bread and water for a month if she bought it. 'I'll take it,' she said firmly.

Sue's thoughts and feelings were very mixed as her train finally chugged into Paddington Station the next day. It was fortunate she had a return ticket as by the time she had raked up every last bit of change she could find she had still been short of seven pounds to pay for David's picture. For the sake of old times, though, Betty was prepared to trust her and handed it over, reverently and care- fully wrapped, on Sue's promise to send the balance as soon as she got back to London. She was elated to have the painting but worried about how she was going to manage for she would really have to scrape the kitty clean to pay for it. It had been sad in a way too catching up with Nanny.

'I felt so sorry for her,' she told Pixie that evening. 'Her sister seems quite ga-ga, not with it at all. She has wandered off a few times, I gathered.'

'Yeah, I guess it must be awful being old,' Pixie said with the calm detachment of one who is quite sure such a fate will never overtake them, 'but I bet your nanny was thrilled to see you.'

'Oh, she was, but I didn't get to see David – I just missed him.'

'David? David who?' You never said anything about a boyfriend down there in Wales.' Pixie sounded indignant.

'That's because he isn't a boyfriend. He is, or was, a friend of my mother,' Sue told her. 'I promised her I would look him up and give him her regards.'

'You mean he was an old flame of your mother's,' Pixie persisted. She was an incurable romantic and their room was already full of the paperback novels she loved.

'Yes – I mean no,' Sue floundered. She didn't like the idea of Pixie or anyone else seeing David in that light. 'Well . . .' How could she explain their relationship? 'I think he was in love with

my mother, in fact I'm sure he was. I thought for a time she might be with him, but nothing came of it, then Tom reappeared in her life. They were married and we were all living in Tasmania before you could say "knife". Anyway,' she finished with a philosophical shrug, 'it was all for the best. David was married. He was nice, though, I liked him.' She paused, remembering, 'I bought one of his paintings while I was there . . .' She began to tear off the wrappings to show Pixie. 'Look!'

'I like it,' Pixie said approvingly, bending closer to look at the figures. 'Who are the people, do you know?'

'I guess so. It's my mother, my brother and me.'

Pixie subjected the painting to a further scrutiny, 'Your mother is beautiful – no wonder he was in love with her. Does she still look as good?'

Sue resisted a sudden urge to snatch the painting back, remembering she had been more than half in love with David herself. Fourteen years old, no longer a child, not yet a woman, she had often resented being treated as a contemporary of her younger brother who at only ten was very definitely still a child. She remembered her mixed feelings towards her mother: on the one hand she couldn't understand why on earth she didn't just fly in the face of all convention and fall wildly in love with David, yet she would have been furious if she had. The return of Tom – who her mother had once loved – into their lives and his subsequent wooing and winning of her which resulted in them all going to Australia had banished her teenage yearnings for David to their rightful limbo. There they had been buried until seeing this painting had brought it all back.

'Does she?' Pixie's impatient voice brought her back to the present.

'Does she what?'

'I was asking you if your mother still looks as good,' Pixie repeated patiently, 'but you were miles away in some dream world of your own.'

'I don't think she has really changed much. Older, I suppose, a bit faded from being out in the sun all day, but yes, I suppose she is much the same.' She looked critically at the painting. 'But I think David made her more beautiful than she was.'

'Well, he would, wouldn't he, he was in love with her,' Pixie pointed out.

Sue didn't answer; instead she returned the painting carefully to its wrappings. 'I'll try and find somewhere to hang it when we move to our flat,' she told Pixie, regretting not the painting itself but that she had put herself in hock to buy it.

CHAPTER TWO

'GUESS what? I've found a job!' Pixie shrugged out of her coat and threw it over one of the two straight-back chairs in the dismal hostel room.

'Great!' was Sue's automatic response, then, 'What do you mean? I thought you had a job, teed up for you by your mother?'

'I did – I chucked it in.'

'Chucked it in?'

'I stuck it for a whole day. It was such a dead-end job. I didn't swot away at shorthand and typing to come over here and take a job where the most responsible thing I would be asked to do was make tea.'

People were full of surprises, Sue reflected. It was hard to believe this was the same Pixie as the weepy girl she had met that first day on board the ship. 'You said you had found another job?'

'Well, I didn't think you would be too keen on sharing a flat with me if I was out of work.'

That hadn't been in Sue's mind at all; she had just been surprised that Pixie could hand in one job and get another in such a short space of time. 'Don't be silly – tell me about your new job.'

'Working for an agency supplying temporary shorthand typists. Better than being stuck in one place – this way I will get much more experience and will soon upgrade to being a secretary.'

'There's a lot more to you than meets the eye, little Pixie.'

Beneath the banter, Sue was awestruck, but then once she dried up on the boat Pixie had shown a surprising tenacity of will and zest for life that on first sight no one would suspect. She was looking prettier than Sue had ever seen her, eyes shining and cheeks slightly flushed. If she would only change her hairstyle, get rid of those steel-framed granny specs, brighten up her clothes and wear a bit of make-up, she would be really attractive, thought Sue.

'Pixie, let's get our hair done.'

'Done? What do you mean?'

'Styled,' Sue said, and ran her fingers through her own hair, which was thick, naturally curly and a colour best described as dark blonde. Sue considered it merely mouse. The curls were an inheritance from her father, the colour from her mother, although hers was naturally lighter and she wore it in a sleek bob. 'I feel a bit like the wild man from Borneo or something.' She looked across the room critically at Pixie. 'We both need a really good stylist.'

Pixie was not working that Saturday so they booked appointments at a smart salon for early in the morning, promising to get moved into their new flat immediately afterwards.

They had collapsed into the two over-stuffed and under-covered armchairs while they waited for the kettle to boil for much needed cups of tea after the settling-in process when Angela and Gina turned up.

Angela herself was wearing her pseudo-sophisticated mien and what looked like a new outfit. She looked round the tiny flatlet with a critical eye. 'A bit cramped . . .' she commented, 'but I suppose it's OK for one. Where are you living, Sue?'

'What do you mean? Here, of course. We decided it would be more sensible to share a flat then live at the hostel.'

'Flat?' Angela's voice rose with her eyebrows. 'I'd call this a bedsitter.'

'I think it's lovely. Much nicer than my hostel.' Gina sounded both soothing and envious.

Sue bit back an angry retort; it was always so easy to quarrel with

Angela. She had often wondered on the ship if she were deliberately provoking or just tactless.

'How did you find us?' she asked.

'I went to the hostel. Pixie had left a forwarding address so here
we are. The boys should be here soon – I told them to come.'

'Boys? What boys?' Sue asked suspiciously, but she found herself
talking to Angela's rump as she leaned out of the window, letting in
a blast of cold damp London air. She was waving to someone down
below. 'Come on up!' she called cheerfully. Behind her Sue
wondered whose flat this was anyway.

Peering over Angela's shoulder before she pulled down the
sash window, Sue saw that one of the boys was Nicholas Thorne,
the young New Zealander from the ship. Because she had not
encouraged him and had firmly kept their relationship on a
friendship level, Sue had not really expected to see him again,
even when she had given him the address of the hostel. Now as
he waved up at her before heading for the entrance, she felt a
flutter of pleasure, noting that he was even more attractive than
she remembered.

She recognized two of the other young men as fellow travellers.
Paul Smith had fallen in a big way for Angela, but his devotion had
been dismissed airily by its object. 'Doesn't mean a thing . . .' she
had insisted. 'Just one of those shipboard romances – you know
what they are like.' None of them, including Angela, did. She also
recognized Tony Something-or-other. He had an Italian-sounding
name, she remembered and his large brown eyes were more often
than not on Gina. The fourth member of the party was a stranger
to everyone, it seemed, but Angela.

'This is Edgar,' she told them all now with a vague wave of her
hand. 'He lives next door to my grandparents. I brought him along
to make up the numbers.'

'Hello, Edgar,' Sue said, hoping to put this rather gauche boy at
his ease. The only one who didn't know everybody, he was hanging
back, then he looked across the room and saw Pixie, and smiled,

watching her return his smile. What a difference a good haircut made, thought Sue.

By accident or design Angela had been very successful in her pairing up. They crammed cheerfully into the small room, drank coffee and caught up on what had happened since they reached London. All of them had found accommodation and most work, with the exception of Angela who didn't seem to want it. 'My grandmother wants me to enjoy myself, look around, be a tourist,' she told them.

Gina expressed envy but no surprise that Pixie had left the Hostel. 'I wish I could find somewhere like this,' she told them, letting her eyes rove round the tiny flat. 'But I'd better stay where I am for the time being. Mother would be upset, she went to a lot of trouble getting me somewhere to stay. Father O'Connor, our parish priest, gave me an introduction for a job too. I start Monday.'

'What's the job?' Sue asked. Everyone but her, it seemed, had everything organized for them. She hadn't even done anything yet about getting into an art school. Nor was she sure that was what she really wanted. It had seemed a good enough reason to come to London when she was in Tasmania, but she had forgotten the British school year began in September, so it wasn't even the right time.

'In a Catholic bookshop.' Puzzled for a moment, Sue came out of her brown study to realize that Gina was answering her question.

'Sounds all right. I wouldn't mind working in a bookshop,' she said for Gina's benefit, then realized she meant it.

Trying to find a course that appealed to her and a place on it over the next week was deflating. She should have done this before she left home, she decided, and the thought brought with it a totally unexpected wave of longing for home, the family, the animals, the wide horizons and the brilliant sunshine. That night she wrote a long letter home to tell her mother about the flat and the course she had finally enrolled on.

27

Two weeks later, searching in her bag for something else Sue came across a scrap of folded paper. She stared blankly for a moment at the address of a real estate agent in Wolverhampton. Of course – the agent who was in charge of David's cottage and who might be able to help her locate him. She stuffed it back where she had found it and promptly forgot all about it for another couple of weeks.

Life in London as a not very affluent student in a cold dank English winter was a far cry from how she had imagined it back in Australia or her memories of schoolgirl holidays. She had a small income from a legacy left by her father which she accessed when she turned twenty-one but it didn't allow for any luxuries.

The painting she had bought on her visit to Nanny hung now on the wall, a constant reminder of the money she had spent so recklessly. As a flashback to what seemed like another life and because the short time she had spent in the art class had convinced her that her talent was very minimal, it depressed her.

The best part of life here were the friends made on the boat; without them she would have been very lonely. Tonight she and Nick had been to the cinema, and as it stretched their slender budget they went back to the flat for coffee.

Sue turned from the corner that held an electric kettle and a gas ring, euphemistically called 'the kitchen', with two mugs of steaming coffee in her hands. Nick was staring at David's painting.

'Say – is this you?' He turned to her with a grin, adding before she could answer, 'You haven't changed much.'

'You'd have to eat your words if I told you it wasn't me,' Sue retorted.

'But I can see it is. It's a nice picture.' Sue winced at this description of the painting. 'I don't know much about art but I do know . . .'

'What I like,' Sue supplied for him. It was a phrase she had heard so often over the years, mostly from people looking at her mother's paintings. It was a pity, she thought, that her mother had given it up. The paintings she did of dogs and horses from photographs were always good likenesses, managing to catch the essential spark that made that particular animal just what it was. They had pleased the owners and kept the wolf from the door when money was tight. 'Yes . . .' she conceded, passing Nick his coffee. 'It is good. It was painted by a friend of my mother's when we were away on holiday.'

'Is it in Tasmania?'

'No, he painted it when we were on holiday in North Wales. That's his cottage.'

She flopped down in one of the battered armchairs.

'I bought it when I went there a few weeks ago to see Nanny . . . no, not my grandmother . . .' She could see that Nick, product of the new world, was about to make the same mistake as Pixie. 'My nanny – she brought me up . . .'

But Nick wasn't listening. 'Did you stay with him?' he asked sharply, a scowl disturbing the smooth surface of his skin.

'Of course not! I told you I was staying with Nanny. I didn't even see him – I bought this in a café where he sells some of his pictures.' Still irritated by what she felt was Nick's unreasonable possessiveness, some demon prompted her to add, 'But I do have to look him up . . .' She allowed a reasonable pause before tagging on, 'My mother specially asked me to.' She reached over for her bag where she had flung it down when they came in a short while ago. 'I've got an address here to chase up.' Finding the crumpled scrap of paper, she smoothed it out and handed it to Nick.

'But this is a real estate agent,' he pointed out. 'I thought you said he was a painter?'

'He is a painter. That's the address of the agent handling the letting of his cottage. I went to see his tenants but they told me they hadn't a clue where he was as they only dealt with the agent.'

'Well, surely you aren't thinking of traipsing on a wild goose chase up to Wolverhampton to find out, are you?'

'Of course not, Nick. I shall write to them.' Sue was irritated by the tone of his voice. 'Why so shirty?' she asked.

29

Nick shrugged. 'I suppose,' he admitted 'I just don't like the idea of you chasing after another man.'

'He is a friend of my mother, her generation, I've already told you that, and anyway, you don't own me, Nick.' She carefully refolded the scrap of paper and returned it to her purse. It was another week before she thought of it again, and another before she did anything about it.

When she finally got a reply she felt a sharp stab of disappointment. They only had a poste restante address in Paris, they told her, no actual address where he could be found. They understood he planned to be away six months at the very minimum, possibly a year.

Well, she supposed, if she wrote to him at the address she had been given he would get it eventually – he must return to Paris at some time to collect his mail. And with that thought, she put him firmly out of her mind.

CHAPTER THREE

STEVIE flopped down at the kitchen table. The large airy room, redolent with comforting cooking smells, was the living heart of the homestead. She pushed back her hair, which fell damply on her forehead; it was unusually humid for Tasmania. She had been baking and the kitchen felt stifling. Opening the window would, she knew, do little to improve things. She could feel her shirt sticking to her back and perspiration trickling between her breasts. Pushing herself up from the table with her hands she crossed to the workbench and flicked on the radio to fill the silence, then poured herself a glass of chilled water.

Michael leaving home to go to college was expected, but she had never really believed that Sue would want to return to England, even when she had talked about it. Had she known how much she would miss her daughter she would have opposed it more. She sighed. What difference would that have made anyway?

When the twins first started school she had missed them but looked forward to extra hours in her busy days. Hours which, deprived of Sue's help, never seemed to materialize. But I miss her company too, not just her help, she told herself, and stifled the thought that maybe she had relied just a little too much on that help.

Sue had first mentioned England in one of their more difficult moments. Stevie tried to gloss over these, telling herself that mother-daughter relationships were notoriously difficult to get right. 'Don't you think it would be a good idea to put them to bed yourself for once?' Sue had snarled when Stevie said she thought the two little boys should be in bed.

'But you always do it while I cook.' Stevie had tried to sound reasonable rather than aggrieved.

'Well, I'm going to England, so you'll have to do it then,' Sue threw at her mother as she shooed her small half-brothers, none too gently, from the room.

Stevie, unwisely she now realized, had tried to ignore this outburst in the hope that that was all it was but Sue had frequently returned to the subject. She intended to study art in London, she told her mother, leaving Stevie wondering if that was what her daughter really wanted to do or whether she was suggesting it because she knew her mother would be sympathetic. Stevie had managed to earn enough to keep the wolf from the door back in England between her second and third marriages by painting animal portraits but had always regretted her own lack of formal training.

The disembodied voice from the radio informing her that it was eleven o'clock reminded Stevie that the mail should be there. She was tempted to leave it till the afternoon when the boys came home from school, but hoping there would be a letter from England she set off down the tree-lined drive to pick up the mail bag from the gate.

The gut feeling that had propelled her from the house was correct. When she unfastened the strap at the neck of the heavy canvas bag and tipped the contents on to the table there among the assorted business letters and bills was a pale blue aerogramme addressed in Sue's distinctive bold, round hand. Stevie flicked on the electric jug – a letter from Sue merited more than a glass of water – and while she waited for it to heat she carefully slit open the aerogramme with a knife to avoid tearing it and perhaps losing some of the message. Finally, coffee in hand, she settled at the table once more to read it.

Sue had crammed several weeks' news into the single sheet, her writing getting smaller and harder to read as she realized she was in danger of running out of space. She wrote at some length about her trip to Wales and her visit with Nanny, and mentioned that she had bought David's painting of them at his cottage. She told her about the tiny flat she was sharing with a friend from the boat, made a casual reference to a boy, and then, squashed in the very bottom corner, said she had given up her course at the art school.

Stevie had never been convinced that studying art was a cogent reason for Sue to leave Tasmania so she was not surprised. She reread the letter, starting at the point where Sue told her about David's painting. She remembered sitting for it; in fact she remembered everything about the cottage in the Welsh mountains which had given her sanctuary that bleak time when she was widowed for the second time.

She had so much more to remember David Jones for with gratitude than the loan of his cottage. His encouragement of her small talent gave her a degree of independence. She more than half suspected he had been in love with her, but he was trapped in a disastrous marriage, and life had buffeted her around so that she had nothing to offer. Briefly she allowed herself to ponder on the outcome if she had responded to his feelings for her.

She drained her now tepid coffee. Dwelling on the might-have-been was a waste of time. Putting Sue's letter aside to reread later, she gave her attention to the rest of the morning's mail.

Stevie had the place to herself today for her husband Tom and her stepson Andrew were away, hoping to purchase a young bull for their own herd of Black Angus cattle. They had been waiting for the annual sale held on this particular stud which was renowned for the quality of its animals. Stevie had chosen to stay home: it seemed an easier option than either taking the twins along with her or making arrangements for a neighbour to collect them from school. A day at a cattle sale was not her idea of a pleasant outing.

There was no shortage of chores – a pile of ironing, a ring round the bath to get rid of – but the tins were full of scones and cookies. She went to the window and tentatively opened it, relieved to find that the air seemed to have lost some of its humidity. The late summer sun was bright and the sky had regained the cerulean blue that she had come to associate with Tasmania. Mount Roland looked close enough to touch and out there in the big yard her favourite mare was drowsily switching away flies as she dreamed equine dreams.

Stevie had a couple of precious hours with no one to answer to but herself: why waste them? She pulled on her scuffed riding boots, grabbed her hat and headed for the horse yards.

By the time she had cantered the length of the longest paddock the cobwebs had gone. Stevie let the reins hang slack on the mare's neck and thought of David Jones and her first meeting with him on the North Wales coast. The idyllic little village was her holiday sanctuary, but he had been born and raised there and came back each summer for a much needed respite. Her first painting was of his cottage. It hung now on Sue's bedroom wall.

Her memories of David were all good and looking back she wondered why she hadn't fallen in love with him. Had some part of her known then that Tom would come back into her life?

Back in the house she flopped in the comfortable old chair in the kitchen, free of cats for once – hopefully they were doing their duty and hunting mice in the feed store. On winter days when the rain came down in heavy vertical streams, folding the house in a misty curtain that blotted out everything, the three of them would be intertwined, forming a tabby striped cushion of fur that covered the entire seat. She leaned back and took a deep draft of her home-made ginger beer and thought about tonight's meal.

Maybe they would get something on the way back. The freezer was well stocked if not.

Thinking of food reminded her that she had not had lunch, so she refilled her glass with ginger beer, admiring the way it sparkled in the glass and relishing the tingle on the tongue, and made herself a cheese and tomato sandwich. She could be a vegetarian, she thought: no greasy washing up, no fatty cooking smells to bring the blowflies in hordes down the chimney. At least in winter when a log fire was burning in the hearth one was spared that invasion, even if the fire itself was almost obscured by wet garments steaming dry in front of it.

Her life today was very different to the days of her first marriage in pre-war England when other people had taken care of all the everyday chores. She had actually complained of having nothing to do. Martin had bought horses and through them Tom, her child-hood sweetheart, had come back into her life and so started in motion the long chain of events that had brought her here, to a Tasmanian farm kitchen and no time to even think of the word boredom.

She picked up Sue's letter again and read it through carefully, trying to find any hidden messages. Was it significant that Nick, the boy from New Zealand she had met on the ship, had asked her to go with him to meet his English relatives?

Glass in hand, she wandered into Sue's room where some of her paintings hung. David's cottage, her first real attempt, and next to it the most recent one of Sue's beloved dog, run over early one morning by the cream lorry, leaving her totally bereft. On the opposite wall was the one she had done of Fairy, her much loved horse from long ago in England.

Sue had shared David's conviction that she had sufficient talent to sell her work. She moved closer and studied the one of the cottage. It looked very amateurish to her now, not in the same class as the animal portraits, but she found her throat tightening and tears pricking her eyes as she stared at it.

'I loved that cottage.' With surprise she heard her own voice expressing the thought aloud.

She moved over to the painting of the old grey mare. She had loved her, more than any horse before or since. 'You gave me a kick-start as an animal portraitist,' she told the horse in the picture.

Gazing into the expressive eyes, she felt for a moment that the animal was alive and willing her to pick up her brushes and start again.

'Why not?' she asked herself out loud. 'With the boys at school I have time.' She opened the cupboard door and soon ran her paints to earth.

No time like now! she told herself, and was soon revelling in the familiar smells as she cleaned the brushes that needed it.

As she hurried out to the car to fetch the boys home from school, she was humming out loud and buzzing inside with a new feeling of optimism.

CHAPTER FOUR

Sue's brief spell as a student ended in a clash of ideas between her and the teacher, who considered her imaginative style 'lightweight'. Sue, on the other hand, thought that to go all out for accuracy was draftsmanship, not art. Things came to a head when the teacher overheard her muttered comment, 'A camera would be a better tool than a drawing pencil if all that is required is realism.'

Although she hadn't particularly enjoyed or benefited from the course, Sue still felt that her departure was the result of a personality clash as much as anything. She waited anxiously for her mother's reply to her letter.

Somewhat at a loose end, she unleashed her energy on the untidy flatlet, collecting paper rubbish and stuffing it in the kitchen waste bin till it all but overflowed. When she had dealt with unwashed coffee mugs, she turned her attention to the furniture. Something was stuck down the side of one of the armchairs: it seemed at first glance to be a wad of paper but when she pulled it out Sue found she had an exercise book folded back on itself in her hand. Without considering if this were a violation of her flatmate's privacy – for one glance had told her that the round, bold hand belonged to Pixie – she sat back on her heels and began to read.

It was obviously a story for young children yet Sue found herself absorbed in the adventures of a little boy whose bright red gumboots were magic: when he made a wish while he was wearing them it was granted.

Without conscious thought, Sue found herself groping for a pencil and putting the little boy in his wonderful boots in the margin. She drew him exactly as he appeared in her head.

'Give me that back!' Sue looked up into Pixie's angry face. She had been concentrating so hard on drawing she had not heard her come in. 'Give me that – it's mine!' she repeated. 'You have no right, absolutely no right at all, to spy into my things like that! What are you doing here anyway? I thought you were in class.'

'Did you write this?' Sue demanded, holding the exercise book just out of reach and ignoring Pixie's command.

'How ... how dare you read my private things?' Pixie sounded on the verge of tears as she made a wild lunge forward and managed to grab the book. Rather than see it torn, Sue let go.

Pixie stared at it in horror. 'You've been scribbling on it!' she accused, putting both hands on it as if she intended ripping it in half.

'No! Oh, Pixie, don't do that – please!' Sue begged. 'It isn't scribble. I'm sorry, really, I just couldn't help drawing your little boy.'

Slowly Pixie relaxed her grip round the book and as it opened from the tight roll she had made of it she studied Sue's sketch. When she looked back at Sue a smile of amazement replaced the anger. 'You've drawn him *exactly* as I imagined him.'

'That's because you described him so well. It's a great story, it ought to be published.'

'Oh yeah, and who would publish it?' Pixie flopped down in the armchair. 'It's just a stupid idea I got and scribbled down to while away the time.' She looked up sharply at Sue. 'Where did you find it?'

'Right there in that chair where you're sitting. I was tidying up.'

'I thought I'd lost it.'

'I wondered what it was and began to read. I'm really sorry I scribbled in it . . .' Pixie flushed slightly as Sue repeated her own words, 'I suppose I just did it without thinking. Why don't you try and get it published?'

'Yeah, but it's just a kids' book, and it needs illustrations . . .' Pixie stopped suddenly and stared at Sue. 'You could do that, Sue! You could do the illustrations. Then we could see if we could find a publisher.'

'Yes, yes we could,' Sue said quietly after a brief hiatus of silence during which this startling idea took root.

'But you wouldn't want to waste time on anything like this . . .' Pixie sounded about as genuine as Uriah Heep. 'You're studying for a great career, the first female Rembrandt or something . . .'

Sue chucked a cushion at her. 'Great careers don't seem like fun to me. Illustrating your story would be. I really enjoyed doing that bit of illicit scribble.' She grinned at Pixie, who chucked the cushion back. 'Anyway, I've left art school, so I would have time.' Sue knew she had neither the talent nor the ambition to be, as Pixie said, a female Rembrandt. She had always enjoyed creating what she called 'fun pictures', brightly coloured Christmas scenes, chocolate-box kittens and puppies and cheerful elves and gnomes along with mythical castles and imaginative fairies. 'I'd much rather illustrate your book,' she admitted. 'Let me show you in colour just how I see your little boy.'

With a few deft strokes she had transferred to paper the small boy in his red boots dreamed up by Pixie. 'But that is *just* how I see him in my mind's eye!' Pixie exclaimed, peering over Sue's shoulder. 'How did you guess?'

'I didn't guess – you described him so well that it would have been impossible to draw him any different. That's a great gift, Pixie, bringing something, or someone to life for other people just by choosing the right words.'

Pixie stared at her with a bemused look. 'Seems to me we both have "something" she murmured aloud. 'Maybe we really should work together . . .' Sue stared back, suddenly aware that the two of them had created a sort of magic.

'Let's start now!' she suggested. 'Tell me the scenes you would like to see illustrated and I'll try and draw them for you.'

For the next two hours, all thought of tidying up gone, they went through the story and by the time they got to the end Sue had a pad covered in rough sketches ready to fill out and colour.

'You never explained why you were here and not in your class,' Pixie said to Sue as they worked.

'I ... disagreed with the teacher.' Sue was evasive. 'So I came home and everything was such a mess I thought I would tidy up,' she explained. 'That's how I found your book.'

'I suppose I should be grateful.' Pixie's smile negated the grudging tone of her voice. 'I thought I'd lost it for ever.'

'Yeah ...' Sue smiled back and wondered why she had ever thought Pixie nondescript: absorbed in something she obviously enjoyed she was really attractive. They were still working when they heard someone at the door.

They both glanced up. 'Help!' Pixie clapped a hand to her mouth. 'That must be Edgar – we're supposed to be going to the pictures.'

'You *are* going to the pictures.' Sue's voice brooked no argument. 'There is nothing you can do till you see how I've carried out your suggestions for illustrations. I'll get on quicker on my own, so let the poor boy in – get yourself ready and off!'

'If you're sure?' Pixie still hesitated but another tap at the door sent her scurrying to open it.

'I'm sure!' Sue assured her, retreating back. 'Hi, Edgar!' She glanced up briefly and saluted him with a paintbrush.

'Shan't be a tick!' Pixie called as she flew into her bedroom to make a quick change of clothes and retouch the make-up she had recently started to use at Sue's urging.

Edgar crossed the room and stood behind Sue, silently watching over her shoulder as she painted in the red boots. She wanted to tell him to back off but before she could say anything he asked, 'Are those just pictures or are they illustrations for a kids' book or something?'

'Yeah, Pixie's book.' Sue responded without thinking, and then turned round in her chair to face him. 'Perhaps I shouldn't have told you – don't say anything to her.'

'Pixie's book? You mean Pixie has written a book?' Sue was relieved that he seemed impressed, not amused or mocking as she had half feared.

'Yeah – a kid's book.'

Sue hardly registered Edgar's quiet 'I see' as she returned her attention to the red boots.

'Edgar wants to read my book.' Pixie announced as they scrambled in the tiny kitchen corner making toast and coffee next morning. 'He says he saw your illustrations yesterday.' Pixie sounded matter of fact, not accusatory or annoyed.

'Yes, he asked me what they were for. I'm afraid I told him.'

'He wants to take the story and the illustrations and show them to his uncle.'

'Show it to his uncle? What on earth for?' Sue could not see why a middle-aged man should want to see the text and illustrations of a book designed for young children.

'Because . . .' Sue could hear the suppressed excitement trembling through her words. 'Uncle Harry works for a publisher! If he thinks it's good enough he'll show it to the children's book editor and we might, just might, get it published.'

Sue gaped at her friend. 'Gosh!' was all she could find to say and, 'Oh, gosh!'

'He says he'll come round and collect it tonight, so I'm trying to get into work early and get some of it typed up. I should be able to finish it during my lunch hour.' Pixie was already putting her dishes in the sink and looking for her coat.

'But I can't possibly get the illustrations finished today,' Sue protested.

'Doesn't matter – Edgar says you have done enough already for them to see what they will be like.'

When Edgar took the folder containing both story and pictures that evening Sue felt as if part of herself were going. Looking at Pixie she could see by her expression that she felt the same. 'Take care of that now, won't you?' she said, nodding at the folder under his arm. He gave her a withering look but didn't bother to answer.

'I'll let you know as soon as I have anything to tell you,' he promised.

CHAPTER FIVE

CHRISTMAS was round the corner and though she had complained in Tasmania about Christmas in the summer, now on this grey day in early December Sue would have given anything for a bit of Tasmanian sunshine. At first it had been fun just wandering the London streets but now she shivered in the dank air and felt at a loose end till she realized she was walking past a gallery. Impulsively she turned in.

She stared at the painting. It was a head and shoulders study of her mother, and she didn't need to look for the artist's signature to see that it was David Jones. It was certainly her mother, there was no doubt about that, but idealized, or so Sue felt. Even allowing for the fact that this must have been done anything from eight to ten years ago, it was her mother – as she was then – and yet . . .

Sue wondered when her mother had sat for it; she would have remembered if she had seen it before. David, she thought, had seen his subject through the eyes of love. She searched for the same feeling on her mother's face, but she was looking into the distance – or the future – and not directly at the artist.

Although she knew she would never be able to afford to buy it, out of sheer curiosity she walked over to the proprietor of the gallery, an attractive woman somewhere around her mother's age.

'Sorry, that one is not for sale. It's here for exhibition only and I guess because he wanted a safe place to hang it for a while,' the woman told her.

'I would like to contact the artist. Do you have an address?'

'No.' The woman answered so swiftly that Sue was sure she had. 'I can tell you that painting is definitely not for sale anyway.' She was studying Sue with an expression of faint puzzlement.

'It is the painter, David Jones, I want to contact. That is my mother.' She nodded at the picture. 'She lives in Australia now, When I came to England she asked me to get in touch with him – they used to be good friends.'

'I see . . .' The proprietor of the gallery chewed her lip slightly, as if weighing up a problem. 'Come into my office and tell me something about yourself and your mother. We'll have a cup of tea . . .' She glanced round; only one other person was wandering round studying the paintings. 'I'll ask my daughter to come out here for a few minutes – she's working in the office at the moment.' Sue followed her through a curtained alcove into a cubby-hole only just large enough to have any pretensions to being a work space. 'Oh, Fiona, could you keep an eye on things out there for a few minutes?'

'Of course, Mother.' As the young woman rose rather clumsily to her feet, Sue saw that she was very pregnant. The older woman watched her, an anxious frown drawing her brows together. 'She should really stop coming in here to help me,' she sighed. 'She will *have* to give it up soon. Problem is, I haven't been able to find anyone to take her place. I need someone with both office and artistic experience and know-how. . . .' She tailed off with another sigh. Then she turned her back on Sue to flick on an electric kettle standing on the shelf.

'I have those qualifications – and – and I need a job.' Sue stopped abruptly with a small intake of breath, her own words taking her by surprise. 'My mother – the one in the painting – is an artist.' She paused briefly for breath. 'I have done a course in art at my local technical college and also a short course in shorthand and typing . . .' The words tumbled out. She stopped suddenly, knowing that she wanted this job more than anything in the world at the moment.

The kettle boiled unheeded as they stared at each other, both equally amazed. 'I couldn't pay much – or even offer you a full-time position.'

'I don't mind; but . . . I may not be suitable . . . You don't know anything about me. . . .' She trailed off and looked at the frantic kettle to hide her embarrassment. The older woman followed her gaze and with a slight shrug flicked the switch to 'off'.

'I'm sorry,' Sue mumbled, and would have left if she had been standing nearer the door.

'No, wait!' An imperious hand gesture kept Sue rooted to the spot. 'We'll talk over tea – or coffee, whichever you prefer.' She looked out into the shop area – the desultory customer wandering round had left. 'Fiona, come and have a coffee.' Throwing Sue a half smile and a silent question to her mother Fiona joined them. She left the door ajar. 'I can see if anyone comes in,' she explained, sitting heavily on a stool near it.

'Why don't you give her a go, Mother? Time, tide and babies wait for no man, you know,' was Fiona's response when Edwina Mancini explained that Sue wanted her job. 'If she started straight away I would still be here to show her the ropes and ease her in for you.' She turned to Sue with a warm smile, which faded to a look of puzzlement. 'Have I met you before?' she asked. 'There is something awfully familiar about you.'

Sue shook her head. 'No, but you see my mother every day.'

'The portrait by David Jones,' the gallery owner explained. 'That is her mother.'

'Well, there you are – marvellous reference!' Fiona laughed. 'Grab her, Mum, while you can!'

Riding back home on the bus, Sue realized that she hadn't got an address for David after all. She began to compose a letter in her head, telling her mother about the gallery and giving her a sanitized version of her change of occupation.

She was writing the letter when Nicholas turned up. 'Hello, Nick . . .' Her hand flew up to her mouth as she remembered they were going out. 'Sorry, I'm not ready – I won't be a tick!'

'You hadn't forgotten, had you? You were the one so keen to see this film.'

'No – no – of course I hadn't forgotten . . .' Sue lied. 'I just didn't realize what the time was. Give me five seconds and I'll be ready!'

She couldn't think why on earth she had wanted to see the film as she sat by Nick, her hand in his, in the darkened cinema. She was impatient to tell him about the decision she had impulsively made and was glad when they were sitting opposite each other in the café where they usually went for a quick snack.

'Good idea!' he said approvingly. 'I could never see how you could just be a student.'

'Not just a student, an art student, Nick!' she protested.

Nick, who had studied engineering and was in England to get some practical experience working on machinery before returning to his parents' large farming property in New Zealand, did not take art very seriously. 'I was always surprised that an independent Aussie like you would be happy living on a parental allowance,' he said.

'I'm not really an Aussie – I was born here in England,' Sue reminded him. 'And I don't get any money from my parents, just a very small income from the money my father left me. I didn't get that till I was twenty-one.'

Nick held up both hands. 'You don't need to explain. I'm sorry for misunderstanding.'

Sue shrugged. 'I didn't explain, so how could you understand?' She hurried on, bursting to tell him of the extraordinary coincidence that had landed her a job. 'I was walking past this gallery and decided to go in, and there was this painting of my mother. The artist was a friend of ours – Mum had actually asked me to look him up but I had no luck finding him. Then I walked into this gallery, just because I was cold and I like galleries, and the first thing I saw was Mum! I don't know when she sat for it, or even if she did. I'd never seen it before, but of course when I realized it was painted by David I asked for his address . . .'

Nick reached across the table and put his hand over hers. 'Did you get it?' he asked.

'No, but I got a job!' Sue turned her hand over in his and smiled across the table at him. 'I hate to admit it, but you are right. I never really wanted to be a student, but knew my mother would accept that as a reason to come. Silly of me – after all, I'm twenty-two now, and it's time I—'

'Grew up?' Nicholas supplied, but his teasing grin took the sting out of his words.

'No! Oh, I suppose so,' she admitted grudgingly. 'But coming over here to study art was really dumb. I enjoy doing things like the pictures for Pixie's story but I'm never going to be a great artist. In fact, I don't even want to be.'

'Why did you think your mother wouldn't mind you coming if you did an art course?'

'Because she always regretted she never did one herself. You know what parents are.'

'Is she an artist?'

'She used to do animal portraits. They were really good – she had a knack of capturing that particular animal's personality.'

'Doesn't she do it now?'

'She's too busy being a farmer's wife and having babies.' She stopped and thought, chewing her lip and frowning slightly. Maybe she felt guilty: that's why she didn't make a fuss about me coming back to England.'

'Guilty for having twins?' Nicholas smiled.

'Don't be silly, for me. I spent so much time helping her I didn't get to do much else. When I suggested coming here to study art I guess she wanted me to have the advantages she missed out on. My stepfather thought it would be a good idea if I left the nest,' she finished with a wry grin as the waitress brought their fish and chips. 'How about you? Are you liking your new job any better?' For a second their glances met and held. What a very nice person he is, she thought, wondering if she was falling in love with him.

'Yes – yes I am, thanks. Did you leave a boyfriend behind in Tassie, Sue?'

She shook her head, startled by his question. 'No one special.' This was true; she had broken up with Ian some weeks before she left. 'How about you? Is there some girl back home in New Zealand awaiting your return to "The land of the long white cloud"?'

'No one special,' he told her.

Tit for tat, Sue thought, wondering if, like her, he was simply speaking the truth. She hoped so. She had had boyfriends in Tasmania but no one special. Looking back she wondered if she had deliberately kept them at arm's length because of the dream she carried in her heart to come back to the land of her birth.

They left the café and went to the gallery, Sue anxious to show Nick where she would be working. She pointed out the painting of her mother. 'See, there it is, in the centre there.'

Nick pressed his nose to the glass and peered inside. 'I can see the likeness,' he murmured. 'She is beautiful.'

'Yes,' Sue conceded, 'but that was several years ago. She looks a bit weather-worn now, she spends so much time outside.' She added that by way of explanation, hoping that he would not take her comment as a jealous one. She sighed, love for her mother sweeping through her. Her hand tightened on Nick's as it lay in hers. To feel homesickness now in any form was absurd: she had worked and planned to get to England and she intended to enjoy it. Falling in love seemed like a good start.

On the dim landing outside their flatlet, Nick kissed her. It was not the first time; there had been many kisses on the boat and since, light and friendly. This was different she thought, as the tip of his tongue slid between her lips and she felt herself respond. Her legs were rubbery and her heart up in her throat, affecting her breathing. 'Nick!' she whispered, then a sudden burst of laughter behind the door stopped her reaching again for his mouth. 'We'd better go in,' she muttered, and moved out of the circle of his arms.

CHAPTER SIX

STEVIE raced through her evening chores while Brian and Barney ate their baked beans. Normally she sat at the table chatting to them and drinking tea, even though she often felt like a fifth leg in their company. They didn't seem to need or want anyone else. In the car they chose to sit in the back together where they carried on their own conversation, making her feel like a taxi driver. Sitting in the front passenger seat was not considered a privilege as it had been by her older children.

Today she welcomed this self-sufficiency that left her free to pursue her own agenda, which, at this moment, was to get through chores so that she would be free to get her paints working for her again.

She had the boys bathed and bedded in record time, but the choocks were not so easy to con into an early night. At last she settled down to organize her painting gear. She had decided to use Sue's bedroom as it was the lightest room in the house and Sue, far away in England, was not in a position to object, or likely to need the room.

Stevie hummed softly to herself as she set up easel and paints. Delving into her ragbag, she fished out an old shirt. Tom had torn a large three-cornered rip in the back negotiating a wire fence. She had consigned it to the ragbag, knowing that the soft cotton flannelette would tear up into wonderful polishing cloths. Now she had a much better use for it. The tear in the back didn't matter – it was the front that was important, and it would make a perfect artist's smock.

She smiled to herself as she rolled up the sleeves above her wrists so that she could use her hands. Donning it reminded her of her indignation when David had told her he had known she was a beginner from the word go. She had felt both foolish and mollified when he explained that it was all her new gear and the fact that she was not enveloped in a paint-daubed garment as she worked.

Sue had said in her letter that David was doing quite well now. A vague statement, telling her very little about her old friend and mentor. Well, he deserved success, she thought, for he had great talent.

She breathed in the heady scent of paint and with a deep sigh of pure satisfaction swept her brush down the paper on her easel, not painting anything in particular but just rejoicing in the feel of the brush in her hand. But she was soon painting in earnest, a picture of her twin sons with one of the working kelpies sitting between them. She had always liked this particular snapshot and when looking around for something to paint realized that this was the perfect study for a much larger picture. Totally absorbed, she didn't hear the old Ford Ute coming up the driveway, only the sweep of its headlights through the glass of the uncurtained window alerted her to the fact that her husband and stepson were home and probably hungry.

She didn't have to ask if they had had a good day – it was written on their faces when she met them in the kitchen.

'You got one, then?' She smiled at Tom as she turned from the fridge her hands full of quick-to-cook steaks. 'A good one – what you wanted?'

'The best – and at a reasonable price too. Wait till you see him. You'll love him!'

Stevie thought that highly unlikely. To her a bull was a dangerous necessity, not something anyone could love, and she doubted her ability to assess the finer points of one.

As she busied herself with the meal, she realized that she too was hungry. She had been so lost in her painting that she had given little thought to feeding herself.

She listened to the men's account of their day, including a bid-by-bid description of the auction. They were eager to tell her how they had succeeded in securing the very bull they wanted, the one who would surely put their stud on the map, for far less than they had been prepared to pay. Finally Tom smiled kindly at her across the table and asked, 'Did you have a good day? Boys behave?'

'Oh yes – to both questions. I rode Lady this morning then decided to get my painting gear out. I set up Sue's room as a makeshift studio . . .' She began to tell him about the picture she had started then realized that he wasn't really listening. Her words petered out on a slight sigh. Tom's interests did not extend much beyond the farm and the horses; she knew he looked upon her painting as something that had filled in her time before she met up with him again.

Andrew, however, had spent enough school holidays with her in the old days to know that it was much more than a hobby, and if he hadn't realized for himself Michael had often told him how his mother earned good fees for painting animals, mostly horses and dogs, from photographs. He had seen her work and thought she was good.

'You can paint our new bull,' he said now. 'How about that, Dad?'

'I can try. I have to confess I've never painted a bull before.' She smiled at him across the table. How lucky she was, in this stepson of hers.

With the two topics of conversation thus linked she had Tom's attention again. 'Good idea!' he approved. 'Tell you what – why don't you paint him on a sign to hang at the gate?'

The twins did their best to get out of school the next morning, begging to stay home and welcome the new bull. Stevie thought the beast could survive without them, assuring them that he would be there to greet them when they got home. She hoped she would be proved correct: she often cursed the laissez-faire attitude of so many Tasmanians usually expressed in the colloquialism, 'She'll be right, mate!', as they did things in their own time, but she had to admit, it usually was.

This time it really was: a cloud of dust was moving up the hill ahead of her when she returned from dropping the boys off at the school gate. She caught glimpses through it of a heavy vehicle rumbling up their hilly drive in bottom gear and knew her model was arriving. She was out there, camera focused, as he was unloaded into a secure yard. By lunchtime she had reeled off a whole film, to drop off at the local pharmacy when she fetched the boys from school. She also managed a few very quick pencil sketches. She was determined to make a success of this job, both for Tom's sake and her own. Already she was feeling a new and vital stirring. She had not realized how much she had missed her painting. One look at that massive head and she knew she would stick with her normal modus operandum and paint from photographs. In the days that followed, she scarcely emerged from her makeshift studio: it just felt so good to be holding a paintbrush again and she was determined that this 'commission' be as good as any she had done.

Tom was delighted with the half-finished sketches she showed him, and when he asked Andrew his opinion before Stevie went on and finished it his son was full of praise. 'I told you she was good, Dad. Some of the paintings she did when I stayed with her were fantastic.' He winked at Stevie. 'What fee are you charging him?'

'Fee? Well, nothing, of course!' Stevie protested. The idea hadn't even crossed her mind.

Andrew shook his head. 'You should charge him top price. When people see that, you'll get asked to do more. You could charge everyone a good fee – you'd soon have the money for a beach shack.'

CHAPTER SEVEN

SUE bent her head over the folder on the desk in the little office behind the gallery. Fiona was leaning over her – as much as she could lean in the last stages of pregnancy – explaining the intricacies of their accounting system. Sue was concentrating hard because she really did want to make a success of this job and looked up at Fiona when she stopped mid-sentence. She appeared to be listening to her mother talking to someone in the gallery, but after a moment she turned her attention back to the accounts and Sue.

'That sounds like Davey,' she said, half to herself. 'I'll put the kettle on – Mother always brings him back here for a cup of coffee.' Sure enough she had barely filled the kettle and was just flicking the switch when the sound of voices was joined by approaching footsteps. The door opened and Madame Mancini came in with a man. Sue looked up and met his eyes. For a moment time stood still: she was a child again in Wales sitting at a rough wooden table on a hillside outside a cottage. She was drinking orangeade and watching her mother and this same man toast each other in red wine. Time telescoped as she relived the flash of insight she had then, when she had known, as she watched his face, that he was in love with her mother. It had invoked a sharp childish fear as she scrutinized her mother's expression followed quickly by relief when all she could find there was friendship and genuine liking. The memory faded and she smiled at the man in front of her.

'Hello, David.'

He stared at her for a long moment. 'Sue! You *must* be Sue! Yes, you *are* Sue!' The warm smile she remembered lit his face. 'Is your mother. . . ?'

Sue shook her head. 'Just me. Mum is still in Tasmania. I'm here to. . . .' She had been about to say she was here to study art but as she had let Madame Mancini and her daughter think she needed the job it would be better to say nothing.

'Shall I make coffee?' she asked as the kettle boiled. 'Do you still take your coffee black with two sugars?' she asked David.

He nodded. 'Yep, hot, strong and sweet – like love.'

Sue smiled; he had always said that.

He smiled back, as if he could read her thoughts. 'What a memory! But you've grown up.'

'Eight years is quite a while,' Sue reminded him.

'You are more like your mother than you were as a child,' he commented as she handed him his cup.

'I don't think I am like her at all.' Sue couldn't agree, even though she knew it was a compliment. Her mother was beautiful, people wanted to paint her, while she was quite ordinary, muted compared to her mother. She was fair, verging on mousy, not ash blonde, and her mother's blue eyes had bypassed her – she had grey ones like her father.

'My mother asked me to look you up, give you her regards and all that.' Sue sipped her coffee and avoided looking at him. She had fulfilled the obligation. She wasn't sure she liked this stirring of memories and, catching her employer looking at her, she didn't think that Madame Mancini altogether approved of the attention David was giving to her. She drained her cup and turned back to her accounts, leaving the others to talk business. When he got up to leave he came and stood by her chair.

'I'd love to catch up with news of you all. We must have dinner or something.' Unsure whether this was a serious suggestion or not, Sue mumbled a vague response.

David nodded. 'I'll be in touch.' Another nod and he was gone.

Sue didn't give a lot more thought to David once she had delivered her mother's message. It might be diplomatic, she thought, to tell her mother she had met him and also break the news that she was working in the gallery that housed her mother's portrait in the same letter. Working here had underlined that she was not cut out to be a great artist. Comparing her work with those, like David, who had more or less made it, she realized that her talent was extremely minimal, and she was happy with that. She was like a pianist who enjoyed playing for her own pleasure, and occasionally that of friends, but had no desire whatsoever to be a concert pianist.

She enjoyed every moment of the time she spent doing the fun illustrations for Pixie's story and, to her surprise, she was also enjoying doing the accounts and clerical work at the gallery. Here her knowledge of art was an asset and the fact that David Jones had painted her mother's portrait and known her as a child elevated her in her employer's eyes.

Edgar arrived that evening, just when both girls were washing their hair. Sue was wearing a towel, turban style, and Pixie was still lathering hers. They could both sense his excitement. The brown paper parcel tucked under his arm looked as if it could be champagne. But he refused to say anything to Sue until Pixie emerged from beneath the taps. When she did they exchanged a quick glance, the same question in both their eyes. Can it be? Dare we hope?

'Champagne, Edgar?' Pixie asked, shaking her head so that droplets of water flew around. She rubbed at her wet hair vigorously then asked directly, 'Have you got news for us?'

'It is champagne, for you both, and the book,' he said, but his eyes were on Pixie.

'You mean *our* book?' Sue asked.

'My story?' Pixie's voice rose to a squeak as she stared at him, looking faintly ridiculous under her mop of wet hair.

'The very same. The children's editor in Uncle Harry's firm loves it. The letter of acceptance is in the mail. I've pre-empted it.'

Then they were all hugging each other and in the excitement and confusion Sue didn't notice that Nick had arrived till she found she was hugging him.

'Is the hair wash part of the celebration?' Nick asked with a grin, then there was a loud pop as Edgar uncorked the champagne and, breathless with excitement, Sue was holding a tumbler beneath the cascading foam.

'Help – more glasses!' she called. Pixie held out three tumblers and a tooth mug. 'Sorry, folks – we don't run to champagne glasses!'

Nick raised the tooth mug on high. 'To success and fame!'

Much later, with the bottle empty and discarded, and everyone full of the scratch meal they had managed to put together, Sue leaned her now dry head on Nick's shoulder. 'With this success Mum shouldn't mind so much about me quitting school,' Sue said to him.

He leaned back and looked into her face. 'How old are you, Sue?'

'Twenty-two,' she told him, surprised by the question. 'You know that.'

Nick pretended to consider. 'Hmmm, twenty-two ... Mature enough, I should have thought, to do what you *want* to do, not what your mother would *like* you to do?'

'Yes, but ...' Sue floundered. How could she explain that she understood the reasons behind her mother wanting her to study art, wanting her to have what she had missed. She sighed with the sudden understanding that life just didn't work out that way – no one could live another's life for them and no one could live by proxy for someone else. With this flash of inner knowing, she relaxed back into Nick's arms. 'You are so right,' she murmured. As his arm tightened round her she felt safe, secure and happy.

But his words had hit a sore spot. She had always prided herself on her independence of spirit, even when she was a small girl. She had never shied away from clashes of will with her mother before, so why now had she been so ready to acquiesce?

She asked herself this that night, wakeful in bed. Sue was more honest than most people in knowing that she was fooling herself when she pretended she was following her mother's wishes. It had seemed an adventure when her mother married Tom and they all set sail for Australia. Life in rural Tasmania, however, had not proved to be as exciting as she had visualized, or maybe the truth was simply that life on a farm was not so different wherever one lived. Tasmania had seemed the Promised Land, but once there England became the place of her dreams and she longed to return. A year or so in England studying art was a far more enticing prospect than life on the farm helping to raise her young half-siblings. The humiliating end to her relationship with Ian Forest was what had really convinced her.

Sue had been going out with Ian Forest ever since high school. His parents farmed the neighbouring property and it had always been more or less taken for granted by all that one day they would get married. So Sue had been shattered when Ian brought home a pretty girl from the city and announced they were marrying in a few weeks. The fact that Wendy was pregnant was added gall, for Sue had always drawn the line at sex with Ian on the grounds that it was cheapening and he would lose his respect for her. Sue was ready to acknowledge now that her pride had been dented, but her heart wasn't even cracked.

She put the light on, found a paper and pen and began a letter to her mother. *Dear Mum . . .*' After a brief hesitation she added, *'and Tom' This is just to let you know I have definitely given up art school. I have got a job working in the gallery that sells David's work – his painting of you (not for sale) has pride of place there. Here's the BIG news: Pixie and I did a kids' book (she wrote the story and I did the illustrations) and it has been accepted for publication! I am quite good at doing colourful and whimsical drawings, so maybe I will get some more illustrating commissions.* She went on to ask about the family and the farm and send snippets of news about London and the weather, finally adding, as a postscript, *Nearly forgot to tell you – I saw David Jones and passed your regards on to him. He sent them back, or rather his regards to you.* As she folded the letter and slipped it into the envelope she remembered reading somewhere that the most important part of any letter was usually in the postscript. Not in this instance, she thought. David Jones was out of her mother's life these days and certainly not in hers.

With the letter written and mailed, Sue felt she could relax and enjoy life as it came, and at the moment it was coming good. Post-war London moving on towards the Swinging Sixties was a pretty good place to be. She liked the independence of their little flat and found Pixie a compatible flatmate, and she had a job she enjoyed and a boyfriend who, while being there when she wanted, did not make too many emotional demands. The exciting prospect of her illustrations being published was the icing on the cake. On these pleasant thoughts she dropped to sleep.

She was met at the gallery next day by an agitated Madame Mancini. 'Ah, Sue! I'm so glad you are here. Fiona is in hospital – I shall have to go in and see her – but you will be able to manage here, won't you? I don't like closing when I am supposed to be open . . .'

'Don't worry, I can cope.' Sue assured her. 'Has she had the baby?'

'Not yet – I took her in last night. Tony, her husband, is away for a couple of nights on business so she stayed with me. I left to come and open up the gallery and see you, then I promised to go back.' She paused and looked at Sue anxiously. 'You are sure you can cope?'

Sue nodded. 'Everything is priced so it shouldn't be too difficult and if any real problems crop up I will just put them on hold till you are back.' She sounded a good deal more confident than she actually felt. Most of her working hours had actually been spent in the small back room doing the paperwork, not in the gallery proper. 'Don't worry about anything here. I'll hold the fort for you.'

Left alone, Sue walked slowly round the gallery studying the paintings and objets d'art on display. She felt very conscious of the portrait of her mother, which it seemed like a living presence that observed her every movement. It had a clear 'Not For Sale' tag on it in lieu of a price and was the centrepiece of a display of other work by David Jones.

This was her mother as she had known her in her teenage years, particularly in the tranquil hiatus between her first stepfather's death and her mother's remarriage and the general turmoil and excitement of their emigration to Australia. Davey had caught something about her mother that was beyond the physical; he had captured the very essence of her. Not for the first time she wondered what her mother had really felt about David in those days. And about Tom, who had such a knack of reappearing at unexpected moments in their lives. Had she really been in love or was she swept along by the thought of a new life in a new country?

Whatever her mother had felt, it was no real concern of hers. She turned her attention to David's other paintings hanging in the gallery. His bold and colourful impressionist style seemed to have developed over the years. She recognized the landscapes and seascapes on and around the Welsh coast and smiled at a small painting of a boy standing back to admire his sandcastle. There was a snapshot of the same scene in the family album: her brother Michael had been as proud of his creation as any architect looking at the cathedral he had visualized and designed. She remembered Davey helping Michael with the building.

Many of the other paintings were of scenes and places she did not recognize, they were vibrant and colourful and looked as if they had been painted in a stronger and more brilliant light than the Welsh ones.

She had returned to the portrait of her mother when the bell jangled as someone pushed the door open. Turning, she found herself face to face with David himself.

CHAPTER EIGHT

'A BEACH shack?' Tom looked at Stevie in surprise. 'Is that what you want? I didn't know.'

'Oh, I don't, not really,' Steve protested. 'It's just that . . . well, Andrew and I were reminiscing about the holidays he spent with me the year I lived on the Welsh coast. I said I missed the sea and sometimes thought it would be nice to have a holiday place on the beach.'

'I see,' Tom said. His hand went up to his chin and he stroked it thoughtfully, as he always did when he was working out a problem. As Stevie wondered what particular teaser filled his mind at the moment he surprised her by acknowledging, 'That's not a bad idea, not bad at all. Have you any suggestions where?'

'Good heavens, Tom, I haven't got as far as thinking about where – I just thought it might be nice to have somewhere by the sea that we could take off to at weekends, while the boys are still young.'

'Big boys as well as little ones enjoy the beach.' Andrew looking toward her closed one eye in a barely perceptible wink before turning to his father. 'Don't they, Dad?'

'Yeah . . .' Tom answered absently, his mind obviously given over to this new project. He looked up and flashed a wide smile at Stevie across the table, and as their eyes met she remembered just why she had married him. 'I think the nearer the better. If we choose somewhere too far away there will be occasions when we just won't go because time will be too short. And the nearest spot, as the crow flies, is the Port Sorrell area near Devonport.'

Stevie smiled. 'Crows in Tasmania must fly pretty crooked – there is no such thing as a straight line between two locations in Tasmania. 'I like Devonport but I don't think I've ever been to Port Sorrell.'

'We'll go this weekend and take a look round. If you like it we can see if there are any places for sale,' Tom promised.

Andrew smiled at her across the table; he had happy memories of a summer holiday spent with her at her rented seaside house on the Welsh coast. He knew, probably better than his father did, how she loved the sea.

Stevie herself had almost forgotten till she stepped out of their solid Holden station wagon at Port Sorrell on Saturday morning.

'Where's Hawley Beach?' she asked, looking up from the Saturday Advocate she was studying as they sat at a picnic table drinking coffee from a thermos.

'Right here – well, almost. Just a little further along. It's almost part of Port Sorrell. Why?'

'There's a cottage advertized there – not actually on the beach front, but it sounds a reasonable price,' Stevie told him, passing the paper over and pointing with her pencil to the advertisement she had been reading.

'Might be worth looking at,' Tom conceded as he drained his plastic picnic mug. 'Come on, boys,' he called, 'let's take a look at this place your mother has found.'

Stevie fell in love with Hawley Beach long before they found the cottage standing a short distance up one of the side roads from the main track that ran along just behind the beach. The sand was firm and golden and the sea lapped gently here. It reminded her so much of Borth-y-Gest, perhaps because it was on an estuary, although there were no mountains behind, or in front of them, just the soft greens and silver of the native gums of the Australian Bush.

The beach was almost deserted, with only a handful of holiday-makers. The cottage itself was set in its own small garden and though out of sight of the sea, it was possible to hear it if one made everyone else keep quiet, closed one's eyes and listened intently. Stevie breathed in deeply, savouring the wonderful mingled scent of seaweed and gum leaves.

'Oh Tom . . .' she sighed. 'It's perfect!'

Tom looked pleased but immediately began to point out the drawbacks. 'It isn't actually on the beach, and the garden could be a drag. It might be awful inside . . .' He grinned sheepishly as he ran out of negative comments.

'Two minutes' walk for us, one minute for running kids,' Stevie countered. 'I think the garden is nice – why should it be a drag?'

'The lawn will have to be cut,' Tom pointed out, 'and we haven't seen inside – it might be dreadful.'

Stevie's answer was to push open the little wicket gate and march firmly up the garden path. She then worked systematically round the windows peering into each in turn. 'Looks fine to me,' she finally said. 'It seems to have four bedrooms – is that possible in such a small place?'

Tom referred to the newspaper in his hand. 'Well, it says so here. It is also for sale as is – furnished.' Stevie held out a hand to him and pulled him close to the window she had just peered through.

'See for yourself,' she told him.

Thirty days later, the shack – Tom pointed out to her that this was the colloquial name for a holiday cottage – was theirs. Settlement day coincided with the completion of her painting of the bull. Two good reasons for the celebration they decided should take place at their new property.

Everybody helped to load the station wagon with all the food and paraphernalia for a barbecue and an overnight stay. It was obvious they were trying to fit a quart into a pint pot so Andrew volunteered to take the surplus, plus Barney, Brian and Tess, the family dog, in his car. He took them straight down to the beach, leaving

Tom and Stevie to unload the cars and take possession of the cottage.

This done, Stevie and Tom changed into swimwear and followed them. Stevie felt the years roll away as she floated on her back. Then she climbed up the hot sand and spread out her beach towel, looking towards the sea where Tess, the twins and Andrew were playing with a large ball in the shallow water. Across the estuary the beach on the far side seemed deserted. It reminded her so much of Borth-y-Gest that she half expected to see Portmeirion, but there was nothing at Bakers Beach but sand and trees. To her left, past the headland, the Bass Strait separated them from mainland Australia. It was an enchanted backwater, much as Borth-y-Gest had seemed on those long ago holidays when her older children had been the age of Brian and Barney. In that moment she felt utterly content with her lot. The purchase of this holiday shack had been an inspiration on Andrew's part, and it would bring a new dimension into all their lives. Tom's pleasure in her painting of his new bull had given her the green light to do more, just as her meeting David on the beach at Borth-y-Gest all those years ago had been the trigger to start her painting seriously in the first place. It was his encouragement that had set her on the path to becoming a successful animal portraitist rather than an amateur dabbler in watercolours. She was glad Sue had met up with him, pleased too to learn he was so successful. She closed her eyes, dropped her head on her folded arms and allowed nostalgic 'might-have-been' thoughts to take over. Where would she have been now if she had given her heart to David instead of to Tom, her old sweetheart? She certainly wouldn't have been lying in the sun on a Tasmanian beach, nor, of course, would she have her twin sons. She had found her 'down under' Borth-y-Gest, her spiritual and physical refuge, and for one crazy moment she wished she could share it with David.

That, of course, was impossible: she had dismissed him from her life when she chose Tom and his way of life. She stood up and snatched up the beach towels, shaking them vigorously and brushing the sand off herself as if she would clear her mind of gritty thoughts as well as her body of sand. She shivered slightly – the day was cooling and called out to the others that they should head back.

CHAPTER NINE

SUE turned away from the portrait, feeling embarrassed and guilty as if she had been caught reading a letter destined for someone else or searching through another person's private belongings. She tilted her chin slightly in an unconscious gesture of defiance as she met David's eyes, catching her breath on a small sound that could almost have been a sob. It broke the tension in the air and David stepped forward with a half smile. 'Do you think it is like her?' he asked.

'You know it is.' She hadn't meant to sound so curt – almost rude. 'It is more than like her.' Trying to soften her words she felt she was only sounding critical. 'What I mean is . . .' Her voice faded. What exactly *did* she mean?

'You think I have made more of her – perhaps made her too beautiful?'

Sue nodded.

'That is the way I saw her.' His eyes took on a far-away look as his inner vision carried him back down the years. 'I wonder, has she changed much?' He sounded as if he were talking to himself, and Sue wondered if he really wanted an answer.

'I suppose she has in some ways, in others not at all.' She frowned slightly, trying to find the right words to explain what she meant. 'She doesn't really look much older, it's just that she has settled into herself somehow. That sounds silly. She is more countrified but I suppose she has to be now she is married to a farmer and she breeds horses. And of course she has Brian and Barney, my twin half-brothers. But, yes, she is still beautiful.'

'Does she still paint?' David asked.

'Not really – that is, not professionally. Just now and again as gifts for people.'

'Animals? People's pets?'

'Yes,' Sue nodded, 'she has a real gift for that. She can catch the true personality of whatever animal she is painting.'

David didn't answer for a few moments then he turned back to the portrait. 'Would you say I have done that with her?' he asked.

'Well . . .' Sue was confused. She felt too closely involved – this was a portrait of her mother they were talking about and the man talking to her was the artist himself. Truthfully she did not think he had entirely caught her mother's essence as she knew her. But then – to be honest – he might have done, as he understood her mother. She tried to put her thoughts into words. 'I think it's a wonderful painting – and I am sure you have captured my mother as you saw her.'

'I feel rather damned with faint praise. You obviously think I have slipped up somewhere.'

'No,' Sue protested, 'I'm not saying that, but we obviously saw her differently. I looked at her with the eyes of a child, whereas you . . .' She bit off the words 'were her lover' and ended lamely, 'As an adult you would see her differently.'

'I was not, you know,' David said quietly as he turned away from the painting.

'Sorry?' Sue asked, confused.

'I was not her lover,' David told her, 'so don't go imagining any exciting scenarios along those lines, my little Sue.'

His use of the diminutive and his tone of voice caught her on the raw. Turning away, she threw over her shoulder at the office door, 'I believe you. My mother is a very sensible woman, and I am no longer little and certainly not yours.' She closed the door of the office firmly between them before remembering that she was 'in charge' and he might have a legitimate reason to be there.

She was still looking at the closed door, annoyed at herself for behaving so childishly and psyching herself up to reopen it, when the knob turned and David's head peered round. 'Don't throw the book – or anything else – at me. I apologize.'

Sue was forced to smile at his expression and the tone of his voice. 'I forgive you,' she told him, forcing herself to add, 'I apologize too. I shouldn't have taken umbrage . . .'

'I have no idea what umbrage is, have you? But I forgive you for taking it anyway.'

'Well, I may well have been "little Sue" when you last saw me, but I am not now.'

'You never really were, so my apology is unreserved,' David assured her as he came into the room. 'Actually . . .' He looked round the room as if Edwina Mancini might be hiding there somewhere. 'I came to see your lady boss. Where is she?'

Sue smiled to herself, not at all sure the lady in question would like being referred to so flippantly. 'She's at the hospital. Fiona went into labour and her husband is not home,' she explained. 'I'm holding the fort until she gets back, and I have no idea when that will be.'

'If you offer me a cup of coffee I'll hold it with you.'

'I don't need you to help me hold a cup of coffee.'

'The fort – goose!'

'I'll put the kettle on . . .' Sue grinned as she moved towards it, adding half under her breath, 'Sir!'

David heard her. 'Touché. You are in charge. I was humbly supplicating, not demanding.'

Sue turned her back and busied herself with the coffee mugs. She had run out of smart retorts.

She passed him his mug, indicating with a nod of her head the bowl of sugar. Her own mug cupped in both hands, she peered at him over the rim. He didn't seem to have aged in the years since she'd left England; in fact if anything he seemed younger. There was a lightness about him, as if he had shed some burden. Maybe, she considered, she had caught up with him – or at least narrowed the gap a little between them. She remembered him as an adult to her child; now she felt if not his equal at least adult to his adult. Covertly studying him, she wondered yet again why her mother had not fallen for him. At fourteen she had been more than half in love with him herself. He was too stocky for conventional good looks and his features were uneven, but he oozed Celtic charm and there was music in his soft Welsh voice which even the overlay of Midlands twang acquired over the years, could not disguise.

'Do you still teach?' She recalled that Nanny had told her he didn't even as she asked.

'Not any more, I gave it up after my wife died. I'm giving myself two years to see if I can make a living without teaching.'

'And are you?'

'Well, I've only had six months so far but yes I am, spurred on, I confess, by my hatred of the constrictions of teaching – set hours, having to live in Wolverhampton.'

Sue smiled, 'I can understand that. I'm a fugitive from the schoolroom myself – only difference is I was a student, not a teacher. I didn't realize when I left home to come here that I would just be leaving one conventional and safe background for another.'

'You're not like your mother. She would always opt for security and conventionality.' His mouth twisted into a tight smile and his eyes were bleak as he spoke, making Sue wonder if he had tried to persuade her mother to toss her bonnet over the windmill and throw in her lot with him.

'I wouldn't say that marrying Tom and setting sail for Australia fell into that category,' she asserted rather tartly at this implied criticism of her mother.

They drained their coffee in silence. 'I had better get some work done,' Sue said as she replaced her mug on the workbench. Right on cue the phone rang. Edwina sounded rattled out of her usual composure. 'Are you managing?' she asked and before Sue could reply rushed on, 'It could be a while before I get back. If you don't think you can cope just close.'

'I can manage,' Sue assured her, at the same time putting her hand over the mouthpiece to ask David if he wanted to talk. He shook his head and Sue, after once more asserting her ability to cope and willingness to do so, replaced the receiver.

'No baby yet?' David asked, adding without waiting for a reply, 'So you're still holding the fort?'

'No baby yet, so, yes, I suppose I am.' She ruffled the papers on the desk to lend weight to her words.

'Well, I had better be on my way.' He made no movement to match his words with action. Sue kept her head studiously bent over the work on her desk, answering him with a non-committal grunt. But her head jerked up when he added, 'Too bad you are too busy to have lunch with me.'

'I didn't say that. Anyway, you didn't ask me.' Too late she saw the gleam in his eye.

'I didn't? It must have slipped my mind. Well, are you?'

'No, of course not.' She was annoyed to feel herself flushing.

'Then I will be back at 12.30. That is lunchtime, according to the sign on the door,' he told her, just as if she had no idea. With a cheery wave he was gone and Sue was left to deal with the paperwork and the trickle of customers, or clients as her employer preferred to call them, who wandered in between then and 12.30.

When he presented himself two minutes before time she was ready and waiting for him.

He took her to an intimate wine bar. 'Hope you like Italian food?' he asked as he pulled out a chair for her.

'I love it,' she told him, the tantalizing smells making her aware of her hunger. 'I don't know whether I should . . .' she demurred when he asked her if she would like a glass of wine.

'One glass, Sue. I'm not aiming to send you back to the gallery three sheets to the wind.'

'All right, just one glass.' She added a belated 'Thank you', realizing that her grudging acceptance sounded ungracious, even childish.

He raised his glass to her. 'To reunions!'

Sue returned the gesture.

'Fill me in, Sue. What has been happening to you all since I last saw you in Barmouth? I see your old nanny from time to time and she told me that your mother married again and swept you all off to the antipodes.'

'That's right. Michael had this school friend who came from Australia, Andrew. You must remember him – he stayed with us a lot in the school holidays.'

David nodded, 'I remember him, nice boy.'

'Well, when his father came to England he turned out to be an old boyfriend of Mum's, from way back when they were kids, actually. Then he went to Australia with his parents. He turned up again in the war, but disappeared again and Mum went and married Uncle Jock. We never heard anything of Tom till he turned up as Andrew's father. He and Mum sort of picked up where they had left off or something. They were both free so they decided to marry, and off we all went to Australia.'

'Did you mind?'

'Gosh, no! I was thrilled! I had always wanted to go to Australia and I liked Tom. Besides, it was an adventure.'

'And how did it work out for you all?' Sue thought he was trying almost too hard to appear casual.

'Oh, it worked out OK I suppose.'

'You suppose? Your mother is happy, isn't she?'

'Oh, yeah, she's fine,' Sue assured him with the blissful sans souciance of youth. 'She and Tom seem to get on really well and she likes the country life. My grandfather was a farmer so she was brought up to it. She has always loved horses and she breeds them now. And she has the twins.'

'What about your stepbrother, or was it brothers? How do you all get along together?'

'Oh, that worked out too. Michael and Andrew always were friends anyway. Michael is going to be a vet and Andrew works the property with Tom. My older stepbrother is an accountant in Melbourne.'

'And you? You've told me about everyone else in the family and not said a word about yourself. What made you come back to England?'

Sue shrugged; she was beginning to feel she was undergoing a cross-examination. 'I wanted to see the old country, have a look at my roots, all that sort of thing.' She paused then asked, 'What about you? As I remember you were a struggling artist teaching for a living in dreary Wolverhampton. Now it seems you are pretty successful. How come?'

'My wife died.' His tone was terse, and Sue remembered that she had been a hopeless invalid or in a mental home or something. 'That freed me from the obligation to live in Wolverhampton and with only myself to think about I took to a wandering lifestyle with my easel on my back.'

'And it paid off?'

'It paid off – but in a way I owe it to your mother.' He paused and his eyes took on a dreamy look as if he were back in the past.

'My mother? How come?'

'I had some paintings in an exhibition. Edwina Mancini came along, she saw the one of your mother and wanted to buy it. I refused to sell, so she asked me if she could hang it in the gallery and if she could sell my other work.' He paused for a moment then shrugged. 'So all my work is now handled by Edwina and she sells me so steadily that I am able to live the life I choose.'

Sue glanced at her watch and bent to pick up her purse and gloves.

'Thanks for lunch,' she said, 'and for filling me in. I will be able to tell Mum that, thanks to her, you are now a famous painter. She asked me to look you up but the only address she had was your cottage in Wales. I went there when I was staying with Nanny.'

'Ah yes, Nanny, how is she? The last time I saw her I thought she had aged a lot, rather quickly.'

'Fine,' she said, 'but yes, you're right. I was shocked by how much she had aged, though of course I hadn't seen her for eight years.' Sue sighed. 'Stupid of me, I know, but somehow I expected her to be just the same.'

'We all tend to hold people in our memory as we last saw them.' David pointed out gently.

'Yes, I suppose so.' Sue conceded. Was that how he remembered her mother? 'Thanks for the lunch – I'd better be going,' she told him, wondering if he would walk back with her to the gallery. He seemed preoccupied in his thoughts.

'Thanks for your company – I enjoyed it,' he said, and let her walk away.

It was almost the end of the day when Edwina Mancini returned to the gallery.

'I have a grandson, Alexander Marcus, to be known as Alex,' she announced excitedly before asking Sue about her day. 'We must celebrate!' she exclaimed before whipping a small cupboard open and producing a half full bottle of sherry with a flourish that reminded Sue of a conjuror producing a rabbit from a hat. She poured two glasses and handed one over to Sue saying as she did so. 'Now, tell me about the day – did you cope? But of course you did.'

'I sold a few things.' Sue detailed them to her. 'And David Jones came in to see you.' Noting the quick flash of interest and the slight flush that touched her employer's throat, she decided it was neither necessary nor diplomatic to mention their lunch together. 'He didn't say there was anything particular that he wanted to see you about – just told me to say he had been in and that he would probably pop in tomorrow.'

'Ah – yes.' Sue tried to read the meaning behind the enigmatic comment. With an inward shrug she finished her drink and began the end-of-day tidy up. Of what interest was it to her if Edwina Mancini had the hots for David Jones, or he for her for that matter?

CHAPTER TEN

'So, how about it, Sue? Would you like to come?'

Sue brought her attention back to Nick, perched on the bar stool next to her.

'Did you hear me? You seem miles away.' The peevish undertone in his voice irritated Sue, but she managed a brief smile as she turned towards him.

'I'm sorry, I am listening,' she lied, 'but it is very noisy here.'

'I was telling you that I have this invitation to go and visit some of Mum's relations in wildest Oxfordshire. I wondered if you would like to come with me.'

'Mmm, I'd love to see Oxford.'

'See, you still aren't listening. I said Oxfordshire, not Oxford. Actually, they live in a little village some miles out of Oxford. They sent me a letter inviting me for a visit and I thought you might like to come with me.'

He added when she didn't reply immediately, 'Aunt Lillian did say bring a friend, so it would be OK.'

'Have you lots of relations here, Nick?'

'Hundreds,' he said, his good humour restored now he had her attention, 'but these particular ones I know quite well. Aunt Lillian and Uncle Robert are my mother's brother and his wife, and they stayed with us in New Zealand for several weeks a couple of years back. I liked them – they were very easy to get along with. I would like you to meet them and they would love having you . . .' His voice took on a pleading note. 'Aunt Lillian really did say – Bring a friend and I am quite sure she meant it. So just say yes and I'll give them a ring and accept. We could go this weekend.'

'If you're sure they wouldn't mind?' Sue was still hesitant but Nick appeared to be really keen to have her go along with him.

'Is that yes?' he asked eagerly.

Sue nodded. 'I'll come,' she told him, wondering why she felt that in agreeing she had made a momentous decision. It was only a one-day visit, for goodness' sake.

'I'll drink to that!' Nick raised his glass, then seeing it was empty, grinned. 'Or I would if I could – we'd better have another round.'

When their glasses had been replenished he raised his again. 'To families!'

Sue smiled and reciprocated. 'To families!' After a moment she added, 'And friends!' Nick loved toasts – she often teased him about it and said it was merely an excuse to drink.

They clinked glasses and as Nick put his down on the counter he asked 'Haven't you any relations here, Sue? You never talk about them.'

She shook her head. 'Not really. Both my parents were only children so I am singularly bereft of aunts, uncles and cousins. I do have a stepbrother and his wife. I suppose I should visit them sometime while I am here. They're doctors – in Shropshire. He's a lot older than me; his father was a lot older than Mum. Yes, I suppose I will go and visit. Mum said I should.'

'Well then, you'd better.' Sue glanced at him sharply, needled by the note in his voice. She couldn't read anything from his expression – he was looking down into his glass.

'You can come with me if I come with you to visit your relatives.'

'Fair enough!' he agreed. 'But it isn't quite the same, is it? I really want to see mine. You'll only be going because Mummy tells you to.'

Sue would have liked to argue but she couldn't think of a good retort. 'I don't know about you but I'm hungry,' she said instead.

'Me, too. I skipped lunch today – too busy.'

Sue stopped herself telling him that she had not skipped lunch but had been taken out. Sliding off the bar stool and slipping her arm through his in one fluid movement, she just said, 'Let's eat.'

Nick told Sue a couple of days later that he had arranged to visit his uncle and aunt that coming weekend.

'This weekend?' Somehow she had not expected she would have such short notice.

'That's OK with you, isn't it?' he asked anxiously. 'If you can't make it I expect I can change it.'

'No, this weekend will be fine, Nick. It's just that I didn't expect you to get anything organized quite so quickly somehow.'

'Well, I didn't have to,' he admitted. 'Aunt Lillian had more or less arranged it. I only had to confirm it and say you were coming.'

'Oh, I see.' Sue thought Nick had probably said he would like to bring a friend but couldn't say anything more definite without consulting with her. She had a sudden sensation of being on a conveyor belt. It was not at all what she wanted, she needed to be in control of her life. Wasn't that the driving force that had brought her to England in the first place?

It was almost time for her to leave the gallery on Friday afternoon when she heard David's voice in conversation with Edwina. She stopped what she was doing for a moment, hands poised over the typewriter she was just about to cover. She could not hear the actual words of their conversation but there was something about the low hum of their voices that was peculiarly intimate, or so it seemed to Sue. Rather ashamed at finding herself in the role of would-be eavesdropper, she switched off her attention and finished her tidying-up operations with rather more efficient bustle and noise than they warranted. She was pulling her outdoor clothes down from the coat stand when the door opened and David came in.

'Ah – I've caught you, then!'

Sue wound her long woollen scarf round her neck so fiercely she almost strangled herself. 'Caught me,' she repeated in a cool distant voice that was totally at odds with the tumultuous feelings engendered by his unexpected appearance in the small office. Inside she was an emotional adolescent, someone who had nothing to do with the cool young woman of twenty-two. She knew she must claim her present-day self or he would think the intervening years had done little, or nothing, to mature her.

'Caught me?' she said again.

'You haven't gone home yet. I can walk you,' he explained.

'I'm not going home, I – I have a – date.' She spoke curtly and then felt sorry as she watched his mobile features fall into an expression of almost comical disappointment.

'Oh – but you must be going somewhere. Can I walk you wherever that is?'

'The nearest underground station. You can walk *with* me if you like, but for heaven's sake stop talking about "walking me". It makes me feel like a dog!'

'I like dogs.'

Sue glared at him but his face was deadpan. 'So do I, but that doesn't mean I want to feel like one.'

He insisted on actually seeing her on to the train, a gallantry that Sue, nurturing her independence, only found irksome. She surprised herself by feeling slightly guilty as the train moved away from the platform and he remained there, watching it leave with one hand raised in salute. It was a relief to hurtle into the enveloping darkness. Damn him, she thought, rather unfairly, as she tried to sort out her feelings. What she really wanted, she thought, was a complete absence of feelings. Feeling and emotion meant involvement and that was the last thing she wanted at this point in time.

If he had been her mother's choice, she would, she supposed, have been prepared to accept him as a stepfather, even tried to forget that she imagined she was in love with him. She reminded herself that he was her mother's friend and contemporary. He had simply invited her to lunch because of that, and old time's sake. But that didn't stop her remembering it with pleasure and thinking of Davey as a very attractive man.

Absorbed by her own thoughts, she jumped up from her seat and leapt down to the platform in the nick of time before the automatic doors closed when she reached the station where she was to rendezvous with Nick. Briefly she enjoyed a fantasy where she was careering round London, ad infinitum and incommunicado, in a carefree bubble of her own creation. She relinquished this for her favourite of seeing someone she knew gliding down the adjacent escalator as she sailed up. Or, more romantic still, someone she didn't know and in the moment of passing, their eyes would meet and they would both know that this was 'it'. She never asked herself what exactly 'it' was.

She saw Nick waiting for her as her head came above the level of the top step, by the bookstand, in the agreed spot. She had joked once that 'Reliable' was his middle name. All the same her heart lifted, then immediately contracted, at the unworthy thought that such reliability left nothing to the imagination.

'Hi!" she greeted him, her warm smile reflecting her real pleasure at seeing him. They were planning to see a film but suddenly the idea of sitting in a cinema for hours failed to appeal. 'Are you particularly keen to see this film?' she asked Nick.

'No, but I thought you were.' He sounded faintly reproachful.

'Well, yes, I was,' she admitted, 'but I've changed my mind. Let's just go and have a meal and talk.'

'Suits me,' Nick said easily and, a few minutes later they were seated opposite each other in a pleasantly intimate little restaurant. 'Anything special you want to talk about or were you just yearning for my company and my scintillating conversation?'

'Something like that,' Sue admitted with a smile. There was an easy camaraderie in their relationship that made being with

Nick very comfortable.

'Do you often see the others from the ship?' she asked him now.

'Meaning who? I see you and Pixie and occasionally the other girls when you throw a party. But if you mean the fellows – then, no, we all seem to have gone our separate ways since we landed.'

'Funny that . . .' Sue mused. 'We girls seemed to bond together from day one, even though we are all so different. Though I must say I never thought I would end up sharing a flat with Pixie – all she did when we first got on the boat was bawl her eyes out. I can remember being quite annoyed with her, but the moment we sailed she mopped up her tears and was a different person. She surprised us all with her hidden depths. Gina was the one I was initially drawn to, but she has so many relations and friends of relations here I haven't seen so much of her.'

'And Angela?'

'Oh, Angela – our gorgeous dumb blonde. I see a bit of her, as you know. We clashed in the first few moments of meeting, but now I don't really mind her. Quite like her, in fact.'

'What did your parents think about you giving up your art course and getting a book published?' Nick always seemed interested in her activities, it was one of the things that endeared him to Sue.

'Not too pleased about the former – at least, Mum wasn't. Ecstatic about the latter.' Sue sighed, remembering the letter she had received from her mother. 'But she can't live my life for me, and I can't live my life to please her.'

'All she probably really wants is for you to have the opportunities and chances she missed out on. Now . . .' His change of subject stopped Sue sinking into introspective melancholy. 'about this weekend. I'll pick you up tomorrow around two o'clock – how will that suit you?'

'Tomorrow? I thought we were going Sunday?'

'Well, yes,' Nick admitted, 'we are invited for the whole day

Sunday, but I thought we could make a weekend of it and spend the night somewhere?'

'Together?' Sue was doubtful. This weekend jaunt was beginning to smack too much of commitment. 'Let's just leave it at Sunday, shall we?'

Nick shrugged. 'If you say so.' He sounded disappointed but did not press the point.

Sue yawned, suddenly tired. 'I think I need an early night,' she told him apologetically.

Angela was pouring out a long sad story to Pixie when Sue got back, and she had a suitcase with her.

'What are you doing here, Angela?' Sue interrupted the monologue.

'It's only for tonight, Sue. I had nowhere to go. I couldn't think of anyone but you two and Pixie said it's OK.'

'I'll make some coffee.' Pixie, looking both helpless and hunted, scrambled to her feet and made for the tiny kitchenette.

'I thought you were living with your grandmother – does she know you are here?' Sue was appalled to hear how grandmotherly she sounded herself.

'Well . . . yes and no.'

'Yes or no?'

'Well, I told her I was coming to stay with you for a few days.' Angela had the grace to look sheepish, Sue noted. For her part she was trying hard not to show her annoyance. Unsuccessfully, it seemed, for Angela's voice rose with righteous indignation. 'Honestly, Sue, you don't know what it was like . . .'

'Suppose you tell me.' All the irritation she had felt when she first met Angela resurfaced; she was totally spoilt and selfish and there was no way she was going to let her stay here for more than a night.

'She kept tabs on me all the time – but ALL the time. It was "Where are you going? Who with? What time will you be back?"

and when I did get back she would be waiting up for me – no matter what time it was. Always fussing and scolding. I decided I couldn't stand it any more – so I told her you and Pixie had asked me to stay for a few days – and here I am.'

Yes, here you are, Sue thought, and sat down heavily. She felt for Angela's grandmother – what a pill to have a pretty young grand-daughter, who was also spoilt and strong-willed, descend on you from the other side of the world. 'I don't know where you are going to sleep,' she grumbled, looking round the cramped living-room.

'Oh, don't worry – I've brought a sleeping bag.'

'Good.' Sue sighed resignedly. That was the last thing it was.

CHAPTER ELEVEN

SUE thumped her pillow after turning it over in a vain attempt to get comfortable. Pixie and Angela were still muttering and whispering, their voices low in deference to her declaration that she was tired and going to bed. She could hear their voices but could not catch the drift of their conversation and wondered what the odd bubble of laughter was about. If Angela was going to be here all weekend she would rather be away with Nick. On the comforting thought that she could change her mind, she dropped to sleep.

'Why the sudden change?' he asked. 'You were quite adamant you wouldn't come last night.'

'It's a woman's prerogative,' she retorted before honesty compelled her to admit, 'Angela had landed on us for the weekend when I got back, complete with sleeping bag. Two is company and three most definitely a crowd in that space.'

'Well, I'm glad you changed your mind, even if the reason is not very flattering.' He sounded put out, Sue thought, but had to let it go for at that moment Edwina came into the office, a worried frown on her face and a sheaf of papers in her hand. They were a backlog of invoices that occupied Sue for most of the morning as she struggled to get them into some kind of order.

Sue was annoyed with herself to find she was listening with half an ear all the time for David's voice in the gallery, and even more annoyed to feel the adrenaline rush when she did. Resolutely she put her head down and concentrated on her work. It was his presence in the doorway that made her look up.

'Oh – hello.' She managed to sound surprised and hoped he would not detect the slight quaver in her voice. With an effort of will she pulled her eyes away from his face and concentrated on the work in front of her.

'I have to go to Wales this afternoon. My tenants are leaving and I want to check all is well before I re-let. I might even spend a short while there.' Sue wondered why he was telling her. 'I thought you might like a lift. I'm going by car – it would save you that tedious train journey. It would be a good chance to stay with whatshername, your old nanny.'

Why on earth had she been so precipitous changing her arrangement with Nick? It would, she supposed, be possible to rearrange, but hardly fair.

'Oh – David – thank you – I would have loved to but I have the whole weekend booked up so it is just out of the question.'

He shrugged. 'Pity,' was all he said. Sue strained to catch some sign of disappointment in his voice, without success. 'He's probably relieved,' she told herself.

Sue was distractedly throwing things into a duffel bag – and out again – when Nick arrived at five minutes to two that afternoon. When she was still doing it ten minutes later he looked pointedly at his watch.

'Oh, come on, Sue. We'll never get off at this rate,' he complained. 'Just chuck a few things in and come.'

'That is exactly what I am doing – the point is what things?' She glared at him over the half-packed bag.

'Oh, anything. If you don't know what clothes you want to wear you can't expect me to tell you.'

'Well, I do. You know your family, what sort of people they are. I mean . . .' She thought about for an example. 'If they are the sort of people that dress for dinner then I have to take suitable clothes.'

'Don't be absurd – no one dresses for dinner these days. They are ordinary people, not characters in a Noel Coward play.' He thought she looked delightful, flushed and dishevelled and slightly grumpy, but he thought his family would expect something a little more feminine than the old jeans she was wearing. 'Just put a decent shirt or jumper in,' he told her. 'No one will see your bottom half at the dinner table anyway.'

Sue glared at him, but turned to her wardrobe and selected her one and only dress and folded it carefully into the open bag. She pulled her pyjamas out from under her pillow and was stuffing them in when Nick said, 'Well, you won't need those anyway.'

'But I thought we were stopping overnight . . .' Sue protested.

'Exactly, that's why—' Nick's words were cut short by the balled-up pyjamas hurling across the room and hitting him squarely in the face.

'If you have any silly ideas about turning this into a dirty weekend you can just forget them.' Sue caught the offending night-wear as they were hurled back at her and stuffed them angrily into the bag. But even as she did so the thought slid across her mind that the weekend might prove more interesting than she had originally envisaged. 'Well, come on, what are you waiting for?' she demanded as she snapped the zip shut, hoisted up her bag and headed for the door.

Behind her Nick shrugged and muttered something to himself about the irrationality of women, fortunately unheard by Sue, and followed her out. His car, a stolid middle-aged Morris Minor, stood sedately at the curb. Up till then Nick had felt quite happy with it, even blessed its reliability, but now, as he opened the door for Sue he wished it were something much more dashing, an MG sports model at least. Maybe, he thought, as he caught sight of her glum expression, Sue thought so too. In fact, it was the whole weekend, not the means of transport, that occupied her thoughts. She couldn't rid her mind of the idea that going to meet close relatives smacked too much of commitment. She was pretty sure Mum would think that too and wished she had never mentioned it in her letter. At least it might distract her from asking too many questions about Davey, who, if she hadn't already accepted Nick's invitation, she could be with right now.

It was not in Sue's nature to remain glum for long and as the car threaded its way out of London her heart lifted and she turned to her companion with a smile. He was, after all, very nice, and not bad-looking either.

They didn't talk much for the first part of the journey. Nick was concentrating on the traffic and Sue deemed it safest to let him do so. When they finally left the city behind he turned to her with a grin. 'Well, at least we are out of London.'

'I'm lost in admiration,' Sue confessed. 'No way could I face driving in that lot.'

'Well, I suppose it is a bit different to Tasmania.'

'Different to New Zealand, too, I should imagine.'

'Somewhat – but at least we all drive on the same side of the road.'

'Where are we heading for?' Sue enquired. 'Have you a map?'

'There's an AA book in the glove pocket,' he told her, 'and at this precise moment we are *en route* for Windsor. We can stop there if you like.'

'Ooh, yes, please!' Sue pulled the AA book on to her lap and flipped through till she found the right page. 'We're nearly there,' she told him, quickly checking the place name of the village they had just passed through with its counterpart on the printed page.

'Can you read a map properly?'

'Of course I can!' Sue was indignant. 'I'm very good at it, as a matter of fact – I've done so much for Mum on both sides of the world. It's a total fallacy spread by men that women are incapable of reading maps.'

'I always knew you were more than just a pretty face!' He half turned towards her, grinning.

'Watch it!' Sue warned. 'If my life wasn't in your hands I should blip you on the head – hard!'

Sue was caught completely by surprise as they drove into Windsor and saw the castle. 'This is the heart of England.' She was embarrassed to be expressing such views, even more by the catch in her voice. Looking at Nick she was surprised to see his face shadowed by disappointment. 'At least I think so,' she added defiantly. 'Doesn't it come up to your expectations?'

'Oh, no – I mean yes – of course it does. It's just that I'd forgotten you were brought up in this country. You've probably been here dozens of times.'

'Not dozens, only once, and that was on a school outing – not nearly as much fun as being here with you, seeing your reaction.'

He smiled then. 'Well, I have to say I agree with you. When we colonials think about England this is one of the places that comes to mind, along with Buckingham Palace and Trafalgar Square. Let's park the car and walk, shall we?'

As they strolled round the old town, Sue found that what she had said to cheer Nick up was in fact true – this was much more fun than her last visit as a schoolgirl.'

'I rather like being a tourist,' she admitted, tucking her arm companionably into his. He responded by tucking his own arm in close so that she received a friendly squeeze.

Nick, Sue reflected, was good to be with, fun and emotionally undemanding. So far at least. Facing him across the cheerful checked cloth in the restaurant where they had chosen to eat she decided with conviction that she wanted to keep it that way. But would Nick?

'I thought you were hungry?' Nick watched her rearrange food on her plate.

'Oh, I was – I am,' she stammered, 'it's just that, well, maybe this is a mistake . . .' She trailed off unhappily, wondering if she had misled him, unwittingly allowed him to expect more from her than she was prepared to give.

He reached across the table and touched her hand. 'The ball is in your court,' he told her. 'I don't want you to do anything you don't feel happy about.' It wasn't strictly true: at that moment he wanted her very much indeed. But because he also liked her so much and truly valued her friendship, he certainly didn't want to rush her and risk losing her altogether.

'Thank you. Nick, I'm grateful.' And she was – wasn't she? She would not have to admit her lack of experience and the fact that she was still a virgin, something that made her feel slightly ashamed. No, ashamed was not the right word, it was more a feeling of rejection, of being insufficiently attractive to tempt anyone to remedy the situation. She repressed the stab of disappointment at his ready acceptance and smiled brightly. 'We'll book separate rooms for the night.'

Nick nodded glumly, thinking they might just as well have arranged to go to his relatives for the night where without a doubt separate rooms would have been allocated without question. On the other hand, while he certainly liked Sue immensely and found her sexually exciting, there was a cautious side of him that warned against too deep an involvement – with her or anyone.

'Where were you planning on spending tonight?' Sue asked as they finished their meal.

'Hadn't thought,' Nick answered, not entirely truthfully. He had given it a good deal of thought, though admittedly he had thought more of the bed than the location.

'Well, I'm tired, I don't know about you.' She yawned rather dramatically to emphasize this statement. 'Let's find somewhere in Windsor – after all, there should be more choice here – then get off in good time in the morning.'

They were given separate but adjoining rooms in the small hotel they settled on. It was adequate but not luxurious and certainly did not run to individual bathrooms – just two to each landing. Finding both unoccupied, they quickly laid claim to them. The dividing wall was so thin that each could hear the sound of the other's ablutions almost as clearly as their own. Sue found this faintly embarrassing; it was almost as if she were not really alone. For Nick it was an erotic experience, made the more so by the heady scent of the bath crystals Sue had flung generously into the water. At first he thought he must be imagining this but when he stretched out in the bath and looked up he saw the dividing wall did not reach the ceiling by several inches. They were virtually bathing in the same bathroom. What a thought! Dwelling on it, Nick felt the beginning of an erection. The combination of warm water, heady perfume wafting in over the badly fitted partition and the splashing sounds that told him Sue was also naked, and only a few feet away, quickened his breath and alerted every nerve in his body.

Sue was blissfully unaware that Nick was straining his ears to catch every sound and interpret it so that he knew just what stage she was at.

'Oh, hi!' He greeted her with elaborate casualness as he achieved his goal of emerging from the bathroom at exactly the same moment as Sue. 'Good bath?'

'Very good, thanks, nice hot water. I feel quite revived.' She smiled, hoping Nick wouldn't read some hidden innuendo into her words.

'Me, too. It seems too early to go to bed now. How about a nightcap?'

'I don't know – is this hotel licensed?' Sue was doubtful.

'Nope, but that's no problem – we folks from the Land of the Long White Cloud are very resourceful, you know, especially if we happen to have been boy scouts.'

'Were you? A boy scout, I mean?' Sue asked, seizing on this scrap of irrelevant information as a subconscious means of avoiding the real issue.

Nick grinned. 'No, but I am resourceful. Come into my room and find out.' He opened his door as he spoke and Sue followed him in, realizing as she did so that the satin kimono her mother had lent her when she left home was not exactly a complete cover-all, even if it did reach from throat to ankles. The wrap-around style had no fastening other than the tie belt, which she had pulled so tight the material moulded her breasts. If she lifted her arms high the wide sleeves revealed that she had nothing underneath, too big a step and the front gaped open. She was sure Nick was well aware of the shortcomings of the garment as a cover-all. As all this went through her mind Nick closed the door with a firm click.

Sue saw that the room was a mirror image of her own, and as she looked round, she realized Nick was looking at her. The glow flowing up her body was not unpleasant but she knew that it was already flooding her cheeks. Nick's eyes rested on the base of the V where the soft material crossed over her breasts. He took a step towards her. 'You invited me in here for a nightcap,' she reminded him.

He crossed quickly to his duffel bag thrown carelessly on the bed and with a flourish produced a bottle of wine.

'You're not very subtle, are you?' Sue smiled in spite of herself as his face fell. 'Lure me into taking my clothes off, persuade me to come to your room, then produce intoxicating liquor.' She looked round. 'What do we use for glasses?'

'Aah – now that's where my boy scout training shows!'

'You said you weren't a boy scout,' Sue reminded him, 'and anyway I doubt if they are trained to . . .' She trailed off, suddenly aware that the verbal badinage they were indulging in sounded very much like invitation and acceptance.

'How's that for forethought?' Nick demanded, flourishing a packet of paper cups triumphantly in front of her. 'And a corkscrew!' he told her as he dived once more in the depths of his bag.

Sue laughed as she flopped down in the only chair, revealing as she did so what Nick privately thought of as 'lengths and lengths of luscious leg'.

The cork came out of the bottle with a satisfactory pop and within minutes they were facing each other with raised paper cups.

They remained like this, frozen by confusion: what should they drink to?

'To us,' Nick mumbled tentatively, his words almost lost in Sue's over-hearty 'Bottoms up!' before she raised the cup to her lips and took a gulp.

Nick's paper cups were designed for lemonade, not wine, and they were soon halfway down the bottle and pleasantly relaxed. Sue was aware of a moistening between her legs and a strong urge to get closer to Nick, to touch him. Wine certainly did something to one's inhibitions, she mused, vaguely recalling something about it 'increasing the desire but reducing the ability'. She thought it was one of Shakespeare's gems. She looked across at Nick sitting on the opposite bed and hoped he was wrong, about the ability bit anyway. When he patted the bed invitingly with his free hand she got straight up and joined him.

'Sue!' His voice came out as a croak as he looked round for a parking place for the cup. Sue, with reckless abandon, drained hers and tossed the empty cup casually on the floor. With it went the last of her inhibitions and she turned into Nick's arms and lifted her face to his.

As his mouth found hers, she responded to the urge in her solar plexus to press her body close to his. As she did her lips parted, allowing his probing tongue to find hers. One hand slid inside the kimono and cupped her breast. Leaning into her, he pushed her back on the bed, his other hand riding up her thigh and pushing aside the soft slippery satin. As his fingers reached for her and tried to enter her she felt the last shred of her self-control dissolving in the exquisite sensation. It was this overriding sense of losing herself that drove her to push him away with all her strength and sit up.

'No . . . don't!' she cried, the surge of panic making her voice sharp, almost strident.

'What do you mean "don't"?' Nick demanded. 'You have been saying "do", "do", if not with your voice then certainly with your body. You can't do that sort of thing . . .' He was breathing heavily as he leaned towards her. 'I want you desperately. I need you – now. If you're worried, you don't have to be – I've come prepared . . .' He fumbled in his pocket for the condom he had put there. But if his words were designed to lull Sue into a sense of safety and security they failed miserably.

'You planned this, didn't you?' She leapt to her feet and pulled the kimono round her, retying the sash belt so vigorously that she gave an involuntary gasp of pain. 'You planned to – to *seduce* me, didn't you? Suppose I had . . . had got pregnant, what then?'

'You wouldn't, I came prepared,' he repeated, and took his hand out of his pocket with the condom, still in its wrapping, lying on his palm.

Sue glared at it, eyes round. 'That makes it worse!' she almost yelled at him. 'It proves you were intending to have your way with me. Well, you made a mistake – a big one. I'm not that kind of girl, and I didn't think you were that kind of boy either. I – I *liked* you!' By now she had reached the door and was yanking it open. 'At least we have separate rooms!' was her parting shot as she closed the door behind her, but not before she heard his reply.

'I liked you too. Now I think you're nothing more than a . . a cock tease!'

CHAPTER ELEVEN

F URIOUS and mortified, Sue nearly turned back. Then her sense of outraged virtue asserted itself. How could he be so crude? This self-righteous attitude upheld her long enough for her to slam and lock her door and crawl between the sheets. Then the tears, mostly of self-pity, welled up.

With masterly self-control she held them back till her jaws ached with the effort. She asked herself sternly where her backbone was, and what was there to weep about when she had behaved so well and Nick so badly. Finally she admitted that she didn't believe a word of her own pep talk and let the tears flow. What Nick had said was true, she had led him on, and she had wanted him, quite desperately. She didn't want to be whatever it was Nick had called her – nor did she want to spend her whole life a desiccated virgin carrying round a great load of sexual hang-ups. But there was no way she was going to crawl back to Nick tonight, however much she cared for him.

Lying wakeful in the strange bed, all too aware of Nick next door, she tried to understand herself. It was not fear of pregnancy, Nick had reassured her on that point. Was she afraid of no longer being desirable if she 'gave in'? Common sense told her that the old saw about men losing interest in a girl once they had sex with her didn't ring true. In her heart she didn't really believe that being a virgin was any big deal. Maybe she was just afraid of being trapped in an intimate and possibly lifelong relationship. She felt her mother's three marriages made her, Sue, something of an expert on the subject, if not from the inside then very nearly so. Each time her mother remarried her children's lives had undergone a radical change. Her mother, she reflected, was addicted to marriage, she didn't seem able to live without a husband. Yet Sue remembered those times when there had been no stepfather around as some of the best, certainly for Michael and herself, and even for her mother. She fell asleep wondering if she could explain all this to Nick.

Over a somewhat stilted breakfast Sue made one or two half-hearted attempts to summarize the thoughts that had kept her wakeful for so long the night before but gave up when each time Nick deftly changed the subject. Once they left the hotel behind things got back on an easier footing between them and she tried again. 'I really am sorry about last night – it wasn't you, or your fault. I – just—'

'Let's just forget it, shall we?' Nick cut her short. 'The golden rule in life is never complain and never explain. If you don't try and explain I promise not to complain, OK?'

Sue nodded. 'I suppose so,' she agreed doubtfully, but she still felt an urge to sort things out, not just for herself but to salve Nick's wounded male ego which she was sure must have suffered a bruising. But a quick sideways glance at his profile and she decided to study their route instead. Reaching for the map she asked, 'What did you say the name of the village was?'

'Appleton. Actually it's in Berkshire, not Oxfordshire. But we will go there via Oxford, City of Dreaming Spires and all that.'

'Appleton? Truly? It sounds more like something out of Enid Blyton than a real place.' Sue stole a quick sideways glance at Nick, hoping to see a return to his normal smiling good humour. He wasn't quite there yet, she decided. 'What is it like? The village, I mean?'

'I wouldn't know – this is my first visit.'

'Oh yes . . .' Of course, she had forgotten. Perhaps she had better keep quiet as her efforts at conversation seemed less than successful.

As they drove through the centre of Oxford, Nick's frown of concentration became a scowl. 'This could be any busy industrial city,' he complained. 'Not a spire, dreaming or otherwise, in sight.'

'Well, it *is* a busy industrial city,' Sue pointed out, 'and the spires often aren't too visible. They are up there in the rain clouds that hover over the place a lot of the time.'

'You sound very knowledgeable – been here before?'

'Mmm .. through it a few times,' she admitted.

'In that case there's no point in lingering,' Nick almost snapped.

Sue bit back the information she had just been about to impart about the location of the colleges and the fascinating second-hand bookshops. It seemed that everything she did or said chipped away at Nick's fragile good humour.

'I keep forgetting that you are a native of the place, not just a tourist like me,' he muttered peevishly.

Sue concentrated on giving him clear directions out of the city towards the village where his relations lived and tried not to think about what a fiasco this whole trip was turning out to be.

'Oh, Nick, what a lovely place! Look at the duck pond right in the middle of the village. It's like something out of a book!'

Her genuine delight was infectious, and Nick turned to her with something more like his normal cheery expression. 'It is. No wonder Uncle Edgar lives here even though he works in Oxford. I think we must be somewhere near their place – it's called Wyre Hall. I gather it's pretty old; seventeenth-century manor house or something.'

'Sounds very grand,' Sue murmured, suddenly doubtful. 'Oh look, what a lovely old house. Perhaps that is it – slow down, there's a name on the gate post.'

Sue leaned out of the window to see the lovely old stone house as Nick turned in to the short drive. It gave the impression of growing from the land around it rather than being built upon it, and as they drew to a halt a pale winter sun came out and gave the house a warm glow. At this time of the year it was naked but Sue could visualize it in late summer when the Virginia creeper that grew up one side of it and over the front door was at its glowing crimson best. It revived long-buried memories of the house where she had been born, memories that were an integral part of her recollections of the time, preserved as idyllic in her mind, when her father was alive. But the wartime years in that house had been happy too; then her mother remarried, and nothing had ever been quite as good again.

She jumped out of the car almost before Nick brought it to a halt outside the front door, which opened immediately to reveal a middle-aged couple with welcome written all over their smiling faces. What at first seemed a whole pack of dogs but which sorted out into two Labradors and a small hairy terrier hurtled towards Sue with such a vociferous welcome that she felt instantly at home.

'Nick, how lovely to see you!' The woman turned to Sue. 'And you, too . . .' She waited for a name to be supplied and Sue guessed that Nick had said merely that he was bringing 'a friend'.

'Oh, this is Sue. She comes from Tasmania – we came over on the same boat.' Nick, aware of his social obligations, explained.

'I'm Nick's Aunt Lillian, and this is my husband, Edgar.' She took Sue by the arm as she spoke. 'Come inside, dear, it's far too cold to stand here. I've hot coffee waiting. Now tell me,' she went on as she steered Sue through the front door, 'is Tasmania in New Zealand? Do you live near Nick?'

Sue smiled. 'No, its part of Australia,' she explained, wondering if her hostess was as ignorant as she made out or if her artless prattling was a good cover for curiosity.

'Tasmania is that little heart-shaped island at the bottom of Australia, Lil,' her husband explained. 'That's right, isn't it, Sue?'

'Yes.' Sue nodded. 'Actually, it's about the size of Scotland,' she felt constrained to add.

'Is that so? Tell me more about it. On paper it looks about the same as the Isle of Wight.' He waved her to a cheerful chintzy armchair close to the glowing log fire. The dogs were already sprawled on the hearth rug and Edgar had to pick his way over them to reach a similar chair on the other side of the hearth. He gave the impression that he really wanted to know.

'Maps can be deceptive. Sometimes they even forget to put Tasmania on at all!' she said smiling. 'It's a good deal further from mainland Australia than the Isle of Wight is from England – about 200 miles away, across the Bass Strait, an all-night crossing.' Sue looked up as Nick's aunt came in with a laden tray of coffee and caught Nick's eye. He was grinning so she shut her mouth quickly – she must sound like a lecturer delivering a travelogue. Edgar moved to help his wife with the coffee. Aware that she only knew them as Uncle Edgar and Aunt Lillian, Sue wished she had found out their surname from Nick.

She let her eyes rove round the room as she sipped her coffee. It was so similar to those she remembered from her childhood that she felt instantly and entirely at home. Even when her mother married again and they had left Wingates to live with Uncle Jock, it had been to a very similar house. Aware that Aunt Lilian was watching her silent appraisal with interest and some amusement, Sue smiled as their eyes met.

'I expect this is very different to what you are used to?' The inflection in Lillian's voice made it a question, not a statement. 'I suppose in a hot climate you live outdoors much more than we do.'

'I suppose we do spend more time out of doors, even though it isn't much warmer in Tasmania than here. I was actually thinking how much this house, and this room, reminded me of the places I lived in as a child.' Sue smiled, hoping her words would not be taken as criticism. 'I was in my early teens when we went to Australia, so I have actually spent more of my life here than there.'

'And which do you prefer?' Lillian stopped short. 'I'm sorry – that was a leading question. You don't have to answer.'

Sue smiled. She liked Nick's relations, very much, and felt that in spite of belonging to different generations she and the older woman were on the same wavelength. Like her, Sue often embarrassed herself by asking questions when it would probably be more polite not to. Andrew, her Tasmanian stepbrother, often told her she was an incurable Sticky Beak. The first time he called her that she had been puzzled and had to ask him what it meant. 'What you Poms would call a Nosey Parker,' he had explained. She remembered laughing and telling him that of the two she would rather be a Sticky Beak than a Nosey Parker. Now she considered the question that had been put to her with a sudden compulsion to answer as honestly as she could.

'If you had asked me that before I left Tassie I should have unhesitatingly said I preferred it there. Now I am here again I have to stop and think and my answer is probably quite different. When I left Tasmania I was "going somewhere", the sensation of "coming home" was totally unexpected. It was a surprise to find things so familiar.' She broke off, embarrassed and rather surprised by her own revelations. Nick, pausing in his conversation with his uncle, rescued her.

'Once a Pom, always a Pom!' His friendly grin robbed his words of any criticism. Sue smiled at him gratefully.

'I guess you're right,' she conceded.

'Would you like to see the rest of the house? And I expect you would like a wash and brush-up before lunch?' Lillian was stacking the coffee cups back on the tray as she spoke. 'I'll just pop these in the kitchen and see how lunch is going.' Her smile at Sue was an invitation to follow.

Sue was surprised to see a plump, middle-aged woman swathed in a cheerful floral apron bending over the open oven to baste the sizzling roast. Straightening up she looked with frank curiosity at Sue before saying, 'Everything is doing nicely, Mrs Beckworth, so when I've washed the coffee cups I'll be off. I've laid the dining-room table for you.'

Sue registered her hostess's name and smiled her gratitude at the woman for the information. She reminded her so much of Mrs

Evans, the kindly housekeeper who had been part of the household she was born into and so much an integral part of her formative years, that she had the strange feeling of being in a time warp. Lillian Beckworth's voice brought her back to the immediate moment. 'Thank you so much Mrs Green, I'm sure I can cope now. It was very good of you to come in today. This is a friend of my nephew – she's from Australia.'

'Best keep away from my boy Charlie, then. Mad keen he is to go to Australia, but I reckon he'd better stay here. It's a mighty long way to go and then wish you hadn't.' She smiled at Sue as she whipped the string of her apron undone, opened a door to a sort of closet and exchanged it for a heavy brown coat and a green beret which she rammed down firmly on her short grey hair.

'It is,' Sue agreed, thinking of the distance that separated her from her own family. She agreed with the sentiment expressed by Mrs Green but wasn't sure which way it applied to her. England was her birthplace and she felt at home here. She didn't regret coming back at all although she missed her family. With a small shock she realized that Lillian Beckworth was looking at her as if waiting for her to reply to something she had said.

'I'm sorry – I – I was . . .' she stammered.

'Miles away,' the older woman said smiling. 'I just have time to show you round before the lunch demands my attention – that is, of course, if you would like to see it?'

'Oh, yes, please!'

The whole house had a comfortable, lived-in appearance. It looked used, Sue thought, and this imparted something of an atmosphere.

'This is the bathroom.' Lillian opened a door off the landing to reveal a comfortable, if somewhat old-fashioned, bathroom. 'There is a cloakroom downstairs as well, but the men are probably using that. I've put a clean hand towel out for you here. Now I had better go and see to that roast. Come downstairs when you are ready – we'll have a glass of sherry before we eat.'

As the day drew on, Sue felt even more at home. When Lillian and Edgar both urged them to come again, and stay the night next time, she found herself assuring them they would, quite forgetting that they were actually Nick's relations and her coming again was dependent on him.

'Do drive carefully,' Lillian fussed as they got into the car. 'It's a long drive there and back in one day – you should have come yesterday and stayed the night.'

Sue smiled. Yes, she thought, they should.

CHAPTER TWELVE

S UE could feel Nick's withdrawal without turning to look at his face. Surely he still wasn't brooding about last night's fiasco?

'I liked your aunt and uncle very much.' Her tone was placatory.

'Yes. They liked you too,' Nick admitted after a pause so lengthy that Sue wondered if he were going to answer at all. He kept his eyes on the road ahead. 'In fact I would say you made quite a hit with them.'

Sue wondered how to reply; to say 'Yes' sounded smug, to deny it absurd. While she was still wondering, Nick spoke again. 'I'm sure my parents will be delighted.'

'Your parents? I don't see . . .' She trailed off, genuinely puzzled by his words and by his obvious disgruntlement.

'I can just see the letter Aunt Lillian will send to them. By the time she has finished writing about you she will have convinced herself that you and I have something serious going. By the time my mother has finished reading the letter she will have us married.'

Sue gave a short laugh, but inwardly she was stung. It was hardly flattering that the thought of marrying her, however remote, should plunge him into such gloom. She almost said something to that effect but checking herself in time merely remarked, 'But that is absurd. We're just good friends.'

'Of course. You made that perfectly clear last night.'

'Oh, Nick, don't be like that. I've said I am sorry. I – it wasn't really anything to do with you, it was me. I guess I've more hang-ups than I realize.'

'Never complain and never explain.' Nick repeated the advice he had given her the night before. The remark provoked in Sue a sudden burst of irritation.

'God, you are a smug, self-centred bastard!' The words burst from her before she could stop them. 'Your mother needn't worry – I wouldn't marry you if you were the only man on earth.'

'I never said she would be worried – quite the reverse. There is nothing she would like more than to see me married to a nice wholesome girl.'

'Oh, thanks – well, that rules me out, anyway. I'm not nice and as for being wholesome ... well, after last night I don't think I'm that either.'

Maddeningly, all her outburst produced from Nick was a shrug, a grin and a 'If you say so.'

The rest of the journey back to London seemed almost unbearably long, passed as it was in a silence broken only occasionally by stiff remarks about the route.

Outside her flat, Sue leapt out of the car almost before Nick pulled in at the kerb. She rushed round to the back, only to find that the boot was locked and she had to wait for him to unlock it. 'Thanks,' she mumbled ungraciously as she snatched her bag from him. 'And ... er ... thanks for the weekend,' she forced herself to add.

'I'll be in touch!' Nick called after her retreating figure.

'Don't bother!' Sue called back over her shoulder but her words were lost in the roar of the car accelerating.

Her mood was not improved when she pushed open the door and saw Angela sitting on her divan, mirror in one hand, mascara brush in the other, mouth slightly open as she concentrated on the all-important task of darkening her lashes. Her mouth dropped open even wider when she saw Sue. 'Oh – you're back.' she said.

'And you're still here.' Sue glowered. 'Isn't it about time you went back to Grandma?'

Angela pouted. 'Oh, Sue, surely I can stay a bit longer?' she pleaded. 'I didn't expect you back so soon.'

Sue glared round the tiny flat. Just about every previously exposed inch was now covered with Angela's paraphernalia, mostly frothy and frivolous bits of clothing. This, as far as Sue was concerned, was the last straw. 'No!' she yelled. 'You can't. Collect your things and pack up and go – now!'

'But Sue...' Tears glistened in the other girl's eyes. 'I'm going out – and anyway,' she added with a spark of defiance, 'you aren't the only one living here. It's Pixie's flat too and she said...'

Sue didn't want to hear what Pixie said – although knowing her soft-hearted friend she could guess – but it was true, she didn't have the only say on who was here and who wasn't. Suddenly she felt too depressed and too tired to argue any more. 'OK, you can stay till tomorrow – if you clear all this stuff off here.' She crossed to her bed and threw her bag down on it. 'Then back to Grandma.'

Alone after Angela had left with her date Sue stowed her clothes away with little care. She wondered where Pixie was – also out on a date she supposed. She prowled the tiny flat restlessly; it was barely eight o'clock, and she hadn't expected Nick to abandon her so early in the evening. She had imagined them having a meal together in one of the cosy little Italian restaurants they both loved. Gloomily she made herself a hot drink and a cheese sandwich, not because she was particularly hungry –the large lunch and lavish afternoon tea with Nick's relations had been more than filling – but it was something to do, something to take her mind off the uncomfortable thought that she had not behaved either well or in a mature manner over the weekend. If she hadn't liked the Beckworths so much she would have regretted ever going.

She listened to the nine o'clock news on the radio, depressing as usual, then, still alone, decided to take herself and her disgruntled thoughts to bed with a good book. But the book wasn't as good as promised; it failed to divert her thoughts from her own problems. She felt really bad about Nick, and tried to console herself with the reminder that she never actually promised anything. It didn't work – she liked him too much and really enjoyed his company. She didn't want to face the alternative. Instead she reminded herself that a girl had every right to give or withhold according to her feelings at the time.

In spite of herself, she dropped off to sleep and didn't see the others until they were all scrambling to get off to work the next morning. She extracted a promise from Angela that she would have her stuff cleared out and be gone by the time she came home from work. Catching Pixie's eye, she had the feeling that her friend thought she was being hard. Too bad, she thought, and hurried to catch the tube.

For the first time since she had begun to work there, the rarefied atmosphere of the gallery failed to charm her. She made mistakes in her accounting and Edwina Mancini picked her up with a sharpness she felt was unwarranted. Tired and dispirited she glanced at the clock: thank heavens, only another ten minutes to go. It was the first time she had eagerly counted the minutes till it was time to pack up for the day.

Sue was already shrugging into her outdoor things when she heard David's voice in the gallery. She paused, coat half on and half off, wondering if he would come into the office, aware that her heart was thudding. When he pushed open the door, however, she greeted him casually. 'Oh, hello, I thought you were in wildest Wales.'

'No, I postponed it.'

'Oh?' The monosyllable came out as a question in spite of herself.

'I hoped you might be free this coming weekend and would like to make the trip to see Nanny?'

'I – yes – I – I would love to see her. I've been feeling a bit guilty – I haven't been for ages. But the train journey . . .' Sue stopped, feeling embarrassed. She was stammering and burbling, and she felt her cheeks flushing. She avoided looking directly at David.

'I would appreciate your company. It's a helluva long journey to take alone. How was your weekend? Good, I hope?'

'Oh, yes, thank you. Very good,' Sue answered primly. She waited, hoping David was going to suggest a meeting before the weekend, but all he said was, 'Fine. I'll be in touch before the weekend. I'm sure Nanny will be delighted to see you and she will be pleased to have plenty of notice of your coming.' With a brief goodbye he was gone, leaving Sue with a vague sense of irritation at his implied instruction to let Nanny know at once that she was coming. It was unnecessary – she knew the old lady liked plenty of warning, just as she knew how pleased she would be to have her.

Later in the week David stuck his head round the office door to tell her that he would pick her up at eight on Saturday morning. Sue tried not to think of Nick, whose absence and silence had been obvious enough for Pixie to ask, 'Is everything all right between you and Nick?' somewhat tentatively on Thursday evening. Pixie liked him, and thought he and Sue ideally suited. 'You haven't broken up or anything, have you?'

'No, of course not,' Sue snapped. Pixie had touched a tender spot; shafts of remorse were still needling at odd moments.

'Well, I haven't seen hair nor hide of him since the weekend.'

'He's probably busy.'

'Did you quarrel when you were away together, or were his relations so utterly horrific you simply couldn't bear to see him again?' Pixie's voice was casual but the quick glance she shot at Sue was keen.

'They were really nice – lovely people – and the house was beautiful and the village they live in is like something out of a book—'

'You quarrelled,' Pixie interrupted. 'What about?' she went on inexorably.

'I told you we didn't,' Sue lied, 'and if we did I wouldn't tell you what it was about.'

106

' 'Course you did.' Pixie was not fooled. 'Why don't you tell Auntie all about it?'

'I've told you we didn't, and I'm not telling you anything – so – so mind your own business!' Sue hurled a cushion across the room at Pixie, who fielded it deftly, rolled her eyes and murmured something about 'the lady doth protest too much' before throwing it back. 'OK, I'll shut up for now, but if you do want to talk . . .' Pixie could see that Sue was beginning to look genuinely upset so contented herself with knowing that her supposition had been correct, and hoped they would have the good sense to make it up. 'How about you and I go to the cinema on Saturday? It just so happens I haven't got a date so we could console each other.'

'Oh, Pixie, I'd love to but I've promised to go and visit Nanny this weekend. It's ages since I've been and . . . and . . .' Her voice tailed off.

'And what?'

'Well, David has offered me a lift.' Sue sounded defiant. Pixie didn't like her seeing David, she thought he was too old for her. It had been a mistake telling her that when she first knew him as a child he had been in love with her mother, as Pixie had immediately said that he was only interested in her as a way back to her mother. When Sue said she didn't think that was true Pixie had retorted that he must be seeing her as a substitute for her mother – and that was worse.

'I see,' Pixie said quietly. Sue was surprised, and relieved, that she didn't heap more good advice on her. 'Well, be careful – remember he is old enough to be your father and don't let him side-track you with any waffle.'

This made Sue smile. Whatever David did or said, he never waffled.

Sue was looking forward to going to Borth-y-Gest to visit Nanny. It would be a treat too to travel by car instead of embarking on that long and tedious rail journey. She was also, though she dismissed this as very secondary, looking forward to David's company.

She felt a frisson of excitement as she took her place in the passenger seat. David was really very attractive and success had given him an aura that had been lacking, or she had not been aware of, in the old days. Not for the first time the thought slid through her consciousness that this was the man her mother should have chosen. But then, she reflected, Mum was staid and conservative; she could never have gone into a relationship where marriage was out of the question. When it came to choosing men she went for safety, not romance. Not that it always worked out that way: Mum's second marriage had hardly turned out a sinecure yet they had known one another just about for ever. She wondered how her mother could have been so naïve as not to realize that her second stepfather was a pansy. She shuddered slightly as she remembered him. Things hadn't been so bad at first, but the rapid downhill run had started when she and Michael reached puberty. He had made no attempt to hide his dislike of her then. As far as her brother was concerned, she reflected now with the wisdom of several years' distance, he probably liked him too much.

'Mmm ... sorry?' Sue turned to her companion. They had left the city behind; she must have been lost in her daydream for quite a while. 'Sorry, Davey, what did you say?'

'I was just asking about your mother. Have you heard from her recently?'

'She writes every week.'

'Is that a bad thing?' David wondered at the faint note of criticism in Sue's voice.

'No, it's just that a week isn't long enough for a letter to get here, an answer to be written and get back, so we are always sort of answering one letter behind, if you see what I mean. It doesn't make for a smooth conversational flow in our correspondence.'

'Yes, I see what you mean. Have you thought of leaving a longer time between receiving a letter and replying? That might be better.'

'It might,' Sue said doubtfully.

'You still haven't told me how she is.'

'Oh, she's fine. She loves Tasmania.'

'Does she still paint?'

Sue frowned slightly and shook her head. 'She's too busy being a farmer's wife.'

'That's a pity. She was very good in her field.' Sue looked at him sharply. Was there a hint of superiority in his tone? She found herself bridling on her mother's behalf.

'She was. And she earned good money from it at a time when we needed it. But Tom never really took her painting seriously. To him it was a "nice little hobby" and, as I said, she is so busy now.' Out of the blue she felt a twinge of guilt for her desertion of her mother.

As if he had picked up her thoughts, David said, 'She must miss you: I liked to see you together – you always seemed good friends, more like sisters than mother and daughter.'

Sue glanced at him in surprise – how perceptive he was. The thought once more flitted through her mind that her mother had been a fool. If it had been her . . .

'That's probably because she was pretty young when I was born and it was Nanny who did the mothering of me, not her. We have our clashes, but yes, we do get on pretty well these days.'

They stopped just inside the Welsh border for lunch. David hadn't mentioned her mother again but they seemed to find plenty to talk about. She asked him where he went to paint.

'France mostly. Sometimes Italy, occasionally Spain. But I go where the spirit moves me, and it usually seems to move me to France.'

'Any particular area?'

'Yes, northern France mostly. I expect it's my Celtic blood – I feel at home there. Normandy, Brittany, Cornwall, Wales: all much the same, just divided by bits of water.'

'That's a refreshing view of geography.'

'Not so much geography as history, I suspect. Whatever – we are all Celts. I have heard it said that a Breton can understand a Cornishman.'

'So that's where most of your paintings originate?' Sue said thoughtfully, but as she spoke it wasn't his colourful landscapes that she was thinking about but the painting of her mother that held pride of place in the gallery. As she looked at the man sitting across the table from her she was pierced by a sharp and totally unexpected stab of jealousy and vowed to try and keep the conversation off her mother for the remainder of their journey together.

She needn't have worried; David seemed no more anxious to harp on the past than she was. She listened to his voice with its lilting Welsh accent with intense pleasure. It held so much music for her that it didn't really matter what he was actually saying and more than once she had to collect herself and ask him to repeat something he had said.

The journey came to an end all too soon and he was drawing the car up at the gate to Nanny's cottage. 'I'm going back tomorrow afternoon so if you would like a ride home?' He had intended to stay at least a week and was surprised to hear himself make the offer, but he knew that if Sue wanted to keep her job at the gallery she would need to be there on Monday morning. Cursing himself for his quixotic offer, he hoped she would turn it down.

Her face lit up. 'Honestly, Davey? I thought you planned on staying longer but yes, please, I would really appreciate a lift back. Will you come in and see Nanny?'

He shook his head. 'Not today – besides, she'll be longing to get you to herself. I'll see her tomorrow when I pick you up. Mid-afternoon sometime.' He pulled the car door shut and drove away. Sue still had her hand raised in farewell when the door opened behind her.

Sue caught her breath as she turned to the house. 'You made me jump,' she explained quickly, before Nanny guessed that it was she herself that had caused the quick intake of breath. There only seemed about half as much of her, Sue thought; she had both shrunk and aged in the weeks since she had last visited. She forced a bright smile and quickly stepped forward to give the old woman a hug, conscious of her frailty. Where was the sturdy, buxom Nanny who had so often hugged her?

Inside, even the cottage felt different. Less full. Sue looked round. Where was Nanny's sister?

'I'm on my own now, dear,' the old lady explained as she closed the door behind them. She sighed. 'My sister is in a Home. I felt badly letting her go, but I just couldn't cope any longer. She kept wandering off and people had to look for her.'

Sue, remembering the taciturn old lady with a Zimmer frame she had seen on her last visit, wondered how on earth she had managed to wander anywhere out of Nanny's orbit. As children, it was something she and Michael had found almost impossible. But Nanny, while not using a frame, now walked slowly and with the aid of a stick. She knew she should have come sooner and more often. To her dismay, she found that her guilt gave way to impatience, even irritation, as the long evening wore on. Nanny was very deaf, or forgetful, or a mixture of both, and kept asking her to repeat things. She stubbornly refused help and Sue found it agonizing being forced to sit and watch her struggle with preparations for a meal. Unable to bear being an idle guest any longer, she insisted on clearing away and washing up.

Afterwards Nanny produced her treasured photograph albums and led Sue in a long slow walk down memory lane. Stifling a yawn, she thought about David and wondered what he was doing.

She soon found herself climbing the narrow twisting staircase to the bedroom she had occupied on every visit, leaving Nanny pottering about downstairs. The tide was in and the sound of the sea breaking rhythmically on the beach across the road soon lulled her to sleep.

CHAPTER THIRTEEN

ONE of the best things about barbecues, Stevie reflected, as she laid out plates, salads, bread rolls and the ubiquitous tomato sauce, was that it was about the only time men did the cooking. Probably because cooking barbecues was not like real cooking – another case of 'men and their toys'. Whatever, she wasn't about to argue, and flopping into a beach chair she sipped gratefully at a cold beer. Only one thing marred the perfection of this moment – the absence of her two older children. Thinking about Sue, she felt a shaft of irritation with her daughter for being so sparse with her information – merely writing that she had run into Davey and he was quite successful these days. She wanted to know what 'quite successful' really meant, and was he still teaching, and what about his wife?

'Come and get it, folks!' Andrew called, bringing her back swiftly to the here and now. She was as ready for it as anyone else, she realized, as she jumped up to help the boys get started. When Tom smiled into her eyes over the steak he had just dropped on to her plate, she smiled back. 'Just as I like it – well done,' she approved, and David Jones was forgotten as she dipped the servers into the big bowl of salad.

How very little time they had on their own, Andrew thought, when he saw the glance that passed between his father and step-mother. Recalling the warm welcome Stevie had always given him in those far-off boarding school days in England, he felt a rush of affection and concern for her.

'Why don't you two take a stroll along the beach in the moonlight?' he offered impulsively. 'I'll see the boys into bed.'

Stevie's face lit up momentarily. 'But what about you? Don't you want to go out somewhere?' she said vaguely, wondering where there was to go round here.

Andrew grinned. 'I'll give you half an hour – three quarters maximum – then when you get back I'll head off and explore the nightlife of Devonport or whatever.'

Stevie smiled her thanks, and thought again how blessed she was in her stepson. It was fresh and cool on the beach, the air coming off the sea bringing with it a tang of seaweed. Stevie took a deep breath, grateful for the cardigan she had thrown round her shoulders. 'I just love the smell of the sea.' She sighed as she slid her hand into that of her husband.

Tom glanced sideways at her. When Andrew made the suggestion, his 'moonlit beach' seemed poetic licence, but now in the fading light Stevie looked both young and vulnerable and he felt a wave of tenderness not unmingled with guilt. It can't have been easy for her coming out here to a new country, especially when Brian and Barney were born less than a year after they arrived in Tasmania. Delightful though they were, most of the time, they had certainly done nothing to make life easy for Stevie. His memory flashed back to those days just before the war when he had first gone back to England. What a shock it had been to find his childhood friend married to a man old enough to be her father.

He had taken the job looking after their horses because he needed money. He hadn't expected, or intended, to fall in love with Stevie. Remembering those days when no one, least of all her husband, had expected her to do anything that might be classed as work, he mentally took his hat off to the capable person she had become. He was glad they had this holiday place, she deserved it. He stood still and pulled her round to face him, then drew her close against his body and bent his head towards her upturned face. Andrew's promised moonlight shone now on her hair so that it appeared the pale ash blonde he remembered. The silver hairs among the gold helped the illusion.

'Let's go back,' he murmured against her cheek as they drew apart from a kiss that would have done credit to lovers half their age.

'Yes . . .' But she made no move away from the circle of his arms. 'I think we have had our allotted thirty minutes. I hope the boys have behaved with Andrew,' she added, the thought bringing her back to everyday life so that now she did turn out of his arms and head back to the cottage.

They found the twins in bed and Andrew singing lustily, if not very tunefully, in the shower as he readied himself to sample whatever nightlife Devonport had to offer.

'Don't wait up for me,' he told them with a grin as he left some fifteen minutes later. Tom assured him he had no intention of doing so, and the timbre in his voice caused Stevie to experience an unexpected and almost forgotten flutter of pleasurable anticipation.

She was not disappointed. Their lovemaking was slow and unhurried and deeply satisfying. As she drifted off to sleep, Stevie felt cocooned, not only by Tom's arm round her but by the walls of the little holiday home temporarily keeping at bay the hassles and worries of everyday life.

By the afternoon of the next day the spell, along with the weather, began to break and Stevie could see that Tom's thoughts were back on the home property, his everyday worries beginning to intrude. Looking at the lowering sky she reluctantly agreed there was little point in prolonging their stay and began packing up, a task which, minus the pleasurable anticipation of the previous day, seemed much more onerous.

Driving home through the fertile farmlands of the north-west coast, Stevie reflected that this area was well designated the 'vegetable garden of Australia'. The rich red soil grew some of the finest potatoes in the world and the canning factories were hard put to coping with the truckloads of peas streaming in from the farms, leaving behind them a trail of dropped vines which following motorists collected. Stevie had been brought up in the country among farming communities, but this was something quite new.

She sometimes reflected with gratitude on the war years that had forced her into a more hands-on approach to farm life. They stood her in good stead now. She certainly would never have been able to cope had she come straight from her pre-war life as Martin's wife. Domestic help had been plentiful then and her most onerous duties had been arranging flowers and exercising the horses. Recalling that only falling pregnant with Sue had stopped her walking out of her comfortable home and secure marriage to come here with Tom so long ago made her think that maybe the fates, or 'someone up there', had known what was best. Looking back she certainly had no regrets: not only had she Sue but Michael as well, and here she was in Tasmania with Tom after all.

Thinking of Sue, she wondered how her weekend had gone. She had written something about going with the boy she met on the boat to visit his family. In her day that would have meant their relationship was serious, but since the war things had changed and everything was more casual and relaxed these days. She sighed as the car turned off the sealed road on to the rough laneway that led to their property and began to think of tonight's meal instead.

CHAPTER FOURTEEN

SUE slept late after the long car journey. She shivered as she drew back the curtains and was almost tempted to crawl back between the sheets but it was already a few minutes past nine. Sea and sky were a uniform grey and the horizon had vanished in sea mist. She shivered again before dressing as quickly as she could, her mind on the warmth downstairs rather than the chill here in her room.

It was little, if any, warmer downstairs; the fire in the open grate had gone out and not yet been relit. It was very quiet. Sue was surprised not to find Nanny pottering about her kitchen getting breakfast, a habitual early riser, she must be sleeping in for once. She filled and switched on the electric kettle before dealing with the fire, smiling to herself as she thought of surprising the old lady with a warm room and a cup of tea. Searching for paper and kindling Sue headed for the scullery, and stopped short with a horrified gasp. 'Nanny!'

The old lady was sprawled out on the flagstone floor. 'Nanny . . .' Sue repeated, dropping to her knees by her. Tentatively she reached out a finger and touched her cheek. It felt cold and clammy. Stuffing her hand into her mouth to stifle the scream she could feel rising in her throat, Sue scrambled to her feet. She was shaking uncontrollably, and not just from cold.

'No! Oh no!' Even as the exclamation burst from her lips in a hoarse rasp she knew her protestations were useless. Nanny had died alone while Sue had slept secure in a warm bed, listening to the lullaby of the sea. Inevitably guilt kicked in as she recalled her inner impatience the previous evening, watching the old lady with her precious photographs. She clapped her hand over the one already covering her mouth as if to keep her rising panic under control. Her wild thoughts flew from her mother, too far away to be of practical help, to Davey right here in the village.

She was unaware of the clammy mist that enveloped her as she ran, gasping for breath, up the rough hillside path leading to David's cottage. She called his name in harsh rasping sobs, barely recognizing the sound as coming from herself, as her fists thudded on the door. She was sobbing incoherently when the door opened and, propelled by the momentum of her actions, she was caught by strong male arms.

'It's Nanny!' She sucked in her breath on a gasp. 'She is – I think she is dead.' Even in the hysteria of the moment she knew there was no doubt.

'Hold on!' he shouted, loosing his grip suddenly so that she had to grab the door frame for support. Seconds later he was back and she realized he had only turned away to collect his car keys. 'Get in,' he rapped as he pushed her towards the vehicle. In one fluid movement he was in beside her and the engine sprang to life. Sue burst into tears of sheer relief that the responsibility had been shifted as they sped back through the village.

One look at the prone figure and Davey knew there was nothing he could do to help her. He turned to Sue, whose teeth were chattering with damp and shock. 'Go and get some dry clothes on. I'll make a cup of tea.' He looked round. 'Did she have a phone? I'll have to. . . .'

Sue looked vague for a moment. The phone, of course – she had forgotten about its existence in her shock and panic. She need not have run wildly through the damp morning. 'Yes – in the kitchen.'

As she stumbled upstairs in search of warm, dry clothes, she heard David explaining the situation to someone and giving the address.

The rest of the day passed in a nightmare blur. The police and the doctor turned up together. 'Her heart was in a bad way,' the latter explained as he signed the death certificate without demur. 'I've been expecting something like this for ages. She shouldn't have been here on her own . . .' At this point he looked somewhat reproachfully from Sue to David and back to Sue, unsure of their connection with the old lady. 'She insisted she must keep the home going for her sister . . .' He shrugged. 'I tried to tell her there was little likelihood of her returning . . . She is quite . . .' Another shrug and another unfinished sentence. Sue thought him cold and unfeeling and his habit of leaving his remarks in mid-air grated on her. But his words reminded her that Nanny did have a sister some-where. She would need to be told what had happened.

'Can you tell me where her sister is?' she asked the doctor.

'In the workhouse.' His reply this time was succinct. Sue gasped at the Dickensian word. The doctor permitted himself a thin smile at her reaction. 'They don't call it that now – it's known as Garth Martin, the old people's home, but that is what it is.'

Telling Nanny's sister proved to be another ordeal. Sue thought she had little or no idea who she was, where she was, or even that she had a sister. When the frail old woman snatched her hand with a grip that astonished her by its strength and intensity and screeched into her face, 'You're her little Sue – she loved you!', she instinctively pulled free, eyes stinging, throat aching.

David's moral support and practical assistance upheld her over the next couple of days. He ferreted out Nanny's few relatives, most of them distant in every way, and when no one else seemed willing to do it, he organized the funeral. He left Sue to call her mother in Tasmania while he gave the cottage a quick once over. 'Better leave it spruce for whoever among her "nearest and dearest" inherits it,' he told her as he pulled an ancient vacuum out from the recess under the stairs.

The thought of having a legitimate excuse to talk with Stevie almost tempted him to suggest reversing the chores, but he was not into masochism. So Sue called home herself.

'Davey has been wonderful – I can't imagine what I would have done without him.' The words spilled from her, followed by such a long pause from the other end that she asked anxiously, 'Mum? Are you still there, Mum?'

'I'm still here – just wondering how David Jones came to have anything to do with it?'

'He was at his cottage. I didn't know anyone else to go to ... I wish you had been here, Mum. It – it was awful!' Her voice broke, then she gulped and added, 'I should have come more often. I feel really bad about it.'

'I wish I had been there too. If only I could have come back – brought the twins – seen her again.' There was a pause, then she added, almost to herself, 'She was so much a part of my life I feel ...' Sue guessed she found the words hard to find but after a brief pause she said briskly, 'Thank you for letting me know. Bye, darling.' As she lowered the receiver, Sue imagined she heard her mother add softly, 'Give my regards to Davey.'

She turned to David. 'Mum sent her regards to you.' She thought he hadn't heard and began to repeat the message.

'Yes. I heard you.' His voice was curt but softened as he added 'I expect you want to stay on for the funeral?'

Sue looked at him in surprise. She hadn't thought that was in question. It was arranged for the next day but one.

'But of course you do,' he answered for her. 'I would stay, but I have to be back in London.'

'You have done more than enough. I can't tell you how grateful I am. I have no idea how I would have managed without you. There's really no need for you to stay.' Brave words, but in her heart Sue felt the full weight of her bereavement and her aloneness.

She had a vague idea that the family was expected to feed those who attended funerals. As far as Nanny's family went it seemed she was almost it. Certainly no one had come forward with any offers of help with arrangements or catering. She decided the best thing would be to ask at the café if they could help with some light refreshments. 'Thanks for everything, David. Have a good trip home and please – if you see her – tell Edwina I will be back in a couple of days.' She had already telephoned to explain why she would be away from the gallery.

'You'd have coped if I hadn't been here,' he assured her, retreating back.

Tears pricked her eyes and her throat ached. She told herself she was being silly, she couldn't expect Davey to continue wet-nursing her. All the same she felt deserted. She couldn't really blame him; she had leaned on him so much since the awful discovery of Nanny's body. If only, she thought yet again, if only her mother had been here.

Sue turned away from the grave momentarily, blinded by a shaft of sunlight that pierced the clouds and caught the tears shimmering in her eyes. She put up her hand and brushed at her lashes then stopped in astonishment. David was standing on the periphery of the small band of mourners staring at her. She stared back, wondering if he was an apparition.

'What made you come back so soon?' she wanted to know as David turned the car inland away from the sea.

'I never left,' he admitted, half turning to her with a rather shamefaced smile.

'Oh, I see.' Sue's voice was tight.

'No, you don't, you don't see at all. People always say that when they haven't a clue.'

'All right then, I don't see;' she snapped. 'Explain.' Physically tired and emotionally drained, the last few days had certainly not proved the pleasant little break she had envisaged when she left London. Sue was in no mood to play mind games, or, she told herself, to be treated like a child, even if he wanted to behave like a school teacher.

Her words fell into a silence that lasted so long that she wondered if he intended to answer, even if he had heard. Well, she was too exhausted to care, so she leaned back and closed her eyes. When he said, 'I changed my mind. Men are allowed to do that as well as women,' she could only give a non-committal grunt in reply.

He stole a glance at her, she looked young and defenceless as well as exhausted, and somehow very like her mother as he remembered her. How could he explain to her his sudden need to distance himself from emotional involvement? He had never had any intention of abandoning her, but she had touched something inside him, and he was afraid of falling in love with her, just as he had with her mother years ago. Even more afraid that he was simply reigniting his feelings for Stevie. If that were so it could only bring heartache to both of them. Remembering how he had felt then, forced to stand by and watch her choose another man and go out of his life, he had fought shy of deep emotional involvement ever since – with anyone.

All this and more went through his mind as he searched for the right words. A soft whistling sigh escaped Sue and he shot another glance at her and saw he needn't bother: she was asleep.

Sue stirred when he pulled the car into the parking lot. After a few moments she opened her eyes and sat upright, looking round her.

'Sorry if I woke you. I need a break, something to eat, something to drink, stretch my legs, men's room.' He tagged on the last with a wry grin.

Sue stretched and yawned 'Me too,' she admitted. 'Well, perhaps not the men's room. I'll settle for the ladies. Have I been asleep long?'

'Quite a while – we're about halfway back to London.' He was out of the car by now and opening the passenger door. 'Come on – let's see what this place has to offer. I guess we've missed lunch but a pot of tea and a bun would go down nicely.'

'Aah, I feel better now,' Sue sighed as she took her place once more beside him in the car. The little town had come up with all their requirements and the tearooms they found had produced hot buttered tea-cakes, sandwiches, a plate of homemade cakes and a huge pot of tea. 'That will last me till breakfast!'

'That's a pity,' David remarked as he settled into the driving seat and turned on the ignition. 'I was planning to take you out to dinner when we got back to London. But there really isn't much point if you won't want anything to eat.'

'I guess I could probably manage something by then.' Sue half turned towards him as she spoke and to her surprise met his eyes as he glanced at her. She gave a quick intake of breath and hoped she was smiling, not treating him to what felt like a 'goofy grin'. She had been totally unprepared for the physical reaction that the brief eye contact sparked. It was as if a tiny electric shock rippled through her entire being and for a brief moment everything about and around David and the immediate interior of the car glowed. As she blinked and turned away, the world swung back to normal. She had never felt the magnetic pull of physical attraction so strongly before.

Looking at him across the small table in the womblike atmosphere of the restaurant David had chosen, Sue guessed the charges would be as high as the lights were low. She was awkwardly aware of an intensity in their relationship. It stemmed from that odd moment in the car, and she wasn't sure she welcomed it. Yet at the same time she knew that nothing had really changed. She had always thought him attractive, always liked him, and never quite understood why her mother chose Tom. With a flash of insight she decided that what Stevie had really chosen was marriage and security, things Davey was in no position to offer in those days, already married and just one of many unknown artists. Looking up from the menu, Sue saw that he was looking at her in a way she would have sold her soul for as a pubescent teenager.

David, for his part, was wondering why it had taken him so long to realize that Sue was no longer just the child of the woman he had once cared for. Even when he had played the white knight and gone to her rescue back there in Wales, it had been primarily because she was Stevie's daughter. The affection he had felt for Sue all those years back and his liking for the old woman they called Nanny had come into it, but he had still done it primarily with Stevie in his thoughts. He had wanted to snatch the phone from Sue and talk to her, had even felt noble for resisting the urge; now, confronted with this new, beautiful grown up Sue, with her sudden flashes of uncanny likeness to her mother, he wasn't sure of anything any more.

Sue glanced up from the menu she was studying to find him looking at her with a curious intensity.

'Have I a smudge on my nose or something?'

'No, of course not – you look quite lovely . . . I was thinking I would like to paint you.'

'Oh.' Sue was astonished; she had never seen herself as a possible artist's model. 'I doubt a painting of me would bring you the same kudos as the one you did of my mother.' She tossed down the menu. 'Oh, I don't know what to have. You choose for me,' she said petulantly.

'Meat or fish?' David asked.

Sue, wondering what it would be like to pose for Davey, was momentarily confused. She shrugged, indicating her indifference, and he picked up their conversation where it had been interrupted.

'I painted your mother because she has a classical, timeless kind of beauty. I want to paint you for other reasons.'

'Are you saying I'm not a beauty like my mother? Well, you can save your breath – I already know that.'

'That is not what I said at all, and if it sounded like it, then I'm sorry.' He wanted to tell her to stop behaving like an adolescent, but the waitress hovered patiently, pencil poised over her pad for their order. He looked up at the girl. 'We are having a bit of trouble coming to a decision. What would you recommend?'

She didn't bother to look at the menu, just leaned slightly forward and said in a low, confidential voice, 'Well, sir, the roast beef is very good. I wouldn't have the chicken or the fish.' As she straightened up she flashed David a slightly guilty smile, as if the two of them were conspirators. Sue saw her tongue flick out quickly over her lips and noticed her colour heighten slightly. She felt her own lips stiffen and was annoyed with herself for this momentary stab of jealousy. What an ugly word for such a transient emotion, but when with feigned indifference she looked round at the other diners she had to admit that there was no one else in the room who had one iota of the sex appeal of her companion.

Turning her attention back to David, she saw a flicker of amusement in his eyes. Damn the man, he seemed capable of reading her every thought. 'You were about to tell me why you wanted to paint me,' she reminded him.

'You have an interesting face.'

'Oh, thanks, that's really flattering.'

'Actually it is, so there is no need for that tone of voice. Your face is alive, interesting, full of character. Most girls your age are just blandly pretty. They do not have half your attraction.'

'Oh.' Sue felt her response was totally inadequate. Had he really said he found her attractive? She dropped her eyes, flicking her tongue over suddenly dry lips, aware that she was behaving in just the same way as the waitress had a few moments earlier. Was this how all women responded to David? Had her mother felt the same way all those years ago?

The arrival of the wine waiter with an interesting-looking bottle distracted them both. When the two men had gone through the required ritual of tasting, nodding sagely and pouring, she raised her glass to him.

He responded with a similar gesture. 'To whom or to what are we drinking?' he asked with a smile.

Sue shrugged; she hadn't thought. 'How about to you and your career?'

'And you and yours? Shall we just say to us?'

Once more Sue found she could not think of a response so she simply raised her glass and drank. The toast sounded so intimate, almost suggestive, that she found it difficult to actually verbalize. She was saved by the arrival of their first course.

In spite of her protest that after the huge afternoon tea she would be unable to eat anything, Sue found she was hungry, and the roast beef was, as the waitress had promised, excellent.

David glanced across the table with approval. He hated taking a woman out for a meal only to be informed that she was on a diet. In his book good food was one of the pleasures of life and definitely to be enjoyed. Sue obviously subscribed to the same belief, he thought. For a fleeting instant he remembered her mother, she had been older than Sue was now when he first met her, yet in some ways there was a curious innocence about her so that she seemed younger. He dismissed the memory. The stirring in his loins now was nothing to do with the woman he had once been in love with and everything to do with her daughter.

CHAPTER FIFTEEN

WHEN David dropped her off at her flat he rested his hands on her shoulders, looked into her face and kissed her lightly on the cheek. It was an avuncular rather than romantic gesture, deliberately so. The moment when they had each raised their glass in a toast to the other had been charged with emotion, and desire, swift and fierce, had flared between them. It was a flame he did not wish to fan. He liked Sue and tonight he had seen her for what she was – a sexually attractive young woman. He knew too that she was drawn to him. But he had loved her mother, and that made the very thought of a sexual relationship with Sue out of the question.

Sue watched him climb back into his car after lifting her bag from the boot. He refused her offer of coffee, and got quickly back into the driver's seat. She watched his tail-lights disappear then with a sigh turned to her own door. She felt that a watershed had been reached in their relationship, and wasn't sure if it was a good thing. The status quo had been pleasant and safe.

'Hello, there, you're back then?' Pixie looked up from the book she was reading to state the obvious. When Sue raked the room for any sign of Angela, she added, 'Don't worry, she's gone. I told her that if you came back and found her still here I wouldn't be responsible for the consequences.'

'Good . . .' Sue smiled in relief, but at the same time she felt a twinge of guilt even though their small two-person flat was definitely over-crowded with three, especially when one was Angela.

'Actually I think she was quite relieved to be able to return to the luxury of life with Grandma without losing face.' Pixie grinned and ran her hands absently through her hair, which had obviously just been shampooed. She was wearing a towelling robe at least two sizes too large. 'What about you? I expected you to stagger in looking limp and wan after your harrowing week – instead you are positively glowing. How did you get back, anyway? You *would* be limp and wan if you had come by train.'

'I . . . I had a lift,' Sue explained hesitantly. Pixie was all too perspicacious at times and she didn't want to talk about David.

'Don't tell me – I can guess. The painter chap, your mother's old flame.'

'Yes, I did come with him, and he is not my mother's old flame.'

'He was last time you mentioned him . . .' Pixie could be very aggravating at times, Sue thought. 'Well, he has certainly made you look all candle-eyes. You didn't look like that when you came back from your naughty night with Nick.'

'It was not a naughty night – far from it,' Sue snapped, hurling a cushion across the room in response to Pixie's 'Aaah, that explains things . . .'

The cushion returned to her. 'By the way, he wants you to get in touch.'

Sue pulled a face. 'Does he?' she muttered tonelessly. Nick and her involvement, or non-involvement, with him had not been in her mind the last few days.

David however presented quite a different problem – he lived in her thoughts. She lay wakeful in bed, recalling every glance, each touch, however casual, and dropped to sleep fantasizing about how differently she would behave if she ever found herself in the same situation with him that she had been in with Nick.

The alarm roused her to a bleak grey morning, not quite foggy. The stresses of the last few days seemed to have caught up with her and she felt as dull and heavy as the day itself as she made her way to the gallery. Edwina Mancini appeared more annoyed by her absence over the last few days than pleased to have her back as she pointed out the large pile of invoices and other papers on the desk.

'We have been very busy while you were away. I have had no time to deal with the paperwork. I may have to ask you to work extra hours to make up the time you missed,' she remarked rather sourly. Sue wondered if she knew that David had been with her, and that was the real cause of her ill humour. She sat down and began to sort through the work that had mounted up in her absence. Each time the door between the office and gallery opened, giving her a glimpse of David's portrait of her mother, it unnerved her, as if Stevie was there in the flesh keeping an eye on her. Common sense told her this was absurd. It was only a painting.

Sue worked doggedly on towards lunchtime, one ear listening for the sound of David's voice in the gallery. It didn't come. She ate a solitary sandwich and drank a gritty coffee alone and finally at the end of the day struggled home, tired and dispirited, on an over-crowded tube train. She had been so sure he would turn up at the gallery – she had been wrong. By the time she got home she had come to the conclusion that she had imagined the way he had made her feel, even possibly the dinner itself. Tired, disgruntled and with the niggling beginning of a headache she found the flat empty, with only a scrawled note from Pixie – 'Out – back later – or late!' – to welcome her. She screwed it up and threw it in the waste bin. Discovering their food supplies consisted of rather stale bread and barely enough cheese to fit on a mousetrap she decided on a bath and an early night.

She was wallowing in rose-scented hot water and self-pity when she heard the unmistakable sound of the doorbell. She tried to ignore it, but the thought that it might be David changed her mind. Pixie had left her voluminous bathrobe hanging on the door so she shrugged herself into it.

'Oh – it's you!'

'Yes, it's me. I see you aren't ready.'

'Ready?' It seemed she had missed something.

'I told Pixie I would be round tonight – I thought we could go out for a meal. I told her that too.'

'You did?' Sue thought of Pixie's scrappy note: it had certainly not mentioned Nick. Then she thought of the tired bread and cheese and her stomach complained. She opened the door wider to let him in. 'I – I won't be a moment,' she promised.

True to her word she was dressed in record time, with hair brushed and a perfunctory application of make-up. This was Nick who she liked but was not in love with so there was no need for more.

It was just starting to rain as they let themselves out. Making a dash for Nick's car at the kerb, she didn't see the other car pulling into the street.

David watched Sue scramble into the old Morris Minor, hurrying to get out of the rain. Her face was turned to the boy getting into the driver's seat and she was laughing. His heart turned over then settled like lead. This, he supposed, was the boyfriend she had casually mentioned once or twice. If he remembered correctly he was a New Zealander and they had met on the boat coming over. After a few moments he turned the car round and left the street. He was, he told himself, a fool to imagine that a girl of Sue's age could be the least interested in a man of his age, especially one who had once been in love with her mother.

Nick and Sue were back in the flat companionably drinking coffee when Pixie came in. To Sue's surprise she was alone.

'Oops!' Pixie put a hand over her mouth in mock guilt. 'I forgot to tell you Nick was coming round tonight.' Sue thought she looked anything but guilty, especially when she rattled on cheerfully, 'Still, it doesn't matter – you seem to have got together in spite of my lapse.' She giggled and Sue decided she had drunk more than was good for her, wherever she had been.

'Have some coffee.' Sue managed to make it sound more like a command than an invitation. Pixie was quite sober enough to catch the intonation, and lit up enough to refuse it.

'Thanks – no. I'd rather have something stronger.'

'Well, then, you are out of luck,' Sue snapped. Pixie had flopped down into an armchair and was smiling at them both. Nick was smiling back, he liked Pixie and was surprised by Sue's somewhat pompous attitude.

'In that case I think I will take myself to bed and leave you two to it.'

Sue glared at her. God, she was irritating at times. She was glad she was not carrying a torch for Nick otherwise she would have found her behaviour impossible. Pixie seemed to have forgotten that as her bed was a divan in this room, she would not be leaving them to anything if she went to bed.

Nick drained his coffee, set the mug down and got to his feet, grinning. 'I guess I had better be off.' He gave Sue a look that plainly asked if she was going to see him out. But Sue was not in the mood for goodnight kisses with anyone. Why couldn't Nick be content to keep their friendship on a strictly platonic level? As David was. She remained where she was.

'Goodnight, then.' Nick's grin faded to be replaced by a scowl. He still lingered, but when Sue remained where she was, he left with a gruff 'goodnight'.

When he had gone Sue got up to take the coffee mugs to the sink. She turned round to find Pixie glaring at her like an avenging angel ready to let fly, which she did, leaving Sue to gape at her in utter astonishment.

'Sue Colville, I think you are absolutely the pits!' she stormed. 'You treat Nick like dirt and the silly fool keeps coming back for more. Doesn't he ever look in a mirror and see what a nice-looking guy he is? And nice to know too! Why doesn't he wake up and see there are plenty more fish in the sea – and not such cold ones as you, either! God, if he ever did . . .' She stopped, afraid of what she might say next. Sue was staring at her, mouth agape, looking enough like the fish Pixie had accused her of being to make her laugh. Sue was not amused, all that registered with her was that Pixie had accused her of being cold.

'How dare you say that about me?' she demanded. It seemed to her totally unfair and undeserved. On the contrary, she felt a mass of jangled emotions. The shock of Nanny's death, the unexpected comfort offered by David, culminating in that odd sensation in the car and again in the restaurant. 'You don't know how I feel – you don't understand anything.'

'I see more than you think. I see you stringing Nick along, with not so much as a goodnight peck on the cheek. I'll bet my cotton socks you were the pure and chaste ice maiden that night you had away with him – all because you've got the hots for someone old enough to be your father, your mother's cast-off!' She spat the last words out, then suddenly shrugged as if all the fight had gone now she had had her say. 'I'm sorry...' Her tone of voice was completely different now and she really did sound sorry. 'I shouldn't have let fly like that – it's none of my business, after all. It's just that, well, Nick really is such a nice guy, I don't like to see him hurt. And you too – I'm *fond* of you and I don't like what you are doing to yourself. You're so screwed up if you got this painter fellow chances are you would....'

But Sue never heard what Pixie thought she would do; her outburst had touched a raw nerve and without warning she burst into tears.

'Hey – gosh – I'm sorry, I didn't mean to upset you. It's just that, well, I suppose it was the look on Nick's face that got me, plus the fact that I had drunk enough to not care what I said.' She finished with a sheepish grin. 'I really am sorry. Let's forget it, shall we?'

Sue subsided into the nearest chair, gulping and sniffing as she groped wildly for a handkerchief. Pixie threw her the tea towel, forcing a spluttering laugh out of her, but she mopped her streaming eyes gratefully. 'Don't be sorry.' She hiccupped the words out. 'I'm crying because... because I'm so afraid you are right. I *am* cold – a cold fish. I must be – I'm nearly twenty-three and still a virgin!' She finished on such a wail of despair that Pixie laughed aloud.

'Well, if that's all that is worrying you why didn't you remedy it when you had the chance?'

'I don't kno-o-w!' Sue's reply was a long drawn-out wail. She sniffed again and mopped up her still-flowing tears with the tea towel. 'I got cold feet or something, I suppose. I don't want to be like my mother!'

'If you are trying to tell me your mother is a virgin, then I just don't believe it.'

This brought a faint grin to Sue's lips and she threw the tea towel at Pixie. 'Of *course* she isn't; just the opposite.'

'Oh?' Sue managed to inject a world of meaning into the single syllable.

'What I mean is, Mum keeps getting married. She can't seem to exist without being someone's wife. It's .. it's as if she can't see herself as a real person unless she has a husband.' Sue sighed. 'I'm putting this awfully badly. I find it hard to explain but I am so terrified of ending up like her, dependent on some man to prove to me that I exist. I want to be me in my own right.'

Pixie was silent, thoughtfully chewing at a hangnail. 'Well, yes, I can see what you mean, but don't you think you are exaggerating, overreacting? After all, your mother may have genuinely loved all the men she married.'

'Only three,' Sue said defensively. 'You make her sound like some Hollywood star with marriage mania and at least six scalps to her credit.'

'OK, OK – since we seem to be analyzing your mother as a way of getting to the bottom of your hang-ups, let's work through them,' Pixie suggested. 'Number one?'

'That was my father.' Sue frowned slightly, trying to recall him clearly. 'He was years and years older than her. She must have married him for security.'

'What can you remember of them together? What did you feel about your father?' Pixie was beginning to enjoy her role as psychological counsellor.

'I adored him, and I think he adored her. I'm not too sure about her feelings. But yes, I think she must have cared for him. They seemed happy together and as far as I remember she was devastated when he died.' She paused, taking her mind back to those sad days. 'I always felt she blamed me. I was only four but I can remember the dreadful guilt I felt.'

'Blamed you? But why? How could you be to blame at four years old?'

'He caught measles from me. It killed him.' This, Sue realized, was the first time she had ever admitted to anyone, even herself, how her father's death had affected her. She closed her eyes and sighed, feeling as if she were letting go of some heavy burden she had carried for most of her life.

'There you are – confession is good for the soul. I bet you haven't admitted that to many people.'

Sue shook her head. 'Never – to anyone.'

'Keep going. Tell me about your first stepfather?'

'Mum didn't actually marry him for years, but he was always around. The local doctor, my father's friend and contemporary. We called him Uncle Jock. Michael and I both liked him – then.' Sue was silent so long remembering the past that Pixie found it necessary to give another verbal prod.

'And later?'

'Later .. Well, later was a different ball game altogether,' Sue said drily. She found the last thing she wanted to talk about was her first stepfather. 'He killed himself. It – oh, it was just awful.'

'But before all that, between my father dying and Mum marrying Uncle Jock, there was the war. Mum was fantastic then. She'd never really done anything before: I mean, she had a housekeeper to run the house, Nanny to look after Michael and me, someone to do the garden. But when the war started she was amazing – she grew vegetables, kept poultry, even milked a cow. She drove us about in a pony and cart, then she took in evacuees from London. I enjoyed the war, and the funny thing is I think she did too. That was when Tom arrived on the scene.'

'Your current stepfather, husband number three?'

Sue nodded. 'They had known one another before, as children, before his father emigrated to Australia. I remember him turning up one summer day during the war; I thought he was terribly romantic in his big Aussie hat and army uniform. He spent all his leave with us. I thought they would get married: hoped they would. Then he disappeared . . .' Her voice died away as she remembered. 'We didn't see or hear anything of him for years, so Mum married Uncle Jock. Then by one of those incredible coincidences that are only supposed to happen in fiction, Michael met Tom's son at boarding school, and because of that Mum and Tom met again. Of course Uncle Jock was dead by then.'

Pixie stifled a yawn: Sue had rattled off this history of her family as if it were a text learned by heart. She wished she hadn't veered away from discussion of her first stepfather – somehow Pixie thought that was the clue to Sue's feelings about men today. Perhaps he had molested her as a child? Never afraid to jump in where angels feared to tread, she asked bluntly, 'This Uncle Jock, or whatever you called him, did he, you know, make advances to you?'

Sue laughed bitterly. 'Molest me? Oh no. I might feel better if he had.'

Pixie couldn't imagine that. She raised her eyebrows in cynical enquiry. 'How come?'

'Well,' Sue said at last, 'everything was fine at first – we moved into his house and sold our own. Then gradually as time went on he got more and more critical, not only of us but of Mum as well. I sometimes thought she was scared of him. She certainly took care not to upset him in any way if she could help it. He was nicer to me than he was to Michael, I suppose, but as we both grew older he changed, seemed as if he couldn't stand us near him as we approached puberty. Then he arranged for us both to go to boarding school. Mum was unhappy about that, we could see, but actually neither of us really minded – in some ways it was better than home. He had got so critical of Michael and I felt that somehow he found me disgusting as I showed signs of becoming a woman.'

'What the hell did he expect a little girl to become?' Pixie interrupted.

'Mum took us every summer to the North Wales coast to stay with Nanny, who had retired there with her sister, and that's where we met David. We were there when we got the news that Uncle Jock was dead. It was awful.' She paused again, her eyes dark with memory. Pixie, realizing that Sue was telling her something that she had kept bottled up for years, managed to stifle a yawn.

'Go on,' she dutifully prodded.

'He killed himself because there was a story around that he had been . . . interfering with little boys.'

Pixie stopped herself saying 'Good riddance' and made a sympathetic grunt instead. 'How awful for your mother,' she remarked after a pause.

'Yes, I suppose it was. At least it explained why he didn't want Michael and me around. He didn't like me because I was a woman and he was in danger of liking Michael too much.'

'I still can't see the connection between your stepfather's sexual preferences and your virginity,' Pixie complained.

'He made me feel that I was unclean and unattractive and no one would want me and I was afraid to trust my own judgement. If Mum could make such a dreadful mistake, so could I.'

Pixie burst out laughing. 'Good God, Sue, you beat all! Talk about looking for hang-ups!'

'That's not all.' Sue sounded defensive. 'When Mum was free she had it made – a career she enjoyed and no one to criticize or make demands, and David in love with her to boot. Then she married

Tom. End of freedom, end of career, with learning about life in Australia, helping on the farm and having twins she had no time for herself. I don't want to get tied up like that – I want to be me, not Mrs Somebody, just an extension of somebody else, living their life and not my own.'

'Taking a lover is an act of freedom, not of bondage. Think of it that way,' Pixie advised, yawning openly now. 'And at the same time ponder on this precious virginity of yours. What's so special about it, anyway?'

Sue gaped at her. This was Pixie talking, who she had always thought of as a model of conventional rectitude. Someone who would date, get engaged, get married, have sex, strictly in that order. Maybe there was something in her advice, maybe she should think about it. Having hang-ups because a homosexual had been offended by her womanhood was plain stupid.

Losing her virginity, however, was not quite as simple as all that. She had made it so clear to Nick that sex was not on the agenda that it was difficult to put it back on – and anyway, did she want to? David, on the other hand, made her pulse race and heightened all her senses – but could she forget that he had once loved her mother?

CHAPTER SIXTEEN

S TEVIE was grief-stricken when Sue told her Nanny was dead. She had come into her life with Sue's birth, employed by Martin to care for the new baby and relieve his young wife of any pressure of work. But Stevie had needed something to do, not an extension of her hours of idleness. Nanny had understood this and had never tried to exclude her from her own baby's daily routine, as so many professional nannies did. Gradually a very real friendship had grown up between them that, over the years, transcended the employer/employee status. When Sue was four years old and nearly old enough to cope without a nanny, her brother Michael was born and Nanny stayed on.

Then Martin died, and Nanny once again gave Sue support far beyond the work she did. In the war years they coped with evacuees together along with wartime problems and shortages. Stevie had never known her mother, but Nanny filled the void.

When Jock died it was Nanny's love and support that Stevie leaned on, although she was now living on the Welsh coast in retirement with her sister. Stevie missed her terribly when she married Tom and went to Tasmania and often thought longingly how wonderful it would have been if she could have gone with them.

Sue's visits would have given her enormous pleasure, Stevie knew, and she was so glad her daughter had taken the trouble to go.

The young did not always realize how much happiness they could give to the old. She sometimes thought Nanny had a soft spot for Sue because she saw Stevie's initial lack of enthusiasm for her baby daughter. What she couldn't know was that if Sue had not decided to make her entrance to the world at that particular point in time Stevie would have left Martin and married Tom then and all their lives would have been different. That was more than twenty years ago, all water under the bridge. Today, she and Sue had, she believed, as good a relationship as any mother and daughter, notwithstanding the quickly suppressed hint of relief she felt when Sue announced her intention of returning to England.

The strong odour of sheep and sheep dip wafting up to her as she dropped the men's work clothes into the washing machine brought Stevie back to the here and now. She had promised herself thirty minutes of creativity while the machine dealt with the washing.

The smell of paints as she dipped her brush in turned her thoughts to Davey. What would she have done if he had asked her to be his mistress? She had known for a long time that he was in love with her, and she was a little in love with him. If there had been no Tom . . . But of course there was and she had carried a torch for him too long to drop it. Besides Tom was free, Davey was not, and in those days she was very conventional. She glanced at her watch. Nearly ten minutes of her precious thirty gone in useless daydreaming. The past was the past and there it could stay. She made her decision then and must stand by it now. She screwed up her eyes to stare at her painting and began mixing colours.

Stevie knew that she was getting maudlin and that the time she had allowed herself was running away. Tom tolerated rather than applauded her painting, even though she earned money from it. He tended to consider it a hobby and as such it should never take precedence over 'real' work: the farm, the children and, of course, himself. With a sigh she wiped her brushes and hurried to peg out the washing before she collected the twins from school. She would have to learn to use her time better than indulging in daydreams about the past.

'Mum, we've got a note for you.' Brian and Barney spoke in unison. After a good deal of rummaging in both school bags it was produced. Stevie read it with a sinking heart: yet another cake for the Mothers' Club. More inroads on painting time. The boys were explaining to her that it was for a cake stall and each child, they emphasized, was expected to bring a contribution. Which meant she had to produce two separate cakes.

It was just her luck, she thought gloomily, to land up in a community that seemed to be composed of cordon bleu cooks, she who had been brought up and then married into a household where she scarcely knew what a wooden spoon was, let alone how to use one. She had learned a lot, of course, but light sponges and super scones still eluded her. She had once sent a bought cake when her sponges refused to rise and the hens hadn't laid enough eggs for another. She doubted if the boys would ever forgive her. They looked at her anxiously now. 'You will make them, won't you?' Barney asked.

She smiled. 'Of course.'

Relieved, they resumed their normal chatter. As she doled out afternoon tea and started on the vegetables for the evening meal, Stevie realized how much she missed her daughter in practical ways. Sue had done so many of these regular chores, as well as taking the boys off her hands. With a pang of guilt she thought of the many times she had taken her help, and her company, for granted. Only now that she was gone, and she remained, the only female in a totally male household, did she realize how much her daughter's presence had meant. Briefly she envied her youth and freedom.

'Come on – eat those biscuits then you can go out and play.' Both boys looked up, surprised. They were usually expected to do simple chores, such as collecting the eggs. They looked at one another, crammed the last bits of biscuit in their mouths, swilled them down with milk and escaped before she changed her mind. But they were not quick enough.

'Hi ...' she called after them, 'Don't forget to feed the chicks and collect the eggs!'

Stevie sighed; it was not fair to take her frustration out on them. They were good kids really. It was not their fault there were two of them. She felt dissatisfied with herself for being dissatisfied. After all, she had got what she wanted, hadn't she? Even as she thought this she could hear Nanny's voice in her head saying to her, just as she had done over the years to her own children: *Be careful what you wish for in case you get it.* Well, she had always wanted Tom, and now she had him she should be over the moon. Which she was – most of the time. It was just that she hadn't bargained for all the other things that came with him. Certainly not the endless cooking.

Stupid though it seemed, she hadn't realized just how far Tasmania was from England. She suddenly felt more isolated than she had in the early days of her marriage.

'You cannot spend the entire day feeling sorry for yourself,' Stevie told herself and walked over to the radio to find something to take her out of herself.

As she took her place at the table later she saw Tom watching her, a slight frown on his face, as if something puzzled him. She met his eyes and smiled. The look vanished and he smiled back. 'How's the painting going?' he surprised her by asking. Her heart gave an unexpected bump, shocking her with the spurt of desire that caught her unawares. But all she said was, 'Slowly – but well.' She smiled again. Yes, she had got what she wanted, and tonight she would enjoy it.

Tom was surprised when she turned to him that night and ran her hand slowly down his body till she came to his pyjama cord. Deftly she undid it and ran her fingers over the soft skin of his belly till she could entwine them in his pubic hair. Before she could go any further, he turned to her with a low moan, his arousal meeting her searching fingers. Stevie was swept up by a tide of love and desire and wondered briefly how she could have forgotten, even for a moment, what this man meant to her.

CHAPTER SEVENTEEN

M AKING an intellectual decision to sacrifice one's virginity was
one thing, Sue discovered, but actually setting about it was
another. She was romantic enough to want to be swept away on a
tide of passion; doing it (or not doing it) this way put it in the same
league as buying a new pair of shoes.

If anyone else had suggested she go out and deliberately sacrifice
what was supposed to be a girl's strongest card, she would probably
have rejected it out of hand. Because it was so unexpected from
Pixie it seemed to have a sort of veracity. What a fool she had been,
Sue thought now, to miss her chance when she and Nick had spent
the night away. She finally dropped into a restless sleep on the
uncomfortable thought that maybe Pixie was right to think her
cold and unfeeling. Perhaps she was right too in her suggestion that
taking a lover was an act of freedom.

After a night of confused and disturbing dreams in which Nick
loomed large she woke feeling more tired than when she went to
bed. However, her dreams had left her feeling warm towards Nick.
She looked forward to seeing him again, and when she did she
would put things right. She didn't ask herself quite what she meant
by that, perhaps their relationship would move naturally to the
next phase, whatever that might be.

These vaguely romantic thoughts were filling her mind instead
of the hard facts of the business side of the gallery when her atten-

tion was caught by her own name in the conversation filtering in through the closed door to the office. Realising it was a conversation between her employer and David, Sue would not have been human if she had not let her hands rest on the typewriter keys to still the clatter.

'No ... no, David, I will not let Sue off early to lunch with you ...' Edwina Mancini was saying in a tone that made it clear she was finding both the request, and the person making it, a bore. 'You seem to have the strange idea that because I choose to give the portrait you did of her mother pride of place here in the gallery that you have some sort of rights on her time. The time that I happen to pay for – at the moment.' She paused and David's voice, muted now as if he had moved further away, said something she couldn't hear. A few seconds later his face appeared round the door.

'I came to see if you would have lunch on me, but you can't get off early and I can't wait, so ...' He shrugged. 'So dinner instead?'

Sue nodded her acceptance, then wondered why she had to be so compliant. She smiled wryly to herself, recalling her original plan for the evening. Accepting David's invitation wasn't quite the way to make things better with Nick.

'Sue, come back!' David said sharply across the dinner table.

'I haven't gone anywhere,' she protested, as he dragged her attention back to him and the present.

'Not physically, no. But your mind has been anywhere but with me all evening.'

'Oh no, it has been on you,' she protested with perfect truth. If you only knew, she thought.

'Tell me what you were thinking about then,' he demanded.

'Oh, this and that,' she prevaricated before surprising him by asking, 'Can we go back to your place afterwards? I would like to see it.'

David made no attempt to hide his pleasure. 'I'd like to show it to you, but whenever I have suggested it before, however tentatively, you have always retired into outraged virtue and only just stopped short of accusing me of evil designs.'

'Do you?' Sue asked softly. 'I hope so,' she tagged on in her head.

'Do I what?' David, she felt, was being deliberately obtuse, but she smiled, noticing that his face had a fuzzy appearance. She wondered vaguely whether this was something to do with him or the wine and drained her glass.

'I don't want coffee,' she said abruptly, although he hadn't asked. On some level she had made a decision and needed to act on it before she changed her mind.

When he stood back to let her into his flat-cum-studio Sue looked round with interest. Basically it was just a large attic room, but it had a north-facing window and a skylight, a perfect artist's pad. She could imagine how light it would be in the daytime, even in mid-winter London. He swiftly drew a curtain across the window but there was nothing to draw across the skylight and the unusually clear night sky, dominated by a sickle moon, fitted into the frame so that it appeared to be just another canvas. Sue crossed the room and began to mount the steps to the mezzanine floor with the exaggerated care of one who has drunk rather too much but is still sober enough to know they have. David watched from below.

The large divan, with brightly coloured rugs and quilts thrown loosely over it, mesmerized her. With an effort she looked at the rest of the small space: the bedside table held a reading lamp and a pile of books, and there was a chest of drawers topped with a small oval swing mirror and a chair with clothes thrown down on it. The careless clutter of the room did nothing to lessen its charm in her eyes.

'Will you make love to me?' She might have been asking for the coffee she had refused in the restaurant.

'Why?' he demanded, the starkness of the monosyllable throwing her off balance.

'Because . . . because I would like you to.' She turned to face him but when he didn't answer she turned away again, mumbling, 'But perhaps you don't find me sexually attractive?' The slight tremor in her voice was not intended but it touched something in David that her bold request had failed to do.

He stared up at her, seeing a desirable woman, not the child he had once known, not the daughter of a woman he had once loved and wanted. The past slid away and he was only in the present, throbbing with his need of her.

Sue stepped forward, intending to descend the steps, but then he was on the top stair and she had no choice but to stay where she was.

'Oh, I find you sexually attractive,' he rasped, gripping her upper arms and pushing her backwards. She gasped, as much at the harshness in his voice as from his grip on her arms. When she felt the bed hit the back of her knees she had no alternative but to fall back on it.

As he came down on top of her, Sue struggled to free herself. He fumbled with his clothes and began to tear at hers, her futile struggles intensifying his efforts. When he tried to push her legs apart, her breath caught in a sob, stopping him when he would have driven into her. She was behaving in a manner totally at odds with her cool demand that he make love to her.

As swiftly as it had flared, his desire turned to anger. He let her go and stood up. Christ – he had all but raped her.

'What the hell are you playing at?' he demanded. 'One minute you behave like a whore and when I respond you turn into an outraged virgin.'

Sue looked up at him, hair dishevelled, make-up smudged by tears. ' I . . . I'm sorry . . .' she mumbled incoherently. 'I am, but I didn't want to be any more. I thought . . .' She sniffed, looking so like the young girl he had first known that guilt overcame him again, making his voice sharper than he intended.

'Are you telling me that you deliberately set me up to deflower you?' he demanded.

She nodded and sniffed again. 'What an old-fashioned word.' A frail smile wobbled on her lips. 'Suits an old-fashioned girl like me, I suppose.'

'Being a virgin is nothing to be ashamed of. Neither is not being, if you go about it in the right way. You should have told me what you wanted, not behaved like a harlot,' he protested, aware that in his eagerness to assuage his own conscience he was using yet another old-fashioned word.

'I didn't think you would do it – in cold blood,' Sue muttered.

David looked down at her, rumpled, tear-stained and half naked, and was astonished to feel himself hardening again so soon. 'Try me.' He spoke softly now, for this time he felt tenderness mingling with his desire.

She searched his face for a long minute then moved closer. 'Please,' she whispered softly, 'will you teach me to make love.'

And that was exactly what he did. Without haste this time, he used his hands to gently caress every part of her body. Not till she was relaxed and pliant in his arms did he use his lips, kissing her first on the mouth, then the nipples and finally moving slowly down her body till he reached the warm sensitive spot between her thighs. When he finally entered her she was ready for him, quivering and gasping, and her cry as she climaxed was one of exquisite pleasure, not pain. Sighing, David drew her to him, pulled the covers up over them both and they slept till a pale wintry sun replaced the moon in the square of glass above them.

Sue stared up at the skylight in confusion. How had the window come to be over her head? She looked round her and saw David's dark head on the pillow beside her. Idly she noticed for the first time the few silver hairs threaded amongst the dark ones then, as memory and realization hit, she sat up so suddenly that his eyes opened and stared at her. For a second they mirrored her own confusion, then with a smile he pulled her towards him and kissed her lightly on the lips.

'Hello.' he said simply. 'Still here, then?'

'Yes – but I'm going.' Suiting the action to the words, she swung her legs over the side of the bed and padded over to the chair where her clothes lay. With morning had come memory of the way in which she had propositioned David the night before and with memory came embarrassment.

'Don't be in such a hurry. There is no need. You don't even have to go to work.'

'I know – but . . .' She trailed off. But what?

'At least have some breakfast first.' David got out of bed and pulled on a robe. 'I'll put coffee on, or would you prefer tea?'

'No, coffee is fine,' Sue assured him, and realized she had accepted his invitation to breakfast.

'Water should be hot if you want a shower,' he called over his shoulder as he made his way down to make coffee.

By the time Sue had quickly showered and dressed, wishing she had a change of clothes, an electric percolator was bubbling away, filling the flat with the smell of coffee. Toast, marmalade and cereal were all laid out.

'Gosh that looks good. I'm really hungry.'

'That's the effect of sex,' David assured her. Sue found she was blushing.

'I'm sorry . . .' she mumbled as she filled a bowl with corn-flakes.

'Sorry? What for? I'm the one who should be saying that. I fear I was less than gentlemanly – but you should have told me.'

Sue was not sure how to answer so she filled her mouth with cornflakes. After a moment when he was still looking at her she said, 'Told you that I was a virgin you mean? But then you might not have done anything.'

'Oh, I would . . .' he said softly. 'I would but I would have been much more gentle, more considerate, from the beginning.' He sipped his coffee thoughtfully, looking at her as if trying to puzzle out a problem. 'What bothers me is why you had to ask me. What is wrong with that husky-looking boyfriend of yours? Surely he would have been more than ready to oblige?'

Sue buttered a piece of toast with intense concentration. 'Well, yes, probably.'

David finally broke the silence with, 'So, why me?'

Sue shrugged in an attempt at nonchalance. 'Why not?' she countered. She had no intention of giving anyone, least of all David, a blow-by-blow account of that evening with Nick. The silence grew uncomfortable as he waited for an answer. She mumbled, 'I thought you would be experienced.'

David sipped his coffee slowly before answering. 'Well...' he said at last. 'I am not sure whether that is a compliment, but I do have this theory about sex. It is so important that a first experience should be good because it can colour your attitude and make or break your whole sex life for years, if not for ever...' He trailed off.

'Yes, I had a sort of inkling of that and after— Well, I thought you being experienced would be the best person.'

'I have this theory,' he went on, as if she had not said anything, 'that experienced men should initiate young women and vice versa. I usually keep it to myself, it goes down like a lead balloon in polite society.' He grinned. 'Another lesson or two and you will be ready to teach that young man of yours how to make love to a desirable woman.'

'He is not that young man of mine,' Sue protested, then after a moment, 'Am I?'

'I'm sure he thinks he is,' David assured her.

'But am I?' Sue persisted. 'A desirable woman?'

Disconcertingly she felt that David was considering his answer. She would have liked a quick affirmation, and when he didn't give it immediately her lack of self-esteem kicked in. 'You don't have to answer,' she muttered, turning away.

'Of course you are...' Sue was startled by the roughness both in his voice and in the hand that caught her arm above the elbow and swung her round to face him. 'And well you know it. Far too attractive to go round inviting older men to rape you! God damn it, Sue, I've known you since you were a child. I'm old enough to be your father . . .' He paused and Sue wondered if, like her, he was thinking that he could have been her stepfather. He let her arm drop.

'I know you were once in love with my mother. Is that why you were reluctant?'

'I was not reluctant,' David corrected. 'Just inhibited by my natural morals, and the disparity in our ages.'

'I like mature men.'

'Well, I don't like immature girls.' David knew he was being cruel, but in the sudden surge of anger that shot through him he didn't care. She was very attractive; more, she was beautiful. His body told him the former, his artist's eye the latter, and she had blatantly asked him to make love to her. He would have been a quixotic fool to refuse. But he did not want the added complication in his life of her falling in love with him.

'You are five years younger than Mum. She was twenty-two when I was born, so that makes you seventeen years older than me – like you said, old enough to be my father. But I am a woman, therefore old for my years, you are a man, therefore young for yours, so I would say that makes us about equal, wouldn't you?' Sue looked directly into his eyes and added softly, 'That has dealt with the age business, so either you still yearn for Mum . . . or . . .'

'So if I do still "yearn for" your mother, as you put it, does that matter? I couldn't have her then, and certainly not now.' He paused, remembering she had left something unsaid. 'Or what . . . what else were you going to say?'

Sue shrugged. 'It could only mean that I left you cold, that you found me totally undesirable.' She was horrified to hear the slight tremor in her voice. The situation was humiliating enough already without her being reduced to pathetic begging. Realizing that he still held her arm she tried to pull away, but his response was only to tighten his grip.

He caught her hand with his free one as she tried to pull away. 'I find you utterly and completely desirable. To even suggest that you leave me cold is blatant stupidity. As for your mother, I don't waste time crying for the moon. I think of her, quite often, with warmth and affection. I remember her as a wonderful model and a good friend, one of the best. There was never more between us. I would have liked it, of course, but it was not to be. I was married and your mother – well, she just never seemed to think of me in that way at all.'

'It was always Tom, I think.' Sue spoke gently, hearing the wistful note in his voice. She thought of her own father and wondered if he too had felt like that. 'I had better get back.' Her voice was brisk as she tried to shake off the maudlin feeling that threatened to take over. She made a half-hearted attempt to free herself of his grip. 'I guess I have made a big enough fool of myself for one session.'

'You haven't made a fool of yourself,' he told her, leaning closer to give her what he meant to be a light kiss on the cheek, but something misfired between the intention and the action. Instead of the chaste, almost paternal peck he intended he found he was drawing her close and his arms were encircling her as his lips sought hers. Sue heard, or thought she did, flattering words muttered in the form of a curse, before she let her body meld with his and returned his kiss.

Without warning he pushed her away, ending the kiss as swiftly as he had begun it. 'This has to stop . . .' he told her. 'Now . . .'

'But . . .' Sue found herself protesting, she didn't want anything to stop. For her it had just begun.

David dropped his hands and walked away from her. 'No!' His voice was sharp. 'It has to end – now,' he repeated. 'What . . . happened last night was a once only.' He saw she was about to protest again and held up his hand. 'No, Sue, I mean it. Once only, it shouldn't have happened. I haven't seen your mother for what, seven, eight years? It doesn't matter, there is no way I could have a long-standing affair with her daughter. You must understand, the memory of our friendship would always stand between us. Besides,' he added with unrelenting honesty, 'I enjoy my freedom, I don't want to be tied down in any way. I know what that is like, I had years of it. Now I can be a vagabond, with no one else to think about. I can go where I like, do what I like and paint to my heart's content.'

Sue dropped her eyes from his face feeling the dull pain of rejection.

'Don't look like that! I don't want to hurt you, I like you far too much. I liked you as a child and I find you enchanting as a woman. It is because I care so much for you that I want you to be free too, not tied to someone old enough to be your father.' He saw her wince at the phrase and smiled slightly. 'Like it or not it's true. You need a young man, your own contemporary. You are a very lovely young woman – go and seduce that handsome young New Zealander.'

Sue tilted her chin and looked round for the few belongings she had brought with her the previous night. 'I'll try!' With an effort she controlled the quaver in her voice. 'And . . . thank you!'

'Don't thank me! Never thank a man for making love to you. Like I said, you're a very lovely young woman . . . with much to offer.' He paused and a mischievous smile broke slowly across his features. 'Now you've broken out of your shell and, I hope, discarded some of those incredible inhibitions and old-fashioned notions that were tying you in knots. You are lovely, Sue. Whatever kept you untouched till the age of twenty-two?'

She smiled, a small bleak smile. 'What you just said: inhibitions and old-fashioned notions, I guess.'

They looked at one another for a moment, then with a slight shrug David said, 'Come on, I'll take you home.'

Sue glanced at her watch: just after ten-thirty. She had been here not quite twelve hours, that was all, yet she felt aeons older, both in years and wisdom. She sighed, mirrored his shrug, and turned towards the door.

He was able to pull up at the kerb just outside her flat. In her hurry to get inside and terminate what she was beginning to think of as an embarrassing experience, Sue failed to notice Nick's car parked a little further down the street. With swift perfunctory thanks and a brief wave she hurried away.

Nick and Pixie were sitting opposite each other cradling mugs of coffee when she walked in. The charged silence told Sue they had been talking about her. She was embarrassed about being dressed for a night out in the middle of the morning. A flicker of amusement touched Pixie's face and as her eyes met Sue's she gave an almost imperceptible shrug expressing her helplessness to improve the situation.

She watched Nick's mouth tighten and his eyes harden as they travelled from her face to her feet then back again to rest there with the blankness of a stranger. She had lost him, and it hurt terribly, far more than she could have imagined. She stepped towards him, holding out her hand in a vague gesture of supplication, but he ignored it as he leapt to his feet, a dull flush staining his cheeks. In a voice all the more deadly for being totally devoid of expression or emotion, he stated flatly, 'You've been out all night!'

Sue could only stare at him as he pushed past her to the door repeating, his voice now taught with pain, 'All night ... with ... him!'

There was an awful finality in the slamming door and the clatter of his feet on the drab linoleum of the stairs.

CHAPTER EIGHTEEN

After a moment's stunned silence, Sue wheeled on Pixie, 'All right, so it looks bad, but David is an old friend . . .' It was neither excuse nor explanation.

Pixie raised her eyebrows. 'I thought he was your mother's friend.'

'He was . . . he is . . . He is a family friend,' Sue floundered.

'Old enough to be your father.' Sue felt she would scream if she heard that phrase just once more. 'But I bet he wasn't being fatherly last night.' Pixie's grin smoothed the barb in her words and reminded Sue that this was her friend and confidante.

'We-e-ell . . . not really . . . although you could say . . .'

'Come clean, Sue. What did happen last night? If you did what I think you did then I reckon you probably paid a high price. You'd better hope it was worth it.'

'What do you mean?' Sue's voice came out as a hoarse whisper.

'You know what I mean. Nick. Unless you have a pretty good story to account for last night you've lost him.'

'I never thought about Nick.' Even as she spoke Sue wondered how she could have just forgotten about him; worse, it had not even crossed her mind that he would be upset, even that he would find out. If anything she had, as David had suggested, seen herself making love with Nick and astonishing him this time with her expertise as a lover. How on earth could she have been so stupid, so utterly naïve? She felt tears welling up, choking her till, with a wail and a hiccup, they spilled over and rained down her face. 'I've been such a fool!'

'Put some sensible clothes on and have a nice hot coffee,' ordered the ever-practical Pixie, getting up to reheat the water as she spoke.

'Now,' she said a few minutes later, handing a steaming mug to Sue, now in sweater and slacks suitable for a Saturday morning at home, 'tell me what you were up to last night.' She looked across at Sue over the rim of her own mug. 'Not the sordid details, just the gist of things.'

Sue told her, finishing by saying, 'David has this theory. He thinks older men should initiate young women and vice versa.'

'Neat,' Pixie interjected. 'I must say I never heard a man suggest that one before to get his own way!'

'He wasn't – getting his own way. I mean. It wasn't like that, really, Pixie. I was the one asking for it.' Sue could feel a hot flush creeping up her neck as she spoke. What on earth had come over her? 'I think,' she mumbled, clasping at a slender straw to save her pride, 'that maybe I drank too much.'

'You mean he plied you with drink?'

'Oh, Pixie, you make him sound awful – and me such an idiot.'

'Not really. On your own admission you didn't want to be a virgin any more so David obliged. That's it in a nutshell.'

Sue nodded. 'It's not that simple. He doesn't want me – and I've lost Nick. Oh, Pixie!' Sue almost choked as the sob rising in her throat met the coffee going down.

'Well, you have handled things rather badly,' Pixie agreed. 'If only you hadn't marched in wearing last night's glad rags and "sated with sex" written all over you, Nick would never have guessed anything. The root of all this bother is the ridiculous hang-ups both you and Nick have about sex. You are probably ideally suited.'

'What do you mean?' Sue sniffed.

'Well, look at you and your absurd ideas about virginity. You seem to think it is shameful to still be one, while Nick thinks it's shameful not to be. Whatever have you been doing with your life up to now, Sue? As for Nick, well, he is just like most men – full of romantic ideas that virginity is something special that a girl hangs on to until she meets the "ideal man" and then, and only then, she relinquishes it!' Pixie paused for breath, then her face broke into a rueful grin. 'Why don't you just tell me to shut up? Here I am going on like a women's magazine agony aunt and you just take it!'

'It's true, that's why! Everything you say is true. I have been such a fool.'

'Why put it in the past tense? You still seem a fool to me.' Pixie grinned. 'Now you've got some sensible clothes on, let's go out and find some fresh air and something to eat.'

Edwina Mancini was in a strange mood when Sue arrived at the gallery the following morning, fluctuating between distant and cool and agitated. Sue did her best to concentrate on her work but found herself floating off into daydreams in which she made love to David. She wondered if her employer had tuned into her thoughts or, worse still, knew somehow what had really happened. It was disconcerting that these daydreams invariably ended with memories of Nick's hurt, angry face. She even caught herself wondering how she would have felt surrendering her virginity (she mentally winced at the old-fashioned phrase, even as she used it) to Nick.

She was already missing his companionship and friendship, and she didn't really expect to hear anything of David, so when Edwina told her she no longer needed her services she settled into a good dose of Monday morning blues.

'I'm so sorry . . .' Edwina told Sue, looking so truly shattered that she almost felt more sorry for her than she did for herself, 'but I did make it clear that the position was only until my daughter was ready to take on the books again, didn't I?'

'Yes, you did,' Sue agreed ruefully. 'I shall miss it – I've really enjoyed working here.' At least, Sue thought, she understood now why her boss had been so strange and uptight when she arrived, and it was nothing to do with Davey.

'When—' Sue began, but Edwina cut her short.

'Would it – could you – or would it be presumptuous on my part, I wonder – would you be prepared to stay on in a part-time capacity?' She peered anxiously at Sue. 'Of course I wouldn't be able to pay you so much. Would that make it difficult?'

Even while she was speaking Sue was working out ways and means of living on a tighter budget. It would be hard, unless she could find another part-time job. She would meet that problem later. 'Thank you – I'd like to stay on.'

'Good, that's settled, then.' Sounding relieved, Madame Mancini left the office and returned to the gallery, leaving Sue thinking there was surely more to be discussed. What hours would she actually be expected to work and by how much would her wages be cut? Worrying about this turn of events, it was a while before her mind registered that the voice beyond the door belonged to David.

With their last encounter still vividly alive she wasn't sure whether to walk boldly out into the gallery with some excuse of asking Edwina some detail about the work she was typing up or to slide under the desk and hide herself completely in case he came in. In the end she did nothing and was working diligently, or appearing to, when David stuck his head round the door with a cheery 'Hi!'

'Oh – hello!' With an effort Sue forced a tone of casual surprise into her greeting. She found it impossible to keep her eyes downcast on the keys and after a brief silence was forced to look up at him. As he was looking down at her she met his gaze directly and to her annoyance felt a warm flush creeping up her neck and throat.

'I just popped in to say goodbye,' he told her casually.

'Goodbye? Where are you going?'

'Abroad, to the Continent. I feel like a change of scene, and I need to get some more work done, as Edwina has just pointed out to me. I thought you might like to have dinner with me before I go.'

'Where? When?' Sue shot back, shaken by the emotion his words engendered in her.

'Where and when you like. . . .'

'I wasn't talking about dinner. I meant where exactly are you going, and when?'

'France – the Loire – in a week, maybe ten days. I've a sudden yen to paint chateaux.'

'I've never been to France at all,' Sue told him glumly.

'Better come with me then.' David spoke so casually that it was a few minutes before Sue, lost in her own gloomy thoughts, actually took in the words.

'Don't be silly – I can't.'

'No such word.'

'Well, I can't. There's my job, my flat. Well, I can't.'

'Your job is not important. Edwina will probably give you the flick anyway – her daughter is ready to come back and she won't keep you then.'

'She's asked me to stay part-time,' Sue was needled into retorting.

David shrugged. 'Oh well . . . As for the flat, surely you or Pixie can find a temporary tenant while you are away?'

'How long for?' she asked.

David shrugged again. 'As long or as short as you like.' He was making it clear that there would be no strings attached, she thought. She would like to see France. What better guide than Davey, who knew it so well.

'You make it sound tempting.' She spoke her thoughts aloud. What she didn't add was that a complete break would take her away from constant reminders of Nick. In a different setting she might banish his hurt and angry face from her mind. Only now when she had, it seemed, lost his friendship, did she realize what it had meant to her.

'Think about it. Tell me when you meet me for dinner tomorrow night.' David spoke absently as if his mind were already on the other side of the English Channel.

Sue felt a frisson of resentment at his cavalier attitude in just assuming she would be free to meet him when he chose, but supposed she would, if only to tell him that the notion of her heading off to France with him, just like that, was absurd.

But was it? she asked herself as she heard him leave the gallery and endeavoured to immerse herself in her interrupted work. Of course it was. She answered her own question inside her head and with determination lost herself in the accounts she had been asked to get straight.

When she got back to the flat she found Gina there stirring a large saucepan on the gas ring while Pixie chopped onions and tomatoes through a haze of tears. She had forgotten that tonight they were having a sort of reunion party for the group who had met on the ship. It had actually been her own idea, several weeks before. It had seemed a good idea then, but now she wondered what on earth had induced her to suggest such a crazy thing. Pixie grabbed a tea towel and mopped at her onion-induced tears.

'Gina is making spaghetti bolognese, and we've got some bottles of Chianti to go with it.' She gestured expansively to the raffia-wrapped squat bottles sitting on the draining board. But we need some bread. Could you—'

'I'll get some French sticks.' Sue turned back to the door, glad to escape the preparations for a party she was in no mood to enjoy.

When she got back with the long crispy rolls, it seemed as if things were already underway. Through the young people crowded into the tiny flat she could see Nick opening a bottle of wine. She paused momentarily and watched him; he was too busy concentrating on what he was doing to notice her or anyone else. Then he looked up and she saw the pleasure at seeing her dim and her heart which had leapt in that first instant became a leaden ball. The hurt and disappointment she felt was so strong. It took her by surprise; she hadn't realized how much Nick's good opinion of her meant. She took the bread over to the rest of the food and began to slice it, her back to the room, and Nick.

'Right, everyone. Grub's up!' Gina called, turning round from the stove with a huge bowl of spaghetti in her hands. There was a concerted sigh and an appreciative sniffing of the air as she placed it on the small coffee table in the centre of the room.

'Aren't we the lucky ones to have a genuine Italian to cook our spaghetti,' someone remarked facetiously.

'A few times removed, via Australia,' Gina retorted.

Nick filled an odd assortment of glasses ranging from crystal to a tooth mug with the garnet red wine. They toasted England, Australia, good food and wine but mostly themselves and in a silence punctuated by the clink of cutlery on china settled down to the serious business of eating.

She didn't quite know how it happened but Sue found herself next to Nick. She hadn't engineered this and she was sure he hadn't. She suspected that the rest of the group, who tended to think of them as a pair, had done it without quite realizing. Sue was prickingly aware of him next to her. If she listed the slightest bit his way she would actually be leaning against him.

The silence between them was deafening. 'Nick . . .' Sue finally ventured. 'Can't we talk?'

'I'm not stopping you,' he mumbled without looking up. It was not very encouraging.

'I can explain,' she began.

Again the pause was so long she wondered if he was bothering to listen. 'I doubt it,' he said at last. 'Anyway, explanations of the obvious are hardly necessary.'

'You're just jumping to conclusions,' she began angrily, then realized that he was, but unfortunately the correct ones. 'Oh, you just don't understand . . .' she wailed in despair. She wanted to tell him that what she had done had been, in an odd sort of way, as much for him as herself. She couldn't bear the thought of another dreadful fiasco like the awful night in Windsor. A fiasco for which she felt entirely to blame.

She turned sideways now and looked at him. His mouth was set in a tight line, studiously refusing to look at her. He had never annoyed her so much, nor had she ever felt his attraction so strongly. She needed to remove herself from his orbit, not just here and now in this room but in the wider scheme of things. She jumped to her feet, passing round more food and drink, chattering brightly about anything, and in the deep recesses of her mind France beckoned.

'I'll come, providing Pixie can find someone to take my place. I couldn't leave her with the whole of the rent to pay,' she told David over the dinner table the following evening. 'You are right, of course, about Madame Mancini . . . she has already reduced my hours . . .' She broke off, realizing that the response she was getting from David was not quite what she had expected – or hoped for. 'You did mean it, didn't you, when you said about France? You know . . .' She floundered on in the face of his silence. 'About me coming with you to France?'

He hadn't meant it, in fact he had almost forgotten he had ever said it, but seeing the expression on her face he couldn't tell her that. Instead he asked with almost brutal directness, 'Can you afford it?'

Her head shot up and she looked him in the face. 'Yes,' she said simply, and she could. Her mother and stepfather had been generous, she had the legacy from her father, and she had been earning.

When she told Pixie, her friend raised her eyebrows. 'When I suggested you lighten up, let your stiff morals relax a bit, I certainly didn't expect you to plunge into a disastrous relationship with a man old enough to be your—'

'He is not old enough to be my father!' Sue jumped in angrily, before she actually said it. 'And it is not a disastrous relationship. In fact, it is not a relationship at all – not in the way you think. David has been a family friend for years. He is a nice person.'

Pixie just went on looking at her in the peculiarly irritating way she had at times. Sue tried to ignore it. 'I'm sure Angela will be more than happy to move in while I am away.'

'Yes, I expect so,' Pixie agreed, but when Sue left for France it was not Angela but Nicholas who moved in with Pixie.

CHAPTER NINETEEN

Sue pulled her coat tighter against the brisk sea breeze blowing off the English Channel and felt, rather than saw, David move closer. She wasn't sure whether it was that or the poignancy of the sight of the famous white cliffs of Dover receding into the mist that choked her with emotion. She shivered and he turned her away from the rail and shepherded her downstairs.

David hunched down into his corner, and somewhat to her chagrin, dropped to sleep as the train left the port and headed for Paris. She supposed he had done the journey so many times over the years that it no longer held either novelty or interest, but to her it was all new and she found herself constantly turning to him with an excited exclamation or question on her lips only to see his face blanked in sleep. Occasionally he stirred, even murmured some incoherent utterance, but he was lost to her until, with perfect timing, he opened his eyes and smiled as the train sped through the suburbs of Paris.

They were spending a couple of days in Paris before moving on to Tours, the principal city of Touraine, David told her that no way could she come to France and just shoot through Paris on her very first visit. By the time they reached the small hotel David had booked them in for the night she could only collapse on the bed, ready to flake out. However after a reviving catnap she was ready to see something of Paris. She knocked hopefully on his door and found him unpacking.

'Why don't you fly?' she asked David, idly watching him putting out his toiletries. 'Wouldn't it be easier?'

'Easier, yes, but not so interesting.'

'You slept all the way from the boat; how can that be interesting?'

'It was for you, I am sure, and for me, well, I prefer the gradual induction to France, or more specifically Paris. By plane it is all too abrupt, too sudden, not good for the system at all.'

'Mmm . . .' she was not at all sure she quite understood just what he meant and too tired at the moment to work it out.

Sue felt as if she was wandering through a dreamscape as they strolled through the night streets of the city. It was only when she was sitting opposite David in the intimate little bistro he took her to, and her stomach rumbled in response to the tantalizing smells wafting from the kitchen, that she realized all this was for real – and she was hungry.

Studying the menu, Sue recognized that her limited amount of schoolgirl French was woefully inadequate. She looked up and saw David watching her with a smile.

'Shall I order for us both?'

'Please – but no snails or frogs' legs.'

David ran his eye swiftly down the printed page. 'None on this menu so you are safe,' he assured her.

She expressed her admiration, tinged with surprise, when he rattled off their order in what sounded like Frenchman's French then had a discussion about the wine.

'I spend a lot of time in this country,' he pointed out, 'and anyway, it's easy for a Welshman to speak French.'

'It is? How come?'

'Well,' David explained, 'if you hear Welsh spoken and then someone speaking French and listen to the rhythm, the lilt, rather than the actual words, you will notice a similarity. Both tend to go up at the end of a sentence. English on the other hand goes down.'

'There speaks a man from the land of music.' Sue's tone was amused, but she found herself listening with a new ear to the French being spoken all around them and to her own voice as she and David carried on a conversation in English. David's, she noted, had much the same cadence when he talked to her as when he spoke to the waiter in French. She wished someone had pointed this out to her when she was grappling with dreary French grammar in school. It was the rhythm of his speech rather than the Welsh accent as such, she realized, that made David's voice so attractive.

Over the next two days David took on the role of tour guide and Sue that of tourist, and while she appreciated his knowledge she began to feel after a while that she was on a school trip. Each night when, pleasantly weary and sated with good food and wine, they returned to their rooms, Sue wondered if this would be the night he would come into her room or ask her into his.

'Tomorrow we move on to Tours.' They had spent a particularly strenuous day sightseeing. Sue was almost asleep on her feet and actually grateful that David expected no more of her that day. 'Tour?' she mumbled sleepily. 'But I thought we were going to the Loire Valley, for you to paint chateaux or something. I didn't think we were going to tour.'

'Tours, not tour,' David corrected her. 'The main city of Touraine. Didn't you learn anything in school? Your geography is pitiful.'

Sue flushed. 'I know – I just wasn't thinking.'

'I can't holiday for ever – I need to paint.'

'Yes, I know that too. I'm sorry to have taken up so much of your time.' Her voice was cool and she turned away from him to her own door.

'I'm sorry, I didn't mean to sound like – well, like I did.' He caught her by the arm and swung her round to face him and she found herself looking directly into his face. For what seemed a long time they stood like that, Sue tinglingly aware of his hands on her arms, of the closeness of his body. For a moment she thought he was going to kiss her, maybe even ... but as suddenly as he had caught hold of her arm he dropped his hands to his sides and with a crisp 'Goodnight – sleep well' turned into his own room.

Sue opened her door with a sigh, unsure which was the strongest – her physical weariness or her feeling of rejection.

CHAPTER TWENTY

STEVIE'S first job in the morning was to milk the house cow. It was something she enjoyed, given a good cow, like old Clover. She had discovered the therapeutic qualities of this daily chore when it was part of her war effort in England; like a meditation it charged her for whatever the day might bring.

She let her head rest on the smooth warm flank, her hands working automatically. The rhythmic sound of the cow chewing her breakfast and the steady ping-ping of the milk hitting the bucket was as soothing as a grandfather clock ticking, and almost as hypnotic. She did most of her serious thinking at this time of day, and this morning was no exception. She thought of Tom and the good sex they had enjoyed the previous night, the best for a long time. She felt a warm tremor float up her body as she remembered the explosion of feeling that he had brought her to. It was a long time since she had experienced anything like it, or Tom had been patient enough to bring her to such a climax.

Into these pleasant thoughts her daughter intruded. Her recent letters had been affectionate and full of chatter and yet, in spite of their apparent openness, Stevie had the oddest feeling that something was being withheld. Well, Sue was grown-up now and under no obligation to tell her anything – or, come to that, even write at all. She was pleased Sue had come across David, and grateful to him for helping her daughter through the tough time of Nanny's sudden death. He was, she understood, quite successful these days. Almost famous, in fact.

Resting her face on Clover's soft flank, Stevie let her mind wander back to the months she had spent at Borth-y-Gest when David had loaned her his cottage. What a sanctuary that had been; she had been almost grateful enough at the time to give him what he wanted.

She smiled to herself as she remembered him quoting Omar Khayyam – 'A jug of wine, a loaf of bread – and thou' – as he raised the glass of red wine he was sipping in salute. The returning children had brought things down to earth with a bump. She wondered now what would have happened if they had not come back just then: would she still have made up the camp stretcher for him or would she have invited him into her own bed? But of course they had, and she had not.

'We might have made love, and that would have changed the course of history,' she confided to the cow. 'Sue says his wife died,' she murmured into Clover's flank. 'I wonder if he married again.'

She got up from the milking stool with a sigh. Clover had finished her food, her udder was empty and Sue's bucket more than half full. Inside her family would be waiting for their breakfast.

As soon as she had the house to herself and the essential chores out of the way Stevie went to her studio. She had almost forgotten that it was Sue's room as the probability of her returning in the near future to claim it back seemed remote. Studying the portrait of the dog she was currently working on and comparing it with the photos of the animal, Stevie sank into herself, experiencing the familiar feeling of both relaxation and a heightening of her physical senses as she began to mix paints. She wished she could tell Davey that she was painting again. Once again this talent that he had encouraged her to develop was coming to her rescue just as it had in the dark days after Jock's suicide. She decided to ask Sue for his address.

The tip of her tongue slid out between her teeth, as it always did when she concentrated, and her face creased slightly as she thought about her daughter. She was just being over-anxious, she assured herself. Impulsively she decided the best way to put the niggling anxiety about Sue to rest would be to speak to her. She only remembered the ten hours time difference when she had dialled the number. It must be about midnight of the previous night there.

'Hello . . .' a sleepy male voice answered.

There was what seemed a long pause, filled with faint static and the echo of her own voice, when she asked for Sue.

'Perhaps I have the wrong number?' she continued anxiously, guilty at having dragged a stranger from his bed at some ungodly hour. 'I'm so sorry—'

She would have replaced the receiver but the voice cut in quickly, 'No – no, you haven't got the wrong number. Sue does live here, only – well, the thing is she isn't here at the moment, she . . .' The voice faded out, leaving Stevie wondering if they had been cut off.

'Hello? Hello, are you still there?' she asked.

'Yes – yes – just a moment. I'll put Sue's friend on.' She could hear a scuffle and thought she caught a female voice breathing 'Who is it?', then a girl's voice came on the line.

'Hello, this is Pixie. I'm sorry, Sue isn't here. She's away at the moment, in France—'

'In France? On holiday?' Sue had not mentioned France in her letter. 'This is her mother speaking.'

'Sue's mother!' She should have found out who was calling before she blurted out where Sue was. If she hadn't told her mother the odds were she didn't want her to know. 'Yes, she . . . er . . . she went with an . . . er . . . friend. It was rather a spur of the moment decision. I expect you will get a postcard from her any day.'

'Nicholas – the New Zealand boy? Is that who she went with?' Stevie asked.

'Nick? Er . . . no, I don't think so. I'm not sure . . . Yes I think she did.' Pixie threw Nick a desperate glance and flapped a hand at him in a 'keep quiet – calm down' gesture. Anxious to terminate this conversation in which she seemed to be floundering in ever deeper waters, she rushed on, 'She'll be in touch, I'm sure, Mrs . . .' God, she had even forgotten the woman's name now; all she knew was that it was not the same as Sue's surname.

When she replaced the phone she looked helplessly at Nick. 'Sorry,' she muttered.

'You let her think I was in France with Sue, didn't you?' Nick accused. 'Whatever for, Pixie? Why did you do that?'

'Well, I could hardly tell her the truth, could I?' she protested. 'And anyway, if you had stayed on the phone instead of handing over to me she would have known you weren't in France, wouldn't she?' She glared at Nick then, turning on her heel, flounced back to bed, but she couldn't resist throwing back over her shoulder as she went, 'Just like a man – ask a woman to get you out of a sticky corner then blame her for how she does it. Anyway, if you hadn't been here there wouldn't have been any confusion. Have you found anywhere yet?'

'Yes, I was going to tell you but you were asleep when I got in. I'm really grateful to you, Pixie, for letting me doss down here when I was stuck.'

'Thank Sue, not me, she's the one that went to France,' She replied sleepily.

On the other side of the world, Stevie replaced the phone slowly on its rest, wishing she had never picked it up in the first place. Far from allaying the smouldering niggle of anxiety, she had merely fanned it into flame. Telling herself that her daughter was now a grown woman and her own person she went back to her painting but now nothing seemed to go right. She had broken the spell. It was only when she finally dried her brushes that she remembered that one of the reasons she had telephoned Sue was to ask her for Davey's address.

Time, Stevie was finding, was a commodity in very short supply these days. Looking after two men and two young boys plus all the extra chores she seemed to be expected to do as a Tasmanian farmer's wife occupied her most of the time and drained her of nearly all her energy. She was becoming increasingly frustrated as since she had painted Tom's new bull for the stud sign at the gate she had received several requests to do signs and portraits for other people, and the work was banking up on her.

'I'll need you to drive the truck for us after lunch. I want to get in those few bales of late hay before it rains,' Tom told her as he reached for the cheese platter and cut himself a wedge.

Stevie felt her bile rising. 'Why me?' she gritted. It seemed that whenever she found time to paint she was asked to down tools to satisfy other people's demands.

Tom looked at her in surprise. 'Because there is no one else, and like I said – I don't want it rained on.'

Stevie looked up at the window; the sky was a cerulean blue and the late summer sun was blazing as if it never intended to stop. She had counted on another hour to maybe even finish the dog portrait before she had to fetch the boys home from school.

'Can't you manage without me?'

'No, there is no one else. There isn't much – we should get it done by the time you have to fetch the kids.' He scraped his chair back. 'See you in the paddock – about ten minutes' time.' With that he was gone.

Andrew, rising from the table to follow him, smiled at Stevie. 'Sorry!' He shrugged helplessly.

She jumped up, crashed the dishes into the sink and turned the tap on full blast.

Driving the old truck round the paddock was neither arduous nor challenging, simply a matter of stopping and starting to order while Andrew hoisted the bales on to the tray and Tom arranged them. Stevie stewed. Why was it that men never saw any value or importance in anything a woman did unless it was of direct benefit to them? There were, of course, the few exceptions that proved the rule. David would have realized that her painting mattered, but that was because painting was the most important thing in his own life.

Maybe she should have stuck with independence when Tom erupted into her life again and not let him persuade her to marry him and come to this godforsaken part of the world. At this point in her thoughts her own innate honesty reminded her that he hadn't had to do much persuading. She had been more than willing to join him here on his Tasmanian farm, which wasn't, after all, so godforsaken. Most of the time she thought how lucky she was to live in such a lovely spot. She felt considerably more cheerful as she reminded herself that it would soon be vacation time and Michael would be home from veterinary college. She looked at her watch as the last bale was picked up and saw it was time to go to the school.

With grim satisfaction she laid out cold cuts and salad for tea. She could hardly be expected to cook meals and work in the paddock.

She left the twins to get themselves into bed, trying not to imagine the desultory lick and a promise they would give themselves, and escaped once more to what she was fast coming to think of as 'her sanctuary'. Here she worked till the painting was finished, then dropped into bed, almost too tired to sleep, beside an already snoring Tom.

CHAPTER TWENTY-ONE

S UE folded her clothes and pushed them into her bags
wondering, not for the first time, how it was that the same
garments could take up so much more room repacking than when
they were originally packed. She finally managed to close up the
bags, still feeling resentful, not at her luggage but smarting from
David's rebuke which, mild though it was, made her once again
child to his adult.

She had left him downstairs settling the account and it was
taking him so long that she wondered if he had forgotten her and
already left for Tours. She was standing in the open doorway of her
room when he bounded up the stairs looking, she thought, as if he
had won the lottery. She was about to say this when he forestalled
her. 'Come on, let's get going – give me those bags and I'll pack
them in the car.'

'Car? I thought we were going by train?'

'Changed my mind – hired a car instead.' He looked as excited as
a small boy. 'Come on, Sue, let's get on our way.'

She snatched up her handbag from the bed, glanced round to
make sure nothing was left behind, picked up the last piece of
luggage and followed him down to the street where a neat Renault
waited at the kerb.

As they set off through the busy city streets, Sue was consumed
with sheer terror. Horns blasted her ears with a cacophony of sound

and all the traffic seemed to be heading straight at them. She was about to tell David that he was driving on the wrong side of the road when she remembered that here it was the right side, literally. A quick sideways glance at him reassured her that he did, apparently, know what he was doing. In fact, he was negotiating the traffic with skill and confidence. By the time they reached the outer suburbs of the city she was able to relax and even enjoy herself.

David turned and grinned at her. 'You can relax,' he told her. 'I've spent a lot of time in this country, and driven through most of it.'

'Yes ...' she murmured and settled back to appreciate the scenery. 'It looks so ... French.' She was at a loss for a better description.

'What did you expect France to look like?' David spoke lightly but Sue felt she detected that irritating 'adult to rather stupid child' note in his voice.

When they reached Tours, David drove straight to a family pension near the centre of the city which he said he had been told was good and at this time of the year would not be booked up. The large house was built directly on to the pavement but at the side was a walled garden with a heavy wooden door opening on to the street. It seemed one had to go through this to get to the pension itself and as they closed it behind them it was like stepping into another world. The garden was an oasis of tranquillity in the midst of the busy town. Unfortunately at this time of the year it was too chilly to linger there.

David was itching to start painting and with that end in view they headed off straight after the continental breakfast they took in the company of the other guests each morning. Sue would have been happy to linger over the hot chocolate, fresh croissants and cherry jam, but David wanted to find a suitable spot to set up his easel.

Sue wondered why he had been so eager to come to this part of France as his interest in the many fantastic chateaux in the region only seemed to extend to their appearance in the landscape while she longed to see inside. When she learned from a leaflet in the vestibule that she could join a guided tour taking in several of the nearest chateaux, she called up all her reserves of schoolgirl French and booked.

She was entranced and amazed, the magnificent buildings themselves were for the most part so well preserved, unlike the mostly ruined castles of England and Wales. Outwardly they gave the landscape an almost Disneyish feel, inside she wandered spellbound. She bought sketching materials and as she drew, from life or from photos, she wished Pixie were there to add her stories.

The days passed pleasantly enough; having something of her own to do she was less lonely than watching David, who scarcely noticed whether or not she was there. She wondered why he had suggested she come, and even more why she had accepted.

She started letters to Nick and Pixie but ended up sending an innocuous 'wish you were here' postcard instead. As she dropped it into the letter box she realized how true that was. It would have been fun if they had both been here, but it was Nick she was lonely for. Nick who was now occupying her space in the tiny flat. As a sharp knife of jealousy twisted in her heart she hoped Edgar was spending plenty of time there too.

'I'm glad you are able to amuse yourself,' David remarked one evening as they lingered over the excellent local wine always served with dinner. 'I should have felt guilty if I had thought you were at a loose end while I was working.'

Sue looked at him in astonishment. What did he think she had been doing before she began sketching? She had the feeling that he was relieved she had gone her own way the last few days. She was no doubt nothing more than an irritating distraction, certainly not the painter's muse and inspiration she had romantically imagined herself when they left England.

'I wish we could see a bit more of the area. Couldn't you ... couldn't we ...' She broke off hesitantly. David painting in France was a different person, she was beginning to realize, than David temporarily resting on his laurels in England. For most of the time she was lonely, often bored, and all the time she missed Nick. It was like a steady dull ache. How stupid she had been to think that new scenes would erase his image from her mind.

David too wondered what demon of idiocy had induced him to suggest that Sue tag along with him on what was, after all, a serious working trip. Her youth made him feel old, and he tried to concentrate on his work, then blamed himself for neglecting her. He cursed himself for being all shades of a fool for acceding to her extraordinary request. It had in some odd way tied him to her while at the same time dulled his desire for her. She was not, he thought bitterly, in the least like her mother at all.

'I'll finish the painting I am working on tomorrow,' he told her. 'How about we take the car and go explore the day after that?' It was a somewhat grudging offer made out of his sense of guilt.

'Oh, David, that would be wonderful!' Sue sparkled at the prospect. He could not help but respond to her enthusiasm; he smiled and reached his hand to her across the table. Sue felt her heart skip as she met his eyes and without thinking she reached out and touched his hand. He turned it over, palm up, in hers, and responded with a light pressure then withdrew it. She felt rebuffed, but the brief touch had ignited sexual desire and in her room that night she tossed and turned, her body a reflection of her thoughts which went backwards and forwards over the events of the last few weeks. If only she could rewrite the script.

When she woke the next morning the sun was streaming through the window. She yawned, stretched and finally slid out of bed. In spite of her late sleep, she felt anything but eager to greet the new day. She had carried the turmoil of her thoughts into sleep and dreamed a confusing scenario that featured both Nick and David. She turned her face into the shower and felt somewhat clearer when she stepped out and began to dress.

She hurried downstairs but there was no sign of David. A glance at her watch told her she had indeed slept late, but the knowledge did not dispel her feeling of abandonment, a feeling so strong that to her embarrassment she felt hot tears pricking behind her lids. She closed her eyes, willing them away.

Sue's eyes flew open when she realized that the little waitress was standing looking down at her and asking if she was ready for breakfast. She smiled, nodded, and did her best to concentrate as the girl went on to tell her something. When she caught the word '*père*' she realized that she was telling her that David had breakfasted and left, and also that she thought he was her father.

'Monsieur left early – he said you understand. He had painting things. He asked for packed lunch,' the girl continued. '*Vous comprenez?*' she asked anxiously as she placed the coffee and croissants on the table.

Sue nodded and reached for the coffee. She understood, she would be on her own all day. She tried to suppress the sharp stab of disappointment and resentment forcing her thoughts ahead. David had promised that he would spend the next day with her sight-seeing, so she hoped that was why he had left so early today. She filled in her time in desultory sketching and returned in what she hoped was good time to shower, change and be ready for dinner.

She stopped in confusion when she saw him talking and laughing with a couple around his own age – at least the man was. Three glasses and an almost empty bottle were between them. Anxious to shower and change, Sue tried to slip past them but David called out, 'Sue, come and have a drink.'

Reluctantly she changed course, aware with every step that brought her closer that the other woman was exquisitely and expensively dressed. It was obvious that she had not spent her day out in the open air as Sue had. Her eyes quickly raked Sue from head to toe and back again. 'Yes, come and join us,' she purred, edging nearer to David to make room for Sue between herself and her companion.

'I must go and change, have a shower . . .' Sue stammered. The newcomer had made her feel not only scruffy and ungroomed but also young and painfully lacking in sophistication. She did not know whether to be relieved or hurt when she caught David's eye and he just shrugged in a 'just as you please' gesture. She turned away and headed for the stairs.

Sue stepped into the shower and turned it on full blast, hoping the warm jets of water would dispel her depression along with the accumulated grime of the day. She soaped herself vigorously and turned her face up to the spray. She felt fresh and clean as she towelled herself dry, but even this feeling of physical well-being failed to lift her spirit. In her head she knew she was being foolish and dramatizing a perfectly ordinary situation as she made up with extra care. She took a deep breath, pasted a smile on her face, and went to join David and his friends.

He began to pull out a chair for her but again the woman moved next to him leaving a space between herself and her companion. The man smiled at Sue and with a rueful shrug moved his chair slightly to allow her room to join them. He looked round and snapped his fingers for another glass. In spite of herself, Sue was impressed. She had always admired the men she saw, usually in films, who did this and summoned taxis with the same ease and nonchalance. 'I'm Lance,' he told her, filling the new glass and pushing it across the table to her without bothering to enquire if that was what she wanted. 'And you?'

'Sue – Sue from down under,' David supplied, smiling apologetically at Sue, aware of his omission in not making introductions all round. 'Lance and Leah – old friends of mine.'

'Not so old,' Leah quickly cut in. 'Well, not me anyway.'

'Down under? Are you Australian?' Lance turned to Sue with interest.

'Well, yes and no. I come from Australia but I was born in England and I'm living there now.'

'Australia . . . I've always wanted to go there . . .' Lance sighed. 'Are there really kangaroos and exotic parrots everywhere, and is it as hot and dusty as it looks in all the films?'

Sue smiled. 'Well, there certainly are plenty of kangaroos, though in Tasmania we only have wallabies, and the parrots can be quite a pest to farmers.'

'I prefer this hemisphere. Australia is all sun, snakes and flies,' Leah interrupted with a somewhat theatrical shudder. 'And Tasmania is a backwater, about fifty years behind the times.' Sue resented this criticism of her adopted country and was about to rise hotly to its defence when Lance leaned towards her and in a soft voice confided; 'Leah comes from Tasmania, but she tries to forget it.'

'Oh,' was all Sue could think of in reply. She did not, she decided, like the woman one bit.

She had turned her back on Sue. 'What are you working on now, David? Are you painting all these chateaux?' she purred.'

'Not really – I've been painting landscapes, people. Sue has been sketching the chateaux.'

Leah pouted, obviously not in the least interested in Sue's activities, but Lance immediately asked, 'You are an artist too?'

'Not really, certainly not in David's league,' she said deprecatingly.

'Few people are.' he commented. Sue liked him and wondered how he had got himself tied up with someone as shallow as Leah appeared. She watched her place a scarlet-tipped hand on David's arm. *You can have them both – I don't want either of them,* Sue was tempted to reassure her, watching the slight petulant twist to her mouth as she asked, 'Where shall we go for dinner? We are all having it together, aren't we?'

If Sue hoped for even an instant that David would say they had already made arrangements, she was doomed to disappointment. 'Great idea!' he exclaimed with more enthusiasm than she really felt necessary. 'There's a little place just up the road.'

'You mean walk?' Sue smiled at the dismay in Leah's voice. She caught Lance's eye and knew he was enjoying her amusement.

'He means walk,' Lance confirmed. 'Let's go, I'm hungry.'

The 'little place up the road' really was a small, intimate restaurant that served excellent food. It usually took David and Sue about five minutes to get there; with Leah it took ten. Sue found she was walking with Lance while Leah hung on to David's arm and complained about the distance. Noting the height of her heels and general inadequacy of her shoes for walking anywhere, Sue was not surprised. What did surprise her was David's tolerance.

Sue felt she was failing miserably in her attempt to drum up anything like a party spirit in herself, probably because the other three had enjoyed at least an hour, if not more, drinking before she joined them. They were, to the casual onlooker two couples, but long before they even reached the restaurant Sue knew the other three were a threesome and she was the odd one. The curious thing was she didn't really mind. What she did mind was her heightened awareness of the age gap between herself and David. Lance and to a lesser extent Leah were his contemporaries. As they settled at the table she caught Lance looking at her and guessed that he was wondering just what her relationship was with David. Leah ignored him and monopolized David's attention, leaving Sue with a few speculations of her own.

'Whoops-a-daisy!' Lance was hardly stone cold sober himself but able enough to catch Sue's arm as she swayed on her feet when the cool night air flowed over her. She clung to him unashamedly and placed her feet with exaggerated care on a sidewalk that seemed to have changed its smooth surface to cobblestones while they had their meal. With a slurred 'goodnight,' she concentrated on finding the haven of her room.

By the time she woke next morning the sun was high in the sky, her mouth felt as if it was full of cottonwool balls and her head was like lead. She groaned, squinting blearily at her watch, and saw that it was almost ten o'clock.

With an effort and another groan Sue sat up and swung her legs, which she was relieved to discover now worked normally, over the side of the bed, and padded to the shower. It was wonderful, she reflected a short while later what could be achieved by water. Clean, dressed and freshly made up, she felt equal to the day and anyone she might come across.

She found Lance reading the *Daily Telegraph* with a bored expression on his face. He threw it to one side when he saw her, indicated the coffee on the table in front of him and asked, 'Coffee?'

Sue nodded and waited for him to make some comment about the previous evening, but to her relief he remained silent. 'Please!' she managed, adding with a weak smile, 'I guess I need it.' She glanced round, wondering where David and Leah were.

'David is, of course, off painting somewhere,' Lance told her, drawing the empty cup already on the table towards him and pouring her coffee. 'Anything to eat?' He nodded towards a solitary croissant which was beginning to look past its best. Sue repressed a shudder. 'Not at the moment, thanks.'

'He left early – a couple of hours ago at least. Leah went with him,' he added as if as an afterthought.

'Oh!' Sue let the monosyllable fall into the silence between them. Recalling the hours she had spent alone while David painted, she wondered bitterly whose idea that had been. Catching the hurt in her voice and touched by the disappointment flitting across her face, Lance had a brief moment's regret that he was, however unwittingly, the cause and not the object of it. Sue, looking up, caught the expression on his face before it resumed its normal mask of casual indifference to the world at large. She felt his sympathy and a shaft of anger laced with fear shot through her, prompting her to say, somewhat crisply, 'David is a free agent. I don't own him.'

Lance shrugged. 'The same goes for Leah ... and they have known each other for a long time. She used to model for him.'

'I see,' Sue replied, not really seeing at all. 'I thought ...' she began, not really sure what she had thought other than Leah and

Lance were a well-bonded couple. 'I thought perhaps you and David were old friends.'

'Not at all – I hardly know him. But he and Leah . . .' He trailed off, like Sue unsure of how much to put into words. He shrugged slightly. 'Can't say I was too thrilled to meet up with him, then when I realized he was with you I thought . . .' He shrugged again, raising his eyebrows in a gesture indicative of his inability to express, or even know, exactly what he thought.

Sue wanted to tell him that she was not with David in the way he meant but when she said as much she only made herself sound like a worshipper trailing after a guru.

'David used to be a great friend of my mother,' she tried to explain to Lance.

'I understand.' He patted her hand in an avuncular manner; Sue realized that all she had achieved was to spell out the fact that she was a whole generation younger. Irritated by his assumptions, she wanted to yell at him, *No, you don't understand – and would you please give me my hand back?*

She pushed back her chair and jumped to her feet. 'I'm going for a walk.' She strode out on to the sunlit street, whipping jumbled thoughts into line as she went. She had spent so much time in her own company since they arrived here that she did not know quite why it bothered her that David had gone off with Leah. She half smiled as she turned the words round; she was sure that in actual fact it was Leah who had gone with David. She looked foolish, pathetic even, but then so did Lance, who was equally abandoned, arguably more so. If she had liked him better she might have felt sorry for him. She repressed the uncomfortable thought that if, as Lance had said, David and Leah were friends from way back, it was both childish and unsophisticated of her to mind. Realizing that she had walked almost into the centre of the town, she turned and retraced her steps while she still had her bearings. David and Leah were still out.

Her head ached with an insidious dull throb, an uncomfortable reminder of her behaviour the previous evening – she really had drunk more wine than was good for her. With something halfway between a groan and a sigh she flopped down on the bed.

'Sue – Sue, are you OK?' From some distant spot David's voice reached her through the layers of muzzy consciousness that enveloped her like a fog.

'What do you want?' Her voice sounded grumpy, even to her own ears. She forced her eyes open and looked up into David's face, surprisingly close; he was sitting on the edge of her bed. He looked anxious and rather paternal, and she felt embarrassed and young. She closed her eyes again, then tried to push herself up to a sitting position. At least when she opened them again she was level with him, but as she sat up he stood and once again was looking down on her.

'I was tired . . .' Her voice was defensive. 'I've been out for a walk. I must have dropped to sleep.' She moved her head tentatively, relieved to find that she had slept off the headache. As she swung her legs over the side of the bed, she dropped her gaze to avoid looking directly into his face and mumbled an apology for her behaviour the previous evening.

David held one hand up in a gesture intended to stifle her words. Sue thought he looked like a cleric bestowing a blessing. She suppressed a smile, for she could see he was being seriously forgiving.

'Say no more,' he abjured her. 'Everybody should get drunk now and then, stops the ego getting inflated.' He smiled. 'Subject closed, OK?' Sue nodded, feeling about six years old. 'Let's get some lunch then, if you are hungry.' Sue nodded again, realizing that, yes, she was hungry, and followed David downstairs.

There was no sign of either Leah or Lance as they crossed the vestibule. Sue found she was almost running to keep up with David, who seemed in a great hurry to get out of the *pension*. Once out in the street he dropped his pace and she caught up with him. She was about to ask what the rush was when David half turned to her and mumbled, 'I think we need to talk, Sue.'

Sue thought so too, but she wasn't at all sure that they both wanted to talk about the same thing so she just grunted.

They walked in silence and when David abruptly turned into a little bistro she almost went on without him.

Their lunch of steaming vegetable soup and hot crusty rolls accompanied by red house wine in a carafe was already in front of them before he volunteered any more.

'I think you should go home.'

'Home . . . do you mean Australia?' Sue asked in the blank voice of someone who has just had a door slammed in their face.

'No, no – I didn't mean that. I just meant back to London.'

'I . . . see . . .' Sue picked up the soup spoon she had let fall at his words and tentatively sipped at what now seemed a very tasteless dish. She felt almost physically hurt and she didn't see at all.

She crumbled her roll and dipped her spoon once more into the bowl in front of her. 'I'm sorry. I shouldn't have come. I'm really sorry.'

'No, no, I'm the one to be sorry, not you. I've treated you really badly . . .' He trailed off, leaving Sue wondering just what he meant.

'Is – is it because of Leah?'

'No, no. It has nothing to do with her.' He paused, looking into his own soup as if he might find inspiration there. 'No – her arrival could perhaps be viewed as a bit of a catalyst but it certainly wasn't the cause for anything.'

'Me then. . . ?' Sue's voice was scarcely above a whisper. 'I know you don't really fancy me, in spite of . . .' Her voice cracked. 'I shouldn't have come,' she repeated.

He reached across the table and caught her hand. 'Don't feel that. It's not true. I like you very much. I think you are quite lovely, in fact, but . . .'

'But now Leah has turned up, you don't want me.'

'Oh, Sue! It's not like that at all!' He brought his hand down on the table so hard to emphasize his words that his soup spoon rattled against the dish. 'Sure, I like Leah a lot and I know her well, but she is with Lance and. . . .'

'And?' Sue prompted.

'You are different – you are Stevie's daughter. I should never have done what I did even though I had the best of intentions.' He broke off and smiled ruefully. 'Don't think I didn't enjoy it and don't, not for one half second, ever think you are not attractive, because you are . . .' He looked at her across the table and shrugged in a gesture of helplessness, hopelessness, she wasn't sure which, He smiled a rather crooked smile then picked up his soup spoon.

'Lance told me Leah used to model for you,' Sue said with studied casualness.

'Yes, she did. But can we drop her from this conversation? She has no relevance to it.

Sue raised her eyebrows and when the silence had gone on longer than she could bear, asked in a level voice, 'Just why do you think I should go back to England?'

David sighed, then leaned towards her, and in the patient tones of someone explaining something to a rather dim pupil said, 'Because you shouldn't be here, you are wasting your time. I am here to work—'

'And I'm just playing and being a nuisance to you. Is that what you are saying?' Sue interrupted.

'No, it is not what I am saying – well, not really. You are on the fringes of my conscience, and I don't need that. We had a good time in Paris, you've had a holiday, seen a bit of France – now, please, Sue, go back to London, do something with your life, go back to art school, get another job, but *do something*.'

'This has nothing to do with Leah turning up?' Sue asked suspiciously.

'Absolutely nothing. It's just that, oh hell, I feel bad about what happened, almost as if I committed some dreadful sin, like incest.'

'But I asked you to . . . do what you did,' she reminded him, 'and when you didn't want to do it again I thought that you didn't like me.'

'I've told you, I liked you, and what we did, very much. But. . . .'

'You knew me too well; it felt like incest,' she reminded him. 'Does that mean that you still carry a torch for Mum?'

David considered this. 'I don't know, I don't honestly know. But I do know that I felt in some way as if I was betraying the friendship she and I had shared, the feelings I had for her then. That didn't make me feel good, but don't ever think badly of yourself. Go back to London, to your life there, move on with the memory you and I share tucked safely away, learn from it, but don't let it intrude in your life. And take a tip from someone who knows: when you meet that "certain someone" don't let them slip away because you have pride or a conscience or anything else.'

'Oh, David, I'm sorry, but it wasn't your fault, it was always Tom for Mum, probably even when she was married to my father, certainly through her second marriage. When he turned up back in her life the way he did then nothing else seemed to register with her.' She reached out and touched his hand. 'You are a good man, David, really good. I wish—'

'Let the past go, Sue, for both us. We have to move on.' He sighed, then asked crisply, 'Have you got enough money to get you back to London?'

She nodded. 'Yes, but thanks. Don't worry about me – only do me a favour, please, David?' Her voice had sunk almost to a whisper.

'If I can.'

She looked across the table at him, swallowed hard then dropped her gaze from his face. 'Tell me, please, why . . . why you've not . . . Well, is it something about me . . . or what?'

She thought he wasn't going to answer, then she felt his fingers touch her clenched fist as it lay on the table top and slowly looked up. His face was kind and concerned, the years seemed to slide back and she was a child again.

'Oh, Sue! No – no – don't ever think I don't find you attractive. I did and I do. You are a very special young woman, you deserve the best, and I hope you find it.'

'Thank you,' she said smiling, 'I'll go back tomorrow. After that beautiful little speech anything else would be an anti-climax.'

It was a disappointment to discover that Lance and Leah had not moved on. She had hoped to have David to herself for this last evening, but as before they were a party of four for dinner.

Leah, Sue thought sourly, looked like a model straight from the catwalk yet she had probably thrown on the first dress that came to hand. Sue had agonized for ages over what to leave unpacked for this last evening. Her gloomy feeling of inadequacy made her believe Leah's rather banal conversation pearls of wit while she became tongue-tied.

Had she not been so absorbed in her own gloomy thoughts, Sue would have realized that the other girl's conversation was mostly rather shallow gossip about people that she and David both knew. Lance didn't know them either so this had the effect of isolating David and Leah in an intimate little world of their own.

She was careful not to drink much at all this time and, making the excuse that she had a train to catch next day, escaped early to her room.

CHAPTER TWENTY-TWO

FEELING like a wrung-out rag, unwashed and totally exhausted afer two train journeys in France and one in England and a choppy night crossing in between, Sue headed for the little flat that represented home. She fumbled in her bag for her key and, unable to find it, rang the bell. With an effort she focused on the days of the week. She thought it was Saturday – with any luck that would mean Pixie would be home.

'Sue! What – where. . . ?' Pixie stammered before changing her focus to peer over Sue's shoulder to the street behind her. 'Where's David. . . ?'

Sue shook her head, stared blankly for a moment at her friend then, to her intense chagrin, burst into noisy, gulping sobs.

'You had better come in.' Pixie pulled her firmly through the door, steered her to the nearest chair and, in the absence of anything else, thrust a tea towel into her hands.

When she realized what she was mopping up her tears with Sue managed a weak smile. 'I'm not going to cry that much,' she protested, hoping she was speaking the truth. 'I'm just so tired – and I've made such a mess of things. I'm sorry.' She mumbled into the folds of linen cloth. 'I suppose I shouldn't have come here. I didn't know where else to go.' She dabbed at her swollen eyelids, thrust the tea towel back at Pixie, sniffed and made for the door.

'Nick isn't here – he went ages ago,' Pixie told her 'It was only temporary, because he was suddenly stuck with nowhere to live.'

'Oh, yes, but . . . I thought . . .' Sue floundered to a stop. There was something about Pixie's shuttered expression that stopped her saying any more.

Pixie smiled ruefully and shook her head. 'Go on – you can say it. I know what you are thinking all right, but you are wrong, quite wrong, about Nick anyway.' Something about her friend's woebegone expression alerted Sue.

'You. . . ?' she began, then stopped, unable to ask the question in her mind. She needn't have worried. Pixie, it seemed, was ready to tell her anyway.

'Nick is one of the best people you could ever meet, in every way, and you treated him abominably. I thought maybe I could pick up the pieces when you went off with that . . . that artist fellow. I should have known no one existed in Nick's world but you, and you didn't care a damn!' As if unable to sit still, or sit near Sue, Pixie crossed the tiny kitchen corner and somewhat noisily began making coffee.

'I'd better go.' Sue got up and moved towards the door.

'Oh, don't be such a fool!' Pixie grabbed her by the sleeve. 'Sit down. There is no point at all in you and I fighting over N— this. We've been friends for too long, and collaborators – think of our book, we could do another. Nick is on his way home; we probably won't hear any more from him – either of us.' Her voice faded on a wobble.

Sue sat down again with a thump. 'He's gone back to New Zealand?'

Nodding bleakly, Pixie handed Sue a steaming mug of coffee and sat down opposite her, cradling her own mug in her hands. 'That's what I said.' She stared down into her coffee, finally saying, almost to herself, 'I loved him, he loves you, Edgar loves me, and you love that artist fellow, so what are you doing back here?'

'Because I don't love him, not that way.' Pixie looked up and Sue saw disbelief, hurt and anger chase across her face. 'He didn't ditch me if that is what you are thinking.' Sue felt too exhausted to care; she felt she had aged ten years in the last two weeks. 'Why did Nick go back? I thought he planned to stay about two years?'

'He was shattered when you went off to France. I was stupid enough to tell him who you had gone with. I thought he might see the light, or more specifically, me . . . I thought maybe I could pick up the pieces and put him together again. I couldn't – and now I never will. When I realized you were all he cared about I pointed out that if you really want something, or someone, you have to go get them. I thought he might go and get you, but then he got an SOS from New Zealand. His father was very ill, so . . .' Pixie shrugged, then got up and moved over to the pantry cupboard. 'I'm going to marry Edgar. The poor dear doesn't know it yet – but I am. You hungry?'

'Starving,' Sue admitted as her stomach rumbled in corroboration.

Pixie's spiel had at least stemmed her flow of tears. Was she right when she said she thought Nick might have come looking for her? If only he had!

'Vegetable or mushroom?'

'What? – oh, soup. Mushroom, please.' Pixie was standing in front of her with a can in each hand.

'So, what are you going to do now?' Pixie asked as she placed a bowl of soup in front of Sue.

'Are you really going to marry Edgar?' she asked.

Pixie shrugged. 'Why not? He loves me and I like him very much. We'll rub along very nicely.'

Sue looked at her friend drinking soup in the same single-minded way she did most things. Yes, she thought, they would. She felt more than a little envious.

'Oh my God! I clean forgot . . .' Pixie dropped her spoon with a clatter into her dish. 'Your mother rang, I said you were on holiday in France and she seemed a bit surprised. Hadn't you told her?'

Sue shook her head. 'But I sent her a postcard from Paris.'

'Big deal,' Pixie remarked laconically. She thought Sue casual in her attitude to her family, especially her mother who, on the few occasions she had spoken briefly to her on the phone, sounded so nice. 'You should ring her and tell her you are safely back here,' she couldn't resist suggesting. Pixie had seen David's painting of Sue's mother in the gallery and thought the whole thing very romantic; she was sure he must have been in love with her when he painted it but Sue closed up like a clam when she voiced the thought.

'Yeah – tomorrow.' Sue didn't feel up to a heart-to-heart with her mother at the moment. 'It's the middle of the night in Australia right now.'

'Tomorrow never comes,' Pixie muttered cryptically.

'You are turning into a real mother hen,' Sue told her sourly.

But Pixie was right, Sue found an excuse the next day not to call home, and the next and the next.

Sue found time hanging heavily on her hands. When she went to see Madame Mancini and learned that there was no chance of her being reinstated in her old job she almost regretted dropping out of college. She missed Nick, more than missed him, almost mourned for him, for now he had returned to New Zealand she felt he had gone out of her life for ever. She missed David, and she even missed Angela, who had been taken on some holiday or other by her grandmother. She met Gina for lunch one day but she was in the all-absorbing early stages of a new romance and in no mood to listen to the details of anyone else's love life, especially when it was as arid as Sue's.

'Boys like Nick don't grow on trees,' she told Sue sternly, 'and he was mad about you.'

'I wasn't in love with him,' Sue protested. 'At least, I didn't think I was.'

'Pouf!' Gina dismissed such airy flim-flam with one of her flamboyant gestures. 'Pixie was in love with him, but she couldn't keep him, even when you threw him into her lap.'

'Is that true? Was she really?'

Gina looked at her pityingly. 'You are a hopeless pair.' She shrugged.

That evening Sue showed Pixie the drawings of the chateaux, hoping they might inspire her to write a story to fit them. But Pixie looked at them, duly admired them, and shook her head.

'I don't know, Sue, my imagination seems to have deserted me. Writer's block, don't they call it? Or maybe I just can't be bothered.'

The couldn't-care-less tone of her voice, so unlike Pixie who had, if anything, been the most enthusiastic of the two of them over their original book, made Sue look at her sharply.

'Did you sleep with Nick when he stayed here?' she asked.

'It's none of your bloody business!' Pixie slammed the china she was carrying to the sink down so hard on the draining board that a cup bounced onto the floor and broke. She stooped to retrieve the pieces and when she straightened up Sue saw the gleam of tears. 'You are nothing better than ... than a dog in the manger!' she accused. 'You didn't want him yourself but you resent anyone else—'

Sue was all contrition. 'Pixie, please! I didn't mean anything – it was a stupid thing to say and you are right, it isn't any of my business.' Then why, she wondered, did she feel such a searing pain at the thought of Nick and Pixie together, or Nick and anyone for that matter?

Sue closed the folder on her sketches with a sigh. 'Oh well, it was just a thought. I don't suppose they are much good anyway.' If only she could inspire Pixie to work with her again.

Pixie was immediately sorry. 'Of course they are good – it's me. Let me have another look.' She reached for the folder. 'Do they really look like castles straight from a fairy tale? I will try, I promise, to think of a story to fit them. After all, we did agree to give the publisher an option on our next book. We can't do that unless we write one.'

Sue put them away until the time when Pixie's imagination was in full flight again.

Next day she signed on at the agency that specialized in supplying temporary office staff where Pixie worked and found the challenge of not knowing where, or even if, she were going to work each day cathartic. They seemed to have slipped back into the old pattern and she was totally unprepared when Pixie asked her in a tight voice, 'What are you planning to do?'

'Do?' Sue asked blankly. 'In what way?'

'Well, what I really meant was, where are you planning to stay?'

Sue hadn't planned, she had just assumed – wrongly, it seemed, for Pixie's next words pulled her up short.

'I mean, are you looking for somewhere else because Angela will be back soon.'

'Angela . . .' Sue repeated the name blankly as if she had never heard it before. 'B-but . . .' Sue stammered. 'I thought . . .'

'I told you, her grandmother has taken her away somewhere, on a tour of relatives, I think. Anyway, I promised her she could come here if she wanted – it's about the only place her grandmother will let her live. She seems to think I'm a good influence or something. You can stay here if you like, but it didn't seem to work when the two of you were here together before, and anyway there really isn't room for three in this place.'

Sue gaped. This was a new Pixie, strong and determined, not the sweet, compliant, rather mousy person she had first met on the ship.

'Why didn't you tell me that when I first arrived? I would have had a bit more time to find somewhere else.'

Pixie shrugged. 'I don't know. I suppose I didn't think you would want to stay.'

'I thought we were friends.' Sue felt hurt and let down. 'Why wouldn't I want to stay here?' She drained her mug, got up abruptly, and walked over to the sink. 'I'll start looking first thing in the morning.' She didn't think she could face up to being cramped in this tiny flat again with Angela, especially if she was the one who had to doss down in a sleeping bag on the floor.

192

She tossed and turned for what seemed an age that night, thinking about the way things had gone recently and wishing she could turn the clock back. She felt that she had made just about every mistake in the book, starting with the disastrous night she and Nick had spent when they visited his relatives. She recalled how she had liked them, and that made her think what a nice person Nick himself was. She finally dropped into an uneasy sleep, dreaming a garbled dream in which he figured.

She reached out and fumbled for the alarm clock, then, when it failed to stop even when her hand found the button, she realized the ring was coming from the phone. She stumbled out of bed, stubbing her toe in the process.

Pixie, looking far more awake than she felt, was saying 'I'll call her' into the mouthpiece. Seeing Sue, she thrust it in her direction. 'Your stepfather,' she mouthed.

Sue snatched the phone, sudden panic squeezing her heart. 'Tom...?' she breathed, her voice husky with sleep and panic. Something had to be wrong – he never rang her. 'Tom...' she repeated, her voice now sharp with fear. 'What is it?'

'Hello, Sue,' he maddened her by replying calmly. 'Don't get in a panic but we are in a bit of strife here. Your mother doesn't know I have called you—'

'What's the matter, Tom? Has something happened to Mum? Is she sick?' Sue felt like screaming with impatience and anxiety.

'No, not sick, but she's had an accident...'

'An accident? What sort of an accident? Is she hurt badly?'

'No, not serious. She's broken her ankle, that's all.'

'What do you mean, that's all? How did she do it? Is it bad?'

'If you would stop interrupting me I might be able to tell you.' Tom's patience was giving out. 'She tripped, coming down a step, simple as that. Point is she is in plaster, can't do much, can't drive or anything. I thought – well, I wondered – could you come home for a while?' He paused. 'We need you, Sue.'

'But Tom, it takes weeks to get back! Even if I could get a passage straight away, by the time I get there Mum will probably be OK.'

'You could fly – I'll telegraph the fare to your bank. If you are prepared to be on standby for a flight you'll get one, but you just might be able to get one anyway. See what you can do, and I'll have the money there for you.'

Well, Sue thought as she slid back under the bedclothes, here was the solution to all her problems: somewhere to live and something to do. Tom's plea, *We need you*, was balm to her wounded feelings. She could guess how her mother would be chafing at her enforced immobility but there was no gain-saying it was extraordinarily fortuitous timing.

It seemed that all the fates were conspiring to get Sue back to Tasmania, for she was able to get a flight leaving London late the very next night. She tried not to see the relief that flitted across Pixie's face when she told her. The day was spent in frantic packing. It was lucky, she reflected, that she had not succeeded in finding somewhere to live. She said as much to Pixie as she hugged her goodbye. 'Give my love to Angela,' she called, and discovered she really meant it, as she clambered into the taxi after her bags.

The novelty of flying soon wore off and Sue arrived in Melbourne washed out and disorientated by the long flight and thankful for a couple of hours' break on terra firma before boarding another plane for Tasmania.

By the time she touched down at Launceston Airport, Sue had worked out an abridged and censored version of her relationship with David that would be suitable for her mother's ears. She was pretty certain she would be asked about him.

In spite of, or maybe because of, her travel weariness, she greeted her younger brother Michael with a wide smile when she saw him waiting for her.

'Gee, Sue, it's really good of you to come.' Sue smiled; she didn't think it necessary to tell him that it had actually suited her. He stowed her gear into the Holden Ute. 'This bust ankle has knocked

Mum for six. You know how she is, always busy, everything under control, her life organized to the nth degree!' Sue wondered if her mother would care for Michael's report. She guessed that the rest of the family, who relied on her mother so much, were the ones really knocked for six. A smile twitched at the corners of her mouth as her brother brought her up to date with happenings at home.

From her seat beside Michael, Sue drank in the Tasmanian countryside. Everything – landscape, houses – struck her as vibrant and colourful, in stark contrast to the drab greys of London, only slightly relieved in places by evidence of spring breaking through. Even France, where spring came earlier, had not stirred her as this landscape did. She had thought she was returning home when she went to England; now she knew this was home.

'How does it feel to be back?' Michael turned to her with a grin as he turned into the rough, unsealed lane that led to the homestead. 'Maybe I should have asked you instead what it felt like to go back to England. I want to go myself as soon as I qualify.'

Her first impulse was to say 'Don't'. Instead she made an honest attempt to answer his question. 'It felt exciting at first,' she admitted, 'much like it felt coming here. Everything was different, exciting . . .'

She trailed off, remembering those early days, and the fun of finding a flat with Pixie and setting up home. For a moment she thought almost longingly of her friend, then remembered how their friendship had lost some of its spark. 'I was lucky,' she told her brother. 'I met up with such a nice group on the ship, all of us young and full of dreams, and we stayed friends when we arrived. I think it might be more difficult to go by yourself by air and be all on your own when you got there.'

'But you knew people there too,' Michael reminded her. 'Nanny was alive then, and you met up with David too.'

'Yes,' she admitted, 'that's true. But Nanny isn't there any more and David spends a lot of his time in France.'

'Is that what you were doing in France?' Michael looked sideways at her, his voice teasing but his eyes keen. Sue was spared having to answer – they had reached the house and the greetings of excited dogs and children filled the air.

CHAPTER TWENTY-THREE

Tom, Stevie thought, sometimes expected too much of her. As the boys grew older they demanded more, not less, of her time, she sometimes felt like a one-woman taxi service. She seldom had time to ride her beloved mare these days, and when she did she was always in a rush. Today was no exception – as usual she was hurrying with her saddle over one arm and her bridle draped over the other, and did not notice the rein dragging round her foot. Not until she tripped and found herself sprawling on the concrete yard. A searing pain shot through her ankle and she heard a distinct crack. She knew before she tried to stand that it was broken. The tears that sprang to her eyes were caused as much by rage and sheer disappointment as physical pain.

Tom turned immediately from the horse he was saddling when he heard her yelp of agony. One glance at her twisted ankle and white face and he was at her side. Yelling instructions to Andrew to carry on as best he could, he picked her up bodily in his arms, put her in the Holden and without more ado headed for the hospital.

It was while he was waiting for Stevie to be treated that he decided Sue must come home. He knew her mother would never ask that of her so it was up to him to get her here. Having ascertained that he had ample time, Tom went straight to the bank and arranged for the transfer of sufficient funds to Sue's account to cover the cost of an air ticket, one way. He didn't tell Stevie what he had done – time enough for that when he knew Sue was on her way.

Dimmed by pain and the effect of pain-killing drugs, the next twenty-four hours passed in such a haze that when she emerged Stevie felt the time had dropped into a black hole somewhere, and she with it.

Facing reality was no less painful; how was she going to cope? More pertinent, how on earth would her all-male household manage without her, or rather with her, for she felt she was just an added burden to them. No one, she told herself, was indispensable; if she died they would have to get along without her. This thought neither cheered nor helped, she fretted, agonized and tortured herself with futile guilt feelings. Then when she couldn't do the myriad things she wanted to do, she sank into a morass of frustration and self-pity that was totally alien to her nature.

Stevie was ensconced on the old day bed in the kitchen near the phone shelling peas when Sue rang from Melbourne to say what time she would arrive at Launceston Airport.

'Sue!'

'Hello, Mum, how are you?'

'Fine, just fine,' Stevie lied. There seemed little point in telling her that she was laid up with a broken ankle, for what could she do on the other side of the world?

'That's great!' Sue played along with the fiction for a few moments, chatting idly about inconsequential things before adding, when her mother asked if she were back from her holiday in France, 'Could someone meet me at Launceston Airport?'

'W-what? Where are you?' Stevie stammered, totally confused.

'In Melbourne, about to catch the Launceston plane. Can you meet me?'

Stevie had no alternative but to answer truthfully, 'Well, no, Sue I can't . . .'

'Can't?' Sue interrupted. 'What do you mean?' Tom had asked her not to tell her mother that he had rung and asked her to come. She felt she was doing a pretty good cover-up job.

'I've broken my ankle,' Stevie confessed after a pause. 'So stupid, and such a nuisance to everyone. I can't drive at the moment, but I'll get someone to meet you, don't worry. Just tell me the time you get in. Oh, Sue, darling, how wonderful you are here!' It seemed too good to be true. Had an SOS been sent? A glance at the time told her it was almost morning tea time. When the men came in and failed to show surprise that Sue had rung, she was sure of it.

'Sue here? That's great – she couldn't have come at a better moment.' Tom sounded genuine enough but Stevie did not miss the look he exchanged with Michael, home on vacation. 'Yeah, great,' he repeated. 'You'd better go and collect your sister from the airport, Michael.'

The hours dragged and long before it was possible Stevie strained her ears for the sound of the vehicle on the long drive leading to the house. Forgotten were the tensions in their relationship, she was only aware of how much she had missed her daughter. She cursed the plaster on her leg that prevented her running to the door in welcome as Michael rounded the last bend and drew to a halt in a swirl of gravel. Her heart thudded as the car doors slammed and she caught her breath on something between a laugh and a sob as they came in together, the latter caused by the sudden stab of regret that their father had not lived to see them grow up. They looked such a fine pair together. It was so long since she had thought of Martin that she had to gulp over the tight ball of emotion in her chest and for a second she saw her son and daughter through a mist of tears.

Then she opened her arms. 'Sue!' she cried. 'How wonderful to see you!'

'Mum!' Sue crossed the room in a single bound to the old day bed where Stevie lay with her plastered leg resting on a cushion. 'Oh, Mum!'

Michael looked across at his mother and sister locked together and felt a momentary and quite unexpected prick of jealousy. He glanced at his watch. 'Is anyone getting the twins from school?' he asked. 'Or should I go?'

'Oh, Michael, would you?' Stevie gave a small guilty laugh. 'Do you know, I had quite forgotten them in the excitement of Sue coming home!' She turned to Sue as Michael left to collect his young half-siblings. 'How about a nice cup of tea before those two tearaways get home and shatter the peace?' She nearly added, *And you can tell me all about everything*, but a glance at her daughter's face reminded her that she was a grown woman now and there would be no confidences unless she chose to give them.

Sue seemed far more interested in talking about what had been happening here than her experiences in England and was anxious to know just how Stevie had broken her ankle. The warm feeling when they had first greeted each other did not seem to have dissipated. Stevie hoped they could avoid the wary tenseness that seemed to characterize so many mother/daughter relationships.

There was so much she wanted to talk about: why Sue had given up the art course that had been her main reason for going to England, the job she had taken, the children's book she and her friend Pixie had done, about her meeting up with David. But most of all about the young man from New Zealand she had met on the boat going to England.

The last was the only thing she got any answers about, and that in a most unexpected way. They had just finished their evening meal and Sue had announced that she was taking an early night in the hope it would cure her jet lag when the phone rang. Tom, who had answered it, held out the receiver towards Sue. 'For you!'

'Me?' Sue asked in astonishment. 'Who on earth?' She wondered who in the world knew she was here in Tasmania, other than Pixie, and she could think of no earthly reason why she should call her.

'It's a man,' Tom told her, shaking the phone lightly. 'Come on,' he added impatiently, 'it's long distance.'

When Sue took the phone and spoke a tentative 'hello' into the mouthpiece, she was astonished to hear Nick's familiar voice on the line. 'Nick?' she breathed in amazement.

'Hello, Sue. How are you?' He sounded as if he really wanted to know.

'Fine – fine – but where are you? Why have you rung?'

'I'm back home in New Zealand. Dad was taken ill so I came back.' There was a pause, then he rushed on. 'I heard from Pixie you were on the way back. I – I just rang on the off chance you were already here.'

'Thanks,' Sue said, feeling guilty and inadequate. 'How good of Pixie.' She meant to sound sarcastic but Nick took her remark at face value.

'She said she needed to make something up to you – something like that. I expect you know what she meant. How is your mother?'

'Fine, apart from her ankle. I suppose Pixie told you that too.' Sue realized that her mother could not help hearing and would guess that she was here because she had been sent for. Why did Pixie have to put her oar in? 'Are you still there, Nick?' The silence seemed to go on for ever.

'I'm still here. I – I had to ring to see if you are all right, but this call is costing. I'd better go . . . can I write to you?' The question came in a rush.

'I guess so.' Sue wondered if that was the reason for his call.

'I haven't got your address,' Nick pointed out, recalling her just as she was about to replace the receiver. There was a thoughtful look on her face as she stood still for a moment before turning back to the room. She wondered what Pixie had said to him, and why she had bothered anyway. But she was glad she had; she had not expected ever to hear anything of Nick again, nor to feel so pleased that she had.

Sue finally turned back towards the room and looked across towards her mother. Stevie was reading the paper Michael had picked up with the mail, and she heard her give a sharp intake of breath then hold the paper closer and reread a news item. When she looked up at Sue her face had paled. 'Whatever is it, Mum?'

Stevie held out the paper towards her pointing as she did so to a news paragraph and a picture of an attractive young woman. Even as she took the paper from her mother's outstretched hand a shock of recognition ran through Sue. Leah. But what was her picture doing in the Hobart daily paper?

When she read the accompanying paragraph, the shock waves that engulfed her turned her legs to jelly so that she sank down helplessly in the nearest chair. A low moan escaped her lips and absurdly, in the midst of her horror, she thought, That's what Nick meant – that's why he rang. It was only much later that it occurred to her that to have been concerned about her at all was some measure of his feeling for her. Dazed, she read through the news item again, forcing her senses to take in the meaning of the words.

Tasmanian actress killed in fatal car crash in France, she read. There were a few brief details about Leah and her career, which it described as 'promising,' and then went on to add, almost as a postscript, *Her companion was David Jones, a painter who has recently gained some recognition in England. Both died instantly in the accident, a head-on collision with a truck. Leah Collis was driving at the time.*

'What the hell was he doing, letting her drive? She probably forgot they drive on the other side of the road there!' Sue burst out angrily. 'David was used to driving in France.'

Looking up from the paper still gripped in her hand, Sue looked across the room and met her mother's intent gaze on her. Even through the tears swimming in her own eyes she could see the question in her mother's. Their gaze locked and held for a moment while the other members of the family looked from one to the other, puzzled by the sudden tension in the room.

Sue was forced to admire her mother's self-control as she turned to Michael. 'There is a news item in the paper about David Jones. You remember him from those childhood holidays in Wales? He has been killed, in France. He was with Leah Collis.'

'Of course I remember him. I liked him, he was good to us kids.' He didn't add that at one time he had hoped he might be their stepfather. 'But what was he doing in France with Leah Collis?'

'They were on holiday,' Sue snapped. 'If you don't mind, I'm going to bed. I am just about whacked – the journey and everything.' She went across to her mother and kissed her lightly on the cheek. 'Goodnight, Mum. I'll be up bright-eyed and bushy-tailed all ready to take over the reins.'

'Goodnight, Sue. It's very good of you to come home and help out.' Unconsciously her slight emphasis on the last two words was a direct reaction to Sue's suggestion that she would take over. 'Oh, by the way, I'm afraid you will have to have the sleep-out. I commandeered your room as a studio – it has the best light.'

'That's fine by me. I like the sleep-out,' Sue told her, forcing a smile. 'Goodnight all. I'm off before I drop on the spot.'

Turning, she left the room, still feeling stunned by the news she had just heard. The sleep-out was an enclosed verandah that ran along the whole of one side of the house, roomier than any of the bedrooms. It was fine in the summer, but a bit chilly in winter.

Michael had put her bags there; she unpacked only what she needed for the night and slid between the sheets with a sigh of relief.

But the change in time zones, jet lag, and most of all the news about David, kept sleep at bay. When she finally dropped off her cheeks were wet with tears.

CHAPTER TWENTY-FOUR

W HEN Sue made her way to the kitchen after anything but a restorative night she found her mother leaning heavily on one of her crutches while she struggled to make breakfast.

'Oh Mum, let me do that, you sit down.'

Thankfully Stevie dropped into the nearest chair. She looked up at her daughter with a rueful smile. 'I won't ask if you slept well because I can see you didn't. In fact, you don't look much more capable than I am of running this house. Maybe two half women will cope as well as one complete woman. We'll do our best, shall we?'

Sue looked her mother in the face. 'Yes,' she said, 'we'll do our best.' And she knew they both meant much more than just getting breakfast.

'Can you go and see if those twins are getting dressed?' Stevie asked. 'They'll be late for school if they don't hurry.'

When Sue returned to the kitchen a few minutes later with the two little boys scrubbed and dressed, looking far better than they were likely to do for the rest of the day, she found Michael just coming in with a pail half full of warm foaming milk. 'I've milked old Clover this morning for you,' he told Sue magnanimously, indicating the bucket.

'Thanks.' Sue's voice was dry as she took in the implication of his words and thought ruefully of the convenience of milk in a bottle. She had forgotten just how much her mother did. Driving back home after dropping the twins off at the school gate, she remembered how hard her mother had worked during the war years. She had milked a cow then too. She had also 'dug for victory' with a vengeance and kept the household in fresh vegetables, in addition to coping with austerity and finding time for evacuated children as well as her own. But she had help – Nanny and dear old Mrs Evans, who had helped run the house since her mother married her father.

It had not occurred to Sue before to wonder if her mother was really happy here with Tom on his Tasmanian farm. She supposed she was, and hoped so; it was not a life of ease but beautiful enough to make up for the hard work. On a clear morning like this, Mount Roland was visible in all his glory, not wrapped in a cloak of grey mist.

'God, Mum, I'm sorry.' Sue was overcome with guilt when she found Stevie perched on a kitchen stool with her crutches propped up against the sink beside her, peeling potatoes. 'Let me do that – that's what I'm here for.'

'You've come halfway round the world just to peel potatoes?' She turned to Sue with a wry smile. 'Let me do the things I can do, please. The men won't be in for morning tea – they've gone away to the far paddock marking lambs.'

Sue gave a small grimace at this euphemistic description. As a teenage newcomer to Tasmanian rural life, she had been horrified when she learned that 'marking' lambs meant putting tight rubber rings round the small creatures' tails and testicles, if they had them, so that, deprived of a blood supply, they atrophied and dropped off. When she expressed her concern, Tom had dryly asked her if she would prefer to go out with a knife and cut them off. Years later when her brother became a veterinary student, she had asked him about it and he had told her that it did seem as humane a way of any of performing these necessary operations; after a short period of initial discomfort they didn't seem to worry. 'Only thing is, there's no lambs' tail pie with this method,' he teased.

She was older and not so squeamish now, but all the same she was glad she had not been called on to help. 'Are you ready for coffee?' she asked her mother as she helped herself to Weeties and put bread in the toaster.

'It's always the right time for me to have coffee,' Stevie admitted. 'I've nearly finished these potatoes so we'll have one together.'

Sue, waiting for the water to boil, was pretty sure that her mother would initiate a heart-to-heart over the coffee and was not certain she either wanted or could cope with it just yet. With that thought came grief, sharp and searing, as she remembered; when she turned back to the table with coffee for them both her eyes were misted with tears.

Stevie appeared not to notice as she struggled to a chair at the kitchen table. She stirred the mug Sue passed her and didn't look at her daughter when she spoke. 'Tell me about David.' Her voice was soft but left no doubt in Sue's mind that she expected an answer.

Sue looked up and met her eyes across the table. 'Wh-what about David?' she mumbled, unable to hold her mother's gaze. 'What do you want me to tell you – that it's all my fault he's dead?' Her voice rose on a note of hysteria before, to both their consternation, she gulped and burst into tears.

'I'm sorry,' Stevie said quietly. 'Of course that is not what I want you to tell me. For one thing I'm sure it is not true, and for another I had no intention of prying. I apologize. David was once a very good friend to me. I was shocked to learn of his death and I just wanted to know something about him, something good. Tell me about his success.'

But Sue was lost in a morass of self-pity and guilt. 'But it is true, Mum, if it hadn't been for me he wouldn't be dead. I feel so awful about it all.'

'Sue, don't upset yourself. Drink your coffee.' Stevie felt a great need to distance herself from whatever load of guilt Sue was weighed down by. She had a strong feeling that whatever story her daughter had to tell she would rather not hear it. It was true David had been a good friend, the very best, but their relationship had been plagued with too many ifs and buts. 'It said in the paper that he was a well-known English painter, or words to that effect. An Australian paper wouldn't write that about him unless he was very well known in his own country.'

Sue sniffed, mopped at her eyes and took a gulp of coffee. 'Yes,' she said, 'he was. He gave up teaching – you know how he hated it – after his wife died, and painted full-time. The gallery where I worked sold his pictures. David said the painting of you was his lucky piece – it attracted people like a magnet and when they found they couldn't buy that they bought something else of his. We sold his pictures like the proverbial hot cakes at the gallery.'

'And of course you met him there?' Stevie interjected softly.

'Yes.'

'And fell in love with him?'

'I – I suppose so. No, I don't think so.'

Stevie raised her eyebrows but only said, 'What about David?'

Sue shook her head. This she could answer. 'No, no he didn't.'

Stevie wanted to ask what had really brought her daughter back to Tasmania, her broken ankle or her own unrequited love, but she remained silent. In fact the only sound for the next several minutes was that of Sue eating her breakfast and Stevie drinking coffee.

'One of the hardest things in being a parent' – Sue glanced up, unsure whether her mother was addressing the remark to her or simply thinking aloud – 'is watching your children make the same mistakes you made yourself, and being powerless to stop them.'

'Powerless?' Sue interjected. 'I should have thought—'

'They simply don't believe that you have been there before them and might just possibly have learned a thing or two,' Stevie continued, apparently unaware of Sue's interruption. She turned and looked at Sue directly. 'I am not prying and I am not lecturing, Sue. I simply want to put on record that I do not like being lied to.'

'Lied to? What are you talking about?'

'Oh, Sue!' Stevie sighed and made a move to get up from the table then remembering her disability, abruptly sat down again. 'Why did you let me think you went to France with that nice New Zealand boy when it was David you were with? Did you think I would mind, that I still hankered after him, or was your relationship with him something that you were ashamed of? No, don't tell me...' She held up her hand in a silencing gesture. 'You are twenty-two, a grown woman, what you choose to do and who you choose to do it with is entirely your own business. However, if it makes any difference, there was never anything but friendship between David and I. A very good friendship, but I was never in love with him.'

Sue gulped and dropped her spoon with a clatter as she fought back the tears that seemed so ready to fall these days. 'Oh, Mum...' she wailed, feeling and sounding more like a two-year-old than the woman her mother had just pointed out she was. 'I've been such a fool. I know it wasn't really my fault but somehow I feel responsible for David's death ... I've been so stupid... Such a fool...'

Stevie smiled wryly. 'I think that is enough breast-beating. If it will make you feel better, tell me about it, woman to woman, but only if you want to. But first make some more coffee.'

Now it was Sue's turn to summon the ghost of a smile as she got up to replenish their cups. 'I don't know where to begin,' she admitted.

'I usually find the beginning is as good a place as any.' Stevie deliberately kept her voice level, surprised that her daughter was prepared to share any confidence with her and afraid to jeopardize the moment by a show of emotion.

'I should never have gone to France – he didn't really want to take me, then after we met Leah and Lance he more or less sent me packing....' Sue trailed off miserably. 'I just feel so awful about him dying and everything....' Her voice was barely audible.

'But how could it possibly be your fault? You weren't even there.' Stevie's voice was gentle. 'I understand how you feel about David dying, believe me, I really do, but to blame yourself is crazy.'

'You don't understand.' Stevie repressed a sigh and thought that if only she had a pound for every time she had heard that said to her she would be a rich woman indeed. 'I shouldn't have gone. I knew he was going there to work and I hindered him. If I hadn't been there he would probably have moved on and then he would never have met Lance and Leah. She used to model for him, did you know?'

Stevie shook her head. 'No, I didn't. Who is Lance?'

'Oh, some man. He was with Leah.'

'Then why—?'

'Why was Leah alone in the car with David?' Sue supplied. 'And why on earth did David let her drive? She was probably drunk,' she finished bitterly, forgetting for the moment that she herself had not been exactly stone cold sober when they were all out together.

'Sue,' Stevie said in what she hoped was a firm, no-nonsense, down-to-earth voice, 'agonizing and blaming yourself is pointless. Nothing can bring David back or reverse the clock. I think you are being unnecessarily hard on yourself taking on board the blame for his death. What I don't understand is why you were in France with him – and not with Nick, as I was led to believe.'

'Oh, Mum, stop harping on about that. I was sparing your feelings when I let you think I was with him. I thought—'

'If you thought there was anything other than friendship between David and I then, as I have already told you, you were wrong. By the time I met him I had learned something, the hard way, about getting involved with someone I didn't truly love – in that way.'

'Didn't you love my father?' Sue shot at her. Stevie held up her hands in despair. So much for her heart-to-heart with her daughter; it seemed to have only led to a cross-examination of her own life.

'Yes, I did. Very much. He was a good, kind man. But because he was so much older than I was. . . .' She trailed off helplessly. 'I'm afraid I married him for the wrong reason. He offered me security.' She spoke softly, almost to herself.

'Is that why you married Uncle Jock, another older man?' Stevie looked up at the note of accusation in her daughter's voice.

'That – and for you and Michael. I felt you both needed a father.'

'And what a success he was!' Sue answered bitterly. 'Maybe that was what attracted me to David – like you I thought older men represented security.'

Stevie sighed and inwardly cursed her plaster and crutches that made it almost impossible for her to rise from the table with anything like grace and dignity.

'Oh, Sue, this is getting us nowhere. I told you I don't want to pry into your life and equally I don't want to have to justify my own. If you had something going with David, if you planned to marry him, whatever, it is your own affair.' Stevie felt heavy with failure; were she and Sue destined for all time to be at cross purposes with each other?

'I didn't have anything going with him – not any more.' The sulky tone in her daughter's voice made Stevie look at her sharply, but she said nothing. 'And I certainly wasn't planning to marry him.'

Stevie repressed a sigh of relief. But she still did not understand. 'But . . .' She stopped herself before she destroyed the fragile confidence between them by asking more questions.

'I had sex with David – once. I asked him to take my virginity – and he obliged.' Her voice was truculent and her eyes hard and defiant as she looked at her mother.

Stevie bit the inside of her lip to suppress a crazy desire to laugh. 'It all sounds a bit . . . clinical . . . to me.' She looked down at her hands resting on the table top to hide the amusement in her eyes.

'No, it wasn't, it was quite wonderful actually.' Sue's face and voice both softened as she remembered. 'I shall always remember and be grateful. He gave me confidence in myself. He made me see that there is nothing wrong in being a woman. He made me proud of my own body.'

Stevie looked up now, startled by Sue's words and touched when she saw the tears glistening in her eyes. 'It's wonderful being a woman.' She spoke softly. 'And you have a beautiful body, you . . .' She was about to add *You should enjoy it* but stopped abruptly – this wasn't the way mothers were supposed to counsel their daughters. 'Whatever made you think otherwise?'

'Who indeed but your last husband – my first stepfather.' She looked at Stevie pityingly and it felt to her as if there was a sudden role reversal. 'You must have known what he was, even when you married him. You can't have not realized?'

'No, I didn't,' Stevie whispered. 'When – well, when we were married, I thought it was something about me personally he didn't like.'

'Oh, Mum! Didn't you realize that was why he pushed us off to boarding school? He couldn't bear the sight of me developing into a woman and Michael had to go because he represented temptation. Luckily Michael came out of it unscathed, he could well have been that poor kid he killed himself over. . . .' Stevie winced and closed her eyes as she remembered the appalling culmination to her second marriage. 'I grew up feeling that there was something about me inherently repulsive to men. If you had explained to me. . . .' Stevie could only murmur sympathetically. 'David changed that – but too late to save my relationship with Nick.'

'But he rang you?' Stevie was puzzled.

'You can't put a messed-up relationship together – it's like Humpty Dumpty.'

'You can try.'

'Not this mess. I was such a fool. Trouble was I didn't have any idea what Nick meant to me until it was too late. Now he thinks I was in love with David.'

'Then why did he ring you?'

'Because he is a kind person and he thought I would have heard about David and be broken up. I am upset, very upset, of course I am, and feel it was my fault that I set the chain of events going that led to his death.'

'Sue, I may be very stupid and obtuse but I am getting more and more confused. Maybe you should tell me the whole story,' Stevie suggested tentatively.

'Oh, Mum, I've been such a fool!' Sue wailed, she told her about the disastrous weekend with Nick and how she had imagined herself in love with David and begged him to take her to France. 'I foisted myself on him,' she admitted, 'even when he made it clear that what we had done was a one-off thing. I'd come to my senses by the time he packed me off back to London.' She didn't add that when she got there it was to find that she no longer had a place in the group of friends, and Nick wasn't even there, which was probably as well – she didn't think she could have borne to have seen him with Pixie.

Stevie listened in silence. 'Nick rang you here,' she finally volunteered. It seemed to her that was an odd thing for a man to do if he didn't care.

'Oh, that was just because he is such a caring person. He knew I would be upset to learn about David.'

'Hmmm.' Stevie had her own views about that. 'How did Leah come into the story?' she asked.

'We bumped into them – her and the man trailing round with her. David had known her before – I told you she used to model for him.' She added thoughtfully, 'we didn't really quarrel over her, or anything else. I guess she was just the catalyst that brought me to my senses. I realized that I wasn't in love with David, that I never had been. To be honest, it was a relief really when David suggested I went back to London. So I left and David was killed.'

'Stop it, Sue. One was not dependent on the other. It was not in any way your fault he was killed. Wallowing in guilt is a pointless exercise. You weren't even in the same country as him when it happened. It's sad, yes, very. Tragic, in fact, that he should die like that just when he was getting the recognition he had striven so hard for, for so long, but it was not – repeat, not – your fault.' Stevie shuddered as the thought struck her that it could just as easily have been Sue with him in that car when it drove headlong into a lorry.

'He never let me drive – said I would forget what side of the road we were supposed to be on and get us both killed.' She gave a shaky little laugh that was more tears than amusement. 'He let Leah drive and that's what must have happened.'

'Make another cup of coffee,' Stevie told her. 'Dry your eyes and try and forget it. Oh, I know that isn't easy,' she added, seeing the protest rising to her daughter's lips, 'but loss, death, tragedy comes into all our lives. However sad, dwelling on it does no good. We have to put it behind us as best we can and just get on with the business of living. You are lucky in a way to have discovered the true nature of your feelings before this all happened. Now let's have that coffee – sermonizing over, I promise!'

CHAPTER TWENTY-FIVE

Stevie was as good as her word. There was no more sermonizing; in fact, David Jones' name was scarcely mentioned, apart from when Sue was looking at her mother's paintings and they remembered how it had been David who had encouraged her so much in the early days.

Sue was delighted to find that her mother had taken up her brush again and exclaimed in admiration at the work she had done recently.

'You're better than ever,' Sue told her, 'but how on earth do you find time to do it?' Since coming home Sue had been amazed at the amount of work her mother seemed to get through in a day. She felt more than one sharp twinge of guilt at her own defection in leaving home to go to England and could understand her mother's concern when she had given up the art course that she had actually gone to London to take. When she tried to talk about this, her mother merely brushed her protestations to one side.

'We all have to make our own way in life,' she told Sue. 'I realize that because you happen to be my daughter that does not give me the right to dictate what you should do with your life. You are a stronger person than I ever was. Until I married Tom I always went for the easy option. I looked for security in marriage. The only real security is in yourself, in your own strength of spirit. I'm afraid it took me a long time to learn that.'

Sue was surprised, and pleased, to get regular letters across the Tasman from Nick. They were friendly and chatty, full of interesting details about life in New Zealand. Sue thought it sounded very like Tasmania. Nick's parents had a large sheep station in the South Island and Nick had gone back when his father had a stroke that disabled him. Sue wondered how he felt about giving up his time in London to help his parents out. She realized they were in much the same position, only the need for her to help her mother was likely to be of shorter duration.

She remembered how they had both smiled in England when people spoke of Australia and New Zealand in one breath as if they were the same country. As for Tasmania, no one seemed to quite know just where that belonged. One person had even asked her if it was part of New Zealand. She wished it were, she felt almost as far apart from Nick as if one of them were still in England.

She enjoyed his letters and looked forward to them, even more to his occasional phone call. She seemed to be getting to know him better than she had when they met regularly.

'Oh, he's just a friend, Mum. Our relationship is strictly platonic.' Stevie thought she sounded just a little too emphatic and when she glanced at Sue the expression on her face seemed a little too blank – or was this wishful thinking on her part?

Sue felt a little hurt that she heard so little from Pixie, but was surprised to hear from Angela. She told her that she had to leave the flat because she had 'fallen pregnant', making it sound, Sue thought, that this was an unfortunate accident that she herself had no part in. *I hope,*' she wrote, *that you didn't mind me giving Nick your phone number. We all knew that you would be upset about David Jones. Pixie said I should leave well alone, but that was because she wanted him herself* . . . Sue stopped reading and caught her breath. The scatty tone of the letter was typical Angela, but was she right or exaggerating as usual? She rattled on about the nice Italian boy that Gina had met in Italy. *So*, she finished, *if Pixie decides to stay here, you will be the only one to go home*. Sue reread the letter then folded it thoughtfully and returned it to its envelope, wondering if Angela was really as scatty as she had always believed. She had been pretty stupid herself not to realize the depth of Pixie's feelings for Nick. She wondered if it had been returned, and what had happened between them when she was in France. She tried to tell herself that it didn't matter, it was none of her business anyway, but all the time she knew it did matter and cursed herself over again for the stupid way she had behaved with Nick. She had treated him very badly and wondered why he had bothered to get in touch with her. After all, New Zealand was a long way from Tasmania.

In the quiet of her own room she reread Angela's letter and those that she had received from Nick, but all she detected was the sort of friendship that might be formed between penfriends in different countries. She found herself counting the time since she had last heard; the gap was longer than between his other letters, maybe that was it. She didn't deserve his friendship.

Then, just when she had made up her mind that she would never hear from him again, he rang and told her that he was coming over to Tasmania. 'Dad is sending me over to the ram sale in Launceston,' he told her. 'He isn't fit to come himself, although he is making good progress.'

'Oh, Nick . . .' Sue breathed, suddenly aware of the tightness in her breath and the odd way her heart was thumping. 'That is terrific!'

'Yeah . . .' Disappointment gripped her at the tone of his voice, he sounded anything but pleased. 'To tell you the truth I'm a bit worried,' he explained. 'I don't know nearly enough about the finer points of a good ram to dare to bid anything like the figure the best will get.'

'Tom, my stepfather, always goes to that sale – he puts rams in. He knows what is good,' Sue told him.

'Dad says I don't have to worry: he has sent for a catalogue and he will mark the rams he wants and the price I can go up to,' he told her.

'Then you've no worries.'

'No, I suppose not.' Nick still sounded doubtful. 'Any chance I can see you?' he asked after a pause.

'I guess so,' Sue said softly, cursing herself even as she spoke for not sounding even one tenth as excited as she felt at the prospect of seeing him again so soon.

When Sue explained to her mother why Nick had rung she insisted that she ring him straight back and offer accommodation. 'Michael will be back at college then,' she pointed out, 'so he can have his room.'

Tom lowered the evening paper and looked at Sue over the top. 'I'm more than willing to see he gets good rams at the right price. Tell him to tell his father that.'

As the time drew nearer for Nick's visit, Sue began to wish the invitation to stay had never been proffered, still less accepted. Waiting for his plane to land at Launceston Airport, she felt anything but full of joyful anticipation, on the contrary her hands were cold and clammy and all she could think was that she would rather be anywhere else in the world than where she was at this moment.

Then she saw him walking towards her among the incoming passengers. He seemed to stand out, almost as if he were illuminated, among a crowd of people who were just a blur. There was that painful thudding of her heart again and she realized she couldn't move.

She stood still, waiting for him to reach her. 'Hello, Nick.' The intensity of her inner turmoil made her stiff and formal when she greeted him.

'Hello, Sue,' he replied, his eyes searching her face. Then

suddenly his features broke into a smile and Sue, in spite of herself, smiled back. This was the Nick she knew. She barely managed to restrain the urge to fling her arms round him and hug and kiss him.

The angst Sue had fought as she waited for Nick's plane dissolved as they drove back to the farm. It seemed they had recaptured the easy camaraderie that had marked their relationship on the boat and in those early days in London. But when she caught him watching her when he didn't think she was aware, Sue was reminded that time had moved on. At these moments she felt deep hungry pangs of regret. What a blind stupid fool she had been, she castigated herself. Seeing him here in her own home, interacting with her family who obviously liked him, brought home to her the sheer stupidity of her own behaviour. She had virtually handed him over to Pixie on a plate. It didn't occur to her to wonder why, if that was so, he was here in Tasmania.

'How's Pixie?' she emerged from her brown study to ask across the dinner table. When conversation stopped and everyone turned in surprise, she realized that she had cut into a conversation on an entirely different subject.

'Sorry ...' she mumbled with a movement of her hand, intended to indicate they should ignore her and continue. No one took any notice.

'Pixie?' Nick stared at her. 'I don't know – doesn't she write to you?'

'No, I haven't heard from her in ages. Since I came back home,' Sue mumbled. She could feel her neck and throat flushing with embarrassment. Sure that everyone was looking at her, she looked down at her plate.

As suddenly as they had stopped talking the family began chattering again. Sue hadn't the faintest idea what they were saying but under cover of the noise, cautiously raised her eyes. Nick was looking directly at her. With the colour now burning in her cheeks, she found it totally impossible to lower her gaze. The conversation round her came to her as a distant hum, the people round the table receded and became a blur; she was only aware of Nick saying, 'Angela gave me your phone number. I've had no contact since I left the flat.'

'Oh.' The single syllable came out as something between a gasp, a sigh and a squeak. Confused, Sue pushed her chair back from the table murmuring, 'I'll make coffee.'

Sue put down her empty coffee cup and quietly walked out on to the verandah round the house. Through the window she could see Nick talking to Tom. I bet they are talking sheep, she told herself sourly. She could see her mother looking round, no doubt wondering where she was. Nick looked up and seemed to catch her mother's eye, then she reached across and dropped her hand on Tom's arm and leaned forward and said something to him. He jumped up immediately to help her to her feet.

Sue turned away from the little tableau; for an instant she had seen the love and concern on Tom's face and realized with something like a shock that he really did love her mother. How could she have been so blind and so stupid for so long not to grasp that her mother and stepfather were actually still in love? I'm not only dumb I'm selfish, she told herself. I should be happy for them, but I'm not – I'm jealous!

She turned her back on them, leaned against the verandah railing and looked up at the stars. It was a clear bright night but she saw them through a haze of tears. Her hands tightened on the railing and her throat ached with the effort to control herself when she heard footsteps on the wooden boards. She couldn't let him find her snivelling in self-pity.

'Sue – I'm sorry.'

'*You* are sorry!'

'I shouldn't have come.' He missed the intonation in her voice. 'It was wrong of me to accept your mother's invitation. I know she gave it on the assumption that I, that you ... we ...' His words trailed off into the night. 'I have put you in a difficult situation. I'll make some excuse and leave tomorrow.'

She whirled on him now, only to find he had turned away; in a moment he would be back in the house making plans to leave.

'Nick!' He turned, his face pale in the moonlight. Sue reached out a hand in a desperate gesture she was not aware of making. 'Is that why you came, because you . . . Oh, God, I feel so awful . . . I . . . I've been such a bitch . . . I can't understand why you came.'

'Do you want me to go?' he asked at last.

'No, of course I don't, it . . . it's wonderful having you here.'

'Do you really mean that?' He took a step closer and his voice had an odd sort of tremor. Sue could only nod.

'Do you know why I'm here?' he asked.

'To buy rams,' she replied with a lopsided grin.

'They are the excuse.' His smile was broad as he reached out for her hand. Sue closed her fingers over his and moved into his arms as he gently drew her towards him. She turned her face to his, eager for his kiss. 'There is something I have to tell you,' he began, but before he could finish his lips were on hers, his tongue moving between them as her body melded into his.

'You were saying. . . ?' she murmured when her lips were finally free.

Sue felt his body tense. 'I'm not going back to England.' He spoke softly, almost without expression, but she knew this was not an idle remark. 'Is there any, just the faintest, possibility that you might stay in this hemisphere too?'

'I think there is a distinct possibility, but it really depends on you.'

Her last few words were almost lost as, pulling her tighter into the circle of his arms, his lips and tongue once more claimed hers. 'New Zealand is very like Tasmania,' he told her when they drew apart briefly for air.

Somewhere in the recesses of her being, Sue registered that this remark was probably a proposal. She sighed; it had been quite a trip, but she was truly home now.

Handbook of
3D Machine Vision

Optical Metrology and Imaging

SERIES IN OPTICS AND OPTOELECTRONICS

Series Editors: **E Roy Pike**, Kings College, London, UK
Robert G W Brown, University of California, Irvine, USA

Handbook of
3D Machine Vision

Optical Metrology and Imaging

Edited by
Song Zhang

CRC Press
Taylor & Francis Group
Boca Raton London New York

CRC Press is an imprint of the
Taylor & Francis Group, an **informa** business
A TAYLOR & FRANCIS BOOK

CRC Press
Taylor & Francis Group
6000 Broken Sound Parkway NW, Suite 300
Boca Raton, FL 33487-2742

Printed on acid-free paper
Version Date: 20121220

International Standard Book Number: 978-1-4398-7219-2 (Hardback)

Library of Congress Cataloging-in-Publication Data

Handbook of 3D machine vision : optical metrology and imaging / author/editor Song Zhang.
  pages cm. -- (Series in optics and optoelectronics ; 16)
  Includes bibliographical references and index.
  ISBN 978-1-4398-7219-2 (alk. paper)
  1. Imaging systems. 2. Three-dimensional imaging. 3. Computer vision. I. Zhang, Song.

  TK8315.H36 2013
  006.3'7--dc23   2012037858

**Visit the Taylor & Francis Web site at
http://www.taylorandfrancis.com**

**and the CRC Press Web site at
http://www.crcpress.com**

Contents

Preface

In August 2010, John Navas and I were sitting in a restaurant, across the road from the San Diego Convention Center, brainstorming the idea of a book on the recent hot topic of three-dimensional (3D) machine vision. We found that the success of any 3D vision technique is founded upon the capabilities of its real-world measurement strategy, and thus a new book covering a wide variety of existing 3D measurement approaches might generate significant interest.

With the release of *Avatar* and other 3D movies and the emergence of 3D TVs and monitors, 3D imaging technologies have started penetrating into our daily lives. The popularity of Microsoft Kinect now enables the general audience easily to capture and access 3D measurements of the real world. However, the Kinect has many limitations, and therefore it becomes increasingly important to know how to choose an optimal 3D imaging technique for a particular application. Yet, with numerous 3D vision methods and no single comprehensive resource for understanding them, the process of choosing a method becomes very frustrating.

This book strives to fill this gap by providing readers with the most popular 3D imaging techniques in depth and breadth. The book focuses on optical methods (optical metrology and imaging), which are the most popular due to their noninvasive and noncontact nature. We start the book (Chapter 1) with stereo vision, as it is a well-studied method. Because of the fundamental difficulty of stereo matching, adding random speckle patterns or space–time varying patterns substantially improves the results of stereo vision; this approach is covered in Chapters 2 and 3. Stereo particle image velocimetry (PIV) will also be discussed in this book (Chapter 4) as a major experimental means in fluid dynamics. Chapter 5 presents the structured-light technique, an extremely popular method in the field of computer science due to its ease of implementation and robustness. However, structured light is usually restricted to macroscale measurement.

Chapter 6 will discuss digital holography, which is capable of performing micro- to nanoscale measurement. Precisely measuring dynamically deformable natural objects (i.e., without surface treatment) is vital to understanding kinematics, dynamics, mechanics, etc. Grating, interferometry, and fringe projection techniques have been successfully used for these types of applications; Chapters 7–9 will cover these methods. All these aforementioned techniques require triangulation to recover a 3D shape; yet, some techniques do not. Chapters 10 and 11 present two representative methods. Moreover, Chapters 12–14 cover 3D measurement techniques that are not restricted to surface capture: 3D ultrasound (Chapter 12), optical coherence tomography (OCT, Chapter 13), and 3D endoscopy (Chapter 14).

Finally, the ultimate goal behind the development of novel 3D imaging techniques is to conquer the challenges we face daily and improve our quality of life. For this reason, the book cannot be complete without dedicating one chapter to a representative application. Therefore, Chapter 15 covers the promising field of biometrics, which may prove essential to security and public safety.

I am deeply indebted to the inventors and/or the major players of each individual technology for contributing the chapter on that particular method. I thank the authors for their time and willingness to work with me, and I genuinely believe that their efforts will be greatly appreciated by readers. I am extremely grateful to John Navas for his tremendous help in originating and navigating the book to its current form and Jennifer Ahringer and Rachel Holt for their incredible effort in publishing this book in a timely fashion. I sincerely thank my professional mentor, Dr. James Oliver, at Iowa State University, who has provided constant encouragement and support over the past few years, which ultimately made me believe that I could edit this book during my early career! I also thank my students, especially Laura Ekstrand, for spending many hours helping me organize this book. Last, but not least, I wholeheartedly thank my wife, Xiaomei Hao, for allowing me to occupy myself many nights and weekends on this book without any complaint. Without all of these wonderful people, this book would not be possible.

I hope that this book is a handy *handbook* for students, engineers, and scientists as a reference for learning the essence of 3D imaging techniques and a time-saver for choosing the optimal method to study or implement. Most of the images are currently printed in black and white, but you can download the color figures from the CRC website for better clarity.

Song Zhang
Iowa State University

The Editor

Dr. Song Zhang is an assistant professor of mechanical engineering at Iowa State University. His research interests include investigation of the fundamental physics of optical metrology, new mathematical and computational tools for 3D shape analysis, and the utilization of those insights for designing superfast 3D imaging and sensing techniques. He has often been credited for developing the first high-resolution, real-time 3D imaging system. Recently, he has developed a 3D imaging system that could achieve kilohertz with hundreds of thousands of measuring points per frame by inventing the defocusing technology.

Dr. Zhang has published over 40 peer-reviewed journal articles, authored four book chapters, and filed five US patents (granted or pending). Among all the journal papers he has published, seven were featured on the cover pages, and one was highlighted as "Image of the Week" by Optics InfoBase. Numerous media have reported his work, and rock band Radiohead has utilized his technology to produce a music video House of Cards. He serves as a reviewer for over 20 international journals, as a committee member for numerous conferences, and as cochair for a few conferences. He won the NSF CAREER award in 2012.

Contributors

Anand Asundi
Nanyang Technological University
    of Singapore
Singapore

Seung-Hae Baek
Graduate School of Electrical
    Engineering and Computer
    Science
Kyungpook National University
Daegu, Korea

Hujun Bao
State Key Lab of CAD & CG
Zhejiang University
Hangzhou, China

Jeff Bax
Imaging Research Laboratories
Robarts Research Institute
Graduate Program in Biomedical
    Engineering
London, Ontario, Canada

Wenjing Chen
Opto-Electronics Department
Sichuan University
Chengdu, China

Bernard Chiu
City University of Hong Kong
Hong Kong, China

Chee Oi Choo
Nanyang Technological University
    of Singapore
Singapore

Brian Curless
University of Washington
Seattle, Washington

Maria De Marsico
Department of Computer Science
University of Rome
Rome, Italy

Kapil Dev
Nanyang Technological University
    of Singapore
Singapore

Laura Ekstrand
Department of Mechanical
    Engineering
Iowa State University
Ames, Iowa

Aaron Fenster
Imaging Research Laboratories
Robarts Research Institute,
    Department of Medical Imaging
Graduate Program in Biomedical
    Engineering, Department of
    Medical Biophysics
London, Ontario, Canada

Sergio Fernandez
Institute of Informatics and
    Applications
University of Girona
Girona, Spain

Jason Geng
IEEE Intelligent Transportation
    System Society
Rockville, Maryland

Yan Hao
Nanyang Technological University
    of Singapore
Singapore

Hui Hu
Department of Aerospace
    Engineering
Iowa State University
Ames, Iowa

Yuan Hao Huang
Singapore–MIT Alliance for
    Research and Technology
    (SMART) Center
Singapore

Nikolaus Karpinsky
Department of Mechanical
    Engineering
Iowa State University
Ames, Iowa

Shoji Kawahito
Shizuoka University
Shizuoka, Japan

Michael K. K. Leung
Department of Electrical and
    Computer Engineering
Ryerson University
Toronto, Canada

Yusheng Liu
Aerospace Image Measurement
    and Vision Navigation Research
    Center
National University of Defense
    Technology
Changsha, China

Michele Nappi
Biometric and Image Processing
    Laboratory (BIPLab)
University of Salerno
Fisciano (SA), Italy

Yukitoshi Otani
Center for Optical Research and
    Education
Utsunomiya University
Utsunomiya, Japan

Soon-Yong Park
School of Computer Science and
    Engineering
Kyungpook National University
Daegu, Korea

Grace Parraga
Imaging Research Laboratories
Robarts Research Institute,
    Department of Medical Imaging
Graduate Program in Biomedical
    Engineering, Department of
    Medical Biophysics
London, Ontario, Canada

Daniel Riccio
Biometric and Image Processing
    Laboratory (BIPLab)
University of Salerno
Fisciano (SA), Italy

Joaquim Salvi
Institute of Informatics and
    Applications
University of Girona
Girona, Spain

Steven M. Seitz
University of Washington
Seattle, Washington

Yang Shang
Aerospace Image Measurement
    and Vision Navigation Research
    Center
National University of Defense
    Technology
Changsha, China

Noah Snavely
University of Wisconsin
Madison, Wisconsin

Beau A. Standish
Department of Electrical and
Computer Engineering
Ryerson University
Toronto, Canada

Xianyu Su
Opto-Electronics Department
Sichuan University
Chengdu, China

Catherine E. Towers
School of Mechanical Engineering
University of Leeds
Leeds, United Kingdom

David P. Towers
School of Mechanical Engineering
University of Leeds
Leeds, United Kingdom

Yajun Wang
Department of Mechanical
Engineering
Iowa State University
Ames, Iowa

Qu Weijuan
Nanyang Technological University
of Singapore
Singapore

Li Zhang
University of Wisconsin
Madison, Wisconsin

Qican Zhang
Opto-Electronics Department
Sichuan University
Chengdu, China

Song Zhang
Department of Mechanical
Engineering
Iowa State University
Ames, Iowa

1

Stereo Vision

Soon-Yong Park and Seung-Hae Baek

CONTENTS

Stereo vision has been of interest to the computer and robot vision community. This chapter introduces fundamental theories of stereo vision such as stereo calibration, rectification, and matching. Practical examples of stereo calibration and rectification are also presented. In addition, several stereo matching techniques are briefly introduced and their performance is compared by using a couple of reference stereo images.

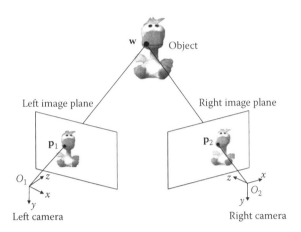

FIGURE 1.1
Stereo correspondence problem.

1.1 Introduction

Stereo vision is motivated from the human vision system, which can perceive depth properties of a scene. The human vision system obtains two different images of a scene from the slightly different views of the eyes and interprets the images for depth perception. Because depth perception is one of the powerful abilities of the human vision system, stereo vision has many application areas, such as three-dimensional (3D) scene reconstruction, object recognition, entertainment, robot navigation, etc. To obtain the depth information of a scene from a pair of images, it needs to solve one of the inherent problems in stereo vision, called the *correspondence problem.* Because two different image planes are defined in stereo vision, the projections of an object into the planes are represented with respect to different image coordinates. Therefore, the correspondence problem can be defined as determining the coordinate difference between the images of the object. Solving the stereo correspondence problem is called *stereo matching.* The result of stereo matching is commonly represented by a disparity map whose intensity represents the coordinate difference between corresponding image points, called *disparity.*

In general, a stereo vision system consists of two identical vision cameras, which capture the left and right images of an object. A conventional configuration of a stereo vision system is shown in Figure 1.1. A 3D point $\mathbf{W}$ on the surface of a real object is projected into the image planes of the cameras. Thus, two two-dimensional (2D) points, $\mathbf{p}_1$ and $\mathbf{p}_2$, on the image planes are the projections of point $\mathbf{W}$. As mentioned in the previous paragraph, the correspondence problem is to find points $\mathbf{p}_1$ and $\mathbf{p}_2$ between stereo images. Finding stereo correspondences needs a huge number of computations because the disparity of every image point should be determined to obtain a 2D disparity or depth map. For example, if the resolution of each image is $N \times M$, a brute force approach for finding all correspondences needs $(N \times M)^2$ computations.

To reduce the computation complexity of the stereo matching problem, the 3D geometry of a stereo vision system should be considered so that stereo matching is restricted to certain image areas. To know the stereo geometry, calibration of a stereo vision with respect to a reference coordinate system is needed. A direct calibration method is presented to obtain a geometric relationship between the two cameras, which is represented by 3D Euclidean transformations, rotation, and translation. From the stereo calibration, we know that stereo correspondences are related by a 2D point-to-line projection, called *epipolar geometry.*

The epipolar geometry between the stereo images provides a very strong constraint to find stereo correspondences. The epipolar constraint is essential in stereo matching because an image point in one image has its conjugate point on an epipolar line in the other image, while the epipolar line is derived by the original point. Therefore, the computation complexity and time of stereo correspondences can be greatly reduced. If the epipolar lines are parallel to the horizontal image axis, stereo matching can be done in an effective and fast way since the correspondences between stereo images lie only along the same horizontal line. For this reason, it is better to convert nonparallel epipolar lines to parallel ones. In terms of stereo configuration, this is the same as converting a general stereo configuration to the parallel stereo configuration, which is called *stereo rectification.* Rectification of stereo images transforms all epipolar lines in the stereo images parallel to the horizontal image axis. Therefore, in the rectified stereo images, corresponding image points are always in the same horizontal lines. This geometric property also greatly reduces computation time for stereo matching.

For many years, various stereo matching techniques have been introduced. Most stereo matching techniques are categorized into two types. In terms of matching cost and energy aggregation, they are categorized as either local or global stereo matching techniques. Local stereo matching techniques use image templates defined in both stereo images to measure their correlation [14,15]. Common techniques are SAD (sum of absolute difference), SSD (sum of squared difference), and NCC (normalized cross correlation).

In the template-based method, a cost function is defined based on the similarity between two image templates of their left and right images. Suppose an image template is defined from the left image and many comparing templates are defined along an epipolar line in the right image. Then a matching template from the right image is determined in the sense of minimizing the matching cost. Local matching techniques are useful when only some parts in an image are of interest for obtaining the depth map of the area.

By the way, most recent investigations in stereo vision address global error minimization. In global matching methods, a cost function is defined in terms of image data and depth continuity [14]. The data term measures the similarity of matching templates, while the continuity term additionally measures the global matching cost based on the disparities of adjacent image pixels. In other words, the disparity of an image point is determined not only from its image properties but also from disparity continuities around it. The global approaches produce more accurate results than the local methods. However, high computation time is needed. Examples of global matching are belief propagation (BP) [3,10,12], semiglobal matching (SGM) [7,8], graph cut (GC) [2], and cooperative region (CR) [19], among others.

In terms of the density of a disparity map, stereo matching techniques are divided into two categories: dense and sparse matching methods. The dense matching method decides the disparity of every image pixel, thus producing a disparity map in which resolution is the same as that of stereo images. Obtaining the disparity of every pixel produces very dense depth information. However, the dense matching method needs high computation time. On the other hand, the sparse matching method computes the disparities of only some image pixels. Feature-based stereo matching techniques belong to this method. Image features are relevant subjects in an image such as corners or edges. Therefore, obtaining disparities of feature points is easier and more robust than obtaining featureless points.

This chapter presents fundamental theories and practices of stereo vision. In Section 1.2, the stereo geometry is presented to define the epipolar geometry and constraint. In Section 1.3, calibration of a stereo vision system, which describes the geometric relationship between two independent camera coordinate systems, is presented. In Section 1.4, rectification of stereo images, which aligns epipolar lines along the same horizontal lines, is presented. Section 1.5 shows some practical examples of stereo calibration and rectification. In Section 1.6, two simple methods to compute 3D coordinates from a pair of stereo correspondences are presented. In Section 1.7, basic theories of several stereo matching techniques are briefly introduced and their performances are compared using standard stereo test images.

1.2 Stereo Geometry

In this section, the epipolar geometry of a stereo vision system is presented in order to understand the *epipolar constraint*. In a pair of stereo images, two corresponding points in the left and right images are always on the epipolar lines, which are defined in the stereo image planes. Figure 1.2 shows the geometry of a stereo vision system. Here, O_1 and O_2 are the centers of the left and right cameras, respectively. In the two image planes Π_1 and Π_2, 2D image points p_1 and p_2 are the projections of a 3D point W to each image plane. Since W is projected toward the center of each camera, p_1 and p_2 lie on the projection lines from W to both centers.

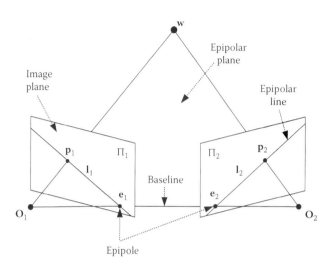

FIGURE 1.2
Stereo geometry.

In Figure 1.2, it is noted that three points, **W**, O_1, and O_2, form a 3D plane that intersects the two image planes. Here, the plane is called the epipolar plane and the intersection lines are called epipolar lines l_1 and l_2 in both image planes. As shown in the figure, two image points are on the epipolar lines, which is an important and strong constraint for finding matching points between the stereo images. For example, in the left image plane, p_1 is the projection of **W** and its conjugate point in the right image plane is on the epipolar line l_2. Therefore, it is possible to search the matching point only on the line l_2, instead of searching all areas in the right image plane.

As shown in Figure 1.2, two image points p_1 and p_2 in the left and right image planes can be represented by either 2D vectors which are represented with respect to two different image coordinate systems or 3D vectors which are represented with respect to two different camera coordinate systems. In other words, p_1 and p_2 are 2D vectors in the image planes as well as 3D vectors in the camera coordinate systems. Now consider p_1 and p_2 as 3D vectors with respect to the left and right camera coordinate systems. In this case, the z component of p_1 and p_2 is the focal length of each camera. If the rotation and translation between two camera systems are **R** and **t**, respectively, p_2 is transformed from p_1 such that

$$p_2 = Rp_1 + t \tag{1.1}$$

Here, the rotation and translation represent the transformations from the left to the right camera coordinate systems. Because **t** is the translation vector from the left to the right cameras, the cross product of $\mathbf{t}$ and $\mathbf{p}_2$ is orthogonal to $\mathbf{p}_2$. Let $\mathbf{Tp}_2$ be the cross product of $\mathbf{t}$ and $\mathbf{p}_2$, where

$$
T = \begin{bmatrix} 0 & -t_z & t_y \\ t_z & 0 & -t_x \\ -t_y & t_x & 0 \end{bmatrix}
\tag{1.2}
$$

In this equation, T is a 3×3 matrix and t_x, t_y, t_z are the x, y, z components of $\mathbf{t}$. Therefore, $\mathbf{Tp}_2$ is a matrix representation of the cross product of two vectors.

Since three vectors, $\mathbf{p}_1$, $\mathbf{p}_2$, and $\mathbf{T}$, are in the same epipolar plane, the relations between the vectors are expressed by the following equations such that

$$
\mathbf{p}_2 \cdot (T\mathbf{p}_2) = 0
\tag{1.3}
$$

$$
\mathbf{p}_2 \cdot (T(R\mathbf{p}_1 + \mathbf{t})) = 0
\tag{1.4}
$$

$$
\mathbf{p}_2 \cdot (T(R\mathbf{p}_1)) = 0
\tag{1.5}
$$

and

$$
\mathbf{p}_2^T E \mathbf{p}_1 = 0
\tag{1.6}
$$

Here, a 3×3 matrix $\mathbf{E}$ is called *essential matrix* and is expressed as

$$
E = TR
\tag{1.7}
$$

From Equation (1.6), it is found that

$$
\mathbf{l}_2 = E\mathbf{p}_1
\tag{1.8}
$$

which means that

$$
\mathbf{p}_2^T \mathbf{l}_2 = 0
\tag{1.9}
$$

because $\mathbf{p}_2$ is on the right epipolar line $\mathbf{l}_2$. This provides a very strong constraint in finding correspondences between stereo images. If an image point $\mathbf{p}_1$ is defined, its correspondence exists only in the right epipolar line $\mathbf{l}_2$. If an image point in the right image plane is not on the epipolar line, it is not possible for the point to be a correspondence. To decide if an image point $\mathbf{p}_2$ in the right image plane is on line $\mathbf{l}_2$, their dot product should be zero. However, in reality, the dot product will not be perfect zero because of the discrete property of the image coordinates. Therefore, if the dot product is very close to zero, the image point can be regarded as on the epipolar line.

Similarly, the left epipolar line is derived by

$$\mathbf{l}_1 = \mathbf{p}_2^T\mathbf{E} \tag{1.10}$$

and

$$\mathbf{l}_1\mathbf{p}_1 = 0 \tag{1.11}$$

It is more convenient that any image point be represented with respect to the pixel coordinate system, rather than to the image coordinate system. To represent an image point in the pixel coordinates, it is necessary to convert the image coordinate system to the pixel coordinate system such that

$$\mathbf{p}_1' = \mathbf{K}_1\mathbf{p}_1 \tag{1.12}$$

$$\mathbf{p}_2' = \mathbf{K}_2\mathbf{p}_2 \tag{1.13}$$

In the preceding equations, $\mathbf{K}_1$ and $\mathbf{K}_2$ are the intrinsic matrices of the left and the right cameras; $\mathbf{p}_1'$ and $\mathbf{p}_2'$ are the coordinates of $\mathbf{p}_1$ and $\mathbf{p}_2$ in the pixel coordinate systems, respectively. Using Equations (1.12) and (1.13), Equation (1.6) is transformed as

$$\mathbf{p}_2'^T\mathbf{F}\mathbf{p}_1' - 0 \tag{1.14}$$

In this equation, $\mathbf{F}$ is called the *fundamental matrix* and it can be derived as

$$\mathbf{F} = \left\{\mathbf{K}_2^{-1}\right\}^T \mathbf{E}\mathbf{K}_1^{-1} \tag{1.15}$$

In Equation (1.14), the image vectors are represented in the pixel coordinates, which is intuitive in obtaining epipolar lines also in the pixel coordinates. In contrast, the unit of vectors in Equation (1.6) follows the metric system. Therefore, to use the essential matrix, we need to convert the pixel coordinate system to the metric system by scaling and translating the center of the pixel coordinate system. For this reason, Equation (1.14) is used more often than Equation (1.6) in stereo vision.

To obtain the fundamental matrix using Equation (1.15), it is necessary to know the essential matrix in advance. If there are no geometric or calibration parameters between the left and the right cameras, the fundamental matrix cannot be derived. To overcome this inconvenience, some studies use the correspondences between stereo images to derive the fundamental matrix. Because the fundamental matrix is singular, it is possible to derive the matrix using only pixel coordinates of several matching points.

Let $\tilde{p}'_1 = [u\,v\,1]^T$ and $\tilde{p}'_2 = [u'\,v'\,1]^T$. Then, Equation (1.14) can be written with two image vectors and a square matrix such that

$$[u'\,v'\,1]\begin{bmatrix} F_{11} & F_{12} & F_{13} \\ F_{21} & F_{22} & F_{23} \\ F_{31} & F_{32} & F_{33} \end{bmatrix}\begin{bmatrix} u \\ v \\ 1 \end{bmatrix} = 0 \tag{1.16}$$

This can be written as

$$[uu'\ uv'\ u\ u'v\ vv'\ v\ u'\ v'\ 1]\begin{bmatrix} F_{11} \\ F_{12} \\ F_{13} \\ F_{21} \\ F_{22} \\ F_{23} \\ F_{31} \\ F_{32} \\ F_{33} \end{bmatrix} = 0 \tag{1.17}$$

In this linear equation, F_{33} can be set 1 because the fundamental matrix is singular. Thus, there are only eight unknowns in this equation. If there are at least eight matched image pairs between the stereo images, we can write a linear equation to solve the elements of the fundamental matrix as follows. The solution of the equation can be easily obtained by using a linear algebra library. This method is called the *eight-point algorithm,* which is very useful not only in stereo vision but also in robot vision.

$$\begin{bmatrix} u_1u'_1 & u_1v'_1 & u_1 & v_1u'_1 & v_1 & u'_1 & v'_1 \\ u_2u'_2 & u_2v'_2 & u_2 & v_2u'_2 & v_2 & u'_2 & v'_2 \\ u_3u'_3 & u_3v'_3 & u_3 & v_3u'_3 & v_3 & u'_3 & v'_3 \\ u_4u'_4 & u_4v'_4 & u_4 & v_4u'_4 & v_4 & u'_4 & v'_4 \\ u_5u'_5 & u_5v'_5 & u_5 & v_5u'_5 & v_5 & u'_5 & v'_5 \\ u_6u'_6 & u_6v'_6 & u_6 & v_6u'_6 & v_6 & u'_6 & v'_6 \\ u_7u'_7 & u_7v'_7 & u_7 & v_7u'_7 & v_7 & u'_7 & v'_7 \\ u_8u'_8 & u_8v'_8 & u_8 & v_8u'_8 & v_8 & u'_8 & v'_8 \end{bmatrix}\begin{bmatrix} F_{11} \\ F_{12} \\ F_{13} \\ F_{21} \\ F_{22} \\ F_{23} \\ F_{31} \\ F_{32} \end{bmatrix} = -\begin{bmatrix} 1 \\ 1 \\ 1 \\ 1 \\ 1 \\ 1 \\ 1 \\ 1 \end{bmatrix} \tag{1.18}$$

1.3 Stereo Calibration

Calibration of a stereo vision system is to determine the 3D Euclidean transformations between the left and the right camera coordinate systems. After the geometrical relationship between two coordinate systems is determined, the relationship can be used for stereo rectification and 3D reconstruction from corresponding image points. In order to calibrate a stereo vision system, it is necessary to define a reference coordinate system, usually called the world coordinate system, so that the camera coordinate systems can be determined with respect to the reference coordinate system.

1.3.1 Pinhole Camera Model

In stereo vision, the pinhole camera model is commonly used. A pinhole camera is modeled by its optical center $\mathbf{O}$ and its image plane Π as shown in Figure 1.3. A 3D point $\mathbf{W}$ is projected into an image point $\mathbf{p}$, which is an intersection of Π with the line containing $\mathbf{O}$ and $\mathbf{W}$. Let $\mathbf{W} = [x\ y\ z]^T$ be the coordinates in the world coordinate system, $\mathbf{p} = [u\ v]^T$ in the image plane (CCD), and $\mathbf{p}' = [u'\ v']^T$ in the pixel plane. The mapping from 3D coordinates to 2D coordinates is the *perspective projection,* which is represented by a linear transformation in *homogeneous coordinates.* Let $\tilde{\mathbf{p}} = [u\,v1]^T$, $\tilde{\mathbf{p}}' = [u'\,v'1]^T$, and $\tilde{\mathbf{W}} = [x\,y\,z1]^T$ be the homogeneous coordinates of $\mathbf{p}$, $\mathbf{p}'$, and $\mathbf{W}$, respectively. Then the perspective transformation is given by the matrix $\tilde{\mathbf{M}}$:

$$\tilde{\mathbf{p}}' = \mathbf{K}\mathbf{p}' \cong \mathbf{K}\tilde{\mathbf{M}}\tilde{\mathbf{W}} \qquad (1.19)$$

where "$\cong$" means equal up to a scale factor. The camera is therefore modeled by a scaling and translating matrix $\mathbf{K}$ and its perspective transformation matrix (PPM) $\tilde{\mathbf{M}}$, which can be decomposed, using the QR factorization, into the product

$$\tilde{\mathbf{M}} = \mathbf{A}\left[\mathbf{R}\,|\,\mathbf{t}\right] \qquad (1.20)$$

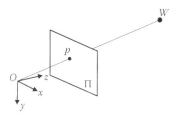

FIGURE 1.3
Pinhole camera model.

The matrices $\mathbf{K}$ and $\mathbf{A}$ depend on the intrinsic parameters only and have the following forms:

$$\mathbf{K} = \begin{bmatrix} k_u & 0 & 0 \\ 0 & k_v & 0 \\ 0 & 0 & 1 \end{bmatrix}, \mathbf{A} = \begin{bmatrix} f_u & \gamma & u_0 \\ 0 & f_v & v_0 \\ 0 & 0 & 1 \end{bmatrix} \tag{1.21}$$

where
f_u, f_v are the focal lengths in the horizontal and the vertical directions
k_u, k_v are the scaling factors from the image plane to the pixel plane
(u_0, v_0) are the coordinates of the principal point in the pixel plane
(u_i, v_i) are the coordinates of the offset of the principal point in the image plane
γ is a skew factor

The camera position and orientation (extrinsic parameters) are represented by a 3×3 rotation matrix $\mathbf{R}$ and a translation vector $\mathbf{t}$, representing a rigid transformation that brings the camera coordinate system onto the world coordinate system.

The PPM can be also written as

$$\tilde{\mathbf{M}} = \begin{bmatrix} \mathbf{q}_1^T & q_{14} \\ \mathbf{q}_2^T & q_{24} \\ \mathbf{q}_3^T & q_{34} \end{bmatrix} = \begin{bmatrix} \mathbf{Q} | \tilde{\mathbf{q}} \end{bmatrix} \tag{1.22}$$

The focal plane is the plane parallel to the image plane that contains the optical center $\mathbf{O}$, and the projection of $\mathbf{W}$ to the plane is 0. Therefore, the coordinate $\mathbf{O}$ is given by

$$\mathbf{O} = -\mathbf{Q}^{-1} \tilde{\mathbf{q}} \tag{1.23}$$

Therefore, $\tilde{\mathbf{M}}$ can be written as

$$\tilde{\mathbf{M}} = \begin{bmatrix} \mathbf{Q} | -\mathbf{QO} \end{bmatrix} \tag{1.24}$$

The optical ray associated to an image point $\mathbf{p}$ is the line $\mathbf{pO}$ that means the set of 3D points $\mathbf{W} : \tilde{\mathbf{p}} \cong \tilde{\mathbf{M}}\tilde{\mathbf{W}}$. In parametric form:

$$\mathbf{W} = \mathbf{O} + \lambda \mathbf{Q}^{-1} \tilde{\mathbf{p}}, \lambda \in \mathbb{R} \tag{1.25}$$

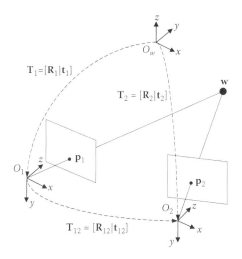

FIGURE 1.4
Stereo calibration.

1.3.2 Direct Calibration

In Figure 1.4, a world coordinate system is defined and two camera coordinate systems are also defined, which are those of the left and right cameras. The 3D transformation from the world to each camera coordinate system is represented as a matrix form $T_i = \left[R_i \mid t_i \right]$, which consists of the rotation and translation from the world to each camera, respectively. Given two transformations, it is easily known that the relation from the left to the right camera coordinate systems is

$$T_{12} = \left[R_{12} \mid t_{12} \right] = T_2 T_1^{-1} \tag{1.26}$$

Therefore, the stereo camera calibration can be regarded as a general camera calibration with respect to a fixed reference coordinate system.

A couple of camera calibration techniques that can determine external and internal parameters of a camera system are already available. In this section, a simple calibration technique called *direct method* is presented. This method calibrates the perspective projection matrix of a camera that contains the intrinsic and extrinsic camera parameters. Projection matrix is a homogeneous transform matrix that maps a 3D point in space into a 2D point in the image plane of a camera. Estimating the projection matrix is the solution of a simple and overdetermined linear system equation, and it can be solved by using the singular value decomposition (SVD) of the linear system. Calibration of a vision camera is considered an estimation of a projective transformation matrix from the world coordinate system to the camera's image coordinate system.

Suppose there is a 3D point with coordinates $\left(X_i^w, Y_i^w, Z_i^w, 1 \right)$ and its projection point with coordinates $(x_c, y_c, 1)$; then a 3×4 projection matrix $\mathbf{M}$ can be written as

$$\begin{bmatrix} u_i \\ v_i \\ w_i \end{bmatrix} = \mathbf{M} \begin{bmatrix} X_i^w \\ Y_i^w \\ Z_i^w \\ 1 \end{bmatrix} \tag{1.27}$$

with

$$x_c = \frac{u_i}{w_i} = \frac{m_{11}X_i^w + m_{12}Y_i^w + m_{13}Z_i^w + m_{14}}{m_{31}X_i^w + m_{32}Y_i^w + m_{33}Z_i^w + m_{34}}$$

$$y_c = \frac{v_i}{w_i} = \frac{m_{21}X_i^w + m_{22}Y_i^w + m_{23}Z_i^w + m_{24}}{m_{31}X_i^w + m_{32}Y_i^w + m_{33}Z_i^w + m_{34}} \tag{1.28}$$

The matrix $\mathbf{M}$ is defined up to an arbitrary scale factor and has only 11 independent entries. Therefore, at least six world 3D points and their 2D projection points in the image plane are needed. If there is a calibration pattern—for example, a checkerboard pattern—$\mathbf{M}$ can be estimated through a least squares minimization technique. Assume there are N matches for a homogeneous linear system like Equation (1.28); then a linear system is given as

$$\mathbf{Am} = 0 \tag{1.29}$$

with

$$\mathbf{A} = \begin{bmatrix} X_1 & Y_1 & Z_1 & 1 & 0 & 0 & 0 & 0 & -x_1X_1 & -x_1Y_1 & -x_1Z_1 & -x_1 \\ 0 & 0 & 0 & 0 & X_1 & Y_1 & Z_1 & 1 & -y_1X_1 & -y_1Y_1 & -y_1Z_1 & -y_1 \\ X_2 & Y_2 & Z_2 & 1 & 0 & 0 & 0 & 0 & -x_2X_2 & -x_2Y_2 & -x_2Z_2 & -x_2 \\ 0 & 0 & 0 & 0 & X_2 & Y_2 & Z_2 & 1 & -y_2X_2 & -y_2Y_2 & -y_2Z_2 & -y_2 \\ \cdot & \cdot & \cdot & \cdot & \cdot & \cdot & \cdot & \cdot & \cdot & \cdot & \cdot & \cdot \\ \cdot & \cdot & \cdot & \cdot & \cdot & \cdot & \cdot & \cdot & \cdot & \cdot & \cdot & \cdot \\ \cdot & \cdot & \cdot & \cdot & \cdot & \cdot & \cdot & \cdot & \cdot & \cdot & \cdot & \cdot \\ X_N & Y_N & Z_N & 1 & 0 & 0 & 0 & 0 & -x_NX_N & -x_NY_N & -x_NZ_N & -x_N \\ 0 & 0 & 0 & 0 & X_N & Y_N & Z_N & 1 & -y_NX_N & -y_NY_N & -y_NZ_N & -y_N \end{bmatrix}$$

and

$$\mathbf{m} = \begin{bmatrix} m_{11}, m_{12}, \mathrm{L}, m_{33}, m_{34} \end{bmatrix}^T$$

Since the rank of $\mathbf{A}$ is 11, $\mathbf{m}$ (or $\mathbf{M}$) can be recovered from an SVD-based technique as the column of $\mathbf{V}$ corresponds to the smallest singular value of $\mathbf{A}$, with $\mathbf{A} = \mathbf{U}\mathbf{D}\mathbf{V}^T$. For more information, see reference 17.

1.4 Stereo Rectification

Stereo rectification determines 2D transformations of stereo image planes such that pairs of conjugate epipolar lines become parallel to the horizontal image axes [4,5]. The rectified images can be considered as new images acquired from new parallel stereo cameras, obtained by rotating the original cameras. A great advantage of rectification is to allow convenient ways in stereo matching. After rectification, all epipolar lines become parallel to the horizontal image axis. Therefore, matching stereo correspondences can be done only on the same horizontal image axis. In this section, a simple stereo rectification method, proposed by Fusiello, Trucco, and Verri [4], is presented. This method utilizes calibration parameters to rectify stereo images and obtain new calibration parameters. This method determines the PPM of each stereo camera by virtually rotating original stereo cameras along the y-axis of each camera's coordinate system.

1.4.1 Epipolar Geometry

Let us consider a stereo vision system composed by two pinhole cameras as shown in Figure 1.5. In the figure, there are two vision cameras with optical centers $\mathbf{O}_1$ and $\mathbf{O}_2$, respectively. Let a 3D point in space be $\mathbf{W}$ and its projection to the left camera's image plane be $\mathbf{p}_1$. Then its corresponding $\mathbf{p}_2$ on the right image plane can be found on the epipolar line $\mathbf{l}_2$, which is the intersection of the right image plane and the epipolar plane of a triangle $\mathbf{WO}_1\mathbf{O}_2$. If two image planes are collinear, the epipolar line $\mathbf{l}_2$ will be collinear with the epipolar line $\mathbf{l}_1$ on the left image plane. However most stereo cameras have a toed-in angle between left and right cameras; therefore, their conjugate epipolar lines are not collinear.

A very special case is when both epipoles are at infinity. This happens when the line $\mathbf{O}_1\mathbf{O}_2$ (the baseline) is constrained in both focal planes, where the image planes are parallel to the baseline. Therefore, any stereo image pair can be transformed so that epipolar lines are parallel and horizontal in each image axis. This procedure is called *stereo rectification.*

1.4.2 Rectification of Camera Matrices

Suppose a stereo vision system is calibrated where the original PPMs $\tilde{\mathbf{M}}_{o1}$ and $\tilde{\mathbf{M}}_{o2}$ are known for the left and right cameras. Rectification estimates

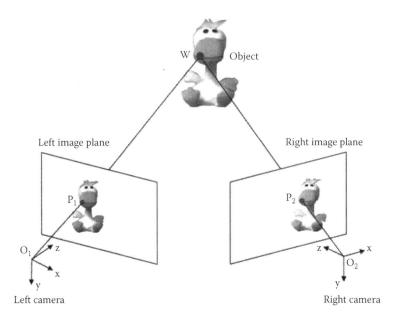

FIGURE 1.5
Epipolar geometry of a stereo vision camera. (Figure from A. Fusiello, E. Trucco, and A. Verri. A compact algorithm for rectification of stereo pairs. *Machine Vision and Applications* 12(1): 16–22, 2000.)

two new PPMs, $\tilde{\mathbf{M}}_{n1}$ and $\tilde{\mathbf{M}}_{n2}$, by rotating the old matrices around their optical centers until focal planes become coplanar.

In order to have horizontal epipolar lines, the baseline must be parallel to the new X axis of both cameras. In addition, corresponding points must have the same vertical coordinate (Y axis). Consequently, the positions of new optical centers are the same as those in the old cameras, the new matrices differ from the old ones by suitable rotations, and intrinsic parameters are the same for both cameras. Therefore, the new PPMs will differ only in their optical centers.

Let us write the new PPMs in terms of their factorization,

$$\tilde{\mathbf{M}}_{n1} = \mathbf{A}\left[\mathbf{R}\middle|{-}\mathbf{R}\mathbf{O}_1\right]$$
$$\tilde{\mathbf{M}}_{n2} = \mathbf{A}\left[\mathbf{R}\middle|{-}\mathbf{R}\mathbf{O}_2\right]$$

(1.30)

The intrinsic parameters matrix $\mathbf{A}$ is the same for both new PPMs and computed arbitrarily in this report as,

$$\mathbf{A} = \frac{\mathbf{A}_1 + \mathbf{A}_2}{2}$$

The rotation matrix **R** is also the same for both PPMs. It can be specified in terms of its row vectors:

$$\mathbf{R} = \begin{bmatrix} \mathbf{r}_1^T \\ \mathbf{r}_2^T \\ \mathbf{r}_3^T \end{bmatrix} \tag{1.31}$$

which are the X, Y, and Z axes of the camera coordinate system.

According to the previous descriptions, each axis is computed as follows:

1. The new X axis is parallel to the baseline: $\mathbf{r}_1 = \dfrac{(\mathbf{O}_1 - \mathbf{O}_2)}{PO_1 - O_2 P}$.

2. The new Y axis is orthogonal to X and to **k**: $\mathbf{r}_2 = \mathbf{k} \wedge \mathbf{r}_1$.

3. The new Z axis is orthogonal to XY plane: $\mathbf{r}_3 = \mathbf{r}_1 \wedge \mathbf{r}_2$.

In number 2, **k** is an arbitrary unit vector and it used to be equal to the Z unit vector in the old left camera coordinate system. In other words, the new Y axis is orthogonal to both the new X and the old left Z.

In order to rectify the left and the right image, it is necessary to compute transformation mapping of the image plane $\tilde{\mathbf{M}}_{oi} = \begin{bmatrix} \mathbf{Q}_{oi} & \tilde{\mathbf{q}}_{oi} \end{bmatrix}$ onto the image plane $\tilde{\mathbf{M}}_{ni} = \begin{bmatrix} \mathbf{Q}_{ni} & \tilde{\mathbf{q}}_{ni} \end{bmatrix}$. For any 3D point **W,** we know that

$$\tilde{\mathbf{p}}_{oi} \cong \tilde{\mathbf{M}}_{oi} \tilde{\mathbf{W}}$$

$$\tilde{\mathbf{p}}_{ni} \cong \tilde{\mathbf{M}}_{ni} \tilde{\mathbf{W}}$$

According to Equation (1.25), the equations of the optical rays are the following:

$$\mathbf{W} = \mathbf{O}_i + \lambda_o \mathbf{Q}_{oi}^{-1} \tilde{\mathbf{p}}_{oi}, \quad \lambda_o \in {}^\circ$$

$$\mathbf{W} = \mathbf{O}_i + \lambda_n \mathbf{Q}_{ni}^{-1} \tilde{\mathbf{p}}_{ni}, \quad \lambda_n \in {}^\circ$$

Hence,

$$\tilde{\mathbf{p}}_{ni} = \lambda \mathbf{Q}_{ni} \mathbf{Q}_{oi}^{-1} \tilde{\mathbf{p}}_{oi}, \quad \lambda \in {}^\circ$$

$$\tilde{\mathbf{p}}_{ni} = \lambda \mathbf{T}_i \tilde{\mathbf{p}}_{oi} \tag{1.32}$$

The transformation $\mathbf{T}_i = \mathbf{Q}_{ni} \mathbf{Q}_{oi}^{-1}$ is then applied to the original stereo images to produce rectified images. Because the pixels of the rectified image correspond to noninteger positions on the original image planes, new pixel positions must be computed by using an image interpolation technique.

FIGURE 1.6
Checkerboard pattern for camera calibration.

1.5 Calibration and Rectification Examples

1.5.1 Calibration Example

To capture stereo images of an object, two cameras that have the same types of image sensors are used in common. Two cameras can be mounted in the parallel or toed-in configuration. In the parallel configuration, the optical axes are parallel to each other. In the toed-in configuration, two optical axes have some angle so that each camera can obtain the image of an object in the center of each image plane, respectively.

To calibrate the stereo camera system, a checkerboard pattern is commonly used. An example of a checkerboard is shown in Figure 1.6. The pattern has two planes that are parallel to the XY and the YZ planes of the world coordinate systems. In each pattern plane, many corners represent a set of 3D points. The top-left corner in the XY plane of the pattern is set as the origin of the world coordinate system. In addition, the coordinates of the other corners can be assigned because the width and the height of each rectangle of the pattern are known in advance. To calibrate the cameras, all 3D coordinates of the corners are assigned as 3D vectors $\mathbf{W}$ and their 2D image coordinates are $\mathbf{p}_1$ and $\mathbf{p}_2$ in the left and right images, respectively. Using the vectors, the intrinsic and extrinsic camera parameters are obtained.

(a)   (b)

FIGURE 1.7
Stereo images of a checkerboard pattern: (a) left image; (b) right image.

Examples of the stereo images of a calibration pattern are shown in Figure 1.7(a) and 1.7(b), which are the left and the right image, respectively. Each image's pixel resolution is 640 × 480. All corner points on the calibration pattern are acquired by a corner detection algorithm. The world coordinates $\mathbf{W}_i$ and the image coordinates $\mathbf{p}_i$ of the inner 96 corner points on both calibration planes are used to compute the projection matrix of each camera. The projection matrix is computed as described in an earlier section. The left and the right projection matrices, $\mathbf{M}_{o1}$ and $\mathbf{M}_{o2}$, which bring a 3D world point to the corresponding image planes, are

$$\mathbf{M}_{o1} = \begin{bmatrix} 7.172 \times 10^{-3} & 9.806 \times 10^{-5} & -5.410 \times 10^{-3} & 1.776 \times 10^{0} \\ 8.253 \times 10^{-4} & 8.889 \times 10^{-3} & 7.096 \times 10^{-4} & 6.427 \times 10^{-1} \\ 8.220 \times 10^{-4} & 6.439 \times 10^{-5} & 7.048 \times 10^{-4} & 1.000 \end{bmatrix} \quad (1.33)$$

$$\mathbf{M}_{o2} = \begin{bmatrix} 7.423 \times 10^{-3} & -4.474 \times 10^{-5} & -5.005 \times 10^{-3} & 1.638 \times 10^{0} \\ 7.078 \times 10^{-4} & 8.868 \times 10^{-3} & 4.957 \times 10^{-4} & 4.270 \times 10^{-1} \\ 7.750 \times 10^{-4} & 6.592 \times 10^{-5} & 7.521 \times 10^{-4} & 1.000 \end{bmatrix} \quad (1.34)$$

$$\begin{bmatrix} \mathbf{R}_{o1} \mid \mathbf{t}_{o1} \end{bmatrix} = \begin{bmatrix} 6.508 \times 10^{-1} & 1.752 \times 10^{-4} & -7.591 \times 10^{-1} & -5.177 \times 10^{-2} \\ -4.517 \times 10^{-2} & 9.982 \times 10^{-1} & -3.850 \times 10^{-2} & -9.596 \times 10^{-1} \\ 7.578 \times 10^{-1} & 5.936 \times 10^{-2} & 6.497 \times 10^{-1} & 9.218 \times 10^{2} \end{bmatrix} \quad (1.35)$$

$$\begin{bmatrix} \mathbf{R}_{o2} \mid \mathbf{t}_{o2} \end{bmatrix} = \begin{bmatrix} 6.970 \times 10^{-1} & -1.556 \times 10^{-2} & -7.168 \times 10^{-1} & -6.884 \times 10^{0} \\ -3.285 \times 10^{-2} & 9.980 \times 10^{-1} & -5.361 \times 10^{-2} & -9.764 \times 10^{1} \\ 7.163 \times 10^{-1} & 6.092 \times 10^{-2} & 6.951 \times 10^{-1} & 9.241 \times 10^{2} \end{bmatrix} \quad (1.36)$$

1.5.2 Rectification Example

Given projection matrices $\mathbf{M}_{oi}$ for the stereo cameras, new projection matrices $\mathbf{M}_{ni}$ are computed as described in Section 1.4.2:

$$\mathbf{M}_{n1} = \begin{bmatrix} -6.571\times10^0 & -9.838\times10^{-2} & 5.033\times10^0 & -1.581\times10^3 \\ -1.417\times10^0 & 8.030\times10^0 & -1.215\times10^0 & -2.058\times10^3 \\ -7.594\times10^{-1} & -5.936\times10^{-2} & -6.478\times10^{-1} & -9.218\times10^2 \end{bmatrix} \quad (1.37)$$

$$\mathbf{M}_{n2} = \begin{bmatrix} -6.571\times10^0 & -9.838\times10^{-2} & 5.033\times10^0 & -1.051\times10^3 \\ -1.417\times10^0 & 8.030\times10^0 & -1.215\times10^0 & -2.058\times10^3 \\ -7.594\times10^{-1} & -5.936\times10^{-2} & -6.478\times10^{-1} & -9.218\times10^2 \end{bmatrix} \quad (1.38)$$

$$\begin{bmatrix} \mathbf{R}_{n1} | \mathbf{t}_{n1} \end{bmatrix} = \begin{bmatrix} -6.490\times10^1 & 5.745\times10^{-4} & 7.607\times10^{-1} & 2.297\times10^0 \\ -4.478\times10^{-2} & 9.982\times10^{-1} & -3.896\times10^{-2} & -9.596\times10^1 \\ -7.594\times10^{-1} & -5.936\times10^{-2} & -6.478\times10^{-1} & -9.218\times10^2 \end{bmatrix} \quad (1.39)$$

$$\begin{bmatrix} \mathbf{R}_{n2} | \mathbf{t}_{n2} \end{bmatrix} = \begin{bmatrix} -6.490\times10^1 & 5.745\times10^{-4} & 7.607\times10^{-1} & 6.783\times10^0 \\ -4.478\times10^{-2} & 9.982\times10^{-1} & -3.896\times10^{-2} & -9.596\times10^1 \\ -7.594\times10^{-1} & -5.936\times10^{-2} & -6.478\times10^{-1} & -9.218\times10^2 \end{bmatrix} \quad (1.40)$$

Transformation matrix $\mathbf{T}_i$ to rectify the stereo pair in the image planes is then estimated as $\mathbf{T}_i = \mathbf{Q}_{ni}\mathbf{Q}_{oi}^{-1}$. For a pixel $\mathbf{p}_o$ in the original image plane and its homogeneous coordinates $\tilde{\mathbf{p}}_o$, a new pixel position $\tilde{\mathbf{p}}_n$ is estimated as

$$\tilde{\mathbf{p}}_n = \mathbf{T}_i\tilde{\mathbf{p}}_o \quad (1.41)$$

The picture coordinate $\tilde{\mathbf{p}}_n = (u', v')$ of the image point $\mathbf{p}_n$ is then obtained by multiplying the scaling and translating matrix $\mathbf{K}$ to the image coordinates:

$$\tilde{\mathbf{p}}'_n = \begin{bmatrix} k_u & 0 & 0 \\ 0 & k_v & 0 \\ 0 & 0 & 1 \end{bmatrix} \tilde{\mathbf{p}}_n \quad (1.42)$$

However when a rectified image is generated in a 2D array of a pixel plane, it is necessary to consider a translation of the principal point. Otherwise, some portions of the rectified image may be lost outside a pixel plane because of an offset between the original principal point (u_{o0}, v_{o0}) and the new principal point (u_{n0}, v_{n0}). In order to translate the rectified image back into the pixel plane, the new principal point (u_{n0}, v_{n0}) must be recomputed by adding the offset to the old principal point. The offset of the principal points can be computed by mapping the origin of the retinal plane onto the new retinal plane:

$$\tilde{\mathbf{o}}_n = \mathbf{T} \begin{bmatrix} u_o 0 \\ v_o 0 \\ 1 \end{bmatrix} \tag{1.43}$$

The new retinal coordinates are

$$\tilde{\mathbf{p}}'_n = \mathbf{K}\left(\tilde{\mathbf{p}}_n - \tilde{\mathbf{o}}_n\right) \tag{1.44}$$

The principal offset is considered only in the x direction because rectifying transformations rotate the image plane around the y axis. In this example, offsets of the principal points on the left and the right retinal planes are $(-0.020231, 0)$ and $(-0.518902, 0)$, respectively.

Figure 1.8(a) and (b) show original stereo images of an object and Figure 1.8(c) and (d) show their rectified images, which are generated by transforming the original images. In addition, the color value of new pixels is determined by using a bilinear interpolation. Rectified images are also shifted so that the new principal points are on or near the image centers.

1.6 3D Reconstruction

Using a rectified stereo image pair, a stereo matching technique can be applied to find stereo correspondences in the same horizontal lines. One of the simple stereo matching methods is normalized cross correlation, which will be described in the next section. Once the disparity of matching image points is determined, the coordinates of a 3D point associated to the matching pixels can be computed. Two simple and general reconstruction methods are presented in this section.

1.6.1 Simple Triangulation

Because stereo images are rectified already, depth computation uses a simple equation for a parallel stereo camera. When there is a disparity d'_u in x direction of the picture plane, the depth D to a 3D point from the stereo camera is

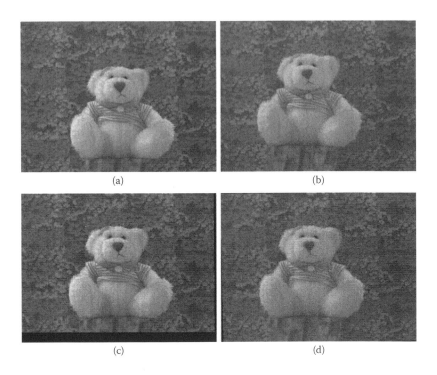

(a)   (b)

(c)   (d)

FIGURE 1.8
Rectification example. (a, b) Original left and right images; (c, d) rectified left and right images.

$$D = \frac{f \cdot B}{d'_u / k_u + \left(u'_{n1} - u'_{n2}\right)} \tag{1.45}$$

where $B = \|\mathbf{O}_1 - \mathbf{O}_2\|$ is the length of the baseline of the stereo camera. For the focal length f of the camera, the intrinsic calibration results f_u, f_v, can be used.

1.6.2 Solution of a Linear Equation

The range for a pair of conjugate points is also reconstructed by using Equation (1.27). Given two conjugate points, $\tilde{\mathbf{p}}_1 = \left(u_1, v_1, 1\right)^T$ and $\tilde{\mathbf{p}}_2 = \left(u_2, v_2, 1\right)^T$, and the two projection matrices, $\tilde{\mathbf{M}}_{n1}$ and $\mathbf{M}'_{n2}$, an overconstrained linear system is written as

$$\mathbf{AW} = \mathbf{y} \tag{1.46}$$

where

$$A = \begin{bmatrix} \left(\mathbf{a}_1 - u_1\mathbf{a}_3\right)^T \\ \left(\mathbf{a}_2 - v_1\mathbf{a}_3\right)^T \\ \left(\mathbf{b}_1 - u_2\mathbf{b}_3\right)^T \\ \left(\mathbf{b}_2 - v_2\mathbf{b}_3\right)^T \end{bmatrix} \quad y = \begin{bmatrix} -a_{14} + u_1 a_{34} \\ -a_{24} + v_1 a_{34} \\ -b_{14} + u_2 b_{34} \\ -b_{24} + v_2 b_{34} \end{bmatrix} \tag{1.47}$$

Then $\mathbf{W}$ gives the position of the 3D point projected to the conjugate points. Column vectors $\mathbf{a}_i$ and $\mathbf{b}_i$ are entry vectors of the new left and the right projection matrices, respectively. Sometimes, the rectified image can be reflected along the vertical or the horizontal axis. This can be detected by checking the ordering between the two diagonal corners of the image. If a reflection occurs, the image should be reflected back to keep the original ordering.

The coordinates of $\mathbf{W}$ are represented with respect to the world system. To represent the point in one of the camera coordinate systems, it needs to convert the point. Suppose the right camera's coordinate system is a reference. Then we can transform the point by simply using the external calibration parameters $[\mathbf{R}|\mathbf{t}]$ of the right cameras. However, two transformations can be considered: One is to the old right camera's coordinates before rectification, and the other is to the new right-hand camera's coordinates after rectification. If the world 3D point is transformed to the old right-hand camera's coordinate system, then

$$P_w = \begin{bmatrix} \mathbf{R}_{o2} & \mathbf{t} \end{bmatrix} \mathbf{W} \tag{1.48}$$

where $[\mathbf{R}_{o2}|\mathbf{t}]$ is the old external calibration parameters of the right camera. Figure 1.9 shows an example of 3D reconstruction from stereo images in Figure 1.8. In Figure 1.9(a), a reconstructed 3D model is represented by point clouds, while Figure 1.9(b) shows its mesh model.

1.7 Stereo Matching

Stereo matching is a technique to find corresponding points between stereo images captured from a pair of cameras. In general, most investigations in stereo matching are categorized as one of two methods. One is local matching and the other is global matching. The local matching method finds corresponding points by comparing image properties only. If the image properties of two image templates, one from the left image and the other from the right, are very similar to each other, the center points of the templates are considered to be matched. Therefore, in the local method, a cost function for

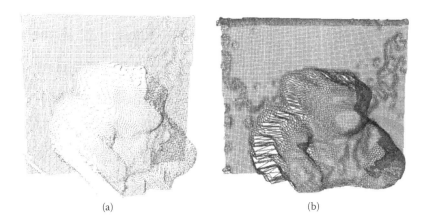

(a)   (b)

FIGURE 1.9
Experimental results of stereo matching. (a) Point clouds of the reconstructed 3D shape; (b) mesh model of the same reconstruction.

measuring the similarity of two templates is designed to use their image properties, such as intensity, color, sharpness, etc. The global matching method uses a global cost function so that it can measure the energy for a point to be matched with another point in terms of image and continuity properties. Recent stereo matching investigations have mostly focused on introducing global matching methods and some of them have yielded very successful results [14,20].

The global matching method measures the energy (or error) cost of a pair of image points in terms not only of image properties but also of disparity differences between neighboring pixels. In general, the disparity value f_p of a pixel **p** is determined in a way to minimize an energy function,

$$E(f) = \sum_{(p,q)\in N} V\left(f_p, f_q\right) + \sum_{p\in P} D_p\left(f_p\right) \qquad (1.49)$$

where N is a set of neighboring pixels and P is a set of pixels in an image. $V(f_p, f_q)$ is the cost of assigning disparity values f_p and f_q to two neighboring pixels, called the discontinuity cost. The second term, $D_p(f_p)$, is the cost of assigning disparity value f_p to pixel **p**, which is the data cost. The correspondence is therefore determined by searching for a point-pair that yields the smallest global energy.

Examples of well-known global matching methods are BP (belief propagation [3,12,21]), GC (graph cut [11,14]), DP (dynamic programming [14,18]), and SGM (semiglobal matching [6–8]). Many variants of them are also introduced to enhance matching performance. Instead of solving the np-hard problem of stereo correspondence, some global matching methods employ multiple scan lines to add cost functions in multiple directions [1,7,8]. A two-way DP technique, introduced by Kim et al. [9], is a simple example. They solve the inter-scan-line inconsistency problem using a bidirectional DP. Recently, they extended their work using several scan directions and edge orientations [16]. Hirschmüller introduced another multi-scan-line matching technique called SGM [7,8]. He generated cost volumes from multiple scan lines and aggregated them to obtain a dense disparity image. Heinrichs [6] has applied the SGM technique to a trinocular vision system for 3D modeling of real objects.

Global matching methods usually produce reasonably accurate results. However, they require more memory space and longer computation time than conventional local approaches. For example, most global matching methods generate disparity or cost space images. In SGM, $(n + 1)$ cost volumes for (n)-scan directions are generated before they are merged to a single cost volume. The size of a cost volume is $N \times M \times D$, where $N \times M$ is the image resolution and D is the disparity range. Therefore, total $(n + 1) \times N \times M \times D$ memory space is needed to process a pair of stereo images. Computation time is therefore also increased with the increasing size of memory space.

In this section, several stereo matching methods, including local and global methods, are briefly described. In addition, their matching performance is compared to help readers understand the difference in matching methods. Using the Middlebury stereo database [20], disparity maps from different matching methods are compared.

1.7.1 Sum of Squared Difference

The SSD matching method is one of the simple stereo matching techniques. This method uses the intensity information around a pixel (x,y) in a reference image to find its matching conjugate in a target image. Since the SSD matching uses image areas around a matching pixel, it is one of the area-based stereo matching techniques. To find correspondences between stereo images, an image window (template) is defined in the reference image. Then, a cost function measures the image difference with another template in the target image.

Figure 1.10 shows a diagram of the SSD stereo matching method. In the figure, two images, $g^{(l)}$ and $g^{(r)}$, are left and right stereo images, respectively. In the left image, an image template at $g^{(l)}(x,y)$ is defined with the width and height of size m. By assuming that two images are obtained from a parallel stereo vision system, epipolar lines in both images are on the same horizontal line. Therefore, correspondence searching can be done in the horizontal epipolar lines. Now let us define a template at $g^{(r)}(x + d,y)$ in the right image, where d is a disparity value. Then, the sum of squared difference between two templates is defined as

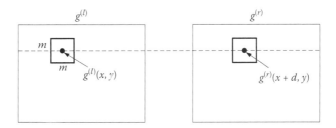

FIGURE 1.10
Stereo matching of image templates in a horizontal epipolar line.

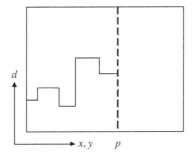

FIGURE 1.11
Scan-line optimization diagram.

$$SSD\left(g^{(l)}, g^{(r)}, x, y, d\right) = \sum_{k=-m/2}^{m/2} \sum_{j=-m/2}^{m/2} \left(g^{(l)}\left(x+k,\ y+j\right) - g^{(r)}\left(x+k+d,\ y+j\right)\right)^2 \quad (1.50)$$

where m is the size of the templates.

To find the matching pixel in the right image, it is necessary to compare $SSD(g^{(l)}, g^{(r)}, x, y, d)$ of all pixels in the horizontal line. In an ideal case, the best matching pixel in the right image yields the least SSD error.

1.7.2 Scan-Line Optimization

The scan-line optimization (SO) method is one of the global matching techniques [13]. The SO technique is very similar to the dynamic programming (DP) technique; however, it differs from the DP in that it does not consider occlusion pixels for cost aggregation. Therefore, its algorithm is simple and intuitive. The basic algorithm of the SO technique is to aggregate the energy of the previous pixel with the cost and continuity functions of the current pixel.

Figure 1.11 shows a general diagram of the SO-based stereo matching method. In the figure, the horizontal axis can be considered a 2D vector axis in which image coordinates (x,y) are two elements. For example, if the search space for correspondence in the right image is restricted to the horizontal line, the vector axis coincides with the horizontal line. In this case, only the x element of the vector is increased for energy aggregation. In addition, the vertical axis of the figure is the disparity axis. The range of the vertical axis is the same with the possible disparity range of pixel **p**. Suppose we need to find the disparity at pixel position **p**(x,y) as shown in Figure 1.11. In the SO method, the disparity of **p** is determined by searching the disparity index, which yields the least energy among the vertical axes.

Suppose the energy aggregation at pixel **p** is $E(\mathbf{p})$ and the matching cost of the pixel to disparity value d is $C(\mathbf{p},d)$. Then the energy aggregation of the current pixel is computed as

$$E(\mathbf{p}) = E(\mathbf{p}-1) + C(\mathbf{p},d) + \rho\left(d_{(\mathbf{p},\mathbf{p}-1)}\right) \tag{1.51}$$

where $\rho(d_{(\mathbf{p},\mathbf{p}-1)})$ is the penalty of disparity change between pixel **p** and **p** − 1. This means that disparity discontinuity increases matching energy along the scan line. Therefore, when aggregating matching energy, the discontinuity penalty should be increased if the disparity values of adjacent pixels are different. Similarly, the discontinuity penalty should be decreased if the disparity values of adjacent pixels are similar. An example of penalty values is shown in Equation (1.52). By combining data and continuity terms in global matching methods, more reliable disparity maps can be obtained:

$$\rho = \begin{cases} \rho_1 & \text{if } 1 \le d_{(p,\,p-1)} < 3 \\ \rho_2 & \text{if } 3 \le d_{(p,\,p-1)} \\ 0 & \text{if } d_{(p,\,p-1)} = 0 \end{cases} \tag{1.52}$$

1.7.3 Semiglobal Matching

In conventional global matching techniques, cost aggregation is done generally in a single matching direction, along the epipolar lines in the left or right image. However, with multiple matching directions, a more reliable disparity map can be obtained even using a simple matching algorithm. For example, Hirschmüller [7] proposes a global stereo matching technique called semiglobal matching (SGM).

Figure 1.12 shows multiple matching directions and a disparity space image in one of the directions. The left side of the figure shows matching directions through which SGM follows. Similarly to other global matching techniques, 8 or 16 matching directions are commonly used. However, the number of matching directions is not proportional to the accuracy of matching results. The right picture shows the disparity relation between **p** and **p**$_{next}$, which are in the same matching direction. In the figure, the current

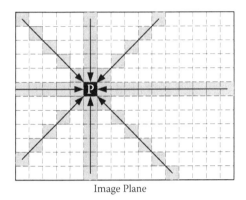

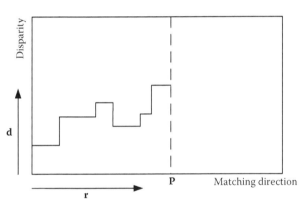

FIGURE 1.12
A general diagram of the semiglobal matching method. (Figures from H. Hirschmüller. *Proceedings of IEEE Conference on Computer Vision and Pattern Recognition,* pages 2386–2393, 2006.)

pixel's disparity d_p is used to calculate the disparity of the next pixel, d_{pnext}. The range of disparity at $\mathbf{p}_{next}$ is from $d_p - 1$ to $d_p + 1$.

In SGM, the disparity of $\mathbf{p}$ is determined so that the accumulation energy of a disparity space image D is minimized along the path depicted in the right-hand figure of Figure 1.12. Let $E(D)$ be the accumulation energy along a matching direction, and $d_\mathbf{p}$ and $d_\mathbf{q}$ be the disparities of $\mathbf{p}$ and $\mathbf{q}$, respectively. Then the accumulation energy is defined as

$$E(D) = \sum_p C(\mathbf{p}, d_\mathbf{p}) + \sum_{q \in N_p} P_1 T \Big[\big| d_\mathbf{p} - d_\mathbf{q} \big| = 1 \Big] + \sum_{q \in N_p} P_2 T \Big[\big| d_\mathbf{p} - d_\mathbf{q} \big| > 1 \Big] \quad (1.53)$$

Here, $C(\mathbf{p}, d_\mathbf{p})$ is the cost of disparity d at pixel $\mathbf{p}$ and P_1 and P_2 are discontinuity penalties.

In Hirschmüller [7], the minimization of the accumulation energy is implemented by a cost aggregation such that

$$L_r(\mathbf{p},d) = C(\mathbf{p},d) + \min\left(L_r(\mathbf{p}-\mathbf{r},d), L_r(\mathbf{p}-\mathbf{r},d-1) + P_1\right.$$
$$L_r(\mathbf{p}-\mathbf{r},d+1) + P_1, \min L_r(\mathbf{p}-\mathbf{r},i) + P_2\right) \tag{1.54}$$

where $L_r(\mathbf{p},d)$ is the accumulated cost of $\mathbf{p}$ with disparity d along the matching direction $\mathbf{r}$. Accumulated costs of all matching directions are then accumulated again to obtain an accumulated cost image

$$S(\mathbf{p},d) = \sum_r L_r(\mathbf{p},d) \tag{1.55}$$

From the accumulation cost image, the disparity of $\mathbf{p}$ can be determined by searching the smallest accumulation cost at each pixel $\mathbf{p}$.

1.7.4 Belief Propagation

Belief propagation (BP) is also one of the global stereo matching methods [3]. The BP algorithm uses a MAP-MRF (maximum a posteriori-Markov random field) model as a global energy model. Let $I = \{I_L, I_R\}$ be a set of stereo images for the input of the MRF model and d^* be the disparity image to obtain from I. Then, the stereo matching problem can be considered as maximizing a posteriori probability such that

$$p(d\mid I) = \frac{p(I\mid d)p(d)}{p(I)} \tag{1.56}$$

$$d^* = \arg\max\, p(I\mid d) \tag{1.57}$$

In the preceding equation, a conditional probability $p(I|d)$ can be represented as

$$p(I\mid d) = e^{\left(-\Sigma_\mathbf{p} D_\mathbf{p}(d_\mathbf{p})\right)} \tag{1.58}$$

where, $D_\mathbf{p}(d_\mathbf{p})$ is the data cost of assigning disparity $d_\mathbf{p}$ at pixel $\mathbf{p}$. In addition, the *prior* term can be represented as

$$p(d) = \frac{1}{Z} e^{\left(-\Sigma V\left(d_p, d_q\right)\right)} \tag{1.59}$$

FIGURE 1.13
(See color insert.) Stereo test images from the Middlebury database (http://vision.middle-bury.edu/stereo/). Top is original images and bottom is disparity images. From left: cone, teddy, and Venus.

where $V(d_p, d_q)$ is the cost of discontinuity between two adjacent pixels **p** and **q**. The MAP problem described in the preceding equation can be considered as the energy minimization problem such that

$$E(d) = \sum_{(\mathbf{p},\mathbf{q}) \in N} V\left(d_\mathbf{p}, d_\mathbf{q}\right) + \sum_{\mathbf{p} \in P} D_\mathbf{p}\left(d_\mathbf{p}\right) \tag{1.60}$$

1.7.5 Performance Comparisons

This section presents comparisons of several stereo matching techniques. In the stereo vision community, the Middlebury stereo database is widely used to compare many matching methods [20]. The Middlebury database provides several stereo images and their ground truth disparity maps. In comparison with the ground truth disparity maps, the matching performance of any comparing method can be evaluated. In this section, three pairs of Middlebury stereo images are used: cone, teddy, and Venus. The original test images are color images; however, they are converted to gray-level images for comparison. Figure 1.13 shows the color and disparity images. The gray level of the disparity image is encoded by a scale factor of 4, from an actual disparity range from 1–63.75 to 1–255. The black pixels in the disparity images are unknown due to occlusions.

Figure 1.14 shows stereo matching results of the three test images. Six different matching methods are evaluated: CR (cooperative region), adapting

FIGURE 1.14
Comparisons of six stereo matching techniques. From top, CR, BP, SGM, GC, DP, and SSD.
(Figures from the Middlebury stereo database, http://vision.middlebury.edu/stereo/.)

TABLE 1.1

Matching Errors of Different Methods

Method	Venus (nonocc, all, disc)	Teddy (nonocc, all, disc)	Cones (nonocc, all, disc)	Ref.
CR	0.11, 0.21, 1.54	5.16, 8.31, 13.0	2.79, 7.18, 8.01	19
(Rank)	(4), (3), (7)	(15), (11), (12)	(15), (4), (19)	
Adapting BP	0.10, 0.21, 1.44	4.22, 7.06, 11.8	2.48, 7.92, 7.32	10
(Rank)	(3), (4), (5)	(7), (6), (8)	(6), (11), (9)	
SGM	1.00, 1.57, 11.3	6.02, 12.2, 16.3	3.06, 9.75, 8.90	7
(Rank)	(67), (66), (76)	(21), (39), (32)	(25), (47), (37)	
GC	1.79, 3.44, 8.75	16.5, 25.0, 24.9	7.70, 18.2, 15.3	2
(Rank)	(89), (94), (72)	(105), (108), (95)	(94), (100), (89)	
DP	10.1, 11.0, 21.0	14.0, 21.6, 20.6	10.5, 19.1, 21.1	14
(Rank)	(112), (112), (101)	(99), (99), (78)	(104), (103), (101)	
SSD + MF	3.74, 5.16, 11.9	16.5, 24.8, 32.9	10.6, 19.8, 26.3	
(Rank)	(100), (101), (79)	(106), (107), (109)	(105), (105), (110)	

Note: Error percentages are calculated over three different areas: nonocclusion (nonocc), discontinuous (disc), and all (all) image areas.

BP (belief propagation), SGM (semiglobal matching), GC (graph cut), DP (dynamic programming), and SSD (sum of squared difference). Disparity results in the top three rows are very close to the ground truth in Figure 1.13. The three methods are all based on global cost minimization and have been introduced recently. Conventional global matching methods in the fourth and fifth rows show reasonable results. The last row is the result of an SSD-based local matching technique. In this result, disparity images are median filtered to remove matching errors.

Table 1.1 shows stereo matching errors evaluated with respect to the ground truth of the Middlebury stereo database. In addition, the performance ranking of each matching method is shown in the table. On the Middlebury stereo vision homepage [20], hundreds of stereo matching methods are compared and their rankings are shown. As mentioned in the previous paragraph, three recent global matching techniques yield very small errors compared with two conventional global and one local matching technique.

1.8 Conclusions

This chapter presents fundamental theories and inherent problems of stereo vision. The main goal of stereo vision is to acquire 3D depth information of a scene using two images obtained from slightly different views. Depth information of a pixel in an image is derived directly from its disparity, which is the coordinate difference with the corresponding pixel in the other image. The epipolar geometry of a stereo vision system and a rectification technique are also presented to explain the epipolar constraint. Several well-known stereo matching techniques that solve the inherent stereo problem in different manners are briefly introduced. Recent stereo matching techniques mostly use global cost functions, which consist of data and continuity terms. It is known that global matching techniques provide better performance than local techniques.

In addition to many existing application areas, stereo vision will bring many new application areas in the future. With the increasing computation power of computers and mobile devices, stereo vision can be applied to autonomous vehicle driving, robot navigation, real-time 3D modeling, etc. Time complexity in stereo matching will not be a problem in the future as it becomes common to use special processing units such as graphics processing units. In the near future, stereo vision will be one of the most used 3D scanning techniques and will be adopted in many commercial products.

References

1. S. Baek, S. Park, S. Jung, S. Kim, and J. Kim. Multi-directional greedy stereo matching. *Proceedings of the International Technical Conference on Circuits/Systems, Computers and Communications,* (1): 753–756, 2008.
2. Y. Boykov, O. Veksler, and R. Zabih. Fast approximate energy minimization via graph cuts. *IEEE Transactions on Pattern Analysis and Machine Intelligence,* 23 (11): 1222–1239, 2001.
3. P. Felzenszwalb and D. Huttenlocher. Efficient belief propagation for early vision. *Proceedings of the IEEE Conference on Computer Vision and Pattern Recognition,* (1): 261–268, 2004.
4. A. Fusiello, E. Trucco, and A. Verri. A compact algorithm for rectification of stereo pairs. *Machine Vision and Applications,* 12 (1): 16–22, 2000.
5. J. Gluckman and S Nayar. Rectifying transformations that minimize resampling effects. *Proceedings of the International Conference on Computer Vision and Pattern Recognition,* (1): 111–117, 2001.
6. M. Heinrichs, V. Rodehorsta, and O. Hellwich. Efficient semi-global matching for trinocular stereo. *Proceedings of Photogrammetric Image Analysis (PIA07),* 185–190, 2007.
7. H. Hirschmüller. Stereo vision in structured environments by consistent semi-global matching. *Proceedings of IEEE Conference on Computer Vision and Pattern Recognition,* 2386–2393, 2006.
8. H. Hirschmüller. Stereo processing by semi-global matching and mutual information. *IEEE Transactions on Pattern Analysis and Machine Intelligence,* 30 (2): 328 341, 2007.
9. C. Kim, K. M. Lee, B. T. Choi, and S. U. Lee. A dense stereo matching using two-pass dynamic programming with generalized ground control points. *Proceedings of IEEE Conference on Computer Vision and Pattern Recognition,* (2): 1075–1082, 2005.

10. A. Klaus, M. Sormann, and K. Karner. Segment-based stereo matching using belief propagation and a self-adapting dissimilarity measure. *Proceedings of IEEE International Conference on Pattern Recognition (ICPR2006)*, (3): 15–18, 2006.

11. V. Kolmogorov and R. Zabih. Computing visual correspondence with occlusions using graph cuts. *Proceedings of the 8th IEEE International Conference on Computer Vision*, (2): 508–515, 2001.

12. S. Larsen, P. Mordohai, M. Pollefeys, and H. Fuchs. Temporally consistent reconstruction from multiple video streams using enhanced belief propagation. *Proceedings of the 11th IEEE International Conference on Computer Vision*, 1–8, 2007.

13. S. Mattoccia, F. Tombari, and L. Di Stefano. Stereo vision enabling precise border localization within a scan line optimization framework. *Proceedings of the 8th Asian Conference on Computer Vision (ACCV2007)*, (2): 517–527, 2007.

14. D. Scharstein and R. Szeliski. A taxonomy and evaluation of dense two-frame stereo correspondence algorithms. *International Journal of Computer Vision*, 47 (1–3): 7–42, 2002.

15. S. D. Sharghi and F. A. Kamangar. Geometric feature-based matching in stereo images. *Proceedings of Information, Decision and Control Conference (IDC99)*, 65–70, 1999.

16. M. Sung, S. Lee, and N. Cho. Stereo matching using multi-directional dynamic programming and edge orientations. *Proceedings of IEEE International Conference on Image Processing*, (1): 233–236, 2007.

17. E. Trucco and A. Verri. *Introductory techniques for 3D computer vision*. Prentice Hall, Englewood Cliffs, NJ, 1998.

18. O. Veksler. Stereo correspondence by dynamic programming on a tree. *Proceedings of IEEE Conference on Computer Vision and Pattern Recognition*, (2): 384–390, 2005.

19. L. Wang, M. Liao, M. Gong, R. Yang, and D. Nistér. High-quality real-time stereo using adaptive cost aggregation and dynamic programming. *Proceedings of the Third International Symposium on 3D Data Processing, Visualization, and Transmission (3DPVT'06)*, 798–805, 2006.

20. Middlebury Stereo webpage. http://vision.middlebury.edu/stereo/

21. Q. Yang, L. Wang, R. Yang, H. Stewenius, and D. Nister. Stereo matching with color-weighted correlation, hierarchical belief propagation and occlusion handling. *Proceedings of the IEEE Conference on Computer Vision and Pattern Recognition*, (2): 17–22, 2006.

2

3D Shapes from Speckle

Yuan Hao Huang, Yang Shang, Yusheng Liu, and Hujun Bao

CONTENTS

One of the major difficulties of reconstructing three-dimensional (3D) shapes from stereo vision is the correspondence problem. Speckle can help in this aspect by providing unique patterns for area-based matching. After applying a high-contrast random speckle pattern on the object surface, disparities map with accuracy up to 0.02 pixels and ultrahigh spatial resolution can be established. The disparity information can then be used for accurate 3D reconstruction by triangulation. This chapter will introduce various algorithms of digital image correlation (DIC) for speckle pattern matching and various algorithms for 3D shape reconstruction from the disparity map. Examples of 3D shape measurement in various fields will also be given.

2.1 Introduction

Conventional stereo vision algorithms (refer to Chapter 1) use image features such as corner, edge, etc., for establishing correspondence in stereo image pairs and reconstructing a 3D scene by triangulation. These methods are efficient and can be implemented in real time for some machine vision applications. In 3D reverse engineering, experimental mechanics, and some other fields where researchers are more concerned about measurement accuracy and spatial resolution, these methods may not be able to satisfy these stringent requirements due to the limited number of feature points available and the matching errors of feature points. Thus, a more accurate 3D reconstruction technique is in demand. As a result, metrology based on speckle has been given intensive attention and is found to provide much better spatial resolution with improved accuracy.

The advantage of using speckle lies in the fact that it provides abundant high-frequency features for establishing accurate correspondence between a stereo image pair. After creating a high-contrast, random speckle pattern on an object surface, each point on the object will be surrounded by a unique intensity pattern that acts as the fingerprint of that point. Thus, accurate and high spatial resolution correspondence can then be established by correlating the intensity patterns. Normally, subpixel matching accuracy of 0.02–0.05 pixel with ultrahigh spatial resolution of 1 pixel can be achieved by proper algorithm design.

The process of establishing accurate correspondence between images with similar speckle patterns is normally called digital image correlation (DIC). Sometimes it is also called electronic speckle photography (ESP), digital speckle correlation (DSC), or texture correlation. There are multiple difficulties in using DIC for accurate 3D reconstruction. Firstly, a proper criterion should be defined to evaluate the level of similarity between speckle patterns. Secondly, the captured stereo speckle patterns are not exactly identical since they are captured from different viewing angles; thus, proper shape adjustment should be enabled to achieve an accurate matching. Thirdly, to achieve subpixel accuracy, proper interpolation schemes should be implemented to construct the intensity values at noninteger pixel positions. Finally, direct searching for the best matching position will require a large amount of computation, especially when accuracy at the order of 0.02 pixel is required; thus, advanced optimization schemes are needed to speed up the algorithm.

In this chapter, the technique of digital image correlation for accurate and efficient speckle matching will be introduced in detail in Section 2.2. Section 2.3 will introduce several triangulation methods for reconstructing a 3D shape from the disparity information obtained in Section 2.2. Section 2.4 gives a few examples for 3D shape measurement and Section 2.5 summarizes the chapter with references for further reading.

2.2 Principles of Digital Image Correlation

It is well known in signal processing that the cross correlation of two wave-forms provides a quantitative measure of their similarity. This basic concept has been explored to compare digital images (two-dimensional [2D] wave-forms) taken from different viewing directions or at different deformed stages to establish point-to-point correspondence and has been named digital image correlation [1–4]. After about 30 years of development, digital image correlation has been well developed and widely applied for in-plane displacement and strain measurement, material characterization, experimental stress analysis, and 3D shape reconstruction from macro to micro scales. Over 1,000 papers on this topic have been published, and the number is increasing every year.

2.2.1 Speckle Generation and Imaging

Before applying digital image correlation algorithm for 3D shape measurement, it is necessary to produce a high-contrast, random speckle pattern on the object surface. For a macro-object, this can be done by first spraying a flat-white paint followed by a flat-black paint on the object, or by using water-color, ink, or other markers. A more convenient way without manual speckle preparation is to project a computer-generated speckle pattern via a digital projector or to direct a laser interference speckle pattern via a diffuser onto the object surface. However, due to brightness deficiency and various electronic noises, a projecting system normally renders a speckle pattern with lower contrast and larger noise than painted speckle and results in lower measurement accuracy. A random laser interference speckle pattern also suffers from low contrast and an additional drawback of requiring a relatively small aperture for capturing larger laser speckle, which will reduce the light intensity and signal-to-noise ratio. Thus, manually painted speckle patterns are preferred for most applications.

For a micro-object, fine toner or other micro- and nanomarking techniques can be applied on the object surface to form a certain pattern. Alternatively, if the natural surface provides apparent intensity variations under high magnification (e.g., some atomic force microscopes, scanning electron microscopes, or optical microscope images), it can be used directly for correlation at the cost of slightly lower measurement accuracy due to the lack of high-frequency speckle components. Normally, resolution of 0.1–0.2 pixel is still achievable with a magnified natural surface. For more details of various practical speckle generation methods, please refer to references [5–10].

After generating a high-contrast speckle pattern, the next step is to image the object with the appropriate optical system. For in-plane displacement and strain measurement of planar objects, normally only one camera is required; it is placed normal to the object surface. Speckle patterns of the planar object before and after a deformation are captured and processed by DIC algorithm to deliver the displacement and strain information. Sometimes a telecentric lens is used if out-of-plane deformation cannot be ignored. For 3D shape or deformation measurement of a nonplanar object, a binocular system is used to capture speckle images of the object simultaneously from two different viewing directions. More details of binocular imaging systems are given in Section 2.3.

2.2.2 Speckle Cell Definition and Matching

After the stereo speckle pairs are captured, the next step is to define a series of points for determination of disparities and a series of speckle cells centered at these points for area-based intensity matching between the left and right stereo images. The size of the speckle cell should be large enough to contain unique speckle features so that correct correspondence can be established. However, it cannot be too large as the disparity information of points inside the cell will be averaged and larger cells will cause more apparent system error. Optimal speckle cells should contain 10–20 speckles.

Figure 2.1(a) shows a pair of typical speckle images for correlation. The left image indicates a point to determine the disparity information and a surrounding speckle cell with proper size. To find out the best matched cell in the right image, the intensity profile of the left speckle cell is shifted within the right-hand image to correlate with corresponding speckle cells and a correlation coefficient (to be defined in Section 2.2.4) is computed and plotted against the disparity values (u,v) as shown in Figure 2.1(b). It can be clearly

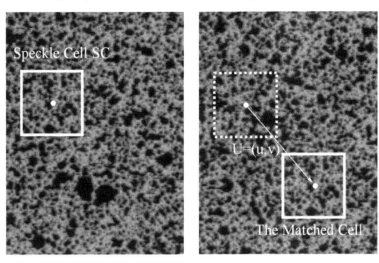

(a)

FIGURE 2.1
(a) Illustration of speckle-cell-based matching; (b) distribution of correlation coefficient by varying disparity (u, v); (c) schematic diagram of speckle cell deformation. (Reproduced from Huang, Y. H. et al. *Optics and Laser Technology* 41 (4): 408–414, 2009. With permission.)

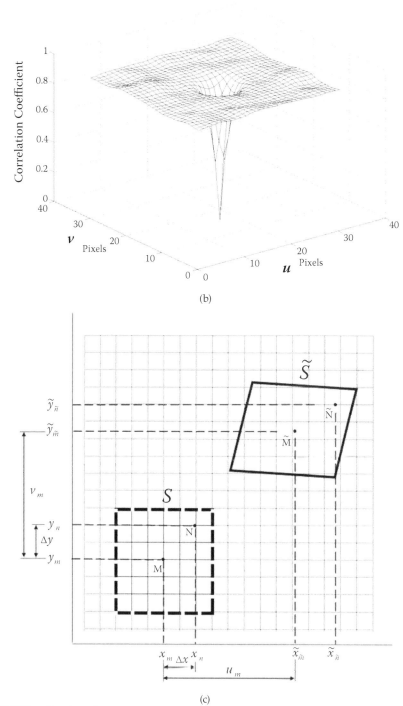

(b)

(c)

FIGURE 2.1 *(Continued)*

observed that the coefficient map presents a sharp minimum that indicates the best matching status. Thus, the corresponding disparity values can be determined from the minimum position for 3D reconstruction

2.2.3 Shape Transformation Function

In a practical imaging system, as the left and right speckle images are captured from different viewing angles or positions, the speckle patterns will undergo certain relative scaling, rotation, and higher order distortion. This will greatly flatten the correlation coefficient peak in Figure 2.1(b) or even cause decorrelation (no apparent peak is found) if pixel-by-pixel comparison is carried out. To avoid such decorrelation problems and improve measurement accuracy, a proper shape transformation function should be considered in the theoretical modeling.

For a point N in a small reference speckle cell S centered at point M (as shown in Figure 2.1c), it would be reasonable to formulate the coordinates $(\tilde{x}_{\tilde{n}}, \tilde{y}_{\tilde{n}})$ of the corresponding point $\tilde{N}$ in the objective speckle cell $\tilde{S}$ using second-order Taylor expansion as

$$\tilde{x}_{\tilde{n}} = x_m + P_1 + P_3\Delta x + P_5\Delta y + P_7\Delta x^2 + P_9\Delta y^2 + P_{11}\Delta x\Delta y \tag{2.1}$$

$$\tilde{y}_{\tilde{n}} = y_m + P_2 + P_4\Delta x + P_6\Delta y + P_8\Delta x^2 + P_{10}\Delta y^2 + P_{12}\Delta x\Delta y \tag{2.2}$$

where
(x_m, y_m) are the coordinates of central point M in, the reference speckle cell
Δx and Δy are the distance of point N from the central point M
$P_1\cdots P_{12}$ are parameters defining the shape transformation

In particular, P_1 and P_2 represent the central point disparity u_m and v_m (as indicated in Figure 2.1c) and are the desired information for 3D reconstruction.

After establishing such point-to-point correspondence between the reference and objective speckle cells, the control parameters $P_1\cdots P_{12}$ can be tuned to achieve a sharp minimum correlation coefficient. However, this direct approach involves tremendous computation as the correlation coefficient map is now established on a 12-dimensional base. Thus, a more efficient method should be implemented to speed up the calculation; this will be shown in Section 2.2.5.

It should be noted that in some ideal applications where the shape change between reference and objective image is quite small, then Equations (2.1) and (2.2) may be simplified to first-order Taylor expansion involving only parameters $P_1\cdots P_6$ to reduce computation. However, in a normal binocular system, if the angle between the two cameras is larger than 30°, the second-order effect will be apparent, especially for term $\Delta x\Delta y$ in Equations (2.1) and (2.2). Thus, the second-order terms should be included for optimal accuracy.

2.2.4 Correlation Coefficient

As shown in previous sections, a correlation coefficient should be defined
to indicate the similarity of reference and objective speckle cells. In the literature, different kinds of coefficients have been defined with different
performance and computation costs [7,12]. Basically, there are two types of
correlation coefficient: one based on the cross-correlation function and the
other on the sum of squared differences. It has been proved that these two
types of coefficients are linearly related and exchangeable [13]. For the case
of stereo matching, if both cameras and the A/D converters are the same, it
can be assumed that the intensity values of the left- and right-hand speckle
patterns are roughly the same. Thus, a simple correlation coefficient can be
defined based on the direct sum of the squared difference formula as

$$C(\vec{P}) = \sum_{N \in S} [I(x_n, y_n) - \tilde{I}(\tilde{x}_{\tilde{n}}, \tilde{y}_{\tilde{n}})]^2 \tag{2.3}$$

where $I(x_n, y_n)$ is the intensity of point N in the reference speckle cell S, and
$\tilde{I}(\tilde{x}_{\tilde{n}}, \tilde{y}_{\tilde{n}})$ is the intensity of the corresponding point in the objective speckle
cell $\tilde{S}$ (refer to Figure 2.1c). The coordinates of $(\tilde{x}_{\tilde{n}}, \tilde{y}_{\tilde{n}})$ are determined by
Equations (2.1) and (2.2) and $\vec{P}$ is a vector containing the control parameters
$P_1 \cdots P_{12}$.

This simple coefficient offers very good matching accuracy with reduced
computation for stereo images. In a case when the left and right images have
apparent intensity scaling and offset with the relationship of $\tilde{I} = \gamma I + \beta$, the
zero-mean normalized form of Equation (2.3) would be preferred at the cost
of larger computation [13], which can be expressed as

$$C(\vec{P}) = \sum_{N \in S} \left[\frac{I(x_n, y_n) - E(I)}{\sigma(I)} - \frac{\tilde{I}(\tilde{x}_{\tilde{n}}, \tilde{y}_{\tilde{n}}) - E(\tilde{I})}{\sigma(\tilde{I})} \right]^2 \tag{2.4}$$

where $E(I)$, $\sigma(I)$ and $E(\tilde{I})$, $\sigma(\tilde{I})$ are the mean intensity and standard deviation values for the reference and objective speckle cells, respectively.

For coefficients in the form of the sum of squared difference, it is obvious
that a smaller coefficient indicates a better matching between the reference
and objective speckle cells. During DIC computation, quite frequently a criterion is required to judge whether or not the parameters $P_1 \cdots P_{12}$ are close
enough to the optimal values. Obviously, the correlation coefficient can serve
as such a criterion. As shown in Figure 2.1(b), where a normalized coefficient
is plotted, it can be seen that the global minimum is quite close to zero, while
the other coefficients outside the minimum cone are quite close to one. Thus,
it would be reasonable to predefine a largest allowed coefficient C_{max} as half
of the average coefficients over a large area. For parameters $P_1 \cdots P_{12}$, which

satisfy the equation $C(\vec{P}) < C_{max}$, it can be presumed that the optimal parameters are close to the current values and can be determined by a nonlinear iteration process (to be introduced in Section 2.2.5).

2.2.5 Nonlinear Optimization

Direct minimization of Equation (2.3) or (2.4) by varying the 12 parameters is $P_1 \cdots P_{12}$ computation intensive. Thus, a more efficient approach has been developed [14]. To determine the minimum position of the correlation coefficient, Fermat's theorem can be applied. This theorem states that every local extremum of a differentiable function is a stationary point (the first derivative in that point is zero), so the following equation should be satisfied at the minimum position:

$$\nabla C(\vec{P}) = 0 \tag{2.5}$$

Equation (2.5) can be solved using the Newton–Raphson (N–R) iteration method as follows:

$$\vec{P}^{k+1} = \vec{P}^{k} - \frac{\nabla C(\vec{P}^{k})}{\nabla \nabla C(\vec{P}^{k})} \tag{2.6}$$

where the expression of $\nabla C(\vec{P})$ and $\nabla \nabla C(\vec{P})$ can be derived from Equation (2.3) as

$$\nabla C(\vec{P}) = \left(\frac{\partial C}{\partial P_i} \right)_{i=1\cdots12} = \left\{ \sum_{N\in S} -2[I(x_n, y_n) - \tilde{I}(\tilde{x}_{\tilde{n}}, \tilde{y}_{\tilde{n}})] \frac{\partial \tilde{I}}{\partial P_i} \right\}_{i=1\cdots12} \tag{2.7}$$

$$\nabla \nabla C(\vec{P}) = \left(\frac{\partial^2 C}{\partial P_i \partial P_j} \right)_{\substack{i=1\cdots12 \\ j=1\cdots12}} = \left\{ \sum_{N\in S} -2[I(x_n, y_n) - \tilde{I}(\tilde{x}_{\tilde{n}}, \tilde{y}_{\tilde{n}})] \frac{\partial^2 \tilde{I}}{\partial P_i \partial P_j} \right\}_{\substack{i=1\cdots12 \\ j=1\cdots12}} + \left\{ \sum_{N\in S} 2 \frac{\partial \tilde{I}}{\partial P_i} \cdot \frac{\partial \tilde{I}}{\partial P_j} \right\}_{\substack{i=1\cdots12 \\ j=1\cdots12}} \tag{2.8}$$

In Equation (2.8), when $\vec{P}$ is close to the correct matching position, $I(x_n, y_n) \approx \tilde{I}(\tilde{x}_{\tilde{n}}, \tilde{y}_{\tilde{n}})$, the first term can be reasonably ignored, which leads to an approximated Hessian matrix of

$$\nabla\nabla C(\vec{P}) = \left(\frac{\partial^2 C}{\partial P_i \partial P_j}\right)_{\substack{i=1\cdots12 \\ j=1\cdots12}} \approx \left\{\sum_{NeS} 2\frac{\partial \tilde{I}}{\partial P_i}\cdot\frac{\partial \tilde{I}}{\partial P_j}\right\}_{\substack{i=1\cdots12 \\ j=1\cdots12}} \tag{2.9}$$

This approximation has been proved to save a large amount of computation and yet deliver a similar result. The expression of

$$\left(\frac{\partial \tilde{I}}{\partial P_i}\right)_{i=1\cdots12}$$

could be further expressed as

$$\left(\frac{\partial \tilde{I}}{\partial P_i}\right)_{i=1\cdots12} = \left(\frac{\partial \tilde{I}}{\partial \tilde{x}_{\tilde{n}}}\cdot\frac{\partial \tilde{x}_{\tilde{n}}}{\partial P_i} + \frac{\partial \tilde{I}}{\partial \tilde{y}_{\tilde{n}}}\cdot\frac{\partial \tilde{y}_{\tilde{n}}}{\partial P_i}\right)_{i=1\cdots12} \tag{2.10}$$

where

$$\frac{\partial \tilde{x}_{\tilde{n}}}{\partial P_i} \text{ and } \frac{\partial \tilde{y}_{\tilde{n}}}{\partial P_i}$$

are readily determined from Equations (2.1) and (2.2) and

$$\frac{\partial \tilde{I}}{\partial \tilde{x}_{\tilde{n}}} \text{ and } \frac{\partial \tilde{I}}{\partial \tilde{y}_{\tilde{n}}}$$

are the intensity derivatives in the objective speckle cell, which can be obtained by an interpolation scheme to be introduced in Section 2.2.6.

It should be noted that Equation (2.6) requires an initial value $\vec{P}^0$ to start the iteration, and the given $\vec{P}^0$ should be close to the correct value; otherwise, the iteration will converge to a local extremum rather than the global minimum. In most cases, the shape transformation between the left and right images is not severe, so only the initial values P_1 and P_2 are provided as (u_m^0, v_m^0), while P_3, P_6 are set to one and the other eight parameters are set to zero (i.e., pure translation). Looking back to the example in Figure 2.1(b), if the initial (u_m^0, v_m^0) are given within the cone of global minimum (the base diameter of the cone is about 12–14 pixels), then the N–R algorithm will quickly converge to the correct disparity values. However, if the initial (u_m^0, v_m^0) are given outside the cone, it will converge to a local minimum and lead to wrong results. Thus, it is essential to provide a proper initial guess for the iteration algorithm.

One way to provide a good initial guess automatically is to evaluate the correlation coefficients of a coarse grid with steps smaller than the cone radius and subsequently a finer grid with a step of 1 pixel around the smallest coefficient obtained from the coarse grid [11]. The location of the minimal coefficient obtained this way is within 1 pixel of the global minimum and can be fed to the algorithm as an initial guess. In the case when the stereo system has been properly calibrated, a search for an initial guess can be conducted along the epipolar line and the computation can be greatly reduced.

When a binocular system with a large intersection angle is used, the second-order effect is apparent and the procedure proposed before that searches for an initial guess by varying P_1 and P_2 only may not be able to give a correct guess (i.e., the criterion $C < C_{max}$ is not satisfied). In such cases, the positions of five local minimum coefficients can be picked up and P_{11} and P_{12} are included in the searching processes for these five points. Hopefully, this will give an initial guess including P_1, P_2, P_{11}, P_{12}, which satisfies $C < C_{max}$.

If the inclusion of P_{11} and P_{12} still fails to give a correct initial guess, manual correspondence must be used for this purpose. By selecting 6–10 feature points around the reference speckle cell and manually identifying their corresponding points in the objective image, the 12 parameters $P_1 \cdots P_{12}$ can then be calculated and provided to the DIC algorithm.

Once a correct speckle cell matching is achieved, the determined parameters $P_1 \cdots P_{12}$ can then serve as the initial guess for adjacent speckle cells. Thus, for a region with smooth disparity change, only one proper initial guess is required. If a region contains some steep disparity changes, the algorithm may result in tremendous error at some points, leading to abrupt increase of the correlation coefficient. A new searching process should be conducted to assign a correct initial guess to those points.

2.2.6 Interpolation Schemes

During the process of stereo matching, the points in the object speckle cell may not reside in integral pixel positions, so it is necessary to interpolate for Gray value and its derivatives (refer to Equation [2.10]) at nonintegral pixel positions. Normally, a higher-order interpolation scheme will give better accuracy and faster convergence, but require more computation. In the literature, bicubic and biquintic spline interpolation have been widely used to render good accuracy (at the order of 0.01 pixel); lower-order schemes such as bilinear interpolation are only used when the accuracy requirement is low.

As the interpolation process accounts for a very large amount of computation for digital image correlation, special attention should be paid to the design of the interpolation scheme. Here a specially designed biquadratic spline interpolation scheme proposed by Spath [15] is recommended where the knots are shifted a half pixel from the nodes, resulting in similar accuracy with normal bicubic spline interpolation while requiring only half of the computation.

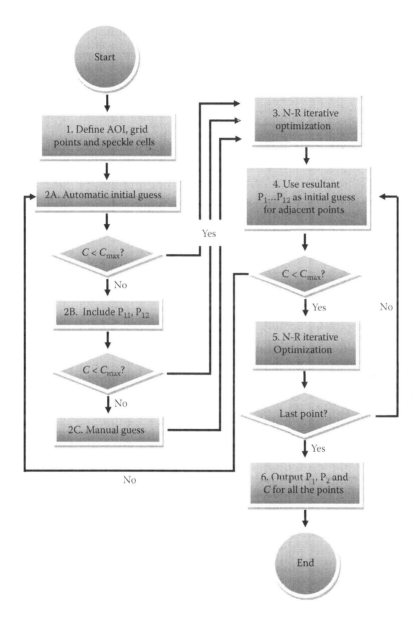

FIGURE 2.2
Flow chart for digital image correlation algorithm design.

2.2.7 Flow Chart Illustration of DIC Algorithm

Figure 2.2 summarizes the whole process of the digital image correlation algorithm described in previous sections. Readers can refer to Sections 2.2.2–2.2.6 for details of each step.

2.2.8 Other Versions of DIC Algorithm

In the literature, researchers have proposed some other versions of DIC algorithms. One of the most intuitive algorithms is the coarse–fine searching algorithm [16], where the integral-pixel correlation coefficients are first calculated by varying u_m, v_m and then subpixel coefficients are further computed around the minimum integral-pixel coefficient by interpolation. Simple as it is, the direct coarse–fine searching algorithm requires a large amount of computation due to the intensive Gray value interpolation involved. Thus, peak-fitting algorithms have been proposed [3,17] to reduce the computation where curve fitting or interpolation is used to establish a continuous correlation coefficient map based on integral-pixel coefficients and the minimum coefficient position is then determined with subpixel accuracy. These algorithms, based on coarse–fine searching and peak fitting, are intuitive and simple. However, because they ignore the shape change between the reference and objective images, they would be most suitable for disparity computation with stereo images captured from a canonical imaging system (parallel stereo cameras). For applications with a nonparallel setup, shape transformation should be considered for optimized accuracy.

Most of the DIC algorithms employ the concept of speckle-cell-based matching. Yet, there is another group of algorithms that are not speckle cell based; they establish whole-field mapping between the reference and objective speckle images using a continuous function [18,19]. Theoretically, such algorithms may eliminate mismatching for individual points due to the continuous constraint and improve the matching accuracy as more information is involved. However, these methods seem not to provide better accuracy according to the reported results, probably because the prescribed continuous function cannot genuinely represent the true displacement or disparity function. Thus, the speckle-cell-based algorithm described earlier dominates in most applications.

2.3 3D Shape Measurement from Stereo DIC

Section 2.2 introduced the DIC method for establishing accurate correspondence between stereo image pairs. This section will introduce the process of 3D reconstruction, which consists of modeling and calibrating the stereo system and subsequently calculating the 3D coordinates of a point from its correspondence information.

2.3.1 Stereo Camera Modeling

A simplified real camera comprises a pinhole and an imaging screen behind it. Rays emitted from the 3D scene will have to travel through the pinhole before

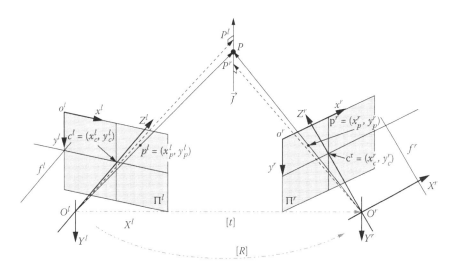

FIGURE 2.3
Pinhole model of a stereo system.

they reach the imaging screen. This will establish a unique projection from a 3D point in the scene to a 2D point on the screen. On the other hand, a 2D point on the screen cannot be uniquely identified in the 3D scene, but rather forms a line that connects the 2D point and the focal point. Thus, stereo cameras are required to uniquely identify a point in the 3D scene from its projections into the left and right imaging screens. The purpose of stereo camera modeling is to establish mathematically the projection of a point in a 3D scene onto the imaging screens and to establish the relation between the left and right cameras.

As shown in Figure 2.3, the imaging screens are placed in front of the pinholes at the symmetric positions for simplicity. Two Cartesian coordinate systems, which are denoted left and right camera coordinates, are established with their origins O^l and O^r residing at the focal points of the left and right cameras (From now on, we use superscripts l and r to represent elements in the left and right camera coordinate systems, respectively). The Z-axes are aligned along the optical axes, and the X-, Y-axes are chosen paralleled to the edges of the corresponding imaging screen Π (refer to Figure 2.3). The imaging screen Π is sampled with periods of h_x and h_y along the x- and y-directions and forms a grid of sensing elements called "pixel," which is the unit for the image coordinate system xoy.

The optical axis intersects with the imaging screen at principal point c with image coordinate (x_c, y_c) in units of pixels. The distance between the focal point O and the principal point c is known as the focal length f. The parameters f, x_c, y_c, h_x, h_y are intrinsic with the camera and called intrinsic parameters (the geometric distortion is ignored temporally for simplicity). These parameters fully determine the projection of a point from the 3D camera coordinate system onto the 2D image coordinate system.

Take the left camera coordinate system $O^l X^l Y^l Z^l$ as an example. A point P in the 3D scene is represented by its coordinates (X_P^l, Y_P^l, Z_P^l). The projection of P onto the imaging screen results in an image point p^l with image coordinates (x_p^l, y_p^l) expressed in the unit of pixels. Using simple triangulation (refer to Figure 2.3), we have

$$\frac{(x_p^l - x_c^l)h_x^l}{X_P^l} = \frac{(y_p^l - y_c^l)h_y^l}{Y_P^l} = \frac{f^l}{Z_P^l} \qquad (2.11)$$

The image coordinates of point p^l can then be expressed in terms of the camera intrinsic parameters and the camera coordinate of point P as

$$x_p^l = \frac{f^l X_P^l}{Z_P^l h_x^l} + x_c^l \qquad (2.12)$$

$$y_p^l = \frac{f^l Y_P^l}{Z_P^l h_y^l} + y_c^l \qquad (2.13)$$

Similarly, the same point P in the 3D scene can also be represented in the right-camera coordinate system as (X_P^r, Y_P^r, Z_P^r), which results in similar projection onto the right imaging screen as

$$x_p^r = \frac{f^r X_P^r}{Z_P^r h_x^r} + x_c^r \qquad (2.14)$$

$$y_p^r = \frac{f^r Y_P^r}{Z_P^r h_y^r} + y_c^r \qquad (2.15)$$

Equations (2.12)–(2.15) have fully established the projection of a point P in the 3D scene onto the left and right imaging screens. However, the same point P has been simultaneously represented by (X_P^l, Y_P^l, Z_P^l) in the left camera coordinate system and (X_P^r, Y_P^r, Z_P^r) in the right camera coordinate system. Thus, the relationship between the left and right camera coordinates should be established to relate (X_P^l, Y_P^l, Z_P^l) and (X_P^r, Y_P^r, Z_P^r). This has been done in numerous textbooks [18,19].

Let $[t]$ specify the column vector representing the translation from origin O^l to O^r and $[R]$ specify the orthogonal rotation matrix from left camera coordinate system $O^l X^l Y^l Z^l$ to right camera coordinate system $O^r X^r Y^r Z^r$ (refer to Figure 2.3). Then the coordinates of point P in these two systems, $P^l = (X_P^l, Y_P^l, Z_P^l)$ and $P^r = (X_P^r, Y_P^r, Z_P^r)$, are related by the following formula:

$$P^r = [R](P^l - [t]) \qquad (2.16)$$

Matrix $[R]$ and column vector $[t]$ characterize the relation between the left and right coordinate systems, which is independent of the individual camera projection model. Thus, they are normally called extrinsic parameters. The intrinsic parameters $f^l, x_c^l, y_c^l, h_x^l, h_y^l$ and $f^r, x_c^r, y_c^r, h_x^r, h_y^r$, as well as the extrinsic parameters $[R]$ and $[t]$, fully characterize the stereo pinhole system.

2.3.2 System Calibration

The calibration process intends to determine the intrinsic camera parameters and the extrinsic parameters of a stereo system. These parameters are a prerequisite for full 3D reconstruction based on the disparity data extracted from the stereo image pairs. The accuracy of the calibration parameters has been found to place an essential and nonlinear effect on the reconstruction accuracy [20].

There are generally two categories of camera calibration techniques: One is based on a known reference object and the other is self-calibration. For the reference-object-based calibration, normally a 3D object with known geometry or a 2D object undergoing known translations is used to establish a series of points with precisely known coordinates in a world coordinate system [21,22]. A series of linear equations are then constructed to determine the intrinsic and extrinsic parameters. The self-calibration technique [23,24], on the other hand, does not require any known calibration object, but rather moves the camera on a static scene and captures images. The rigidity of the scene poses some constraints on the camera's intrinsic parameters, and correspondence information between three or more images is sufficient to determine the calibration parameters up to a scaling factor. Other techniques are also available using two- or one-dimensional known objects [25,26] for flexible calibration. Here we introduce the standard calibration method based on 3D objects with known geometry. Readers can refer to Gruen and Huang [27] for a more complete study in the calibration methods and Sun and Cooperstock [28] for an empirical comparison of three widely used calibration techniques.

For calibrating the stereo system shown in Figure 2.3 using a 3D known object, an auxiliary world coordinate system is introduced and the coordinates of N known 3D points are defined based on the world coordinate system as $P_i^w = (X_{pi}^w, Y_{pi}^w, Z_{pi}^w)$, $i = 1 \cdots N$. The rotation matrixes and translation column vectors from the world coordinate system to the left and right camera coordinate systems are defined as $[R^l], [t^l]$ and $[R^r], [t^r]$, respectively, which help to transform point P into the left and right camera coordinates as

$$P^l = [R^l](P^w - [t^l]) \qquad (2.17)$$

$$P^r = [R^r](P^w - [t^r]) \qquad (2.18)$$

By projecting the N points from the left camera coordinate system onto the left image coordinate system according to Equations (2.12) and (2.13), we have $2N$ equations with 14 unknowns (five intrinsic parameters, six independent components in rotation matrix $[R^l]$, and three independent components in the translation vector $[t^l]$). Thus, if the reference object contains more than seven known points, the 14 calibration parameters $f^l, x_c^l, y_c^l, h_x^l, h_y^l$ and $[R^l], [t^l]$ for the left camera system can be determined from the overdetermined linear equation group by singular value decomposition [29]. Similarly, the 14 calibration parameters $f^r, x_c^r, y_c^r, h_x^r, h_y^r$ and $[R^r], [t^r]$ from the right camera system can also be determined from the same series of known points using Equations (2.18), (2.14), and (2.15). The rotation matrix $[R]$ and translation vector $[t]$ can be subsequently obtained from Equations (2.16)–(2.18) as

$$[R] = [R^r][R^l]^T \qquad (2.19)$$

$$[t] = [R^l]([t^r] - [t^l]) \qquad (2.20)$$

So far the stereo camera system is fully calibrated and ready for measuring a 3D scene from the stereo 2D projections.

2.3.3 Conventional 3D Shape Reconstruction

Three-dimensional reconstruction using the correspondence information of the left and right images and the calibration parameters of the stereo system is straightforward. Grouping Equations (2.12)–(2.15) and the vector in Equation (2.16), we have seven linear equations in total. Within all the parameters in these seven equations, since the correspondence positions $p^l = (x_p^l, y_p^l)$, $p^r = (x_p^r, y_p^r)$, the intrinsic parameters $f^l, x_c^l, y_c^l, h_x^l, h_y^l, f^r, x_c^r, y_c^r, h_x^r, h_y^r$, and the extrinsic parameters $[R], [t]$ are all known, we have only six unknowns: (X_P^l, Y_P^l, Z_P^l) and (X_P^r, Y_P^r, Z_P^r). Thus, the six unknowns can be determined from the overdetermined equation group by least-squares optimization.

A more intuitive geometric solution is also given in Cyganek and Siebert [18] and Trucco and Verri [19]. Referring to Figure 2.3, based on the calibration parameters and the correspondence positions p^l and p^r, the equations of lines $O^l p^l$ and $O^r p^r$ can be written (in the left camera coordinate system, for example). These two lines may not intersect with each other due to various modeling and measurement errors associated with a practical system. Let the two reconstructed lines $O^l p^l$ and $O^r p^r$ be represented by the two dashed lines (as shown in Figure 2.3) adjacent to their perfect positions $O^l P$ and $O^r P$. It is intuitive and straightforward that there exists a unique line perpendicular to both dashed lines simultaneously and intersecting the two dashed lines at points P^l and P^r. The middle point of segment P^lP^r is then chosen as the optimal 3D estimation P_E, which forms minimal distances to both reconstructed dashed lines.

The coordinates of points P^l and P^r can be determined by the following equation:

$$k^l[O^lp^l]^T + k\vec{j} = [t] + k^r[R]^T[O^rp^r]^T \tag{2.21}$$

where

$[O^lp^l]^T$ is the column vector connecting O^l and p^l expressed in the left camera coordinate system

$[O^rp^r]^T$ is the column vector connecting O^r and p^r expressed in the right camera coordinate system

$[t] + k^r[R]^T[O^rp^r]^T$ is the column vector connecting O^r and P^r expressed in the left camera coordinate

$\vec{j}$ is a column vector perpendicular to both O^lP^l and O^rP^r, as shown in Figure 2.3, and can be expressed in the left camera coordinate system as

$$\vec{j} = [O^lp^l]^T \times [R]^T[O^rp^r]^T \tag{2.22}$$

and the scaling factors k^l, k^r, k can be determined by solving vector Equation (2.21).

Finally, the coordinate of P^l expressed in the left camera coordinate system is $k^l[O^lp^l]^T$, the coordinate of P^r expressed in the left camera coordinate system is $[t] + k^r[R]^T[O^rp^r]^T$, and the reconstructed 3D point P_E is

$$P_E = (k^l[O^lp^l]^T + [t] + k^r[R]^T[O^rp^r]^T)/2 \tag{2.23}$$

Once P_E is determined in the left camera coordinate system, it can be transformed to any other coordinate system by a proper rotation matrix and translation vector. An algorithm for this approach can be found in Ahuja [30].

2.3.4 Improved 3D Shape Reconstruction Using Back-Projection

The reconstruction methods introduced in Section 2.3.3 tend to obtain the correspondence information beforehand by the stereo matching method introduced in Section 2.2 and then conduct the 3D reconstruction accordingly. As the stereo images captured by the left and right cameras are related by the intrinsic and the extrinsic parameters of the stereo system, the incorporation of such information during the speckle matching process will help to improve the matching accuracy as well as reduce computation time.

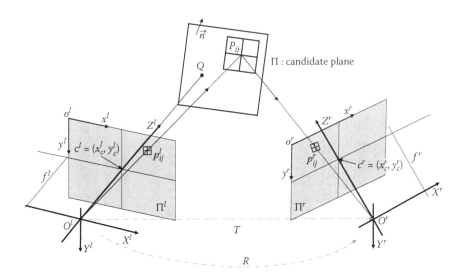

FIGURE 2.4
Process of back-projection of pixels within a speckle cell.

The incorporation of the calibration parameters will help to design a specific shape function from the constraint posed by the epipolar geometry and perspective transformation of the stereo system. This can be fulfilled by a back-propagation model [7,31].

As shown in Figure 2.4, after capturing the left and right speckle image, the DIC process is not directly applied to determine the disparities. On the contrary, a small speckle cell from the left speckle image is back-projected into the 3D scene to hit the object surface. As the cell has a very small area, the object surface at this area can be approximated by a plane Π. The intersection between the candidate plane and each ray emitted from the left speckle cell will then be determined and projected onto the right imaging screen to form a corresponding objective speckle cell. The correlation coefficient between the reference speckle cell in the left image and the back-projected objective speckle cell in the right image is then minimized by varying the parameters for the candidate plane Π.

The candidate plane Π can be defined in the left camera coordinate system using a unit vector $\vec{n} = (n_1, n_2, n_3)$, denoting its surface normal, and a point $Q = (0, 0, Z_Q)$, denoting the intersection position of the left optical axis with the candidate plane Π. For each point P^l within the candidate plane Π, its coordinates (X_P^l, Y_P^l, Z_P^l) should satisfy the following equation:

$$[P^l Q^l] \cdot \vec{n} = 0 \tag{2.24}$$

where $[P^l Q^l]$ is the vector connecting P^l and Q^l.

Expanding Equation (2.24) explicitly yields

$$n_1 X_P^l + n_2 Y_P^l + n_3(Z_P^l - Z_Q^l) = 0 \qquad (2.25)$$

By combining Equations (2.12), (2.13), and (2.25), the coordinates of the back-projected point $P^l = (X_P^l, Y_P^l, Z_P^l)$ can be expressed explicitly in the left camera system as

$$X_P^l = \frac{n_3 Z_Q^l (x_p^l - x_c^l) h_x^l}{n_1(x_p^l - x_c^l)h_x^l + n_2(y_p^l - y_c^l)h_y^l + n_3 f^l} \qquad (2.26)$$

$$Y_P^l = \frac{n_3 Z_Q^l (y_p^l - y_c^l) h_y^l}{n_1(x_p^l - x_c^l)h_x^l + n_2(y_p^l - y_c^l)h_y^l + n_3 f^l} \qquad (2.27)$$

$$Z_P^l = \frac{n_3 Z_Q^l f^l}{n_1(x_p^l - x_c^l)h_x^l + n_2(y_p^l - y_c^l)h_y^l + n_3 f^l} \qquad (2.28)$$

These coordinates are then transformed into the right camera coordinate system using Equation (2.16) to obtain $P^r = (X_P^r, Y_P^r, Z_P^r)$; the coordinates of the back-projected point $p^r = (x_p^r, y_p^r)$ on the right imaging screen are subsequently obtained using Equations (2.14) and (2.15).

After all pixels p_{ij}^l within the left speckle cell are back-projected onto the right imaging screen to obtain the corresponding position p_{ij}^r, a sum of the square difference correlation coefficient $\bar{C}(\vec{P})$ can then be established using Equation (2.3) and minimized using the N–R iteration method discussed in Section 2.2.5. The controlling parameters $\vec{P}$ now contain only three independent parameters, n_1, n_2, and Z_Q^l (n_3 can be determined from n_1, n_2); thus, less computation is required by the nonlinear optimization process. In addition, the back-projection model has incorporated the epipolar constraint and an improved shape function. This approach can potentially deliver 3D reconstruction results with higher accuracy.

It should be noted that the procedure of back-projection is unique to the area-based matching process. Since the feature points are sparse, this approach cannot be implemented for feature-based stereo matching.

2.3.5 A Simplified Case: Canonical Stereoscopic System

When the two cameras in the stereo setup have only a relative translation t_x in X direction without any rotation [32], or a single camera is given a pure translation t_x in X direction [33] to capture two different images, a simplified system called canonical setup results. In this simplified case, if identical cameras are used, we have $x_c^l = x_c^r = x_c$ (same principal point position), $h_x^l = h_x^r = h_x$ (same pixel dimension), $f^l = f^r = f$ (same focal length), $Z_P^l = Z_P^r = Z_P$ (same

Z coordinate), and $X_P^l - X_P^r = t_x$ (X coordinate difference is equal to baseline length t_x). Subtracting Equation (2.12) from Equation (2.14) and taking into account the previously mentioned identity, we have

$$Z_P = \frac{t_x f}{(x_p^l - x_p^r)h_x} = \frac{\text{Constant}}{x_p^l - x_p^r} \tag{2.29}$$

This means that the Z coordinate (which is the shape) of a point P is in inverse proportion to the X disparity of the image points, implying a much simpler calibration and measurement process. This simple relationship can also be deduced from a geometric point of view [18].

2.4 Application Examples

Thanks to the high-contrast speckle pattern and accurate speckle matching algorithm, 3D DIC has enabled stereo vision systems for reconstruction of 3D shapes with high accuracy. During the last two decades, 3D DIC has found numerous applications in various fields.

Pan and coauthors [34] used 3D DIC for measuring the surface profile of a carbon fiber composite satellite antenna with a diameter of 730 mm. The reconstructed profile in Figure 2.5(a) shows good agreement with measurements taken from a commercial 3D coordinate measuring machine (CMM) and the maximum discrepancy is less than 2% of the maximum height. Orteu et al. [35] developed a four-camera system with the DIC algorithm and applied the system for measurement of a 3D profile (refer to Figure 2.5b) and deformation of sheet metal during the process of single point incremental forming. In comparison with the commercial HandyScan laser scanning system, accuracy of better than 0.05 mm has been reported.

A very interesting application of 3D DIC had also been reported by Morgan, Liu, and Yan [36], where a canonical setup with a narrow baseline was employed. A narrow baseline system is compact and suitable for measuring large-scale objects; it also helps to avoid occlusion in a steep region. However, measurement sensitivity has been inevitably reduced by the employment of a narrow baseline. Thus, high-accuracy subpixel methods should be enabled for disparity computation. In their experiment measuring the surface profile of a model landscape (as shown in Figure 2.6), accuracy as high as 0.015 pixel was obtained and the root mean square error of the reconstructed 3D shape was less than 1% of the maximum height. Real 3D terrain had also been obtained by the authors using satellite stereo images;

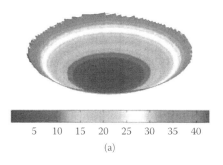

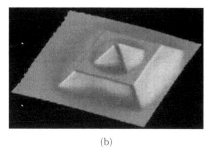

5 10 15 20 25 30 35 40

(a) (b)

FIGURE 2.5
Three-dimensional profile measurement of (a) a satellite antenna (reproduced from Pan, B. et al. *Strain* 45:194–200, 2009; with permission); (b) a sheet metal part produced by single point incremental forming (reproduced from Orteu, J. J. et al. *Experimental Mechanics* 51:625–639, 2011; with permission).

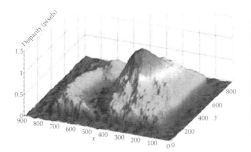

FIGURE 2.6
Surface profile measurement of (a) a model landscaped; (b) its photography for comparison. (Reproduced from Morgan, G. L. K. et al. *IEEE Transactions on Geoscience and Remote Sensing* 48 (9): 3424–3433, 2010. With permission.)

the results agreed well with publically available measurement results and showed better spatial resolution.

Due to its inherent nature of high accuracy, the 3D DIC method has been extensively used in the fields of experimental mechanics for 3D profile, 3D deformation measurement, and material characterization [37–39]. It has also been extended for microscale measurement using stereo images for light microscopes [40] or scanning electron microscopes [41].

2.5 Summary

The techniques for reconstructing an accurate 3D profile from stereo speckle image pairs have been introduced and the algorithms described in fine detail to facilitate the work of researchers interested in applying 3D DIC for measurement. Due to length limits, we have focused on the most essential part of this topic while ignoring some other contents. Readers can refer to other literature for error analysis and elimination [42] and 3D shape measurement from speckle projection [43]. A more complete description of 3D DIC can also be found in Sutton, Orteu, and Schreier [44].

References

1. M. A. Sutton, W. J. Wolters, W. H. Peters, W. F. Ransons, and S. R. McNeill. Determination of displacements using an improved digital correlation method. *Image Vision Computing* 1:133, 1983.
2. M. A. Sutton, H. A. Bruck, and S. R. McNeill, Determination of deformations using digital correlation with the Newton-Raphson method for partial differential corrections. *Experimental Mechanics* 29:261, 1989.
3. M. Sjodahl and L. R. Benchert. Electronic speckle photography: Analysis of an algorithm giving the displacement with subpixel accuracy. *Applied Optics* 32:2278–2284, 1993.
4. H. Lu and P. D. Cary. Deformation measurements by digital image correlation: Implementation of a second-order displacement gradient. *Experimental Mechanics* 40:393–400, 2000.
5. D. J. Chen, F. P. Chiang, Y. S. Tan, and H. S. Don. Digital speckle-displacement measurement using a complex spectrum method. *Applied Optics* 32:1839–1849, 1993.
6. M. Sjodahl. Electronic speckle photography—Increased accuracy by nonintegral pixel shifting. *Applied Optics* 33:6667–6673, 1994.
7. M. A. Sutton, S. R. McNeill, J. D. Helm, and Y. J. Chao. 2000, Advances in two-dimensional and three-dimensional computer vision. In *Photomechanics,* ed. P K Rastogi, 323–372. Berlin: Springer, 2000.
8. D. Garcia, J. J. Orteu, and L. Penazzi. A combined temporal tracking and stereo-correlation technique for accurate measurement of 3D displacements: Application to sheet metal forming. *Journal of Materials Processing Technology* 125–126:736–742, 2002.
9. T. A. Berfield, J. K. Patel., and R. G. Shimmin. Micro- and nanoscale deformation measurement of surface and internal planes via digital image correlation. *Experimental Mechanics* 47 (1):51–62, 2007.
10. M. Dekiff, P. Berssenbrügge, B. Kemper, C. Denz, and D. Dirksen. Three-dimensional data acquisition by digital correlation of projected speckle patterns. *Applied Physics* B 99:449–456, 2010.
11. Y. H. Huang, L. Liu, T. W. Yeung, and Y. Y. Hung. Real time monitoring of clamping force of a bolted joint by use of automatic digital image correlation. *Optics and Laser Technology* 41 (4):408–414, 2009.
12. B. Pan, K. Qian, H. Xie, and A. Asundi. Two-dimensional digital image correlation for in-plane displacement and strain measurement: A review. *Measurement Science Technology* 20:062001, 2009.

13. B. Pan, H. M. Xie, Z. Q. Guo, and T. Hua. Full-field strain measurement using a two-dimensional Savitzky–Golay digital differentiator in digital image correlation. *Optical Engineering* 46:033601, 2007.

14. G. Vendroux and W. G. Knauss, Submicron deformation field measurements: Part 2. Improved digital image correlation. *Experimental Mechanics* 38 (2):86–92, 1998.

15. H. Spath. *Two-dimensional spline interpolation algorithms.* Wellesley, MA: A. K. Peters, pp. 49–67, 1995.

16. W. H. Peters and W. F. Ranson. Digital imaging techniques in experimental stress analysis. *Optical Engineering* 21:427–431, 1981.

17. B. C. Wattrisse, A. Muracciole, and J. M. Nemoz-Gaillard. Analysis of strain localization during tensile tests by digital image correlation. *Experimental Mechanics* 41:29–39, 2001.

18. B. Cyganek and J. P. Siebert. *An introduction to 3D computer vision techniques and algorithms.* New York: Wiley, 2009.

19. E. Trucco and A. Verri. *Introductory techniques for 3-D computer vision.* Englewood Cliffs, NJ: Prentice Hall, 1998.

20. W. E. L. Grimson. Why stereo vision is not always about 3D reconstruction. Memo 1435, MIT Artificial Intelligence Laboratory, 1993.

21. O. Faugeras. *Three-dimensional computer vision: A geometric viewpoint.* Cambridge, MA: MIT Press, 1993.

22. R. Y. Tsai. A versatile camera calibration technique for high-accuracy 3D machine vision metrology using off-the-shelf TV cameras and lenses. *IEEE Journal Robotics and Automation* 3 (4):323–344, 1987.

23. Q. T. Luong and O. D. Faugeras, Self-calibration of a stereo rig from unknown camera motions and point correspondences. INRIA Technical Report 2014, 1993.

24. M. I. A. Lourakis and R. Deriche, Camera self-calibration using the Kruppa equations and the SVD of the fundamental matrix: The case of varying intrinsic parameters. INRIA Technical Report 2121, 2000.

25. Z. Y. Zhang. A flexible new technique for camera calibration. *IEEE Transactions on Pattern Analysis Machine Intelligence* 22:1330–1334, 2000.

26. Z. Y. Zhang. Camera calibration with one-dimensional objects. *IEEE Transactions on Pattern Analysis and Machine Intelligence* 26 (7):892–899, 2004.

27. A. Gruen and T. S. Huang, eds. *Calibration and orientation of cameras in computer vision,* Springer Series in Information Sciences. New York: Springer, 2001.

28. W. Sun and J. R. Cooperstock. An empirical evaluation of factors influencing camera calibration accuracy using three publicly available techniques. *Machine Vision and Applications* 17 (1):51–67, 2006.

29. W. H. Press, S. A. Teukolsky, W. T. Vetterling, and B. P. Flannery. *Numerical recipes in C: The art of scientific computing,* 3rd ed. Cambridge, England: Cambridge University Press, 2007.

30. N. Ahuja. *Motion and structure from image sequence.* New York: Springer–Verlag, 1993.

31. J. D. Helm, S. R. McNeil, and M. A. Sutton. Improved three-dimensional image correlation for surface displacement measurement. *Optical Engineering* 35:1911–1920, 1996.

32. P. Synnergren. Measurement of three-dimensional displacement fields and shape using electronic speckle photography. *Optical Engineering* 36 (8):2302–2310, 1997.

33. Y. H. Huang, C. Quan, C. J. Tay, and L. J. Chen. Shape measurement by the use of digital image correlation. *Optical Engineering* 44 (8):087011, 2005.

34. B. Pan, H. M. Xie, L. H. Yang, and Z. Y. Wang. Accurate measurement of satellite antenna surface using three-dimensional digital image correlation technique. *Strain* 45:194–200, 2009.

35. J. J. Orteu, F. Bugarin, J. Harvent, L. Robert, and V. Velay. Multiple-camera instrumentation of a single point incremental forming process pilot for shape and 3D displacement measurements: Methodology and results. *Experimental Mechanics* 51:625–639, 2011.

36. G. L. K. Morgan, J. G. Liu, and H. S. Yan. Precise subpixel disparity measurement from very narrow baseline stereo. *IEEE Transactions on Geoscience and Remote Sensing* 48 (9):3424–3433, 2010.

37. J. D. Helm, M. A. Sutton, and S. R. McNeill. Deformations in wide, center-notched, thin panels, part I: Three-dimensional shape and deformation measurements by computer vision. *Optical Engineering* 42 (5):1293–1305, 2003.

38. J. J. Orteu. 3-D computer vision in experimental mechanics. *Optics and Lasers in Engineering* 47:282–291, 2009.

39. S. B. Park, C. Shah, J. B. Kwak, C. Jang, S. Chung, and J. M. Pitarresi. Measurement of transient dynamic response of circuit boards of a handheld device during drop using 3D digital image correlation. *Journal of Electronic Packaging—Transactions of the ASME* 130–044502-1-3, 2008.

40. H. W. Schreier, D. Garcia, and M. A. Sutton. Advances in light microscope stereo vision. *Experimental Mechanics* 44 (3):278–288, 2004.

41. N. Cornille. Accurate 3D shape and displacement measurement using a scanning electron microscope. PhD thesis. INSA, France, and University of South Carolina, Columbia, June 2005.

42. M. Bornert, F. Brémand, P. Doumalin, J. C. Dupré, M. Fazzini, M. Grédiac, F. Hild, et al., Assessment of digital image correlation measurement errors: Methodology and results. *Experimental Mechanics* 49:353–370, 2009.

43. H. J. Dai and X. Y. Su. Shape measurement by digital speckle temporal sequence correlation with digital light projector. *Optical Engineering* 40 (5):793–800, 2001.

44. M. A. Sutton, J. J. Orteu, and H. W. Schreier. *Image correlation for shape, motion and deformation measurements: Basic concepts, theory and applications.* New York: Springer.

3

Spacetime Stereo

Li Zhang, Noah Snavely, Brian Curless, and Steven M. Seitz

CONTENTS

3.1 Introduction

Very few shape-capture techniques work effectively for rapidly moving scenes. Among the few exceptions are depth from defocus [9] and stereo [5]. Structured-light stereo methods have shown particularly promising results for capturing depth maps of moving faces [6,11]. Using projected light patterns to provide dense surface texture, these techniques compute pixel correspondences and then derive depth maps by triangulation. Products based on these triangulation techniques are commercially available.*

Traditional one-shot triangulation methods [3,12] treat each time instant in isolation and compute spatial correspondences between pixels in a single pair of images for a static moment in time. While they enable reconstructing moving scenes, they typically provide limited shape detail and resolution. Better results may be obtained by considering how each pixel varies over time and using this variation as a cue for correspondence, an approach we call *spacetime stereo.*

---

* For example, see www.3q.com, www.eyetronics.com, and www.xbox.com/en-US/kinect.

3.2 Spacetime Stereo Matching Metrics

In this section, we formulate the spacetime stereo problem and define the metrics that are used to compute correspondences. Consider a Lambertian scene observed by two synchronized and precalibrated video cameras.* Spacetime stereo takes as input the two rectified image streams $I_l(x,y,t)$ and $I_r(x,y,t)$ from these cameras. To recover the time-varying three-dimensional (3D) structure of the scene, we wish to estimate the disparity function $d(x,y,t)$ for each pixel (x,y) in the left image at each time t. Many existing stereo algorithms solve for $d(x,y,t)$ at some position and moment (x_0,y_0,t_0) by minimizing the following error function:

$$E\big(d_0\big)= \sum_{(x,y)\in W_0} e\big(I_l\big(x,y,t_0\big),I_r\big(x-d_0,y,t_0\big)\big) \qquad (3.1)$$

where d_0 is a shorthand notation for $d(x_0,y_0,t_0)$, W_0 is a spatial neighborhood window around (x_0,y_0), and $e(p,q)$ is a similarity measure between pixels from two cameras. Depending on the specific algorithm, the size of W_0 can vary from being a single pixel to, say, a 10×10 neighborhood, or it can be adaptively estimated for each pixel [8]. A common choice for $e(p,q)$ is simply

$$e\big(p,q\big)=\big(p-q\big)^2 \qquad (3.2)$$

In this case, Equation (3.1) becomes the standard sum of squared difference (SSD). Better results can be obtained in practice by defining $e(p,q)$ to compensate for radiometric differences between the cameras:

$$e\big(p,q\big)=\big(s{\cdot}p+o-q\big)^2 \qquad (3.3)$$

where s and o are window-dependent scale and offset constants to be estimated. Other forms of $e(p,q)$ are summarized in Baker and Matthews [1].

Spacetime stereo seeks to incorporate *temporal appearance variation* to improve stereo matching and generate more accurate depth maps. In the next two subsections, we will consider how multiple frames can help to recover static and nearly static shapes and then extend the idea for moving scenes.

---

* Here we assume the two cameras are offset horizontally. However, our formulation can be used for any stereo pair orientation.

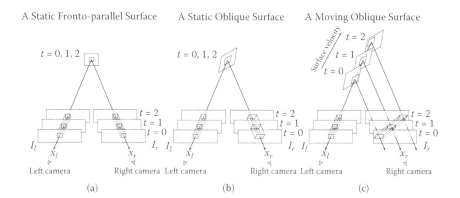

FIGURE 3.1

Illustration of spacetime stereo. Two stereo image streams are captured from stationary cameras. The images are shown spatially offset at three different times, for illustration purposes. For a static surface (a, b), the spacetime windows are "straight," aligned along the line of sight. For an oblique surface (b), the spacetime window is horizontally stretched and vertically sheared. For a moving surface (c), the spacetime window is also temporally sheared (i.e., "slanted"). The best affine warp of each spacetime window along epipolar lines is computed for stereo correspondence.

3.2.1 Static Scenes

Scenes that are geometrically static may still give rise to images that change over time. For example, the motion of the sun causes shading variations over the course of a day. In a laboratory setting, projected light patterns can create similar but more controlled changes in appearance.

Suppose that the geometry of the scene is static for a period of time $T_0 = [t_0 - \Delta t, t_0 + \Delta t]$. As illustrated in Figure 3.1(a), we can extend the spatial window to a spatiotemporal window and solve for d_0 by minimizing the following sum of SSD (SSSD) cost function:

$$E(d_0) = \sum_{t \in T_0} \sum_{(x,y) \in W_0} e\left(I_l(x,y,t), I_r(x - d_0, y, t)\right) \tag{3.4}$$

This error function reduces matching ambiguity in any single frame by simultaneously matching intensities in multiple frames. Another advantage of the spacetime window is that the spatial window can be shrunk and the temporal window can be enlarged to increase matching accuracy. This principle was originally formulated as spacetime analysis in Curless and Levoy [4] and Kanade, Gruss, and Carley [7] for laser scanning and was applied by several researchers [2,13] for structured-light scanning. However, they only consider either a single-frame spatial window or a single-pixel temporal window and their specialized formulation is only effective for single stripe illumination. Here we are casting this principle in a general spacetime stereo framework that is valid for any illumination variation.

We should point out that Equations (3.1) and (3.4) treat disparity as being constant within the window W_0, which assumes the corresponding surface is frontoparallel. For a static but oblique surface, as shown in Figure 3.1(b), a more accurate (first order) local approximation of the disparity function is

$$d(x,y,t) \approx \hat{d}_0(x,y,t) \overset{\text{def}}{=} d_0 + d_{x_0} \cdot (x - x_0) + d_{y_0} \cdot (y - y_0) \tag{3.5}$$

where d_{x_0} and d_{y_0} are the partial derivatives of the disparity function with respect to spatial coordinates x and y at (x_0, y_0, t_0). This local spatial linearization results in the following SSSD cost function being minimized:

$$E(d_0, d_{x_0}, d_{y_0}) = \sum_{t \in T_0} \sum_{(x,y) \in W_0} e(I_l(x,y,t), I_r(x - a_0, y, t)) \tag{3.6}$$

where $\hat{d}_0$ is a shorthand notation for $\hat{d}_0(x,y,t)$, which is defined in Equation (3.5) in terms of (d_0, d_{x_0}, d_{y_0}) and is estimated for each pixel. Nonzero d_{x_0} and d_{y_0} will cause a horizontal stretch or shrinkage and vertical shear of the spacetime window, respectively, as illustrated in Figure 3.1(b).

Figure 3.2 shows the experimental results obtained by imaging a small sculpture (a plaster bust of Albert Einstein) using structured light. Specifically, stripe patterns based on a modified Gray code [14] are projected onto the bust using a digital projector and 10 stereo image pairs are captured. The 10 image pairs are matched with a spacetime window of $5 \times 5 \times 10$ (5×5 pixels per frame by 10 frames). The shaded rendering reveals details visually comparable to those obtained with a laser range scanner.

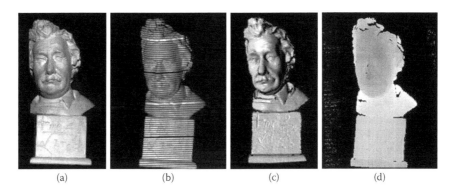

| (a) | (b) | (c) | (d) |

FIGURE 3.2
Spacetime stereo reconstruction with structured light. (a) Einstein bust under natural lighting. (b) One image taken from the set of 10 stereo image pairs captured when the bust is illuminated with modified Gray code structured-light patterns [14]. (c) Shaded rendering of geometric reconstruction. (d) Reconstructed disparity map where pixel intensities encode surface depth.

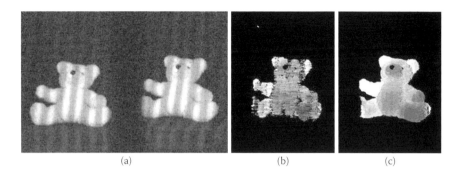

(a)   (b)   (c)

FIGURE 3.3

Spacetime stereo reconstruction with loosely structured light using transparency and desk lamp. (a) One out of the 125 stereo pair images. (b) Disparity map for a traditional stereo reconstruction using a single stereo pair. (c) Disparity map for spacetime stereo using all the 125 stereo pairs.

Figure 3.3 shows the experimental results obtained by a simpler imaging system with much looser structured light. Specifically, for illumination, an ordinary desk lamp is shined through a transparency printed with a black and white square wave pattern onto the subject (a teddy bear) and the pattern is moved by hand in a free-form fashion. During the process, 125 stereo pairs are captured. Both single-frame stereo for one of the stereo pairs using a 5 × 1 window and spacetime stereo over all frames using a 5 × 1 × 125 window are tried. Figure 3.3 shows marked improvement of spacetime stereo over regular single-frame stereo.

3.2.2 Quasi-Static Scenes

The simple SSSD method proposed in the previous section can also be applied to an interesting class of time-varying scenes. Although some natural scenes, like water flow in Figure 3.4, have spatially varying texture and motion, they have an overall shape that is roughly constant over time. Although these natural scenes move stochastically, people tend to fuse the image stream into an average shape over time. We refer to this class of natural scenes as *quasi-static*. By applying the SSSD method from the previous section, we can compute a temporally averaged disparity map that corresponds roughly to the "mean shape" of the scene. In graphics applications where a coarse geometry is sufficient, one could, for instance, use the mean shape as static geometry with time-varying color texture mapped over the surface.

Figure 3.4 shows experimental results of applying spacetime stereo to a quasi-static scene: a small but fast moving waterfall. Specifically, 45 stereo image pairs are captured and both traditional stereo for one of the image pairs and spacetime stereo for all 45 image pairs are tried. As Figure 3.4 shows, spacetime stereo produces much more consistent results than traditional stereo does.

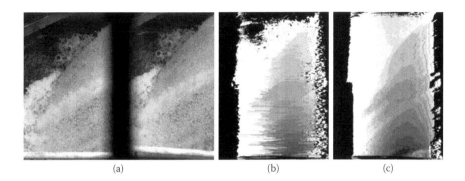

(a)   (b)   (c)

FIGURE 3.4
Spacetime stereo reconstruction of quasi-static rushing water. (a) One out of the 45 stereo pair images. (b) Disparity map for a traditional stereo reconstruction on one image pair. (c) Disparity map for spacetime stereo on all 45 stereo image pairs.

3.2.3 Moving Scenes

Now we consider the case where the object is moving in the time interval T_0 = $[t_0 - \Delta t, t_0 + \Delta t]$, as illustrated in Figure 3.1(c). Because of the object motion, the window in the left video is deformed in the right sequence. The temporal trajectory of window deformation in the right video is determined by the object motion and could be arbitrarily complex. However, if the camera has a high enough frame rate relative to the object motion and there are no changes in visibility, we can locally linearize the temporal disparity variation in much the same way we linearized spatial disparity in Equation (3.5). Specifically, we take a first-order approximation of the disparity variation with respect to both spatial coordinates x and y and temporal coordinate t as

$$d(x,y,t) \approx \tilde{d}_0(x,y,t) \stackrel{def}{=} d_0 + d_{x_0}\cdot(x-x_0) + d_{y_0}\cdot(y-y_0) + d_{t_0}\cdot(t-t_0) \quad (3.7)$$

where d_{t_0} is the partial derivative of the disparity function with respect to time at (x_0, y_0, t_0). This local spatial–temporal linearization results in the following SSSD cost function to be minimized:

$$E(d_0, d_{x_0}, d_{y_0}, d_{t_0}) = \sum_{t\in T_0}\sum_{(x,y)\in W_0} e(I_l(x,y,t), I_r(x-d'_0,y,t)) \quad (3.8)$$

where $\tilde{d}_0$ is a shorthand notation for $\tilde{d}_0(x,y,t)$, which is defined in Equation (3.7) in terms of $(d_0, d_{x_0}, d_{y_0}, d_{t_0})$ and is estimated for each pixel at each time. Note that Equation (3.7) assumes a linear model of disparity within the spacetime window (i.e., $(d_0, d_{x_0}, d_{y_0}, d_{t_0})$ is constant within $W_0 \times T_0$).

We use the term *straight window* to refer to a spacetime window whose position and shape are fixed over time, such as the windows shown in

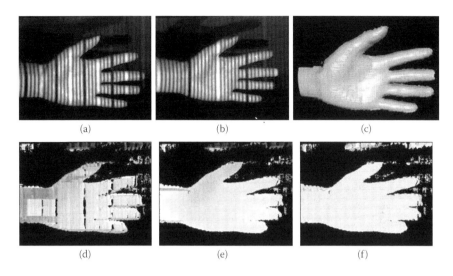

FIGURE 3.5

Spacetime stereo reconstruction of moving hand with structured light. (a, b) Two images taken from one of the cameras. The hand is moving away from the stereo rig, which is why it is getting smaller. (c) Shaded rendering of the reconstructed model using slanted window spacetime stereo. (d) Disparity map with straight spacetime windows. (e) Disparity map with slanted spacetime windows. (f) Temporal derivative of disparity. Since the hand is translating at roughly a constant speed, the disparity velocity is fairly constant over the hand.

Figure 3.1(a, b). If the position of the window varies over time, we say that the spacetime window is *slanted*, such as the one in the right camera in Figure 3.1(c).

Figure 3.5 and Figure 3.6 show two experimental results for moving scenes. In Figure 3.5, the modified Gray code patterns are projected onto a human hand that is moving fairly steadily away from the stereo rig. In this case, the disparity is changing over time, and the straight spacetime window approach fails to reconstruct a reasonable surface. By estimating the temporal derivative of the disparity using slanted windows, we obtain a much better reconstruction, as shown in Figure 3.5.

In Figure 3.6, spacetime stereo and one-shot stereo are compared for reconstructing moving scenes. Specifically, a short sequence of stripe patterns is generated randomly and projected repeatedly to a deforming human face. To demonstrate the effect of extruding the matching window over time, a $9 \times 5 \times 5$ spacetime window and a 15×15 spatial window, which have the same number of pixels, are chosen to compare spacetime stereo and frame-by-frame stereo on reconstructing facial expressions. Notice that the spacetime reconstruction generates significantly more accurate results, as shown in Figure 3.6. The video format of this comparison is available at http://grail.cs.washington.edu/projects/ststereo/, which also shows that spacetime stereo results in temporally much more stable reconstruction than frame-by-frame stereo.

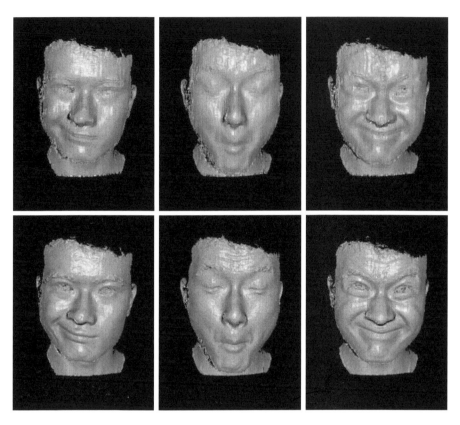

FIGURE 3.6
Comparison of spacetime and frame-by-frame stereo for a moving face reconstruction. Top row: three face expressions reconstructed using a 15×15 spatial window. Bottom row: the same face expressions reconstructed using a $9 \times 5 \times 5$ spacetime window. Notice that although both the spatial and spacetime windows have the same number of pixels, spacetime stereo results in a more detailed reconstruction.

3.3 Global Spacetime Stereo Matching

One major artifact of spacetime stereo matching is that it produces quite noticeable ridging artifacts, evident in Figure 3.8(e). It has been suggested [16] that these artifacts are due primarily to the fact that Equation (3.8) is minimized for each pixel independently, without taking into account constraints between neighboring pixels. Specifically, computing a disparity map with M pixels introduces $4M$ unknowns: M disparities and $3M$ disparity gradients. While this formulation results in a system that is convenient computationally, it is clearly overparameterized, since the $3M$ disparity gradients are a function of only M disparities. Indeed, the estimated disparity gradients may not agree with the estimated disparities.

For example, $d_x(x,y,t)$ may be quite different from its central difference approximation, $1/2\big(d(x+1,y,t)-d(x-1,y,t)\big)$, because $d_x(x,y,t)$, $d(x+1,y,t)$, and $d(x-1,y,t)$ are independently estimated for each pixel. This inconsistency between disparities and disparity gradients results in inaccurate depth maps, as shown in Figure 3.8(e, i).

In this section, spacetime stereo is reformulated as a global optimization problem to overcome this inconsistency deficiency. Specifically, the global spacetime stereo method computes the disparity function while taking into account gradient constraints between pixels that are adjacent in space and time. Given image sequences $I_l(x,y,t)$ and $I_r(x,y,t)$, the desired disparity function $d(x,y,t)$ minimizes

$$\Gamma\big(\{d(x,y,t)\}\big)\overset{\Delta}{=}\sum_{x,y,t}E\big(d,d_x,d_y,d_t\big) \tag{3.9}$$

This is subject to the following constraints[*]:

$$d_x(x,y,t)=\frac{1}{2}\big(d(x+1,y,t)-d(x-1,y,t)\big)$$

$$d_y(x,y,t)=\frac{1}{2}\big(d(x,y+1,t)-d(x,y-1,t)\big) \tag{3.10}$$

$$d_t(x,y,t)=\frac{1}{2}\big(d(x,y,t+1)-d(x,y,t-1)\big)$$

Equation (3.9) defines a nonlinear least squares problem with linear constraints. This problem can be solved using the Gauss–Newton method [10].

Figure 3.8 shows the improvement using global spacetime stereo by comparing it to the spacetime stereo matching method presented in the previous section, as well as standard frame-by-frame stereo. The experiment's data are captured by a camera rig of six synchronized video streams (four monochrome and two color) running at 60 Hz, shown in Figure 3.7. Three of the cameras capture the left side of the face, and the other three capture the right side. To facilitate depth computation, two video projectors are used that project grayscale random stripe patterns onto the face. The projectors send a solid black pattern every three frames, and surface color texture is captured at these frames. A video of a pair of depth map sequences reconstructed from both left and right sides of a moving face using global spacetime stereo is available at http://grail.cs.washington.edu/projects/stfaces/.

---

[*] At spacetime volume boundaries, we use forward or backward differences instead of central differences.

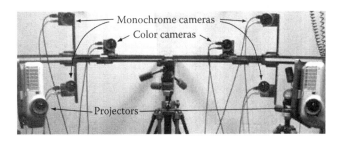

FIGURE 3.7
A camera rig consists of six video cameras and two data projectors. The two monochrome cameras on the left constitute one stereo pair, and the two on the right constitute a second stereo pair. The projectors provide stripe pattern textures for high-quality shape estimation. The color cameras record video streams used for optical flow and surface texture.

3.4 From Depth Map Videos to Dynamic Mesh Models

Using the camera rig in Figure 3.7, spacetime stereo methods capture both shape and texture for a dynamic surface. The captured shapes are represented as depth maps. These depth maps have missing data due to occlusions. Also, they lack correspondence information that specifies how a point on the 3D surface moves over time. For face modeling applications in graphics, these limitations make it difficult to re-pose or reanimate the captured faces. In Zhang et al. [16], one method is presented to compute a single time-varying mesh that closely approximates the depth map sequences while optimizing the vertex motion to be consistent with pixel motion (i.e., optical flow) computed between color frames.

In Figure 3.9, eight examples of mesh models for two subjects are shown. Each mesh has about 23,728 vertices. The sequence for the first subject has 384 mesh models and that for the second has 580 meshes. In Figure 3.10, eight examples of the mesh sequence for the third subject are shown. This sequence consists of 339 meshes and each mesh has 23,728 vertices. Notice that, in Figure 3.9(i, j) and Figure 3.10(i, j), close-up views of some of the face meshes are shown, which demonstrates the ability to capture fine features such as the wrinkles on a frowning forehead and near a squinting eye. These subtle shape details are extremely important for conveying realistic expressions because the human visual system is well tuned to recognize human faces. The uniqueness of the system is its capability to capture not only these shape details, but also how these shape details change over time. In the end, the system is an automatic, dense, and markerless facial motion capture system.

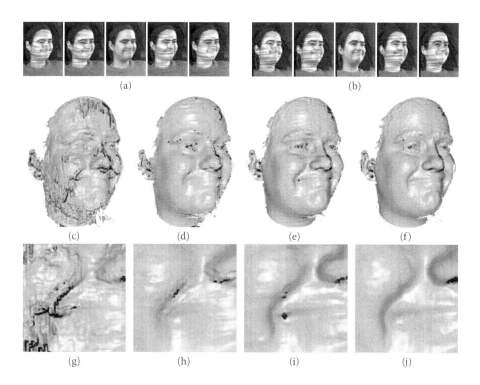

FIGURE 3.8

Comparison of four different stereo matching algorithms. (a, b) Five consecutive frames from a pair of stereo videos. The third frames are nonpattern frames. (c) Reconstructed face at the third frame using traditional stereo matching with a 15×15 window. The result is noisy due to the lack of color variation on the face. (d) Reconstructed face at the second frame using stereo matching with a 15×15 window. The result is much better because the projected stripes provide texture. However, certain face details are smoothed out due to the need for a large spatial window. (e) Reconstructed face at the third frame using local spacetime stereo matching with a $9 \times 5 \times 5$ window. Even though the third frame has little intensity variation, spacetime stereo recovers more detailed shapes by considering neighboring frames together. However, it also yields noticeable striping artifacts due to the parameterization of the depth map. (f) Reconstructed face at the third frame using our new global spacetime stereo matching with a $9 \times 5 \times 5$ window. The new method removes most of the striping artifacts while preserving the shape details. (g–j) Close-up comparison of the four algorithms around the nose and the corner of the mouth.

3.5 Discussion

In this chapter, spacetime stereo methods are presented to capture time-varying 3D surfaces. We discuss limitations of the methods and suggest future works. The spacetime stereo matching techniques are based on window warping using a locally linear disparity variation model, which fails near discontinuity boundaries. For example, rapid lip movements during speech result in temporal depth discontinuities in the scanned sequence. It

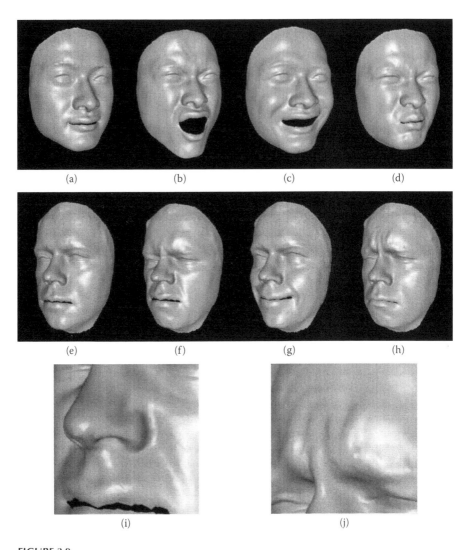

FIGURE 3.9
(a–h) Eight examples of the template tracking results for two subjects. (i) A close-up view of the skin deformation near the nose in the "disgusted" expression shown in (f). (j) A close-up view of the wrinkles on the "frowning" forehead of (h).

is desirable to improve spacetime stereo algorithms for better performance near spatial and temporal discontinuities. Specifically, the window should be adaptively selected based on local spacetime shape variation. In the extreme case of large shape variation over time due to fast motion, the algorithm should automatically switch to one-shot stereo. Kanade and Okutomi [8] proposed an adaptive window selection theory for one-shot stereo assuming a front-parallel disparity model; adaptive window selection for a locally linear disparity model in spacetime remains an important topic for future research.

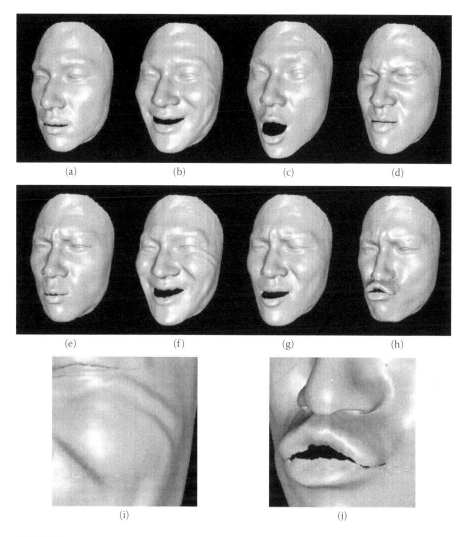

FIGURE 3.10
(a–h) Eight examples of the template tracking results for the third subject. (i) A close-up view of the wrinkles near the left eye in (f). (j) A close-up view of the pouting lips in (h).

Stereo matching algorithms involve various parameters, such as window sizes in spacetime stereo and regularization weight in Markov random field (MRF) stereo. In practice, different data sets require different parameters for optimal performance. Learning parameters automatically is therefore of great importance for these algorithms to be deployed in automated vision systems for real applications. The problem of learning optimal parameters for MRF stereo matching is studied in Zhang and Seitz [15]. How to apply this mechanism to spacetime stereo and other visual reconstruction algorithms is a very interesting problem for future research.

Although the accuracy of spacetime stereo is good enough for several applications (e.g., face modeling and animation), a current limitation is speed. It takes 2–3 minutes to compute a disparity map. Some applications, such as 3D shape recognition of faces, expressions, and poses for natural human computer interfaces, require 3D reconstruction techniques that operate in real time. An important future research avenue is to design new techniques and accelerate existing techniques to fulfill both the speed and accuracy requirements for real-time 3D reconstruction.

References

1. S. Baker and I. Matthews. Lucas–Kanade 20 years on: A unifying framework. *International Journal of Computer Vision* 56 (3): 221–255, March 2004.
2. J.-Y. Bouguet and P. Perona. 3D photography on your desk. *Proceedings International Conference on Computer Vision* 43–50, 1998.
3. K. L. Boyer and A. C. Kak. Color-encoded structured light for rapid active ranging. *IEEE Trans. on Pattern Analysis and Machine Intelligence* 9 (1): 14–28, 1987.
4. B. Curless and M. Levoy. Better optical triangulation through spacetime analysis. *Proceedings International Conference on Computer Vision* 987–994, June 1995.
5. O. Faugeras. *Three-dimensional computer vision.* Cambridge, MA: MIT Press, 1993.
6. P. S. Huang, C. P. Zhang, and F. P. Chiang. High speed 3-D shape measurement based on digital fringe projection. *Optical Engineering,* 42 (1): 163–168, 2003.
7. T. Kanade, A. Gruss, and L. Carley. A very fast VLSI range finder. *Proceedings International Conference on Robotics and Automation* 39: 1322–1329, 1991.
8. T. Kanade and M. Okutomi. A stereo matching algorithm with an adaptive window: Theory and experiment. *IEEE Transactions on Pattern Analysis and Machine Intelligence* 16 (9): 920–932, 1994.
9. S. K. Nayar, M. Watanabe, and M. Noguchi. Real-time focus range sensor. *IEEE Transactions on Pattern Analysis and Machine Intelligence,* 18 (12): 1186–1198, 1996.
10. J. Nocedal and S. J. Wright. *Numerical optimization.* New York: Springer, 1999.
11. M. Proesmans, L. Van Gool, and A. Oosterlinck. One-shot active 3D shape acquisition. *Proceedings International Conference on Pattern Recognition* 336–340, 1996.
12. M. Proesmans, L. Van Gool, and A. Oosterlinck. One-shot active 3d shape acquisition. *International Conference on Pattern Recognition* 336–340, 1996.
13. K. Pulli, H. Abi-Rached, T. Duchamp, L. Shapiro, and W. Stuetzle. Acquisition and visualization of colored 3D objects. *Proceedings International Conference on Pattern Recognition* 11–15, 1998.
14. L. Zhang, B. Curless, and S. M. Seitz. Spacetime stereo: Shape recovery for dynamic scenes. *Proceedings IEEE Conference on Computer Vision and Pattern Recognition* 367–374, 2003.
15. L. Zhang and S. M. Seitz. Parameter estimation for MRF stereo. In *IEEE Computer Society Conference on Computer Vision and Pattern Recognition,* 2005.
16. L. Zhang, N. Snavely, B. Curless, and S. M. Seitz. Spacetime faces: High-resolution capture for modeling and animation. *ACM Annual Conference on Computer Graphics* 548–558, August 2004.

4

Stereo Particle Imaging Velocimetry Techniques: Technical Basis, System Setup, and Application

Hui Hu

CONTENTS

4.1 Introduction

Particle image velocimetry (PIV) [1] is an imaging-based flow diagnostic technique that relies on seeding fluid flows with tiny tracer particles and observing the motions of the tracer particles to derive fluid velocities. For PIV measurements, a sheet of laser light is usually used to illuminate the region of interest. The tracer particles scatter the laser light as they move through it. Photographic film or digital cameras are used to record the positions of the tracer particles at two different times separated by a prescribed

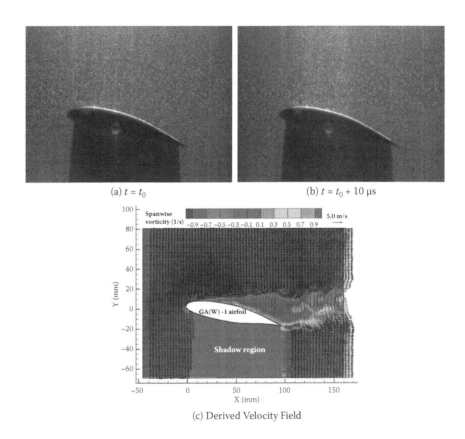

(a) $t = t_0$ (b) $t = t_0 + 10\ \mu s$

(c) Derived Velocity Field

FIGURE 4.1
(See color insert.) A pair of PIV images and the corresponding velocity distribution. (Hu, H. and Yang, Z. 2008. *ASME Journal of Fluid Engineering* 130 (5): 051101. With permission.)

time interval. The displacements of individual tracer particles—or, more often, groups of tracer particles—are determined by a well-developed computer-intensive PIV image processing procedure. The displacements over a known time interval provide the particle velocity vectors. The velocity of the working fluid is deduced based on the assumption that the tracer particles move with the same velocity as local working fluids. Figure 4.1 shows a typical PIV image pair and the corresponding flow velocity distribution derived from the images as the result of the PIV measurements.

A "classical" PIV technique, as shown in Figure 4.1, is a two-dimensional (2D) measuring technique. It is only capable of measuring two components of flow velocity vectors in the plane of the illuminating laser sheet. The out-of-plane component of velocity vectors is lost, while the in-plane components are affected by an unrecoverable error due to the perspective transformation [2]. Recent advances in the PIV technique have been directed toward obtaining all three components of fluid velocity vectors in a plane or in a volume simultaneously to allow wider applications of the PIV technique to study more complex flow phenomena. Several advanced PIV techniques have been developed successfully in recent years, including the holographic PIV (HPIV) technique [3,4], three-dimensional (3D) particle-tracking velocimetry (3D-PTV) [5], tomographic PIV [6], and the stereo PIV (SPIV) to be described in the present study.

Holographic PIV [3,4] utilizes holography techniques for image recording, which enables the determination of all three components of velocity vectors throughout a volume of fluid flow. Of the existing PIV techniques, HPIV is capable of the highest measurement precision and spatial resolution [7]. However, HPIV is also the most complex PIV technique and requires significant investment in equipment and optical alignments as well as the development of advanced data processing techniques. Continuous efforts are still required to make HPIV a practical PIV technique for various complex engineering applications [8–10].

Three-dimensional PTV [5] and tomographic PIV [6] techniques typically use three or more cameras to record the positions of the tracer particles in the measurement volume from different observation directions. Through 3D image reconstruction, the locations of the tracer particles in the measurement volume are determined. By using particle-tracking (for 3D-PTV) or 3D correction-based image processing algorithms, the 3D displacements of the tracer particles in the measurement volume are determined. It should be noted that the positions of almost all the tracer particles in the measurement volume are required to be recorded by each image recording camera for the 3D-PTV or tomographic PIV measurements. Thus, it becomes very difficult, if not impossible, to distinguish the positions of the tracer particles if the image density of the tracer particle in the measurement volume becomes too high. Therefore, the measurement results of 3D-PTV and tomographic PIV systems usually suffer from poor spatial resolution to elucidate the small-scale vortex and flow structures in the fluid flows.

The stereo PIV technique is the most straightforward and easily accomplished method to achieve simultaneous measurements of all three components of velocity vectors in the laser illuminating plane. It uses two cameras at different view axes or with an offset distance to do stereoscopic image recording. In the view reconstruction, the corresponding image segments in the image planes of the two cameras are matched to reconstruct all three components of the velocity vectors in the measurement plane. Stereo PIV measurements can have much higher in-plane spatial resolution compared to the 3D-PTV and tomographic PIV methods. It can provide thousands of flow velocity vectors in the measurement plane.

In the sections that follow, the technical basis of stereo PIV technique is introduced briefly at first. Three basic optical arrangements commonly used for this type of image recording are compared and the advantages and disadvantages of each optical arrangement are briefly described. A general in situ calibration procedure is described to determine the mapping functions between the 3D physical space in the objective fluid flow and the image planes of the cameras used for stereoscopic image recording. The flow chart to reconstruct the three components of the velocity vectors in the measurement plane of physical space from the 2D displacement vectors detected by the two cameras is also given. Finally, the feasibility and implementation of the stereo PIV technique are demonstrated by performing simultaneous measurements of all three components of flow velocity vectors in an airflow exhausted from a lobed nozzle/mixer to reveal the unique 3D flow features in the lobed jet mixing flow.

4.2 Technical Basis of the Stereo PIV Technique

The technical basis of stereo PIV measurements is how to reconstruct all three components of displacement vectors in the measurement plane of physical space from the two projected planar displacement vectors detected by the two cameras. Figure 4.2 shows the schematic on how and why the three components of displacement vectors in the measurement plane of the physical space can be reconstructed from the two projected planar vectors in the image planes detected by the two cameras. The origin, O, is a known point within the measurement plane (i.e., laser illuminating plane), which is visible by both of the cameras, with the physical coordinate of (x_0, y_0, z_0). Assuming an orthogonal, global coordinate system, the X- and Y-axes are aligned with the laser sheet, while the Z-axis is normal to the laser sheet plane.

The two cameras view the area of interest within the light sheet plane from the points $L_1 = (x_1, y_1, z_1)$ and $L_2 = (x_2, y_2, z_2)$. Based on the pinhole lens assumption, the measured displacements of three-dimensional displacement (dx, dy, dz) in the physical space are (dx_1, dy_1) and (dx_2, dy_2) in the image planes of the two cameras. Given the ensemble averaging nature of the PIV measurements and the fact that the illuminating laser sheet thickness is several orders smaller than the observation distance, the displacement vectors can be assumed to be within a zero thickness plane in the physical space. The angles enclosed by the viewing ray and the light sheet normal direction (parallel to the Z-axis direction) are α_1 and α_2 for the respective viewing directions projected on the X–Z plane. Correspondingly, β_1 and β_2 define the angles within the Y–Z plane. Because the viewing distance typically is much greater than the displacement vector, the angle differences along the displacement vector, $\delta\alpha$ and $\delta\beta$, are ignored. Following the work of Brucker [11], the three components of the displacement vector can be reconstructed using the following equations:

$$dx = \frac{dx_2 \tan\alpha_1 - dx_1 \tan\alpha_2}{\tan\alpha_1 - \tan\alpha_2} \qquad (4.1)$$

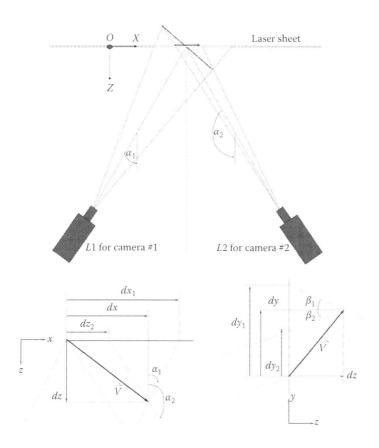

FIGURE 4.2
The schematic for the reconstruction of three components of the displacement vector for stereo PIV measurements.

$$dy = \frac{dy_2 \tan\beta_1 - dy_1 \tan\beta_2}{\tan\beta_1 - \tan\beta_2} \tag{4.2}$$

$$dz = \frac{dx_2 - dx_1}{\tan\alpha_1 - \tan\alpha_2} \tag{4.3}$$

or

$$dz = \frac{dy_2 - dy_1}{\tan\beta_1 - \tan\beta_2} \tag{4.4}$$

These equations can be applied to any stereo imaging geometry. However, the numerators may approach zero as the viewing axes become collinear in either of their two-dimensional projections. For example, the two cameras arranged in the same vertical position as the field of view make the angles β_1, β_2 and their tangents (i.e., $\tan\beta_1$ and $\tan\beta_2$) very small. Clearly, the dz can only be estimated with higher accuracy by using Equation (4.4), while dy has to be rewritten using Equation (4.3), which does not include $\tan\beta_1$ and $\tan\beta_2$ in the nominator [7]:

$$dy = \frac{dy_1 + dy_2}{2} + \frac{dz}{2}(\tan\beta_2 - \tan\beta_1)$$

$$= \frac{dy_1 + dy_2}{2} + \frac{dx_2 - dx_1}{2}\left(\frac{\tan\beta_2 - \tan\beta_1}{\tan\alpha_1 - \tan\alpha_2}\right) \quad (4.5)$$

4.2.1 Stereoscopic Image Recording

As in conventional 2D PIV measurements, a laser sheet is usually used to illuminate the flow field in the region of interest for stereo PIV measurements. The tracer particles seeded in the objective fluid flow will scatter the laser light when they pass through the illuminated plane. For stereo PIV measurements, the images of the tracer particles are recorded stereoscopically by using two image-recording cameras. As shown in Figure 4.3, three basic approaches are usually used for the stereo image recording in stereo PIV measurements: the lens translation method, general angle displacement method, and angle displacement arrangement with Scheimpflug condition.

4.2.1.1 Lens Translation Method

In the lens translation method, the two cameras used for stereoscopic image recording are placed side by side with the image planes and camera lens principal plane parallel to the measurement plane (laser sheet), as shown schematically in Figure 4.3(a). Such implementation is the most straightforward approach used for stereoscopic image recording. Because of the parallel geometry, the ratio of the image distance to object distance (i.e., the magnification factor) is constant across the entire acquired PIV images. Therefore, the 2D displacement vectors in the image planes of the two cameras are readily combined to reconstruct the three components of displacement vectors in the measurement plane without the additional manipulations necessary in a variable magnification.

However, it should be noted that when the lens translation method is applied to a liquid flow, the change of the refractive index at the liquid–air interface will cause a variable magnification over the image field [2]. For such cases, the merit of the paralleling arrangement described before will not be valid anymore. Furthermore, the lens translation method has the drawback of the

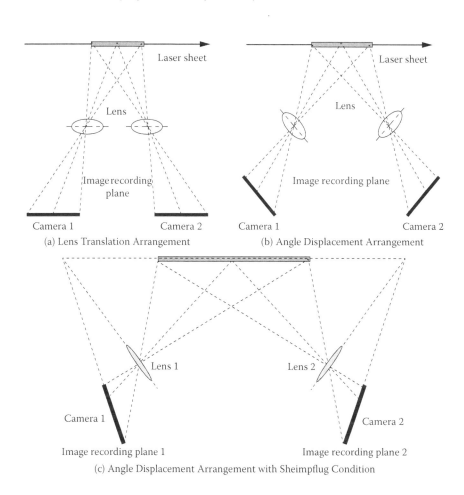

(a) Lens Translation Arrangement

(b) Angle Displacement Arrangement

(c) Angle Displacement Arrangement with Sheimpflug Condition

FIGURE 4.3

The camera configurations for stereoscopic PIV image recording.

limited common area in the flow field viewed by both cameras. A large angle between the cameras is usually desirable in order to have good measurement accuracy for the measurements of the out-of-plane component of the displacement vectors [12,13]. As a result, the camera image sensors are usually moved close to the outer edge of the image circle. Since the outer edge of the image area is used for stereo image recording, the image quality may decrease and the lens aberrations may become serious in the recorded images [14].

4.2.1.2 General Angle Displacement Method

For the general angle displacement approach, as shown in Figure 4.3(b), the two cameras view the same region of interest with an angle displacement. The image planes of the two cameras and the principal planes of the camera lenses are rotated with respect to the laser illuminating plane. Compared with the lens translation arrangement described before, the general angle displacement approach can have a much larger overlapped view region, which means a much larger measurement window for the stereo PIV measurements. It can also provide a better image quality since the image sensors are placed near the lens optical axis. However, the main disadvantage of such an arrangement is that the planes with the best focus are parallel to the image planes of the cameras—not in the measurement plane illuminated by the laser sheet. As a result, in order to have the entire measurement window in focus, smaller lens apertures (i.e., larger f-number) are usually needed to increase the depth of focus in the particle image recording, which will result in lower PIV image intensity. Ensuring enough signal-noise-ratio (SNR) in the acquired PIV images will require more powerful lasers for illumination and increase the diffraction limited image of the tracer particles when using small lens apertures (i.e., large f-number). This will impose additional requirements on the illumination system for stereo PIV measurements or cause larger measurement uncertainties.

4.2.1.3 Angle Displacement Arrangement with the Scheimpflug Condition

As described in Prasad and Jensen [15], if the tilted image sensor plane and the lens principal plane can intersect with the measurement plane at a common line to satisfy the Scheimpflug condition [16], the measurement plane in the physical space can be focused onto the image plane of the camera perfectly. As shown in Figure 4.3(c), an angle displacement arrangement with the Scheimpflug condition utilizes the Scheimpflug principle for stereoscopic image recording. This can overcome the disadvantage of conventional angle displacement configuration and provide the best focus for the entire measurement window in the stereo image recording.

The angle displacement arrangement with the Scheimpflug condition approach allows one to keep the best focus plane in the laser illuminating plane while having the cameras view the measurement plane from an off-axial angle; this allows the lens apertures of the cameras to be operated with the same aperture settings as a conventional 2D PIV system. It also enables the image sensors to be near the optical axis of the camera lenses so that the quality of the acquired PIV images can be much better compared to the lens translation approach. Due to its great advantage in stereoscopic image recording, the angle displacement arrangement with the Scheimpflug condition approach is the most commonly used approach in stereo PIV measurements.

4.3 Determination of Mapping Functions between Physical and Image Planes

As described earlier, while angle displacement approaches have the advantage of providing a larger measurement window for stereo PIV measurements,

FIGURE 4.4
The perspective effect of the angle displacement arrangement.

perspective distortions will be introduced in the recorded images since the image planes of the cameras are tilted with respect to the illuminating laser plane (i.e., the measurement plane) for stereoscopic image recording. As shown in Figure 4.4, a rectangular grid in the measurement plane will become trapezoid in the acquired images of the two cameras. A calibration procedure is needed to determine the mapping function between the measurement plane in the measurement plane of the physical space and the image planes of the cameras in order to correct the perspective distortions for quantitative stereo PIV measurements. So far, two approaches have been suggested to determine the mapping functions between the image planes of the cameras and the measurement plane in the physical space. They are usually called the mechanical registration approach and the mathematical registration approach [17].

For the mechanical registration approach [2,15], ray tracing is performed to establish the relationship between the image planes of the cameras and the measurement plane in the physical space. The point sources are located on a square grid in the measurement plane of the physical space and the positions of their images on the two image planes are determined by using a ray tracing technology based on a linearly optical assumption. It should be noted that the mechanical registration method is applicable only for the flow measurements with relatively simple configurations. For example, when the mechanical registration method is used, the air–liquid interface must be parallel to the measurement plane; liquid prisms are usually needed at the interface to compensate for the aberrations due to the different refractive indexes of the air and the liquid flow [15]. It would be very difficult, if not impossible, to use the mechanical registration method when complex nonlinear distortions (such as curved air–liquid interfaces) exist between the measurement plane and the image planes of the cameras.

Compared with the mechanical registration approach described before, the mathematical registration method is more general and can efficiently establish the relationship between the image planes of the cameras and the measurement plane in the physical space This is usually conducted by performing a general in situ calibration procedure based on the acquisition of one or several images of a calibration target plate—say, a Cartesian grid of small dots—at the center of the illuminating laser sheet (i.e., measurement plane [7]) or across the depth of the laser sheet [12,13,18]. The images of the acquired calibration target plate are used to determine the magnification matrices of the image recording cameras, and the mapping functions between the image planes of the two cameras and the measurement plane are determined mathematically [17]. This can account for various distortions between the measurement plane and the image planes of the cameras.

So far, a number of mathematical models have been suggested to represent the relationship between the measurement plane in physical space and the image planes of the two cameras used for stereoscopic image recording. The three most commonly used models will be compared in the following context.

4.3.1 Parallel Projection Model

Based on the parallel projection assumption of perfect lenses, Lawson and Wu [12,13] suggested using a linear function to express the relationship between the measurement plane in the physical space and the image planes of the two cameras used for stereoscopic image recording, which is expressed as

$$X^{(c)} = M^{(c)}(z\sin\alpha^{(c)} + x\cos\alpha^{(c)}) \tag{4.6}$$

$$Y^{(c)} = M^{(c)}y \tag{4.7}$$

where $c = 1$ and 2 for the left and right cameras, respectively. While $X^{(c)}$ and $Y^{(c)}$ are in the image planes of the cameras, x, y, z are in the physical space. $M^{(c)}$ is the magification factor, which is given by

$$M^{(c)} = \frac{d^{(c)}}{d_0 - z\cos\alpha^{(c)} - x\sin\alpha^{(c)}} \tag{4.8}$$

Differentiating Equations (4.7) and (4.8) in terms of $x, y,$ and z leads to particle image displacement ($\Delta X^{(c)}$ and $\Delta Y^{(c)}$) in the image planes equal to

$$\Delta X^{(c)} = a^{(c)}\Delta x + b^{(c)}\Delta z \tag{4.9}$$

$$\Delta Y^{(c)} = c^{(c)}\Delta x + d^{(c)}\Delta y + e^{(c)}\Delta z \tag{4.10}$$

The displacement of the tracer particle in the physical space ($\Delta x, \Delta y, \Delta z$) can be solved from Equation (4.9) and Equation (4.10), which gives

$$\Delta x = \frac{b^{(2)}\Delta X^{(1)} - b^{(1)}\Delta X^{(2)}}{a^{(1)}b^{(2)} - a^{(2)}b^{(1)}} \tag{4.11}$$

$$\Delta y = \frac{c^{(1)}\Delta Y^{(1)} + c^{(2)}\Delta Y^{(2)}}{2} \tag{4.12}$$

$$\Delta z = \frac{a^{(2)}\Delta X^{(1)} - a^{(1)}\Delta X^{(2)}}{a^{(2)}b^{(1)} - a^{(1)}b^{(2)}} \tag{4.13}$$

where the parameters $a^{(c)}$, $b^{(c)}$, and $c^{(c)}$ in the equations are determined from the geometrical parameters of the system setup or calculated from the calibration images obtained by an in situ calibration procedure. When the displacements in the two image planes of the cameras ($\Delta X^{(1)}$, $\Delta Y^{(1)}$, $\Delta X^{(2)}$, and $\Delta Y^{(2)}$) are known, the displacement of the tracer particles in the measurement plane (Δx, Δy, Δz) can be constructed by using Equation (4.11) to Equation (4.13).

It should be noted that the linear model described here is based on the parallel projection assumption, which is valid only for perfect optics and cannot account for nonlinear distortions such as the effects of imperfect lenses or other optical elements used for stereoscopic image recording. This may cause significant errors in stereo PIV measurements for cases where the nonlinear distortions cannot be ignored.

4.3.2 Second-Order Mapping Approach

Willert [7] suggested a more robust approach to determine the mapping function between the measurement plane in the physical space and the image planes of the two cameras that can account for the nonlinear optical distortions in the stereoscopic image recording. In this approach, second-order functions are used to express the relationships between the measurement plane and the image planes of the cameras, which are written as

$$x = \frac{a_{11}X_{(c)} + a_{12}Y_{(c)} + a_{13} + a_{14}X_{(c)}^{2} + a_{15}Y_{(c)}^{2} + a_{16}X_{(c)}Y_{(c)}}{a_{31}X_{(c)} + a_{32}Y_{(c)} + a_{33} + a_{34}X_{(c)}^{2} + a_{35}Y_{(c)}^{2} + a_{36}X_{(c)}Y_{(c)}} \tag{4.14}$$

$$y = \frac{a_{21}X_{(c)} + a_{22}Y_{(c)} + a_{23} + a_{24}X_{(c)}^{2} + a_{25}Y_{(c)}^{2} + a_{26}X_{(c)}Y_{(c)}}{a_{31}X_{(c)} + a_{32}Y_{(c)} + a_{33} + a_{34}X_{(c)}^{2} + a_{35}Y_{(c)}^{2} + a_{36}X_{(c)}Y_{(c)}} \tag{4.15}$$

where $c = 1$ and 2 for the left and right cameras, respectively, and the x–y plane is in the measurement plane. $X_{(c)}$ and $Y_{(c)}$ are in the image planes of the cameras. While $a_{33} = 1$ for these equations, the other 17 coefficients are determined by an in situ calibration procedure. As described in Willert [7], by using this approach, only one calibration image is needed with the calibration target plate located at the central plane of the illuminating laser sheet. However, it should be noted that Equations (4.14) and (4.15) can only be used for the coordinate mapping between the measurement plane and the image planes of the cameras. Since variable z, which is in the direction normal to the measurement plane in the physical space, does not appear in the equations, the relationships between the displacement vectors of the tracer particles in the physical space $(\Delta x, \Delta y, \Delta z)$ and the 2D displacements in the image planes $(\Delta X_L, \Delta Y_L)$ and $(\Delta X_R, \Delta Y_R)$ cannot be obtained directly by using the equations. As a result, it is necessary to rely on Equation (4.1) to Equation (4.5), which are based on the pinhole lens assumption, to reconstruct the three components of the displacement vectors in the physical space; this limits the applications of this approach for stereo PIV measurements.

4.3.3 General Multidimensional Polynomial Function Mapping Approach

A more general multidimensional polynomial function mapping approach, suggested by Soloff et al. [18], can compensate various optical distortions such as inaccurate optical alignment, lens nonlinearity, refraction by optical windows, or fluid interfaces involved in the stereo PIV measurements.

It is assumed that the general relationship between the physical space in the objective fluid flow (x, y, z) and the image planes of the cameras (X^1, Y^1) and (X^2, Y^2) can be described by a general mapping function:

$$X^{(c)} = F^{(c)}(x_i) \qquad (4.16)$$

where $c = 1,2$ for the left and right cameras, respectively, for stereoscopic image recording, and $i = 1,2,3$ for the x, y, and z directions in the physical space of the objective fluid flow.

Between the time interval of $t = t_0$ and $t = t_0 + \Delta t$ for stereo PIV image acquisition, tracer particles at the original positions of x_i move to new positions of $x_i + \Delta x_i$. The displacements of their images in the image planes can be expressed as

$$\Delta X^{(c)} = F^{(c)}(x_i + \Delta x_i) - F^{(c)}(x_i) \qquad (4.17)$$

Performing the Taylor series expansion in this equation and volume averaging over the interrogation cells, the first-order relationships between the displacements in the image planes of the cameras $\overline{\Delta X_i^{(c)}}$ and the displacement in the physical space $(\overline{\Delta x_j})$ should be

$$\overline{\Delta X_i^{(c)}} \cong F_{i,j}^{(c)}(x)\overline{\Delta x_j} \qquad i = 1,2 \qquad j = 1,2,3 \qquad (4.18)$$

Equation (4.18) provides a set of equations for each camera used for stereo PIV measurements. Writing out both sides of the equations in full and augmenting their yields, it will be

$$
\begin{pmatrix}
\overline{\Delta X_1^{(1)}} \\
\overline{\Delta X_2^{(1)}} \\
\overline{\Delta X_1^{(2)}} \\
\overline{\Delta X_2^{(2)}}
\end{pmatrix}
=
\begin{pmatrix}
F_{1,1}^{(1)} & F_{1,2}^{(1)} & F_{1,3}^{(1)} \\
F_{2,1}^{(1)} & F_{2,2}^{(1)} & F_{2,3}^{(1)} \\
F_{1,1}^{(2)} & F_{1,2}^{(2)} & F_{1,3}^{(2)} \\
F_{2,1}^{(2)} & F_{2,2}^{(2)} & F_{2,3}^{(2)}
\end{pmatrix}
\begin{pmatrix}
\overline{\Delta x_1} \\
\overline{\Delta x_2} \\
\overline{\Delta x_3}
\end{pmatrix}
\qquad (4.19)
$$

$$
F_{i,j}^{(c)} = \frac{\partial F_i^{(c)}}{\partial x_j} \qquad c = 1,2 \qquad i = 1,2 \qquad j = 1,2,3 \qquad (4.20)
$$

or

$$
\overline{\Delta X_i^{(c)}} \cong (\nabla F)\overline{\Delta x} \qquad (4.21)
$$

In Equation (4.19), the four terms $\overline{\Delta X_1^{(1)}}$, $\overline{\Delta X_2^{(1)}}$, $\overline{\Delta X_1^{(2)}}$, $\overline{\Delta X_2^{(2)}}$ on the left side are the displacements in the image planes for the left and right cameras. They can be determined by using an image processing procedure. The 12 terms in the transformation matrix (∇F) are the derivatives of the general mapping function.

The three-dimensional displacement $\overline{\Delta x_1}$, $\overline{\Delta x_2}$, and $\overline{\Delta x_3}$ in the physical space can be obtained by solving the set of four equations given previously. It should be noted that Equation (4.19) is overdetermined (i.e., there are only three unknown variables with four equations). A least squares method can be used to solve the equations to determine the displacement vectors of the tracer particles in physical space (Δx_1, Δx_2, and Δx_3).

In order to determine the general mapping function between the physical space and the image planes of the cameras used for stereoscopic image recording, a target plate with arrays of dots at a prescribed gap interval, as shown in Figure 4.5, is usually used for the in situ calibration. The front surface of the target plate is aligned with the center plane of the laser sheet, and the images of the calibration target plate are acquired with the target plate translated at several locations across the depth of the laser sheets, as shown schematically in Figure 4.6.

Since any function can be expressed as a multidimensional polynomial function mathematically, the mapping functions between the 3D physical space in the objective fluid flow and the 2D image planes of the two cameras used for stereo image recording can be expressed as multidimensional polynomial functions. For example, the polynomial functions can be chosen to be fourth order in the plane parallel to the illuminating laser sheet plane and second order along the direction normal to the laser sheet plane. This can be expressed as

FIGURE 4.5
The calibration plate used in the present study.

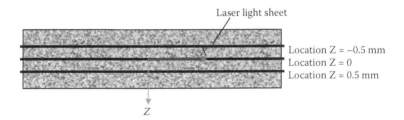

FIGURE 4.6
The locations of the calibration plate for the in situ calibration.

$$F(x, y, z) = a_0 + a_1 x + a_2 y + a_3 z + a_4 x^2 + a_5 xy + a_6 y^2$$

$$+ a_7 xz + a_8 yz + a_9 z^2 + a_{10} x^3 + a_{11} x^2 y + a_{12} xy^2$$

$$+ a_{13} y^3 + a_{14} x^2 z + a_{15} xyz + a_{16} y^2 z + a_{17} xz^2$$

$$+ a_{18} yz^2 + a_{19} x^4 + a_{20} x^3 y + a_{21} x^2 z^2 + a_{22} x^1 y^3$$

$$+ a_{23} y^4 + a_{24} x^3 z + a_{25} x^2 yz + a_{26} xy^2 z + a_{27} y^3 z$$

$$+ a_{28} x^2 z^2 + a_{29} xyz^2 + a_{30} y^2 z^2$$

(4.22)

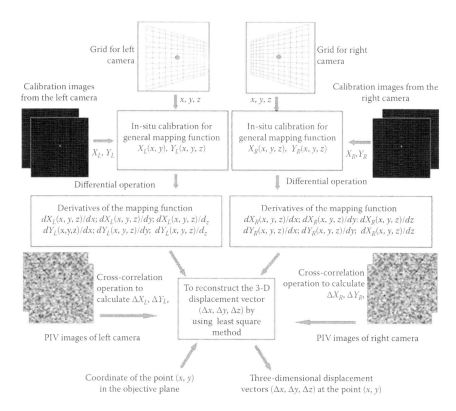

FIGURE 4.7
Illustration of the steps to reconstruct the three components of the displacement vectors in the measurement plane (Dx, Dy, Dz) for stereo PIV measurements.

In this equation, the x- and y-directions are in the plane parallel to the laser sheet plane; the z-direction is normal to the laser sheet plane. The 31 coefficients a_0 to a_{31} in the equation can be determined from the acquired calibration images.

Figure 4.7 shows the flow chart typically used to reconstruct all three components of the displacement vectors of the tracer particles (Δx, Δy, Δz) in the physical space by using the general multidimensional polynomial mapping function described before. As shown in Figure 4.7, in order to obtain the general mapping functions between the 3D physical space and the image planes of the two cameras, the images of the calibration target plate with a grid of dots (as shown in Figure 4.5) are captured at several locations across the thickness of the illuminating laser sheet (as shown in Figure 4.6). The coordinates of the marker grids (i.e., arrays of dots) in the physical space are known, and the coordinate values of the marker grids in the image planes of the left and right cameras can be determined quantitatively by using an image processing procedure.

It should be noted that, as shown in Equation (4.22), there are only 31 unknown coefficients for each image recording camera to determine the relationship between the 3D physical space in the objective fluid flow and the image plane of the camera. The acquired images of the marker grids on the calibration plate at several different locations across the laser sheet will make the number of equations that can be used to determine the 31 coefficients in the several thousands. By using a least squares method [19], the 31 coefficients for each image recording camera can be determined with optimum values.

Once the general mapping functions are determined through the in situ calibration procedure, differentiating the general mapping functions in terms of x, y, and z leads to 12 coefficients of the transformation matrix (∇F) given in Equation (4.19). The derivatives of the mapping functions represent the gradients of the particle image displacements in the image planes of the two cameras due to the displacements of the tracer particles in the physical space.

A sample of the 12 gradients for the two image recording cameras obtained by an in situ calibration procedure is given in Figure 4.8 and Figure 4.9. These gradients are the amount of the particle image displacement, in pixels, in the X- or Y-direction in the image planes caused by a 1.0 mm displacement of the tracer particles along x-, y-, or z-direction in the physical space. For example, at the point of (0,0,0) in the measurement plane of the physical space, the 12 gradient values are

$$L\,dX/dx = 11.1035 \quad L\,dY/dx = 0.0485 \quad R\,dX/dx = 11.1029 \quad R\,dY/dx = -0.0104 \quad (4.23)$$

$$L\,dX/dy = 0.0029 \quad L\,dY/dy = 12.1847 \quad R\,dX/dy = -0.0278 \quad R\,dY/dy = 12.1586 \quad (4.24)$$

$$L\,dX/dz = 5.1942 \quad L\,dY/dz = -0.0112 \quad R\,dX/dz = -4.8357 \quad R\,dY/dz = 0.0311 \quad (4.25)$$

For the values given in Equation (4.23), this indicates that a 1.0 mm displacement at the point of (0,0,0) along the x-direction in the measurement plane of the physical space will cause an image displacement of 11.1035 pixels along the X-direction and 0.0485 pixels along the Y-direction in the image plane of the left camera. An image displacement of 11.1029 pixels along the X-direction and 0.0104 pixels along the Y-direction will be detected in the image plane of the right camera.

Equation (4.24) indicates that a 1.0 mm displacement at the point of (0,0,0) along the y-direction in the measurement plane of the physical space will result in image displacements of 0.0029 pixels along the X-direction and 12.1847 pixels along the Y-direction in the image plane of the left camera. An image displacement of −0.0278 pixels along the X-direction and 12.1586 pixels along the Y-direction will be detected in the image plane of the right camera.

From Equation (4.25), it can be seen that a 1.0 mm displacement at the point of (0,0,0) along the z-direction in the measurement plane of the physical space will lead to an image displacement of 5.1942 pixels along the X-direction and

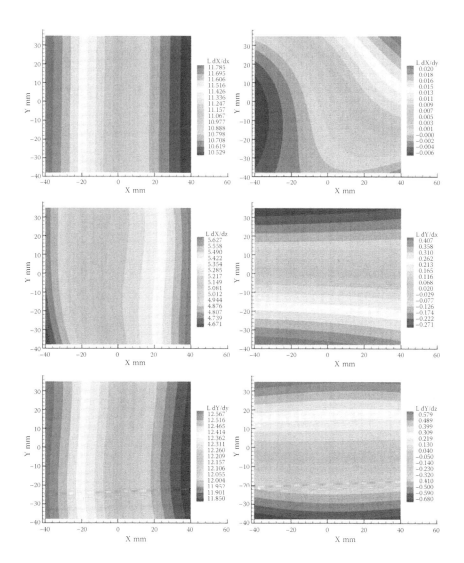

FIGURE 4.8
(See color insert.) The gradients of the left-hand image recording camera for stereo image recording.

−0.0112 pixels along the Y-direction in the image plane of the left camera. An image displacement of −4.8357 pixels along the X-direction and 0.0311 pixels along the Y-direction will be detected in the image plane of the right camera.

Once the general mapping functions are determined through the in situ calibration procedure, the stereo PIV system is ready to be used to conduct quantitative measurements in fluid flows. After the images of the tracer particles in the objective fluid flows are recorded stereoscopically by using the two cameras, the next step for stereo PIV measurements is to reconstruct the

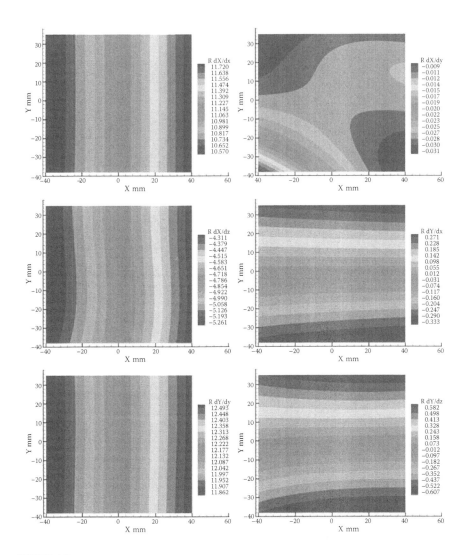

FIGURE 4.9
(See color insert.) The gradients of the right-hand image recording camera for stereo image recording.

three components of the displacement vectors of the tracer particles (Δx, Δy, Δz) based on the 2D particle image displacements (ΔX_L and ΔY_L) and (ΔX_R and ΔY_R) detected by the left and right cameras. The 2D particle image displacements in each image plane can be calculated separately by using a routine PIV image processing procedure, which is the same as that used for conventional 2D PIV measurements.

Figure 4.10 shows a pair of typical PIV raw images along with the 2D particle image displacements (ΔX_L and ΔY_L) and (ΔX_R and ΔY_R) detected by the left and right cameras; these were obtained in an experimental study to characterize a turbulent lobed jet mixing flow [20]. Based on the 2D particle image displacements (ΔX_L and ΔY_L) and (ΔX_R and ΔY_R), along with the distributions of the 12 gradients as shown in Figure 4.8 and Figure 4.9, the three components of the displacement vectors of the tracer particles in the measurement plane ($\Delta x, \Delta y, \Delta z$) can be reconstructed by solving Equation (4.19) with a least squares method. The reconstructed 3D flow velocity distribution in the measurement plane is given in Figure 4.10(d).

4.4 Using the Stereo PIV Technique to Study a Lobed Jet Mixing Flow

A lobed nozzle/mixer (Figure 4.11), which consists of a splitter plate with convoluted trailing edge, is considered a very promising fluid mechanic device for efficient mixing of two co-flow streams with different velocity, temperature, and/or species [21,22]. Lobed nozzles/mixers have been given a great deal of attention by many researchers in recent years, and they have also been widely used in various engineering applications. For example, for some commercial aeroengines, lobed nozzles have been used to reduce both take-off jet noise and specific fuel consumption (SFC) [23]. In order to reduce the infrared radiation signals of military aircraft, lobed nozzles have also been used to enhance the mixing process of the high-temperature and high-speed gas plume from aeroengines with ambient cold air [24]. More recently, lobed nozzles have also emerged as attractive approaches for enhancing mixing between fuel and air in combustion chambers to improve the efficiency of combustion and reduce the formation of pollutants [25].

In addition to the continuous efforts to optimize the geometry of lobed mixers/nozzles for better mixing performance and to widen the applications of lobed mixers/nozzles, extensive studies about the mechanism of why the lobed mixers/nozzles can substantially enhance fluid mixing have also been conducted in recent years. Based on pressure, temperature, and velocity measurements of the flow field downstream of a lobed nozzle, Paterson [26] revealed the existence of large-scale stream-wise vortices in lobed mixing flows induced by the special geometry of the lobed nozzles/mixers. These vortices were suggested to be responsible for the enhanced mixing.

Werle et al. [27] and Eckerle et al. [28] found that the stream-wise vortices in lobed mixing flows follow a three-step process by which these vortices form, intensify, and then break down and suggested that the high turbulence resulting from the vortex breakdown would improve the overall mixing process. Elliott et al. [29] suggested that there are three primary contributors to the mixing processes in lobed mixing flows. The first is the span-wise

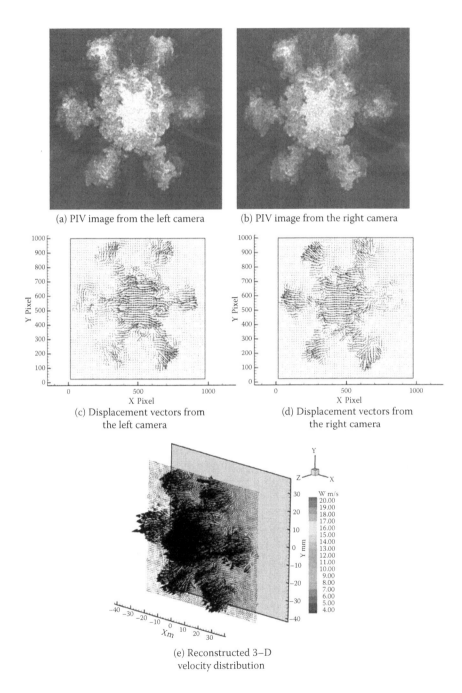

(a) PIV image from the left camera

(b) PIV image from the right camera

(c) Displacement vectors from the left camera

(d) Displacement vectors from the right camera

(e) Reconstructed 3–D velocity distribution

FIGURE 4.10
Stereo PIV measurement results in a lobed jet mixing flow.

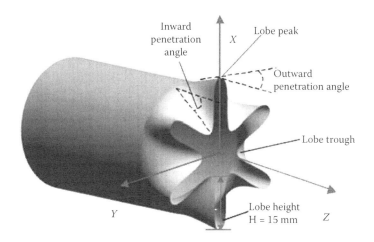

FIGURE 4.11
Schematic of the lobe nozzle/mixer used in the present study.

vortices, which occur in any free shear layers due to the Kelvin–Helmholtz instability. The second is the increased interfacial contact area due to the con-voluted trailing edge of the lobed mixer. The last element is the stream-wise vortices produced by the special geometry of the lobed mixer.

Although the existence of unsteady vortices and turbulent structures in lobed mixing flows has been revealed in previous studies by qualitative flow visualization, the quantitative, instantaneous, whole-field velocity and vorticity distributions in lobed mixing flows were not obtained until the work of Hu et al. [30]. These researchers used both planar laser induced fluorescence (PLIF) and conventional 2D PIV techniques to study lobed jet mixing flows. Based on the directly perceived PLIF flow visualization images and quantitative PIV velocity, vorticity, and turbulence intensity distributions, the evolution and interaction of various vortical and turbu-lent structures in the lobed jet flows were discussed. It should be noted that the conventional 2D PIV system used in Hu et al. [30] is only capable of obtaining two components of velocity vectors in the planes of illuminating laser sheets. The out-of-plane velocity component is lost while the in-plane components may be affected by an unrecoverable error due to perspective transformation [2].

Meanwhile, for the highly 3D turbulent flows like lobed jet mixing flows, conventional 2D PIV measurement results may not be able to reveal the 3D features of the complex lobed jet mixing flows successfully. A high-resolu-tion stereo PIV system, which can provide all three components of veloc-ity vectors in a measurement plane simultaneously, is used in the present study to quantify the turbulent jet mixing flow exhausted from a lobed nozzle/mixer.

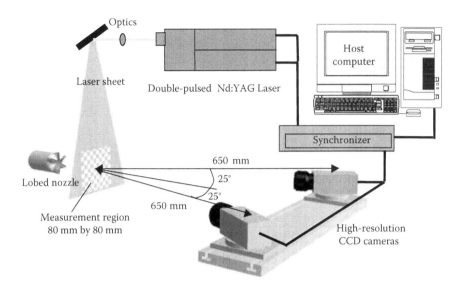

FIGURE 4.12
Experimental setup used for the stereo PIV measurements.

4.4.1 Experimental Setup for Stereo PIV Measurements

Figure 4.12 shows the schematic of the experimental setup used in the present study to achieve stereo PIV measurements. An air jet flow is exhausted from a circular nozzle/mixer at the speed of $U_0 = 20.0$ m/s. The jet flow is seeded with ~1 μm oil droplets by using a droplet generator. Illumination is provided by a double-pulsed Nd:YAG laser (NewWave Gemini 200) adjusted on the second harmonic and emitting two pulses of 200 mJ at the wavelength of 532 nm with a repetition rate of 10 Hz. The laser beam is shaped to a sheet by a set of mirrors with spherical and cylindrical lenses. The thickness of the laser sheet in the measurement region is about 2.0 mm for the present study. Two high-resolution digital cameras used to perform stereoscopic PIV image recording are arranged in an angular displacement configuration. With the installation of tilt-axis mounts, the lenses and camera bodies are adjusted to satisfy the Scheimpflug condition. The cameras and the double-pulsed Nd:YAG lasers are connected to a workstation (host computer) via a synchronizer, which controls the timing of the laser sheet illumination and the charged coupled device camera data acquisition.

A general in situ calibration procedure (described before) is used in the present study to determine the mapping functions between the image planes of the two cameras and the measurement plane in the fluid flow. The mapping function used is taken to be a multidimensional polynomial, which is fourth order for the X- and Y-directions parallel to the laser sheet plane and second order for the Z-direction normal to the laser sheet plane, as expressed in Equation (4.22). The 2D displacements in each image plane of the two cameras are obtained by a frame-to-frame cross-correlation technique involving successive frames of patterns of particle images in an interrogation window of 32 pixels × 32 pixels. An effective overlap of 50% of the interrogation windows is employed in the PIV image processing. Following the flow chart shown in Figure 4.7, by using the mapping functions obtained by the in situ calibration procedure and the 2D displacements in the two image planes detected by the two cameras, the 3D flow velocity vectors in the laser illuminating plane are reconstructed (shown in Figure 4.10).

4.4.2 Measurement Results and Discussion

Figure 4.13 and Figure 4.14 give the stereo PIV measurement results in two typical cross planes of the lobed jet mixing flow, which include typical instantaneous velocity fields, simultaneous stream-wise vorticity distributions, ensemble-averaged velocity, and stream-wise vorticity fields. The ensemble-averaged velocity and stream-wise vorticity fields given in the

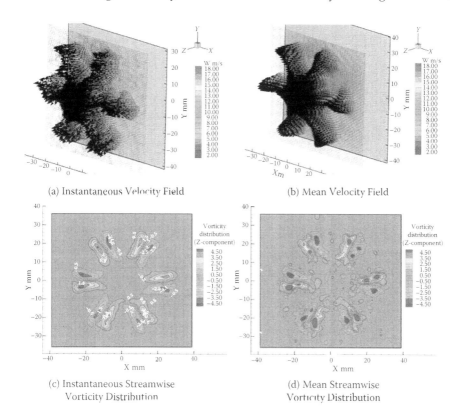

(a) Instantaneous Velocity Field

(b) Mean Velocity Field

(c) Instantaneous Streamwise
Vorticity Distribution

(d) Mean Streamwise
Vorticity Distribution

FIGURE 4.13
(See color insert.) Stereo PIV measurement results in the $Z/D = 0.25$ ($Z/H = 0.67$) cross plane.

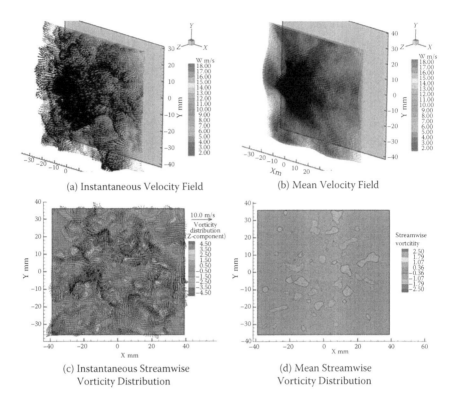

(a) Instantaneous Velocity Field

(b) Mean Velocity Field

(c) Instantaneous Streamwise
Vorticity Distribution

(d) Mean Streamwise
Vorticity Distribution

FIGURE 4.14
(See color insert.) Stereo PIV measurement results in the Z/D = 3.0 (Z/H = 8.0) cross plane.

figures are calculated based on 500 frames of instantaneous stereo PIV measurement results.

As shown clearly in Figure 4.13, the high-speed core jet flow is found to have the same geometry as the lobed nozzle in the Z/D = 0.25 (Z/H = 0.67) cross plane (almost at the exit of the lobed nozzle). The "signature" of the lobed nozzle in the form of a six-lobe structure can be seen clearly from both the instantaneous and ensemble-averaged velocity fields. The existence of very strong secondary streams in the lobed jet flow is revealed clearly in the velocity vector plots. The core jet flow ejects radially outward in the lobe peaks and ambient flows inject inward in the lobe troughs. Both the ejection of the core jet flow and the injection of the ambient flows are generally following the outward and inward contours of the lobed nozzle, which results in the generation of six pairs of counter-rotating stream-wise vortices in the lobed jet flow. The maximum radial ejection velocity of the core jet flow in the ensemble-averaged velocity field is found to be about 5.0 m/s, which is almost equal to the value of $U_0 \bullet \sin(\theta_{out})$. A big high-speed region can also be seen clearly from the ensemble-averaged velocity field; this represents the high-speed core jet flow in the center of the lobed nozzle.

The existence of the six pairs of large-scale stream-wise vortices due to the special geometry of the lobed nozzle can be seen clearly and quantitatively from the stream-wise vorticity distributions shown in Figure 4.13(c) and Figure 4.13(d). The size of these large-scale stream-wise vortices is found to be on the order of the lobe height. Compared with those in the instantaneous stream-wise vorticity field (Figure 4.13c), the contours of the large-scale stream-wise vortices in the ensemble-averaged stream-wise vorticity field (Figure 4.13d) are found to be much smoother. However, they have almost the same distribution pattern and magnitude as their instantaneous counterparts. The similarity between the instantaneous and ensemble-averaged stream-wise vortices suggests that the generation of the large-scale stream-wise vortices at the exit of the lobed nozzle is quite steady.

As revealed from the stereo PIV measurement results given in Figure 4.14, the lobed jet mixing flow is found to become so turbulent that the "signature" of the lobed nozzle can no longer be identified easily from the instantaneous velocity fields as the downstream distance increases to Z/D = 3.0 (Z/H = 8.0). The flow field is fully filled with many small-scale vortices and turbulent structures. The ensemble-averaged velocity field in this cross plane shows that the distinct high-speed region in the center of the lobed jet flow has dissipated so seriously that iso-velocity contours of the high-speed core jet flow have become small concentric circles. The ensemble-averaged secondary streams in this cross plane become so weak (the maximum secondary stream velocity is less than 0.8 m/s) that they cannot be identified easily from the ensemble-averaged velocity vector plot.

From the instantaneous stream-wise vorticity distribution in the Z/D = 3.0 (Z/H = 8.0) cross plane given in Figure 4.14(c), it can be seen that there are many small-scale stream-wise vortices in the lobed jet mixing flow that almost fully fill the measurement window. However, the maximum vorticity value of these instantaneous small-scale stream-wise vortices is found to be at the same level of those in the upstream cross planes. Due to serious dissipation caused by the intensive mixing between the core jet flow and ambient flow, almost no apparent stream-wise vortices can be identified from the ensemble-averaged stream-wise vorticity distribution (Figure 4.14d) in the Z/D = 3.0 (Z/H = 8.0) cross plane anymore.

Based on the stereo PIV measurement results at 12 cross planes, the 3D flow field in the near downstream region of the lobed jet mixing flow is reconstructed. Figure 4.15 shows the ensemble-averaged velocity vector distributions in the lobed jet mixing flow viewed from upstream and downstream positions. The corresponding velocity iso-surfaces of the reconstructed 3D flow field are also given in Figure 4.15. The velocity magnitudes of the iso-surfaces are 4.0, 8.0, 12.0, and 16.0 m/s, respectively. It can be seen clearly that the high-speed core jet flow has the same geometry as the lobed nozzle (i.e., six-lobe structure) at the exit of the lobed nozzle/mixer. Due to the "stirring effect" of the large-scale stream-wise vortices generated by the lobed nozzle,

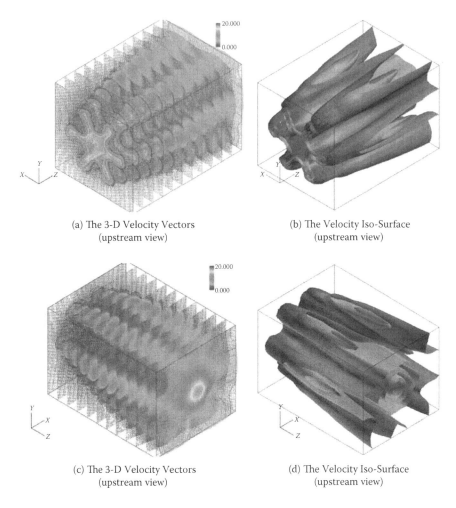

(a) The 3-D Velocity Vectors
(upstream view)

(b) The Velocity Iso-Surface
(upstream view)

(c) The 3-D Velocity Vectors
(upstream view)

(d) The Velocity Iso-Surface
(upstream view)

FIGURE 4.15
(See color insert.) Reconstructed three-dimensional flow fields of the lobed jet mixing flow.

the six-lobe structure of the core jet flow is rounded up rapidly. At $Z/D = 3.0$ ($Z/H = 8.0$) downstream, the iso-surfaces are found to become concentric cylinders, which are very similar to those in a circular jet flow.

The unique flow structures in the lobed jet mixing flow are revealed clearly and quantitatively from the stereo PIV measurement results. By elucidating the underlying physics, our understanding about the important physical process pertinent to the mixing enhancement in lobed mixing flow can be improved significantly. This will enable us to explore and optimize design paradigms for the development of novel mixers/nozzles for various engineering applications.

4.5 Summary

The technical basis of the stereo PIV technique, which is capable of achieving simultaneous measurements of all three components of flow velocity vectors in fluid flows, has been described in the present study. Three basic optical arrangements most commonly used for stereo image recording were introduced along with a brief description about the advantages and disadvantages of each optical arrangement. A general in situ calibration procedure to determine the mapping functions between the 3D physical space in the objective fluid flow and the image planes of the cameras used for stereoscopic image recording was described in detail. The study also gave the flow chart and steps needed to reconstruct the three components of the displacement vectors in the measurement plane of the physical space by using the 2D displacement vectors in the image planes detected by the two cameras and the multidimensional polynomial mapping functions.

The feasibility and implementation of the stereo PIV technique were demonstrated by achieving simultaneous measurements of all three components of flow velocity vectors in an air jet flow exhaust from a lobed nozzle/mixer. The evolution of the large-scale stream-wise vortices and the unique 3D flow structures in the lobed jet mixing flow were revealed clearly and quantitatively from the stereo PIV measurement results. Based on these results, the underlying physics related to the enhanced mixing processes in lobed mixing flows can be elucidated more clearly and quantitatively.

References

1. Adrian, R. J. 1991. Particle-image technique for experimental fluid mechanics. *Annual Review Fluid Mechanics* 261–304.
2. Prasad, A. K. and Adrian, R. J. 1993. Stereoscopic particle image velocimetry applied to fluid flows. *Experiments in Flows* 15:49–60.
3. Barnhart, D. H., Adrian, R. J., and Papen, G. C. 1994. Phase-conjugate holographic system for high-resolution particle image velocimetry. *Applied Optics* 33:7159–7170.
4. Zhang, J., Tao, B., and Katz, J. 1997. Turbulent flow measurement in a square duct with hybrid holographic PIV. *Experiments in Fluids* 23:373–381.
5. Virant, M. and Dracos, T. 1997. 3D PTV and its application on Lagrangian motion. *Measurement Science and Technology* 8:1539.
6. Elsinga, G. F., Scarano, F., Wieneke, B., and van Oudheusden, B. W. 2006. Tomographic particle image velocimetry. *Experiments in Fluids* 41:933–947.
7. Willert, C. 1997. Stereoscopic digital particle image velocimetry for application in wind tunnel flows. *Measurement Science and Technology* 8:1465–1479.

8. Meng, H., Pan, G., Pu, Y., and Woodward, S. H. 2004. Holographic particle image velocimetry: From film to digital recording. *Measurement Science and Technology* 15:673–685.

9. Svizher, A. and Cohen, J. 2006. Holographic particle image velocimetry system for measurement of hairpin vortices in air channel flow. *Experiments in Fluids* 40:708–722.

10. Katz, J. and Sheng, J. 2010. Applications of holography in fluid mechanics and particle dynamics. *Annual Review Fluid Mechanics* 42:531–555.

11. Brucker, C. 1996. 3-D PIV via spatial correlation in a color-coded light sheet. *Experiments in Fluids* 21:312–314.

12. Lawson, N. J. and Wu, J. 1997. Three-dimensional particle image velocimetry: Error analysis of stereoscopic techniques. *Measurement Science Technology* 8:894–900.

13. Lawson, N. J. and Wu, J. 1997. Three-dimensional particle image velocimetry: Experimental error analysis of a digital angular stereoscopic system. *Measurement Science Technology* 8:1455–1464.

14. Bjorkquist, D. C. 1998. Design and calibration of a stereoscopic PIV system. *Proceedings of the Ninth International Symposium on Application of Laser Techniques in Fluid Mechanics,* Lisbon, Portugal, 1998.

15. Prasad, A. K. and Jensen, K. 1995. Scheimpflug stereocamera for particle image velocimetry in liquid flows. *Applied Optics* 34:7092–7099.

16. Larmore, L. 1965. *Introduction to photographic principles.* New York: Dover Publications, Inc.

17. Hill, D. F., Sharp, K.V., and Adrian, R. J. 1999. The implementation of distortion compensated stereoscopic PIV. *Proceedings of 3rd International Workshop on PIV,* Santa Barbara, CA, Sept. 16–18, 1999.

18. Soloff, S. M., Adrian, R. J., and Liu, Z. C. 1997. Distortion compensation for generalized stereoscopic particle imaging velocimetry. *Measurement Science Technology* 8:1441–1454.

19. Watanabe, Z., Natori, M., and Okkuni, Z. 1989. Fortran 77 software for numerical computation. Maruzen Publication, ISBN4-621-03424-3 C3055.

20. Hu, H., Saga, T., Kobayashi, T., and Taniguchi, N. 2002. Mixing process in a lobed jet flow. *AIAA Journal* 40 (7):1339–1345.

21. McCormick, D.C. and Bennett, J. C., Jr. 1994. Vortical and turbulent structure of a lobed mixer free shear layer. *AIAA Journal* 32 (9):1852–1859.

22. Belovich, V. M. and Samimy, M. 1997. Mixing process in a coaxial geometry with a central lobed mixing nozzle. *AIAA Journal* 35 (5):838–84l.

23. Presz, W. M., Jr., Reynolds, G., and McCormick, D., 1994. Thrust augmentation using mixer-ejector-diffuser systems. AIAA paper 94-0020, 1994.

24. Hu, H., Saga, T., Kobayashi, T., Taniguchi, N., and Wu, S. 1999. Research on the rectangular lobed exhaust ejector/mixer systems. *Transactions of Japan Society of Aeronautics & Space Science* 41 (134):187–194.

25. Smith, L. L., Majamak, A. J., Lam, I. T., Delabroy, O., Karagozian, A. R., Marble, F. E., and Smith, O. I. 1997. Mixing enhancement in a lobed injector. *Physics of Fluids* 9 (3):667–678.

26. Paterson, R. W. 1982. Turbofan forced mixer nozzle internal flowfield. NASA CR-3492.

27. Werle, M. J., Paterson, R. W., and Presz, W. M., Jr. 1987. Flow structure in a periodic axial vortex array. AIAA paper 87-6l0.

28. Eckerle, W. A., Sheibani, H., and Awad, J. 1993. Experimental measurement of the vortex development downstream of a lobed forced mixer. *Journal of Engineering for Gas Turbine and Power* 14:63–71.
29. Elliott, J. K., Manning, T. A., Qiu, Y. J., Greitzer, C. S., Tan, C. S., and Tillman, T. G. 1992. Computational and experimental studies of flow in multi-lobed forced mixers. AIAA 92-3568.
30. Hu, H., Saga, T., Kobayashi, T., and Taniguchi, N. 2000. Research on the vortical and turbulent structures in the lobed jet flow by using LIF and PIV. *Measurement Science and Technology* 11 (6):698–711.

5

Basic Concepts

Sergio Fernandez and Joaquim Salvi

CONTENTS

Shape reconstruction using coded structured light is considered one of the most reliable techniques to recover object surfaces. With a calibrated projector–camera pair, a light pattern is projected onto the scene and imaged by the camera. Correspondences between projected and recovered patterns are found and used to extract three-dimensional (3D) surface information. Among structured light (SL) techniques, the combination of dense acquisition and real time constitutes an active field of research. To achieve density and real time, most of the work present in the literature is based on the projection of a single one-shot fringe pattern, where depth is extracted analyzing phase deviation of the imaged pattern. However, the algorithms employed to unwrap the phase are computationally slow and can fail in the presence of depth discontinuities and occlusions. This chapter presents an up-to-date review and a new classification of the existing techniques. Moreover, a proposal for a new one-shot dense pattern that combines De Bruijn and fringe pattern projection to obtain an absolute, accurate, and computationally fast 3D reconstruction is presented. Finally, the proposed technique is compared to some of the already existing methods, obtaining both qualitative and quantitative results. The advantages and drawbacks of the proposed technique are discussed.

5.1 Introduction

Three-dimensional measurement constitutes an important topic in computer vision, with different applications such as range sensing, industrial inspection of manufactured parts, reverse engineering (digitization of complex, free-form surfaces), object recognition, 3D map building, biometrics, clothing design, and others. The developed solutions are traditionally categorized into contact and noncontact techniques. Contact techniques, used for a long time in reverse engineering and industrial inspections, present slow performance and high cost due to the necessity of using mechanically calibrated passive arms [68].

On the other hand, noncontact techniques (both active and passive) achieve higher accuracy without the necessity of touching the object, which is highly recommended in many applications. In passive approaches, the scene is first imaged by two or more calibrated cameras and correspondences between the images are found to extract the 3D shape. This implies that the density of the reconstruction is directly related to the texture of the object, obtaining poor results in the presence of textureless surfaces [4, 32]. Methods based on structured light (active techniques) came to cope with this issue, substituting one of the cameras by an active device (a projector) which projects a structured-light pattern onto the scene. This active device is modeled as an inverse camera and can be calibrated correspondingly [55]. The projected pattern imposes the illusion of texture onto an object, increasing the number of correspondences [56], thus being able to obtain dense reconstructions even for textureless surfaces.

This chapter analyzes the different coding strategies used in active structured light, focusing on the improvements presented in the last years. The classification of the different SL approaches presented in the work of Salvi, Batlle, and Mouaddib [57] is considered to this end. Furthermore, a new proposal of one-shot dense reconstruction is presented that combines De Bruijn and fringe pattern projection to obtain an absolute, accurate, and computationally fast 3D reconstruction. This new technique is compared to some SL representative techniques, providing both quantitative and qualitative results. Finally, in the conclusions we analyze the main positives and drawbacks of the technique.

5.2 Classification

Coded structured light (CSL) is based on the projection of one pattern or a sequence of patterns that univocally determines the code word of a projecting pixel (or feature) within a nonperiodic region. Coded structured light has produced many works during the last decades and some recopilatory works can be found in the literature. This is the case of the surveys presented by Batlle, Mouaddib, and Salvi [4] and Salvi et al. [58], which analyzed the different CSL techniques existing in temporal and spatial multiplexing domains from 1998 until 2004, respectively. Regarding frequency multiplexing, Su [62] reviewed the Fourier transform (FT) techniques proposed until 2001. However, there is no previous work comparing the three approaches. Therefore, a classification extracting and analyzing attributes common in all the approaches is missing. This is overcome in the present survey, which also incorporates the most recent contributions done in CSL in the last years.

Table 5.1 shows a new classification of the existing pattern projection techniques. The main distinction has been done regarding the sparse or dense 3D reconstruction achieved. Patterns providing sparse reconstruction present a digital profile with the same value for the region represented by the

TABLE 5.1

Proposed Classification Embracing Every Group of CSL

			Shots	Cameras	Axis	Pixel Depth	Coding Strategy	Subpixel Acc.	Color
SPARSE	Spatial multiplexing								
	De Bruijn	Boyer and Kak	1987	1	1	C	A	Y	N
		Salvi et al.	1998	1	1	C	A	Y	Y
		Monks et al.	1992	1	1	C	A	Y	N
		Pages et al.	2004	1	1	C	A	Y	N
	Nonformal	Forster	2007	1	1	C	A	Y	N
		Fechteler and Eisert	2008	1	1	C	A	Y	N
		Tehrani	2008	2	1	C	A	N	Y
		Maruyama and Abe	1993	1	2	B	A	N	Y
		Kawasaki et al.	2008	1	2	C	A	N	Y
		Ko	1995	1	2	G	A	N	Y
		Koninckx and Van Gool	2006	1	2	C	P	Y	Y
	M-array	Griffin et al.	1992	1	2	C	A	Y	Y
		Morano et al.	1998	1	2	C	A	Y	Y
		Pages et al.	2006	1	2	C	A	Y	N
		Albitar et al.	2007	1	2	B	A	N	Y

		Author	Year								
Time multiplexing	Binary codes	Posdamer and Altschuler	1982	>2	1	1	1	B	A	N	Y
		Ishii et al.	2007	>2	1	1	1	B	A	N	Y
		Sun	2006	>2	2	1	1	B	A	Y	Y
	N-ary codes	Caspi et al.	1998	>2	1	1	1	C	A	N	N
	Shifting codes	Zhang et al.	2008	>2	1	1	1	C	A	Y	N
		Sansoni et al.	2000	>2	1	1	1	G	A	Y	N
		Guhring	2001	>2	1	1	1	G	A	Y	Y
DENSE	Single phase shifting (SPS)	Srinivasan et al.	1985	>2	1	1	1	G	A	Y	Y
		Ono et al.	2004	>2	1	1	1	G	P	Y	Y
		Wust et al.	1991	1	1	1	1	C	P	Y	N
		Guan et al.	2004	1	1	1	1	G	P	Y	Y
	Multiple phase shifting (MPS)	Gushov and Solodkin	1991	>2	1	1	1	G	A	Y	Y
		Pribanic et al.	2009	>2	1	1	1	G	A	Y	Y

TABLE 5.1 (*Continued*)

Proposed Classification Embracing Every Group of CSL

				Shots	Cameras	Axis	Pixel Depth	Coding Strategy	Subpixel Acc.	Color
DENSE	Frequency multiplexing	Single coding frequency	Takeda and Mutoh	1983	1	1	1	G	P	Y	Y
			Cobelli et al.	2009	1	1	1	G	P	Y	Y
			Li et al.	1990	2	1	1	G	P	Y	Y
			Hu and He	2009	2	2	1	G	P	Y	Y
			Chen et al.	2007	1	1	1	C	P	Y	N
			Yue	2006	1	1	1	G	P	Y	Y
			Chen et al.	2005	2	1	1	G	P	Y	Y
			Berryman et al.	2008	1	1	1	G	P	Y	Y
			Gdeisat et al.	2006	1	1	1	G	P	Y	Y
			Zhang et al.	2008	1	1	1	G	P	Y	Y
			Lin and Su	1995	2	1	1	G	P	Y	Y
			Huang et al.	2005	>2	1	1	G	P	Y	Y
			Jia et al.	2007	2	1	1	G	P	Y	Y
			Wu and Peng	2006	1	1	1	G	P	Y	Y
			Fernandez et al.	2000	1	1	1	C	A	Y	N
	Spatial multiplexing	Grading	Carrhill and Hummel	1985	1	1	1	G	A	Y	N
			Tajima and Iwakawa	1990	1	1	1	C	A	Y	N

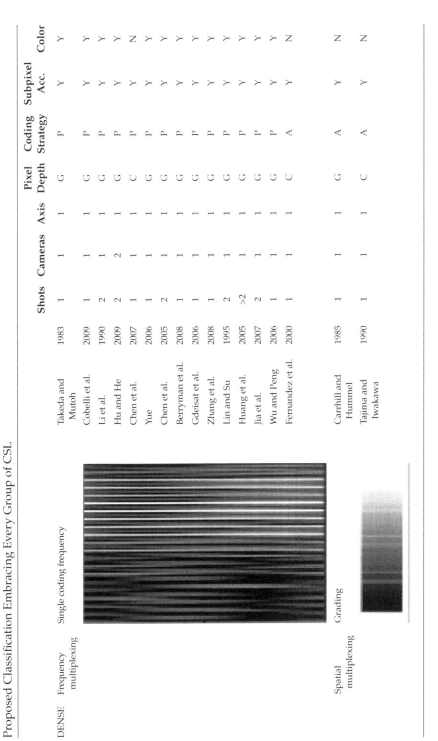

same code word. The size of this region largely determines the density of the reconstructed object. On the other hand, dense reconstruction is achieved by projecting a sequence of digital patterns superposed over time to obtain full pixel coverage or with a smooth profile pattern, where every pixel has a unique code word within the nonperiodicity region. Both approaches achieve dense reconstruction. A posteriori subclassification is done regarding spatial, time, and frequency multiplexing. Columns on the right indicate the value of some intrinsic attributes common to all the patterns. These attributes are

- *Number of projected patterns* determines whether the method is valid or not for measuring moving objects.
- *Number of cameras* uses stereo vision (two or more cameras) coupled to a noncalibrated pattern used only to get texture on the surface pattern, or a unique camera coupled to a calibrated projector.
- *Axis codification* codes the pattern along one or two axes.
- *Pixel depth* refers to the color and luminance level of the projected pattern (B, G, and C stand for binary, grayscale, and color, respectively).
- *Coding strategy* refers to the periodicity of the set of patterns projected on the surface (A stands for absolute and P stands for periodic).
- *Subpixel accuracy* determines whether the features are found considering subpixel precision, thus providing better reconstruction results (yes or no).
- *Color* determines whether the technique can cope with colored objects (yes or no).

5.3 Sparse Reconstruction Methods

In sparse reconstruction methods the pattern presents a digital profile, and spatial or temporal multiplexing is employed to image the scene. Spatial multiplexing techniques code the pattern using the surroundings of a given feature, while temporal multiplexing creates the code word by the successive projection of patterns onto the object. In addition, some methods combine spatial and temporal information to take advantage of both techniques.

5.3.1 Spatial Multiplexing

Spatial multiplexing groups all techniques where the code word of a specific position is extracted from surrounding points. Intensity or color variations are used to create the code word. Three different coding strategies can be distinguished within this group: De Bruijn patterns, nonformal coding, and M-arrays.

5.3.1.1 De Bruijn-Based Techniques

De Bruijn sequences are a set of pseudorandom values with specific properties between them. A k-ary De Bruijn sequence of order n is a circular sequence d_0, d_1, d_{n^k-1} (length n^k) containing each substring of length k exactly once (window property of k). De Bruijn sequences can be constructed by taking a Hamiltonian or Eulerian path of an n-dimensional De Bruijn graph (see Fredricksen [18] for more details). This algorithm allows us to create univocal stripe sequences in the pattern and is able to extract the position by looking at the color of the stripes placed in the same window.

Several proposals can be found using De Bruijn sequences, with both striped and multislit patterns. First proposals of De Bruijn-based striped patterns are found in the method developed by Boyer and Kak [7]. In this approach, RGB (red, green, blue) space was used to code the sequence of stripes. Being c_i^k the color of the stripe i in the subpattern k, the distance between two subpatterns k and l is given by

$$d = \sum_{i=1}^{N} \delta_i \tag{5.1}$$

where

$$\delta_i = \begin{cases} 0 & \text{if } c_i^k = c_i^l \\ 1 & \text{otherwise} \end{cases} \tag{5.2}$$

The pattern proposed by Boyer and Kak [7] contains more than 300 stripes colored by three different colors. Color detection was done with a stripe indexing algorithm preceded by a Hamming filtering. However, no color calibration was pursued to suppress the effect of different albedo, leading to some errors due to leakage from the blue to the green channel.

A different approach was followed by Monks, Carter, and Shadle [41], where a multislit-based De Bruijn sequence was projected. Six colors were used to color the slits, separated by black gaps. The slit colors were chosen so that every subsequence of three colors appeared only once. Colors were chosen in the hue channel (hue, saturation, and intensity [HSI] space), despite the fact that projection was performed in RGB and transformed back to HSI once the image was captured by the camera. Full saturation and full intensity were chosen in the SI (saturation/intensity) channels. A previous color calibration step was performed by the authors in order to determine the transfer function of the optical system. Once the system was calibrated, captured colors were corrected before applying fringe detection. A minimum cost matching algorithm was used in the decoding step in order to find the most probable matching between projected and recovered patterns, considering that some slits might be imaged partly occluded or badly segmented [58].

To simplify the peak detection process, Salvi et al. [56] created a grid of horizontal and vertical colored slits. Every crossing of the two slits was

FIGURE 5.1
(See color insert.) Pattern proposed by Pages et al. RGB pattern and luminance channel. (Pages, J. et al. *17th International Conference on Pattern Recognition, ICPR 2004* 4:284–287, 2004. With permission.)

extracted by simple peak intensity detection. Hue channel was again used (in HSI space) to encode the colors. Three colors were assigned for the horizontal lines and another three for the vertical lines, using a De Bruijn third-order sequence. The decoding step was done back in HSI space, showing negligible errors scanning planar surfaces under scene light control. However, some problems were encountered due to the sensitivity of the hue channel under different albedo of the illuminated object.

Some years later, Pages et al. [46] and Pages, Salvi, and Forest [47] proposed an alternative approach to traditional striped- or multislit-based patterns. They combined a striped pattern in the hue channel with a multislit pattern in the intensity channel (see Figure 5.1), which defined dark and bright areas within the same color stripe. Therefore, the high resolution of classical striped patterns and the accuracy of multislit patterns were combined. The half-illuminated stripes were colored according to a De Bruijn sequence for a subpattern of n stripes, while bright slits were colored equally within the same subpattern. In the experiments, a 128-striped pattern with four colors and a window property of three encoded stripes was applied. Using this codification, their approach doubled the resolution of traditional De Bruijn stripe-based techniques.

5.3.1.2 Nonformal Coding

Nonformal coding comprises all the techniques having nonorthodox codification, in the sense that the pattern is designed to fulfill some particular requirements. Both one-axis and two-axes encoding are suitable for these methods. One-axis coding methods are based on striped or multislit patterns. This is the case of Forster's [17] and Fechteler and Eisert's [15] proposals, which created color-based patterns in which two adjacent colors must differ in at least two color channels in the receptor device (red, green, and blue). This condition is not usually accomplished in De Bruijn sequences. Forster used a striped pattern, while Fechteler and Eisert employed a multislit pattern. In Fechteler and Eisert, a parabola was fitted in every RGB channel (or combination of channels for nonpure RGB colors, the option selected by Forster). Optionally, surface color was acquired by projecting an extra white pattern. Tehrani, Saghaeian, and Mohajerani [65] applied the idea of color slits to reconstruct images taken from two camera views, using 10 hue values to create the slit pattern (the difference between colors was maximal for adjacent slits).

There are also some proposals based on two-axes encoding. For instance, Maruyama and Abe [39] proposed a pattern of randomly cut black slits on a white background. In this approach, coding information was held in the length of the slits and their position within the pattern. Every recorded segment had its own length, which could be similar for several segments. The code word corresponding to a segment was determined by its own length and the lengths of its six adjacent segments. The main drawback of this method is that the length of segments is affected by the projector–object and object–camera distances, as well as by the camera optics, therefore reducing the reliability of the system.

Another solution based on stripe lengths was recently developed by Kawasaki et al. [32], who established a pattern of horizontal and vertical lines. In this work, the uniqueness of a specific location was coded in the spacing between horizontal lines (in blue); vertical lines (in red) were equally spaced. A peak detection algorithm was applied to locate the crossing points (dots) in the recovered image, and a posteriori comparison with distances to neighboring dots determined their positions in the projected pattern.

Ito and Ishii [29] did not use stripes or slits for coding; instead, they used a set of square cells (like a checkerboard) that had one out of three possible intensity values. Every node (intersection between four cells of the checkerboard) was associated with the intensity values of the forming cells. In order to differentiate nodes with the same subcode, epipolar constraints between the camera and the projector were employed.

The idea of using epipolar constraints was also applied in the work presented by Koninckx and Van Gool [35]. They proposed an adaptive system where green diagonal lines ("coding lines") were superimposed on a grid of vertical black lines ("base pattern"). If a coding line was not coincident with an epipolar line, intersections created with the base pattern would all have lain on different epipolar lines on the camera image. This determines a unique point in the projected pattern being able to perform the matching and the triangulation. A greater inclination of diagonal lines gave a higher density of the reconstruction, but a lower noise resistance. Therefore, the density of reconstruction could be chosen depending on how noisy the environment was, giving an adaptive robustness versus accuracy.

5.3.1.3 M-arrays

First presented by Etzion [14], M-arrays (perfect maps) are random arrays of dimensions $r \times v$ in which a submatrix of dimensions $n \times m$ appears only once in the whole pattern. Perfect maps are constructed theoretically with dimensions $rv = 2^{nm}$, but for real applications, the zero submatrix is not considered. This gives a total of $rv = 2^{nm} - 1$ unique submatrices in the pattern and a window property of $n \times m$. M-arrays represent in a two-dimensional space what De Bruijn patterns are in a one-dimensional space (see references

14 and 38 for more details). Choosing an appropriate window property will determine the robustness of the pattern against pattern occlusions and object shadows for a given application. Morita, Yajima, and Sakata [43] proposed a two-projection-based technique where an encoded matrix of black dots on a white background was projected; in the second projection some black dots were removed according to a binary-encoded M-array.

There are different approaches to represent nonbinary M-arrays, which are classified regarding the approach used to code the M-array: colored dots (color based) or geometric features like circles and stripes (feature based). For instance, Griffin, Narasimhan, and Yee [21] generated an array of 18×66 features using an alphabet of four words—1, 2, 3, 4—comparing color- and feature-based approaches. As the second approach is not color dependent, better results were obtained in the presence of colored objects. Morano et al. [42] used a brute force (not De Bruijn based) algorithm to generate the pattern. An iterative algorithm, adding one new code word and checking it against all the previous ones, was performed. If all the distances between values were at least equal to the specified minimum Hamming distance, the new word was accepted and the next iteration was followed, until the pattern was created. The directions in which the pattern was created are indicated in Figure 5.2.

This algorithm was used a posteriori by Pages et al. [45] to design a 20×20 M-array-based pattern with an alphabet of three symbols and a window property of 3×3. A color approach was used for the dots' codification, using red, green, and blue in order to separate them in the camera sensor. The decoding algorithm analyzed the four neighbors of every dot. Once this was done, a comparison between all possible combinations of eight neighbors was performed in order to locate the recorded dot univocally in the projected pattern and perform the triangulation.

A different approach was followed by Albitar, Graebling, and Doignon [2], who used a 3×3 window property and three different symbols (black circle, circumference, and stripe) to represent the code word. As no color codification was employed, this solution presented robustness against colored objects. In the detection step, orientation of the projected pattern was extracted from the direction of the projected stripes. Once this was done, location of the symbols in the projected pattern was accomplished. Albitar et al. employed this method to create a 3D scan for medical imaging purposes (scanning of parts of the body), stating that this one-shot technique was robust against occlusions (up to a certain limit) and suitable for moving scenarios.

5.3.2 Time Multiplexing

Time multiplexing methods are based on the code word created by the successive projection of patterns onto the object surface. Therefore, the code word associated with a position in the image is not completely formed until all patterns have been projected. Usually, the first projected pattern corresponds to the most significant bit, following a coarse-to-fine paradigm. Accuracy

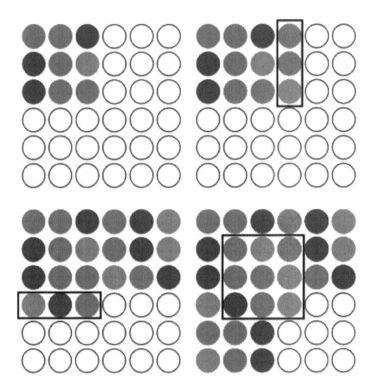

FIGURE 5.2
(See color insert.) Code generation direction followed by Morano et al. with colored spots representation. (Morano, R. A. et al. *IEEE Transactions on Pattern Analysis and Machine Intelligence* 20 (3): 322–327, 1998. With permission.)

directly depends on the number of projections, as every pattern introduces finer resolution in the image. In addition, code word bases tend to be small, providing higher resistance against noise. There are several approaches in sparse time multiplexing, which are explored here.

5.3.2.1 Temporal Binary Codes

These codes were first proposed by Posdamer and Altschuler [48] in 1982. A sequence of patterns with black and white stripes was projected onto the object. The number of stripes increased by two in every pattern, following a coarse-to-fine strategy. Therefore, the length of the code word was given by 2^m bits, where m was the total number of projected patterns. An edge detection algorithm was employed to localize the transition between two consecutive stripes (black/white or vice versa). Moreover, Hamming distance between the code words of two adjacent points could be maximized to reduce errors in the detection step, as was proposed by Minou, Kanade, and Sakai [40].

5.3.2.2 Temporal n-ary Codes

Based on the use of n-ary codes, Caspi, Kiryati, and Shamir [9] proposed a color-based pattern where n^m stripes were coded in RGB space. The parameters to set were the number of colors to be used (N), the number of patterns to be projected (M), and the noise immunity factor alpha (α). For the calibration step, Caspi et al. proposed a reflectivity model given by the following equation:

$$\underbrace{\begin{bmatrix} R \\ G \\ B \end{bmatrix}}_{\vec{C}} = \underbrace{\begin{bmatrix} a_{rr} & a_{rg} & a_{rb} \\ a_{gr} & a_{gg} & a_{gb} \\ a_{br} & a_{bg} & a_{bb} \end{bmatrix}}_{A} \underbrace{\begin{bmatrix} k_r & 0 & 0 \\ 0 & k_g & 0 \\ 0 & 0 & k_b \end{bmatrix}}_{K} \vec{P} \underbrace{\left\{ \begin{bmatrix} r \\ g \\ b \end{bmatrix} \right\}}_{\vec{c}} + \underbrace{\begin{bmatrix} R_0 \\ G_0 \\ B_0 \end{bmatrix}}_{\vec{C}_0} \tag{5.3}$$

where

$\vec{c}$ is the projected instruction for a given color

$\vec{P}$ is the nonlinear transformation from projected instruction to the projected intensities for every RGB channel

A is the projector–camera coupling matrix

K is the reflectance matrix (constant reflectance in every RGB channel is assumed)

$\vec{C}_0$ is the reading of the camera under ambient light

5.3.2.3 Temporal Hybrid Codes

In order to reduce the number of projections, Ishii et al. [28] proposed a system where temporal and spatial coding were combined. The level of spatial or temporal dependence was given by the speed and accuracy requirements. For a given pixel $p(x, y)$ at time t of the projected pattern, the value was determined by using the following equation:

$$I(x, y, t) = G\left(\hat{I} \frac{x}{m} + t^\circ (\operatorname{mod} n), y \right) \tag{5.4}$$

where

$$G(k, y) = G\left(\hat{I} \frac{2^k y}{I_y} + \frac{1}{2} \circ (\operatorname{mod} 2) \right) \tag{5.5}$$

G is a binary image obtained from a camera at time t

n is the space code size

m is the light pattern width in the x direction

I_y is the image size in the y direction

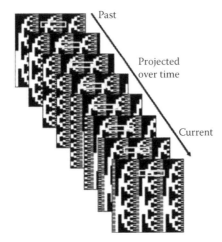

	2	3	4	5	6	7	0
2	3	4	5	6	7	0	1
3	4	5	6	7	0	1	2
4	5	6	7	0	1	2	3
5	6	7	0	1	2	3	4
6	7	0	1	2	3	4	5
7	0	1	2	3	4	5	6
0	1	2	3	4	5	6	7

FIGURE 5.3
Spatiotemporal algorithm proposed by Ishii et al. (Ishii, I. et al. *IEEE/RSJ International Conference on Intelligent Robots and Systems (IROS)*, 925–930, 2007. With permission.)

There were n selectable code values for a pixel at time t, depending on the importance of temporal encoding or spatial encoding. As shown in Figure 5.3, combination of temporal and spatial information can be done from total temporal encoding (represented by $p = 1$) to total spatial encoding (given by $p = 8$). The parameter p is called the space coding weighter, as it provides an idea of how temporal or spatial the codification is.

5.4 Dense Reconstruction Methods

This group of techniques provides 3D reconstruction of all the pixels captured by the image device. It is constituted by discrete or continuous shifting patterns, frequency patterns, and spatial grading, showing continuous variations on intensity or color throughout one axis or two axes. Among these methods, the use of periodic and absolute patterns can be found. Periodic patterns are used in time multiplexing shifting methods and in frequency multiplexing. Additionally, absolute patterns are based on spatial grading.

5.4.1 Time Multiplexing

The same concept of time multiplexing in sparse reconstruction techniques is applied for dense reconstruction approaches. Dense time multiplexing is represented by shifting techniques with discrete and continuous patterns.

5.4.1.1 Discrete Shifting Methods

There are some discrete implementations that use the shifting of patterns to obtain dense reconstructions. This is the case of Sansoni, Carocci, and Rodella [59], Guhring [23], and Zhang, Curless, and Seitz [72]. The proposals of Sansoni et al. and Guhring projected a set of black and white striped patterns (as in binary codes). Afterward, the work of Sansoni et al. projected four shifted versions of the last pattern, while Guhring's proposal projected shifted versions of a slit-based pattern covering every pixel in the image. Binary patterns provided an absolute location of the information given by shifted patterns, avoiding ambiguities in the decoding step. Using a different strategy, Zhang et al. employed color to project De Bruijn sequences, which are smoothed and shifted versions of the same pattern. The smoothing process provided subpixel accuracy to this method. In order to avoid errors due to occlusions and discontinuities, multipass dynamic programming (a variance of the dynamic programming proposed by Chen et al. [10]) was employed to match observed to projected patterns.

5.4.1.2 Continuous Phase-Shifting Methods

When projecting a sinusoidal grating onto a surface, every point along a line parallel to the coding axis can be characterized by a unique phase value. Any nonflat 3D shape will cause a deformation in the recorded pattern with respect to the projected one, which is recorded as a phase deviation. This phase deviation provides information about the illuminated shape. By matching the recovered image with the projected pattern, the object shape is recovered. The pattern must be shifted and projected several times in order to extract the phase deviation (this is not the case with frequency multiplexing approaches). Due to the grayscale nature of the projected patterns, they present advantages like resistance to ambient light and resistance to reflection variation. Depending on the number of frequencies used to create the pattern, we can distinguish between simple and multiple phase-shifting (PS) methods.

5.4.1.2.1 Single Phase Shifting

Single phase-shifting (SPS) techniques use only one frequency to create the sequence of patterns. In order to recover phase deviation, the pattern is projected several times; every projection is shifted from the previous projection by a factor of $2\pi/N$, with N the total number of projections, as shown in the following equation (superindex P indicates the projected pattern):

$$I_n^p\left(y^p\right) = A^p + B^p \cos\left(2\pi f_0 y^p - 2\pi n/N\right) \tag{5.6}$$

where A^p and B^p are the projection constants and (x^p, y^p) are the projection coordinates, $n = 0, 1, \ldots N$. The received intensity values from the object surface, once the set of patterns is projected, is

$$I_n(x, y) = \alpha(x, y) \left[A + B \cos\left(2\pi f_o y^p + \phi(x, y) - 2\pi n/N\right) \right] \qquad (5.7)$$

As can be observed from Equation (5.7), it suffers of intensity and phase deviation; it is necessary to cancel the effect of a different albedo ($\alpha(x, y)$) to extract the phase correctly. This is shown in the following equation:

$$\phi(x, y) = \arctan \left[\frac{\sum_{n=1}^{N} I_n(x, y) \sin\left(2\pi n/N\right)}{\sum_{n=1}^{N} I_n(x, y) \cos\left(2\pi n/N\right)} \right] \qquad (5.8)$$

From a minimum of three projected shifted patterns it is possible to create a relative phase map and to reconstruct the phase deviation caused by the object shape. However, the arctangent function returns values in the range $(-\pi, \pi]$ and therefore a phase unwrapping procedure is necessary to work with a nonambiguous phase value out of the wrapped phase. This is the reason why these patterns provide effective dense reconstruction only under the restriction of smoothed surfaces.

Phase-shifting methods have been used in a variety of applications during the last years. For instance, Ono et al. [44] created the so-called correlation image sensor (CIS), a device that generates temporal correlations between light intensity and three external reference signals on each pixel using phase shifting and a space–temporal unwrapping. Some approaches using phase shifting have also been developed from the work proposed by Srinivasan, Liu, and Halious [61].

One of the drawbacks of phase-shifting methods is the necessity to project several patterns in time, which is more than the theoretic minimum of three patterns considered for real conditions. A solution to reduce the total time required in the projection step is to multiplex the patterns either in color space or in frequency. Following this idea, Wust and Capson [70] proposed a method that projected three overlapping sinusoidal patterns shifted 90° and coded in red, green, and blue. Therefore, in this way the camera recorded phase deviation of every pattern in a different color channel and a normal phase extraction algorithm, like the one shown in the following equation:

$$\Phi(x, y) = \arctan \left(\frac{I_r - I_g}{I_g - I_b} \right) \qquad (5.9)$$

where $\Phi(x, y)$ is the phase of a given pixel, and I_r, I_g, and I_b are the red, green, and blue intensities, respectively.

A different approach was proposed by Guan, Hassebrook, and Lau [22], where the patterns were combined in frequency using the orthogonal

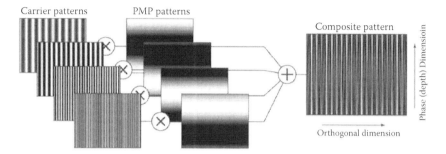

FIGURE 5.4
Composite pattern formed by the multiplexation of modulated phase shifting profilometry (PMP) patterns using the algorithm of Guan et al. (Guan, C. et al. *Optics Express* 11 (5): 406–417, 2003. WIth permission.)

dimension, as shown in Figure 5.4. Basically, traditional band pass filtering was performed on the recorded pattern, as is theoretically done in communications for frequency multiplexing. This step filters noise without suppressing the information hold in the surroundings of the carriers. In particular, Guan et al. [22] used a maximally flat magnitude Butterworth filter. Once this step was done, a normal phase extraction was performed over the obtained patterns. This method provided higher signal-to-noise ratio than color multiplexing approaches and it was not dependent on the surface color. However, some errors arose in the presence of a different albedo and abrupt shape variations.

5.4.1.2.2 Multiple Phase Shifting

The use of more than one frequency in phase shifting comes to cope with the uncertainty created in the extracted wrapped phase. As stated in the remainder theorem [52], an absolute phase map can be computed from two different relative phase maps with frequencies that are relative prime numbers. This principle was used by Gushov and Solodkin [24] for interferometry, where an interferometer able to deal with vibrations or relief parameters was constructed. More recently, Pribanic, Dapo, and Salvi [49] presented a technique based on multiple phase shifting (MPS) where only two patterns were used to create the relative phase maps. Two sinusoidal patterns were shifted and projected in time, in order to recover phase deviation (see Figure 5.5). From these sets of images it was possible to obtain two relative phase maps, using normal phase-shifting decoding algorithms (as shown in Equation 5.8). With this, the absolute phase map was recovered. This map can be directly compared to the ideal phase-shifting map, providing correspondences for the triangulation step. The algorithm was tested for different pairs of frequencies over a flat surface. Finally, the reconstruction of a footprint and a face were pursued, providing small 3D reconstruction errors.

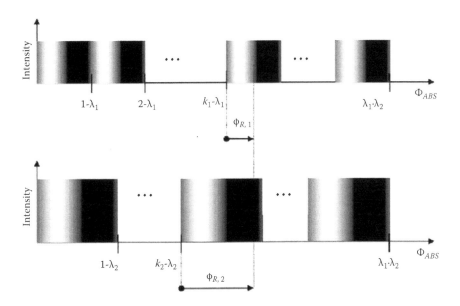

FIGURE 5.5
Pair of projected sinusoidal patterns with two different frequencies (k is the number of periods).

5.4.2 Frequency Multiplexing

Frequency multiplexing methods group all the techniques where phase decoding is performed in the frequency domain rather than in the spatial domain. There are different approaches depending on the frequency analysis performed on the image. Traditionally, Fourier methods have been used for this purpose, although wavelet-based methods have also been studied.

5.4.2.1 Fourier Transform

Fourier transform (FT) was introduced to solve the necessity of having a phase-shifting-based method for moving scenarios. FT was first proposed by Takeda and Mutoh [64], who extracted depth from one single projected pattern. A sinusoidal grating was projected onto the object, and the reflected deformed pattern was recorded. The projected signal for a sinusoidal grating was represented by

$$I_n^p\left(y^p\right) = A^p + B^p \cos\left(2\pi f_\phi y^p\right) \tag{5.10}$$

Once reflected onto the object, the phase component was modified by the shape of the object, thus giving an intensity value expressed as

$$I\left(x,y\right) = \alpha\left(x,y\right)\left[A + B\cos\left(2\pi f_\phi y^p + \phi\left(x,y\right)\right)\right]_p \tag{5.11}$$

The phase component must be isolated to extract shape information. This was achieved performing a frequency filtering in the Fourier domain. The background component was suppressed and a translation in frequency was done to bring the carrier component (which holds the phase information) to the zero frequency axis. When the following sequence of equations is applied, the phase can be extracted from the signal. First, the input signal was rewritten as

$$I(x,y) = a(x,y) + c(x,y)e^{2\pi i f_0 y^p} + c^*(x,y)e^{-2\pi i f_0 y^p} \tag{5.12}$$

where

$$c(x,y) = \frac{1}{2}b(x,y)e^{i\phi(x,y)} \tag{5.13}$$

where $c^*(x,y)$ is the complex value of constant $c(x,y)$. Finally, the phase component was extracted from the imaginary part of the following equation:

$$\log[c(x,y)] = \log\left[\left(\frac{1}{2}\right)b(x,y)\right] + i\phi \tag{5.14}$$

The obtained phase component range is $(-\pi, \pi]$, and it is necessary to apply an unwrapping algorithm in order to obtain a continuous phase related to the object. Once the phase was unwrapped, the relative depth information was extracted using

$$h(x,y) = L \cdot \frac{\Delta\phi(x,y)}{\left(\Delta\phi(x,y) - 2\pi f_0 d\right)} \tag{5.15}$$

where L is the distance to the reference plane and d is the distance between the camera and the projector devices.

FT has been widely used in industrial applications. For instance, Cobelli et al. [13] used FT for global measurement of water waves. In their work, two sources of noise were considered in the filtering step. The first one was related to illumination inhomogeneities of background variations over the field of view, which remains present as an additive variation. The second one was due to the local surface reflectivity. As this reflection varies much more slowly than the sinusoidal modulation impinged on the surface, it can also be treated as background noise. Thus, both sources of noise can be suppressed using the background component filtering procedure proposed by Takeda and Mutoh [64]. Due to the periodic nature of the projected pattern,

this method was constrained by the maximum reconstructible slope given
by

$$\left| \frac{\partial h(x,y)}{\partial x} \right|_{max} < \frac{L}{3d} \qquad (5.16)$$

In order to increase this slope limitation, Li, Su, and Guo [36] proposed the
so-called π-phase-shifting FT. Two sinusoidal patterns were projected using
this method; the second one was a half-period shifted version of the first one.
This solution multiplies by three the detectable range in depth slope. This
principle was used by Hu and He [25] to scan moving objects that had uniform velocity (as in an assembly line). In their work, two scan line cameras
were used, and one single pattern was projected. The distance between the
two cameras corresponded to half the period of the grating. As the velocity of
the object was known, matching two scannings of the same point at different
instants of time could be done. This procedure avoids the projecting of two
patterns and takes advantage of the uniform motion present in assembly lines.

There are some proposals that combine both π-phase-shifting FT patterns
in one single projected pattern using color or frequency multiplexing. For
instance, Chen et al. [11] used color space to project a bicolor sinusoidal fringe
pattern consisting of the sum of π-phase-shifting FT patterns represented by
blue and green patterns. Another approach was considered by Yue, Su, and
Liu [71]. In this work the same principle used by Guan et al. for phase shifting
was developed for FT. Appropriate carrier frequencies were chosen regarding
the characteristics of the projector and camera used, assuming that the Nyquist
sampling theorem was satisfied. These frequencies were kept away from zero
frequency as much as possible. When the results are analyzed, the standard
deviation error is slightly lower than for normal FT, while accuracy remains
unaltered.

In case of scanning coarse objects where discontinuities and speckle-like
structures can appear, two-dimensional (2D) FT filtering must be used [62], as
it permits better separation of the desired information from noise. This is due
to the fact that noise is normally in two dimensions distributed in a fringe
pattern, having a spectra scattered in a 2D frequency domain. For instance,
Hung and more recently Lin and Su [37] proposed a method for 2D FT scanning where the filtering step, aimed to prevent frequency spreading, was performed using a 2D Hanning window. However, some other filters that have
similar characteristics can also be used. This is the case of Chen et al. [12],
who applied a Gaussian filter. Two-dimensional FT filtering has been used
by Berryman et al. [6] to create a low-cost automated system to measure the
three-dimensional shape of the human back, obtaining an accuracy of ±1 mm.

Spatial phase detection (SPD) constitutes an alternative to FT that was initially proposed by Toyooka and Iwaasa [67]. The analysis of the received
signal (Equation 5.17) is done using the sine and cosine functions, as can be
observed in Equations (5.18) and (5.20).

$$I(x,y) = \alpha(x,y)\left[a + B\cos\left(2\pi fy^p + \phi(x,y)\right)\right] \tag{5.17}$$

$$I_c(x,y) = \alpha(x,y)\left[A + B\cos\left(2\pi fy^p + \phi(x,y)\right)\right]\cdot\cos\left(2\pi fy^p\right) \tag{5.18}$$

$$= \alpha(x,y)\cdot A\cos\left(2\pi fy^p\right) + \frac{1}{2}\alpha(x,y)\cdot B\cos\left(4\pi fy^p + \frac{1}{2}\alpha(x,y)\cdot B\cos\left(\phi(x,y)\right)\right) \tag{5.19}$$

$$I_s(x,y) = \alpha(x,y)\left[A + B\cos\left(2\pi fy^p + \phi(x,y)\right)\right]\cdot\sin\left(2\pi fy^p\right) \tag{5.20}$$

$$= \alpha(x,y)\cdot A\sin\left(2\pi fy^p\right) + \frac{1}{2}\alpha(x,y)\cdot B\sin\left(4\pi fy^p + \frac{1}{2}\alpha(x,y)\cdot B\sin\left(\phi(x,y)\right)\right) \tag{5.21}$$

Now, $\phi(x, y)$ varies more slowly than any term containing f, so only the last term in each new function is a low-frequency term. This part of the function can then be extracted by low-pass filtering. Regarding Euler's formula for the sine and cosine functions and the principles of Fourier transform applied on sinusoidal functions [50], this step provides similar results to obtaining the real and the imaginary components of the Fourier transform applied to the incoming signal. Therefore, the last step is to extract the phase component from these components, which is obtained by applying the arctangent function:

$$\phi(x,y) = \arctan\left[\frac{r(x,y)*I_s(x,y)}{r(x,y)*I_c(x,y)}\right] \tag{5.22}$$

where $r(x, y)$ represents a low-pass filter and $*$ denotes convolution. It is important to note that Toyooka and Iwaasa use integration to extract the phase terms, whereas other authors using related spatial domain methods apply different low-pass filters [5]. As in FT, this method suffers from leakage distortion when working with fringe patterns, as no local analysis is performed to avoid spreading errors due to discontinuities and different albedo.

5.4.2.2 *Window Fourier Transform*

The task of suppressing the zero component and avoiding the frequency overlapping between background and data (the leakage distortion problem) has also been studied using other frequency-based approaches.

This is the case of the windowed Fourier transform (WFT; also called the Gabor transform), which splits the signal into segments before the analysis in frequency domain is performed. The received signal is filtered applying the WFT analysis transform shown in Equations (5.23) and (5.25).

$$Sf(u,v,\xi,\eta) = \int_{-\infty}^{\infty}\int_{-\infty}^{\infty} f(x,y)\cdot g(x-u,y-v)\cdot\exp(-j\xi x - j\eta y)\,dx\,dy \text{ is } (x,y) \quad (5.23)$$

(ξ, η) are the translation and frequency coordinates, respectively, and $g(x, y)$ is the windowing function

When $g(x, y)$ is a Gaussian window, the WFT is called a Gabor transform; that is,

$$g(x,y) = \frac{1}{\sqrt{\pi\sigma_x\sigma_y}}\cdot\exp\left(-\frac{x^2}{2\sigma_x^2} - \frac{y^2}{2\sigma_y^2}\right) \quad (5.24)$$

where σ_x and σ_y are the standard deviations of the Gaussian function in x and y, respectively.

Equation (5.23) provides the four-dimensional (4D) coefficients $Sf(u, v, \xi, \eta)$ corresponding to the 2D input image. The windowing permits the WFT to provide frequency information of a limited region around each pixel. The Gaussian window is often chosen as it provides the smallest Heisenberg box [34]. Once the 4D coefficients are computed, the phase can be extracted. There are two main techniques for phase extraction in WFT: windowed Fourier filtering (WFF) and windowed Fourier ridge (WFR). In WFF the 4D coefficients are first filtered, suppressing the small coefficients (in terms of its amplitude) that correspond to noise effects. The inverse WFT is then applied to obtain a smooth image:

$$\overline{f(x,y)} = \int_{-\infty}^{\infty}\int_{-\infty}^{\infty}\int_{-\eta_1}^{\eta_h}\int_{-\xi_1}^{\xi_h} \overline{Sf(u,v,\xi,\eta)}\cdot g_{u,v,\xi,\eta}(x,y)\,d\xi\,d\eta\,du\,dv \quad (5.25)$$

where

$$\overline{Sf(u,v,\xi,\eta)} = \begin{cases} Sf(u,v,\xi,\eta) \text{ if } |Sf(u,v,\xi,\eta)| > \text{threshold} \\ 0 \text{ if } |Sf(u,v,\xi,\eta)| < \text{threshold} \end{cases} \quad (5.26)$$

The estimated frequencies $\omega_x(x, y)$ and $\omega_y(x, y)$ and corresponding phase distribution are obtained from the angle given by the filtered WFF, as explained in Kemao [34]. In WFR, however, the estimated frequencies are extracted from the maximum of the spectrum amplitude:

$$\left[\omega_x(u,v),\omega_y(u,v)\right] = \arg\max_{\xi,\eta}|Sf(u,v,\xi,\eta)| \quad (5.27)$$

The phase can be directly obtained from the angle of the spectrum for those frequency values selected by the WFR (phase from ridges) or integrating the frequencies (phase by integration). Phases from ridges represent a better solution than phases from integration (despite some phase correction that may need to be applied [34]), as phases from integration errors are accumulated and lead to large phase deviations.

Using WFT, Chen et al. [11] proposed its use (Gabor transform) to eliminate the zero spectrum. However, as was demonstrated by Gdeisat, Burton, and Lalor [19], Chen and colleagues' technique was not able to eliminate the zero spectrum in fringe patterns that have large bandwidths or in cases where the existence of large levels of speckle noise corrupts the fringe patterns. This is mainly caused by an erroneous selection of the width and shape of the window for the Fourier analysis. The window size must be small enough to reduce the errors introduced by boundaries, holes, and background illumination; at the same time, it must be big enough to hold some periods and hence allow the detection of the main frequency to perform an optimal filtering. This problem is studied in the work of Fernandez et al. [16], where an automatic algorithm for the optimal selection of the window size using adapted mother wavelets is proposed. However, in applications where the frequency varies considerably during the analysis (in space or in time), this trade-off is difficult to achieve and noise arises due to an incorrect frequency detection.

5.4.2.3 Wavelet Transform

Wavelet transform (WT) was proposed to solve the aforementioned trade-off. In WT the window size increases when the frequency to analyze decreases, and vice versa. This allows removal of the background illumination and prevents the propagation of errors produced during the analysis, which remain confined in the corrupted regions alone [19]. Additionally, the leakage effects are reduced, avoiding large errors at the edges of the extracted phase maps. The continuous wavelet transform (CWT) is a subfamily of WT that performs the transformation in the continuous domain. Moreover, it is common to use CWT with complex wavelets for the analysis of the fringe patterns [1]. The one-dimensional (1D)-CWT algorithm analyzes the fringe pattern on a row-by-row basis, whereas the 2D-CWT algorithm is an extension of the analysis to the two-dimensional space. In 2D analysis, a 4D transform is obtained from WT. (The daughter wavelets are obtained by translation, dilation, and rotation of the previously selected mother wavelet).

Once this is performed, phase extraction is pursued using the phase from ridges or the phase by integration algorithms, also named phase estimation and frequency estimation (similarly to WFT). As in WFT, it has been proven that the phase from ridges provides better results than the phase from integration, due to the accumulative effect in the phase from the integration algorithm [1]. The work done by Gdeisat et al. [19] applied a two-dimensional wavelet function to the recovered image, based on the phase from ridge extraction. Rotation and scale were considered jointly with x and y coordinates resulting in a four-dimensional wavelet transform. To apply the transformation, the mother wavelet $\psi(x, y)$ must satisfy the admissibility condition. Under this condition Gdeisat et al. used a differential of Gaussian as the mother wavelet; Zhang, Chen, and Tang [73] employed a 2D complex Morlet wavelet. Four subimages were created at one iteration of the wavelet decomposition algorithm corresponding to the low and high frequencies in both axes. The phase component was extracted from the ridge information present in the corresponding high-frequency subimage. The task of choosing appropriate values for rotation and scale parameters determined the results of filtering and phase extraction.

Related to this, a novel method for choosing the adaptive level of discrete wavelet decomposition has been proposed by Zhang et al. [73]. They have achieved higher accuracy in the principal frequency estimation and low-frequency energy suppression against traditional zero suppression algorithms used in FT. More recently, Salvi, Fernandez, and Pribanic [54] proposed a colored one-shot fringe pattern based on 2D wavelet analysis. This work proposes a color-based coding strategy to face the problem of phase unwrapping. Using a combination of color fringes at some specific frequencies with a unique relation between them, it is possible to obtain the absolute phase without any uncertainties in the recovered depth. However, there are some problems related to the relationship between the window size and the frequency of the fringes. In WT, the window size increases when the horizontal or vertical fringe frequencies decrease.

This can be troublesome for the analysis of some fringe patterns where the carrier frequency is extremely low or high, as was pointed out by Kemao et al. [33]. Moreover, in computational applications, a dyadic net is used to generate the set of wavelet functions. That is, the size of the wavelet is modified by the factor 2^j. This can lead to some problems in applications like fringe pattern analysis, where the change in the spatial fringe frequencies throughout the image is not high enough to produce a relative variance of 2^j in the size of the optimal wavelet.

5.4.2.3.1 The Problem of Phase Unwrapping

Phase unwrapping represents a crucial step in frequency multiplexing techniques. In absence of noise, if all phase variations between neighboring pixels are less than π, the phase unwrapping procedure can be reduced to add the corresponding multiple of 2π when a discontinuity appears. Unfortunately, noise, local shadows, undersampling, fringe discontinuities, and irregular surface brightness make the unwrapping procedure much more difficult to solve. Plenty of approaches have been presented [3, 69]. For instance, phase unwrapping based on modulation follows an iterative algorithm, starting from the pixel with higher intensity value and comparing it to the pixels inside a 3 × 3 surrounding square region. The comparison step is done one by one, queuing the affected pixels from maximum to minimum intensity.

This method can also be applied when dealing with moving objects, substituting the searching area to a 3 × 3 × 3 voxel.

Additionally, Wu and Peng [69] presented a phase unwrapping algorithm based on region growing. The phase was unwrapped from the smoothest area to the surroundings according to a linear estimation. In order to decrease the error, a quality map was used to guide the unwrapping. The map can be defined in different ways as far as it provides quality information. For instance, second-order partial derivative can be used to determine the pixels to unwrap—that is, those pixels having this value lower than a specified threshold. Statistical methods can also be used to consider the variance within a mask for every pixel. Finally, Gorthi and Lolla [20] projected an extra color-coded pattern, which can be univocally identified once the image is captured, thus giving rough information about the required phase to add or subtract in the unwrapping step. A further explanation of different unwrapping methods used in profilometry can be found in Judge and Bryanston-Cross [31].

5.4.2.3.2 *Alternatives to Sinusoidal Grating*

Not all frequency transform methods use sinusoidal fringes for the projected pattern. As Huang et al. [27] stated, structured-light techniques based on sinusoidal phase-shifting methods have the advantage of pixel-level resolution, large dynamic range, and few errors due to defocusing. However, the arctangent computation makes them relatively slow. As an alternative, they used three 120° phase-shifted trapezoidal fringe patterns. The phase deviation was extracted from the so-called intensity ratio image:

$$r(x,y) = \frac{I_{med}(x,y) - I_{min}(x,y)}{I_{max}(x,y) - I_{min}(x,y)} \quad (5.28)$$

where $I_{min}(x,y)$, $I_{med}(x,y)$, and $I_{max}(x,y)$ are the minimum, median, and maximum intensities of the three patterns for the image point (x, y). Image defocus does not cause major errors when using a sinusoidal pattern, as it is still sinusoidal when the image is defocused. However, errors caused by blurring have to be taken into account when dealing with trapezoidal patterns. Modeling these errors as a Gaussian filtering, Huang and colleagues' experiments yielded defocusing errors not bigger than 0.6%. More recently, another approach using triangular patterns has been proposed by Jia, Kofman, and English [30]. This approach used only two triangular patterns shifted half the period, making it more feasible to be implemented in real-time applications. Ronchi grating has also been used in pattern projection as an alternative to sinusoidal grating. This is the case of Lin and Su [37], who proposed an algorithm where only one pattern was needed. Phase information was obtained taking the imaginary part of

$$\Delta\Phi(x,y) = \log\left[\hat{I}(x,y)\hat{I}_0^*(x,y)\right] \quad (5.29)$$

where $\hat{I}(x,y)$ and $\hat{I}_0(x,y)$ are the recorded illuminance from the setup and the reference plane, respectively. A Ronchi grating was also used by Spagnolo et al. [60] in real applications, in order to recover 3D reconstructions of artwork surfaces.

5.4.3 Spatial Multiplexing (Grading Methods)

Grading methods refer to all techniques containing the entire code word for a given position only in the pixel value. Therefore, the resolution can be as high as the pixel resolution of the projector device is. However, these methods suffer from high sensitivity to noise and low sensitivity to surface changes, due to the short distances between the code words of adjacent pixels. This is the reason why some authors use methods introducing temporal redundancy, projecting the same pattern several times. As a drawback, note that restriction to static scenarios is imposed when more than one pattern is projected. There are two main techniques based on grading methods: grayscale-based patterns and color-based patterns. Regarding grayscale-based methods, Carrihill and Hummel [8] proposed a linear grayscale wedge spread going from white to black, along the vertical axis. The authors achieved a mean error of 1 cm, due to the high sensitivity to noise and nonlinearity of the projector device. In color-based patterns, the pixel is coded using color instead of grayscale values. As a drawback, color calibration is required. Tajima and Iwakawa [63] presented a rainbow pattern codified in the vertical axis. In order to project this spectrum, a nematic liquid crystal was used to diffract white light. Two images were projected to suppress the effect of colored surfaces.

5.5 One-Shot Dense Reconstruction Using De Bruijn Coding and WFT

As can be observed, the main contributions in SL done during the last years rely on the fields of real-time response (that is, one-shot pattern projection) and dense projection. Some one-shot techniques obtain dense reconstruction; this is the case of many frequency multiplexing-based techniques and spatial grading. However, both groups present some problems in 3D reconstruction. The former fails under presence of discontinuities and slopes of the 3D surface, suffering from errors due to the periodicity of the projected fringes in the unwrapping step. Additionally, the latter presents low-accuracy results due to the high sensitivity to noise and low sensitivity to surface changes. Moreover, as can be extracted from the work of Salvi et al. [57], the best results in terms of accuracy are obtained by De Bruijn-based techniques for one-shot pattern projection.

However, De Bruijn codes are present only in sparse reconstruction algorithms. The new method presented in this section attempts to solve this problem. The proposed algorithm uses a De Bruijn codification integrated with a fringe pattern projection and consequent frequency analysis. Therefore, it is possible to obtain the accuracy provided by a classical De Bruijn stripe pattern and the density of the reconstruction provided in fringe pattern analysis. To this end, a set of colored fringes is projected on the object. The color of these fringes is established following a De Bruijn codification. The analysis of the recovered image is done in two different ways: one for De Bruijn decoding and another for windowed Fourier transform. A general scheme of the proposed algorithm is shown in Figure 5.6.

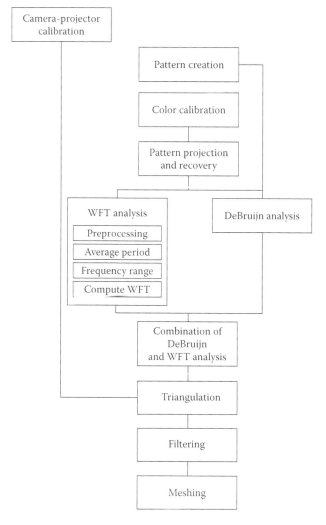

FIGURE 5.6
Diagram of the proposed algorithm.

5.5.1 Camera–Projector Calibration

Many camera calibration techniques can be found in the literature [2–5]. However, projector calibration has not been so widely studied, mainly due to the more limited field of application, which has dealt with custom application-oriented solutions. As Berryman et al. [6] stated, there are three different ways of modeling a projector. Among them, the plane structured-light model, which approximates the projector as the inverse of the pinhole camera model, is the most common. The establishment of 2D–3D point correspondences required for the projector calibration is not straightforward and usually requires specific projector calibrating patterns and nonautomatic image processing algorithms. Our proposal makes use of three different patterns: the printed checkerboard calibrating pattern (CCP), the projector calibrating pattern (PCP), and the projected CCP onto the PCP. For comparison, we have manufactured two PCPs. The first consists of a white plane in which a checkerboard pattern has been printed at one of the corners of the plane (PCP1). The second consists of a white plane in which a checkered row of points has been printed all along the perimeter of the plane (PCP2). Both patterns are shown in Figure 5.7.

First, the camera is calibrated using the printed CCP and Bouguet's implementation of Zhang's technique [2]. The camera is modeled according to the pinhole camera model, where a given 2D image point, $\hat{m} = [u, v, 1]$, and a 3D object point, $\hat{M} = [X, Y, Z, 1]$, are related by $s\hat{m} = A \cdot [R t] \hat{M}$, where s is an arbitrary scale factor and A and $[R\ t]$ are the camera intrinsic and extrinsic matrices, respectively. Also, lens distortion is modeled considering both linear and nonlinear distortion up to six levels of radial and tangential distortion.

FIGURE 5.7
The left column shows the printed CCP. The middle column shows the PCP1 (top) and PCP2 (bottom). The right column shows one view of the projected CCP on PCP1 and PCP2, respectively.

Second, we place the world coordinate system at the camera center and we face the projector calibration. The projector projects another CCP (similar to the one used for camera calibration) on the white area of the PCP. Then, the PCP is shown to the camera making sure that it is placed at many different positions and orientations, as done in camera calibration, and an image I_i is taken for every PCP pose i.

Third, for every I_i, the PCP printed pattern is segmented and the PCP corner points in pixels extracted. Since the metric distance among these corner points on the PCP is known, the homography between the 2D corner points on the image and the 2D corner points on the PCP is computed. A proper algorithm considering both linear and nonlinear distortion is applied.

Fourth, for every I_i, the CCP pattern projected on the white area of the PCP is segmented and the CCP corner points on the image extracted. Using the previous homography, the projection of these corner points on the PCP is computed, obtaining a set of 3D corner points in metrics. Their 2D correspondences in pixels are known since they are given by the corners on the CCP image projected by the projector device. The same pinhole model described for camera calibration is applied for the calibration of the projector. Therefore, Zhang's method is performed using the 2D–3D correspondences for all I_i, $i = 1...n$, thus obtaining the optimized intrinsic and extrinsic parameters for the projector. Note that radial and tangential distortion parameters are computed considering nondistorted 2D points and distorted projected 3D points inversely to those used for camera calibration.

5.5.2 Pattern Creation

The first step in any SL technique is focused on the creation of the pattern to be projected on the measuring surface. The sequence of colors used in the fringes is selected using a De Bruijn-based sequence generator. As was mentioned in previous sections, a k-ary De Bruijn sequence of order n is a circular sequence $d_0, d_1, ..., d_{n^k-1}$ (length n^k) containing each substring of length k exactly once (window property of k). In our approach we set $n = 3$ as we work only with red, green, and blue colors. Moreover, we set the pattern to have 64 fringes—a convention given the pixel resolution of the projector and the camera. Therefore, $n^k \geq 64$, so we set the window property to $k = 4$. An algorithm performing the sequence generation provides us an arbitrary De Bruijn circular sequence $d_0, d_1, ..., d_{80}$.

The next step is to generate the colored fringes according to the color sequence. To this end, an HSI matrix is created and converted to RGB space. The intensity channel matrix is created from a sinusoidal vector with values from 0 to 255 and $n = 64$ periods in total for the image height. This vector defines every column in the intensity channel matrix. The hue channel matrix is created using the previously computed De Bruijn sequence. For all the pixels corresponding to the same period in the intensity channel matrix, this matrix is assigned to the same value of the De Bruijn sequence, starting

FIGURE 5.8
(See color insert.) Pattern of the proposed method; $m = 64$ sinusoidal fringes are coded in color using a De Bruijn code generator algorithm.

from the first element. Finally, the saturation channel matrix is set to the maximum value for all the pixels. The proposed pattern containing $m = 64$ fringes can be observed in Figure 5.8.

5.5.3 Color Calibration

Once the deformed pattern is captured by the camera, the first task is to split the three color channels obtained from the camera and perform a color enhancement to reduce the effect of albedo and cross talk in every color channel. To cope with this, a previous color calibration has been pursued. Different proposals of color calibration can be found in the literature [9, 41, 47, 51]. The most exhaustive work for SL was proposed by Caspi et al. [9], who developed a precise color calibration algorithm based on linearizing the projector–camera matrix and the surface reflectance matrix specific to every scene point projected into a camera pixel.

A simpler version of this method has been performed in our work. The proposed algorithm uses least-squares to linearize the combination matrix corresponding to the projector–camera pair and the surface reflectance matrices, in terms of response to color intensity, for each pixel in the received image and each color channel (red, green, and blue). For every pixel and every color channel, the projected intensity is increased linearly and the corresponding captured color is stored.

Figure 5.9 shows the projected and captured color values. As can be observed, the red channel suffers the higher cross talk effects, mainly when projecting green onto the image. This is compensated by the transformation matrix. A linear regression is computed that yields a matrix estimation of the projected color values for every received value. Having the set of three

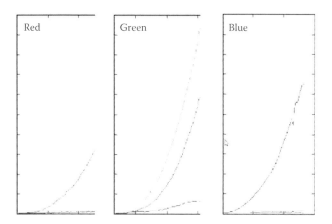

FIGURE 5.9
(See color insert.) Received color intensities for projected increasing values of red, green, and blue, respectively.

received color values—R_0, G_0, B_0—the estimated projected values R, G, B are given by Equation (5.30). It is important to note that this calibration has been done under the assumption that all objects have a reflectance similar to the flat-white Lambertian plane used for calibration, as only Lambertian white surface objects were analyzed.

$$\begin{bmatrix} R_0 \\ G_0 \\ B_0 \end{bmatrix} = \begin{bmatrix} a_{rr} & a_{rg} & a_{rb} \\ a_{gr} & a_{gg} & a_{gb} \\ a_{br} & a_{bg} & a_{bb} \end{bmatrix} \begin{Bmatrix} R \\ G \\ B \end{Bmatrix} \tag{5.30}$$

The matrix of Equation (5.30) represents the whole system (projector–camera) and aims to subtract the effect of cross talk between color channels. However, as it approximates the system as a linear transformation between projected and received images, some errors will persist due to nonlinearities. This is the reason why De Bruijn vocabulary was minimized to three colors, in order to maximize the Hamming distance between different colors in the hue channel.

5.5.4 Pattern Projection and Recovery

Once the deformed pattern is recovered by the camera and the color calibration has been pursued, an image processing step is applied. First, the color calibrated (corrected) RGB image is transformed to the HSV space. Afterward, a mask is created regarding the information held in the V plane. A closure morphological operation is applied, followed by a binarization. Those pixels exceeding the value given by the Otsu thresholding algorithm are selected as active pixels for the mask. Finally, the mask is applied separately to the corrected RGB image and to the V matrix. The masked V matrix is used in the WFT analysis, whereas the masked RGB image is the input of the De Bruijn detection algorithm.

5.5.5 Windowed Fourier Transform Analysis

A dense 3D reconstruction of the imaged scene (subjected to the robustness of the phase unwrapping) can be obtained extracting the phase of the recovered image. There are five different techniques used traditionally for phase extraction: phase measurement profilometry (PMP), SPD, FT, WFT, and WT. Among them, only those based on frequency analysis (FT, WFT, and WT) project one single shot and thus are able to work with moving objects. Regarding these frequency-based techniques, the main differences among them are related to the section of the imaged pattern that is considered in the frequency analysis. In the state of the art, FT performs a global analysis, which is appropriate for stationary signals with poor spatial localization. However, this is not the case in CSL, which is by nature limited in space and thus nonstationary. This fact led to the use of the other two frequency-based transforms (WFT and WT), which analyze local information in the imaged pattern.

WFT and WT are constituted by two main steps: windowing the imaged pattern in local patches and computing the transform at every local patch. The crucial point in these techniques relies on the necessity of selecting an optimal window size, which constitutes a trade-off between resolution in space and resolution in frequency. To this end, theoretical and practical comparisons were performed in the work of Fernandez et al. [16]. As stated in this work, the main difference between both techniques is the way the window size is set, depending on whether it has a fixed or a variable value. WT performs better with signals that have a wide range of frequencies with shorter correlation times for the higher frequencies than for the lower frequencies. This is the case in natural scenes, where low-frequency components usually last for longer durations than high-frequency components.

However, in fringe patterns, their periodicity and spatial extension do not depend on the selected frequency. Nevertheless, they mostly present spatial-harmonic components around the selected frequency. This is the reason why, despite many authors' claim of the goodness of WT [1, 19], some recent works state the best suitability of WFT [26, 34]. Another point to consider is the resistance to noise. It has been demonstrated [26] that, for noiseless fringe patterns, the frequency components can be accurately recovered in either small or large windows, regardless of the frequency value. However, in the presence of higher noise on the imaged fringe pattern, an optimal selection of the window size is crucial for filtering the noise while preserving the main frequency components.

Under these circumstances, the fixed window size of WFT performs better than the variable window size of WT. This is mainly due to the dyadic net used in practical applications of WT. This net changes the window size for adjacent levels of dilation geometrically (by two) and is excessive for some applications where the main frequency stands close to a fixed value (as in fringe pattern analysis). This is the reason why the WFT technique was selected for the analysis of the recovered pattern.

Another point to consider is the importance of selecting a window with good localization in both frequency and space, in order to perform an optimal analysis of the fringes. This point was also studied in the work of Fernandez et al. [16]. As a result, the Morlet wavelet adapted to WFT presented a better localization in the frequency domain than the others and was thus more suitable for demodulating fringe patterns with slow phase variations and relatively low signal-to-noise ratios. It must be mentioned that the adaptation of the Morlet wavelet to the use in WFT includes a normalization in frequency and size as, to preserve the value of energy provided by the WFT algorithm, a change in the window size must be compensated with an increment of the modulus of the signal. Finally, the ability to adapt the size of the wave envelope relative to the wave period must be considered. In wavelet analysis, this parameter is used to create a set of complex mother wavelets within the same wavelet family. In WFT, this is equivalent to changing the size of the window, as the preset frequency does not change with this size. Further information can be found in Fernandez et al. [16].

5.5.5.1 Preprocessing the Image

The preprocessing step consists of salt-and-pepper filtering and histogram equalization. This reduces the noise present in the captured image and enhances the image contrast for a later frequency component extraction, respectively. Finally, a DC filter is applied to extract the DC component of the image. This step delivers an enhanced image where the fringes are perceived more clearly.

5.5.5.2 Setting the Average Period and the Standard Deviation

This step represents the main idea of the automatic selection of the window. The algorithm extracts an approximated value of the number of periods existing in every line along the coding axis of the image. To do so, a local maximum extraction is performed for both maximum and the minimum values in every line along the coding axis. The algorithm avoids false positives by suppressing those local maxima that are not followed by a local minimum. Once the number of periods is extracted for every image column, an average of the global period, the corresponding frequency, and its variance are computed. This variance represents the uncertainty in the estimated frequency and is crucial to perform a global analysis of the image.

Regarding this point, a discussion about whether the selection of global or local variance for patches in the image is required needs to take place.

In principle, a local selection seems to be more appropriate, as it can distinguish frequencies of different patches. However, it requires more computation because the WFT must be applied in every patch. Using a global WFT and the appropriate range for the analytic frequencies, a trade-off to delete noisy frequencies and to preserve the ones related to the real shape must be set. This reduces the total number of WFTs to one, thus reducing the computational time.

5.5.5.3 Setting the Range of Frequencies and the Window

The selection of the appropriate range of frequencies is done according to the variance and the average values of the period. For instance, considering the range $[f_m - 3 \cdot std(f), f_m + 3 \cdot std(f)]$ in both x and y axes, the 95% of detected frequencies are analyzed, according to the central limit theorem [53]. The frequencies outbounding this range are considered outliers. In practice, this range can be reduced to $[fm - 2 \cdot std(f), fm + 2 \cdot std(f)]$ (90% of the frequencies are represented) without a significant loss in accuracy.

Another variable to consider is the window size related to the number of periods of the sinusoidal signal. In contrast to the mother wavelets in WT, WFT does not require the number of periods to be linked to the sinusoidal oscillation of the signal. In WT, the number of periods determines a mother wavelet within the same wavelet family and usually goes from one up to three or four periods, allowing information about the frequency to be held without losing local information. In WFT, though, the number of periods can be directly set from the definition of the signal. Our algorithm has tested from one up to three periods, determining the optimal value by the ridge extraction algorithm (WFR).

5.5.5.4 Computing the WFT

Once all the parameters are defined, the set of signals that have different sinusoidal frequencies and windows are convolved with the enhanced image. As a result, a 4D matrix is obtained (having dimensions of x and y axes, window size, and frequency). The WFR algorithm is then applied to compute the most likely values of window (w_x, w_y) and the corresponding phase value, delivering the wrapped phase in the interval $[-\pi, \pi]$.

5.5.6 De Bruijn

The corrected RGB image consists of a set of sinusoidal deformed color fringes coded following a certain De Bruijn structure. The aim of this step is to extract the color lines associated with every deformed color fringe. As mentioned, in the state of the art, multislit and striped 1D De Bruijn-based patterns can be found in the literature. When a multislit pattern is projected and reflected on the scene, the lines get smoothed, resulting in a Gaussian shape for every line in the recovered pattern. This scenario is similar to the one resulting after the projection of sinusoidal fringes, where the fringes are also sinusoidal (Gaussian like) when they are imaged by the camera. Therefore, our recovered pattern can be seen as a slit-based pattern in terms of the decoding process.

Following this idea, the localization of the maxima in every line must be found. This is done with subpixel accuracy, assuring that the total number of maxima found at every column does not exceed the number of fringes present in the pattern. The positions and color values of the maxima are used in the matching algorithm, which solves the correspondences through dynamic programming. Afterward, correspondences in every column are compared with the surrounding columns in order to detect errors in the matching procedure (due to an erroneous color extraction or a wrong matching process). The correction is done assuming color smoothness for single pixels in the image regarding the value of the surrounding pixels.

5.5.7 Combination of De Bruijn Pattern and Wrapped Phase Pattern

Having, on one hand, the wrapped phase of the recovered pattern and on the other hand the correspondences of the De Bruijn lines for every fringe in the pattern, the next step is to merge them into a correspondence map containing all the pixels present in the recovered pattern. This is done assuming that the subpixel accuracy provided by the De Bruijn slit-based decoding algorithm is better than the precision provided by the WFT. Therefore, the maxima of the fringes found in the De Bruijn decoding are used as ground truth where the fringe pattern is fitted in. Errors in the fringe pattern may cause some fringes to be wider or thinner than the distance between the corresponding maxima. This is caused by the 2D nature of the WFT algorithm, which may include some frequencies of adjacent positions in the Fourier transform, leading to an erroneous phase value for that position.

This effect is corrected by shrinking or expanding the wrapped phase according to the De Bruijn correspondences for the maxima. A nonlinear fourth-order regression line is used to this end. This process is done for every column in the image, obtaining the modified wrapped-phase map. Finally, an interpolation is done in the correspondence map in order to find the correspondences of every pixel to its maximum. That is, for every column, the modified wrapped-phase map between two maximum positions goes from $-\pi$ to π; therefore, a direct correlation is set between these values and the position of the projected and the recovered color intensities.

5.5.8 Triangulation

Every pair of (x, y) projector–camera coordinates given by the matching step is an input in the triangulation module, which also makes use of the extrinsic and intrinsic parameters provided by the calibration module. The output is a cloud of points in (x, y, z) representing the shape of the reconstructed object.

5.5.9 Filtering

A post-triangulation filtering step is necessary due to some erroneous matchings that originate outliers in the 3D cloud of points. Two different filtering steps are applied regarding the constraints given by the statistical 3D positions and the bilaterally based filter:

- *Three-dimensional statistical filtering:* In the 3D space, the outliers are characterized by their extremely different 3D coordinates regarding the surrounding points. Therefore, pixels that have 3D coordinates different from the 95% of the coordinates of all the points are considered for suppression. This is done in two steps for all the points in the 3D cloud. First, the distance to the centroid of the cloud of points is computed for every pixel. Afterward, those pixels with a distance to the centroid greater than two times the standard deviation of the cloud of points are considered outliers.

- *Bilateral filtering:* Still, there can be some misaligned points after applying the statistical filtering. In this case it would be propitious to apply some anisotropic filtering that filters the data while preserving the slopes. Of course, 3D points must be modified only when they present isolated coordinates that do not correspond to the shape of a reconstructed 3D object. To this end, an extension to 3D data of the 2D bilateral filter proposed by Tomati and Manduchi [66] was implemented. The bilateral filter is a nonrecursive anisotropic filter whose aim is to smooth the cloud of points (up to a given value), while preserving the discontinuities, by means of a nonlinear combination of nearby image values. Equations (5.31) and (5.32) are the distance mask and the height mask for a given set of points X, Y, Z around the selected 3D point; the corresponding filtered height value is computed. Afterward, points with a height value different from the output of more than a given threshold are considered points to be filtered out, and height is substituted by the filtered value.

$$G(x, y) = \exp\left(-\left((x - x_c)^2 + (y - y_c)^2\right) \middle/ (2 * \sigma_1^2)\right) \qquad (5.31)$$

$$H(z) = \exp\left(-(z - z_c)^2 \middle/ (2 * \sigma_2^2)\right) \qquad (5.32)$$

5.5.10 Meshing

Finally, a meshing step is applied to obtain a surface from the 3D cloud of points. To do this, a 2D bidimensional Delaunay meshing algorithm is applied to the 3D coordinates with respect to the camera in order to avoid duplicities in the depth value, as this cannot occur from the camera point of view.

5.6 Results

In the field of structured light, the performance of the different techniques has been compared in many different ways over the years, as can be found in the literature. The main difficulty is to set some fixed parameters to evaluate the goodness of a proposed method with respect to the others. In this chapter we proposed a new technique for one-shot dense structured light. Therefore, a comparison with some other techniques requires compulsory testing not only of the main architecture premises of this proposal (number of shots and density of the reconstruction), but also of some parameters common to all SL approaches. However, it would be too much in terms of time and computational requirements to test every single technique and compare it to the others; therefore, six representative techniques corresponding to the main groups existing in SL were selected. Table 5.2 shows these techniques and briefly explains their characteristics.

Three discrete coding techniques and three continuous coding techniques have been chosen for comparison. It is important to mention that all the methods presented here have been implemented directly from the corresponding papers (original code not available), and the parameters have been set in order to obtain optimal reconstruction results. Among sparse spatial multiplexing, one-axis coding was chosen as it presents an easier decoding algorithm than two-axes coding. Among them, the technique of Monks et al. [41] presents a colored slit, pattern-based technique that provides bigger

TABLE 5.2

Selected Methods with Their Main Attributes

Group		Method	Characteristics	Ref.
DC	Spatial m.	Monks et al.	De Bruijn slits pattern; six hue colors (1 pattern)	41
DC	Time m.	Posdamer et al.	Stripes patterns; 7 bits Gray code (24 patterns)	48
DC	Time m. (PS)	Guhring	Time multiplexing + shifting (16 patterns)	23
CC	Time m. (PS)	Pribanic et al.	Multiple phase shifting (18 patterns)	49
CC	Frequency m.	Li et al.	Sinusoidal pattern, π-phase shifting (two patterns)	36
CC	Spatial m.	Carrihill and Hummel	Grading grayscale pattern (one pattern)	8

vocabulary than grayscale approaches as well as easier detection and matching than stripe patterns techniques.

For sparse time multiplexing, the Posdamer algorithm [48] was selected for being a well-known, effective technique in time multiplexing. Dense time multiplexing using shifting codes was proposed by Sansoni et al. [59] and Guhring [23] to obtain dense reconstruction. Between them, Guhring's method was selected because it uses slit shifting, which is easier to segment than the fringe shifting used by Sansoni et al. Also, the technique presented by Pribanic et al. [49] was selected for being the latest dense time multiplexing technique using multiple phase shifting. In frequency multiplexing, the π-phase-shifting FTP method proposed by Li et al. [36] provides higher resistance to slopes than the traditional FTP of Takeda and Mutoh [64], without the necessity to perform wavelet filtering or having to deal with the blurring associated with nonsinusoidal patterns. Chen et al. [11] and Yue et al. [71] use the same π-phase-shifting FTP, multiplexing the patterns into one single projection.

However, the main idea remains unaltered, and therefore the simpler solution proposed by Li et al. is still a good representative to evaluate the performance of these techniques. The grayscale spatial grading proposed by Carrihill and Hummel [8] was chosen against the rainbow pattern implemented by Tajima and Iwakawa [63], which employs a nematic liquid crystal. Finally, the proposed one-shot dense reconstruction algorithm of this chapter was implemented and compared to these techniques.

The setup used for the tests was composed of an LCD video projector (Epson EMP-400W) with a resolution of 1024 × 768 pixels, a camera (Sony 3 CCD), and a frame grabber (Matrox Meteor-II) digitizing images at 768 × 576 pixels with 3 × 8 bits per pixel (RGB). Both camera and video projector were calibrated using the projector camera calibration method developed by Fernandez et al. [55]. The baseline between camera and projector was about 1 m. The results and time estimates were computed using a standard Intel Core2 Duo CPU at 3.00 GHz and 4 GB RAM memory. The algorithms were programmed and run in MATLAB® 7.3.

5.6.1 Quantitative Results

Quantitative results have been analyzed reconstructing a white plane at a distance of about 80 cm from the camera. Principal component analysis (PCA) was applied to obtain the equation of the 3D plane for every technique and for every reconstruction. This technique is used to span the 3D cloud of points onto a 2D plane defined by the two eigenvectors corresponding to the two largest eigenvalues. The results of the experiment are shown in Table 5.3. Observe that the algorithm of Li et al. [36] is conceived to measure deviation of smooth surfaces with respect to the reference plane; therefore, a plane is not conceived to be reconstructed by depth deviation.

Among the techniques obtaining sparse reconstruction, the De Bruijn one-shot projection algorithm developed by Monks et al. [41] presents the

TABLE 5.3

Quantitative Results

Technique	Average (mm)[a]	Standard (mm)[b]	3D Points[c]	Patterns[d]	Ref.
Monks et al.	1.31	1.19	13,899	1	41
Posdamer et al.	1.56	1.40	25,387	14	48
Guhring	1.52	1.33	315,273	24	23
Pribanic et al.	1.12	0.78	255,572	18	49
Li et al.	—	—	—	1	36
Carrihill and Hummel	11.9	5.02	202,714	1	8
Proposed technique	1.18	1.44	357,200	1	

[a] Average deviation of the reconstructing error.
[b] Standard deviation of the reconstructing error.
[c] Number of 3D points reconstructed.
[d] Number of projected patterns.

best results, in terms of average error and standard deviation, against the traditional time multiplexing represented by Posdamer and Altschuler [48]. Dense reconstruction techniques can be divided into one-shot and multiple pattern projection techniques. Among one-shot techniques, the proposed technique defeats the other implemented technique, based on spatial grading. The technique proposed by Carrihill and Hummel [8] obtains the poorest results due to the low variance existing between adjacent pixels in the projected pattern. In contrast, Fourier analysis represented by the proposed technique presents a lower error rate, thanks to the frequency filtering process that is performed in the analysis.

Among multiple pattern projection techniques, the method developed by Pribanic et al. [49] gives the best results in terms of sensitivity to noise, as can be extracted from the values of average error and standard deviation. Regarding the computing time, it can be observed that methods obtaining dense reconstructions (Guhring, Pribanic et al., Li et al., Carrihill and Hummel, and the proposed algorithm) need to compute more 3D points, requiring higher computational time. However, our proposal does not need to compute many images and no unwrapping algorithm is required. This makes our technique faster in terms of computational time. Among methods providing sparse reconstruction, the color calibration step makes Monks and colleagues' algorithm slower than that of Posdamer and Altschuler (also affecting the proposed technique) even though it preserves the same order of magnitude. Still, real-time response is achievable working with the appropriate programming language and firmware.

5.6.2 Qualitative Results

The reconstruction of a real object permits one to analyze the performance of the programmed techniques in terms of accuracy and noise sensitivity. The reconstructed object used to perform the qualitative analysis of the results is a ceramic figure placed at a distance of about 80 cm from the camera. In order to show the results, both 3D cloud of points and surfaces are used. The surface has been generated performing a 2D Delaunay triangulation over (x, y) coordinates.

As can be observed in Figures 5.10, 5.11, 5.12, and 5.13, the best results are obtained with time multiplexing shifting approaches (Guhring [23] and Pribanic et al. [49]). These techniques obtain the best accuracy results and also provide dense reconstruction. Furthermore, both algorithms perform well in the presence of surface slopes, as can be observed in some of the details of the reconstructed object (see, for instance, the ears of the horse). However, more than one projection is necessary to reconstruct the object and this makes them unable to cope with moving scenarios. This is also the case of Posdamer and Altschuler [48], which suffers from some noise in the recovered cloud of points caused by nonlinearities of the camera, which produces some leakage from white to black fringes that can lead to some errors in the position of the recovered edges.

Among one-shot techniques, De Bruijn-based coding presents the best results in terms of accuracy. This is the case of the Monks et al. algorithm [41], which employs De Bruijn color coding to obtain a dynamic sparse reconstruction. Another approach, proposed by Li et al. [36], employs frequency multiplexing (π-phase shifting). This also provides one-shot dense reconstruction. However, high frequencies are lost in the filtering step, causing the loss of some information in the surface details. Moreover, traditional frequency multiplexing approaches can work only on smooth surfaces with slopes not exceeding three times the value given in Equation (5.16).

It is important to mention that the method chosen for phase unwrapping employs a qualitative map to determine the region where the unwrapping should start. Our proposal, also based on frequency analysis, combines it with De Bruijn coding to provide the best performance, in terms of accuracy density of the reconstruction, for one-shot techniques. It obtains results similar to those of Monks et al. [41], but dense reconstruction is achieved. This provides a final 3D shape where details appear much better defined. Moreover, it is robust against slopes in the shape, which is not the case for other frequency-based approaches. Finally, the grading technique proposed by Carrihill and Hummel [8] showed high sensitivity to noise and low sensitivity to changes in depth, caused by the low range existing between adjacent pixels.

5.7 Conclusion

In this chapter, an up-to-date review and a new classification of the different techniques existing in structured light have been proposed, based on the

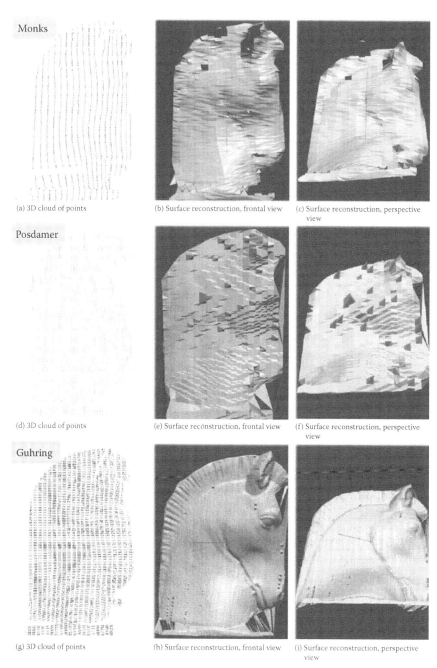

Monks

(a) 3D cloud of points

(b) Surface reconstruction, frontal view

(c) Surface reconstruction, perspective view

Posdamer

(d) 3D cloud of points

(e) Surface reconstruction, frontal view

(f) Surface reconstruction, perspective view

Guhring

(g) 3D cloud of points

(h) Surface reconstruction, frontal view

(i) Surface reconstruction, perspective view

FIGURE 5.10

Results of Monks et al. [41], Posdamer and Altschuler [48], and Guhring [23], respectively. (Monks, T. P. et al. *IEEE 4th International Conference on Image Processing*, 327–330, 1992; Posdamer, J. L. and M. D. Altschuler. *Computer Graphics and Image Processing* 18 (1): 1–17, 1982; Guhring, J. *Videometrics and Optical Methods for 3D Shape Measurement* 4309:220–231, 2001.)

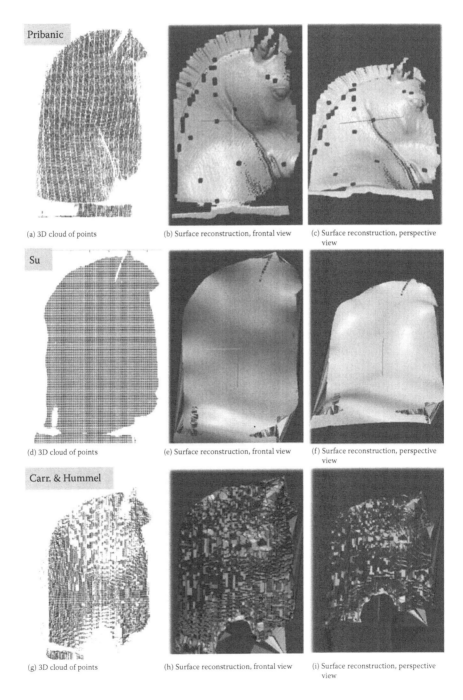

(a) 3D cloud of points   (b) Surface reconstruction, frontal view   (c) Surface reconstruction, perspective view

(d) 3D cloud of points   (e) Surface reconstruction, frontal view   (f) Surface reconstruction, perspective view

(g) 3D cloud of points   (h) Surface reconstruction, frontal view   (i) Surface reconstruction, perspective view

FIGURE 5.11
Results of Pribanic et al. [49], Su et al. [36], and Carrihill and Hummel [8], respectively.

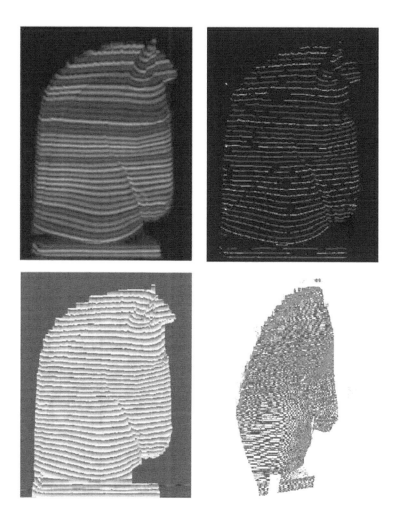

FIGURE 5.12
(See color insert.) Proposed algorithm: input image (top left), extracted color slits (top right), combined slits and WFT fringes (bottom left), and 3D cloud of points (bottom right).

survey of Salvi et al. [57]. The classification was done regarding the sparse or dense 3D reconstruction of the imaged scene. A subclassification regarding the spatial, frequency, or time multiplexing strategies was done. Moreover, a new proposal for one-shot dense 3D reconstruction has been presented that combines the accuracy of De Bruijn spatial multiplexing with the density of reconstruction obtained using frequency multiplexing in fringe projection.

This proposal was implemented jointly with some representative techniques of every group in the classification. Both quantitative and qualitative comparisons were performed, extracting advantages and drawbacks of each technique. The results show that the best results are obtained with time multiplexing shifting approaches, which obtain dense reconstruction

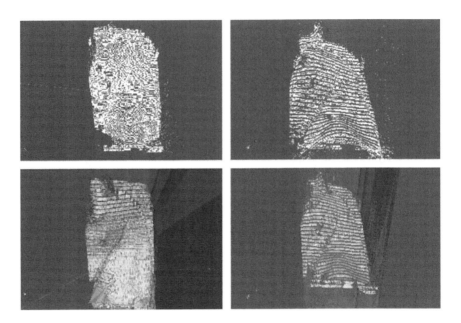

FIGURE 5.13
Different views of the 3D reconstruction using the proposed algorithm. 3D cloud of points (upper row) and 3D mesh (lower row).

and excellent accuracy. However, they are only valid for static scenarios. Among one-shot techniques, our proposed method achieves the best results in terms of accuracy, comparable with other De Bruijn-based spatial coding. Moreover, our proposal achieves dense reconstruction and absolute coding. Additionally, other frequency multiplexing methods provide dense reconstruction for moving scenarios, but present high sensitivity to nonlinearities of the camera, reducing the accuracy and sensitivity to details in the surface, and they can fail in the presence of big slopes.

Among spatial multiplexing approaches able to work in moving scenarios, the use of De Bruijn codes gives good accuracy in the reconstruction, but at the expense of having discrete reconstruction and high sensitivity to changes in color surface or background illumination. Regarding this point, it is important to mention that the background illumination is filtered in the proposed technique by the frequency analysis step.

Summarizing the main contributions done in structured light in the last years, it is important to mention that most of the work has been concerned with frequency multiplexing approaches, trying to increase the robustness in the decoding step and the resistance to slopes under the constraint of moving scenarios [11, 19, 71, 73]. Time multiplexing in phase shifting has arisen also to overcome the problem of slopes in the objects [49]. Hybrid techniques have been the main contribution in both time multiplexing and spatial multiplexing approaches [15, 17, 28, 32, 45], preserving the principles proposed in previous work. Under this scenario, the proposal made in this chapter of merging De Bruijn and frequency-based one-shot patterns achieves a dense reconstruction, with the robustness in the decoding step provided by frequency analysis jointly with the accuracy given by spatial De Bruijn-based patterns. This combination gives us a one-shot absolute dense pattern with the highest accuracy achievable for moving scenarios.

Acknowledgments

This work has been partly supported by the FP7-ICT-2011-7 project PANDORA—Persistent Autonomy through Learning, Adaptation, Observation and Replanning (Ref 288273)—funded by the European Commission and the project RAIMON—Autonomous Underwater Robot for Marine Fish Farms Inspection and Monitoring (Ref CTM2011-29691-C02-02)— funded by the Spanish Ministry of Science and Innovation. S. Fernandez is supported by the Spanish government scholarship FPU.

References

1. A. Z. A. Abid. Fringe pattern analysis using wavelet transforms. PhD thesis, General Engineering Research Institute (GERI). Liverpool John Moores University, Liverpool, UK, 2008.
2. C. Albitar, P. Graebling, and C. Doignon. Design of a monochromatic pattern for a robust structured light coding. *IEEE International Conference Image Processing ICIP* 6: 529–532, 2007.
3. A. Baldi, F. Bertolino, and F. Ginesu. On the performance of some unwrapping algorithms. *Optics and Lasers in Engineering* 37 (4): 313–330, 2002.
4. J. Batlle, E. Mouaddib, and J. Salvi. Recent progress in coded structured light as a technique to solve the correspondence problem: A survey. *Pattern Recognition* 31 (7): 963–982, 1998.
5. F. Berryman, P. Pynsent, and J. Cubillo. A theoretical comparison of three fringe analysis methods for determining the three-dimensional shape of an object in the presence of noise. *Optics and Lasers in Engineering* 39 (1): 35–50, 2003.
6. F. Berryman, P. Pynsent, J. Fairbank, and S. Disney. A new system for measuring three-dimensional back shape in scoliosis. *European Spine Journal* 17 (5): 663–672, 2008.
7. K. L. Boyer and A. C. Kak. Color-encoded structured light for rapid active ranging. *IEEE Transactions on Pattern Analysis and Machine Intelligence* 9 (1): 14–28, 1987.
8. B. Carrihill and R. Hummel. Experiments with the intensity ratio depth sensor. *Computer Vision, Graphics, and Image Processing* 32 (3): 337–358, 1985.

9. D. Caspi, N. Kiryati, and J. Shamir. Range imaging with adaptive color structured light. *IEEE Transactions on Pattern Analysis and Machine Intelligence* 20 (5): 470–480, 1998.

10. C. S. Chen, Y. P. Hung, C. C. Chiang, and J. L. Wu. Range data acquisition using color structured lighting and stereo vision. *Image and Vision Computing* 15 (6): 445–456, 1997.

11. W. Chen, P. Bu, S. Zheng, and X. Su. Study on Fourier transforms profilometry based on bi-color projecting. *Optics and Laser Technology* 39 (4): 821–827, 2007.

12. W. Chen, X. Su, Y. Cao, Q. Zhang, and L. Xiang. Method for eliminating zero spectrum in Fourier transform profilometry. *Optics and Lasers in Engineering* 43 (11): 1267–1276, 2005.

13. P. J. Cobelli, A. Maurel, V. Pagneux, and P. Petitjeans. Global measurement of water waves by Fourier transform profilometry. *Experiments in Fluids* 46 (6): 1037–1047, 2009.

14. T. Etzion. Constructions for perfect maps and pseudorandom arrays. *IEEE Transactions on Information Theory* 34(5, Part 1): 1308–1316, 1988.

15. P. Fechteler and P. Eisert. Adaptive color classification for structured light systems. *IEEE Computer Society Conference on Computer Vision and Pattern Recognition Workshops* 1–7, 2008.

16. S. Fernandez, M. A. Gdeisat, J. Salvi, and D. Burton. Automatic window size selection in windowed Fourier transform for 3D reconstruction using adapted mother wavelets. *Optics Communications* 284 (12): 2797–2807, 2011.

17. F. Forster. A high-resolution and high accuracy real-time 3D sensor based on structured light. *Proceedings 3rd International Symposium on 3D Data Processing, Visualization, and Transmission* 208–215, 2006.

18. H. Fredricksen. A survey of full length nonlinear shift register cycle algorithms. *SIAM Review* 195–221, 1982.

19. M. A. Gdeisat, D. R. Burton, and M. J. Lalor. Eliminating the zero spectrum in Fourier transform profilometry using a two-dimensional continuous wavelet transform. *Optics Communications* 266 (2): 482–489, 2006.

20. S. S. Gorthi and K. R. Lolla. A new approach for simple and rapid shape measurement of objects with surface discontinuities. *Proceedings SPIE* 5856: 184–194, 2005.

21. P. M. Griffin, L. S. Narasimhan, and S. R. Yee. Generation of uniquely encoded light patterns for range data acquisition. *Pattern Recognition* 25 (6): 609–616, 1992.

22. C. Guan, L. Hassebrook, and D. Lau. Composite structured light pattern for three-dimensional video. *Optics Express* 11 (5): 406–417, 2003.

23. J. Gühring. Dense 3-D surface acquisition by structured light using off-the-shelf components. *Videometrics and Optical Methods for 3D Shape Measurement* 4309: 220–231, 2001.

24. V. I. Gushov and Y. N. Solodkin. Automatic processing of fringe patterns in integer interferometers. *Optics and Lasers in Engineering* 14 (4–5): 311–324, 1991.

25. E. Hu and Y. He. Surface profile measurement of moving objects by using an improved π-phase-shifting Fourier transform profilometry. *Optics and Lasers in Engineering* 47 (1): 57–61, 2009.

26. L. Huang, Q. Kemao, B. Pan, and A. K. Asundi. Comparison of Fourier transform, windowed Fourier transform, and wavelet transform methods for phase extraction from a single fringe pattern in fringe projection profilometry. *Optics and Lasers in Engineering* 48 (2): 141–148, 2010.

27. P. S. Huang, S. Zhang, F. P. Chiang, et al. Trapezoidal phase-shifting method for three-dimensional shape measurement. *Optical Engineering* 44:142–152, 2005.

28. I. Ishii, K. Yamamoto, K. Doi, and T. Tsuji. High-speed 3D image acquisition using coded structured light projection. *IEEE/RSJ International Conference on Intelligent Robots and Systems (IROS)*, 925–930, 2007.

29. M. Ito and A. Ishii. A three-level checkerboard pattern (TCP) projection method for curved surface measurement. *Pattern Recognition* 28 (1): 27–40, 1995.

30. P. Jia, J. Kofman, and C. English. Two-step triangular-pattern phase-shifting method for three-dimensional object-shape measurement. *Optical Engineering* 46:083201, 2007.

31. T. R. Judge and P. J. Bryanston-Cross. A review of phase unwrapping techniques in fringe analysis. *Optics and Lasers in Engineering* 21 (4): 199–240, 1994.

32. H. Kawasaki, R. Furukawa, R. Sagawa, and Y. Yagi. Dynamic scene shape reconstruction using a single structured light pattern. *IEEE Conference on Computer Vision and Pattern Recognition, CVPR* 1–8, 2008.

33. Q. Kemao. Windowed Fourier transform for fringe pattern analysis. *Applied Optics* 43 (17): 3472–3473, 2004.

34. Q. Kemao. Two-dimensional windowed Fourier transform for fringe pattern analysis: Principles, applications and implementations. *Optics and Lasers in Engineering* 45 (2): 304–317, 2007.

35. T. P. Koninckx and L. Van Gool. Real-time range acquisition by adaptive structured light. *IEEE Transactions on Pattern Analysis and Machine Intelligence* 28 (3): 432–445, 2006.

36. J. Li, X. Su, and L. Guo. Improved Fourier transform profilometry for the automatic measurement of three-dimensional object shapes. *Optical Engineering* 29 (12): 1439–1444, 1990.

37. J. F. Lin and X. Su. Two-dimensional Fourier transform profilometry for the automatic measurement of three-dimensional object shapes. *Optical Engineering*, 34: 3297–3297, 1995.

38. F. J MacWilliams and N. J. A. Sloane. Pseudo-random sequences and arrays. *Proceedings of the IEEE* 64 (12): 1715–1729, 1976.

39. M. Maruyama and S. Abe. Range sensing by projecting multiple slits with random cuts. *IEEE Transactions on Pattern Analysis and Machine Intelligence* 15 (6): 647–651, 1993.

40. M. Minou, T. Kanade, and T. Sakai. A method of time-coded parallel planes of light for depth measurement. *Transactions of IECE Japan* 64 (8): 521–528, 1981.

41. T. P. Monks, J. N. Carter, and C. H. Shadle. Color-encoded structured light for digitization of real-time 3D data. *IEEE 4th International Conference on Image Processing*, 327–330, 1992.

42. R. A. Morano, C. Ozturk, R. Conn, S. Dubin, S. Zietz, and J. Nissano. Structured light using pseudorandom codes. *IEEE Transactions on Pattern Analysis and Machine Intelligence* 20 (3): 322–327, 1998.

43. H. Morita, K. Yajima, and S. Sakata. Reconstruction of surfaces of 3-D objects by M-array pattern projection method. *Second International Conference on Computer Vision* 468–473, 1988.

44. N. Ono, T. Shimizu, T. Kurihara, and S. Ando. Real-time 3-D imager based on spatiotemporal phase unwrapping. *SICE 2004 Annual Conference* 3: 2544–2547, 2004.

45. J. Pages, C. Collewet, F. Chaumette, J. Salvi, S. Girona, and F. Rennes. An approach to visual serving based on coded light. *IEEE International Conference on Robotics and Automation, ICRA* 6: 4118–4123, 2006.

46. J. Pages, J. Salvi, C. Collewet, and J. Forest. Optimized De Bruijn patterns for one-shot shape acquisition. *Image Vision and Computing* 23: 707–720, 2005.

47. J. Pages, J. Salvi, and J. Forest. A new optimized De Bruijn coding strategy for structured light patterns. *17th International Conference on Pattern Recognition, ICPR 2004* 4: 284–287, 2004.

48. J. L. Posdamer and M. D. Altschuler. Surface measurement by space-encoded projected beam systems. *Computer Graphics and Image Processing* 18 (1): 1–17, 1982.

49. T. Pribanic, H. Dapo, and J. Salvi. Efficient and low-cost 3D structured light system based on a modified number-theoretic approach. *EURASIP Journal on Advances in Signal Processing* 2010: article ID 474389, 11 pp., 2009.

50. J. G. Proakis, D. G. Manolakis, D. G. Manolakis, and J. G. Proakis. *Digital signal processing: Principles, algorithms, and applications,* vol. 3. Englewood Cliffs, NJ: Prentice Hall, 1996.

51. J. Quintana, R. Garcia, and L. Neumann. A novel method for color correction in epiluminescence microscopy. *Computerized Medical Imaging and Graphics,* 35(7–8): 646–652, 2011.

52. P. Ribenboim. *Algebraic numbers,* ed. R. Courant, L. Bers, and J. J. Stoker. New York: John Wiley & Sons, 1972.

53. J. A. Rice. *Mathematical statistics and data analysis.* Belmont, CA: Duxbury Press, 1995.

54. J. Salvi, S. Fernandez, and T. Pribanic. Absolute phase mapping for one-shot dense pattern projection. *IEEE Workshop on Projector–Camera Systems* (in conjunction with IEEE International Conference on Computer Vision and Pattern Recognition) 64–71, 2010.

55. J. Salvi, S. Fernandez, D. Fofi, and J. Batlle. Projector–camera calibration using a planar-based model. Submitted to *Electronics Letters,* 2011.

56. J. Salvi, J. Batlle, and E. Mouaddib. A robust-coded pattern projection for dynamic 3D scene measurement. *Pattern Recognition Letters* 19 (11): 1055–1065, 1998.

57. J. Salvi, S. Fernandez, T. Pribanic, and X. Llado. A state of the art in structured light patterns for surface profilometry. *Pattern Recognition* 43 (8): 2666–2680, 2010.

58. J. Salvi, J. Pages, and J. Batlle. Pattern codification strategies in structured light systems. *Pattern Recognition* 37 (4): 827–849, 2004.

59. G. Sansoni, M. Carocci, and R. Rodella. Calibration and performance evaluation of a 3-D imaging sensor-based on the projection of structured light. *IEEE Transactions on Instrumentation and Measurement* 49 (3): 628–636, 2000.

60. G. S. Spagnolo, G. Guattari, C. Sapia, D. Ambrosini, D. Paoletti, and G. Accardo. Contouring of artwork surface by fringe projection and FFT analysis. *Optics and Lasers in Engineering* 33 (2): 141–156, 2000.

61. V. Srinivasan, H. C. Liu, and M. Halious. Automated phase-measuring profilometry: A phase mapping approach. *Applied Optics* 24: 185–188, 1985.

62. X. Su and W. Chen. Fourier transform profilometry: A review. *Optics and Lasers in Engineering* 35 (5): 263–284, 2001.

63. J. Tajima and M. Iwakawa. 3-D data acquisition by rainbow range finder. *Pattern Recognition, 1990. Proceedings 10th International Conference* 1: 309–313, 1990.

64. M. T. K. Takeda and M. Mutoh. Fourier transform profilometry for the automatic measurement of 3-D object shapes. *Applied Optics* 22: 3977–3982, 1983.

65. M. A. Tehrani, A. Saghaeian, and O. R. Mohajerani. A new approach to 3D modeling using structured light pattern. *Information and Communication Technologies: From Theory to Applications, 2008. ICTTA 2008* 1–5, 2008.

66. C. Tomasi and R. Manduchi. Bilateral filtering for gray and color images. *Sixth International Conference on Computer Vision, 1998* 839–846.

67. Y. Iwaasa and S. Toyooka. Automatic prolometry of 3-D diffuse objects by spatial phase detection. *Applied Optics* 25 (10): 1630–1633, 1986.

68. J. Vanherzeele, P. Guillaume, and S. Vanlanduit. Fourier fringe processing using a regressive Fourier-transform technique. *Optics and Lasers in Engineering* 43 (6): 645–658, 2005.

69. L. S. Wu and Q. Peng. Research and development of fringe projection-based methods in 3D shape reconstruction. *Journal of Zhejiang University-Science A* 7 (6): 1026–1036, 2006.

70. C. Wust and D. W. Capson. Surface profile measurement using color fringe projection. *Machine Vision and Applications* 4 (3): 193–203, 1991.

71. H. M. Yue, X. Y. Su, and Y. Z. Liu. Fourier transform profilometry based on composite structured light pattern. *Optics and Laser Technology* 39 (6): 1170–1175, 2007.

72. L. Zhang, B. Curless, and S. M. Seitz. Rapid shape acquisition using color structured light and multi-pass dynamic programming. *Proceedings of the 1st International Symposium on 3D Data Processing, Visualization, and Transmission (3DPVT)* Padova, Italy, June 19–21, 2002, pages 24–36, 2002.

73. Q. Zhang, W. Chen, and Y. Tang. Method of choosing the adaptive level of discrete wavelet decomposition to eliminate zero component. *Optics Communications* 282 (5): 778–785, 2008.

6

Digital Holography for 3D Metrology

Anand Asundi, Qu Weijuan, Chee Oi Choo, Kapil Dev, and Yan Hao

CONTENTS

6.1 Introduction to Digital Holography

6.1.1 Holography and Digital Holography

Holography is a well established technique for three-dimensional (3D) imaging. It was first introduced by D. Gabor in 1948 [2] in order to improve the resolution of the electron microscope. Light scattered from an object is recorded with a reference beam in a photographic plate to form a hologram. Later, the processed photographic plate is illuminated with a wave identical to the reference wave, and a wave front is created that is identical to that originally produced by the object. As the development of laser, holography is applied in optical metrology widely. The phase of the test object wave could be reconstructed optically but not measured directly until the introduction of digital recording devices for the hologram recording. The digital recorded hologram can be stored in the computer and the numerical reconstruction method used to extract both the amplitude and phase information of the object wave front. By digital holography, the intensity and the phase of electromagnetic wave fields can be measured, stored, transmitted, applied to simulations, and manipulated in the computer.

For a long time, it has been hard to extract the phase from a single off-axis hologram because the phase of the test object is overlapped with the phase of the illuminating wave and the off-axis tilt. Off-axis digital holographic interferometry (double exposure) can easily remove the phase of the illuminating wave and the off-axis tilt by subtraction of the holograms with and without the test object to provide a correct phase measurement. Since the mid-1990s, it has been extended, improved, and applied to many measurement tasks, such as deformation analysis, shape measurement, particle tracking, and refractive index distribution measurement [3] within transparent media due to temperature or concentration variations and bio-imaging application. The drawback of this method is the necessity of recording multiple holograms, which is not suitable in real-time dynamic phase monitoring. In 1999, Cuche, Bevilacqua, and Depeursinge proposed that not only amplitude but also phase can be extracted from a single digital hologram [4]. The introduction of the concept of a digital reference wave that compensates the role of the reference wave in off-axis geometry has successfully removed the off-axis tilt of the optical system. Since then, the numerical reconstruction method for the digital hologram has been thoroughly developed [5–7].

The limited sampling capacity of the electronic camera gives impetus to finding different approaches to achieve microscopic imaging with digital holography and thus revives digital holographic microscopy (DHM) [8]. DHM, by introduction of a microscope objective (MO), gives very satisfactory measurement results in lateral resolution and in vertical resolution. Nevertheless, MO only in the object path introduces a phase difference between the object wave and reference wave. The phase difference will render the phase measurement a failure if a powerful numerical phase compensation procedure is lacking [9, 10].

Numerical phase compensation is based on the computation of a phase mask to be multiplied by the recorded hologram or by the reconstructed wave field in the image plane. In the early days, the phase mask was computed depending on the precisely measured parameters of the optical setup. It was then multiplied by the reconstructed wave front. The correct phase map was obtained by a time-consuming digital iterative adjustment of these parameters to remove the wave front aberration [11–13]. To exclude the necessity of physically measuring the optical setup parameters, a phase mask is

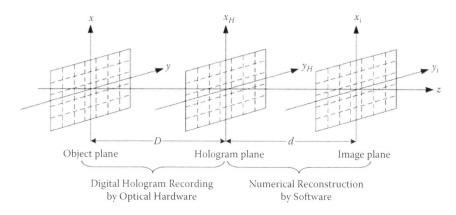

FIGURE 6.1
Digital hologram recording and numerical reconstruction.

computed in a flat portion of the hologram, where the specimen is flat and used for the aberration compensation. This was proposed by Ferraro et al. [14] and then developed by Montfort et al. [15] using a polynomial fitting procedure to adjust the parameters for one dimension at first and then for two dimensions. Numerical compensation, however, makes the reconstruction algorithm complex by the iterative adjustment and extrapolation of the fitted polynomials in different areas. For the special case of the microlens shape (spherical shape), this may result in false compensation [16]. In the case of the compensation in the reconstruction plane, the phase mask has to be adapted when the reconstruction distance is changed.

It is also possible to compensate the phase difference between the object wave and reference wave physically. There are examples, such as the Linnik interferometer [17] and Mach–Zehnder interferometer [18, 19], that can physically solve the problem by introducing the same curvature in the reference wave. Previously, it was difficult to align all the elements precisely to acquire the correct compensation. Now it is easy with the help of real-time phase monitoring software. With the help of the software, we also find that when the two phases between the object wave and the reference wave are matched, the fringe pattern of the hologram is a straight parallel line. A lens or a diverging spherical wave can be used in the reference wave to achieve a quasi-spherical phase compensation [16, 20]. Phase aberration-free DHM can be achieved by a common-path DHM system based on a single cube beam splitter (SCBS) interferometer [21] using an MO [22] or diverging spherical wave [23] to provide magnification to the test specimen. Since the object beam and reference beam share the same optical path, the wave front curvatures can physically compensate each other during the interference.

Digital holography is recording a digitized hologram by using an electronic device (e.g., a charge coupled device [CCD]) and later numerical reconstruction with a computer; both the amplitude and the phase of an optical wave arrive from a coherently illuminated object. Thus, both the hardware and software are needed in digital holography. As shown in Figure 6.1, there are three planes: object plane, hologram plane, and image plane. From the object plane to the hologram plane, the recording of a digital hologram is done by the optical interferometer—namely, optical hardware of digital holography. The CCD or complementary metal oxide semiconductor (CMOS) arrays are used to acquire the hologram and store it as a discrete digital array. From the hologram plane to the image plane, the numerical reconstruction is done by the computer software with a certain algorithm to calculate the diffraction propagation of the waves. In this section, DH from the object plane to the hologram plane—namely, the digital hologram recording process—will be introduced in detail.

As is well known, each optical wave field consists of an amplitude distribution as well as a phase distribution, but all detectors can register only intensities. Consequently, the phase of the wave is missing in the recording process. Interference between two waves can form certain patterns. The interference pattern can be recorded. Its intensity is modulated by phases of the involved interference wave fronts. Interference is the way of phase recording. In conventional holography, the interference pattern is recorded by a photographic plate. In digital holography, the interference pattern is recorded by a digital device. Different from the optical reconstruction of the processed photographic plate, numerical reconstruction will be performed in digital holography. In digital hologram recording, an illuminating wave front modulated by an unknown wave front coming from the object, called object wave O, is added to the reference wave R to give an intensity modulated by their phases. The intensity $I_H(x, y)$ of the sum of two complex fields can be written as

$$I_H(x,y) = |O+R|^2 = |O|^2 + |R|^2 + RO^* + R^*O \tag{6.1}$$

where RO^* and R^*O are the interference terms with R^* and O^* denoting the complex conjugate of the two waves. Thus, if

$$O(x,y) = A_O \exp\left[-j\varphi_O(x,y)\right] \tag{6.2}$$

$$R(x,y) = A_R \exp\left[-j\varphi_R(x,y)\right] \tag{6.3}$$

where A_O and A_R are the constant amplitude of the object wave and reference wave, respectively; $\varphi_O(x, y)$ and $\varphi_R(x, y)$ are the phase of the object wave and reference wave, respectively. The intensity of the sum is given by

$$I_H(x,y) = A_O^2 + A_R^2 + A_O A_R \cos\left[\varphi_R(x,y) - \varphi_O(x,y)\right] \tag{6.4}$$

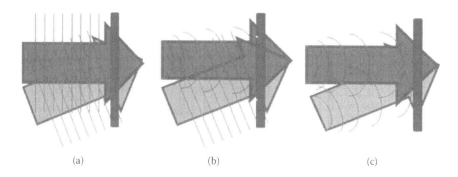

(a)   (b)   (c)

FIGURE 6.2
Interference between two waves: (a) two monochromatic plane waves; (b) one monochromatic diverging spherical wave and one monochromatic plane wave; (c) two monochromatic diverging spherical waves.

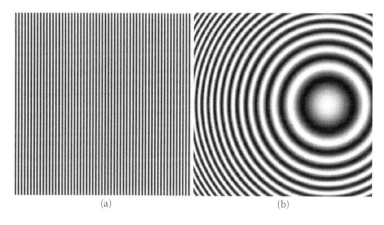

(a)   (b)

FIGURE 6.3
Interference pattern from two waves: (a) two monochromatic plane waves; (b) one monochromatic diverging spherical wave and one monochromatic plane wave.

It is obvious that the intensity depends on the relative phases of the two involved interference waves. In order to get sufficient information for the reconstruction of the phase of the test object, one needs to specify the detailed characters of the involved waves.

The wave fronts involved in an interferometer depend on the configurations of the optical interferometer. If two monochromatic plane waves interfere with each other, as shown in Figure 6.2(a), the interference pattern will always be straight lines, as shown in Figure 6.3(a). For digital holographic microscopy systems, as an imaging lens combination (condenser lens, MO, and tube lens) is used in the object beam path, the output wave front is a spherical one. If in the reference beam path a plane wave is used, as shown in Figure 6.2(b), the interference pattern will be closed or unclosed circular fringes, as shown in Figure 6.3(b). The spherical phase from the object beam

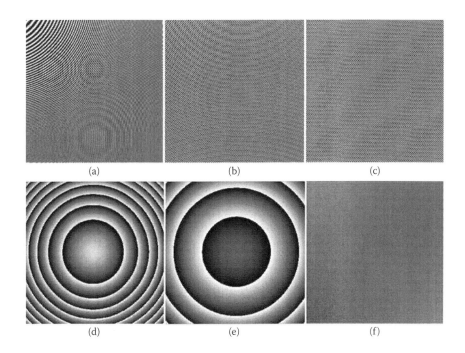

FIGURE 6.4
System phase of holograms in different fringe patterns: (a, b) hologram with circular fringe pattern; (c) hologram with straight fringe pattern; (d) system phase of hologram in (a); (e) system phase of hologram in (b); (f) system phase of hologram in (c).

path plays the important role in the phase modulation of the intensity. If the reference beam path uses a spherical wave, the interference pattern can be straight lines or circular lines depending on the relative positions of the two point sources of the diverging spherical waves. Detailed illustrations are given next.

If two diverging spherical waves are involved in the interference, the fringe patterns of the off-axis digital hologram are shown in Figure 6.4(a)–(c). In fact, the fringe of the interference pattern is decided by the final phase of the system. In order to illustrate this more clearly, the hologram is reconstructed to give the system phase. From the holograms shown in Figure 6.4(a)–(c), the reconstruction of the system phase by using a plane reconstruction reference wave normal to the hologram plane is shown in Figure 6.4(d)–(f). This confirms that different recording conditions give different system phases. In Figure 6.4(d)–(f), the spherical phase curvatures of the system phases are decreasing. In Figure 6.4(f), the system phase is constantly flat. In such a case, there will be no other phase introduced to the phase of the test object if it is involved. This is a very special case in the hologram recording process.

A specific theoretical analysis of the involved spherical wave fronts' interference in DHM is given as follows. We assumed that the reference wave is generated by a point source located at coordinates $(S_{Rx}, S_{Ry}, (z_R^2 - S_{Rx}^2 - S_{Ry}^2)^{1/2})$ and that the illuminating wave is generated by a point source located at coordinates $(S_{Ox}, S_{Oy}, (z_O^2 - S_{Ox}^2 - S_{Oy}^2)^{1/2})$. z_R and z_O are, respectively, the distance between the source points of the reference and illuminating waves and the hologram plane. Using quadratic-phase approximations to the spherical waves involved, the reference wave front in the hologram plane is thus given by

$$R(x,y) = \exp\left\{-j\frac{\pi}{\lambda z_R}\left[(x - S_{Rx})^2 + (y - S_{Ry})^2\right]\right\} \tag{6.5}$$

The illuminating wave is modulated by the phase of the object. In the hologram plane it is given by

$$O(x,y) = A_O \exp\left\{-j\frac{\pi}{\lambda z_O}\left[(x - S_{Ox})^2 + (y - S_{Oy})^2\right]\right\}\exp\left[j\varphi(x,y)\right] \tag{6.6}$$

where A_O is the unit amplitude and $\varphi(x,y)$ is the phase introduced by the test object. The corresponding intensity distribution in the pattern of the interference between the two waves is

$$I_H(x,y) = 1 + |A_O|^2$$

$$+ A_O \exp\left[-j\frac{\pi}{\lambda}\left(\frac{S_{Rx}^2}{z_R} - \frac{S_{Ox}^2}{z_O} + \frac{S_{Ry}^2}{z_R} - \frac{S_{Oy}^2}{z_O}\right)\right]$$

$$\times \exp\left[-j\frac{\pi}{\lambda}\left(\frac{1}{z_R} - \frac{1}{z_O}\right)(x^2 + y^2) + j\frac{2\pi}{\lambda}\left(\frac{S_{Rx}}{z_R} - \frac{S_{Ox}}{z_O}\right)x\right.$$

$$\left. + j\frac{2\pi}{\lambda}\left(\frac{S_{Ry}}{z_R} - \frac{S_{Oy}}{z_O}\right)y\right]\exp\left[-j\varphi(x,y)\right] \tag{6.7}$$

$$+ A_O \exp\left[j\frac{\pi}{\lambda}\left(\frac{S_{Rx}^2}{z_R} - \frac{S_{Ox}^2}{z_O} + \frac{S_{Ry}^2}{z_R} - \frac{S_{Oy}^2}{z_O}\right)\right]$$

$$\times \exp\left[j\frac{\pi}{\lambda}\left(\frac{1}{z_R} - \frac{1}{z_O}\right)(x^2 + y^2) - j\frac{2\pi}{\lambda}\left(\frac{S_{Rx}}{z_R} - \frac{S_{Ox}}{z_O}\right)x\right.$$

$$\left. - j\frac{2\pi}{\lambda}\left(\frac{S_{Ry}}{z_R} - \frac{S_{Oy}}{z_O}\right)y\right]\exp\left[j\varphi(x,y)\right]$$

The interference term of interest includes combinations of a spherical wave front, tilt in the x direction, tilt in the y direction, and a constant phase. One may not be able clearly to discern them directly from the interference pattern. Its Fourier transform gives the Fourier spectra distribution of

$$I_H^F(f_x, f_y) = \delta(f_x, f_y)$$

$$+ j\lambda \frac{z_R z_O}{z_O - z_R} \exp\left[j\pi\lambda \frac{z_R z_O}{z_O - z_R}(f_x^2 + f_y^2) \right]$$

$$\otimes \delta\left(f_x - \frac{1}{\lambda}\left(\frac{S_{Rx}}{z_R} - \frac{S_{Ox}}{z_O} \right), f_y - \frac{1}{\lambda}\left(\frac{S_{Ry}}{z_R} - \frac{S_{Oy}}{z_O} \right) \right) \otimes \mathrm{FFT}\left\{ \exp\left[j\varphi(x, y) \right] \right\} \quad (6.8)$$

$$+ j\lambda \frac{z_R z_O}{z_O - z_R} \exp\left[-j\pi\lambda \frac{z_R z_O}{z_O - z_R}(f_x^2 + f_y^2) \right]$$

$$\otimes \delta\left(f_x + \frac{1}{\lambda}\left(\frac{S_{Rx}}{z_R} - \frac{S_{Ox}}{z_O} \right), f_y + \frac{1}{\lambda}\left(\frac{S_{Ry}}{z_R} - \frac{S_{Oy}}{z_O} \right) \right) \otimes \mathrm{FFT}\left\{ \exp\left[-j\varphi(x, y) \right] \right\}$$

where $\otimes$ denotes the convolution operation.

It is obvious that the spectrum of the interference term of interest (the virtual original object) consists of three parts:

$$j\lambda \frac{z_R z_O}{z_O - z_R} \exp\left[j\pi\lambda \frac{z_R z_O}{z_O - z_R}(f_x^2 + f_y^2) \right]$$

$$\delta\left(f_x - \frac{1}{\lambda}\left(\frac{S_{Rx}}{z_R} - \frac{S_{Ox}}{z_O} \right), f_y - \frac{1}{\lambda}\left(\frac{S_{Ry}}{z_R} - \frac{S_{Oy}}{z_O} \right) \right)$$

and

$$\mathrm{FFT}\left\{ \exp\left[j\varphi(x, y) \right] \right\}$$

These three parts determine the shape of the spectrum. The first term is a spherical factor, which results in the spherical spectrum extending out. The second term is a delta function, indicating the position of the spectrum as

$$\left[\left(\frac{S_{Rx}}{z_R} - \frac{S_{Ox}}{z_O} \right), \left(\frac{S_{Ry}}{z_R} - \frac{S_{Oy}}{z_O} \right) \right]$$

The third term is the information of the test object.

The difference between z_R and z_O results in a different hologram pattern and thus different frequency spectra distribution in the hologram frequency domain. If $z_R > z_O$,

$$\frac{z_R z_O}{z_O - z_R} < 0$$

The spherical wave front of the interference term of interest is a converging one. This means the divergence of the spherical wave front coming from the illuminating wave front or the imaging MO is smaller than that of the reference wave front. In the interference term, the conjugate of the reference wave front is a converging one. Consequently, a converging wave front is left in the DHM system. If $z_R = z_O = z$, then

$$\frac{1}{z_R} - \frac{1}{z_O} = 0$$

The spherical wave front disappears and leaves only the tilt and constant phase. The pattern of the hologram is a set of straight fringes, which is described by the following equation:

$$
\begin{aligned}
I_H(x,y) = 1 + |A_O|^2 \\
+ A_O \exp\left[-j\frac{\pi}{\lambda}\left(\frac{S_{Rx}^2 - S_{Ox}^2 + S_{Ry}^2 - S_{Oy}^2}{z} \right) \right] \\
\times \exp\left[j\frac{2\pi}{\lambda}\left(\frac{S_{Rx} - S_{Ox}}{z} \right)x + j\frac{2\pi}{\lambda}\left(\frac{S_{Ry} - S_{Oy}}{z} \right)y \right]\exp\left[-j\varphi(x,y) \right] \\
+ A_O \exp\left[j\frac{\pi}{\lambda}\left(\frac{S_{Rx}^2 - S_{Ox}^2 + S_{Ry}^2 - S_{Oy}^2}{z} \right) \right] \\
\times \exp\left[-j\frac{2\pi}{\lambda}\left(\frac{S_{Rx} - S_{Ux}}{z} \right)y - j\frac{2\pi}{\lambda}\left(\frac{S_{Ry} - S_{Oy}}{z} \right)y \right]\exp\left[j\varphi(x,y) \right]
\end{aligned}
\tag{6.9}
$$

This means the spherical wave front coming out from the illuminating wave front or the imaging lens combination is totally compensated by the reference wave front during interference. Consequently, a plane wave front should be left in the DHM system. Its Fourier transform gives the Fourier spectra distribution as follows:

$$
\begin{aligned}
I_H^F(f_x, f_y) = \delta(f_x, f_y) \\
+ \delta\left(f_x - \frac{S_{Rx} - S_{Ox}}{\lambda z}, f_y - \frac{S_{Ry} - S_{Oy}}{\lambda z} \right) \otimes \mathrm{FFT}\left\{ \exp\left[j\varphi(x,y) \right] \right\} \\
+ \delta\left(f_x + \frac{S_{Rx} - S_{Ox}}{\lambda z}, f_y + \frac{S_{Ry} - S_{Oy}}{\lambda z} \right) \otimes \mathrm{FFT}\left\{ \exp\left[-j\varphi(x,y) \right] \right\}
\end{aligned}
\tag{6.10}
$$

If there is no test object, the spectrum of interest will be a delta function with a sharp point distribution. When a different object is testing, the convolution in Equation (6.10) will make the sharp point distribution a complicated shape.

If $z_R < z_O$, then

$$\frac{z_R z_O}{z_O - z_R} > 0$$

The spherical wave front of the interference term of interest is a diverging one. This means the divergence of the spherical wave front coming from the illuminating wave front or the imaging lens combination is bigger than that of the reference wave front. Consequently, a diverging wave front is left in the DHM system.

In conclusion, when $z_R \neq z_O$, the left spherical wave front can be either diverging or converging, depending on the relative position of the two point sources. This means the spherical wave front coming from the illuminating wave front or the imaging lens combination cannot be physically compensated by the reference wave front during interference. When an individual interference term of interest is considered, a system phase with a spherical curvature is presented. For numerical reconstruction, a collimated reference wave is used in the off-axis digital holographic microscopy setup [11–14, 24] due to the simplicity of the digital replica of such a reference wave. Thus, no other spherical phase will be introduced to the whole interference term of interest. For the wanted phase of the test object, the system's spherical phase must be numerically compensated.

When $z_R = z_O$, the spherical wave front can be removed by the physical matching of the involved object and reference wave front. Thus, the phase directly reconstructed from the hologram is the phase introduced by the test object without any other further numerical process.

From the preceding analysis, it is obvious that the shape of the spectrum can indicate whether the wave front aberration between the object and reference waves can be physically compensated during the hologram recording. The numerical reference wave front should be carefully chosen to ensure that no other phase factor is introduced to the reconstructed object phase. One can monitor the shape of the spectrum to judge whether the spherical phase curvature is totally compensated in the setup alignment process.

As an example, the difference in Figure 6.4(a) and (b) is obvious in the off-axis extent. But it is hard to tell the difference from Figure 6.4(b) and (c) directly due to the almost similar fringe pattern. In this case, the frequency spectra in the spatial frequency domain may provide useful information about the difference between the two digital holograms. Fourier transform of the holograms has been undertaken to give the frequency spectra distribution in the spatial frequency domain as shown in Figure 6.5(a)–(c). In

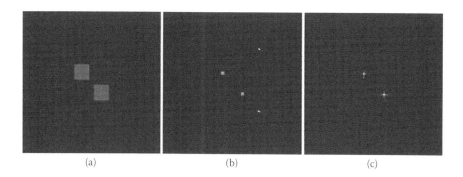

FIGURE 6.5
Fourier spectra of holograms in different fringe patterns: (a) Fourier spectra of hologram in Figure 6.4(a); (b) Fourier spectra of hologram in Figure 6.4(b); (c) Fourier spectra of hologram in Figure 6.4(c).

Figure 6.5(a)–(c), the position of the spectrum is not changed. But the size of the spectrum is decreased from a rectangular shape to a point. This indicates that the status of the physical phase curvature matches between the involved object wave front and reference wave front for the configured interferometer.

Consequently, in the digital hologram recording process, the selection of the configuration of the optical interferometer is important for a successful phase measurement. If the two interference wave fronts match each other, the system phase will not affect the phase measurement of the test object. If the two interference wave fronts do not match, the final system phase must be compensated by using numerical methods to provide the correct phase measurement of the test object. In the following section, numerical reconstruction of the recorded digital hologram will be introduced in detail.

6.1.2 Numerical Reconstruction Algorithms

The digital hologram recording is described by Equation (6.4). Then digital hologram reconstruction is achieved by illumination with a numerical reference wave C. The reconstructed wave front in the hologram plane is then given by

$$CI_H(x,y) = C\left(|O|^2 + |R|^2\right) + CRO^* + CR^*O \qquad (6.11)$$

For in-line recording geometry, the zero order and the two twin images are superposed with one another. It is hard to separate the object information of interest from one single hologram, which limits its application in real-time inspection. For off-axis recording geometry, the separation of the three terms enables further operation to the digital hologram, such as apodization and spatial filtering [25]. After that, the terms to reproduce the original wave front $\psi^H(x,y) = CR^*O$ in the hologram plane are achieved and propagated to the image plane to have a focused image $\psi^I(x,y)$.

Two different numerical reconstruction algorithms are using to calculate the scalar diffraction between ψ^H and ψ^I: the single Fresnel transform (FT) formulation in the spatial domain and the angular spectrum method (ASM) in the spatial frequency domain.

Numerical reconstruction by the Fresnel transform method gives a central reconstruction formula of digital holography as the following:

$$\psi^I\left(n\Delta x_i, m\Delta y_i\right)$$

$$= e^{j\pi d\lambda\left(\frac{n^2}{N^2\Delta x_H^2} + \frac{m^2}{M^2\Delta y_H^2}\right)} \sum_{k=0}^{N-1}\sum_{l=0}^{M-1} \psi^H\left(k\Delta x_H, l\Delta y_H\right) R^* \left(k\Delta x_H, l\Delta y_H\right) e^{\frac{j\pi}{d\lambda}\left(k^2\Delta x_H^2 + l^2\Delta y_H^2\right)} e^{-2j\pi\left(\frac{kn}{N} + \frac{lm}{M}\right)} \tag{6.12}$$

where

$m, n, k,$ and l are $M \times N$ matrixes denoting the address of the sampling pixel in x and y direction, respectively

d is the hologram reconstruction distance

$\Delta x_i, \Delta y_i, \Delta x_H,$ and Δy_H are the sampling pixel size of the image plane and the hologram plane in x and y directions, respectively, and are related by

$$\Delta x_i = \frac{d\lambda}{N\Delta x_H}, \Delta y_i = \frac{d\lambda}{M\Delta y_H}$$

Numerical reconstruction of ψ^H by the angular spectrum method needs a Fourier transform and an inverse Fourier transform:

$$\begin{cases} \psi^I\left(n\Delta x_i, m\Delta y_i\right) = \frac{\exp(jkd)}{j\lambda d}\text{FFT}^{-1}\left\{\text{FFT}\left\{\psi^H\left(k\Delta x_H, l\Delta y_H\right)\right\} \cdot G\left(k\Delta\xi, l\Delta\eta\right)\right\} \\ G\left(k\Delta\xi, l\Delta\eta\right) = \exp\left[j\frac{2\pi d}{\lambda}\sqrt{1 - (\lambda k\Delta\xi)^2 - (\lambda l\Delta\eta)^2}\right] \end{cases} \tag{6.13}$$

where $G\left(k\Delta\xi, l\Delta\eta\right)$ is the optical transfer function in the spatial frequency domain; $\Delta\xi$ and $\Delta\eta$ are the sampling intervals in the spatial frequency domain. The relation between the sampling intervals of the hologram plane and that of the image plane is

$$\Delta x_i = \frac{1}{N\Delta\xi} = \Delta x_H \text{ and } \Delta y_i = \frac{1}{M\Delta\eta} = \Delta y_H.$$

Using the single Fresnel transform formulation, the resolution of the reconstructed optical wave field depends not only on the wavelength of the illuminating light but also on the reconstruction distance. And it is always lower
than the resolution of the CCD camera. While using the angular spectrum
method, one can obtain the reconstructed optical wave field with maximum
resolution the same as the pixel size of the CCD camera.

Nevertheless, both the single Fresnel transform formulation and the ASM
can give correct reconstruction of the recorded hologram if the distance
between the hologram plane and image plane, d, is not too small. If d is such
a small value that

$$d \gg \sqrt[3]{\frac{\pi}{4\lambda}\left[\left(x_i - x_H\right)^2 + \left(y_i - y_H\right)^2\right]_{max}^2} \tag{6.14}$$

the assumption of scalar diffraction, cannot be satisfied, the calculation of
the light diffraction propagation between ψ^H and ψ^I will give the wrong
results. This means the reconstruction distance of the single Fresnel transform formulation cannot be set as zero. The angular spectrum method can
give correct reconstruction of the recorded hologram at any reconstruction
distance.

The procedure of digital hologram reconstruction by using the angular
spectrum method is shown in Figure 6.6. It is composed of the following steps:

1. Make the digital hologram a Fourier transform to get a superposition of the plane wave front with a different direction.
2. The spectrum of the virtual image is filtered out and moved to the
   center of the coordinate system.
3. Multiply by the optical diffraction transform function in the frequency domain to calculate the propagation of the light waves.
4. Perform an inverse Fourier transform to the wave front to get its
   distribution at the spatial domain.

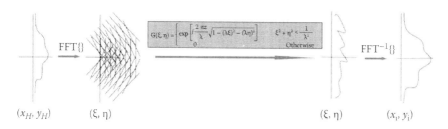

FIGURE 6.6
Digital hologram reconstruction by angular spectrum method.

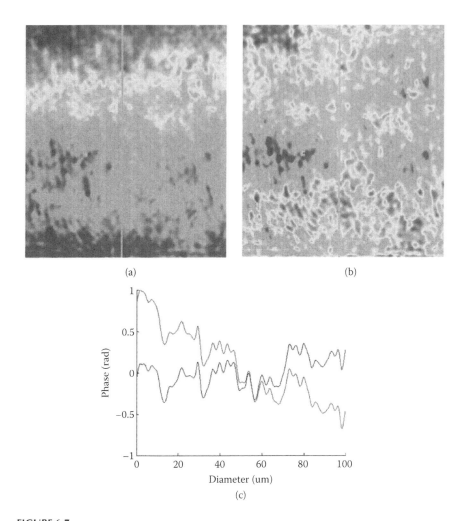

FIGURE 6.7
(See color insert.) (a) Phase with subpixel tilt; (b) phase without subpixel tilt; (c) phase profile comparison along the dark lines in (a) and (b).

It should be noted that in step 2 there are two ways to move the selected spectrum to the center of the coordinate system. One way is to use a plane wave to illuminate the hologram at a certain angle. This angle will offset the off-axis tilt of the selected spectrum. The other way is by direct geometrical movement of the selected spectrum, pixel by pixel. This may cause a problem called subpixel tilt since the discrete pixel always has a certain size. If there is subpixel tilt in the phase, the only way to remove it is a plane wave illumination at a small angle. As for the subpixel tilt shown in Figure 6.7(a), a plane wave is used to illuminate the hologram at a small angle to give the phase reconstruction shown in Figure 6.7(b). The phase profile comparison is given in Figure 6.7(c).

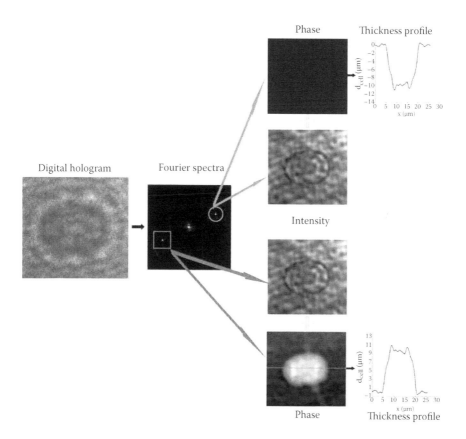

FIGURE 6.8

Digital hologram reconstruction by selecting different spectra: (a) digital hologram of a divid ing Vero cell; (b) Fourier spectra of hologram (a); (c) phase from the minus order; (d) intensity from the minus order; (e) phase from the plus order; (f) intensity from the plus order; (g) thick ness profile from the phase in (c); (h) thickness profile from the phase in (f).

In step 2, the spectrum of the virtual image is mentioned. One may ask whether there is any difference between the reconstruction results of the spectrum of the virtual image and that of the real image. The reconstruc tion results of dividing Vero cells are shown in Figure 6.8 to give a clear illustration of the difference. The digital hologram is shown in Figure 6.8(a). Its Fourier spectra are shown in Figure 6.8(b). The reconstruction distance for the spectrum selected by the white circle is $-d$. It should be the virtual image of the test object. The reconstructed phase and intensity are shown in Figure 6.8(c) and (d). The reconstruction distance for the spectrum selected by the white rectangle is d. It should be the real image of the test object. The reconstructed phase and intensity are shown in Figure 6.8(e) and (f). It is obvious that the intensities from the two different spectra are the same as each other and the phases are opposite to each other.

6.1.3 Phase to Profile

Reflection digital holography is widely used for deformation and displacement measurement. The relation between the shape of the test object and the achieved phase is

$$\varphi(x,y) = \frac{4\pi}{\lambda} d(x,y,z) \tag{6.15}$$

where $\varphi(x,y)$ is the achieved phase distribution $d(x,y,z)$ and is the profile of the test object. The depth or height one can measure is

$$-\frac{\lambda}{2} < d(x,y,z) < \frac{\lambda}{2}$$

Transmission digital holography can be applied to refractive index measurement. Light transmitting the test transparent object experiences a change of the optical path length and thereby a phase variation. The interference phase due to refractive index variations is given by

$$\Delta\varphi(x,y) = \frac{2\pi}{\lambda} \int_{-l}^{l} n(x,y)\,dz \tag{6.16}$$

where $n(x,y)$ is the wanted refractive index. The light passes the medium in the z-direction and the integration is taken along the propagation direction. Given the thickness of the specimen, the phase distribution can be transferred to refractive index distribution or, given the refractive index of the specimen, the phase distribution can be transferred to thickness. As shown in Figure 6.7(g) and (h), the detected phase of the dividing Vero cell is transferred to a cell thickness with an average refractive index of 1.37.

6.2 Digital Holoscopes

6.2.1 Reflection Digital Holoscope

Three configurations have been developed for the compact reflection digital holoscope. The premise behind these configurations includes the need to make measurements on-site or during processes such as etching or thin-film coating. The goal is to incorporate the system in a noninvasive manner for real-time quantitative measurements with nanometer axial sensitivity.

(a)

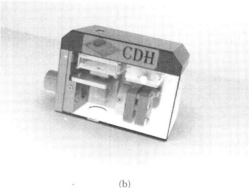
(b)

FIGURE 6.9

(a) Product prototypes for compact digital holoscopes showing scanning system on translation stage and portable system that can be placed directly on sample in foreground; (b) prototype of an integrated CDH system.

Figure 6.9(a) shows three of the models. The one mounted on the translation stage enables measurement of large samples using a scanning image system. The items in the foreground are two portable systems that can be placed directly on the specimen to be measured. Finally, the system in Figure 6.9(b) shows a drawing of the new system, which is about 30% smaller than the previous versions with the camera integrated into the system.

6.2.1.1 Calibration (Height Calibration by Comparison with AFM)

A calibration of the system was performed to ensure correct measurements as well as to highlight the accuracy and repeatability of the measurement. One of the concerns here is that there is no specific calibration target that can provide a whole-field calibration of the system. Hence, this study compares the compact digital holoscope (CDH) results of available targets such as the U.S. Air Force (USAF) or internally fabricated microelectromechanical systems (MEMS) step-height target with an atomic force microscope (AFM) scan. The concern here is that the line used for the AFM scan and the line selected from the CDH image may not be exactly the same. Hence, some errors may arise but it gives good ballpark data.

Figure 6.10(a) shows the results of a USAF target measured using the CDH system along with a typical line scan plot from this image. Figure 6.10(b) shows the result from the AFM scan. The AFM scan area plot is also shown, but this one covers a smaller area and took a longer time to scan as compared with the DH result. The results indicate good correlation between the CDH results and the AFM scan. The CDH was then used to test a step-height sample fabricated using the MEMS etching process. The sample was designed

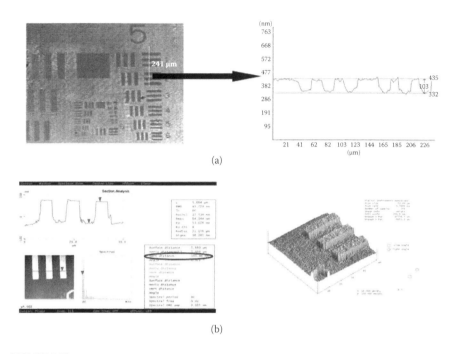

(a)

(b)

FIGURE 6.10
(a) CDH phase image of the USAF target and a line scan plot along the marked line showing the profile; (b) AFM line scan plot as well as the area plot of a small segment.

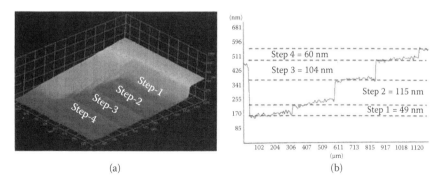

(a)   (b)

FIGURE 6.11
Profiling of MEMS etched target: (a) whole-field profile map; (b) line scan plot.

with etch heights of 50, 100, 100, and 60 nm. The color-coded 3D phase image is shown in Figure 6.11(a) and the line scan profile along a typical section is shown in Figure 6.11(b). The heights match quite well; however, during the etching process, the etch depth is determined by the time of etch rather than any measurement. CDH provides an elegant way to monitor the etch depth during the etching process in real time.

(a) (b) (c)

FIGURE 6.12
(See color insert.) Profile of accelerometer: (a) bare, unmounted; (b) mounted on ceramic substrate; (c) mounted on plastic substrate.

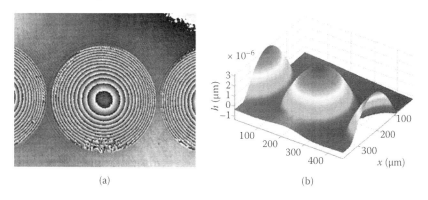

(a) (b)

FIGURE 6.13
(a) Phase of reflection microlens array in pitch 250 mm modulo 2p; (b) height map of the microlens array.

6.2.1.2 MEMS Inspection

A typical example of the use of the CDH for MEMS inspection involved the testing of a MEMS accelerometer mounted onto different substrates holding the related electronics. In the process of bonding the accelerometer to the substrate, deformation or distortions occur that would adversely affect the performance of the accelerometer. Figure 6.12(a) shows the profile of a bare accelerometer and Figure 6.12(b) and (c) the profile for the accelerometer mounted on ceramic substrate and on plastic substrate. The distortion in Figure 6.12(c) as compared to Figure 6.12(b) is quite evident and indicative of the poorer performance of the accelerometer on plastic substrates.

6.2.1.3 Reflective Microlens Array Characterization

A 4 mm × 14 mm × 0.5 mm reflective planoconvex linear microlens array from SUSS micro-optics with a 250 μm pitch was tested by use of the CDH system. Figure 6.13(a) shows the wrapped phase map of a single microlens

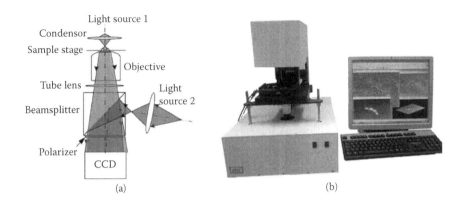

FIGURE 6.14
(a) Schematic of transmission mode DHM setup for short coherence light source; (b) packaged DHM setup for transmission specimen.

and Figure 6.13(b) shows the 3D unwrapped height map of the corresponding microlens.

6.2.2 Transmission Digital Holoscope

A DHM system built in the Michelson interferometer configuration is proposed by using an adjustable lens in the reference beam to perform the quasi-physical spherical phase compensation. It is built for using a light source with a short coherence length. As shown in Figure 6.14(a), an adjustable lens is put in the reference beam path. The coherence length of the light source may limit the position-adjustable capability of the reference wave. In such a case, the adjustable lens can be used to change the phase curvature to fulfill the spherical phase compensation in the hologram recording process.

6.2.2.1 Quantitative Mapping of Domain Inversion in Ferroelectric Crystal

A very interesting electrochromism effect has been observed during the ferroelectric domain inversion on RuO_2-doped $LiNbO_3$ crystals [26, 27]. They have become a new kind of material for investigation in domain inversion engineering. Digital holographic microscopy has been successfully applied to in situ visualization, monitoring, quantitative measurement, and analysis of the domain inversion in ferroelectric crystals. Here, DHM is applied for domain inversion investigation of RuO_2-doped $LiNbO_3$ crystals.

The refractive index and thickness of the ferroelectric crystals under a uniform voltage will change because of the electro-optic (EO) effect and the piezoelectric effect. These changes cause a phase retardation of a normally transmitted wave field. For a crystal wafer with antiparallel domain structure, the refractive index will change according to its polarization. The

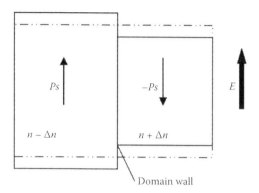

FIGURE 6.15
Schematic of the variation of the ferroelectric crystal under external voltage.

spontaneous polarization of the crystal sample is along its optical axis, the crystallographic c axis. If we applied the external electric field along the optical axis, there is a refractive index variation $\Delta n < 0$ in the part with spontaneous polarization and a refractive index variation $\Delta n > 0$ in the other part with reversed polarization, as shown in Figure 6.15. Additionally, the external electric field causes the thickness variation of the crystal due to the piezoelectric effect. The phase retardation experienced by the normally transmitted wave field when the external electric voltage is applied can be calculated by the following formula [28]:

$$\Delta\varphi = 2\left[\frac{2\pi}{\lambda}\Delta n D + \frac{2\pi}{\lambda}(n_0 - n_w)\Delta D\right] = \frac{2\pi}{\lambda}\left[-\gamma_{13}n_0^3 + 2(n_0 - n_w)k_3\right]U \quad (6.17)$$

where
$\Delta n \propto \gamma_{13}\, U/d$
$n_0 = 2.286$ (when $\lambda = 632.8$ nm) is the refractive index of the original crystal
$n_w = 1.33$ is the refractive index of water
U is the electric voltage
D is the thickness of the crystal along its optical axis
γ_{13} is the linear EO coefficient
k_3 is the ratio between the linear piezoelectric tensor and the stiffness tensor [29]
ΔD is the piezoelectric thickness change

The phase retardation experienced by the object wave field during poling can be calculated.

The sample holder used for the experiments is illustrated by Figure 6.16. The crystal sample, which is a z-cut, 0.5-mm-thick, double-side-polished

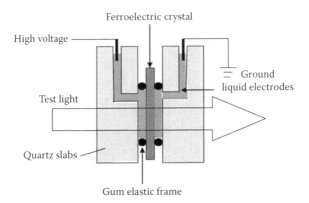

FIGURE 6.16
Schematic of the sample crystal holder.

RuO_2:$LiNbO_3$ substrate, is mounted between two rectangular gum elastic frames, which are clamped among two quartz slabs. The two cavities filled with water act as liquid electrodes. The crystal sample has an area of 36.00 mm^2 (6.0 mm × 6.0 mm) contacting the liquid electrodes, which provide the homogeneous electric field. A high-voltage supply is used for an electric pulse or continuous external field with 20.0 kV and 2.0 mA maximum output. The switching current caused by the charge redistribution within the crystal is monitored by a microamperemeter.

In the domain inversion, one stable domain nucleus is observed. The phase variation during the whole nucleus growth is obtained. The bottom of the nucleus is a hexagonal shape. As the nucleus grows, the top becomes sharper and sharper, as shown in Figure 6.17. The top view of the domain nucleus in 400 s is shown in Figure 6.18. The hexagonal shape is not very clear due to the nonuniform distribution of the top phase. The phase profiles in different times are given along the white line in Figure 6.18(a) as shown in Figure 6.18(b) and (c). From the comparison, as the domain nucleus grows, the phase retardation increases. The speed of the increment of the phase retardation is different. Along line 3, the phase increment is the fastest. The unequal increment speed indicates that the shape of the domain nucleus will change from a hexagonal shape to a different one during its growth. The reason for this variation is very complex. One reasonable explanation is the redistribution of the poling electrons in the domain inversion. It is related closely to the initial property of the crystal.

6.2.2.2 Characterization of Transmission Microlens Array

Microlens arrays have numerous and diverse applications and are employed in coupling light to optical fibers, increasing the light collection efficiency

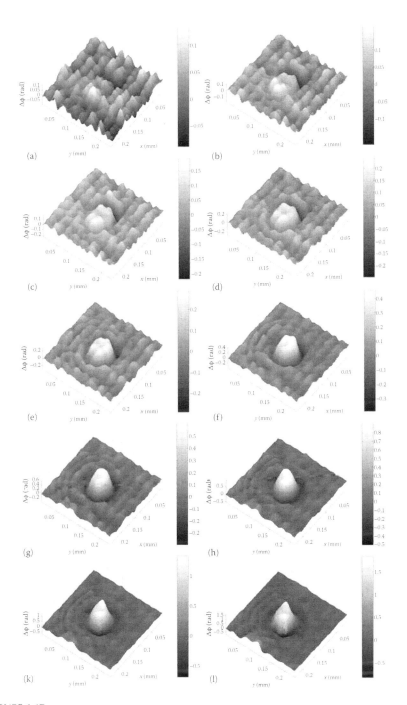

FIGURE 6.17
The growth of the domain nucleus in the crystal. (a) 1 s; (b) 20 s; (c) 30 s; (d) 50 s; (e) 100 s; (f) 150 s; (g) 200 s; (h) 250 s; (k) 300 s; (l) 400 s.

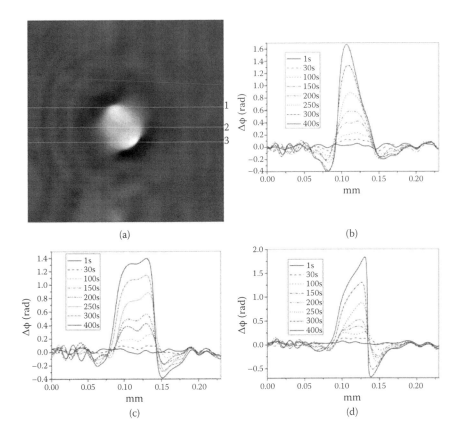

FIGURE 6.18
Evolution of phase profile of domain nucleus: (a) 2D image; (b) along line 1; (c) along line 2; (d) along line 3.

of CCD arrays, compact imaging in photocopiers and mobile-phone cameras, and enabling integral photography in 3D imaging and displays [30]. Precise control of the shape, surface quality, and optical performance of the microlenses is required, as well as the uniformity of these parameters across the array. A common-path DHM system based on a single cube beam splitter (SCBS) interferometer [21] uses an MO [22] to provide magnification to the test specimen (Figure 6.19). Since the object beam and reference beam share the same optical path, the wave front curvatures can physically compensate each other during the interference. This provides a better way for microlens characterization as well as uniformity inspection across a whole array.

A 1 mm × 12.8 mm × 1.2 mm refractive planoconvex linear microlens array from SUSS micro-optics with a 127 μm pitch was tested by the previously described DHM system. With a known refractive index of the lens material, the geometrical thickness of the lens can be deduced from the quantitative

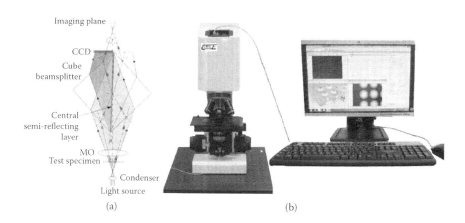

FIGURE 6.19
(a) Schematic of transmission mode common-path DHM used for 3D imaging of linear micro-lens array; (b) packaged CPDHM setup.

phase map as well as the lens shape, height, and radius of curvature (ROC), if the lens has a flat face (e.g., a planoconvex lens). When light is transmitted through the lens, the optical path length will be changed according to the height and refractive index of the lens. By using DHM, the optical path length change can be easily achieved from the phase map of the wave front. Given the refractive index, one can calculate the height of the test lens according to the following equation:

$$h = \frac{\lambda}{2\pi} \frac{\varphi}{\left(n_L - n_S\right)} \tag{6.18}$$

where
λ is the wavelength of the light
φ is the phase given by the SCBS microscope
n_L is the refractive index of the lens
n_S is the refractive index of the medium around the test lens

As shown in Figure 6.20, the linear microlens array can be tested in different magnifications as required.

The microscope is calibrated by using the 0.1 mm/100 div calibration microstage for the actual magnification it can provide. For example, the calibration results for a 40× microscope objective is shown in Figure 6.21. The total pixel used in the y direction is 960 with a pixel size of 4.65 μm. The length of the calibration microstage is 130 μm. Consequently, the magnification of the system is about 34×.

Given that the refractive index is 1.457 at 633 nm, the height profile of the single microlens is shown in Figure 6.22(b). It was drawn from the height

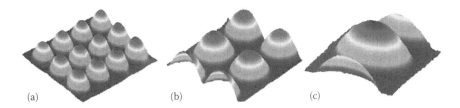

(a)   (b)   (c)

FIGURE 6.20
Three-dimensional imaging of linear microlens array in different magnifications.

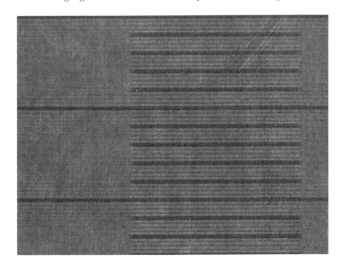

FIGURE 6.21
Magnification calibration of the 40× microscope objective.

map along with the same position as the solid line in Figure 6.22(a). Given the height profile of the lens, the ROC can be calculated by the following equation:

$$ROC = \frac{h}{2} + \frac{D^2}{8h} \qquad (6.19)$$

where h is the height and D is the diameter of the microlens. The maximum height of the microlens, h, is read as 5.82 µm. The diameter, D, is read as 121 µm. Thus, the calculated ROC is 317 µm. It is slightly different from the ROC value of 315 mm provided by the supplier.

6.2.2.3 Characterization of Diffractive Optical Elements on Liquid Crystal Spatial Light Modulator

A diffractive optics element (DOE) is a passive optical component containing complex micro- and nanostructure patterns that can modulate or transform

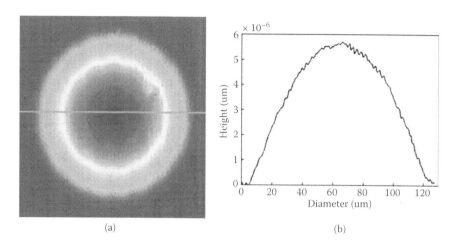

FIGURE 6.22
(See color insert.) (a) Height map of a single microlens; (b) height profile along the solid line in (a).

the light in a predetermined way. DOE works on the principle of interference and diffraction to represent desired optical elements, in contrast to refraction of light from conventional optical element. In general, DOEs fabricated on glass with wavelength-sized features involve time-consuming microfabricated semiconductor foundry resources. A computer-generated DOE displayed on the liquid crystal spatial light modulator (LCSLM) is an active and dynamic replacement of physical optical components. Diffractive optical lens and microlens array on the LCSLM with variable focal lengths and diameter make them important in many applications, including adaptive optics, optical tweezers, retinal imaging, diffraction strain sensors, etc. The computer-generated diffractive microlens array displayed on the LCSLM can replace the static physical lens array in the Shack–Hartmann wave front sensor (SHWS) and the multipoint diffraction strain sensor (MDSS) for wave front sampling. However, it is difficult to investigate the quality of these lenses by traditional metrology since the wave front profile is modulated by liquid crystal molecules on application of an electric field instead of the solid surface of the optical components. Thus, the characterization of diffractive optical microlens array on the LCSLM is necessary to quantify the effect on exiting optical wave fronts.

LCSLMs are polarization-sensitive devices and, depending on the incident polarization and wavelength, amplitude and phase of the exiting optical wave front are modulated. The diffractive microlens array displayed on the LCSLM can be characterized easily after characterizing the maximum phase modulation from the LCSLM using the DH method. The advantage of phase modulation characterization using the proposed DH over other existing methods is that the full-field quantitative phase value is calculated from the single digital hologram and thus the phase map of the full active region of the twisted nematic (TN)-LCSLM can be visualized and quantified.

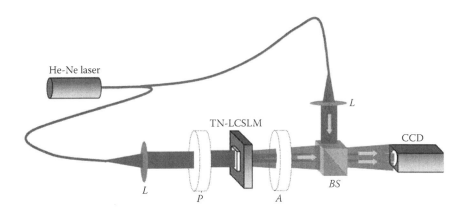

FIGURE 6.23
Digital holography experimental setup for HOLOEYE 2002 TN-LCSLM phase modulation characterization. BS = beam splitter, P = polarizer, A = analyzer, L = collimation lens, CCD = charge coupling device.

The TN-LCSLM is sandwiched between a pair of polarizers in order to separate two modes of modulation that are generally coupled. The complex wave front coming out of the polarizer–SLM–analyzer combination bears the amplitude and phase information that is evaluated quantitatively using the DH method. When an object wave interferes with a known reference wave, the recorded interference pattern is called a hologram. The amplitude and phase information of the object wave are encoded in the interference pattern. In DH, a hologram is recorded directly in digital form using CCD and numerically reconstructed for quantitative evaluation of amplitude and phase information acquired from the entire active area of TN-LCSLM.

The experimental setup to characterize phase modulation from the transmissive HOLOEYE LC2002 TN-LCSLM that uses the Sony LCX016AL liquid crystal microdisplay is shown in Figure 6.23. The TN-LCSLM active area of 21 mm × 26 mm contains 832 × 624 square pixels with pixel pitch of 32 μm and has a fill factor of 55%. HOLOEYE LC2002 has a twisted arrangement of nematic liquid crystal molecules between inner ends of two conductive glass plates. The output of a He-Ne laser (632.8 nm) is coupled into a bifurcated single mode fiber. A collimated beam coming from one fiber arm, called an object beam, is passed through the polarizer–SLM–analyzer combination and illuminates the entire active area of the TN-LCSLM. The complex object wave front, modulated according to the input conditions of the TN-LCSLM, interferes with the collimated reference beam coming from the second fiber arm using a beam splitter and the digital hologram recorded by the CCD sensor and is given by

$$H(n_x, n_y) = \left| O(n_x, n_y) \right|^2 + \left| R(n_x, n_y) \right|^2 + O^*(n_x, n_y) R(n_x, n_y)$$

$$+ O(n_x n_y) R^*(n_x, n_y)$$

(6.20)

where

$n_x = 0,1,\ldots N_x - 1$ and $n_y = 0,1,\ldots N_y - 1$ are the pixel indices of the camera

$N_x \times N_y$ is the size of the CCD sensor in pixels

$O(n_x, n_y)$ is the object wave

$R(n_x, n_y)$ is the collimated reference wave

Since the active area of the TN-LCSLM comprises two-dimensional (2D) arrays of liquid crystal (LC) cells, the object wave, after passing through the TN-LCSLM active area, diffracts into a number of plane waves whose direction of propagation depends on the grating period and size of the LC cell. Using the Fresnel approximation, the complex object wave $O(x, y)$ at CCD plane (x, y) diffracted from SLM plane (x', y') is given by

$$O(x,y)\frac{e^{ikz}}{i\lambda z}\iint t(x',y')\exp\left[i\frac{2\pi}{\lambda z}\left\{(x-x')^2+(y-y')^2\right\}\right]dx'dy' \qquad (6.21)$$

Here, k denotes the propagation constant and z is distance between the SLM and CCD planes, λ is wavelength of object wave, and $t(x', y')$ is the TN-LCSLM transmittance. It should be noted here that the TN-LCSLM transmittance does not include any contribution from the nonactive area of the TN-LCSLM since it provides constant phase change only.

After recording the digital hologram, the convolution method of numerical reconstruction is used to extract quantitative amplitude and phase information from the recorded hologram. This method provides the same resolution of reconstructed image as that of a CCD sensor and is more effective for smaller recording distances. The numerically reconstructed real image wave $U_{real}(n_x', n_y')$ can be written as

$$U_{real}(n_x',n_y') = \Im^{-1}\left[\Im\left\{H'\left(n_x',n_y'\right)\times R\left(n_x',n_y'\right)\right\}\times\Im\left\{g\left(n_x',n_y'\right)\right\}\right] \qquad (6.22)$$

where

$n_x' = 0,1,\ldots N_x' - 1$ and $n_y' = 0,1,\ldots N_y' - 1$ are the pixel indices of the reconstructed image

$N_x' \times N_y'$ is the new size of the preprocessed hologram $H'(n_x', n_y')$

$\Im$ represents the Fourier transform operator

$R(n_x', n_y')$ is the numerically defined reconstructed plane wave

$g(n_x', n_y')$ is the impulse response function of coherent optical system

Finally, the phase value is quantitatively evaluated directly from the reconstructed real image wave as

$$\Delta\phi\left(n_x',n_y'\right) = \arctan\left[\operatorname{Im}\left\{U_{real}\left(n_x',n_y'\right)\right\}\middle/\operatorname{Re}\left\{U_{real}\left(n_x',n_y'\right)\right\}\right] \qquad (6.23)$$

As stated earlier, the amplitude and phase mode of modulation are coupled in the TN-LCSLM and can be separated by choosing particular orientation of the polarizer and analyzer. In order to characterize the TN-LCSLM for phase-mostly modulation, the active area is divided into two equally separated regions called the reference and modulation regions. The grayscale value addressed in the reference region is kept at 0 whereas, in the modulation region, the addressed grayscale value can be varied from 0 to 255 in equal steps. Now, the orientation of polarization axes of both polarizer and analyzer is adjusted with respect to the TN-LCSLM in such a way that the reconstructed intensity image does not show any difference in contrast of two regions from the digital hologram recorded when the reference region is addressed with 0 grayscale value and the modulation region is addressed with 255 grayscale value. At this position of the polarizer and analyzer orientation axes, the transmissive TN-LCSLM operates in phase-mostly mode and hence shows no intensity or amplitude modulation. In our experiment, phase-mostly modulation of the TN-LCSLM is attained with polarizer and analyzer orientation of 15° and 145°, respectively. It should be noted here that the addressed contrast and brightness value on the TN-LCSLM is 255.

Figure 6.24(a) shows the digital hologram recorded when the polarizer–LCSLM–analyzer combination is operated in the phase-mostly mode. Figure 6.24(b) shows the numerically reconstructed intensity image, which depicts that the TN-LCSLM is operated in phase-mostly mode since there is no difference in contrast between the two regions separated by a line due to diffraction. Figure 6.24(c) shows the numerically reconstructed quantitative phase image and Figure 6.24(d) indicates the phase step height of $1.26\,\pi$ measured on the two regions when the TN-LCSLM is addressed with 0 and 255 grayscale values in two equally separated regions.

The DH method to characterize the phase modulation of the TN-LCSLM is also very helpful in characterizing diffractive optics such as single digital lens or digital lens array. This digital lens array is a diffractive optical element computed using the iterative Fourier transform algorithm (IFTA). This digital diffractive lens array is addressed onto the TN-LCSLM active area and the phase modulation in the transmitted optical wave front is analyzed using the DH method in a manner similar to that done previously. First, single lenses with different focal lengths of 8, 120, and 160 mm are displayed on the active area of the TN-LCSLM and tested. The numerically reconstructed phase map for these diffractive optics lenses and the line profile through the center along the diameter are shown in Figure 6.25. The maximum phase modulation measured for three different diffractive optics lenses with different focal lengths is the same and is equal to maximum phase modulation of the TN-LCSLM evaluated earlier. However, the more detailed line profile through the center along the diameter for each lens is slightly different in shape and profile from one to another due to difference in focal lengths and the aberrations existing for practical use of the TN-LCSLM.

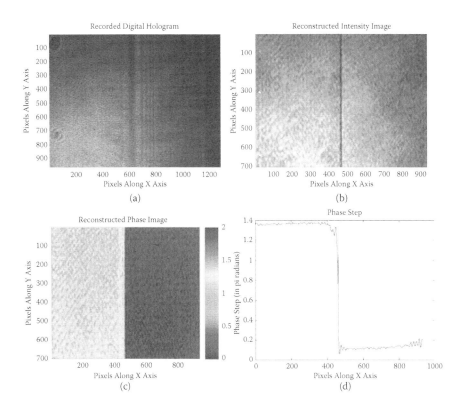

FIGURE 6.24
(See color insert.) (a) Recorded digital hologram numerically reconstructed; (b) intensity image; (c) phase image; (d) phase step height measured from digitally recorded hologram with the TN-LCSLM addressed with 0 and 255 grayscales in two equally separated regions.

Figure 6.26(a) shows the diffractive lens array—all with focal length of 80 mm. The lens array is displayed onto the active area of the TN-LCSLM and the quantitative modulated phase is extracted from the recorded digital hologram. The phase modulation value from the different lenses is the same, however; it was found that if the number of diffractive lenses is increased in an array, the phase modulation from individual digital lenses is decreased due to increase in phase modulation from the lens background. Figure 6.25(b) and (c) show the numerically reconstructed intensity and phase images from the recorded digital hologram, respectively. Figure 6.25(d) shows the phase line profile through the center along the diameter of individual lenses; this can be compared to other lenses in the lens array to ensure the quality of the array. The final results can be used as a quantitative qualification of the DOE lenses or as feedback to revise and improve the previous DOE lens design.

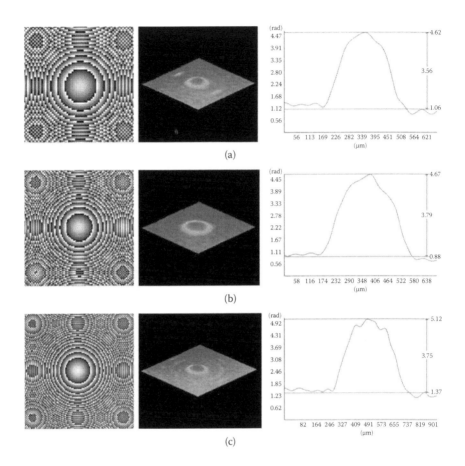

FIGURE 6.25
(See color insert.) Diffractive optics lens with focal lengths with their numerical phase reconstruction using DH method and line profile traced at the center in respective order: (a) 80 mm; (b) 120 mm; (c) 160 mm.

6.2.3 Resolution Enhancement in Digital Holography

6.2.3.1 *Resolution Enhancement Methods*

Compared to conventional holography, DH [31–33] has many advantages, including access to quantitative amplitude and phase information. However, the lateral resolution of DH is limited by the digital recording device. Factors contributing to lateral resolution limitation have been investigated [34–37].

Much research work on the lateral resolution enhancement has been reported. One direct method is to introduce MO into the DH system [38–49]. The drawback of this method is the reduction of the field of view. The MO introduces unwanted curvature and other aberrations that need to be compensated to get correct results.

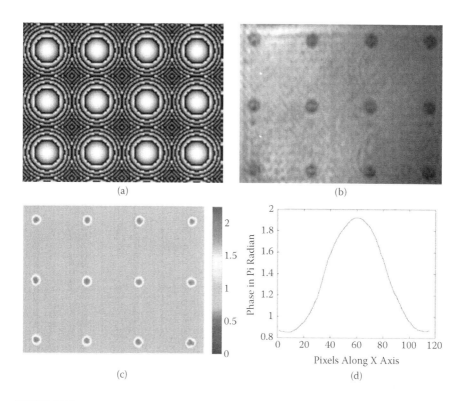

FIGURE 6.26
(a) Diffractive lens array with focal length of 80 mm; (b) numerically reconstructed intensity; (c) phase distribution from the lens array using the DH method; (d) line profile of distribution along the diameter of a typical microlens from the array.

Another method to enhance lateral resolution is to use the aperture synthesis method, which can be categorized into three approaches. One translates the CCD position and records multiple holograms at different positions to collect more object information at a larger diffraction angle. The second approach changes the illuminating light angle or translates the illuminating point source with a fixed CCD position to record multiple holograms. By changing the illuminating light direction or translating the illuminating point source, different diffraction angles of object information can be projected onto and recorded by the CCD. In the third method, the specimen is rotated with a fixed CCD position and illuminating angle. Different diffraction angles of the object are recorded onto the CCD. Larger diffraction angles correspond to higher object frequencies and larger numerical apertures. Better lateral resolution can be expected. After recording, the information recorded by different holograms in aperture synthesis methods needs to be integrated. References 1 and 50–57 illustrate the first aperture synthesis approach of translation of CCD positions.

FIGURE 6.27
Nine holograms taken by shifting CCD. The original hologram is in the middle. (Yan, H. and A. Asundi. *Optics and Lasers in Engineering,* 2011. With permission.)

Here we use reference 1 as an example to illustrate this method. In the experiment, nine holograms are taken, as in Figure 6.27, with the original hologram located at the center. Before stitching, the hologram aperture is 5.952 mm in width and 4.464 mm in length. After stitching, the CCD aperture is expanded to 8.952 mm in width and 7.464 mm in length. The reconstructed intensity images before and after stitching are shown in Figure 6.28. Figure 6.28(a)–(c) are before stitching and Figure 6.28(d)–(f) are after stitching. Figure 6.28(b) and (e) are the images in the highlighted square area of Figure 6.28(a) and (d), respectively, which present the G4 and G5 groups of the USAF target. Figure 6.28(c) and (f) are the images in the highlighted square area of Figure 6.28(b) and (e), respectively, which show the G6 and G7 groups of the USAF target. Lateral resolution is enhanced from about 6.960 and 8.769 μm in x and y directions, respectively, as in Figure 6.28(c), to about 4.385 μm in the x direction and 4.922 μm in the y direction, as in Figure 6.28(f). The field of view is enlarged at the same time, as seen by comparison of Figure 6.28(a) and (b).

References 58–64 illustrate the second aperture synthesis approach by changing the illumination light direction or translating the illuminating point source. As an example, we use reference 60, which reported a super-resolving approach for off-axis digital holographic microscopy in which a microscope objective is used. In this approach, the single illumination point source shifts in sequential mode and holograms are recorded at each shift position. Holograms recorded at different illumination positions are superimposed. Each shift of the illumination beam generates a shift in the object spectrum in such a way that different spatial-frequency bands are transmitted through the objective lens as seen in Figure 6.29. The lateral resolution

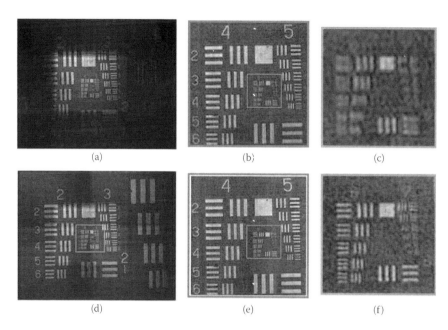

(a)　　　　　　　　(b)　　　　　　　　(c)

(d)　　　　　　　　(e)　　　　　　　　(f)

FIGURE 6.28
Reconstructed intensity images before and after stitching: (a–c) images reconstructed from a single hologram; (d–f) images reconstructed from the stitched hologram. (Yan, H. and A. Asundi. *Optics and Lasers in Engineering*, 2011. With permission.)

was enhanced by a factor of 3× in the x and y directions, and 2.4× in the oblique directions. Finally, reconstruction with lateral resolution of 1.74 μm, as in Figure 6.30, was demonstrated. The setup is a phase step digital holographic setup.

References 65 and 66 illustrate the third aperture synthesis approach by specimen rotation. Of the three methods of aperture synthesis, the first one by translation of CCD has a limitation on the object spatial frequency recorded by the hologram. When CCD is away from the optical axis, the light of higher object spatial frequency is collected with larger angle light diffraction on the CCD. The sampling interval sets a limitation on the maximum frequency to avoid spectrum overlapping. The other two methods do not suffer this limitation as the angles of the light projected on the CCD are not affected by the object spatial frequency. In the second method, object spatial frequency recorded by the CCD is controlled by the illumination light angle. Larger illumination angles diffract higher object frequency onto the CCD. In the third method, the object spatial frequency recorded by the CCD is controlled by the rotation angle of the object. Larger object rotation diffracts higher object frequencies onto the CCD. However, as the object position and phase are also changed during the rotation, additional work to compensate the position and phase change is needed.

FIGURE 6.29
Fourier transform of the addition of different recorded holograms. (Mico, V. et al. *Journal of the Optical Society of America A—Optics Image Science and Vision* 23:3162–3170, 2006. With permission.)

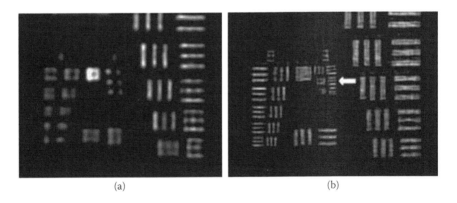

(a)   (b)

FIGURE 6.30
(a) Image obtained with 0.1 NA lens and conventional illumination; (b) super-resolved image obtained with the synthetic aperture. The G9E2 corresponding to the resolution limit using the proposed method is marked with an arrow. (Mico, V. et al. *Journal of the Optical Society of America A—Optics Image Science and Vision* 23:3162–3170, 2006. With permission.)

6.2.3.2 Differences between Hologram Stitching and Zero Padding

Some people think that hologram stitching provides a similar effect to that of zero padding [67]. Their standpoint is that if the size of the modified hologram after zero padding and stitching is the same, the NA should be the same. The fields of view with hologram stitching and zero padding are the same.

But hologram stitching does not really provide an effect similar to that of zero padding, as demonstrated in the practical experiment shown in Figure 6.31. The first column shows the reconstruction from an original recorded hologram (a) of size 1280 × 960 pixels. No padding or stitching is used here. The

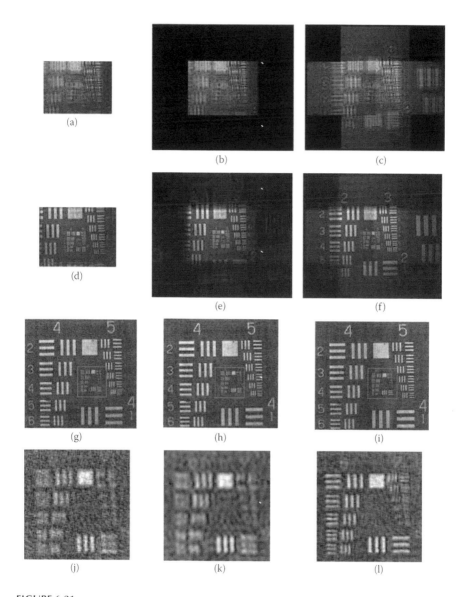

FIGURE 6.31
Reconstruction of original hologram: (a) zero-padded hologram; (b) stitched hologram; (c) using transfer function method.

second column shows the reconstruction from a zero padded hologram (b) from the original hologram (a). This hologram (b) is 2600 × 2280 pixels with zero padding. The third column shows the reconstruction from a stitched hologram (c) of 2600 × 2280 pixels. Hologram (c) is stitched by five single holograms. Each of them is 1280 × 960 pixels. The size of the modified hologram after zero padding (Figure 6.31b) and stitching (Figure 6.31c) is the same.

In reconstruction, the transfer function (or convolution) method is used. Figure 6.31(d)–(f) are the full-field reconstructed images of holograms (a), (b), and (c), respectively. Figure 6.31(g)–(i) show group 4 and group 5 in Figure 6.31(d)–(f), respectively. Figure 6.31(j)–(l) show group 6 and group 7 in Figure 6.31(g)–(i) (inside the white squares), respectively.

From the comparison of Figure 6.31(j)–(l), it can be seen that the resolution capability in (l) by hologram stitching is twice the resolution in (j) from the original hologram and the resolution in (k) from the zero padded hologram. The resolution difference in (j) and (k) is not obvious. Therefore, the lateral resolution of hologram stitching and zero padding is not the same. Hologram stitching provides better lateral resolution than just zero padding.

The aperture size that determines the resolution is not the zero padded hologram size, but rather is the aperture size before zero padding. Suppose that if the original hologram is of size $2D$, it is zero padded to size L, where L is larger than $2D$. The system lateral resolution is $\lambda z/2D$, but not $\lambda z/L$. If the zero padded hologram is used to perform reconstruction, each pixel of the reconstructed image is of the size $\lambda z/L$. But the pixel size of the reconstructed image is not the lateral resolution. They are two different concepts. In the zero padding method, $2D$ is not changed. But, by hologram stitching, the value of $2D$ increases and therefore lateral resolution can be improved.

From the physical view, zero padding does not collect additional information in the system, especially the lights of larger diffraction angles. Only the collection of lights with larger diffraction angles can provide more details of the object and therefore better resolution. Hologram stitching is one way to collect lights of larger diffraction angles. Therefore, it can provide better resolution while zero padding cannot.

Zero padding is usually used in the Fresnel reconstruction method rather than the transfer function method. In Figure 6.32, we use the Fresnel reconstruction method to reconstruct the same holograms in Figure 6.31(a)–(c). Holograms in Figure 6.32(a)–(c) are identical to Figure 6.31(a)–(c), respectively. Figure 6.32(d)–(f) are the full-field reconstructed images of holograms Figure 6.32(a)–(c), respectively. Figure 6.32(g)–(i) show group 4 and group 5 in Figure 6.32(d)–(f), respectively. Figure 6.32(j)–(l) show group 6 and group 7 in (g)–(i) (inside white squares), respectively.

From the comparison of Figure 6.32(j)–(l), it can be seen that the resolution capability in Figure 6.32(l) by hologram stitching is twice the resolution in Figure 6.32(k) by zero padding of the hologram. From the comparison of Figure 6.32(j) and (k), it seems that zero padding in Figure 6.32(k) provides better lateral resolution than without zero padding in Figure 6.32(j). But if we compare Figure 6.32(j) and (k) with Figure 6.31 (j) and (k), it can be noticed that Figure 6.31(j) and (k) and Figure 6.32(k) can provide nearly the same resolution. The resolution of Figure 6.32(j) is worse. Figure 6.31(j) and Figure 6.32(j) are reconstructed from the same hologram. The difference between them is only the reconstruction method. The reason for this is that, under certain parameters, the Fresnel reconstruction causes the loss of lateral

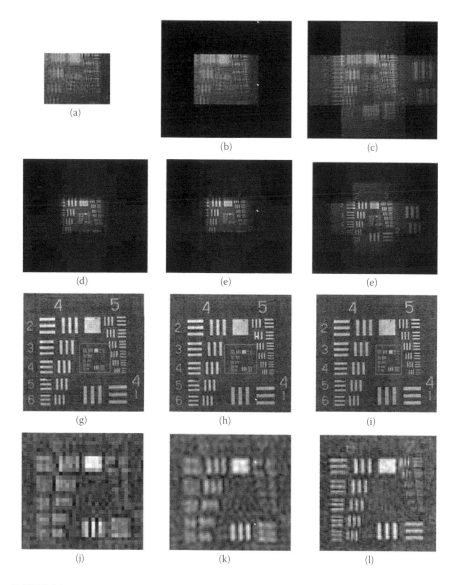

FIGURE 6.32
Reconstruction of original hologram: (a) zero-padded hologram; (b) stitched hologram; (c) using Fresnel method.

resolution; zero padding in the Fresnel reconstruction method can help to avoid this loss. But the transfer function method does not have such problems. Zero padding essentially can help to present the information recorded in the hologram fully, but it cannot add information to the image. Hence, it can only improve the lateral resolution to the value $\lambda z/2D$ where $2D$ is the hologram size before zero padding but cannot exceed it. This improvement by zero padding is reconstruction method dependent. On the other hand, in both Figure 6.31 and Figure 6.32, it can be seen that hologram stitching provides better lateral resolution than just zero padding.

6.3 Conclusion

Digital holography has been shown to have widespread applications for 3D profilometry with nanoscale sensitivity. For reflective surfaces as encountered in MEMS and the microelectronics industry, the compact digital holoscope is a portable system that can be used for in situ process measurement as well as characterizing and inspection of microsystems and devices. For transparent objects such as microlenses and other optical elements, the system can characterize these components. Indeed, some novel applications of the transmission system for ferroelectric and liquid crystal based diffractive optical element testing have been demonstrated. Finally, optical systems suffer from a lack of spatial resolution. While the axial resolution is high (~10 nm), the spatial resolution is diffraction limited. A novel approach, which enables smaller objects to be monitored, has been shown to enhance this spatial resolution.

References

1. H. Yan, and A. Asundi. Studies on aperture synthesis in digital Fresnel holography. *Optics and Lasers in Engineering* 50:(4)556–562 (2011).
2. D. Gabor. A new microscopic principle. *Nature* 161:777–778 (1948).
3. S. Kostianovski, S. G. Lipson, and E. N. Ribak. Interference microscopy and Fourier fringe analysis applied to measuring the spatial refractive-index distribution. *Applied Optics* 32:7 (1993).
4. E. Cuche, F. Bevilacqua, and C. Depeursinge. Digital holography for quantitative phase-contrast imaging. *Optics Letters* 24:291 (1999).
5. F. Zhang, I. Yamaguchi, and L. P. Yaroslavsky, Algorithm for reconstruction of digital holograms with adjustable magnification. *Optics Letters* 29:1668–1670 (2004).
6. S. D. Nicola, A. Finizio, G. Pierattini, P. Ferraro, and A. D. Alfieri. Angular spectrum method with correction of anamorphism for numerical reconstruction of digital holograms on tilted planes. *Optics Express* 13:9935–9940 (2005) (http://www.opticsinfobase.org/oe/abstract.cfm?uri=oe-13-24-9935).
7. L. Yu, and M. K. Kim. Pixel resolution control in numerical reconstruction of digital holography. *Optics Letters* 31:897–899 (2006).

8. W. Haddad, D. Cullen, J. C. Solem, J. M. Longworth, A. McPherson, K. Boyer, and C. K. Rhodes. Fourier-transform holographicmicroscope. *Applied Optics* 31:4973–4978 (1992).

9. T. Colomb, F. Montfort, J. Kühn, N. Aspert, E. Cuche, A. Marian, F. Charrière, et al. Numerical parametric lens for shifting, magnification, and complete aberration compensation in digital holographic microscopy. *Journal Optical Society America* A 23:3177 (2006).

10. T. Colomb, E. Cuche, F. Charrière, J. Kühn, N. Aspert, F. Montfort, P. Marquet, and A. C. Depeursinge. Automatic procedure for aberration compensation in digital holographic microscopy and applications to specimen shape compensation. *Applied Optics* 45:851 (2006).

11. E. Cuche, P. Marquet, and A. C. Depeursinge. Simultaneous amplitude-contrast and quantitative phase-contrast microscopy by numerical reconstruction of Fresnel off-axis holograms. *Applied Optics* 38:6994–7001 (1999).

12. A. Stadelmaier, and J. H. Massig. Compensation of lens aberrations in digital holography. *Optics Letters* 25:3 (2000).

13. D. Carl, B. Kemper, G. Wernicke, and G. V. Bally. Parameter-optimized digital holographic microscope for high-resolution living-cell analysis. *Applied Optics* 43:9 (2004).

14. P. Ferraro, S. D. Nicola, A. Finizio, G. Coppola, S. Grilli, C. Magro, and A. G. Pierattini. Compensation of the inherent wave front curvature in digital holographic coherent microscopy for quantitative phase-contrast imaging. *Applied Optics* 42:1938–1946 (2003).

15. F. Montfort, F. Charrière, T. Colomb, E. Cuche, P. Marquet, and A. C. Depeursinge. Purely numerical compensation for microscope objective phase curvature in digital holographic microscopy: Influence of digital phase mask position. *Journal Optical Society America* A 23:2944 (2006).

16. W. Qu, C. O. Choo, Y. Yingjie, and A. Asundi, Microlens characterization by digital holographic microscopy with physical spherical phase compensation. *Applied Optics* 49:6448–6454 (2010).

17. D. Malacara, ed. *Optical shop testing*. New York: Wiley (1992).

18. C. Mann, L. Yu, C -M. Lo, and M. Kim. High-resolution quantitative phase-contrast microscopy by digital holography. *Optics Express* 13:8693–8698 (2005).

19. Z. Ya'nan, Q. Weijuan, L. De'an, L. Zhu, Z. Yu, and L. Liren. Ridge-shape phase distribution adjacent to 180° domain wall in congruent LiNbO3 crystal. *Applied Physics Letters* 89:112912 (2006).

20. W. Qu, C. O. Choo, V. R. Singh, Y. Yingjie, and A. Asundi. Quasi-physical phase compensation in digital holographic microscopy. *Journal Optical Society America* A 26:2005–2011 (2009).

21. J. A. Ferrari, and E. M. Frins. Single-element interferometer. *Optics Communications* 279:235–239 (2007).

22. Q. Weijuan, Y. Yingjie, C. O. Choo, and A. Asundi. Digital holographic microscopy with physical phase compensation. *Optics Letters* 34:1276–1278 (2009).

23. Q. Weijuan, K. Bhattacharya, C. O. Choo, Y. Yingjie, and A. Asundi. Transmission digital holographic microscopy based on a beam-splitter cube interferometer. *Applied Optics* 48:2778–2783 (2009).

24. B. Kemper, and G. V. Bally. Digital holographic microscopy for live cell applications and technical inspection. *Applied Optics* 47:10 (2008).

25. E. Cuche, P. Marquet, and C. Depeursinge. Spatial filtering for zero-order and twin-image elimination in digital off-axis holography. *Applied Optics* 39:4070 (2000).

26. Q. Xi, D. A. Liu, Y. N. Zhi, Z. Luan, and A. L. Liu. Reversible electrochromic effect accompanying domain-inversion in LiNbO3:Ru:Fe crystals. *Applied Physics Letters* 87:121103 (2005).

27. Y. N. Zhi, D. A. Liu, Y. Zhou, Z. Chai, and A. L. Liu. Electrochromism accompanying ferroelectric domain inversion in congruent RuO2:LiNbO3 crystal. *Optics Express* 13:10172 (2005).

28. S. Grilli, P. Ferraro, M. Paturzo, D. Alfieri, P. D. Natale, M. D. Angelis, S. D. Nicola, A. Finizio, and A. G. Pierattini. In-situ visualization, monitoring and analysis of electric field domain reversal process in ferroelectric crystals by digital holography. *Optics Express* 12:1832 (2004).

29. M. Jazbinsek, and M. Zgonik. Material tensor parameters of LiNbO3 relevant for electro- and elasto-optics. *Applied Physics* B 74:407–414 (2002).

30. H. Takahashi, N. Kureyama, and T. Aida. Flatbed-type bidirectional three-dimensional display system. *International Journal of Innovative Computing, Information and Control* 5:4115–4124 (2009).

31. U. Schnars. Direct phase determination in hologram interferometry with use of digitally recorded holograms. *Journal of the Optical Society of America A—Optics Image Science and Vision* 11:2011–2015 (1994).

32. U. Schnars, and W. Juptner. Direct recording of holograms by a CCD target and numerical reconstruction. *Applied Optics* 33:179–181 (1994) (<Go to ISI>://A1994MX44500005).

33. U. Schnars, and W. P. O. Juptner. Digital recording and numerical reconstruction of holograms. *Measurement Science & Technology* 13:R85–R101 (2002) (<Go to ISI>://000178298700001).

34. D. P. Kelly, B. M. Hennelly, N. Pandey, T. J. Naughton, and W. T. Rhodes. Resolution limits in practical digital holographic systems. *Optical Engineering* 48 (9)095801-1-13 (2009) (<Go to ISI>://000270882000012).

35. L. Xu, X. Y. Peng, Z. X. Guo, J. M. Miao, and A. Asundi. Imaging analysis of digital holography. *Optics Express* 13:2444–2452 (2005) (<Go to ISI>://000228180800024).

36. H. Z. Jin, H. Wan, Y. P. Zhang, Y. Li, and P. Z. Qiu. The influence of structural parameters of CCD on the reconstruction image of digital holograms. *Journal of Modern Optics* 55:2989–3000 (2008) (<Go to ISI>://000261381800008).

37. A. A. Yan Hao. Resolution analysis of a digital holography system. *Applied Optics* 50:11 (2011).

38. T. Colomb, J. K. Kuhn, F. Charriere, C. Depeursinge, P. Marquet, and N. Aspert. Total aberrations compensation in digital holographic microscopy with a reference conjugated hologram. *Optics Express* 14:4300–4306 (2006) (<Go to ISI>://000237608600011).

39. F. Charriere, J. Kuhn, T. Colomb, F. Montfort, E. Cuche, Y. Emery, K. Weible, P. Marquet, and C. Depeursinge. Characterization of microlenses by digital holographic microscopy. *Applied Optics* 45:829–835 (2006) (<Go to ISI>://000235387400003).

40. B. Rappaz, P. Marquet, E. Cuche, Y. Emery, C. Depeursinge, and P. J. Magistretti. Measurement of the integral refractive index and dynamic cell morphometry of living cells with digital holographic microscopy. *Optics Express* 13:9361–9373 (2005) (<Go to ISI>://000233334900026).

41. F. Charriere, N. Pavillon, T. Colomb, C. Depeursinge, T. J. Heger, E. A. D. Mitchell, P. Marquet, and B. Rappaz. Living specimen tomography by digital holographic microscopy: Morphometry of testate amoeba. *Optics Express* 14:7005–7013 (2006) (<Go to ISI>://000239861100004).

42. C. Liu, Y. S. Bae, W. Z. Yang, and D. Y. Kim. All-in-one multifunctional optical microscope with a single holographic measurement. *Optical Engineering* 47 (8)087001-1-7 (2008) (<Go to ISI>://000259865500025).

43. F. Charriere, A. Marian, F. Montfort, J. Kuehn, T. Colomb, E. Cuche, P. Marquet, and C. Depeursinge. Cell refractive index tomography by digital holographic microscopy. *Optics Letters* 31:178–180 (2006) (<Go to ISI>://000234665000013).

44. P. Marquet, B. Rappaz, P. J. Magistretti, E. Cuche, Y. Emery, T. Colomb, and C. Depeursinge. Digital holographic microscopy: A noninvasive contrast imaging technique allowing quantitative visualization of living cells with subwavelength axial accuracy. *Optics Letters* 30:468–470 (2005) (<Go to ISI>://000227371800006).

45. F. Montfort, T. Colomb, F. Charriere, J. Kuhn, P. Marquet, E. Cuche, S. Herminjard, and C. Depeursinge. Submicrometer optical tomography by multiple-wavelength digital holographic microscopy. *Applied Optics* 45:8209–8217 (2006) (<Go to ISI>://WOS:000241888200006).

46. F. Charriere, T. Colomb, F. Montfort, E. Cuche, P. Marquet, and C. Depeursinge. Shot-noise influence on the reconstructed phase image signal-to-noise ratio in digital holographic microscopy. *Applied Optics* 45:7667–7673 (2006) (<Go to ISI>://WOS:000241084300017).

47. F. Charriere, A. Marian, T. Colomb, P. Marquet, and C. Depeursinge. Amplitude point-spread function measurement of high-NA microscope objectives by digital holographic microscopy. *Optics Letters* 32:2456–2458 (2007) (<Go to ISI>://WOS:000249327600062).

48. I. Yamaguchi, J. Kato, S. Ohta, and J. Mizuno. Image formation in phase-shifting digital holography and applications to microscopy. *Applied Optics* 40:6177–6186 (2001) (<Go to ISI>://WOS:000172713000005).

49. A. Stern, and B. Javidi. Improved-resolution digital holography using the generalized sampling theorem for locally band-limited fields. *Journal of the Optical Society of America A   Optics Image Science and Vision* 23:1227–1235 (2006), (<Go to ISI>://000237303600029).

50. T. Kreis, M. Adams, and W. Juptner. Aperture synthesis in digital holography. In *Interferometry XI: Techniques and analysis,* ed. K. Creath and J. Schmit, 69–76, Bellingham, WA: SPIE (2002).

51. J. H. Massig. Digital off-axis holography with a synthetic aperture. *Optics Letters* 27:2179–2181 (2002) (<Go to ISI>://000179795000011).

52. L. Martinez-Leon, and B. Javidi. Improved resolution synthetic aperture holographic imaging. Art. no. 67780A. In *Three-dimensional TV, video, and display VI,* ed. B. Javidi, F. Okano, and J. Y. Son, A7780–A7780 (2007).

53. D. Claus. High resolution digital holographic synthetic aperture applied to deformation measurement and extended depth of field method. *Applied Optics* 49:3187–3198 (2010) (<Go to ISI>://000278265600027).

54. F. Gyimesi, Z. Fuzessy, V. Borbely, B. Raczkevi, G. Molnar, A. Czitrovszky, A. T. Nagy, G. Molnarka, A. Lotfi, A Nagy, I. Harmati, and D. Szigethy. Half-magnitude extensions of resolution and field of view in digital holography by scanning and magnification. *Applied Optics* 48:6026–6034 (2009) (<Go to ISI>://000271374000044).

55. J. L. Di, J. L. Zhao, H. Z. Jiang, P. Zhang, Q. Fan, and W. W. Sun. High resolution digital holographic microscopy with a wide field of view based on a synthetic aperture technique and use of linear CCD scanning. *Applied Optics* 47:5654–5659 (2008) (<Go to ISI>://000260726000013).

56. L. Martinez-Leon, and B. Javidi. Synthetic aperture single-exposure on-axis digital holography. *Optics Express* 16:161–169 (2008) (<Go to ISI>://000252234800019).

57. T. Kreis, and K. Schluter. Resolution enhancement by aperture synthesis in digital holography, *Optical Engineering* 46 (5)055803-1-7 (2007) (<Go to ISI>://000247812900042).

58. S. A. Alexandrov, T. R. Hillman, T. Gutzler, and D. D. Sampson. Synthetic aperture Fourier holographic optical microscopy. *Physical Review Letters* 97 (16):168102 (2006), <Go to ISI>://000241405400066.

59. T. R. Hillman, T. Gutzler, S. A. Alexandrov, and D. D. Sampson. High-resolution, wide-field object reconstruction with synthetic aperture Fourier holographic optical microscopy. *Optics Express* 17:7873–7892 (2009) (<Go to ISI>://000266381900017).

60. V. Mico, Z. Zalevsky, P. Garcia-Martinez, and J. Garcia. Synthetic aperture super-resolution with multiple off-axis holograms. *Journal of the Optical Society of America* A—Optics Image Science and Vision 23:3162–3170 (2006) (<Go to ISI>://000242326400019).

61. C. J. Yuan, H. C. Zhai, and H. T. Liu. Angular multiplexing in pulsed digital holography for aperture synthesis. *Optics Letters* 33:2356–2358 (2008) (<Go to ISI>://000260970800025).

62. L. Granero, V. Mico, Z. Zalevsky, and J. Garcia. Synthetic aperture super-resolved microscopy in digital lensless Fourier holography by time and angular multiplexing of the object information. *Applied Optics* 49:845–857 (2010) (<Go to ISI>://000274444100013).

63. P. Feng, X. Wen, and R. Lu. Long-working-distance synthetic aperture Fresnel off-axis digital holography. *Optics Express* 17:5473–5480 (2009) (<Go to ISI>://000264747500064).

64. V. Mico, Z. Zalevsky, P. Garcia-Martinez, and J. Garcia. Superresolved imaging in digital holography by superposition of tilted wave fronts. *Applied Optics* 45:822–828 (2006) (<Go to ISI>://000235387400002).

65. R. Binet, J. Colineau, and J. C. Lehureau. Short-range synthetic aperture imaging at 633 nm by digital holography. *Applied Optics* 41:4775–4782 (2002) (<Go to ISI>://000177327100003).

66. Y. Zhang, X. X. Lu, Y. L. Luo, L. Y. Zhong, and C. L. She. Synthetic aperture digital holography by movement of object. In *Holography, diffractive optics, and applications II*, Pts 1 and 2, ed. Y. L. Sheng, D. S. Hsu, C. X. Yu, and B. H. Lee, 581–588 Bellingham, WA: SPIE (2005).

67. S. D. N. Pietro Ferraro, A. Finizio, G. Pierattini, and G. Coppola. Recovering image resolution in reconstructing digital off-axis holograms by Fresnel-transform method. *Applied Physics Letters* 85 (14)2709–2711 (2004).

7

3D Dynamic Shape Measurement Using the Grating Projection Technique

Xianyu Su, Qican Zhang, and Wenjing Chen

CONTENTS

Three-dimensional (3D) shape measuring techniques, using a combination of grating projection and a most frequently used mathematical tool—Fourier fringe analysis—have been deeply researched and are increasing in number. These kinds of techniques are based on the idea of projecting and superposing a carrier fringe pattern onto the surface of the tested object and then reconstructing its corresponding 3D shape from the deformed fringe pattern modulated by the height of the tested object and captured by a camera from another view direction. In this chapter, the basic principles and some proof-of-principle applications of 3D dynamic shape measurement using grating projection and Fourier fringe analysis will be demonstrated to review our research results of this combined approach. This chapter mainly focuses on this technology and its applications that we have developed over the past 10 years. Section 7.1 gives a brief introduction of 3D shape measurement using grating projection. Section 7.2 describes the basic principles of 3D dynamic shape measurement using grating projection and Fourier fringe analysis. Section 7.3 demonstrates some typical applications that we achieved. Section 7.4 expresses the fundamental concept of the time-average fringe method for vibration mode analysis and its experimental results. In the last section, we discuss the advantages and challenges of this technique and the current development of real-time measurement in this research field.

7.1 Introduction

Optical noncontact 3D shape measurement based on grating projection (namely, structured illumination) is concerned with extracting the geometric information from an image of the measured object. With its excellence in high speed and high accuracy, it has been widely used for industry inspection, quality control, biomedical engineering, dressmaking, and machine vision [1,2].

By means of two-dimensional (2D) grating projection, we have the possibility of recovering 3D shape information with the advantages of speed and full field. Many varieties of projected grating, such as black and white grating, grayscale grating, color-coded grating, and Gray-coded binary fringe sequences (which can be also classified as Ronchi, sinusoidal, and saw tooth grating), have been proposed and used in 3D shape measurement [3]. Actually, a more commonly used fringe is 2D Ronchi or sinusoidal grating.

There are two types of projection units. The first uses a conventional imaging system to make an image of the mask, precisely produced from a well designed pattern onto the surface of the tested object. The new type of projection unit uses a programmable spatial light modulator (SLM)—for example, a liquid crystal display (LCD) or digital micromirror device (DMD)—to control the spacing, color, and structure of the projected grating precisely.

Meanwhile, several methods of fringe analysis have been exhaustively studied for 3D shape measurement of a static object, including the moiré technique (MT) [4], phase-measuring profilometry (PMP) [5,6], Fourier transformation profilometry (FTP) [7–10], modulation measurement profilometry (MMP) [11], spatial phase detection (SPD) [12,13], etc. For 3D dynamic shape measuring, a set of grayscale random stripe patterns is projected onto a dynamic object and then the time-varying depth maps are recovered by the space–time stereo method [14]. Some researchers have succeeded in establishing a high-speed projection unit by removing the DMD's color wheel to increase the rate at which three-step phase-shifting grayscale gratings are projected to 180 Hz; they have achieved some wonderful applications using this system [15].

Among these techniques, FTP, originally conceived and demonstrated by Takeda, Ina, and Kobayashi [7], is one of the most used methods because only one or two fringes are needed, full-field analysis, high precision, etc. In FTP, a Ronchi grating or a sinusoidal grating is projected onto an object, and the depth information of the object is encoded into the deformed fringe pattern recorded by an image acquisition sensor. The surface shape can be decoded by calculating Fourier transformation, filtering in the spatial frequency domain, and calculating the inverse Fourier transformation.

Compared with MT, FTP can accomplish a fully automatic distinction between a depression and an evaluation of the object shape. It requires no fringe order assignments or fringe center determination, and it requires no interpolation between fringes because it gives height distribution at each pixel over the entire field. Compared with PMP and MMP, FTP requires only one or two images of the deformed fringe pattern, which has become one of the most popular methods in real-time data processing and dynamic data processing.

After Takeda et al., the FTP method and its applications were extensively studied [16–28]. Many researchers worked to improve one-dimensional (1D) FTP method and extend its application. W. W. Macy [16] expanded 1D FTP to 2D FTP, and Bone discussed fringe pattern analysis issues using a 2D Fourier transform [17,18]. Two-dimensional Fourier transform and 2D filtering techniques were successfully introduced into specific applications [19–22]. In order to extend the measurable slope of FTP, a sinusoidal projection technique and π-phase-shifting grating technique, by which the measurable slope of height variation was nearly three times that of the original FTP, were proposed [9]. Some modified FTP permits the tested objects to have 3D steep shapes, discontinuous height step, and/or spatially isolated surfaces, or 360° entire shape [23–26]. The phase error introduced by the application of the Fourier transform method to improve the accuracy of FTP has been discussed in detail [27,28]. In addition, 3D dynamic measurement based on FTP has widely attracted research interest [29,30]. In recent years, 3D Fourier fringe analysis was proposed by Abdul-Rahman et al. [31]. In 2010, an editorial, "Fringe Projection Techniques: Whither We Are?" reviewed the fringe projection techniques and their applications [32]; this was helpful to people interested in 3D measurement based on the fringe projection technique.

We have dedicated our research effort to improving the FTP method, extending its application, and introducing it into 3D dynamic shape measurement over the past 10 years; we have developed some achievements in 3D dynamic shape measurement based on grating projection and Fourier fringe analysis (covered in this chapter and already published in either conference proceedings or journal articles). For more detailed descriptions and discussions of this technique, the references listed at the end of this chapter, especially our three published papers in *Optics and Lasers in Engineering* [10,29,30], are recommended.

7.2 Basic Principles of 3D Dynamic Shape Measurement Based on FTP

Fourier transformation profilometry for 3D dynamic shape measurement is usually implemented as follows. A Ronchi grating or sinusoidal grating is projected onto an object's surface to modulate its height distribution. Then, a sequence of dynamic deformed fringe images can be grabbed by a camera from the other view and rapidly saved in a computer. Next, data are processed by Fourier fringe analysis with three steps.

- By using Fourier transform, we obtain their spectra, which are isolated in the Fourier plane when the sampling theorem is satisfied
- By adopting a suitable band-pass filter (e.g., a Hann window) in the spatial frequency domain, all the frequency components are eliminated except the fundamental component. And by calculating inverse Fourier transform of the fundamental component, a sequence of phase maps can be obtained.
- By applying the phase-unwrapping algorithm in 3D phase space, the height distributions of the measured dynamic object in different time can be reconstructed under a perfect phase-to-height mapping.

7.2.1 Measuring System Based on Grating Projection

The optical geometry of the measurement system for dynamic scenes is similar to traditional FTP. Two options of optical geometry are available in FTP, including crossed optical axes geometry and parallel optical axes geometry. Each has its own merits as well as disadvantages [5]. The crossed optical axes geometry, as shown in Figure 7.1, is easy to construct because both a grating and an image sensor can be placed on the optical axes of the projector and the camera, respectively. It is very popular in FTP. Here, we use it as an example to describe the principle of FTP.

In Figure 7.1, the optical axis $E_p'-E_p$ of a projector lens crosses the optical axis $E_c'-E_c$ of a camera lens at point O on a reference plane, which is normal to the optical axis $E_c'-E_c$ and serves as a fictitious reference to measure the object height $Z(x, y)$. d is the distance between the projector system and the

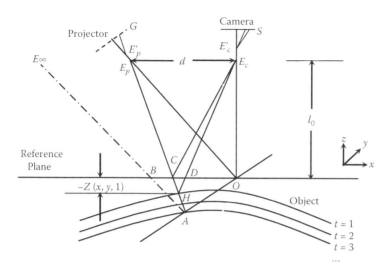

FIGURE 7.1
Crossed-optical-axes geometry of a 3D dynamic shape measurement system based on FTP.

camera system, and l_0 is the distance between the camera system and the reference plane.

By projecting a grating G onto the reference plane, its image (with period p_0) can be observed through the camera in another view and can be represented by

$$g_0(x,y) = \sum_{n=-\infty}^{+\infty} A_n r_0(x,y)\exp\{i[2n\pi f_0 x + n\phi_0(x,y)]\} \qquad (7.1)$$

where
$r_0(x, y)$ is a nonuniform distribution of reflectivity on the reference plane
A_n are the weighting factors of Fourier series
f_0 $(f_0 = 1/p_0)$ is the carrier frequency of the observed grating image in the x-direction
$\phi_0(x,y)$ is the original phase on the reference plane (i.e., $Z(x, y) = 0$)

The coordinate axes are chosen as shown in Figure 7.1. According to this optical geometry, an experimental setup can be established as shown in Figure 7.2.

When the measured object is stationary, the image intensity, which is obtained by the camera, is independent of the time and usually expressed as $g(x, y)$. But when a dynamic object whose height distribution varies with the time is placed into this optical field, the intensity of these fringe patterns is obviously a function of both the spatial coordinates and the time, and it can

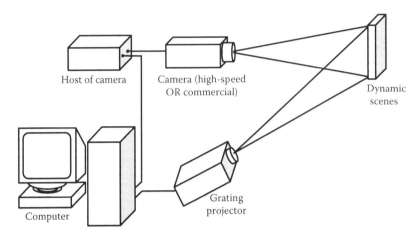

FIGURE 7.2
Schematic diagram of the experimental setup.

be marked as $g(x, y, z(t))$. The phase distribution that implicated the height variation of the measured dynamic object is also a function of the time and can be noted as $\varphi(x,y,t)$. Strictly speaking, in dynamic scenes, x and y coordinates are also changing with time and are much smaller in comparison with z coordinates. Therefore, their changes are usually ignored.

A sequence of the deformed fringe patterns can be grabbed by camera and rapidly stored in a computer. The intensity distributions of these fringe patterns in different time can be expressed as

$$g(x,y,z(t)) = \sum_{n=-\infty}^{+\infty} A_n r(x,y,t) \exp\{i[2n\pi f_0 x + n\phi(x,y,t)]\} \quad (t = 1,2,...,m) \quad (7.2)$$

where $r(x,y,t)$ and $\varphi(x,y,t)$ respectively represent a nonuniform distribution of reflectivity on the object surface and the phase modulation caused by the object height variation in the different time; m is the total number of all fringe images grabbed by the camera.

Fourier transform (filtering only the first-order term ($n = 1$) of the Fourier spectra) and inverse Fourier transform are carried out to deal with each fringe pattern grabbed by the camera at a different time. Complex signals at different times can be calculated:

$$\hat{g}(x,y,z(t)) = A_1 r(x,y,t) \exp\{i[2\pi f_0 x + \phi(x,y,t)]\} \quad (7.3)$$

The same operations are applied to the fringe pattern on the reference plane to obtain the complex signal of the reference plane:

$$\hat{g}_0(x,y) = A_1 r_0(x,y)\exp\{i[2\pi f_0 x + \phi_0(x,y)]\} \tag{7.4}$$

By knowledge of the geometrical and optical configuration of the system in Figure 7.1, the phase variation resulting from the object height distribution is

$$\Delta\phi(x,y,t) = \phi(x,y,t) - \phi_0(x,y) = 2\pi f_0 (\overline{BD} - \overline{BC}) = 2\pi f_0 \overline{CD}$$

$$= 2\pi f_0 \frac{-dZ(z,y,t)}{l_0 - Z(x,y,t)} \tag{7.5}$$

Since the phase calculated by computer gives principal values ranging from $-\pi$ to π, $\Delta\phi(x,y,t)$ is wrapped into this range and consequently has discontinuities with 2π-phase jumps. A phase-unwrapping process is required to correct these discontinuities by adding or subtracting 2π according to the phase jump ranging from π to $-\pi$ or vice versa.

Solving Equation (7.5) for $Z(x, y, t)$, the formula of height distribution can be obtained:

$$Z(x,y,t) = \frac{l_0 \Delta\Phi(x,y,t)}{\Delta\Phi(x,y,t) - 2\pi f_0 d} \tag{7.6}$$

where $\Delta\Phi(x,y,t)$ is the unwrapped phase distribution of $\Delta\phi(x,y,t)$. In practical measurements, usually $l_0 \gg Z(x,y,t)$, Equation (7.6) can be simplified as

$$Z(x,y,t) \approx -\frac{l_0}{2 f_0 d} \Delta\Phi(x,y,t) = -\frac{1}{2\pi\lambda_e} \Delta\Phi(x,y,t) \tag{7.7}$$

where λ_e is the equivalent wavelength of the measuring system. When the measuring system is not perfect, some research work has been carried out to solve the problems.

7.2.2 3D Phase Calculation and Unwrapping

The 3D wrapped phase can be calculated by two approaches. In the first one, the recorded 3D fringe data (time-sequence fringes) are regarded as a collection of many individual 2D fringes, and the wrapped phase can be calculated frame by frame in 2D spatial space according to the sampling time. Directly calculating the multiplication of $\hat{g}(x,y,z(t))$ with $\hat{g}^*(x,y,t=0)$ in each 2D space at different sampling times, the phase distribution $\Delta\phi(x,y,t)$ can be calculated by

$$\Delta\phi(x,y,t) = \phi(x,y,t) - \phi(x,y,0) = arctg\frac{\text{Im}[\hat{g}(x,y,z(t))\hat{g}^*(x,y,t=0)]}{\text{Re}[\hat{g}(x,y,z(t))\hat{g}^*(x,y,t=0)]} \tag{7.8}$$

where *Im* and *Re* represent the imaginary part and real part of $\hat{g}(x,y,z(t))\hat{g}^*$ $(x,y,t=0)$, respectively. By this method, we can obtain a sequence of phase distributions contained in each deformed fringe that include the fluctuation information of a dynamic object. If the sampling rate is high enough, the phase difference between two adjacent sampling frames will be smaller, and it will lead to an easy phase-unwrapping process in 3D space. On the other hand, the fringe analysis could also be done in a single 3D volume rather than as a set of individual 2D frames that are processed in isolation. Three-dimensional FFT and 3D filtering in the frequency domain to obtain the 3D wrapped phase volume are equivalent in performance to 2D fringe analysis [31].

The phase calculation by any inverse trigonometric function (i.e., arc-tangents) provides the principal phase values ranging from $-\pi$ to π; consequently, phase values have discontinuities with 2π phase jumps. For phase data without noise, these discontinuities can be easily corrected by adding or subtracting 2π according to the phase jump ranging from $-\pi$ to π or vice versa. This is called the phase-unwrapping procedure [33–37]. Research on phase-unwrapping algorithm is also an attractive branch in FTP. Some achievements have been gained and employed in special application results [38,39].

Three-dimensional phase unwrapping must be conducted along x, y, and t directions. Compared to 2D phase unwrapping, it can provide more choices of the path for the unwrapping process. Some discontinuity points, which result from noise, shadow, and undersampling and cannot be unwrapped along x or y directions in their own frame, can be unwrapped successfully along the t direction. Therefore, compared with 2D phase unwrapping, 3D phase unwrapping is easier and more accurate.

If the wrapped phase is reliable everywhere and the phase difference between the neighboring pixels in a 3D phase space is less than π (the camera's frame rate is high enough), the unwrapping problem is trivial. The precise phase values in the whole 3D phase field can be obtained by calculating the sum of the phase difference along the t direction under this condition.

In an actual measurement, many factors, such as noise, fringe break, shadow, undersampling resulting from very high fringe density, and under-modulation from very sparse fringe density, make the actual unwrapping procedure complicated and path dependent. Combined with a modulation analysis technique, the 2D phase-unwrapping method based on modulation ordering has been discussed well in references 32 and 35. This 2D phase-unwrapping procedure based on modulation can be extended as a reliability function to 3D phase space. The unwrapping path is always along the direction from the pixel with a higher modulation to the pixel with lower modulation until the entire 3D wrapped phase is unwrapped. The unwrapping scheme is shown in Figure 7.3; the lines with arrows display one of the phase-unwrapping paths based on modulation ordering.

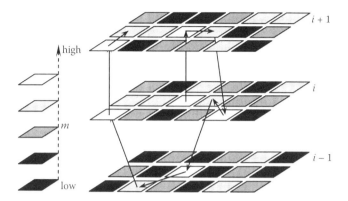

FIGURE 7.3
Sketch map of 3D phase unwrapping based on modulation ordering.

7.2.3 System Calibration

In practice, the system calibration will be completed through two steps. The first is to calibrate the used camera accurately. We adopt Zhang's calibration model [40] to find the intrinsic parameters and extrinsic parameter and the transformation between the (x, y, z) coordinates in a world coordinate system and that in the camera coordinate system. After the camera is well calibrated, the second step is to establish a phase-to-height mapping table, which is used to determine the height of each point of the object. The dual-direction nonlinear phase-to-height mapping technique is usually adopted (see detailed description in reference 41). Generally, the relation between the unwrapped phase and the height $Z(x, y, t)$ can be written as

$$\frac{1}{Z(x,y,t)} = a(x,y) + \frac{b(x,y)}{\Delta\Phi_r(x,y,t)} + \frac{c(x,y)}{\Delta\Phi_r^2(x,y,t)} \qquad (7.9)$$

where, for a sampling instant t, $\Delta\Phi_r(x,y,t) = \Phi(x,y,t) - \Phi_r(x,y)$ is the phase difference between the two unwrapped phase distributions, $\Phi(x,y,t)$ for the measured object and $\Phi_r(x,y)$ for the reference plane. $Z(x,y,t)$ is the relative height from the reference plane; $a(x,y)$, $b(x,y)$, and $c(x,y)$ are the mapping parameters that can be calculated from the continuous phase distributions of four or more standard planes with known heights. The height distribution of the measured object at each sampling instant will be obtained by Equation (7.9), as long as its 3D phase distribution has been unwrapped.

7.2.4 Measuring Accuracy and Measurable Range

Since FTP is based on filtering for selecting only a single spectrum of the fundamental frequency component, the carrier frequency f_0 must separate this spectrum from all other spectra. This condition limits the maximum range measurable by FTP. The measurable slope of height variation of conditional FTP does not exceed the following limitation [8]:

$$\left|\frac{\partial Z(x,y)}{\partial x}\right|_{\max} < \frac{l_0}{3d} \tag{7.10}$$

When the measurable slope of height variation extends this limitation, the fundamental component will overlap the other components, and then the reconstruction will fail. In order to extend the measurable slope of FTP, the sine or quasi-sine projection technique and π-phase-shifting technique can be employed to make only fundamental component exist in a spatial frequency domain [9]. In this case, the lower frequency part of the fundamental component can extend to zero, and the higher part can extend to $2f_0$ without overlaps. The sinusoidal (quasi-sinusoidal) projection and π-phase-shifting technique result in a larger range of the measurement—that is,

$$\left|\frac{\partial h(x,y)}{\partial x}\right| < \frac{L_0}{d} \tag{7.11}$$

The entire accuracy of a measurement system is determined by the system parameter d/l_0 and the grating period p_0. It can be improved by increasing the d/l_0 or decreasing the p_0 according to the maximum variation range of the measured height.

7.3 Some Applications of 3D Dynamic Shape Measurement

According to the speed of object's motion and the requisite precision of time in measurement from low speed to high speed, the measured dynamic objects can be divided into different types: the slow-movement process, the high-movement process, rapid rotation, and the instantaneous process. In our research work, we have proposed corresponding techniques and measurement systems for them.

7.3.1 3D Dynamic Shape Measurement for Slow-Movement Processes

For dynamic processes with slow movement, we have developed a low-cost measurement system in which a conventional imaging system is employed to produce an invariable sinusoidal optical field on the surface of the measured object; a video recording system is used to collect the deformed fringes.

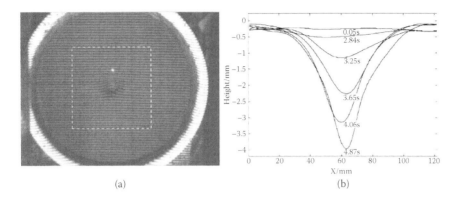

(a)   (b)

FIGURE 7.4
Dynamic measurement of vortex shape. (a) One of the deformed fringes when the stirrer is working; (b) profiles of the reconstructed vortices at different times.

This system succeeds in reconstructing the motion of vortex when the poster paint surface is stirring [42]. The deformed grating image is observed by a low-distortion TV charge-coupled device (CCD) camera (TM560, 25 frames per second [fps]) with a 12 mm focal length lens via a video-frame grabber digitizing the image in 128 × 128 pixels. One of the recorded fringes is shown in Figure 7.4(a). Figure 7.4(b) shows the profiles of the reconstructed vortices; the number under each line is the corresponding sampling instant.

7.3.2 3D Dynamic Shape Measurement for High-Movement Processes

For high-movement processes, a high-speed camera replaces the video recording system to record the deformed fringe rapidly. A measuring system is established to restore the 3D shape of a vibrating drum membrane [43]. A Chinese double-sided drum is mounted into the measuring volume and quickly hit three times. The whole vibration is recorded with 1000 fps in sampling rate speed. The vibration at the central point of the resonant side is shown in Figure 7.5(a).

The height distributions of the vibrating drumhead at their corresponding sampling instants are exactly restored. Figure 7.5(b) gives the profiles of the center row of six sampling instants in one period; the number above each line is the corresponding sampling instant.

Figure 7.5(c) and (d) show the grid charts of two sampling instants, and their sampling instants are given respectively as titles. Observing them, two modes, (1, 0) and (1, 1), can be found in one period of the principal vibration of the drumhead. This indicates that the point we hit is not the exact center of the drumhead. Furthermore, nonlinear effects (such as the uniform surface tension across the entire drumhead) exert their own preference for certain modes by transferring energy from one vibration mode to another.

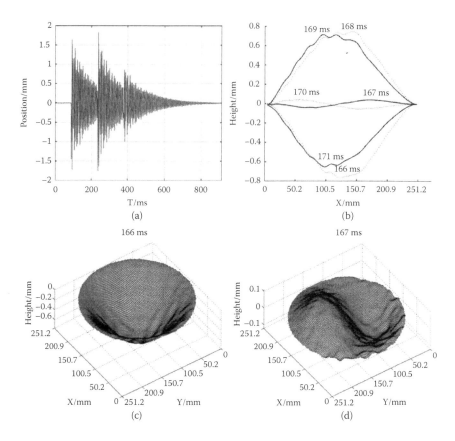

FIGURE 7.5
Three-dimensional dynamic shape measurement for a vibrating drum. (a) Vibration at the center point of the tested drumhead; (b) restored profiles of six sampling instants in one period; (c, d) grid charts of restored height distribution of the vibrating drumhead.

With the advantage of high-speed, full-field data acquisition and analysis, this system could be used in digitizing 3D shapes of those objects in rapid motion.

7.3.3 3D Dynamic Shape Measurement for Rapid Rotation and Instantaneous Process

The stroboscope [44] is an intense, high-speed light source used for the visual analysis of the objects in periodic motion and for high-speed photography [45,46]. The objects in rapid periodic motion can be studied by using the stroboscope to produce an optical illusion of stopped or slowed motion. When the flash repetition rate of the stroboscope is exactly the same as the object movement frequency or an integral multiple thereof, the moving object will appear to be stationary. This is called the *stroboscopic effect*.

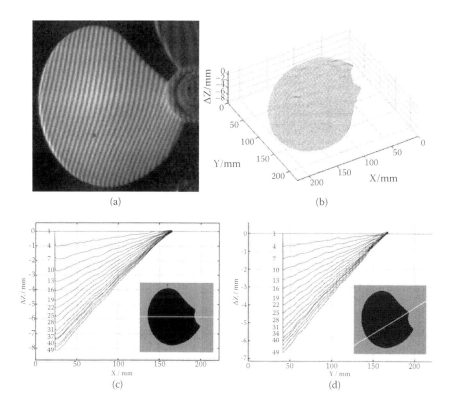

(a)

(b)

(c)

(d)

FIGURE 7.6
Three-dimensional dynamic shape measurement for a rotating blade. (a) Deformed fringes recorded at 50th revolution; (b) deformation (relative to the first revolution) at the 50th revolution; (c, d) deformations (relative to the first revolution) along the line shown in the inset.

Combining active 3D sensing with stroboscopic technology, we present another practical 3D shape measuring system for rapid rotation and instantaneous process, in which a stroboscopic sinusoidal grating is synchronously projected onto the dynamic tested object according to its motion and the deformed fringes are also synchronously collected by an ordinary commercial CCD camera or a high-speed one. The stroboscopic sinusoidal grating can "slow down" or even "freeze" the motion of the tested object and help the camera to shoot a clear, sharp, and instantaneous deformed fringe modulated by the 3D height distribution of a rapid motion object.

The 3D shape and deformation of a rotating blade with 1112 rpm (revolutions per minute) has been recovered by this method [47]. From quiescence to stable rotation, one image is synchronously captured during each revolution, as shown in Figure 7.6(a). Figure 7.6(b) shows the deformation (relative to the first revolution) of the whole reconstructed blade at the 50th revolution. Figure 7.6(c) and (d) show the deformations (relative to the first revolution also) of the reconstructed blades at difference revolutions along the line shown in each inset; the numbers marked on the left sides of the curves are their corresponding revolutions. They distinctly depict the twisting deformations of the blade with increasing speed. The farther the distance from the rotating shaft is, the bigger the deformation is.

Except for high-speed motion objects with obvious and variable repetition, such as rotation and vibration, this technique can also be used in the study of high-speed motion without obvious repetition, such as expansion, contraction, or ballistic flight and high-speed objects with known and invariable frequencies. This method can also be expanded using different detectors or sensors. For example, explosion phenomena with sound signals can be studied using a sound control unit instead of the optical position detector.

7.3.4 3D Dynamic Shape Measurement for Breaking Objects

When the measured dynamic object is deficient of sampling in a time direction or breaking into several isolated parts, the phase unwrapping is difficult. We propose a marked fringe method [48], in which a special mark is embedded into the projected sinusoidal gratings to identify the fringe order. The mark will not affect the Fourier spectra of the deformed fringe and could be extracted easily with a band-pass filter in the other direction. The phase value on the same marked strip is equivalent and known, so these phase values at the marked strips keep the relation of those separated fringes. The phase-unwrapping process of each broken part will be done from the local marked strip. In the experiment to test a breaking ceramic tile, the tile is obviously divided into four spatially isolated blocks and the fringe discontinuity is followed. The introduced marked fringe has been used to ensure that the phase-unwrapping process is error free. The whole breaking process contains 47 frames and lasts 235 ms. Six of these images are shown in Figure 7.7(a). Figure 7.7(b) shows the reconstructed 3D shape of this breaking tile at the corresponding sampling instants in Figure 7.7(a).

For the same purpose, Wei-huang Su [49] created a structured pattern in which the sinusoidal gratings are encoded with binary stripes and color grids. The binary stripes are used to identify the local fringe order, while the color grid provides additional degrees of freedom to identify the stripes. This encoding scheme provides a more reliable performance to identify the fringe orders since it is not sensitive to the observed colors. In Guo and Huang's research work [50,51], a small cross-shaped marker is embedded in the fringe pattern to facilitate the retrieval of the absolute phase map from a single fringe pattern. Another option of the marked fringe is two frequency sinusoidal gratings, in which the jumping line of the low-frequency gratings' wrapped phase could be used as the marked fringes and the same rank of high-frequency deformed grating will be tracked by this marked line.

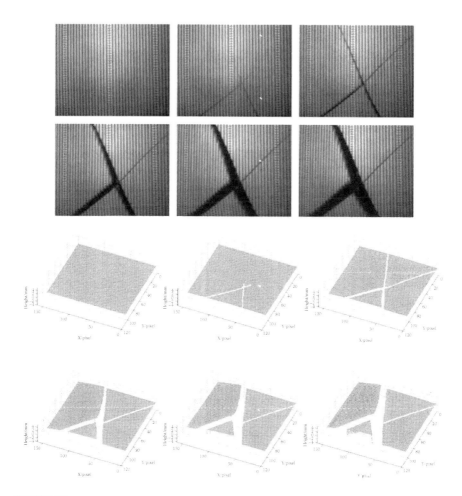

FIGURE 7.7
Three-dimensional dynamic shape measurement for a breaking tile. (a) Six frames of deformed fringe images in the breaking process; (b) the reconstructed 3D shape of the breaking tile at the corresponding sampling instants in (a).

7.4 Time-Average Fringe Method for Vibration Mode Analysis

In 3D dynamic shape measurement based on FTP, a sequence of dynamic deformed fringe images can be grabbed by a high-speed CCD camera and be processed by Fourier fringe analysis. This can efficiently measure a changing shape. When this proposed method is used for vibration analysis, it is a basic request that the time sampling rate of the detector be higher than twice that of the vibration frequency at least. It is difficult for a low-speed CCD or even a higher speed CCD to analyze the vibration with high frequency.

Similarly to time-average holographic technology for vibration analysis, the time-average fringe technology can also be used for the vibration mode analysis [52]. In this method, a sequence of the deformed and partly blurred sinusoidal fringe images on the surface of a vibrating membrane is grabbed by a low sampling rate commercial CCD camera. By Fourier transform, filtering, and inverse Fourier transform, the vibration mode is obtained from the fundamental component of the Fourier spectrum. Computer simulations and experiments have verified its validity. Under different excited vibration frequencies, the vibration modes of a vibrating surface can be qualitatively analyzed. When the excited vibration frequency changes continuously, the changing process of the vibration modes of the membrane is observed clearly.

7.4.1 Fundamental Concept

The time-average fringe method is implemented as follows. A Ronchi or sinusoidal grating is projected onto the surface of a vibrating membrane. A sequence of the deformed and partly blurred fringe images, caused by the changing shape of the tested vibrating membrane, is grabbed by a low sampling rate commercial CCD camera. Then, five steps are applied to implement the data processing.

1. Two-dimensional Fourier transform of the time-average fringe
2. Two-dimensional band-pass filtering (all frequency components of the Fourier spectrum are eliminated except the fundamental component)
3. Two-dimensional inverse Fourier transform of the filtered fundamental component
4. Calculation of the module of the complex signal extracted by 2D inverse Fourier transform
5. The same operation on the grabbed clear fringe pattern while the tested object is static

Ultimately, the vibration mode is obtained from the ratio of the modules of the two complex signals.

The optical geometry of the vibration analysis of a membrane is similar to traditional FTP, as shown in Figure 7.1. When the membrane is static, the intensity distributions of fringe patterns can still be expressed as

$$g_r(x,y) = a_r(x,y) + b_r(x,y)\cos[2\pi f_0 x + \phi_0(x,y)] \tag{7.12}$$

The vibration equation can be written as

$$Z(x,y,t) = A(x,y)\sin(2\pi f t) \tag{7.13}$$

where $A(x,y)$ is the vibration amplitudes and f is the vibration frequency. If the membrane is vibrating and each point of the membrane surface has an out-of-plane displacement, according to Equations (7.7) and (7.12), the varying phase distribution $\varphi(x,y,t)$ caused by the membrane's vibrating can be described as

$$\phi(x,y,t) = \frac{Z(x,y,t)}{\lambda_e} \cdot 2\pi \tag{7.14}$$

The instantaneous intensity distributions of these fringe patterns in difference time can be expressed as

$$g_t(x,y,t) = a_t(x,y) + b_t(x,y)\cos[2\pi f_0 x + \phi_0(x,y,t) + \phi(x,y,t)] \tag{7.15}$$

The Bessel functions are well known:

$$\cos(z\sin\theta) = J_0(z) + 2\sum_{n=1}^{\infty}\cos(2n\theta)J_{2n}(z) \tag{7.16}$$

$$\sin(z\sin\theta) = 2\sum_{n=0}^{\infty}\sin[(2n+1)\theta]J_{2n+1}(z) \tag{7.17}$$

Inserting Equations (7.13) and (7.14) into Equation (7.15) and developing the trigonometric terms into Bessel functions, the instantaneous intensity distributions is given by

$$g_t(x,y,t) = a_t(x,y) + b_t(x,y)\cos[2\pi f_0 x + \phi_0(x,y)] \cdot J_0\left[\frac{2A(x,y)\pi}{\lambda_e}\right]$$

$$+2b_t(x,y)\cos[2\pi f_0 x + \phi_0(x,y)] \cdot \sum_{n=1}^{\infty}\cos[2n\cdot(2\pi ft)]J_{2n}\left[\frac{2A(x,y)\pi}{\lambda_e}\right] \tag{7.18}$$

$$-2b_t(x,y)\sin[2\pi f_0 x + \phi_0(x,y)] \cdot \sum_{n=0}^{\infty}\sin[(2n+1)2\pi ft]J_{2n+1}\left[\frac{2A(x,y)\pi}{\lambda_e}\right]$$

When these deformed fringe patterns are recorded by a low-speed commercial CCD camera with a sampling time T, which is always larger than the vibration period of the membrane, the fringe will be averaged and partly blurred during the sampling time. The averaged fringe intensity at each pixel is then given by

$$g_{averaged}(x,y) = \frac{1}{T}\int\limits_{0}^{T} g_t(x,y,t)dt \qquad (7.19)$$

Finally, by inserting Equation (7.18) into Equation (7.19), we can obtain

$$g_{averaged}(x,y) = a_t(x,y) + b_t(x,y)\cos[2\pi f_0 x + \phi_0(x,y)] \cdot J_0\left[\frac{2A(x,y)\pi}{\lambda_e}\right] \qquad (7.20)$$

After the process of Fourier transform, filtering, and inverse Fourier transform, a complex signal will be calculated:

$$\hat{g}_{averaged}(x,y) = \frac{b_t(x,y)}{2} \cdot J_0\left[\frac{2A(x,y)\pi}{\lambda_e}\right]\exp\{i[2\pi f_0 x + \phi_0(x,y)]\} \qquad (7.21)$$

Meanwhile, the intensity distributions of fringe patterns on the static membrane (shown in Equation 7.12) can be dealt with in the same way and its corresponding complex signal can be noted as

$$\hat{g}_r(x,y) = \frac{b_r(x,y)}{2}\exp\{i[2\pi f_0 x + \phi_0(x,y)]\} \qquad (7.22)$$

Thus, the vibration mode I can be shown as

$$I = \frac{\left|\hat{g}_{averaged}(x,y)\right|}{\left|\hat{g}_r(x,y)\right|} = \left|J_0\left[\frac{2A(x,y)\pi}{\lambda_e}\right]\right| \qquad (7.23)$$

The relation between the vibration mode I and the vibration amplitudes $A(x,y)$ can be found via the zero-order Bessel function.

7.4.2 Experimental Results

A principal diagram of the experimental setup is similar to that in Figure 7.2. The experiment is performed on an aluminum membrane whose edges are tightly fixed on a loudspeaker. A function generator and a power amplifier

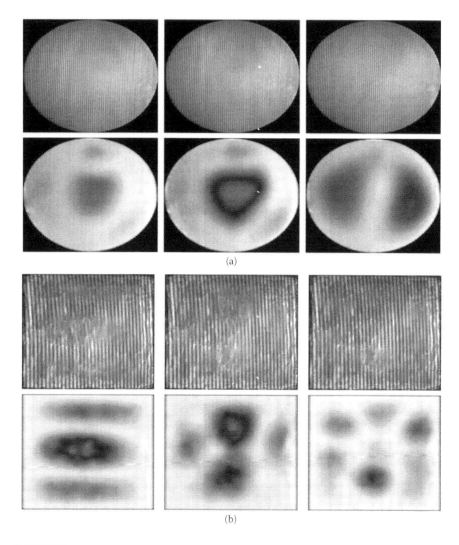

FIGURE 7.8
Deformed fringe images and their corresponding vibration mode: (a) for a circle membrane, mode (0,1) at 73.3 Hz, mode (0,2) at 82.2 Hz, mode (1,1) at 91.1 Hz; (b) for a rectangular membrane, mode (1,3) at 125.7 Hz, mode (3,1) at 163.7 Hz, mode (3,2) at 206.7 Hz.

are used to create a sine wave, which is transferred to the loudspeaker and drives the membrane to vibrate. Under different excited vibration frequencies, the vibration modes of a vibrating circle membrane and a vibrating rectangular membrane can be recovered. Figure 7.8(a) gives three deformed fringe images and their corresponding vibration modes for a circle membrane. Figure 7.8(b) gives three deformed fringe images and their corresponding vibration modes for a rectangular membrane.

The results of the theoretical analysis and experiment indicate that this method of vibration mode analysis using a time-average fringe is valid. This method has the advantage of rapid speed, high accuracy, and simple experimental setup.

7.5 Advantages and Challenges

In this chapter, we mainly reviewed our past 10+ years of research work on 3D dynamic shape measurement using grating projection and Fourier fringe analysis. The basic principles of this method were introduced, and some typical applications, such as the combination of stroboscopic effects and FTP to test the objects in rapid periodic motion, high-speed optical measurement for the vibrating membrane of the drum, dynamic measurement of a rotating vortex, and breaking tile, were also demonstrated. Furthermore, also based on grating projection and Fourier fringe analysis, the time-average fringe method was used to recover the vibration mode of a vibrating membrane. The fundamental concept and some experimental results were also described in this chapter.

There are increasing demands for obtaining 3D information; moreover, it is expected that the trend will be to expand existing techniques to deal with the dynamic process. As a noncontact shape measurement technique, Fourier transform profilometry has dealt well with the dynamic process in recent years, due to its merits of only one fringe needed, full field analysis, and high precision. This 3D dynamic shape measurement using grating projection and Fourier fringe analysis has the advantage of high-speed, full-field data acquisition and analysis. With the development of high-resolution CCD cameras and high frame rate frame grabbers, the method, as proposed here, should be a promising one in studying high-speed motion including rotation, vibration, explosion, expansion, contraction, and even shock wave.

Although this method has been well studied and applied in different fields, there are still some challenges that must be addressed in future work. Real-time 3D shape measurement, which is the key for successfully implementing 3D coordinate display and measurement, manufacturing control, and online quality inspection, is more difficult in a dynamic process. By making full use of the processing power of the graphics processing unit, 3D dynamic shape reconstruction can be performed rapidly and in real time with an ordinary personal computer [15]. A high-resolution, real-time 3D shape measurement, developed by Zhang, took advantage of digital fringe projection, phase-shifting techniques, and some developing hardware technologies and has achieved simultaneous 3D absolute shape acquisition, reconstruction, and display at an ultrafast speed [53]. A measuring system has demonstrated that it can accurately capture dynamic changing 3D scenes and it will be more promising in the future.

The requirements of the environment for dynamic measurement are tougher than 3D static shape measurement—for example, the influence of the varying environmental lights in a stroboscope and of the unexpected motion of peripheral equipment. Moreover, the measurement accuracy is also affected by the object surface color. When the color gratings are used in this proposed measuring system, the accuracy and measurable range can be improved by decreasing the overlapping spectrum. But other problems caused by the color cross and sampling rate of the color camera will affect the measuring accuracy.

Due to the varying objects, the accuracy of 3D dynamic shape measurement is usually less than that of 3D static shape measurement. Generally, the different experimental setups of each measurement will lead to different accuracy. In the applications proposed in this chapter, the accuracy of this kind of method is up to decades of micrometers. The primary task of the future work would be to improve the accuracy of 3D dynamic shape measurement to meet industrial application requirements.

Acknowledgments

First of all, we would like to thank this book's editor, Dr. Song Zhang, for his invitation. Our thanks also go to our colleagues and former graduate students in Sichuan University for their contributions to this research. We would like to thank the National Natural Science Foundation of China (nos. 60527001, 60807006, 60838002, 61177010); most of this work was carried out under NSFC's support.

References

1. Chen, F., Brown, G. M., Song, M. 2000. Overview of three-dimensional shape measurement using optical methods. *Optical Engineering* 39 (1): 10–22.
2. Jähne, B., Haußecker, H., Geißler, P. 1999. *Handbook of computer vision and applications,* volume 1: *Sensors and imaging,* chapters 17–21. San Diego: Academic Press.
3. Salvi, J., Pagès, J., J. Batlle, J. 2004. Pattern codification strategies in structured light systems. *Pattern Recognition* 37 (4): 827–849.
4. Yoshizawa, T. 1991. The recent trend of moiré metrology. *Journal Robust Mechanics* 3 (3): 80–85.

5. Srinivasan, V., Liu, H. C., Halioua, H. 1984. Automated phase-measuring pro-filometry of 3-D diffuse objects. *Applied Optics* 23 (18): 3105–3108.
6. Su, X. Y., Zhou, W. S., von Bally, V., et al. 1992. Automated phase-measuring pro-filometry using defocused projection of a Ronchi grating. *Optics Communications* 94 (6): 561–573.
7. Takeda, M., Ina, H., Kobayashi, S. 1982. Fourier-transform method of fringe-pat-tern analysis for computer-based topography and interferometry. *Journal Optical Society America* 72 (1): 156–160.
8. Takeda, M., Motoh, K. 1983. Fourier transform profilometry for the automatic measurement of 3-D object shapes. *Applied Optics* 22 (24): 3977–3982.
9. Li, J., Su, X. Y., Guo, L. R. 1990. An improved Fourier transform profilometry for automatic measurement of 3-D object shapes. *Optical Engineering* 29 (12): 1439–1444.
10. Su, X. Y., Chen, W. J. 2001. Fourier transform profilometry: A review. *Optics Lasers Engineering* 35 (5): 263–284.
11. Su, L. K., Su, X. Y., Li, W. S. 1999. Application of modulation measurement pro-filometry to objects with surface holes. *Applied Optics* 38 (7): 1153–1158.
12. Toyooka, S., Iwasa, Y. 1986. Automatic profilometry of 3-D diffuse objects by spatial phase detection. *Applied Optics* 25 (10): 3012–3018.
13. Sajan, M. R., Tay, C. J., Shang, H. M., et al. 1998. Improved spatial phase detection for profilometry using a TDI imager. *Optics Communications* 150 (1–6): 66–70.
14. Zhang, L., Curless, B., Seitz, S. 2003. Spacetime stereo: Shape recovery for dynamic senses. *Proceedings of IEEE Computer Society Conference on Computer Vision and Pattern Recognition (CVPR)*, Madison, WI, 367–374.
15. Zhang, S., Huang, P. S. 2006. High-resolution, real-time three-dimensional shape measurement. *Optical Engineering* 45 (12): 123601-1-8.
16. Macy, W. W. 1983. Two-dimensional fringe-pattern analysis. *Applied Optics* 22 (23): 3898–3901.
17. Bone, D. J., Bachor, H. A., Sandeman, R. J. 1986. Fringe-pattern analysis using a 2-D Fourier transform. *Applied Optics* 25 (10): 1653–1660.
18. Bone, D. J. 1991. Fourier fringe analysis: The two-dimensional phase unwrap-ping problem. *Applied Optics* 30 (25): 3627–3632.
19. Burton, D. R., Lalor, M. J. 1989. Managing some of the problems of Fourier fringe analysis. *Proceedings SPIE* 1163:149–160.
20. Burton, D. R., Lalor, M. J. 1994. Multi-channel Fourier fringe analysis as an aid to automatic phase unwrapping. *Applied Optics* 33 (14): 2939–2948.
21. Lin, J-F., Su, X-Y. 1995. Two-dimensional Fourier transform profilometry for the automatic measurement of three-dimensional object shapes. *Optical Engineering* 34 (11): 3297–3302.
22. C. Gorecki. 1992. Interferogram analysis using a Fourier transform method for automatic 3D surface measurement. *Pure Applied Optics* 1:103–110.
23. Su, X., Sajan, M. R., Asundi, A. 1997. Fourier transform profilometry for 360-degree shape using TDI camera. *Proceedings SPIE* 2921: 552–556.
24. Yi, J., Huang, S. 1997. Modified Fourier transform profilometry for the measure-ment of 3-D steep shapes. *Optics Lasers Engineering* 27 (5): 493–505.
25. Takeda, M., Gu, Q., Kinoshita, M., et al. 1997. Frequency-multiplex Fourier-transform profilometry: A single shot three-dimensional shape measurement of objects with large height discontinuities and/or surface isolations. *Applied Optics* 36 (22): 5347–5354.

26. Burton, D. R., Goodall, A. J., Atkinson, J. T., et al. 1995. The use of carrier frequency-shifting for the elimination of phase discontinuities in Fourier-transform profilometry. *Optics Lasers Engineering* 23 (4): 245–257.
27. Chen, W., Yang, H., Su, X. 1999. Error caused by sampling in Fourier transform profilometry. *Optical Engineering* 38 (6): 927–931.
28. Kozloshi, J., Serra, G. 1999. Analysis of the complex phase error introduced by the application of Fourier transform method. *Journal Modern Optics* 46 (6): 957–971.
29. Su, X., Chen, W., Zhang, Q., et al. 2001. Dynamic 3-D shape measurement method based on FTP. *Optics Lasers Engineering* 36: 46–64.
30. Su, X., Zhang, Q. 2010. Dynamic 3D shape measurement: A review. *Optics Lasers Engineering* 48 (2): 191–204.
31. Abdul-Rahman, H. S., Gdeisat, M. A., Burton, D. R., et al. 2008. Three-dimensional Fourier fringe analysis. *Optics Lasers Engineering* 46 (6): 446–455.
32. Siva Gorthi, S., Rastogi, P. 2010. Fringe projection techniques: Whither we are? *Optics Lasers Engineering* 48 (2): 133–140.
33. Su, X. Y., Chen, W. J. 2004. Reliability-guided phase unwrapping algorithm: A review. *Optics Lasers Engineering* 42 (3): 245–261.
34. Judge, T. R., Bryyanston-Cross, P. J. 1994. A review of phase unwrapping techniques in fringe analysis. *Optics Lasers Engineering* 21:199–239.
35. Su, X. Y. 1996. Phase unwrapping techniques for 3-D shape measurement. *Proceedings SPIE* 2866: 460–465.
36. Li, J. L., Su, X. Y., Li, J. T. 1997. Phase unwrapping algorithm-based on reliability and edge-detection. *Optical Engineering* 36 (6): 1685–1690.
37. Asundi, A. K., Zhou, W. S. 1999. Fast phase-unwrapping algorithm based on a grayscale mask and flood fill. *Applied Optics* 38 (16): 3556–3561.
38. Su, X., Xue, L. 2001 Phase unwrapping algorithm based on fringe frequency analysis in Fourier transform profilometry. *Optical Engineering* 40 (4): 637–643.
39. Takeda, M., Abe, T. 1996. Phase unwrapping by a maximum cross-amplitude spanning tree algorithm: A comparative study. *Optical Engineering* 35 (8): 2345–2351.
40. Zhang, Z. 2000. A flexible new technique for camera calibration. *IEEE Transactions Pattern Analysis Machine Intelligence* 22 (11): 1330–1334.
41. Li, W. S., Su, X. Y., Liu, Z. B. 2001. Large-scale three-dimensional object measurement: A practical coordinate mapping and imaging data-patching method. *Applied Optics* 40 (20): 3326–3333.
42. Zhang, Q. C., Su, X. Y. 2002. An optical measurement of vortex shape at a free surface. *Optics Laser Technology* 34 (2): 107–113.
43. Zhang, Q. C., Su, X. Y. 2005. High-speed optical measurement for the drumhead vibration. *Optics Express* 13 (8): 3310–3316.
44. Visionary engineer, Harold Edgerton. 2011. http://web.mit.edu/museum/exhibitions/edgertonexhibit/harolddocedgertonindex.html (accessed Oct. 26, 2011).
45. Asundi, A. K., Sajan, M. R. 1994. Low-cost digital polariscope for dynamic photoelasticity. *Optical Engineering* 33 (9): 3052–3055.
46. Asundi, A. K., Sajan, M. R. 1996. Digital drum camera for dynamic recording. *Optical Engineering* 35 (6): 1707–1713.
47. Zhang, Q. C., Su, X. Y., Cao, Y. P., et al. 2005. An optical 3-D shape and deformation measurement for rotating blades using stroboscopic structured illumination. *Optical Engineering* 44 (11): 113601-1–7.

48. Xiao, Y. S., Su, X. Y., Zhang, Q. C., et al. 2007. 3-D profilometry for the impact process with marked fringes tracking. *Opto-Electronic Engineering* 34 (8): 46–52 (in Chinese).
49. Su, W. H. 2008. Projected fringe profilometry using the area-encoded algorithm for spatially isolated and dynamic objects. *Optics Experiments* 16 (4): 2590–2596.
50. Guo, H., Huang, P. S. 2008. 3-D shape measurement by use of a modified Fourier transform method. *Proceedings SPIE* 7066: 70660E-1–8.
51. Guo, H., Huang, P. S. 2007. Absolute phase retrieval for 3D shape measurement by the Fourier transform method. *Proceedings SPIE* 6762: 676204-1–10.
52. Su, X., Zhang, Q., Wen, Y., et al. 2010. Time-average fringe method for vibration mode analysis. *Proceedings SPIE* 7522: 752257.
53. Zhang, S. 2010. Recent progress on real-time 3D shape measurement using digital fringe projection techniques. *Optics Lasers Engineering* 48 (2): 149–158.

8

Interferometry

David P. Towers and Catherine E. Towers

CONTENTS

8.1 Introduction

Interferometric techniques have found widespread use in three-dimensional (3D) profilometry. When two coherent waves of wavelength λ are brought together such that they have traversed a relative optical path difference Δx, the intensity obtained is given by [1]

$$I = I_{DC} + I_M \cos(S\Delta x)$$

where
S is introduced as a sensitivity parameter
I is the measured intensity
I_{DC} is the constant component of the intensity
I_M is the modulation depth of the interference term

In a conventional Twyman-Green interferometer [2] (see Figure 8.1a), the laser beam is split and the object beam directed to the test object with the

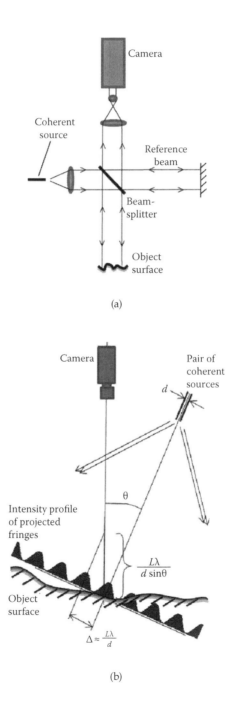

(a)

(b)

FIGURE 8.1

(a) A conventional Twyman–Green interferometer; b) a fringe projection arrangement using coherent illumination.

reflected light used to form the interferogram in combination with the reference beam. With such a configuration, the sensitivity is given by $S = 2\pi(2/\lambda)$ and an interference fringe relates to a topology change of $\lambda/2$. With a sensitivity inversely proportional to the wavelength, these techniques are suitable for inspection of, for example, microelectromechanical system (MEMS) devices, wear of materials, and optical components.

Interference fringes may also be projected onto an object in a triangulation configuration in which the illumination and viewing axes intersect at an angle θ. Assuming that the fringes originate from a pair of coherent sources, in a geometry directly analogous to Young's double-slit experiment [3], the fringe spacing Δ obtained at the object (in the fair-field approximation) is given by $\Delta \approx L\lambda/d$, where L is the distance from the sources to the object and d is the separation of the sources. By utilizing a triangulation configuration, the fringe spacing has a component along the imaging direction such that the sensitivity is given by $S = 2\pi(d\sin\theta/L\lambda)$ and the effective wavelength relates to a topology change of $L\lambda/(d\sin\theta)$. There is free choice over the values for θ and d and hence a wide range of effective wavelengths can be realized.

The field of view of conventional interferometers is normally limited by the aperture of the optical components; however, with fringe projection, this constraint does not apply. Therefore, fringe projection is more applicable for machine vision applications and will be the focus of this chapter. Coherent fringe projection was first proposed as double source contouring with holographic recording [4]. While significant flexibility arose with the advent of multimedia data projectors (see Chapter 9), coherent based fringe projection retains distinct advantages: the ability to filter out ambient light, miniaturization of the fringe projector, and the precisely known geometry of the projected patterns. This chapter will discuss the optical systems for generating projected fringe patterns, the specific calibration issues with coherent systems, and implementation with multiwavelength techniques to give absolute 3D metrology.

8.2 Coherent Fringe Projection Systems: Optical Setups and Characteristics

8.2.1 Twin-Fiber-Based Coherent Fringe Projection

One of the most direct ways to generate coherent fringes is to use a pair of single mode fibers via a single coherent source and directional coupler [5,6]. The two output fibers from the coupler are made parallel and brought close together to form the projected fringes (see Figure 8.2). By mounting one of the fibers from an appropriately oriented linear traverse, the separation of the fibers can be adjusted, thereby controlling the spacing of the projected

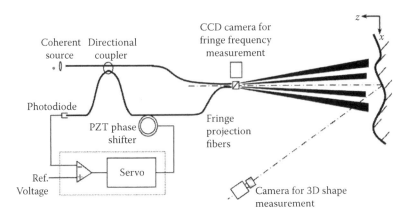

FIGURE 8.2
A twin-fiber-based fringe projector with additional components for sampling and controlling the phase of the projected fringes. (Courtesy of Towers, C. E., Towers, D. P., and Jones, J. D. C. *Optics Letters* 28 (11): 887–889, 2003. Published by Optical Society of America.)

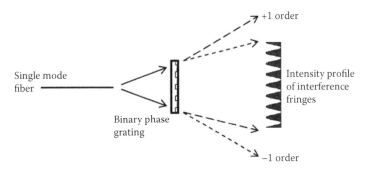

FIGURE 8.3
Interference fringe formation via a binary phase grating.

fringes. The main practical issue with fiber fringe projectors concerns the environmental sensitivity of the fibers. Vibration or thermal changes in the environment modulate the phase of the wave transmitted by the fiber and thereby cause the fringes to sweep across the object surface [7].

8.2.2 Diffraction Grating Fringe Projection

The diffraction orders from a grating can be used to form the two beams needed for fringe projection. This technique was originally introduced using a blazed grating [8], but is better implemented using a binary phase grating, which is optimized to produce only the +1 and −1 diffraction orders, thereby minimizing the energy in the other diffraction orders (see Figure 8.3) [9]. The input beam to the grating can be derived from a single mode optical fiber, thereby maintaining flexibility in positioning. The advantage of the diffraction grating approach is that the interferometer is common path in fiber with the only non-common path elements in air; hence the system is significantly less sensitive to environmental disturbances compared to the twin-fiber approach. However, the projected patterns are sensitive to the quality of the grating and the presence of overlapping diffraction orders, and they lack the precise theoretical form of those formed from a pair of single mode fibers. Phase modulation can be achieved by translating the grating and the fringe spacing can be controlled by varying the separation between the distal end of the fiber and the grating.

There are alternative bulk-optic configurations to form interference fringes that can be projected over an object in a triangulation setup. These include the use of a Michelson interferometer, a Lloyd mirror, or a Wollaston prism; however, as these methods use bulk optic components, they do not have the flexibility of the methods described before.

8.2.3 Sensitivity and Effective Wavelength

The fringe projection configurations described in the previous sections can produce a wide range of sensitivities owing to the choice of θ and d in Figure 8.1. Figure 8.4 presents a family of curves of the effective wavelength $L\lambda/(d\sin\theta)$, with $L = 1.5$ m and $\lambda = 532$ nm. It can be seen that a fringe can represent a surface depth change between >100 mm and <0.5 mm depending on the configuration.

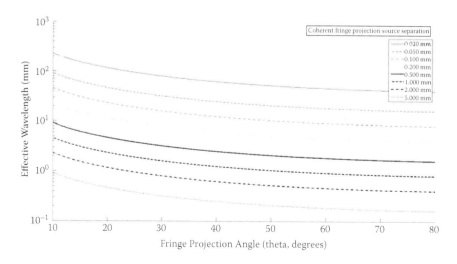

FIGURE 8.4
The effective wavelength of a fringe projection system as a function of triangulation angle and source spacing in a coherent fringe projector.

(a) Fringes from a binary phase grating
    interferometer, the line is 20 mm, with
    approximately 2.4 fringes/mm

(b) Fringes from a twin-fiber
    interferometer with approximately
    0.2 fringes/mm

FIGURE 8.5
Examples of interferometric projected fringes. (Images courtesy of D. Dipresa.)

Examples of the patterns produced using interferometric fringe projection are given in Figure 8.5 using both twin-fiber and grating-based interferometers.

8.3 Interferometric Fringe Processing

The goal of fringe analysis in fringe projection is to determine a 3D coordinate at each pixel on the detector. An interferometric phase in the fringe pattern defines a plane from the projector. When this phase is measured at a particular pixel on the detector, the back propagation of that pixel through the imaging lens will intersect the phase plane at a unique 3D coordinate. This analysis relies on knowing the absolute phase within the projected pattern. As each fringe in the pattern has a similar sinusoidal intensity profile, knowledge of the position within the projected fringes relies on both the integer fringe number, or order, and the wrapped or fractional phase value.

8.3.1 Wrapped-Phase Calculation

The wrapped phase may be determined by carrier-fringe-based methods [10], which require a single image. This is directly compatible with either twin-fiber- or grating-based fringe projectors. The exposure time of the camera can be set according to a compromise between fringe stability (for twin-fiber projectors) and the available optical power. The disadvantage of most single image carrier fringe analysis methods is that ringing can appear in the vicinity of any edges or object discontinuities within the image, giving errors in the calculated phase.

Alternatively, phase-stepping techniques can be applied to determine the fringe phase [11]. Phase stepping requires three or more images in order to determine the fringe phase and hence the data acquisition time is increased. (The interested reader is directed to the work of Surrel for a review of the performance of various phase-stepping algorithms [12].) Phase shifting can be implemented in twin-fiber projectors by winding one of the output fibers around a cylindrical piezoelectric transducer (PZT) and applying a voltage [5]. With open loop adjustment of the phase, the actual phase shifts obtained may be different from those desired due to environmental effects. Phase stabilization can be achieved by monitoring the intensity at the fourth arm of the coupler using a photodiode (see Figure 8.2). The interference signal obtained is derived from waves that are reflected from the distal ends of the output fibers. An error signal is found by subtraction of a fixed reference voltage and a suitably tuned servo can drive the PZT in one of the output arms of the interferometer to fix the phase of the projected pattern in a closed loop mode [13].

It has also been shown that such a configuration can be used to produce exact phase shifts of 90° [13]. While this method demonstrates the potential to use twin-fiber-based projectors in more hostile environments, in practice, instabilities may remain between the projector and object that cannot be compensated by such an approach and hence single image analysis is preferred [14]. Phase-shifting techniques may also be applied to grating-based projectors by translation of the grating. The fringe projection setup and test object must remain stable during the time needed for mechanical translation of the grating and acquisition of the phase-stepped images.

8.3.2 Fringe Order Calculation

For contiguous object surfaces, the simplest approach to determine the fringe order is to utilize a reference marker within the projected field [15]. With *a priori* knowledge of surface continuity, a spatial phase-unwrapping algorithm yields the desired absolute phase distribution [16,17].

For generic artifacts or scenes composed of multiple discrete objects, the fringe order must be determined at each pixel independently. The most robust approach is to use a multiwavelength strategy [18]. Here the "wavelengths" are the effective wavelengths of the projected patterns, rather than optical wavelengths. Two strategies have evolved. The first aims to generate a beat wavelength that spans the field of view of the camera. The wrapped phase at a beat wavelength can be calculated from the difference of two wrapped-phase measurements. For example, if the original effective wavelengths are λ_0 and λ_1, at which wrapped phase measurements of $\Delta\phi_0$ and $\Delta\phi_1$ are obtained respectively, the phase $\Delta\phi_{01}$ at the beat wavelength, Λ_{01} is found from [19]

$$\Delta\phi_{01} = \Delta\phi_0 - \Delta\phi_1 = 2\pi L\left(\frac{\lambda_1 - \lambda_0}{\lambda_1\lambda_0}\right) = \frac{2\pi L}{\Lambda_{01}}$$

where L is the unknown optical path difference. From a single beat fringe there is a unique range of wrapped-phase values that correspond to each fringe order at λ_0 and thus the original fringes can be identified unambiguously.

To appreciate the formation of beat fringes, it is sometimes helpful to make an acoustic analogy. When an orchestra is warming up, each instrument will be tuned to a common frequency. When two players produce notes of slightly different pitch, a low-frequency "beat" is heard between the two. This beat frequency has a long wavelength and the aim in fringe processing is to make it span the desired measurement range of projected fringe orders. In interferometric projected fringe systems such as those depicted in Figures 8.2 and 8.3, it is not possible to obtain a single projected fringe across the field of view directly (e.g., by bringing the twin fibers close to each other). Therefore, the indirect approach using beat analysis is necessary.

The highest dynamic range in fringe projection is obtained when the best wrapped-phase resolution is combined with data over the largest number of projected fringes. However, it has been shown that the noise in the wrapped-phase data, which may be quantified by a standard deviation σ_ϕ, limits the number of projected fringes that can be reliably identified. A number of researchers in this field have presented multiwavelength methodologies for use with fringe projection and the interested reader is referred to the work of Burton and Lalor [20], Nadeborn, Andra, and Osten [21], and Towers, Towers, and Jones [22]. The theory reported in Towers et al. [22] brings together the reliability of calculating the correct fringe order with the phase noise from the interferometer to determine the maximum number of fringe orders measurable and hence defines a framework for optimization. It is shown that the number of fringes N_{f0} at wavelength λ_0 that can be ordered to 6σ reliability (i.e., 99.73%, within each beat fringe at Λ_{01}) is limited by

$$\frac{N_{f0}}{N_{f01}} \leq \frac{2\pi}{6\sqrt{2}\sigma_\phi}$$

Hence, if the phase resolution corresponds to 1/100th of a fringe, the ratio N_{f0}/N_{f01} is limited to ≤ 11.8. For a larger dynamic range, additional measurement wavelengths must be added. An optimal configuration is found when the series of beat wavelengths and the highest resolution effective wavelength, λ_0, form a geometric series with a common ratio given by N_{f0}/N_{f01}. In turn, this defines the number of projected fringes at each wavelength, N_{fi}, by [22]

$$N_{fi} = N_{f0} - \left(N_{f0}\right)^{\frac{i-1}{n-1}}$$

where n is the number of measurement wavelengths, i denotes the ith measurement wavelength, and N_{f0} is the maximum number of projected fringes at the shortest effective wavelength λ_0. For example, with the same phase noise of $1/100^{th}$ of a fringe, but with $n = 3$, the numbers of projected fringes required are $N_{f0} = 121$, $N_{f1} = 120$, and $N_{f2} = 110$. In this case, the beat is formed by N_{f0} N_{f1} and contains one beat fringe. The beat from N_{f0} and N_{f2} gives 11 beat fringes, which, together with $N_{f0} = 121$, form a geometric series. For typical megapixel resolution detectors, three wavelengths of projected fringes are sufficient and give a dynamic range for depth measurement in the region of 10,000:1 (from 100 fringes at a resolution of $1/100^{th}$ of a fringe).

An alternative multiwavelength approach is to use the uniqueness of the set of wrapped-phase values obtained at the measurement wavelengths along with the method of excess fractions [23] or the Chinese remainder theorem [24] to determine the fringe order. Recent results with the method of excess fractions have demonstrated that similar performance can be obtained as from the beat approach but with significantly greater choice of measurement wavelengths [25].

8.4 Automation and Calibration

It is essential to automate the measurement process, particularly with multiwavelength analysis, in order to obtain repeatable results and increase usability. With a twin-fiber interferometer, a PZT driven traverse with a range of up to 100 µm is suitable to adjust the effective wavelength, whereas with grating projection a larger range of motion is typically needed via a piezomotor or other motorized traverse. With three projected fringe frequencies and carrier fringe analysis, a minimum of 3 images is needed, whereas with phase step analysis 12 images are typically necessary. In either case the multiwavelength analysis algorithms require accurate knowledge of the effective wavelength in order to determine the fringe order [22].

The effective wavelength in the projected fringes can be determined by splitting off part of the projected pattern to fall onto a second area detector [13]. This is shown schematically in Figure 8.2 for a twin-fiber setup. A wrapped-phase map from this second camera can be obtained by carrier frequency or phase-shifting analysis and then spatially unwrapped. The resulting phase distribution is then fitted to the exact hyperbolic fringe function in order to recover the fiber separation parameters in all three orthogonal axes. As an example, the data in Figure 8.6 show the fiber separation in the x-axis after the fiber was moved 20 µm using a PZT actuator. The gradual movement of the fiber from the desired position can be seen and is a characteristic of the actuator; however, this behavior is largely repeatable and hence, by timing image acquisition to occur after the initial high rate of change, it is possible to obtain stable results at the desired fiber separations. It is also clear from Figure 8.6 that the fiber separation measurement is highly repeatable with an uncertainty < 50 nm.

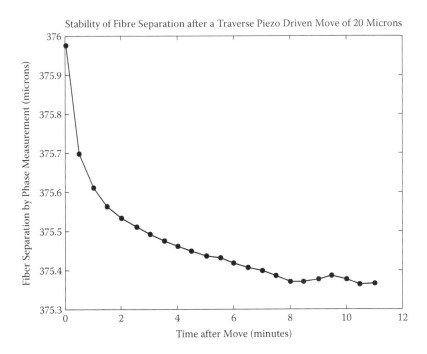

FIGURE 8.6
Fiber separation measurements from a twin-fiber interferometric projector following translation of one fiber using a PZT actuator.

Having obtained the source separation information, the fringes are defined
as hyperbolic functions in 3D space. It is also possible to conduct a camera
calibration for a set of internal and external parameters (see, for example,
Bouguet [26]). Hence, a parametric calibration can be achieved once the triangulation angle, θ, is known. This angle is best found by using a known
artifact (e.g., containing a known step height) and iteratively modifying the
angle until the expected depth parameter is obtained. Alternative techniques
for calibration in fringe projection are discussed in Chapter 9.

8.5 Results

Two sets of example results are shown in Figure 8.7. Figure 8.7(a) shows
the calculated fringe order information on a casting insert that is measured in order to assess wear. The black fringe is the zero-order fringe
with the fringe order increasing positively and negatively on either side
of this. The sharply defined boundaries of each fringe show the quality
of the multiwavelength processing. After calibration, the fringe data are

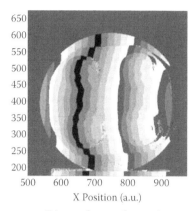

650
600
550
500
450
400
350
300
250
200

500   600   700   800   900

X Position (a.u.)

Fringe order map from twin-
fiber fringes on a casting insert

(a)

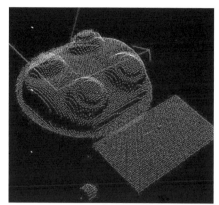

3-D point cloud, showing every
4th pixel in x and y

(b)

Projected fringes on a soft top
vehicle roof in a wind tunnel

(c)

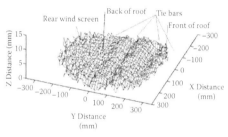

Deformation of soft top vehicle
roof between 0 and 60 mph wind speed

(d)

FIGURE 8.7

Example data from a twin-fiber-based interferometric fringe projection system. (a, b) Reprinted from Towers, C. E. et al., *Optics and Lasers in Engineering* 43: 788–800, copyright 2005, with permission from Elsevier. (c) Reprinted from Buckberry, C. H. et al. *Optics and Lasers in Engineering* 25:433–453, copyright 1996, with permission from Elsevier.

converted into a matrix of xyz coordinates and every fourth pixel is plotted in x and y, as plotted in Figure 8.7(b). The casting insert was mounted on a metal block. A second example is given in Figure 8.7(c), which shows interference fringes projected onto a passenger vehicle soft-top roof in a wind tunnel. The field of view is approximately 1.5 m. The 3D shape of the roof was measured with the wind off and then with a wind speed of 60 mph, and the deformation of the roof was then determined (shown in Figure 8.7d). The fringes were processed using a single image Fourier transform algorithm due to the instability of the setup. The presence of tie bars can be seen in the deformation map where the height change is close to zero, with the material bulging by approximately 5 mm between the tie bars.

The primary difficulty with using coherent light for interferometric fringe projection is the formation of speckle, which appears as noise within the image. Therefore, under the same experimental conditions, a white-light fringe projector will produce a lower noise level compared to a laser-based projector. The main mechanism to control the level of speckle noise is via the imaging lens aperture, or f-number. Increasing the aperture, corresponding to a lower f-number, produces a smaller speckle size and hence increases the number of speckles per pixel on the detector. The benefit of opening the lens aperture is illustrated in Figure 8.8, which shows the noise in the depth measurements to one standard deviation against the f-number for a narrowband 532 nm laser-based fringe projection setup with a field of view of approximately 500 mm. Opening the lens aperture has the disadvantage of reducing the depth of field. Therefore, there is a compromise in setting up an interferometric system between reducing the speckle noise, and hence the noise on the depth measurements, while achieving sufficient depth of field.

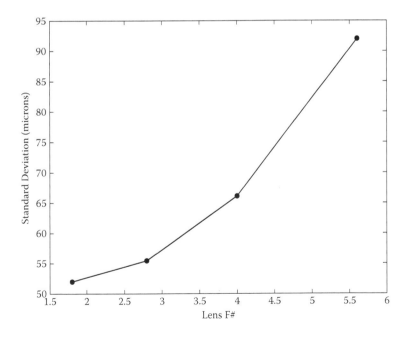

FIGURE 8.8
Resolution of shape data as a function of imaging lens aperture.

8.6 Summary

This chapter has presented the key features of interferometric fringe projection systems employing laser illumination. There are a number of optical configurations that can be used to generate the projected fringes that employ single mode fibers and hence offer considerable flexibility. While white-light-based projectors dominate the research and commercial exploitation of fringe projection, laser-based devices still offer some unique advantages: The projector can be miniaturized to the mounts required for single mode fibers and the use of narrow band filters enables operation in environments with significant levels of ambient light.

References

1. C. Vest. *Holographic interferometry.* New York: Wiley-Blackwell, 1979.
2. P. Hariharan. *Optical interferometry,* 2nd ed. San Diego: Academic Press Inc., 2003.
3. T. Young. Experimental demonstration of the general law of the interference of light. *Philosophical Transactions of the Royal Society of London* 94, 1804.
4. B. P. Hildebrand, K. A. Haines. Multiple-wavelength and multiple-source holography applied to contour generation. *Journal Optical Society of America* 57 (2): 155–157, 1967.
5. J. D. Valera, J. D. C. Jones. Phase stepping in projected-fringe fiber-based moiré interferometry. *Electronics Letters* 29 (20): 1789–1791, 1993.
6. M. J. Lalor, J. T. Atkinson, D. R. Burton, P. Barton. A fiber-optic computer-controlled fringe projection interferometer for surface measurement. *Proceedings Fringe '93, Automatic Processing of Fringe Patterns,* W. Juptner and W. Osten, eds., Akademie Verlag, Berlin, 1993.
7. D. Jackson, R. Priest, A. Dandridge, A. Tveten. Elimination of drift in a single-mode optical fiber interferometer using a piezoelectrically stretched coiled fiber. *Applied Optics* 19 (17): 2926–2929, 1980.
8. G. Schirripa-Spagnolo, D. Ambrosini, Surface contouring by diffractive optical element-based fringe projection. *Measurement Science Technology* 12: N6–N8, 2001.
9. M. Reeves, A. J. Moore, D. P. Hand, J. D. C. Jones. Dynamic shape measurement system for laser materials processing. *Optical Engineering* 42 (10): 2923–2929, 2003.
10. M. Takeda, K. Mutoh. Fourier transform profilometry for the automatic measurement of 3-D object shapes. *Applied Optics* 22: 3977–3982, 1983.
11. J. Schmit, K. Creath. Extended averaging technique for derivation of error-compensating algorithms in phase-shifting interferometry. *Applied Optics* 34 (19): 3610–3619, 1995.
12. Y. Surrel. Additive noise effect in digital phase detection. *Applied Optics* 36 (1): 271–276, 1997.

13. A. J. Moore, R. McBride, J. S. Barton, J. D. C. Jones. Closed loop phase-stepping in a calibrated fibre optic fringe projector for shape measurement. *Applied Optics* 41 (16): 3348–3354, 2002.

14. D. P. Towers, C. H. Buckberry, B. C Stockley, M. P. Jones. Measurement of complex vibrational modes and surface form—A combined system. *Measurement Science Technology* 6: 1242–1249, 1995.

15. S. Zhang, S.-T. Yau. High-resolution, real-time 3D absolute coordinate measurement based on a phase-shifting method. *Optics Express* 14 (7): 2644–2649, 2006.

16. D. C. Ghiglia M. D. Pritt. *Two-dimensional phase unwrapping.* New York: John Wiley & Sons, 1998.

17. D. P. Towers, T. R. Judge, P. J. Bryanston-Cross. Automatic interferogram analysis techniques applied to quasi heterodyne holography and ESPI. *Optics and Lasers in Engineering,* special issue on fringe pattern analysis 14: 239–281, 1991.

18. C. E. Towers, D. P. Towers, J. D. C. Jones. Optimum frequency selection in multi-frequency interferometry. *Optics Letters* 28 (11): 887–889, 2003.

19. Y. Y. Cheng, J. C. Wyant. Two-wavelength phase shifting interferometry. *Applied Optics* 23 (24): 4539–4543, 1984.

20. D. R. Burton, M. J. Lalor. Multichannel Fourier fringe analysis as an aid to automatic phase unwrapping. *Applied Optics* 33: 2939–2948, 1994.

21. W. Nadeborn, P. Andra, W. Osten, A robust procedure for absolute phase measurement. *Optics Lasers Engineering* 24: 245–260, 1996.

22. C. E. Towers, D. P. Towers, J. D. C. Jones. Absolute fringe order calculation using optimized multi-frequency selection in full field profilometry. *Optics Lasers Engineering* 43: 788–800, 2005.

23. M. Takeda, Q. Gu, M. Kinoshita, H. Takai, Y. Takahashi. Frequency-multiplex Fourier-transform profilometry: A single-shot three-dimensional shape measurement of objects with large height discontinuities and/or surface isolations. *Applied Optics* 36: 5347–5354, 1997.

24. C. E. Towers, D. P. Towers, J. D. C. Jones. Time efficient Chinese remainder theorem algorithm for full-field fringe phase analysis in multi-wavelength interferometry. *Optics Express* 12 (6): 1136–1143, 2004.

25. Z. H. Zhang, D. P. Towers, C. E. Towers. Snapshot color fringe projection for absolute three-dimensional metrology of video sequences. *Applied Optics* 49 (31): 5947–5953, 2010.

26. J.-Y. Bouguet. Camera calibration toolbox for MATLAB. http://www.vision.caltech.edu/bouguetj/calib_doc/

9

Superfast 3D Profilometry with Digital Fringe Projection and Phase-Shifting Techniques

Laura Ekstrand, Yajun Wang, Nikolaus Karpinsky, and Song Zhang

CONTENTS

Recent years have seen the rise of digital fringe projection (DFP) techniques and their subsequent employment in diverse areas, including manufacturing, medicine, and homeland security. This chapter focuses on some of the recent advancements in high-speed three-dimensional (3D) optical profilometry with DFP and phase-shifting techniques. Over the past few years, we have developed a high-resolution real-time 3D profilometry system that has achieved simultaneous 3D shape acquisition, reconstruction, and display at 40 Hz with more than 250,000 points per frame. More recently, we have developed novel binary defocusing techniques that give DFP systems the potential to achieve tens of kilohertz 3D profilometry. In this chapter, we will explain the principles of these techniques, discuss their merits and limitations, and present experimental results achieved with these techniques.

9.1 Introduction

Three-dimensional optical profilometry techniques for static or quasi-static events have been extensively studied over the past few decades and have seen great success in video game design, animation, movies, music videos, virtual reality, telesurgery, and many engineering disciplines [1]. Though numerous 3D profilometry techniques exist, they can be classified into two categories: surface contact methods and surface noncontact methods. Both the coordinate measurement machine (CMM) and the atomic force microscope (AFM) require contact with the measuring surface to obtain 3D profiles at high accuracy. This requirement places severe restrictions on the speed of contact methods. They cannot reach kilohertz measurement speed with thousands of points per scan.

Surface noncontact techniques typically utilize optical triangulation methods (e.g., stereo vision [2], space–time stereo [3], structured light [4]), although some can retrieve depth from the same view (e.g., shape from focus/defocus [5,6], time of flight [7]). Triangulation-based systems can recover depth by matching and geometrically relating distinct regions of a scene viewed from different angles. This is usually realized by analyzing two images with a digital image correlation (DIC) algorithm [8]. However, because the DIC approach relies upon the unique features of corresponding region pairs to perform matching, the measurement accuracy is low for surfaces without strong local texture variations.

Speckle technology [9] can resolve this problem by actively projecting or painting the scene with random patterns [10] and then applying the DIC algorithm to recover the depth. Such speckle systems can achieve high temporal resolution (kilohertz or better). However, it is difficult for stereo DIC to reach camera-pixel spatial resolution because the DIC algorithm must match regions larger than one camera pixel. Also, the surface treatment (e.g., paint speckles) often causes surface damage.

Structured-light technology increases the measurement capability by actively projecting known patterns onto the objects [4]. Therefore, it can be used to measure surfaces without strong local texture variations. Though discrete-coded structured-light techniques have been able to achieve tens of hertz [11–13], their spatial resolution is limited to being larger than a single projector pixel. Fringe analysis is a special group of structured-light techniques that uses sinusoidal structured patterns (also known as fringe patterns). Because these patterns have intensities that vary continuously from point to point in a known manner, they boost the structured-light techniques from projector-pixel resolution to camera-pixel resolution.

In the recent past, fringe analysis techniques were instrumental in achieving high-speed and high-resolution 3D profilometry. For instance, a single fringe pattern could be used to recover dynamic 3D shape measurements [14] using the Fourier transform method [15] or the windowed Fourier transform method [16]. However, the Fourier method is limited to measuring surfaces that are "smooth" in both geometry and texture. Other fringe analysis methods [17] use coherent light (laser) or white light interference to generate sinusoidal patterns and have been extensively used in high-precision 3D profilometry. Though laser and interference systems have high accuracy, they typically require mechanical adjustments, making their measurement speed very slow.

The DFP technique uses digital video projectors instead of interference to generate sinusoidal fringe patterns. This technique has the merits of lower cost, higher speed, and simplicity of development, and it has been a very active research area within the past decade [14,18–21]. We developed systems to acquire 3D video at 40 Hz [20] and then later at 60 Hz [22,23]. More recently, various researchers have developed real-time 3D profilometry systems of their own through several different methods [21,24,25]. However, because the speed of switching multiple 8-bit grayscale patterns is limited by the projector's refresh rate, the maximum achievable 3D shape measurement rate is typically 120 Hz [24,26].

To overcome the speed limitation of the conventional DFP technique, we have invented a new method for 3D profilometry [27] that utilizes the defocusing effect of the projector lens to convert black and white stripes to pseudosinusoids. This defocusing technique significantly increases measurement speeds because the projector loads 1-bit binary structured images instead of 8-bit sinusoidal structured images for each 3D frame. This technique shows great potential for capturing 3D profilometry at unprecedented rates and has already enabled us to develop a 667 Hz 3D profilometry system [28] with the digital light processing (DLP) Discovery platform.

Nevertheless, the binary defocusing technique has the following limitations: (1) The DLP Discovery is very expensive, (2) the measurement accuracy is lower, and (3) the measurement depth range is smaller. We are currently striving to overcome these limitations while preserving the technique's merits.

This chapter will introduce the fundamental principles of DFP and provide examples of conventional, real-time, and superfast DFP systems.

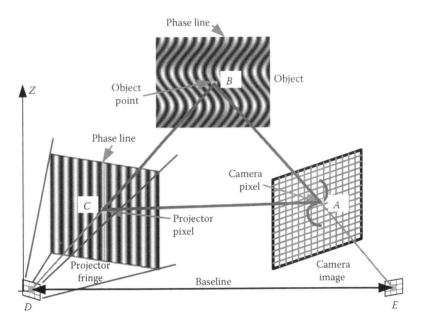

FIGURE 9.1
Schematic diagram of a 3D profilometry system using a DFP technique. (Modified from Zhang, S. *Optics and Lasers in Engineering* 48:149, 2010. With permission.)

9.2 Fundamentals

9.2.1 Digital Fringe Projection Technique

The DFP technique is a special kind of triangulation-based structured-light method where the structured patterns vary in intensity sinusoidally. This structured-light method is similar to a stereo-based method, except that it uses a projector to replace one of the cameras [4]. Figure 9.1 shows the schematic diagram of a 3D profilometry system based on a DFP technique. The image acquisition unit (a), projection unit (c), and the three-dimensional object (b) form a triangulation base. The projector shines vertical (varying horizontally) straight fringe stripes (phase lines) onto the object. The object surface distorts the fringe images from straight phase lines to curved ones. A camera captures the distorted fringe images from another angle. In such a system, the correspondence is established by analyzing the distortion of the structured patterns (fringe patterns) through fringe analysis techniques.

9.2.2 Phase-Shifting Techniques

Phase-shifting algorithms are widely used in optical metrology because of their numerous merits [17]: (1) *point-by-point measurement*, allowing camera-pixel-level spatial resolution; (2) *lower sensitivity to surface reflectivity variations,* facilitating the measurement of very complex objects with strong texture variations; and (3) *lower sensitivity to ambient light,* reducing the requirements on measurement conditions. Numerous phase-shifting algorithms have been developed including three step, four step, double three step, and five step. In general, the fringe patterns for an N-step phase-shifting algorithm with equal phase shifts can be described as

$$I_n(x,y) = I'(x,y) + I''(x,y)\cos(\phi + 2\pi n/N)$$ (9.1)

where $I'(x,y)$ is the average intensity, $I''(x,y)$ the intensity modulation, $\phi(x,y)$ the phase to be solved for, and $n = 1, 2, ..., N$. Solving these equations leads to

$$\phi(x,y) = \tan^{-1}\frac{\sum_{n=1}^{N} I_n(x,y)\sin(2\pi n/N)}{\sum_{n=1}^{N} I_n(x,y)\cos(2\pi n/N)}$$ (9.2)

The phase obtained in Equation (9.2) ranges from $-\pi$ to $+\pi$ with 2π discontinuities. A spatial phase-unwrapping algorithm [29] can be used to obtain the continuous phase, which can be converted to 3D shape data if the system is calibrated [30].

9.2.3 Phase-to-Height Conversion

The simplest system calibration method compares the unwrapped phase map for the 3D object with that for a reference plane taken with the same system. Figure 9.2 illustrates the derivation of this method. The digital micromirror device (DMD) pixel N in the DLP projector illuminates point A on the reference plane and point D on the object. Therefore, the phase value Φ_D at point D is the same as that at point A on the reference plane ($\Phi_A' = \Phi_D$). From the point of view of the CCD (M), the phase value that was at point A on the reference plane now appears to come from point C because of the object ($\Phi_C \leftarrow \Phi_A'$). The phase difference for this particular camera pixel is then $\Delta\Phi_{DC} = \Phi_D - \Phi_C' = \Phi_A' - \Phi_C' = \Delta\Phi_{AC}'$.

Assuming that the line of the device $\overline{MN}$ is parallel to the reference plane, by similar triangles we obtain

$$\frac{d}{CA} = \frac{s - \overline{BD}}{BD} = \frac{s}{BD} - 1 \approx \frac{s}{BD}$$ (9.3)

Here, we assume that, for real measurement, $s \gg \overline{BD}$. Therefore, the depth becomes

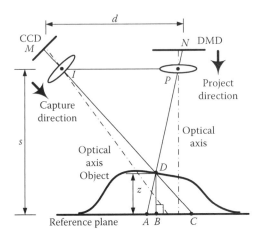

FIGURE 9.2
Calibration with a reference plane to retrieve depth for a 3D object. (Modified from Xu, Y. et al. *Applied Optics* 50:2572, 2011. With permission.)

$$z(x,y) = \overline{BD} \approx \frac{s}{d}\overline{CA} \qquad (9.4)$$

This distance $\overline{CA}$ is proportional to $\Delta\Phi^r_{AC}$. Therefore, for the whole scene,

$$z(x,y) = c_0\left[\Phi(x,y) - \Phi^r(x,y)\right] \qquad (9.5)$$

Here, c_0 is a constant determined by imaging a cube with known dimensions, Φ is the unwrapped phase map for the 3D scene, and Φ^r is the unwrapped phase for the reference plane. This calibration method has relatively low accuracy since it is an approximation, and it cannot provide (x,y) coordinates [25].

9.2.4 Phase-to-Coordinates Conversion

More complex calibration techniques have been developed to achieve better accuracy. Typically, the camera and the projector are calibrated through optimization while imaging a known scene such as a flat checkerboard [31]. For calibration purposes, we can model the DFP system as a stereo vision system, modeling the projector's DMD as an imaging sensor. After calibration, the linear model of the camera and the projector can be represented as

$$P = \begin{bmatrix} f_u & \alpha & u_0 \\ 0 & f_v & v_0 \\ 0 & 0 & 1 \end{bmatrix}\begin{bmatrix} r_{00} & r_{01} & r_{02} & t_x \\ r_{10} & r_{11} & r_{12} & t_y \\ r_{20} & r_{21} & r_{22} & t_z \end{bmatrix} = A[R,t] \qquad (9.6)$$

where

$$A = \begin{bmatrix} f_u & \alpha & u_0 \\ 0 & f_v & v_0 \\ 0 & 0 & 1 \end{bmatrix}; \quad R = \begin{bmatrix} r_{00} & r_{01} & r_{02} \\ r_{10} & r_{11} & r_{12} \\ r_{20} & r_{21} & r_{22} \end{bmatrix}; \quad t = \begin{bmatrix} t_x \\ t_y \\ t_z \end{bmatrix} \quad (9.7)$$

Here, (u_0, v_0) is the coordinate of the principal point, f_u and f_v are the focal lengths along the u and v axes of the image plane, and α is the parameter that describes the skewness of the two image axes. Since these parameters are intrinsic to the lenses and the imaging sensors of the camera and the projector, they form the intrinsic parameter matrix A. The matrix formed by R and t represents the rotation and translation, respectively, from the lens coordinates (x^c, y^c, z^c) to the world coordinates (x^w, y^w, z^w). It should be noted that this linear model does not account for lens distortions; those must be accounted for separately [31].

In the DFP system, the absolute phase map is usually used to establish the relationship between the camera sensor and the projector sensor as a one-to-many mapping (i.e., one point on the camera sensor corresponds to one line on the projector sensor with the same absolute phase value). This constraint was found sufficient to solve for (x^w, y^w, z^w) coordinates from the phase value point by point if the camera and the projector were calibrated in the same world coordinate system [30].

9.3 Real-Time 3D Profilometry with DLP Projectors

As was introduced in Section 9.1, we have developed real-time 3D profilometry systems based upon the DFP technique and DLP projectors. These systems take advantage of the unique projection mechanism of DLP technology, which will be addressed next.

9.3.1 DLP Technology

The core of the DLP projector is the DMD. Each micromirror can rotate between $+\theta_L$ (ON) and $-\theta_L$ (OFF). The grayscale value of each pixel is realized by controlling the ON time ratio: 0% ON time represents 0, 50% ON time means 128, and 100% ON time is 255. Therefore, a DLP projector produces a grayscale value by time modulation [32].

We have carried out a simple experiment to verify the time modulation behavior of one type of DLP projector used in our systems, the PLUS U5-632h. In this experiment, we connected a photodiode to a resistor to

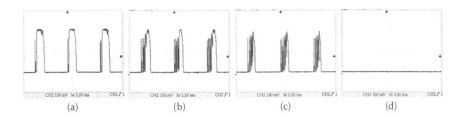

FIGURE 9.3
Examples of DLP time modulation for images with different uniform red values: (a) 255; (b) 128; (c) 64; (d) 0.

sense the output light of the projector. An oscilloscope was used to monitor the voltage of the photodiode system as the projector projected uniform red images at values of 255, 128, 64, and 0. Figure 9.3 shows the resulting oscilloscope output. It should be noted that the large gaps in the voltage data are due to the absence of the green and blue color channels. In Figure 9.3(a) and (d), the light level from the projector appears relatively constant at a high level and a low level, respectively. At a value of 128, as shown in Figure 9.3(b), the light level alternates between low and high, remaining at each level for approximately equal amounts of time. At a value of 64, the light level again alternates between the two levels, but it only jumps to the high level for about one-quarter of the time.

This experiment demonstrates that for images with values between 0 and 255, such as sinusoidal fringe patterns, the entire projection period of the image needs to be captured in order to recover the correct pattern. Therefore, to capture a conventional sinusoidal fringe pattern encoded in the red channel of a 120 Hz color DLP projector correctly, the camera exposure time must be a multiple of 1/360 second.

9.3.2 Principle

As addressed briefly in Section 9.2.2, only three fringe images are required to recover one 3D frame, and these can therefore be encoded in the three primary color channels (red, green, and blue, or RGB) and projected at once. However, the measurement quality degrades if the measured surface has strong color variations. In addition, the color coupling between RG and GB also affects the measurement quality if no filtering is used [33].

Replacing the color fringe patterns with three monochromatic fringe patterns projected in rapid succession eliminates these color-related issues. The unique projection mechanism of a single-chip DLP projection system makes this rapid switching feasible, thus facilitating real-time 3D data capture. Figure 9.4 shows the layout of such a system. In this system, the three phase-shifted images are still encoded in the projector's RGB channels for projection in rapid succession. However, the color filters of the DLP projector are first removed so that the projected fringes are monochromatic. A high-speed

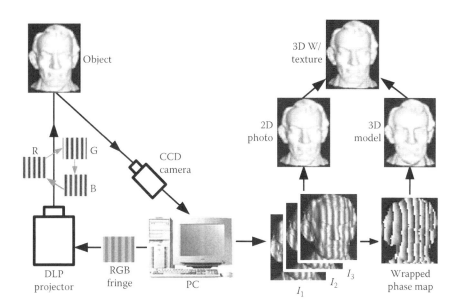

FIGURE 9.4
(See color insert.) The layout of the real-time 3D profilometry system we developed. (Modified from Zhang, S. *Optics and Lasers in Engineering* 48:149, 2010. With permission.)

CCD camera synchronized with the projector is used to capture the three channel images one by one. Applying the three-step phase-shifting algorithm to the three fringe images yields the computed phase and therefore the associated 3D shape measurements. With this type of system, we achieved 3D data acquisition at 40 frames per second (fps) [20] and later at 60 fps [34].

Furthermore, real-time 3D profilometry requires phase wrapping and phase unwrapping in real time. We have developed a fast three-step phase-shifting algorithm that improves the phase-wrapping speed by about 3.4 times [35]. This algorithm essentially approximates the arctangent function with an intensity ratio calculation in the same manner as that of the trapezoidal phase-shifting algorithm [36]. The approximation error is then compensated with a small lookup table.

Phase unwrapping removes the 2π discontinuities from the phase to yield the smooth phase map. Though numerous robust phase-unwrapping algorithms have been developed that include the branch-cut algorithms [37,38], the discontinuity minimization algorithm [39], the L^p-norm algorithm [40], and the least-squares algorithms [41], a conventional robust phase-unwrapping algorithm is usually too slow for real-time processing: It takes anywhere from a few seconds, to a few minutes, to even a few hours to process a standard 640×480 phase map [29]. Moreover, these algorithms are usually very sensitive to noise in the phase map.

We have developed a rapid yet robust phase-unwrapping algorithm by combining the advantages of the rapid scan-line algorithm with those of a robust quality-guided algorithm [42]. In our algorithm, a quality map is first computed from the phase gradient; higher quality points experience less noise and therefore yield lower phase gradients. Thresholds are then used to segregate points into multiple quality levels. Finally, the scan-line algorithm is used to unwrap the points in each quality level, beginning with the highest quality level. In this way, the unwrapping is both fast and accurate.

Finally, real-time 3D profilometry requires real-time conversion of the phase map to 3D coordinates and real-time visualization of the results. We found that it was very challenging to accomplish these tasks with central processing units (CPUs). Since the phase-to-coordinate conversion consists of simple point-by-point matrix operations, it can be efficiently calculated in parallel on a graphics processing unit (GPU). Data transfer rates between the CPU and the GPU do not pose a significant problem since the input data set to the GPU consists of a single phase value at each point instead of computed 3D coordinates. In addition, because the coordinates are computed on the GPU, they can be rendered immediately without accessing CPU data, again preventing a data transfer bottleneck between the CPU and the GPU. The adoption of this GPU technique permits real-time 3D coordinate calculation and visualization [43].

9.3.3 Experimental Results

We have developed a real-time 3D profilometry system that uses a high-speed CCD camera (Pulnix TM-6740 CL) with a 16 mm focal length lens (Fujinon HF16HA-1B). The sensor pixel size is 7.4 µm × 7.4 µm. The maximum data speed for this camera is 200 frames per second (fps) with an image resolution of 640 × 480. The projector (PLUS U5-632h) has an image resolution of 1024 × 768 and a focal length of f = 18.4–22.1 mm. This projector refreshes at 120 Hz, and thus this system can theoretically reach 120 Hz 3D profilometry speed. However, due to the speed limit of the camera and the synchronization requirements between the camera and the projector, we can only capture fringe images at 180 fps. Since three fringe images are needed to reconstruct one 3D shape, the 3D profilometry speed is actually 60 Hz.

With such a high measurement speed, this system can capture high-quality natural facial expressions. Figure 9.5 presents 3D measurements of the forming of a human facial expression. Photographs of the subject's face are included for comparison. As the figure demonstrates, the system captures the facial details quite well. It should be noted that the data were processed with a 5 × 5 Gaussian smoothing filter to reduce the most significant random noise. The system was calibrated using the technique discussed in Section 9.2.4, and the 3D absolute coordinates were obtained by encoding a small cross marker into the projected fringe pattern.

As introduced in Section 9.3.2, this system not only acquires 3D shape measurements in real time, but also simultaneously processes and displays them

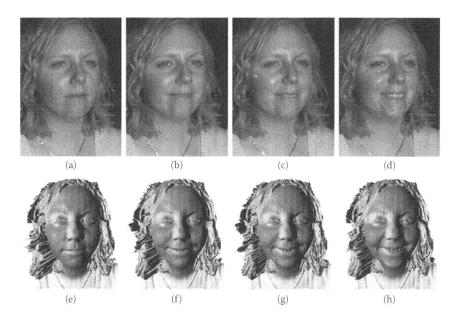

FIGURE 9.5
Real-time 3D shape measurement results using the developed system. (a)–(d) Photographs of the human subject forming a facial expression; (e)–(h) the corresponding 3D facial expressions captured at 60 fps with a spatial resolution of 640 × 480.

at high speed. Figure 9.6 illustrates the real-time measurement of a human subject. The captured 3D geometry is rendered on a computer screen to the subject's left. For this measurement, the simultaneous 3D data acquisition, reconstruction, and display speed achieved was 30 fps.

9.3.4 Discussion

As demonstrated earlier, real-time 3D profilometry can be achieved using the traditional DFP technique by taking advantage of the unique projection mechanism of single-chip DLP. However, such a technique usually requires high-quality fringe images containing at least 8 bits of precision (256 gray-scale values). The following issues arise when using 8-bit sinusoidal patterns with this real-time DFP technique:

- *Projector nonlinearity.* Since the projector is a nonlinear device, gener-ating perfect sinusoidal fringe patterns is very difficult, even though numerous algorithms have been proposed to calibrate and correct such a problem [44–46]. In our research, we have also noticed that the computer's graphics card influences the system nonlinearity and that this influence changes over time, further complicating the problem.

FIGURE 9.6
Simultaneous 3D data acquisition, reconstruction, and display. The system achieved real-time
3D profilometry at a frame rate of 30 fps with an image resolution of 640 × 480 per frame.

- *Synchronization requirement.* As introduced in Section 9.3.1, a DLP
  projector is a digital device that generates images by time integration
  [32]. In order for the camera to image the projected pattern correctly,
  it must be precisely synchronized with the projector and capture the
  entire projection period of the image. Any mismatch will result in
  significant measurement error [47].

- *Minimum exposure time limitation.* The precise synchronization
  requirement limits the camera's exposure time to at least the duration of the projection period of the fringe image. If a fringe image
  is encoded in one color channel of the typical color DLP projector
  (which has a refresh rate of 120 Hz), the minimum exposure time is
  2.78 ms. Since a much shorter exposure time is usually required for
  fast motion capture, this limits the potential of such a real-time DFP
  technique for fast motion capture applications.

If, on the other hand, 1-bit images could be used to generate sinusoidal
fringes, these issues could be avoided or significantly reduced. As mentioned briefly in Section 9.3.1, for a 1-bit image, the micromirrors of the DMD
remain stationary for the whole image projection period, eliminating most of
the synchronization requirements. This led to the development of the binary
defocusing technique for 3D profilometry, which will be addressed next.

9.4 Superfast 3D Profilometry with DLP Discovery Platform

9.4.1 Principle

9.4.1.1 Sinusoidal Fringe Pattern Generation by Defocusing

The aforementioned issues with conventional DFP render it undesirable for use in ultrafast 3D profilometry system development. Our recent research shows that a binary structured pattern becomes pseudosinusoidal when properly defocused [27]. This result is similar to that obtained by Su et al. using a Ronchi grating [48].

Figure 9.7 shows some typical results when the projector is defocused to different degrees while the camera is in focus. The pattern employed here is a basic set of black-and-white stripes referred to as a squared binary pattern (SBM). This figure shows that as the projector becomes increasingly defocused, the binary structured pattern becomes increasingly distorted. Figure 9.7(a) shows the result when the projector is in focus: clear binary structures on the image. As the degree of defocusing increases, the binary structures become less and less clear, and the sinusoidal ones become more and more obvious. However, if the projector is defocused too much, the sinusoidal structures start diminishing, as indicated in Figure 9.7(e). This experiment indicates that a pseudosinusoidal fringe pattern can indeed be generated by properly defocusing a binary structured pattern.

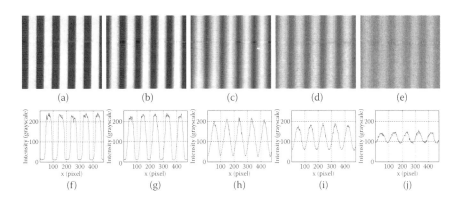

FIGURE 9.7
Example of sinusoidal fringe generation by defocusing a binary structured pattern: (a) the result when the projector is in focus; (b)–(e) the result when the projector is increasingly defocused. (f)–(j) the 240th row cross section of the corresponding image. (Modified from Ekstrand, L. and Zhang, S. *Optical Engineering* 50:123603, 2011. With permission.)

9.4.1.2 Optimal Pulse Width Modulation Technique

The seemingly sinusoidal fringe pattern generated from the SBM pattern retains some of its binary structure in the form of harmonics beyond the fundamental sinusoidal frequency [49]. Some of these harmonics induce errors in the results that limit the depth range for accurate 3D measurement [50]. An alternative approach to the defocusing technique uses fringe patterns generated by optimal pulse width modulation (OPWM), which produces binary fringe patterns by selectively removing regions of the square wave of SBM that would generate the undesired harmonics after defocusing [49]. This technique is used in the field of electrical engineering to generate sinusoidal waveforms [51]. Figure 9.8 shows an SBM pattern in comparison to an OPWM pattern, illustrating the shifting of columns that takes place during the removal of selected harmonics. Indeed, Figure 9.8(b) appears more sinusoidal even prior to defocusing. Therefore, defocused OPWM patterns can serve as an alternative to 8-bit sinusoidal patterns with all of the advantages of binary structured patterns.

9.4.2 Experimental Results

The SBM binary pattern defocusing technique was verified with the measurement of a complex sculpture. Figure 9.9 presents the results of this verification. Figure 9.9(a)–(c) shows the three fringe images employed, which are phase shifted by $2\pi/3$. To produce this phase shift, the pattern was translated in the computer by one-third of its period. The three-step phase-shifting algorithm was then used to obtain the wrapped phase map shown in Figure 9.9(d). After unwrapping via a phase-unwrapping algorithm, the unwrapped phase map was converted to depth values using the simple phase-to-height conversion algorithm given in Section 9.2.3. Figure 9.9(e) presents the recovered 3D results, which are clearly of high quality.

(a)   (b)

FIGURE 9.8
Comparison of computer-generated binary patterns: (a) one of the SBM patterns; (b) one of the OPWM patterns. (From Ekstrand, L. and Zhang, S. *Optical Engineering* 50:123603, 2011. With permission.)

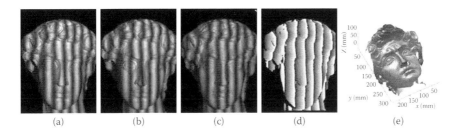

FIGURE 9.9
Three-dimensional shape measurement example using the binary defocusing technique: (a)–(c) three phase-shifted fringe patterns; (d) wrapped phase map; (e) recovered 3D shape.

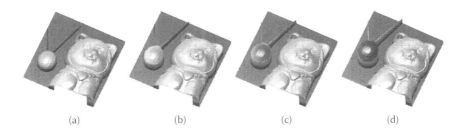

FIGURE 9.10
Three-dimensional shape measurement with the OPWM defocusing technique and a multifrequency phase-shifting algorithm: (a)–(d) 3D frames of a swinging pendulum system next to a stationary 3D sculpture. (Modified from Wang, Y. and Zhang, S. *Optics Express* 19:5149, 2011. With permission.)

In addition to the aforementioned advantages of using binary structured patterns, the defocusing technique also leads to large breakthroughs in 3D profilometry speed. The most recently developed DLP Discovery technology is capable of switching 1-bit images at tens of kilohertz. By applying the new fringe generation technique to this DLP Discovery projection platform, we achieved an unprecedented rate for 3D shape measurement: 667 Hz [28]. Furthermore, using the OPWM technique, we implemented a multifrequency phase-shifting algorithm with fringe image capture at 5000 fps to develop a 3D profilometry system capable of measurements at 556 Hz [52]. In this system, we used a DLP Discovery projection system that included a DLP Discovery board (D4000), an ALP high-speed software package, and an S3X optical module; a high-speed CMOS camera (Phantom v9.1) that captures the fringe images at 5000 fps with an image resolution of 576 × 576; and a synchronization circuit that takes the projection timing signal and generates a timing signal to trigger the camera.

Figure 9.10 presents four 3D frames of a swinging pendulum system simultaneously measured next to a complex 3D sculpture. The measurement quality is clearly very high. These frames were captured with the 556 Hz multifrequency system; it is important to observe that this system is capable of measuring arbitrary step height objects since it utilizes temporal instead of spatial phase unwrapping.

9.4.3 Discussion

Due to the numerous advantages of defocusing binary structured patterns to generate sinusoidal fringe patterns, binary defocusing has the potential to replace the conventional fringe generation technique for 3D profilometry. However, the defocusing technique is not trouble free. A number of challenges need to be overcome before such a technology can be widely deployed:

- *Challenge 1: The hardware system cost is quite high.* Compared to commercially available DLP projectors, the DLP Discovery is approximately 10 to 20 times more expensive. The question is how to attain similar or higher speed 3D profilometry without using such an expensive platform.
- *Challenge 2: The 3D profilometry speed is limited to 10 kHz.* The binary image refresh rate of the DLP Discovery is 32 kHz, which places a limit on its 3D profilometry speed of approximately 10 kHz. The question is whether there is a way to break through this speed bottleneck.
- *Challenge 3: The calibration is difficult.* Since the projector is out of focus, all existing high-accuracy structured-light system calibration techniques that require the projector to be in focus cannot be applied. The question is how to calibrate the system accurately with an out-of-focus projector.
- *Challenge 4: The measurement depth range is much smaller.* The defocused binary structured patterns only become high-quality sinusoidal patterns within a small depth range (less than 10% of the high-contrast projection region). Therefore, any measurements made outside that range will have errors. The question is how to increase the measurement depth range without sacrificing the sensing speed.
- *Challenge 5: The high-order harmonics cause residual errors.* The defocusing technique essentially acts like a low-pass filter, suppressing the high-frequency harmonics present in the binary pattern that cause measurement errors. However, it is difficult to eliminate these harmonics completely. The question is how to remove their residual effects.

Our recent research efforts in developing OPWM [49] seem to hold the most promise for overcoming these challenges. However, the effectiveness of this OPWM technique is limited by the discrete nature of DFP; the digital fringe images cannot be continuously divided to obtain more accurate sinusoids upon defocusing. Therefore, it remains difficult to achieve the same depth range as the conventional DFP method.

9.5 Summary

This chapter has presented some of the recent advances in high-speed 3D optical profilometry with digital fringe projection and phase-shifting techniques. Two high-speed 3D profilometry systems were presented: a real-time 3D profilometry system that achieved simultaneous 3D shape acquisition, reconstruction, and display at 40 Hz with more than 250,000 points per frame; and a superfast 3D profilometry system that achieved 556 Hz measurement speed with the novel binary defocusing techniques. We have explained the principles of these techniques, presented some relevant experimental results, and addressed some challenging issues that we still face.

References

1. G. Geng. Structured-light 3D surface imaging: A tutorial. *Advances in Optics and Photonics* 3 (2):128–160 (2011).
2. U. Dhond and J. Aggarwal. Structure from stereo—A review. *IEEE Transactions Systems, Man, and Cybernetics* 19:1489–1510 (1989).
3. L. Zhang, B. Curless, and S. Seitz. Spacetime stereo: Shape recovery for dynamic scenes. *Proceedings Computer Vision and Pattern Recognition* 2:367–374 (2003).
4. J. Salvi, S. Fernandez, T. Pribanic, and X. Llado. A state of the art in structured light patterns for surface profilometry. *Pattern Recognition* 43:2666–2680 (2010).
5. S. Nayar and Y. Nakagawa. Shape from focus. *IEEE Transactions Pattern Analysis and Machine Intelligence* 16:824–831 (1994).
6. M. Subbarao and G. Surya. Depth from defocus: A spatial domain approach. *International Journal of Computer Vision* 13:271–294 (1994).
7. W. C. Wiley and I. H. McLaren. Time-of-flight mass spectrometer with improved resolution. *Review of Scientific Instruments* 26(12) (1955).
8. F. Ackermann. Digital image correlation: Performance and potential application in photogrammetry. *Photogrammetric Record* 11:429–439 (1984).
9. J. P. Siebert and S. J. Marshall. Human body 3D imaging by speckle texture projection photogrammetry. *Sensor Review* 20(3):218–226 (2000).
10. A. Anand, V. K. Chhaniwal, P. Almoro, G. Pedrini, and W. Osten. Shape and deformation measurements of 3D objects using volume speckle field and phase retrieval. *Optics Letters* 34 (10):1522–1524 (2009).
11. S. Rusinkiewicz, O. Hall-Holt, and M. Levoy. Real-time 3D model acquisition. *ACM Transactions Graphics* 21 (3):438–446 (2002).
12. L. Zhang, N. Snavely, B. Curless, and S. M. Seitz. Space-time faces: High-resolution capture for modeling and animation. *ACM Annual Conference on Computer Graphics* 23(3):548–558 (2004).
13. J. Davis, R. Ramamoorthi, and S. Rusinkiewicz. Space-time stereo: A unifying framework for depth from triangulation. *IEEE Transactions Pattern Analysis Machine Intelligence* 27 (2):1–7 (2005).

14. X. Su and Q. Zhang. Dynamic 3-D shape measurement method: A review. *Optics Lasers Engineering* 48:191–204 (2010).

15. M. Takeda and K. Mutoh. Fourier transform profilometry for the automatic measurement of 3-D object shape. *Applied Optics* 22:3977–3982 (1983).

16. K. Qian. Windowed Fourier transform for fringe pattern analysis. *Applied Optics* 43 (13):2695–2702 (2004).

17. D. Malacara. ed. *Optical shop testing,* 3rd ed. New York: John Wiley & Sons (2007).

18. P. S. Huang, C. Zhang, and F.-P. Chiang. High-speed 3-D shape measurement based on digital fringe projection. *Optics Engineering* 42 (1):163–168 (2002).

19. C. Zhang, P. S. Huang, and F.-P. Chiang. Microscopic phase-shifting profilometry based on digital micromirror device technology. *Applied Optics* 41:5896–5904 (2002).

20. S. Zhang and P. S. Huang. High-resolution real-time three-dimensional shape measurement. *Optics Engineering* 45 (12):123, 601 (2006).

21. K. Liu, Y. Wang, D. L. Lau, Q. Hao, and L. G. Hassebrook. Dual-frequency pattern scheme for high-speed 3-D shape measurement. *Optics Express* 18 (5):5229–5244 (2010).

22. S. Zhang and S.-T. Yau. High-resolution, real-time 3-D absolute coordinate measurement based on a phase-shifting method. *Optics Express* 14 (7):2644–2649 (2006).

23. S. Zhang, D. Royer, and S.-T. Yau. GPU-assisted high-resolution, real-time 3-D shape measurement. *Optics Express* 14 (20):9120–9129 (2006).

24. Y. Li, C. Zhao, Y. Qian, H. Wang, and H. Jin. High-speed and dense three-dimensional surface acquisition using defocused binary patterns for spatially isolated objects. *Optics Express* 18 (21):21, 628–631, 635 (2010).

25. S. Zhang. Recent progress on real-time 3-D shape measurement using digital fringe projection techniques. *Optics Lasers Engineering* 48 (2):149–158 (2010).

26. Y. Gong and S. Zhang. High-speed, high-resolution three-dimensional shape measurement using projector defocusing. *Optics Engineering* 50 (2):023, 603 (2011).

27. S. Lei and S. Zhang. Flexible 3-D shape measurement using projector defocusing. *Optics Letters* 34 (20):3080–3082 (2009).

28. S. Zhang, D. van der Weide, and J. Oliver. Superfast phase-shifting method for 3-D shape measurement. *Optics Express* 18 (9):9684–9689 (2010).

29. D. C. Ghiglia and M. D. Pritt. *Two-dimensional phase unwrapping: Theory, algorithms, and software.* New York: John Wiley & Sons, Inc. (1998).

30. S. Zhang and P. S. Huang. Novel method for structured light system calibration. *Optics Engineering* 45 (8):083, 601 (2006).

31. Z. Zhang. A flexible new technique for camera calibration. *IEEE Transactions Pattern Analysis Machine Intelligence* 22 (11):1330–1334 (2000).

32. L. J. Hornbeck. Digital light processing for high-brightness, high-resolution applications. *Proceedings SPIE* 3013:27–40 (1997).

33. J. Pan, P. S. Huang, and F.-P. Chiang. Color-coded binary fringe projection technique for 3-D shape measurement. *Optics Engineering* 44 (2):023, 606 (2005).

34. S. Zhang and S.-T. Yau. High-speed three-dimensional shape measurement system using a modified two-plus-one phase-shifting algorithm. *Optics Engineering* 46 (11):113, 603 (2007).

35. P. S. Huang and S. Zhang. Fast three-step phase-shifting algorithm. *Applied Optics* 45 (21):5086–5091 (2006).

36. P. S. Huang, S. Zhang, and F.-P. Chiang. Trapezoidal phase-shifting method for three-dimensional shape measurement. *Optics Engineering* 44 (12):123, 601 (2005).

37. J. M. Huntley. Noise-immune phase unwrapping algorithm. *Applied Optics* 28:3268–3270 (1989).

38. M. F. Salfity, P. D. Ruiz, J. M. Huntley, M. J. Graves, R. Cusack, and D. A. Beauregard. Branch cut surface placement for unwrapping of undersampled three-dimensional phase data: Application to magnetic resonance imaging arterial flow mapping. *Applied Optics* 45:2711–2722 (2006).

39. T. J. Flynn. Two-dimensional phase unwrapping with minimum weighted discontinuity. *Journal Optical Society America* A 14:2692–2701 (1997).

40. D. C. Ghiglia and L. A. Romero. Minimum L^p-norm two-dimensional phase unwrapping. *Journal Optical Society America* A 13:1–15 (1996).

41. J.-J. Chyou, S.-J. Chen, and Y.-K. Chen. Two-dimensional phase unwrapping with a multichannel least-mean-square algorithm. *Applied Optics* 43:5655–5661 (2004).

42. S. Zhang, X. Li, and S.-T. Yau. Multilevel quality-guided phase unwrapping algorithm for real-time three-dimensional shape reconstruction. *Applied Optics* 46 (1):50–57 (2007).

43. S. Zhang, D. Royer, and S.-T. Yau. GPU-assisted high-resolution, real-time 3-D shape measurement. *Optics Express* 14 (20):9120–9129 (2006).

44. S. Zhang and P. S. Huang. Phase error compensation for a three-dimensional shape measurement system based on the phase shifting method. *Optics Engineering* 46 (6):063, 601 (2007).

45. S. Zhang and S.-T. Yau. Generic nonsinusoidal phase error correction for three-dimensional shape measurement using a digital video projector. *Applied Optics* 46 (1):36–43 (2007).

46. B. Pan, Q. Kemao, L. Huang, and A. Asundi. Phase error analysis and compensation for nonsinusoidal waveforms in phase-shifting digital fringe projection profilometry. *Optics Letters* 34 (4):2906–2914 (2009).

47. S. Lei and S. Zhang. Digital sinusoidal fringe generation: Defocusing binary patterns vs. focusing sinusoidal patterns. *Optics Lasers Engineering* 48:561–569 (2010).

48. X.-Y. Su, W.-S. Zhou, G. von Bally, and D. Vukicevic. Automated phase-measuring profilometry using defocused projection of a Ronchi grating. *Optics Communications* 94 (13):561–573 (1992).

49. Y. Wang and S. Zhang. Optimum pulse width modulation for sinusoidal fringe generation with projector defocusing. *Optics Letters* 35 (24):4121–4123 (2010).

50. Y. Xu, L. Ekstrand, J. Dai, and S. Zhang. Phase error compensation for three-dimensional shape measurement with projector defocusing. *Applied Optics* 50 (17):2572–2581 (2011).

51. V. G. Agelidis, A. Balouktsis, and I. Balouktsis. On applying a minimization technique to the harmonic elimination PWM control: The Bipolar Waveform. *IEEE Power Electronics Letters* 2:41–44 (2004).

52. Y. Wang and S. Zhang. Superfast multifrequency phase-shifting technique with optimal pulse width modulation. *Optics Express* 19 (6):5143–5148 (2011).

10

Time-of-Flight Techniques

Shoji Kawahito

CONTENTS

10.1 Introduction

Time-of-flight (TOF) range imaging is a three-dimensional (3D) imaging method with moderate accuracy and simple configuration. In the past 20 years, great progress has been made in TOF range imaging. There are two methods for measuring the TOF: direct and indirect. In the direct TOF measurement, the TOF is measured directly in a time domain, and a semiconductor device—the so-called single photon avalanche diode—has enabled all electronic range cameras without any mechanically moving components. Indirect TOF range imaging has been realized by the invention of a lock-in pixel with charge-domain demodulation of the modulated light signal. In the indirect TOF measurement, the TOF is converted to a physical quantity and then the range is calculated by the amount of physical quantity modulation due the TOF and a time reference. The lock-in pixel used for the TOF range imagers is based on the concept of rapid charge transfer in a fully depleted semiconductor, which originated in charge-coupled device (CCD) image sensors and now is realized mostly in CMOS (complementary metal oxide semiconductor) image sensors.

Using the round-trip TOF of light T, the range to an object L is expressed as

$$\text{Mass of 1 aluminum atom} = \frac{27\,\text{g/mol}}{N_A} = 4.5 \times 10^{-23}\ \text{g/atom} \quad (10.1)$$

where c (= 3×10^8 m/s) is the speed of light.

A high time resolution is required for precise range measurement because of the speed of light. For instance, to resolve the depth of 1.5 mm, the TOF to be resolved is 10 ps. Progress in semiconductor integrated circuits technology is enabling a high time resolution of less than 10 ps. Practical applications of the TOF range imager require high tolerance to background light as well as the range accuracy or resolution. The TOF imaging system using a mechanical scanner has relatively high tolerance to background light because of the high light energy concentration to the point of measurement. On the other hand, spatial resolution and speed of imaging are limited by the performance of the scanner. All-electronic 3D imaging systems using an area light projector and an area TOF sensor have practical advantages of cost effectiveness, high reliability due to nonmechanical implementation, higher frame rate, and higher 2D spatial resolution.

This chapter describes possible system configurations for TOF range imaging, but mainly focuses on all-electronic range cameras using direct and indirect TOF measurements. Devices, circuits, and systems for TOF range imaging are described and range resolution and tolerance to background light in indirect TOF measurements are discussed.

10.2 System Configurations for TOF Range Imaging

TOF range imaging methods are categorized into three types, depending on the types of mechanical scanners and photo detectors, as shown in Table 10.1. The *SPD* uses a two-dimensional (2D) mechanical scanner with a single-point detector The *LD* uses a one-dimensional (1D) mechanical scanner with a 1D array detector or a linear imager. An all-electronic (*AE*) type or a mechanical scannerless range imager can be implemented with a 2D array detector or an area imager. The *SPD* and *AE* types are treated hereafter.

TABLE 10.1

System Configurations for TOF Range Imaging

Type	Mechanical Scanner	Detector
SPD	2D	Single point
LD	1D	1D array (linear imager)
AE	Scannerless	2D array (area imager)

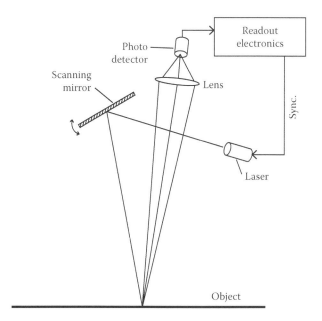

FIGURE 10.1

TOF system using a single-point detector and a laser 2D scanner.

10.2.1 Single-Point Detector with Laser Scanner

Figure 10.1 shows a configuration of the single-point TOF range imaging system. A laser beam is scanned by a 2D scanning mirror and the back-reflected light is received by a photo detector. The 2D spatial position is determined by the amount of the diffraction of the mirror and the depth is measured by the time of flight. The laser pulse generation is synchronized with the readout electronics for the received light to measure the TOF.

The advantage of the single-point detection method is a high tolerance to the background light because the laser power is concentrated at the point of measurement. The range resolution is closely related to the signal-to-noise ratio (SNR). One of the noises is due to background light. In the system shown in Figure 10.1, the photo detector area must cover the field of view of imaging and receives back-reflected background light from all the scanning

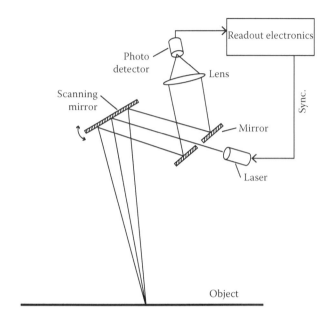

FIGURE 10.2
TOF system using coaxial optical system.

areas. Therefore, even though the laser power is concentrated at the point of measurement, this system is not always ideal for maximizing the SNR.

An optical system shown in Figure 10.2 offers the best solution for minimizing the influence of background light [1]. In this system, the laser beam emitted and light received use a coaxial optical system. This enables the field of view of the photo detector to be concentrated on the measuring point and only a small portion of background light to be influenced to the signal, resulting in a high SNR in the range calculation.

Electronics for the single-point detector to measure the TOF often use a direct measurement of the delay of the back-reflected light pulse in the time domain. The detailed circuit implementation will be discussed in the next section.

10.2.2 Scannerless System with Area Detector and Area Light Projector

Using an area image sensor or a 2D array photo detector, a scannerless TOF range imaging system can be implemented as shown in Figure 10.3. The entire field of view is illuminated by an area light projector and the back-reflected light image is taken by a TOF range camera that has a time-resolving capability in each pixel. One of the methods for time-resolved imaging is to use a gated image intensifier (GII) in front of a CCD camera [2]. A switching of a few nanosecond time windows with a modulation period of 20 to 100 ns is possible using the GII.

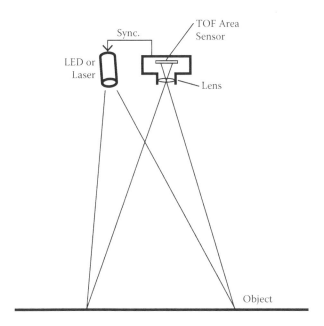

FIGURE 10.3
TOF system with area detector and area light projector.

Another time-resolved imaging method is to use time-resolved CCD or CMOS imagers in which each pixel has a dedicated design for synchronized operation and high-speed photo response to a high-frequency modulated light. Such pixel technology is often called a lock-in pixel [9]. The time-resolved photo response in each pixel is used for measuring the TOF directly or indirectly. The "direct TOF" means that the TOF is measured directly in time domain. The "indirect TOF" means that the TOF is once measured as a result of modulation of physical quantity in the receiver, such as a modulation of photo-generated charge, current, or voltage; then, the TOF is calculated by the conversion of the physical quantity to time-domain signal change using a time reference. The devices, circuits, and systems for the direct and indirect TOF measurements will be described in the following two sections.

10.3 Direct TOF Range Imaging

10.3.1 2D Array Detector with SPAD

A CMOS LSI (large scale integration) technology allows us to implement a 1D or 2D array light receiver with control circuits and makes a direct TOF system without any mechanical scanner but with an area projector possible.

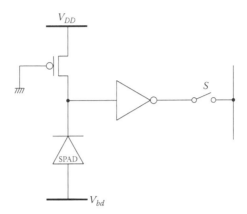

FIGURE 10.4
Single photon avalanche diode.

The scannerless direct TOF system requires photo-charge detection mechanism with very high sensitivity and high-speed response. A single photon avalanche diode (SPAD) working in Geiger mode fulfills this purpose [3–5].

The schematic of the single photon receiver pixel using the SPAD and the operation are shown in Figures 10.4 and 10.5, respectively [6]. When a p–n junction or a SPAD is suddenly reverse biased above its breakdown voltage, there will be no breakdown current until a carrier enters the depletion region. Suppose that a photon is absorbed at this moment in the depletion region. The carriers resulting from the absorption of a photon generate an extremely large number of electron-hole pairs by impact ionization, causing an avalanche multiplication due to a single photon.

A p-channel MOS (pMOS) transistor whose gate-to-source voltage is biased to V_{DD} is connected to the anode terminal of the SPAD. When the avalanche current is larger than the bias current of the pMOS transistor, the cathode terminal voltage of the SPAD goes down and hence the reverse bias is lowered so that the avalanche current is quenched. Once the avalanche current is quenched, the pMOS again recharges the depletion capacitance of the SPAD to V_{DD}. This mode of operation is commonly known as Geiger mode. A CMOS inverter connected at the anode of the SPAD is used as a comparator to generate a logical pulse right after a photon is received. The output of the inverter is connected to a common signal line by a switch S when the pixel is selected for readout.

Figure 10.6 shows the cross-sectional view of the SPAD, which is compatible to CMOS technology. To prevent a premature breakdown due to the high electric field at the periphery of the p+ junction, the p+ layer is surrounded by a guard ring using a relatively lightly doped p-well layer. A planar avalanche multiplication region is created below the p+ junction with a deep n-well region.

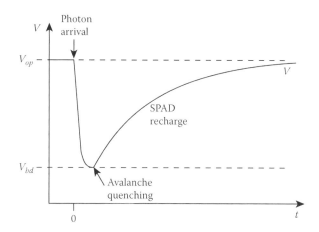

FIGURE 10.5
Operation of Geiger-mode SPAD.

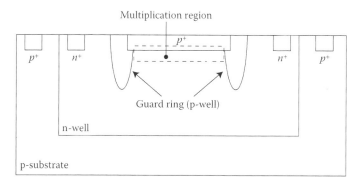

FIGURE 10.6
Cross-sectional view of the SPAD.

10.3.2 Time-to-Digital Converter

A critical component of the direct TOF range imager using the SPAD is the time-to-digital converter (TDC). A direct TOF measurement system using a TDC and operation timing is shown in Figures 10.7 and 10.8, respectively. A TDC can be implemented with a digital counter, which measures the time interval between the transmitted light pulse and the received light pulse. To do this, a gate pulse is generated by the measurement of the time interval (TOF) and the number of clock cycles is counted using the gated high-frequency clock given at a counter. To generate the gating pulse, a flip-flop with set and reset inputs can be used, as shown in Figure 10.7. The flip-flop is set by a trigger pulse for light pulse transmission and is reset by the rising edge of the received light pulse, which is generated by the output of the SPAD.

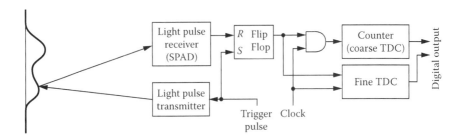

FIGURE 10.7
Direct TOF measurement system using a TDC.

The time resolution of the TDC using a counter is equal to the inverse of the clock frequency, and therefore the range resolution is determined by the clock frequency. For instance, the clock frequency of 1 GHz gives the time resolution of 1 ns and the range resolution of 15 cm. If a range resolution of 1 mm is required, the clock frequency of 150 GHz must be used for the gated counter. An implementation of the gated counter working at 150 GHz is not easy, even if state-of-the-art CMOS technology is used.

For higher time resolution without increasing clock frequency, a subranging technique is often used for the TDC. As shown in Figure 10.7, the counter is used for coarse TDC and a fine TDC measures the subrange of one clock cycle T_c of the coarse TDC.

A typical implementation of the fine TDC is shown in Figure 10.9. A start pulse is given at the input of a delay line consisting of an inverter chain and is activated at the rigging edge of the clock. The outputs of the M-stage inverter chain are latched in a flash register using a stop pulse that is activated at the falling edge of the gating pulse. The register output is expressed as a thermometer code corresponding to the subrange delay T_{SR}, which is expressed as the difference of the TOF to be measured T from its coarse measure given by $N_1 \times T_c$, where N_1 is the number of counts of the counter output. By adding up the ones of the thermometer code, a binary code M_1 is generated. Using the unit inverter delay ΔT, the binary code is expressed as

$$M_1 = \frac{T_{SR}}{\Delta T} = \frac{T - N_1 \times T_c}{\Delta T} \qquad (10.2)$$

If the number of inverter stages is $M = 2^m$, where m is an integer, and an n-bit counter is used, the TDC using the subranging technique has a resolution of $n + m$ bits and the minimum time step of ΔT. The unit delay of an inverter chain using state-of-the-art CMOS technology can be smaller than 10 ps. Therefore, a range resolution of a few millimeters can be realized in the SPAD-based range imager. In actual range measurements, the TDC output is averaged over many samples and the equivalent resolution is improved to smaller than ΔT.

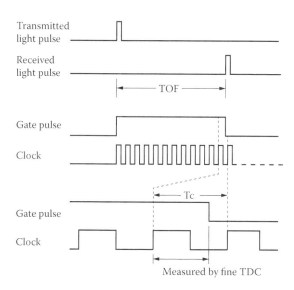

FIGURE 10.8
Operation of the TDC using a subranging technique.

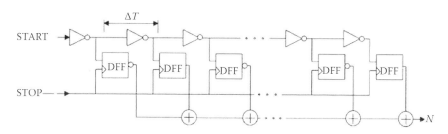

FIGURE 10.9
Time-to-digital converter using a delay line and flash register.

10.3.3 CMOS Implementations

The first TOF range image sensor with SPADs was implemented with a 0.8 µm CMOS process and had 32 × 32 pixels [6]. The pixel occupies the area of 58 × 58 µm² and the active area of the SPAD is 38 × 38 µm². The TDC is not on the sensor chip, but rather is implemented in a separated CMOS chip. Using a light source with a pulse width of 150 ps, the range resolution of 1.8 mm is attained for a distance range of 3 m.

A TOF range image sensor with a large SPAD pixel array of 128 × 128 pixels has been implemented with a 0.35 µm CMOS process and on-chip 10-bit 32-channel TDC [7]. The 10-bit TDC uses a three-level subranging technique with a counter (2 bits), DLL(delayed locked 100p)-based TDC (4 bits), and delay-line-based TDC (4 bits). The time resolution of 97 ps has been achieved with the on-chip TDC. The pixel occupies the area of 25 × 25 μm² and the active diameter of the circular SPAD is 7 μm. A range resolution (standard deviation) of 5.2 mm for the distance range of 3.75 m is attained. Though the range resolution of the TDC with 97 ps time resolution is 1.5 cm, the averaging mechanism of the system improves the range resolution to 5 mm.

10.4 Indirect TOF Range Imaging

10.4.1 Lock-in Pixel for Time-Dependent Charge Detection

In indirect TOF measurement using silicon technology, a lock-in pixel using charge domain processing is used. The first attempt of time-resolved imaging with charge domain processing was reported in Povel, Aebersold, and Stenflo [8] for an application to the 2D polarimeter, in which the modulated light is generated by a piezoelastic modulator and the modulation frequency is 50 kHz. For the application to 3D imaging with millimeter depth resolution, a modulation frequency of higher than 10 MHz is required. Dedicated pixel structures for high-frequency lock-in operation using a CCD have elevated the charge modulation frequency of lock-in pixels to be several 10 MHz [9].

Figure 10.10 shows a conceptual schematic of the charge-domain processing in a lock-in pixel for indirect TOF range imaging. The photo detector has two transfer gates for transferring photo-induced charge into two charge accumulators. When the light pulse is received at the phase as depicted by a solid line, the photo-induced charge is equally divided into two storages. If the light pulse is delayed, as depicted by a dashed line, the charge transferred to the right-side storage is increased while that of the left-side storage is decreased. The difference of the two charges depends on the delay of the light pulse and therefore the range can be measured by the amount of charge. This operation is repeated many times so that sufficient amounts of charge are accumulated in the two storages.

Figure 10.11 shows a cross-sectional view of the two-tap lock-in (range finder) CCD [10]. An incoming light pulse is received in the aperture area of the pixel and is absorbed in bulk silicon through a photo gate (PG). In TOF measurements, near infrared light is commonly used. The PG made of thin polycrystalline silicon is transparent to infrared light.

Two transfer gates $TX1$ and $TX2$ are turned on alternately, as shown in Figure 10.12. If there is no delay time in the received light, a photo-generated charge is equally divided into two storages under the gates $ST1$ and $ST2$. The delay of the received light pulse decreases the charge Q_1 and increases the charge Q_2. With photo current I_p, the light pulse width T_w, and the delay time T_d, these charges are expressed as

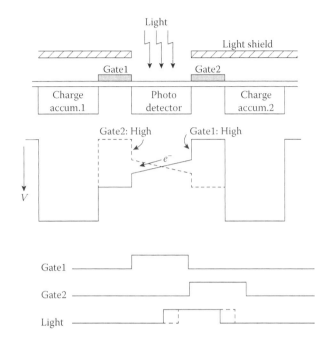

FIGURE 10.10
Operation of a lock-in pixel.

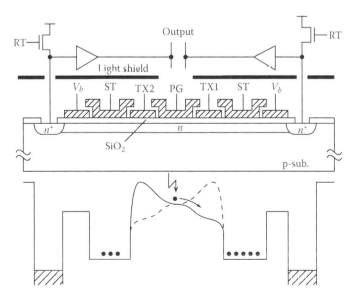

FIGURE 10.11
TOF imager using CCD process.

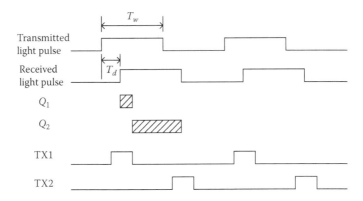

FIGURE 10.12
Operation of two-tap lock-in CCD.

$$Q_1 = I_p\left(T_w/2 - T_d\right) \tag{10.3}$$

$$Q_2 = I_p\left(T_w/2 + T_d\right) \tag{10.4}$$

The delay time can be estimated using Equations (10.3) and (10.4) as

$$T_d = \frac{T_w}{2}\frac{Q_2 - Q_1}{Q_1 + Q_2} \tag{10.5}$$

Using Equation (10.5), the range can be estimated by the charge ratio and a time reference of T_w; it is independent of light intensity.

To read out the two charges, two floating diffusion amplifiers with floating diffusion (floating p–n junction) and a source follower are used. The final voltage outputs V_x, $x = 1$ or 2, are given by

$$V_x = G_{SF}\frac{Q_x}{C_{FD}} \tag{10.6}$$

where G_{SF} is the gain of a source follower amplifier, typically 0.8 to 0.9, and C_{FD} is the floating diffusion capacitance.

10.4.2 Sinusoidal Modulation

Figure 10.13 shows the top view of the four-tap lock-in pixel suitable for TOF range imaging [9]. One pixel consists of a PG, a dump-gate (DG), a dump diffusion (DD), four transfer gates, and a four-phase CCD. Two vertical, four-phase CCD lines are located in each pixel. The four-phase CCD is covered by

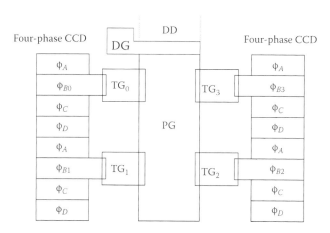

FIGURE 10.13
Four-tap lock-in CCD.

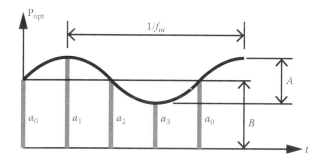

FIGURE 10.14
Timing diagram of the indirect TOF pixel.

a metal layer for light shielding in order to prevent unwanted photo-charge generation during signal readout.

In order to use the four-tap lock-in CCD for TOF range imaging, an LED (light emitting diode) or laser diode is modulated by a sine wave, and the photo charge is sampled in the four taps as shown in Figure 10.14. Using the four sampled signals, the phase delay of the propagated light signal is estimated while reducing the influence of background light.

From the definition of discrete Fourier transform, the amplitude A, offset b, and phase ϕ are given by

$$A = \sqrt{\left(a_0 - a_2\right)^2 + \left(a_1 + a_3\right)^2} \tag{10.7}$$

$$B = \left(\frac{a_0 + a_1 + a_2 + a_3}{4} \right) \tag{10.8}$$

$$\phi = \arctan\left(\frac{a_0 - a_2}{a_1 - a_3}\right) \qquad (10.9)$$

The range L is given by

$$L = \frac{c\phi}{4\pi f_m} \qquad (10.10)$$

where f_m is the modulation frequency of the light.

10.4.3 Small-Duty-Cycle Pulse Modulation

The four-tap lock-in pixel has a capability of canceling offset charge due to background light. However, strong background light such as direct sunlight may produce extremely large amounts of offset charge and it may exceed the full well capacity of the storage.

In order to reduce the background light charge, a lock-in pixel structure for receiving small-duty-cycle light pulses can be used [14]. The top view of a lock-in pixel for the small duty cycle is shown in Figure 10.15. In addition to two transfer gates at the right and left sides of the photo detector, draining gates are located at the top and bottom for high-speed charge draining. The timing diagram of the transfer gates $TX1$ and $TX2$ and draining gate TXD, together with the light pulse received, is shown in Figure 10.16. A small-duty-cycle light pulse is received while $TX1$ or $TX2$ is turned on; in the rest of the cycle, TXD is turned on so that unwanted charge components due to ambient light, stray light, and dark noise are reduced.

This technique allows us to obtain higher tolerance to background light because, for a given average power of the light source, the signal-light power

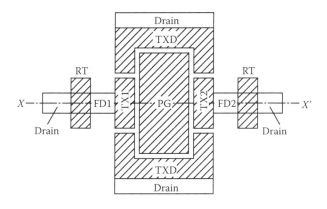

FIGURE 10.15
TOF ranging pixel for small-duty-cycle light pulse.

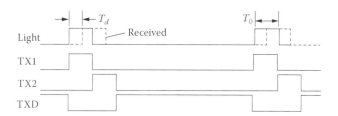

FIGURE 10.16
Timing diagram of the lock-in pixel for small-duty-cycle light pulse.

can be concentrated in a short duration and the signal-light charge is intensified compared with the background-light charge. Because of the property that the maximum rating of the LED (light-emitting diode) can be increased if a small duty cycle is used, this operation also leads to a cost-effective use of LEDs.

10.4.4 CCD and CMOS Implementations

Lock-in pixels for high-modulation frequency need high-speed carrier transfer due to a fringing electric field in a depleted semiconductor region. This idea originated in the CCD. Solid-state image sensors have been attracted by CMOS technology since the mid-1990s; thus, range imagers with lock-in pixels are also often implemented based on CMOS or mixed CCD/CMOS technologies.

The four-tap lock-in pixels have been realized with CCDs [9,11,12] and are most suitable for demodulating the sinusoidally modulated light. However, because each sample needs large storage space for attaining sufficient signal dynamic range, the four-tap approach has a drawback of a low fill factor (2.2% for a wheel-shaped four-tap pixel [12]).

The sensor of the first TOF range camera was based on the one-tap lock-in pixel using mixed CCD/CMOS technology [13]. The cross-sectional view of the one-tap lock-in pixel is shown in Figure 10.17. This pixel has a size of 65 × 21 μm^2 and an optical fill factor of 22% using 2 μm CCD/CMOS technology and is used for a 64 × 25-pixel TOF range imager.

Using the one-tap lock-in pixel, the phase measurement of sinusoidally modulated light is based on a serial acquisition of the four samples shown in Figure 10.14. This leads to a reduced frame rate and may cause errors in fast moving objects. Despite these drawbacks, it was worth demonstrating the first all-electronic solid-state TOF range camera.

The preferred choice of the pixel architecture in practical TOF range imagers is often the two-tap lock-in pixel [15]. It has a symmetrical architecture consisting of photo gates (PGR and PGL), storage gates (IG), output gates (OUTG), and sense diffusions at both sides of the middle photo gate (PGM), instead of using dump diffusion at the left end in the one-tap lock-in pixel. Using advanced CCD/CMOS technology of 0.6 μm rules, the number of pixels of the TOF range imager with two-tap lock-in pixels has been increased to 176 × 144 pixels.

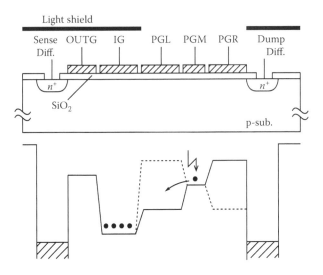

FIGURE 10.17
One-tap lock-in pixel using CCD/CMOS technology.

The architecture shown in Figure 10.17 using a CCD-type charge transfer is preferable for reduced readout noise because reset noise (kTC noise) at the sensing diffusion is canceled by a truly correlated double sampling (CDS) operation. However, such a charge transfer structure requires CCD or mixed CCD/CMOS technology.

To implement lock-in pixels using CMOS technology, a simplified lock-in pixel architecture is often used. Figure 10.18 shows a CMOS-based lock-in pixel using gates on field oxide structure [14]. The pixel uses single-layer polysilicon gates on relatively thick field oxide. To create an n-type buried layer that prevents the interface traps from causing charge transfer delay, one additional mask and an ion implantation process step are used. Because of the thick oxide and buried channel structure on a lightly doped p-type epitaxial layer, a relatively large fringing field is realized by a small voltage swing of 3 V, and a barrierless potential profile at the gap between two gates is also created by the single-layer polysilicon gates. Photo-generated and demodulated charges are directly stored in either of two sensing diffusions. Signal charge storage in the sensing diffusions suffers from reset noise and dark current noise.

However, if a sufficient amount of signal charge is available, the noise level is dominated by the photon shot noise, as discussed in the next section. The lock-in pixel shown in Figure 10.18 is used to implement the pixel whose top view is shown in Figure 10.16 for small-duty light pulse modulation. Thanks to the simplified pixel architecture, a TOF range imager with high spatial resolution of 336×252 pixels has been implemented using 0.35 μm CMOS technology. The pixel size is 15×15 μm^2.

A further simplified lock-in pixel architecture is shown in Figure 10.19 [16]. It uses only two gates for modulating a photo-generated charge. The lock-in

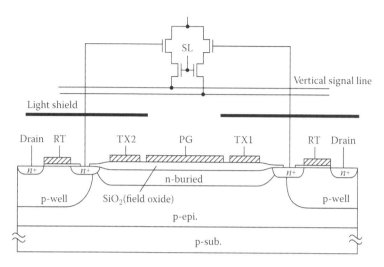

FIGURE 10.18
CMOS-based TOF pixel using gates on field oxide structure.

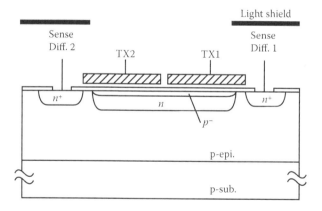

FIGURE 10.19
CMOS-based TOF pixel using two gates on active area and a buried channel.

pixel using two photo gates is also called a photo-mixing device (PMD) [17]. In Figure 10.19, a buried channel is created under the two photo gates and has offsets from the edges of sensing diffusions. This structure is useful for a better demodulation factor at higher modulation frequency.

A pinned photodiode has become a dominant technology for CMOS image sensors and is also useful for lock-in pixels in the TOF range imagers based on standard CMOS image sensor technology. Figure 10.20 shows a lock-in pixel using a pinned photodiode [18]. A photo-generated charge in the pinned photodiode is transferred to sensing diffusion or drained by applying high voltage to the TX and TXD gates, respectively. A prototype TOF range image sensor with 64 × 16 pixels, each of which

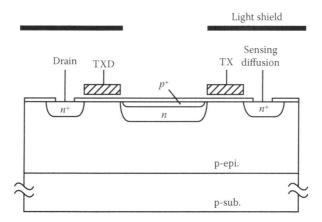

FIGURE 10.20
CMOS-based TOF pixel using two gates on active area and a buried channel.

has the size of $12 \times 12 \ \mu m^2$, has been implemented. Using the modulation frequency of 5 MHz, the range accuracy is 2% to 4% in the distance range of 1 to 4 m.

Lock-in pixels based on CMOS technology described before use a floating diffusion as a charge storage as well as a sensing diffusion and suffer from the reset noise during the readout operation. To overcome this problem, two-stage charge transfer architectures using a pinned photodiode and pinned storage diode can be used [19,20].

10.4.5 Range Resolution and Influence of Background Light and Noise

The range resolution of the indirect TOF range imagers is determined by the different types of noise. In the four-tap lock-in CCD using sinusoidal modulation, the range resolution $\Delta\varphi$ is expressed as

$$\Delta\varphi = \sqrt{\sum_{i=0}^{3} \left(\frac{\partial\varphi}{\partial a_i} \right)^2 a_i} \qquad (10.11)$$

Using Equations (10.7)–(10.10), the range resolution ΔL is expressed as [13]

$$\Delta L = \frac{L}{2\pi}\Delta\varphi = \frac{L}{\sqrt{8}} \cdot \frac{\sqrt{B}}{2A} \qquad (10.12)$$

In this equation, $\sqrt{B}$ means the amplitude of noise fluctuation. Under the influence of read noise and shot noise due to background light, as well as the shot noise of the signal light itself, B in Equation (10.12) is expressed as

$$B = N_s + N_b + N_r^2 \qquad (10.13)$$

where N_s is the number of signal electrons, N_b is the number of electrons generated by background light, and N_r is the equivalent number of electrons due to read noise. Equation (10.13) is based on the fact that the square of shot noise due to photo-generated electrons (variance in Poisson distribution) is equal to the mean number of photo-generated electrons. The signal amplitude A depends on the modulation contrast of the light source C_{mod} and the demodulation contrast of the lock-in pixel device C_{demod} and is expressed as

$$A = C_{mod}C_{demod}N_s \qquad (10.14)$$

Thus, Equation (10.12) can be rewritten as

$$\Delta L = \frac{L}{\sqrt{8}} \cdot \frac{\sqrt{N_s + N_b + N_r^2}}{2C_{mod}C_{demod}N_s} \qquad (10.15)$$

The equivalent number of reset noise electrons is given by

$$N_{reset} = \sqrt{2\frac{V_{th}}{V_s}N_{well}} \qquad (10.16)$$

where V_{th} is the thermal voltage (26 mV at room temperature) and V_s is the maximum signal voltage amplitude. The factor of 2 in Equation (10.16) is due to the noise power doubling effect in the readout operation. Typically, N_{well} ranges from several thousands to one million. For $V_s = 1$ V and $N_{well} = 200{,}000$, N_{reset} is calculated to be approximately 100.

Figure 10.21 shows the range resolution as a function of the signal amplitude for different conditions of background light and read noise.

For $N_s = 100{,}000$ and $N_b = 100{,}000$, the range resolution $\Delta L/L$ is less than 0.1%. In this condition, for example, the resolution of 5 mm is obtained, or a 5 m range. For a small signal, the resolution is highly dependent on the background light and readout noise. For $N_s = 1000$, $\Delta L/L$ is 0.56% and 5.6% for $N_b = 100$ and $N_b = 100{,}000$, respectively. If the readout noise N_r is increased to 100 because of the reset noise, $\Delta L/L$ is increased to 1.5% for $N_s = 1000$ and $N_b = 100$. Range imaging with relatively low signal light, a lock-in pixel architecture for reset noise canceling, offers a better performance in range resolution.

The background light also limits the available well capacity for a signal charge. If N_b is smaller than the well capacity of the charge storage N_{well}, the available well capacity for the signal charge is given by $N_{well} - N_b$. Under a very strong background light, N_b may exceed N_{well} and no residual well capacity is available for the signal.

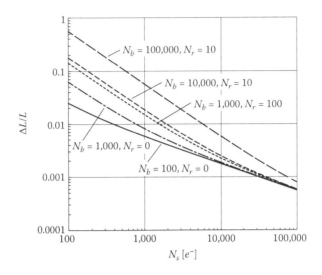

FIGURE 10.21
CMOS-based TOF pixel using two gates on active area and a buried channel.

The well capacity is also important for signal dynamic range and the resulting distance range because the signal intensity of back-reflected light at the focal plane of the image sensor is inversely proportional to the distance to the fourth power. On the other hand, the large well capacity will cause large reset noise. The lock-in pixel architecture with reset noise canceling is a better choice for wide distance range and total high-range resolution.

References

1. http://www.ecoscan.jp/
2. M. Kawakita, K. Iizuka, H. Nakmura, I. Mizuno, T. Kurita, T. Aida, Y. Yamanouchi, et al. High-definition real-time depth-mapping TV camera: HDTV axi-vision camera. *Optics Express* 12 (12): 2781–2794, 2004.
3. A. Rochas, A. R. Pauchard, P.-A. Besse, D. Pantic, Z. Prijic, R. S. Popovic. Low-noise silicon avalanche photodiodes fabricated in conventional CMOS technologies. *IEEE Transactions Electron Devices* 49 (3): 387–394, 2002.
4. A. Rochas, M. Gosch, A. Serov, P.-A. Besse, R. S. Popovic, T. Lasser. R. Rigler. First fully integrated 2-D array of single-photon detectors in standard CMOS technology. *IEEE Photonics Technology Letters* 15 (7): 963–965, 2003.
5. C. Niclass, A. Rochas, P.-A. Besse, E. Charbon. Toward a 3-D camera based on single photon avalanche diodes. *IEEE Journal Selected Topics Quantum Electronics* 10 (4): 796–802, 2004.

6. C. Niclass, A. Rochas, P.-A. Besse, E. Charbon. Design and characterization of a CMOS 3-D image sensor based on single photon avalanche diodes. *IEEE Journal Solid-State Circuits* 40 (9): 1847–1854, 2005.

7. C. Niclass, C. Favi, T. Kluter, M. Gersbach, E. Charbon. A 128 × 128 single-photon image sensor with column-level 10-bit time-to-digital converter array. *IEEE Journal Solid-State Circuits* 43 (12): 2977–2989, 2008.

8. H. Povel, H. Aebersold, J. O. Stenflo. Charge-coupled device image sensor as a demodulator in a 2-D polarimeter with a piezoelastic modulator. *Applied Optics* 29 (8): 1186–1190, 1990.

9. T. Spirig, P. Seitz, O. Vietze, F. Heiger. The lock-in CCD—Two-dimensional synchronous detection of light. *IEEE Journal Quantum Electronics* 31 (9): 1705–1708, 1995.

10. R. Miyagawa, T. Kanade. CCD-based range-finding sensor. *IEEE Transactions Electron Devices* 44 (10): 1648–1652, 1997.

11. T. Spirig, M. Marley, P. Seitz. Multitap lock-in CCD with offset subtraction. *IEEE Transactions Electron Devices* 44 (10): 1643–1647, 1997.

12. P. Seitz, A. Biber, S. Lauxtermann. Demodulation pixels in CCD and CMOS technologies for time-of-flight ranging. *Proceedings SPIE* 3965:177–188, 2000.

13. R. Lang, P. Seitz. Solid-state time-of-flight camera. *IEEE Journal Quantum Electronics* 37 (3): 390–397, 2001.

14. S. Kawahito, I. A. Halin, T. Ushinaga, T. Sawada, M. Homma, Y. Maeda. A CMOS time-of-flight range image sensor with gates-on-field-oxide structure. *IEEE Sensors Journal* 7 (12): 1578–1586, 2007.

15. B. Buttgen, T. Oggier, M. Lehmann, R. Kaufmann, S. Neukom, M. Richter, M. Schweizer, et al. High-speed and high-sensitive demodulation pixel for 3D imaging. *Proceedings SPIE* 6056: 22–33, 2006.

16. D. Stoppa, N. Massari, L. Pancheri, M. Malfatti, M. Perenzoni, L. Gonzo. A range image sensor based on 10 μm lock-in pixels in 0.18 μm CMOS imaging technology. *IEEE Journal Solid-State Circuits* 46 (1): 248–258, 2011.

17. T. Ringbeck, T. Moller, B. Hagebeuker. Multidimensional measurement by using 3-D PMD sensors. *Advances Radio Science* 5: 135–146, 2007.

18. S. J. Kim, S. W. Han, B. Kang, K. Lee, D. K. Kim, C. Y. Kim. A three-dimensional time-of-flight CMOS image sensor with pinned-photodiode pixel structure. *IEEE Electron Device Letters* 31 (11): 1272–1274, 2010.

19. H. J. Yoon, S. Itoh, S. Kawahito. A CMOS image sensor with in-pixel two-stage charge transfer for fluorescence lifetime imaging. *IEEE Transactions Electron Devices* 56 (2): 214–221, 2009.

20. K. Yasutomi, S. Itoh, S. Kawahito. A two-stage charge transfer active pixel CMOS image sensor with low-noise global shuttering and a dual-shuttering mode. *IEEE Transactions Electron Devices* 58 (3): 740–747, 2011.

11

Uniaxial 3D Shape Measurement

Yukitoshi Otani

CONTENTS

11.1 Introduction

Recently, noncontact three-dimensional (3D) profilometry has been required in the field of manufacturing inspection for industry, biometrics, and robot vision. Table 11.1 shows typical 3D methods that have already been proposed for this purpose. We can classify the type of optical axis based on measuring depth data by a stereoscopic or uniaxis method. The stereoscopic method is the most popular for measuring 3D shapes. It uses a parallax where two or more optical axes are imaging, or one is for illuminating specified patterns and the other is imaging. The stereo method has two axes of an optical system with projection and observation and originated as aerophotography. A 3D measurement by the stereo machine is proposed multi-eye which is employed multioptical axes and differential illumination. A moiré topography is an elegant method and an easy-to-understand way to produce a contour map by superimposing gratings [1,2]. Optical sectioning in the pattern projection is the oldest method for noncontact 3D measurement [3]. It has been expanded for different methods and production, such as spot scanning, Gray code, random-dots color pattern, and grating projection [4]. However, it has a drawback in measuring deep holes, steep height, and shadow portions (shown in Figure 11.1). Figure 11.1(a) shows a conventional method. It cannot capture the projected pattern because of different axes.

To overcome this problem, a uniaxis profilometry has been proposed [5–14]. It is necessary to capture the projected patterns coaxially, as shown in Figure 11.1(b). We can categorize methods by focus, interferometry, time of

TABLE 11.1

Typical Methods for Three-Dimensional Measurement

	Specific Method	Specific Examples
Stereoscopic method	Optical triangulation	Stereo: multieye:
		Differential illumination
		Moiré topography
		Pattern projection:
		Light section
		Spot scanning
		Gray code
		Random dots
		Color pattern
		Grating pattern
Uniaxis method	Focus	Shape from focus (defocus)
		Confocal
	Interferometry	Subfringe:
		Phase-shifting method
		Optical heterodyne
		Fourier transform method
		Common path
		Oblique incidence
		Low-coherence
		Wave length scanning
	Time of flight	Short plus
		Modulation
	Polarization	Talbot effect
		Conscopic holography

flight, and polarization. The interferometry is a powerful tool to use to measure with high sensitivity less than wavelength. However, there are some limitations in the size of the measurement area and tilt angle because of optical components. The time of flight is identified as future potential areas of 3D metrology. However, it is still necessary and costly equipment. The polarization method (such as a conoscopic holography) has already been in commercial production but it is still a point measurement. The contrast distribution or intensity change along the focus direction to a sample is detected for distance information. One of the famous methods is the shape form focus of 1994 [5]. It is already used in a variety of robotics areas. The first trial of focus detection by grating projection was proposed in 1997 [6]. There was a limitation of sample size because of measuring on the microscope. A focus method by grating projection for the large objects was proposed and succeeded in measuring large objects [7–14].

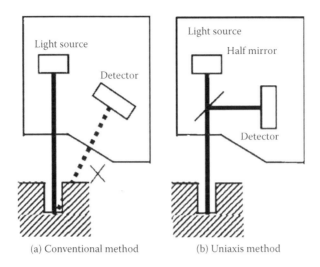

(a) Conventional method   (b) Uniaxis method

FIGURE 11.1
Requirement of uniaxis measurement.

In this section, a uniaxis measurement of a 3D surface is explained within a wide range. Two key components for practical applications are to design a compact measuring system with a telecentric optical system and to detect the contrast with high accuracy by the phase-shifting method. We discuss how to increase accuracy of the grating projection method by detecting the contrast variation by a phase-shifting technique. Its key device is a liquid crystal grating (LCG). The contrast distribution can be changed depending on the pitch, such as frequency of grating, of the LCG. This technique is almost the same as the optical sectioning of the confocal microscope to detect a 3D profile. Finally, we discuss designing a new lens system with a wide measurement area and mounting on the arm robot with six degrees of freedom. We introduce a principle of the focus method using the phase-shifting technique by an LCG and demonstrate measuring the surface profile of samples with a steep profile.

11.2 Principle of the Uniaxial Measurement Method for 3D Profiles

Figure 11.2 shows an optical setup for a uniaxial measurement method 3D shape by the focus method using LCG. We can analyze 3D data from the contrast value. A grating pattern made of liquid grating is projected onto a

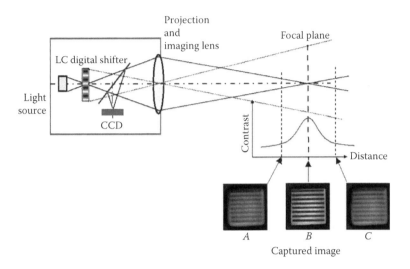

FIGURE 11.2
Optical setup for focus method.

sample and is applied to the phase shifting. In this case, there is no phase change because of one-dimensional measurement.

The contrast variation along an optical axis is theoretically similar to the Bessel function. The maximum contrast means the focus position of the projection lens. Its distribution varies depending not only on the projection and imaging lens but also on the period of the LCG, which is a useful tool for changing the frequency. A measurement range of the system is limited to the dynamic range of the projection lens. The contrast distribution along an optical axis is the relation of the Bessel function along the z-direction. It is written as follows:

$$F(z) = \left\{ \frac{2J_1\left[\pi z\, fF\right]}{\pi z\, fF} \right\} \tag{11.1}$$

where f is grating pitch and F is f-number.

This means the contrast cure is variable by spatial frequency of grating or projection grating pitch. We employ two methods for determining the peak point of the contrast curve. One is a Gaussian fitting, shown in Figure 11.2, and the other is focus changing by a varifocus lens or moving by a robot.

The captured intensity distribution I_i at (x,y) is expressed as

$$I_i = I_0\left(1+V(x,y)\cdot\cos\left\{\varphi(x,y)+\delta_i\right\}\right) \tag{11.2}$$

where I_0, $V(x,y)$, and $\varphi(x,y)$ are an illuminated intensity, a contrast, and initial phase, respectively. δ_i is the shifted phase with $90° \cdot i/4$ ($i = 0, 1, 2, 3$).

The contrast $V(x,y)$ is determined by the four-step phase-shifting principle as

$$V(x,y) = \frac{2\sqrt{\left(I_{0°} - I_{180°}\right)^2 + \left(I_{90°} - I_{270°}\right)^2}}{I_{0°} + I_{90°} + I_{180°} + I_{270°}} \tag{11.3}$$

The relation between a focus length and the contrast $V(x,y)$ is a linear function.

11.3 Experimental Setup and Results

Figure 11.3 shows an experimental setup for the 3D surface profile measurement using liquid crystal grating. The measuring system is designed with a telecentric optical system. The measuring area is expanded to 50 × 50 mm² by using a wide objective lens with 92 mm of diameter. The size of this system is less than notebook size: 275 × 153 mm². The appearance of the system on the arm robot with six degrees of freedom is shown in Figure 11.2(b). The robot is used not only for calibration but also for expanding the working distance. Theoretically, we can measure in the area of 500 × 500 mm² by the arm robot.

The sample can be set on either side, as shown in Figure 11.2. A contrast on the sample is captured by a charge-coupled device camera through a half mirror between the projection part and the detection part (shown in Figure 11.2). The contrast distribution is detected by a four-step phase-shifting technique by LCG without mechanical movement. We checked the accuracy of this method with the grating period of 0.6 mm/line on the sample. Figure 11.4 shows a measured result of calibrated distance versus a measured one. The repeatability is determined as 39 μm with 2 s of measuring time.

Figure 11.5 shows the result of a surface profile of a mechanical part with holes and steep height. The background is a hard board. We succeeded in measuring the steep height comparing the gear surface and background.

Figure 11.6 is a measured result of a cylinder part in midair. The square part at the right-hand bottom is a bump with 10 mm height. Moreover, we can detect the characters with less than 1 mm.

11.4 Conclusions

Measurement of a three-dimensional surface by the profiled uniaxial method by projecting a grating pattern was discussed. The optical axis coincides

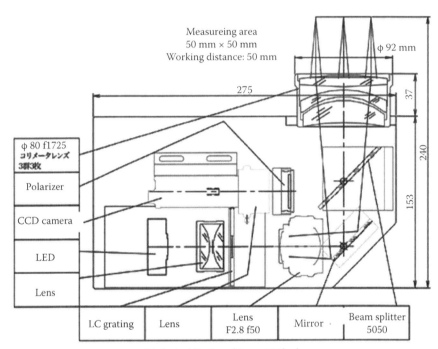

Measureing area
50 mm × 50 mm
Working distance: 50 mm

φ 92 mm

275

37

240

φ 80 f1725
コリメータレンズ
3群3枚

153

Polarizer

CCD camera

LED

Lens

| LC grating | Lens | Lens
F2.8 f50 | Mirror · | Beam splitter
5050 |

(a) Optical Design of Focus Method

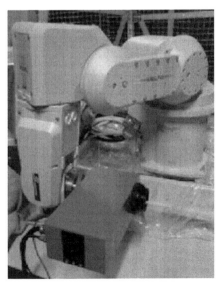

(b) System Appearance

FIGURE 11.3
Experimental setup for the 3D profile measurement on the arm robot.

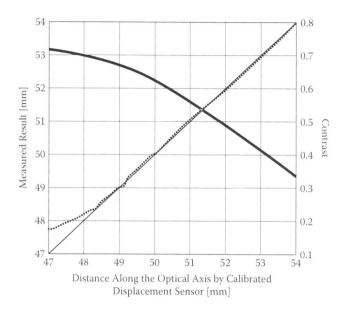

FIGURE 11.4
Accuracy check for distance measurement.

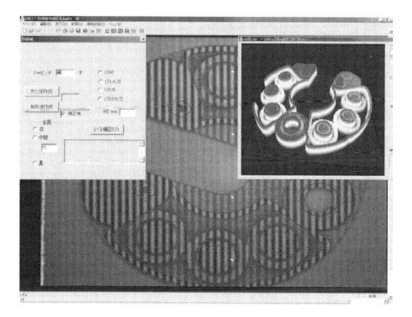

FIGURE 11.5
Measured result of gear sample.

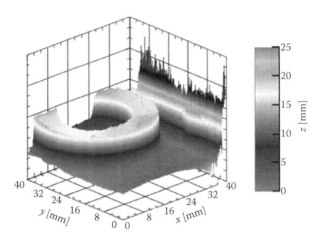

FIGURE 11.6
Measured result of cylinder part.

with a projection and an observation axis. A distance from a projection lens and an object can be determined by a contrast distribution. An advantage of the uniaxial method is measuring for steep shapes and deep holes. Accuracy has been achieved to 36 μm.

Acknowledgment

This work was supported by the Grant for Practical Application of University R&D Results under the matching fund method, New Energy and Industrial Technology Development Organization, Japan. The author would like to express his gratitude to Dr. Mizutani and Dr. Kobayashi.

References

1. D. M. Meadows, W. O. Johnson, J. B. Allen. Generation of surface contours by moiré patterns. *Applied Optics* 9 (4): 942–947 (1970).
2. H. Takasaki. Moiré topography. *Applied Optics* 9 (4): 1467–1472 (1970).
3. G. Schmaltz. *Technische oberflächenkunde.* Berlin: Springer Verlag (1936).
4. T. Yoshizawa, Y. Ohtsuka, et al. *Surface topography and spinal deformity,* 403–410. Stuttgart: Gustav Fischer (1987)
5. S. K. Nayar, Y. Nakagawa. Shape from focus. *IEEE Transactions on Pattern Analysis and Machine Intelligence* 16 (8): 824–831 (1994).

6. M. A. A. Neil, R. Juskaitis, T. Wilson. Method of obtaining optical sectioning by using structured light in a conventional microscope. *Optics Letters* 22 (24): 1905–1907 (1997).

7. M. Ishihara, Y. Nakazato, H. Sasaki, M. Tonooka, M. Yamamoto, Y. Otani, T. Yoshizawa. Three-dimensional surface measurement using grating projection method by detecting phase and contrast. *Proceedings SPIE* 3740: 114–117 (1999).

8. M. Takeda, T. Aoki, Y. Miyamoto, H. Tanaka, R. W. Gu, Z. B. Zhang. Absolute three-dimensional shape measurements using coaxial and coimage plane optical systems and Fourier fringe analysis for focus detection. *Optical Engineering* 39 (1): 61–68 (2000).

9. A. Ishii. 3-D shape measurement using a focused-section method. *Pattern Recognition* 4 (4): 4828 (2000).

10. T. Yoshizawa, T. Shinoda, Y. Otani. Uniaxis range finder using contrast detection of a projected pattern. *Proceedings SPIE* 4190: 115–122 (2001).

11. Y. Mizutani, R. Kuwano, Y. Otani, N. Umeda, T. Yoshizawa. Three-dimensional shape measurement using focus method by using liquid crystal grating and liquid varifocus lens. *Proceedings SPIE* 6000: 6000J-1-7 (2005).

12. R. Kuwano T. Tokunaga, Y. Otani, N. Umeda. Liquid pressure varifocus lens. *Optical Review* 12 (5): 405–408 (2005).

13. K. Yamatani, M. Yamamoto, Y. Otani, T. Yoshizawa, H. Fujita, A. Suguro, S. Morokawa. Three-dimensional surface profilometry using structured liquid crystal grating. *Proceedings SPIE* 3782: 291–296 (1999).

14. Y. Otani, F. Kobayashi, Y. Mizutani, T. Yoshizawa. Three-dimensional profilometry based on focus method by projecting LC grating pattern. *Proceedings SPIE* 7432: 743210 (2009).

12

Three-Dimensional Ultrasound Imaging

Aaron Fenster, Grace Parraga, Bernard Chiu, and Jeff Bax

CONTENTS

12.1 Introduction

X-ray beams used to generate two-dimensional (2D) projection images of the human body have been used since they were studied by Roentgen in 1895. Since 2D x-ray imaging provides only a projection image, complete information of an organ or pathology necessary to diagnose or treat pathology may not be available. In the early 1970s, the development of computed tomography (CT) revolutionized diagnostic radiology. The contiguous tomographic images generated by CT scanners could be assembled into three-dimensional (3D) images and viewed with the aid of computer visualization software. Three-dimensional magnetic resonance imaging (MRI), positron emission tomography (PET), and multislice and cone beam CT imaging have further stimulated the field of 3D medical imaging, stimulating the development of a wide variety of applications in diagnostic and interventional medicine.

In addition to the development of 3D imaging using CT, PET, and MR images, ultrasound (US) imaging has also been extended to 3D imaging [1]. The majority of ultrasound-based diagnostic and interventional procedures are currently performed using 2D imaging; 3D ultrasound (3D US) technology is being improved and applications utilizing that technology has been growing in demand [2–4]. Although 3D US technology is still being improved, it already provides high-quality 3D images of complex anatomical structures and pathology to be used in diagnostic, interventional, and surgical procedures. Researchers and commercial companies are actively pursuing integration of 3D visualization techniques into ultrasound instrumentation as well as specialized biopsy and therapy systems [4–8].

In this chapter, we introduce the different methods for obtaining 3D US images and describe their use in two applications: guided prostate biopsy and monitoring carotid atherosclerosis.

12.2 Benefits of 3D Ultrasound Imaging

Conventional 2D US imaging systems are highly flexible, allowing users to manipulate handheld ultrasound transducers freely over the body in order to generate real-time 2D images of organs and pathology. However, these 2D US systems suffer from the following disadvantages, which 3D US imaging systems attempt to overcome:

- Conventional 2D US imaging systems require users to integrate many 2D images mentally to form an impression of the 3D anatomy and pathology. While this approach can be effective at times, it leads to longer procedures and variability in diagnosis and guidance in interventional procedures.

- Since the 2D US imaging transducer is held and controlled manually, it is difficult to relocate the 2D US image at the exact location and orientation in the body when imaging a patient. Thus, monitoring progression and regression of pathology in response to therapy can be suboptimal, as accurate monitoring requires a physician to reposition the transducer to view the same image of the pathology.

- 2D US imaging does not permit viewing of planes parallel to the skin. Diagnostic and interventional procedures sometimes require an arbitrary selection of the image plane for optimal viewing of the pathology.

- Diagnostic procedures, therapy/surgery planning, and therapy monitoring often require accurate volume delineation and measurements. However, the use of conventional 2D US imaging for measurements of organ or lesion volume is variable and at times inaccurate. Thus, a 3D imaging approach is required to allow accurate and precise volume measurements.

Along with the development of 3D viewing with CT images, 3D US images were demonstrated in the 1970s. The development of commercial 3D US systems took longer to be sold as the first commercial system became available in 1989 by Kretz. However, many researchers and commercial companies have been active over the past two decades and have developed efficient 3D US imaging systems for use in a wide variety of applications [9–15]. While development of commercial CT and MR systems has been rapid, progress in the development of 3D US systems and their routine use has been slow because 3D US systems require significant computational speed for acquiring, reconstructing, and viewing 3D US information in real or near real time on inexpensive systems. Advances in low-cost computer and visualization technology have now made 3D US imaging a viable technology that can be used in a wide range of applications. Most of the major ultrasound system manufacturers are now providing 3D US transducers and viewing software on their imaging platforms.

In the following sections, we describe various approaches used in 3D US imaging systems, with an emphasis on the geometric accuracy of the generation of 3D images as well as the use of this technology in interventional and quantitative monitoring applications.

12.3 3D US Scanning Techniques

Over the past two decades, investigators have explored a wide variety of approaches for generating 3D US images. These include the use of US transducers generating real-time 2D US images in mechanical and freehand scanning and the use of 2D arrays for generating real-time 3D images. Use of conventional transducers to produce 3D US images requires methods to determine the position and orientation of the 2D images within the 3D image volume, while 2D arrays require a 3D scan converter to build the 3D image from the sequence of transmit/receive acoustic signals. In both types of systems, production of high-quality 3D US images without any distortions requires that three factors be optimized:

- The scanning technique must be either rapid (i.e., real time or near real time) or gated to avoid image artifacts due to involuntary, respiratory, or cardiac motion.

- The locations and orientations of the acquired 2D US images must be accurately known to avoid geometric distortions in the generation of the 3D US image. Any geometric errors will lead to geometric distortions and errors of measurement and guidance of needles to targets.

- The scanning apparatus must be simple and convenient to use; therefore, the scanning must be easily added to the examination or interventional procedure.

Although many approaches for production of 3D US images have been explored, current systems make use of one of the following approaches: mechanical scanning, freehand scanning with position sensing, freehand scanning without position sensing, or 2D array scanning for dynamic 3D ultrasound (or four-dimensional [4D] US) imaging.

12.3.1 Mechanical 3D US Scanning Systems

Three-dimensional US systems based on mechanical scanning mechanisms make use of motorized components to translate, tilt, or rotate a conventional 2D US transducer while a sequential series of real-time 2D US images is rapidly acquired by a computer. In this approach the scanning geometry is predefined and precisely controlled by a motor/encoder, allowing the relative positions and orientations of the acquired 2D US images to be known accurately. Thus, the acquired 2D US images and their predefined relative locations and orientation can then be used to reconstruct the 3D US image in real time (i.e., as the 2D images are acquired). These mechanical scanning systems provide great flexibility, allowing the user to adjust the speed of the motor, the number of 2D images to be acquired, and the angular or spatial interval between each acquired 2D image. This flexibility allows the user to optimize the scan time and resolution in the 3D US image through adjustments made to interval spacing between images [16].

Mechanical scanning mechanisms have been particularly successful and have been developed and used in a variety of clinical applications. These include integrated 3D US transducers that house the scanning mechanism within the transducer housing, and external mechanical fixtures that hold the housing of conventional transducers that generate 2D US images.

Many ultrasound manufacturers now offer integrated 3D US transducers that are based on a mechanically swept probe or "wobbler." In these systems an ultrasound transducer is wobbled or swept back and forth inside the handheld housing, while the 2D US-generated planes are reconstructed into the 3D US image. Since these types of 3D transducers are integrated with the ultrasound scanner, the collection and reconstruction of the images can be optimized, allowing generation of two or three 3D images per second. These types of 3D transducers are typically larger than conventional 2D US transducers since they have to accommodate "wobbling" of the transducer. However, they are easier to use than 3D US systems using external fixtures with conventional 2D US transducers.

Since these types of 3D transducers are integrated into the manufacturer's ultrasound system, they require a special US machine that can control them and reconstruct the acquired 2D images into a 3D image. While external mechanical 3D scanning fixtures (discussed later) are generally bulkier than integrated transducers, they can be adapted to hold any conventional US transducer, obviating the need to purchase a special 3D US machine. Since 3D US scanning external fixtures can accommodate any manufacturer's transducer, they can take advantage of improvements in the US machine (e.g., image compounding, contrast agent imaging) and flow information (e.g., Doppler imaging) without any changes in the scanning mechanism.

Three-dimensional mechanical scanning offers the following advantages: short imaging times, ranging from about 3 to 0.2 volumes per second; high-quality 3D images, including B-mode and Doppler; and real-time 3D reconstruction times allowing viewing of the 3D image as it is being acquired. However, 3D mechanical scanners can be bulky and their weight sometimes makes them inconvenient to use. Figure 12.1 shows three basic types of mechanical scanners that are used: linear scanners, tilt scanners, and rotational scanners.

12.3.1.1 *Wobbling or Tilt Mechanical 3D US Scanners*

This approach uses a motorized drive mechanism to tilt or wobble a conventional one-dimensional (1D) US transducer over an angle that can be as large as 60° about an axis parallel to the face of the transducer. The 2D US images that are generated are arranged as a page in an open book with an angular spacing between the 2D images, such as 1.0°. In both the integrated 3D US probe and the external fixture approach, the housing of the transducer remains fixed on the skin of the patient while the US transducer is angulated or wobbled. Since the reconstruction of the 3D image can be performed as the 2D images are acquired, the time to acquire a 3D US image depends on the 2D US image update rate and the number of 2D images used to generate the 3D image.

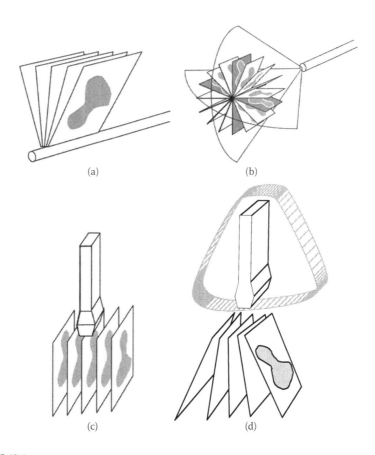

FIGURE 12.1

Schematic diagrams of 3D US mechanical scanning methods. (a) A side-firing TRUS transducer is mechanically rotated and the acquired images have equal angular spacing. The same approach is used in a mechanically wobbled transducer. (b) A rotational scanning mechanism using an end-firing transducer, typically used in 3D TRUS guided prostate biopsy. The acquired images have equal angular spacing. (c) A linear mechanical scanning mechanism in which the acquired images have equal spacing. (d) The mechanically tilting mechanism, but integrated into a 3D US transducer. The US transducer is "wobbled" inside the housing of the transducer.

The 2D US update rate depends on the US machine settings, such as the depth setting and number of focal zones. The number of acquired 2D images is controlled by the choice of the angular separation between the acquired images needed to yield a desired image quality. Typically, these parameters can be adjusted to optimize scanning time, image quality, and the size of the volume imaged [17–22]. The most common integrated 3D probes require special 3D US systems or upgrades that are used for abdominal and obstetrical imaging [15,23–26].

Since the geometry of the acquired 2D US images is predefined, the 3D image reconstruction can be performed in real time while the 2D images are acquired. In this 3D scanning geometry, the resolution in the 3D US image will not be isotropic because it will degrade as the distance from the axis of rotation is increased due to US beam spread in the lateral and elevational directions of the acquired 2D US images. In addition, since the geometry of the acquired 2D images is fan-like, the distance between the acquired US images increases with increasing depth, resulting in a decrease in the spatial sampling and spatial resolution of the reconstructed 3D image [27].

12.3.1.2 Linear Mechanical 3D Scanners

Mechanical 3D scanners, which move conventional transducers in a linear manner, use a motorized drive mechanism to translate the transducer across the skin of the patient. A mechanical housing can hold the transducer perpendicular to the surface of the skin or at an angle for acquiring Doppler images. The 2D images are acquired at a regular but adjustable distance interval so that they are parallel and uniformly spaced (Figure 12.1b). The temporal sampling interval can be chosen to match the 2D US frame rate for the US machine and the translating speed can be chosen to match the required spatial sampling interval, which should be at least half of the elevational resolution of the transducer [16].

Since the acquired 2D US images have a predefined and regular geometry, the 3D image can be reconstructed in real time as the set of 2D US images is acquired. In this scanning approach, the resolution in the 3D image will also not be isotropic. In the direction parallel to the acquired 2D US images (i.e., axial and lateral directions in the 2D images), the resolution of the restructured 3D US image will be the same as the original 2D US images. However, the resolution of the reconstructed 3D image will be equal (if spatial sampling is appropriate) to the elevational resolution of the transducer in the direction perpendicular to the acquired 2D US images. Thus, the resolution of the 3D US image will be poorest in the 3D scanning direction, and a transducer with good elevational resolution should be used for optimal results [28].

The linear scanning is typically used when long scanning distances are needed. Thus, this approach has been successfully used in many vascular B-mode and Doppler imaging applications, particularly for carotid arteries, where scanning distances of about 5 cm are needed (see discussion in Section 12.5) [21,29–37]. Figure 12.2 shows two examples of linearly scanned 3D US images of the carotid arteries made with an external fixture.

12.3.1.3 Endocavity Rotational 3D Scanners

This scanning approach uses an external fixture or internal mechanism to rotate or "wobble" an endocavity probe (e.g., a transrectal ultrasound [TRUS] probe, see Figure 12.1). For endocavity probes using an end-firing transducer, the set of acquired 2D images may be arranged as a fan (Figure 12.1c), intersecting in the center of the 3D US image (see resulting image in Figure 12.3).

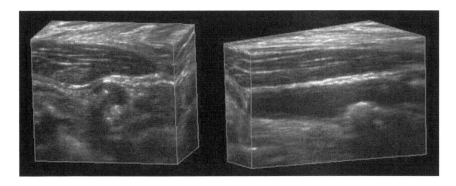

FIGURE 12.2
Examples of 3D carotid US images obtained with the mechanical linear 3D scanning approach. The 3D US images are displayed using the cube-view approach with the faces sliced to reveal the details of the atherosclerotic plaque in the carotid arteries.

For endocavity probes using a side-firing 1D transducer (as used in prostate brachytherapy), the acquired images will also be arranged as a fan, but intersect at the axis of rotation of the transducer (see Figure 12.1a). In this scanning approach, the side-firing probe is typically rotated from 80° to 110° and an end-firing transducer is typically rotated by 180° [22,38,39]. Figure 12.3 shows images generated with an end-firing TRUS transducer using the endocavity 3D scanning approach [21,31,32,38], and guiding 3D US biopsy and therapy [6,8,22,40–43].

In this 3D scanning approach, the resolution of the 3D image will also not be isotropic. The spatial sampling is highest near the axis of the transducer (i.e., axis of rotation) and the poorest away from the axis of the transducer; thus, the resolution of the 3D US image will degrade as the distance from the rotational axis of the transducer increases. Similarly, the axial and elevational resolution will decrease as the distance from the transducer increases. The combination of these effects will cause the 3D US image resolution to vary—highest near the transducer and the rotational axis and poorest away from the transducer and rotational axis.

Three-dimensional rotational scanning with an end-firing transducer is most sensitive to the motion of the transducer and patient during the scanning. Because the acquired 2D images intersect along the rotational axis of the transducer, any motion during the scan will cause a mismatch in the acquired planes, resulting in the production of artifacts in the center of the 3D US image. Artifacts in the center of the 3D US image will also occur if the axis of rotation is not accurately known; however, proper calibrations can remove this source of potential error. Although handheld 3D rotational scanning of the prostate and uterus can produce excellent 3D images (see Figure 12.3), for optimal results in long procedures, such as prostate brachytherapy and biopsy [22,38,44], the transducer and its assembly should be mounted onto a fixture, such as a stabilizer in prostate brachytherapy.

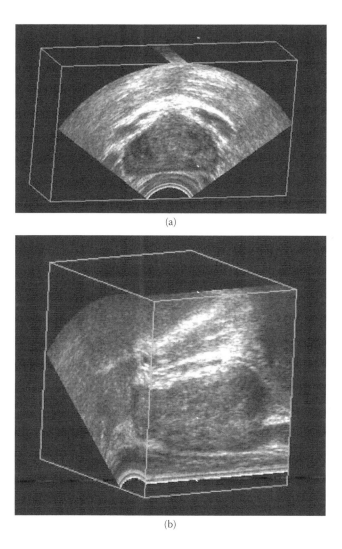

FIGURE 12.3
A 3D US image of the prostate acquired using a side-firing endocavity rotational 3D scanning approach (rotation of a TRUS transducer). The transducer was rotated around its long axis, while 3D US images were acquired and reconstructed. The 3D US image is displayed using the cube view approach and has been sliced to reveal (a) a transverse view and (b) a sagittal view.

12.3.2 Freehand Scanning with Position Sensing

Over the past 20 years researchers have been developing freehand 3D scanning approaches that do not require bulky mechanical scanning devices. Since freehand 2D US transducers do not use mechanical mechanisms to control the movement of the transducer, other means must be used to monitor the position and orientation of the transducer. Many approaches in which a small sensor is mounted on the transducer to allow measurement of the transducer's position and orientation as the transducer is moved over the body have been investigated. These approaches include optical, acoustic, mechanical, image-based (speckle decorrelation), and electromagnetic devices used to track the transducer and hence the 2D images and their relative location and orientation, which are then used to reconstruct the 3D image [45]. Since the transducer is moved freely by the user, the locations and orientations of the acquired 2D images are not predefined. Thus, the user must move the transducer at an appropriate speed to ensure that the transducer's position is sampled so that no significant gaps will result in the reconstructed 3D image. The method used most commonly is the magnetic field sensing approach; several companies provide the sensing technology: Ascension: Bird sensor [46], Polhemus: Fastrack sensor [47], and Northern Digital: Aurora sensor [3].

12.3.2.1 Freehand 3D Scanning with Magnetic Field Sensors

The magnetic field sensor approach for freehand 3D US imaging has been used extensively in many applications, including echocardiography, obstetrics, and vascular imaging [3,46–57]. To allow tracking of the conventional transducer as it is moved over the body, a time-varying 3D magnetic field transmitter is placed near the patient, and a small receiver containing three orthogonal coils (with six degrees of freedom) is mounted on the probe and used to sense the strength of the magnetic field in three orthogonal directions. The position and orientation of the transducer are calculated by measuring the strength of the three components of the local magnetic field. This information, together with the acquired 2D images, is used in the 3D reconstruction algorithm.

The main advantage of this approach is that the position sensor can be small and unobtrusive. However, the accuracy of the tracking can be compromised by electromagnetic interference. Since geometric distortions in the 3D US image can occur if ferrous (or highly conductive) metals are located nearby, metal hospital beds in procedure or surgical rooms can cause significant distortions. Modern magnetic field sensors—particularly ones that use a magnetic transmitter placed between the bed and the patient—produce excellent images and are now less susceptible to sources of error. Nonetheless, to minimize these potential sources of error, the position of the sensor relative to the transmitter must be calibrated accurately and precisely using one of the numerous calibration techniques that have been developed [57–65].

12.3.2.2 Freehand 3D US Scanning without Position Sensing

If spatial accuracy of the 3D US image is not required, reconstruction can easily be produced without position sensing. In this approach, the transducer is assumed to be moved over the body in a predefined scanning geometry and speed. As the user moves the transducer, either in a linear manner or by tilting, the 3D US image is reconstructed from the acquired 2D US images using the assumed scanning geometry and speed. Since position or orientation information is not recorded during the motion of the transducer, the operator must move the transducer at a constant linear or angular velocity so that the 2D images are acquired at a regular interval [31,32]. Since this approach does not guarantee that the 3D US image is geometrically accurate, it must not be used for measurements.

12.3.3 Real-Time 3D Ultrasound Imaging (4D Imaging) Using 2D Arrays

The mechanical or freehand 3D scanning approaches limit the volume acquisition update rate to about two or three volumes per second. To increase the volume update rate, transducers with 2D arrays generating 3D images in real time have been developed. In this approach, a transducer containing a 2D phased array allows the transducer to remain stationary. An electronic approach is then used to control the transmission and receiving of a broadly diverging ultrasound beam away from the array, sweeping out a volume shaped like a truncated pyramid [66–72]. The returned echoes detected by the 2D array are processed to display a set of multiple image planes in real time. This approach allows acquisition of a set of 3D images to occur in real time, generating time-dependent 3D images, known as 4D US imaging. Users can interactively control and manipulate these acquired planes to explore the entire volume while they are being updated in real time. This approach is successfully being used in echocardiology, which requires dynamic 3D imaging of the heart and its valves [73–76]. Since the technology for developing a transducer based on a 2D phased array is very difficult, few companies provide this technology.

12.4. Visualization of 3D Ultrasound Images

The wide use of 3D images produced by CT and MRI systems has stimulated the development of many interactive 3D algorithms to help physicians and researchers visualize and manipulate 3D images. Because US images suffer from shadowing, poor tissue–tissue contrast, and image speckle, the display of 3D US images presents significant visualization problems, unlike 3D displays of CT and MR images. Although many 3D display techniques have been developed, two of the most frequently used techniques for 3D US visualization are multiplanar reformatting (MPR) and volume rendering (VR).

12.4.1 Multiplanar Reformatting

The MPR technique is the most commonly used in 3D and 4D US viewing approaches. In this technique, 2D US planes are extracted from the 3D

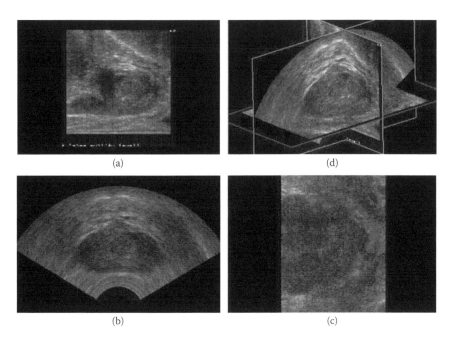

(a)   (d)

(b)   (c)

FIGURE 12.4
The 3D US of the prostate displayed using the multiplanar reformatting approach: (a–c) three orthogonal planes from a 3D image, and (d) the crossed-planes approach. The 3D TRUS image being displayed was acquired using a side-firing transducer using the mechanical rotation approach.

US images and displayed to the user with 3D cubes. Users interact with the images by moving the planes to view the desired anatomy. Three MPR approaches are commonly used to display 3D US images. Figure 12.4(a) illustrates the *crossed-planes* approach, in which multiple planes (typically two or three) are presented in a view that shows their correct relative orientations in 3D. These planes intersect with each other and can be moved in a parallel or an oblique manner to any other plane to reveal the desired anatomy.

A second approach displays the 3D US image using the *cube-view* approach illustrated in Figure 12.4(b). In this approach, an extracted set of 2D US images is texture mapped onto the faces of a polyhedron representing the volume being viewed. Users can select any face of the polyhedron and move it (parallel or obliquely) to any other plane, while the appropriate 2D US image is extracted in real time and texture mapped on the new face. The appearance of a "solid" polyhedron provides users with 3D image-based cubes, which relates the manipulated plane to the other planes [13,77–79]. In a third approach, three *orthogonal planes* are displayed in separate panels with 3D cubes, such as lines on each extracted plane, to designate the intersection with the other planes (Figure 12.4c). These lines can be moved in order to extract and display the desired planes [80,81].

12.4.2 Volume Rendering Techniques

Volume rendering techniques are used to view 3D objects as well as the anatomy using 3D CT and MRI images. However, US images do not typically produce sufficient tissue–tissue contrast to allow easy segmentation or rendering needed for VR rendering, making this approach appropriate only in a few applications of 3D US. Since ultrasound imaging does produce excellent contrast between tissue and fluids (i.e., blood and amniotic fluid), the VR approach is used extensively to view 3D US fetal images [73,75] and 4D US cardiac images [25,74,82]. The VR approach uses ray-casting techniques to project a 2D array of lines (rays) through a 3D image [83–86]. The volume elements (voxels) intersecting each ray are then determined and are weighted, summed, and colored in a number of ways to produce various effects.

The VR technique projects 3D information onto a 2D plane, and thus many VR techniques are not well suited for viewing the details of soft tissues in 3D B-mode ultrasound images. VR techniques are best suited for viewing anatomical surfaces that are distinguishable in 3D B-mode US images, including limbs and fetal face surrounded by amniotic fluid (see Figure 12.5) [80,81], tissue–blood interfaces such as endocardiac surfaces and inner vascular surfaces (see Figure 12.6), and structures where B-mode clutter has been removed from power or color Doppler 3D images [31,32].

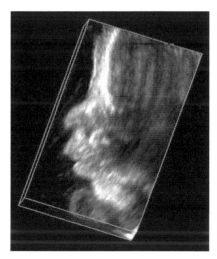 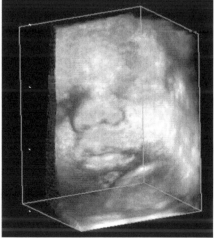

FIGURE 12.5
Two views of a 3D US image of a fetal face that have been volume rendered.

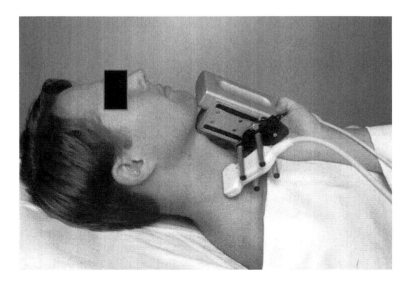

FIGURE 12.6
Mechanically linear scanning approach to produce a 3D US image of the carotid arteries by translating the transducer along the neck by a distance of about 4 cm.

12.5. 3D Ultrasound Imaging of the Carotid Arteries

12.5.1 Motivation

In this section we describe a quickly developing application using 3D US imaging as an example of the use of 3D US. Three-dimensional US imaging of the carotid arteries is used to analyze, quantify, and monitor carotid atherosclerosis. Atherosclerosis is an inflammatory disease in which the inner layer of arteries progressively accumulates low-density lipoproteins and macrophages over a period of several decades, forming plaques [87]. The carotid arteries in the neck supply oxygenated blood to the brain and face and are major sites for developing atherosclerosis. Unstable plaques may suddenly rupture, forming a thrombus causing an embolism, which may ultimately lead to an ischemic stroke by blocking the oxygenated blood supply to parts of the brain. Since carotid arteries are close to the skin, it is relatively easy to acquire high-quality 3D US images of carotid arteries.

The use of 3D US to image the carotid arteries has allowed the development of two sensitive biomarkers of carotid atherosclerosis. Over the past decade *total plaque volume* (*TPV*) and *vessel wall volume* (*VWV*) [33–35,88–91] have emerged as useful US phenotypes of carotid atherosclerosis that quantify plaque burden in 3D. Total plaque volume has been shown to be useful in measuring changes in plaque burden [33–35,92,93] and evaluating the effects of drug therapy [36,94]. More recently, VWV has been shown to provide a more reproducible measure of atherosclerosis burden changes in the carotid arteries. The VWV technique quantifies vessel wall thickness plus plaque within carotid arteries by measuring the volume between the vessel intima and media. It can be implemented more easily in a semiautomated computer segmentation algorithm, resulting in shorter quantification times and greater reliability.

Three-dimensional US-based TPV requires users to distinguish plaque–lumen and plaque–outer vessel wall boundaries, but the measurement of 3D US-based VWV requires the user to outline the lumen–intima/plaque and media–adventitia boundaries, similarly to the measurement of the intima–media (IMT) phenotype [95]. These boundaries are easier to interpret than plaque–lumen and wall boundaries in 3D carotid US images. In this section, we review the method used to acquire 3D carotid US images and discuss its use in the measurement of TPV and VWV.

12.5.2 3D Carotid Ultrasound Scanning Technique

Since imaging of the carotid arteries requires scanning at least a 4 cm of length of the neck, real-time 3D (i.e., 4D) systems using 2D phased arrays optimized for cardiac imaging cannot be used effectively. Thus, investigators have focused on the use of mechanical scanning mechanisms with external fixtures and freehand scanning systems with magnetic field sensors to generate 3D images of the carotid arteries.

We have developed and used a mechanical scanning mechanism with an external fixture (see Figure 12.6) to translate the transducer linearly along the neck of the patient, while transverse 2D US images are acquired at regular spatial intervals [35]. The length of the scan is adjustable and is typically 4 to 6 cm; speed of the scan can be adjusted to minimize the scan time and optimize the spatial resolution. Typically, we acquire 2D US images at 30 frames per second with a spatial interval of 0.2 mm. Thus, a 4 cm scan length will require 200 two-dimensional US images, which can be collected in 6.7 seconds without cardiac gating.

12.5.3 Display of 3D US Carotid Images

The most commonly used method to display 3D carotid US images is the *cube-view* approach, as it is best suited for segmentation of the desired anatomy to quantify TPV and VWV. The user can view transverse images of the carotid arteries with optimal resolution and yet be able to view the vessel and plaque in a longitudinal view to obtain 3D anatomical context [28,78,96]. An example of this approach is shown in Figure 12.7.

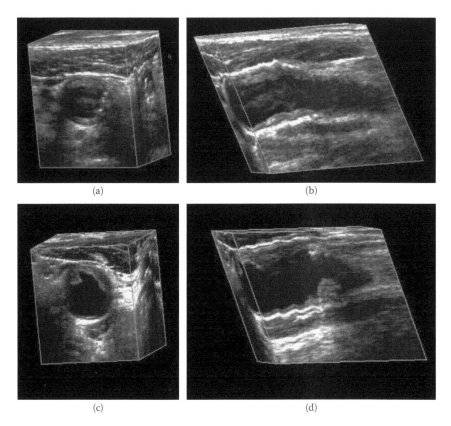

(a)   (b)

(c)   (d)

FIGURE 12.7
Multiplaner views of 3D US images of the carotid arteries. (a) Transverse view of a 3D US image of carotid artery for a subject with moderate stenosis; (b) longitudinal view of a 3D US image of carotid artery.

12.5.4 Use of 3D US to Quantify Carotid Atherosclerosis

12.5.4.1 Total Plaque Volume

Quantification of carotid atherosclerosis burden using the *total plaque volume* requires the operator to manipulate the 3D US image by "slicing" it transverse to the vessel axis, starting from one end of the plaque using an inter-slice distance (ISD) of 1.0 mm. In each cross-sectional image, the plaque is contoured and the result is displaced in the 3D image. The area enclosed by each contour is calculated, and the sequential areas are summed and multiplied by the ISD to obtain the plaque volume. The sum of all plaque volumes in the 3D image provides the TPV.

12.5.4.2 Vessel Wall Volume

This vessel wall volume technique proceeds in a similar way to the measurement of TPV. Each 3D US carotid image is "sliced" transverse to the vessel

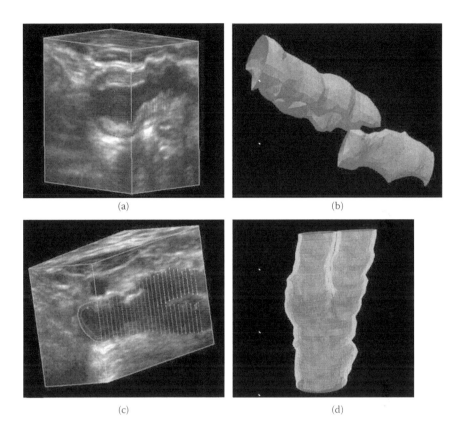

FIGURE 12.8
(See color insert.) Manual segmentation of the CCA, ICA, and ECA lumen and outer wall boundaries from 3D US images are used to calculate the vessel wall volume (VWV). The reconstructed surfaces for the lumen and outer wall boundaries from the manual segmentations are shown.

axis, starting from one end of the 3D US image using an ISD of 1.0 mm. However, unlike the TPV technique, in this approach, the lumen (blood–intima boundary) and the vessel wall (media–adventitia boundary) are segmented in each slice. The area between the lumen and vessel wall is calculated giving the vessel wall area. Sequential areas are summed and multiplied by the ISD to give the VWV (see Figure 12.8).

The VWV measurements are global measurements; however, in monitoring of plaque and vessel wall thickness changes, it is important to analyze these on a spatial point-by-point basis. Chiu et al. [97] proposed extending the VWV phenotype to generating vessel wall thickness (VWT) maps and VWT change maps to quantify and visualize local changes in plaque morphology on a point-by-point basis. Identification of the locations of change in plaque burden may assist in developing treatment strategies for patients. To facilitate the visualization and interpretation of these maps for clinicians,

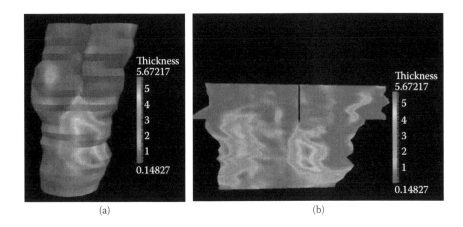

(a)   (b)

FIGURE 12.9
(See color insert.) (a) Vessel wall thickness map for a patient with moderate stenosis. Manual segmentations of the lumen and outer wall boundaries were used to generate the thickness maps (indicated in millimeters). (b) Corresponding flattened thickness map for better visualization.

Chiu et al. [98] proposed a technique to flatten the 3D VWT maps and VWT change maps to 2D (see Figure 12.9a and b).

12.6 3D Ultrasound Guided Prostate Biopsy

12.6.1 Background

Digital rectal exams and prostate-specific antigen (PSA) blood tests are the most common prostate cancer screening methods in men who have no symptoms of the disease. However, a PSA test does not provide sufficient information to provide a definitive diagnosis of prostate cancer. Thus, a histological assessment of tissue cores drawn from the prostate during a biopsy procedure are required to provide a definitive diagnosis. Currently, a physician uses a 2D transrectal ultrasound (TRUS) transducer to guide the needle into the prostate to obtain a biopsy sample. Unfortunately, early stage cancer is not usually visible in ultrasound images. Thus, physicians obtain biopsy samples from predetermined regions of the prostate with a high probability of harboring cancer rather than targeting the lesions directly. Although this approach is commonly used, it has a false negative rate as high as 34%, requiring repeat biopsies to locate the cancer site. Depending on the pathological results, the urologist must either avoid a previously targeted region in the prostate or aim near these sites to obtain additional cores during a repeat biopsy.

Since 2D US images do not provide sufficient information about the 3D location of the biopsy sample, it is difficult for physicians to plan and guide a repeat biopsy procedure. A 3D ultrasound-based navigation system would provide a reproducible record of the 3D locations of the biopsy targets throughout the procedure, allowing guidance of the biopsy to the desired locations in the prostate.

We have developed a mechanical 3D US-guided biopsy system that overcomes the current limitations of a 2D TRUS biopsy procedure while maintaining the procedural work flow, thus minimizing costs and physician retraining [22]. This mechanical system has four degrees of freedom and an adaptable cradle that supports commercially available TRUS transducers. It also allows the acquisition of 3D TRUS images and real-time tracking and recording of the 3D position and orientation of the biopsy needle relative to the 3D TRUS image as the physician manipulates the US transducer.

12.6.2 Mechanically Tracked 3D US System

Our 3D TRUS-guided prostate biopsy system consists of an integrated personal computer, conventional US system with an end-firing transducer, and a mechanical guidance system. Two-dimensional TRUS images are acquired and reconstructed into a 3D TRUS image in real time using the rotational scanning approach (Figure 12.1). The details of the mechanical system have been described elsewhere and are only summarized here [22]. The system uses [99]

- Passive mechanical components for guiding, tracking, and stabilizing the position of a commercially available end-firing TRUS transducer
- Software components for acquiring, storing, and 3D reconstructing (in real time) a series of 2D TRUS images into a 3D TRUS image
- Software that displays a model of the prostate to guide and record the biopsy core locations in 3D

The mechanical assembly consists of a passive four degrees-of-freedom tracking device, an adaptable cradle to accommodate any conventional end-firing TRUS transducer (Figure 12.10). To produce a 3D US image, the transducer is rotated around its long axis (mechanical rotational scanning) to acquire a 3D image, which is then shown in a cube-view display (Figure 12.11).

12.6.3 Biopsy Work Flow

The physician begins the procedure by inserting the TRUS probe into the patient's rectum and aligning the prostate to the center of the 2D TRUS image. A 3D TRUS image of the prostate is acquired by rotating the transducer 180° about its long axis. The boundary of the prostate is then segmented and used

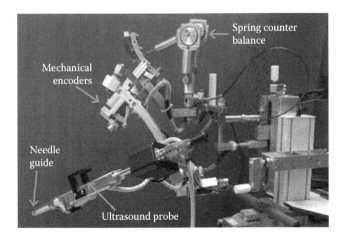

FIGURE 12.10

Photograph of the mechanical tracking system to be used for 3D TRUS guided prostate biopsy. The system is mounted at the base of a stabilizer while the linkage allows the TRUS transducer to be manipulated manually about a remote center of motion (RCM) to which the center of the probe tip is aligned. The spring-loaded counterbalance is used to support the weight of the system fully throughout its full range of motion about the RCM. (Bax, J. et al., *Medical Physics* 35 (12): 5397–5410, 2008. With permission.)

to produce a model of the prostate, which is used in the biopsy navigation display [100–103]. After the model has been displayed, the physician can manipulate the 3D TRUS image on the computer screen and select locations to biopsy. After all of the targets have been selected, the system then displays the 3D biopsy needle guidance interface, which facilitates the systematic targeting of each biopsy location previously selected (Figure 12.12).

Figure 12.12 illustrates the biopsy interface, which is composed of four windows: the live 2D TRUS video stream, the 3D TRUS image, and two 3D model views. The 2D TRUS window displays the real-time 2D TRUS images from the US machine. The 3D TRUS window contains a 2D slice of the 3D prostate image in real time to reflect the expected orientation and position of the TRUS probe. This correspondence allows the physician to compare the 3D image with the real-time 2D image to determine if any prostate motion or deformation has occurred. Finally, the two 3D graphical model windows show orthogonal views (sagittal and coronal) of the 3D prostate model, the real-time position of the 2D TRUS image plane, and the expected trajectory of the biopsy needle.

12.7 Discussion and Conclusions

The utility of 3D US imaging has already been demonstrated in obstetrics, cardiology, and image guidance of interventional procedures. Current 3D US

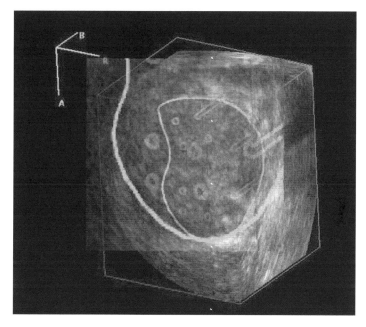

FIGURE 12.11
(See color insert.) A 3D US image of the prostate acquired using an end-firing endocavity rotational 3D scanning approach (rotation of a TRUS transducer), which was used to guide a biopsy using the system shown in Figure 12.10. The transducer was rotated around its long axis, while 3D US images were acquired and reconstructed. The image also showed the segmented boundary of the prostate and the locations of the biopsy cores within the prostate.

imaging technology is sufficiently advanced to allow real-time 3D imaging using 2D array transducers and near real-time 3D imaging with mechanically conventional transducers. Investigators are continuing to establish the utility of 3D US in additional clinical applications using improved image analysis techniques and quantitative measurement approaches. Improved software tools for image analysis are promising to make 3D US a routinely used tool on ultrasound machines. The following are some possible improvements in 3D US imaging that may accelerate its use in routine clinical procedures.

12.7.1 Improved Visualization Tools

Many 3D US imaging applications require interactive visualization tools. However, many approaches are complicated and difficult to use by physicians during busy clinical procedures, particularly interventional procedures. For 3D US to become widely accepted for interventional guidance applications, intuitive tools are required to manipulate the 3D US image and display the result with the appropriate background using the appropriate rendering method. Currently, segmentation, guidance, and volume-rendering approaches using 3D US images require multiple parameters to be

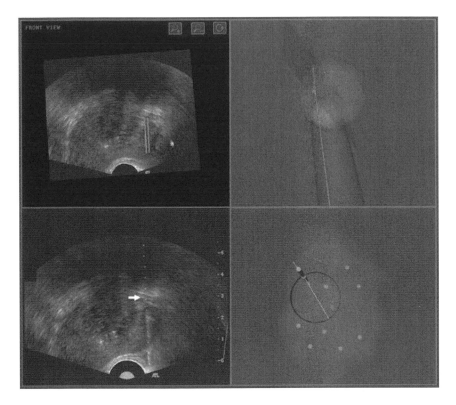

FIGURE 12.12

(See color insert.) The 3D TRUS-guide biopsy system's interface is composed of four windows: (top left) the 3D TRUS image dynamically sliced to match the real-time TRUS transducer 3D orientation; (bottom left) the live 2D TRUS video stream; (right side) the 3D location of the biopsy core is displayed within the 3D prostate models. The targeting ring in the bottom right window shows all the possible needle paths that intersect the preplanned target by rotating the TRUS about its long axis. This allows the physician to maneuver the TRUS transducer to the target (highlighted by the red dot) in the shortest possible distance. The biopsy needle (arrow) is visible within the real-time 2D TRUS image.

optimized and manipulated. Techniques are needed that provide immediate optimal selection of parameters for segmentation, volume rendering, and guidance without significant user intervention.

12.7.2 3D US Segmentation

Over the past decade, many semiautomated and automated segmentation algorithms have been developed for use with 3D US images. Since US images suffer from shadowing and poor tissue contrast, many segmentation approaches are not yet sufficiently robust to be used in routine clinical procedures. Semiautomated segmentation approaches typically require the user to identify the organ or pathology to be segmented (e.g., plaque or prostate), and an algorithm then performs the segmentation. While this approach is easier than manual segmentation, it still requires user interaction. Thus, improvements in segmentation of organs and pathology using robust, accurate, and reproducible algorithms would be highly welcome.

12.7.3 3D US Guided Interventional Procedures

Three-dimensional US imaging has been demonstrated to be useful during interventional procedures, such as biopsy, therapy, and surgery. For example, the 3D TRUS-guided prostate biopsy approach improves the physician's ability to guide the biopsy needle accurately to selected targets and record the biopsy location in 3D. The use of 3D TRUS images allows the physician to view the patient's prostate in views currently not possible in 2D TRUS-based procedures. However, significant work and testing are still required to allow physicians to integrate 3D US imaging efficiently into the interventional procedure. Some required improvements are better 3D registration tools allowing integration of 3D US with images from other modalities, efficient and robust 3D US-based segmentation tools, hands-free methods to control and manipulate the 3D US image and 3D visualization tools to help the physician guide tools within the body.

Acknowledgments

The authors gratefully acknowledge the financial support of the Canadian Institutes of Health Research, the Ontario Institute for Cancer Research, the Ontario Research Fund, the National Science and Engineering Research Council, and the Canada Research Chair program.

References

1. Elliott, S. T. (2008). Volume ultrasound: The next big thing? *British Journal Radiology* 81 (961): 8–9.
2. Downey, D. B., A. Fenster and J. C. Williams (2000). Clinical utility of three-dimensional US. *Radiographics* 20 (2): 559–571.
3. Hummel, J., M. Figl, M. Bax, H. Bergmann and W. Birkfellner (2008). 2D/3D registration of endoscopic ultrasound to CT volume data. *Physics in Medicine and Biology* 53 (16): 4303–4316.
4. Carson, P. L. and A. Fenster (2009). Anniversary paper: Evolution of ultrasound physics and the role of medical physicists and the AAPM and its journal in that evolution. *Medical Physics* 36 (2): 411–428.

5. Chin, J. L., D. B. Downey, G. Onik and A. Fenster (1996). Three-dimensional prostate ultrasound and its application to cryosurgery. *Techniques in Urology* 2 (4): 187–193.

6. Chin, J. L., D. B. Downey, M. Mulligan and A. Fenster (1998). Three-dimensional transrectal ultrasound guided cryoablation for localized prostate cancer in nonsurgical candidates: A feasibility study and report of early results. *Journal Urology* 159(3): 910-914.

7. Smith, W. L., K. Surry, G. Mills, D. Downey and A. Fenster (2001). Three-dimensional ultrasound-guided core needle breast biopsy. *Ultrasound Medicine and Biology* 27 (8): 1025–1034.

8. Wei, Z., G. Wan, L. Gardi, G. Mills, D. Downey and A. Fenster (2004). Robot-assisted 3D-TRUS guided prostate brachytherapy: System integration and validation. *Medical Physics* 31 (3): 539–548.

9. Nelson, T. R. and D. H. Pretorius (1992). Three-dimensional ultrasound of fetal surface features. *Ultrasound Obstetrics and Gynecology* 2: 166-174.

10. Greenleaf, J. F., M. Belohlavek, T. C. Gerber, D. A. Foley and J. B. Seward (1993). Multidimensional visualization in echocardiography: An introduction [see comments]. *Mayo Clinic Proceedings* 68 (3): 213–220.

11. King, D. L., A. S. Gopal, P. M. Sapin, K. M. Schroder and A. N. Demaria (1993). Three-dimensional echocardiography. *American Journal Cardiology Imaging* 7 (3): 209–220.

12. Rankin, R. N., A. Fenster, D. B. Downey, P. L. Munk, M. F. Levin and A. D. Vellet (1993). Three-dimensional sonographic reconstruction: Techniques and diagnostic applications. *American Journal Roentgenology* 161 (4): 695–702.

13. Fenster, A. and D. B. Downey (1996). 3-dimensional ultrasound imaging: A review. *IEEE Engineering in Medicine and Biology* 15: 41–51.

14. Sklansky, M. (2003). New dimensions and directions in fetal cardiology. *Current Opinion Pediatrics* 15 (5): 463–471.

15. Peralta, C. F., P. Cavoretto, B. Csapo, O. Falcon and K. H. Nicolaides (2006). Lung and heart volumes by three-dimensional ultrasound in normal fetuses at 12-32 weeks' gestation. *Ultrasound Obstetrics and Gynecology* 27 (2): 128–133.

16. Smith, W. L. and A. Fenster (2000). Optimum scan spacing for three-dimensional ultrasound by speckle statistics. *Ultrasound Medicine and Biology* 26 (4): 551–562.

17. Gilja, O. H., N. Thune, K. Matre, T. Hausken, S. Odegaard and A. Berstad (1994). In vitro evaluation of three-dimensional ultrasonography in volume estimation of abdominal organs. *Ultrasound Medicine and Biology* 20 (2): 157–165.

18. Delabays, A., N. G. Pandian, Q. L. Cao, L. Sugeng, G. Marx, A. Ludomirski and S. L. Schwartz (1995). Transthoracic real-time three-dimensional echocardiography using a fan-like scanning approach for data acquisition: Methods, strengths, problems, and initial clinical experience. *Echocardiography* 12 (1): 49–59.

19. Downey, D. B., D. A. Nicolle and A. Fenster (1995). Three-dimensional orbital ultrasonography. *Canadian Journal Ophthalmology* 30 (7): 395–398.

20. Downey, D. B., D. A. Nicolle and A. Fenster (1995). Three-dimensional ultrasound of the eye. *Administrative Radiology Journal* 14: 46–50.

21. Fenster, A., S. Tong, S. Sherebrin, D. B. Downey and R. N. Rankin (1995). Three-dimensional ultrasound imaging. *SPIE Physics Medicine Image* 2432: 176–184.

22. Bax, J., D. Cool, L. Gardi, K. Knight, D. Smith, J. Montreuil, S. Sherebrin, C. Romagnoli and A. Fenster (2008). Mechanically assisted 3D ultrasound guided prostate biopsy system. *Medical Physics* 35 (12): 5397–5410.

23. Benacerraf, B. R., C. B. Benson, A. Z. Abuhamad, J. A. Copel, J. S. Abramowicz, G. R. Devore, P. M. Doubilet, et al. (2005). Three- and 4-dimensional ultrasound in obstetrics and gynecology. Proceedings of the American Institute of Ultrasound in Medicine Consensus Conference. *Journal Ultrasound Medicine* 24 (12): 1587–1597.

24. Dolkart, L., M. Harter and M. Snyder (2005). Four-dimensional ultrasonographic guidance for invasive obstetric procedures. *Journal Ultrasound Medicine* 24 (9): 1261–1266.

25. Goncalves, L., J. Nien, J. Espinoza, J. Kusanovic, W. Lee, B. Swope and E. Soto (2005). Two-dimensional (2D) versus three- and four-dimensional (3D/4D) US in obstetrical practice: Does the new technology add anything? *American Journal Obstetrics and Gynecology* 193 (6): S150.

26. Kurjak, A., B. Miskovic, W. Andonotopo, M. Stanojevic, G. Azumendi and H. Vrcic (2007). How useful is 3D and 4D ultrasound in perinatal medicine? *Journal Perinatal Medicine* 35(1): 10-27.

27. Blake, C. C., T. L. Elliot, P. J. Slomka, D. B. Downey and A. Fenster (2000). Variability and accuracy of measurements of prostate brachytherapy seed position in vitro using three-dimensional ultrasound: an intra- and inter-observer study. *Medical Physics* 27 (12): 2788–2795.

28. Fenster, A., D. B. Downey and H. N. Cardinal (2001). Three-dimensional ultrasound imaging. *Physics in Medicine and Biology* 46 (5): R67–99.

29. Pretorius, D. H., T. R. Nelson and J. S. Jaffe (1992). 3-dimensional sonographic analysis based on color flow Doppler and grayscale image data: A preliminary report. *Journal Ultrasound Medicine* 11(5): 225–232.

30. Picot, P. A., D. W. Rickey, R. Mitchell, R. N. Rankin and A. Fenster (1993). Three-dimensional color Doppler imaging. *Ultrasound Medicine and Biology* 19 (2): 95–104.

31. Downey, D. B. and A. Fenster (1995). Three-dimensional power Doppler detection of prostate cancer [letter]. *American Journal of Roentgenelogy* 165 (3): 741.

32. Downey, D. B. and A. Fenster (1995). Vascular imaging with a three-dimensional power Doppler system. *American Journal Roentgenology* 165 (3): 665–668.

33. Landry, A. and A. Fenster (2002). Theoretical and experimental quantification of carotid plaque volume measurements made by 3D ultrasound using test phantoms. *Medical Physics* 10: 2319–2327.

34. Landry, A., J. D. Spence and A. Fenster (2004). Measurement of carotid plaque volume by 3-dimensional ultrasound. *Stroke* 35 (4): 864–869.

35. Landry, A., J. D. Spence and A. Fenster (2005). Quantification of carotid plaque volume measurements using 3D ultrasound imaging. *Ultrasound Medicine and Biology* 31 (6): 751–762.

36. Ainsworth, C. D., C. C. Blake, A. Tamayo, V. Beletsky, A. Fenster and J. D. Spence (2005). 3D ultrasound measurement of change in carotid plaque volume; a tool for rapid evaluation of new therapies. *Stroke* 35: 1904–1909.

37. Krasinski, A., B. Chiu, J. D. Spence, A. Fenster and G. Parraga (2009). Three-dimensional ultrasound quantification of intensive statin treatment of carotid atherosclerosis. *Ultrasound Medicine and Biology* 35 (11): 1763–1772.

38. Tong, S., D. B. Downey, H. N. Cardinal and A. Fenster (1996). A three-dimensional ultrasound prostate imaging system. *Ultrasound Medicine and Biology* 22 (6): 735–746.

39. Tong, S., H. N. Cardinal, R. F. McLoughlin, D. B. Downey and A. Fenster (1998). Intra- and inter-observer variability and reliability of prostate volume measurement via two-dimensional and three-dimensional ultrasound imaging. *Ultrasound Medicine and Biology* 24 (5): 673–681.

40. Downey, D. B., J. L. Chin and A. Fenster (1995). Three-dimensional US-guided cryosurgery. *Radiology* 197 (P): 539.

41. Onik, G. M., D. B. Downey and A. Fenster (1996). Three-dimensional sonographically monitored cryosurgery in a prostate phantom. *Journal Ultrasound Medicine* 15 (3): 267–270.

42. Chin, J. L., D. B. Downey, T. L. Elliot, S. Tong, C. A. McLean, M. Fortier and A. Fenster (1999). Three dimensional transrectal ultrasound imaging of the prostate: Clinical validation. *Canadian Journal Urology* 6 (2): 720–726.

43. Wei, Z., L. Gardi, D. B. Downey and A. Fenster (2005). Oblique needle segmentation and tracking for 3D TRUS guided prostate brachytherapy. *Medical Physics* 32 (9): 2928–2941.

44. Cool, D., S. Sherebrin, J. Izawa, J. Chin and A. Fenster (2008). Design and evaluation of a 3D transrectal ultrasound prostate biopsy system. *Medical Physics* 35 (10): 4695–4707.

45. Pagoulatos, N., D. R. Haynor and Y. Kim (2001). A fast calibration method for 3-D tracking of ultrasound images using a spatial localizer. *Ultrasound Medicine and Biology* 27 (9): 1219–1229.

46. Boctor, E. M., M. A. Choti, E. C. Burdette and R. J. Webster III (2008). Three-dimensional ultrasound-guided robotic needle placement: An experimental evaluation. *International Journal Medical Robotics* 4 (2): 180–191.

47. Treece, G., R. Prager, A. Gee and L. Berman (2001). 3D ultrasound measurement of large organ volume. *Medical Image Analysis* 5 (1): 41–54.

48. Raab, F. H., E. B. Blood, T. O. Steiner and H. R. Jones (1979). Magnetic position and orientation tracking system. *IEEE Transactions Aerospace Electronic Systems* AES-15: 709–717.

49. Detmer, P. R., G. Bashein, T. Hodges, K. W. Beach, E. P. Filer, D. H. Burns and D. E. Strandness, Jr. (1994). 3D ultrasonic image feature localization based on magnetic scanhead tracking: In vitro calibration and validation. *Ultrasound Medicine and Biology* 20 (9): 923–936.

50. Hodges, T. C., P. R. Detmer, D. H. Burns, K. W. Beach and D. E. J. Strandness (1994). Ultrasonic three-dimensional reconstruction: In vitro and in vivo volume and area measurement. *Ultrasound Medicine and Biology* 20 (8): 719–729.

51. Pretorius, D. H. and T. R. Nelson (1994). Prenatal visualization of cranial sutures and fontanelles with three-dimensional ultrasonography. *Journal Ultrasound Medicine* 13 (11): 871–876.

52. Nelson, T. R. and D. H. Pretorius (1995). Visualization of the fetal thoracic skeleton with three-dimensional sonography: A preliminary report. *American Journal Roentgenology* 164 (6): 1485–1488.

53. Riccabona, M., T. R. Nelson, D. H. Pretorius and T. E. Davidson (1995). Distance and volume measurement using three-dimensional ultrasonography. *Journal Ultrasound Medicine* 14 (12): 881–886.

54. Hughes, S. W., T. J. D'Arcy, D. J. Maxwell, W. Chiu, A. Milner, J. E. Saunders and R. J. Sheppard (1996). Volume estimation from multiplanar 2D ultrasound images using a remote electromagnetic position and orientation sensor. *Ultrasound Medicine and Biology* 22 (5): 561–572.

55. Gilja, O. H., P. R. Detmer, J. M. Jong, D. F. Leotta, X. N. Li, K. W. Beach, R. Martin and D. E. J. Strandness (1997). Intragastric distribution and gastric emptying assessed by three-dimensional ultrasonography. *Gastroenterology* 113 (1): 38–49.

56. Leotta, D. F., P. R. Detmer and R. W. Martin (1997). Performance of a miniature magnetic position sensor for three-dimensional ultrasound imaging. *Ultrasound Medicine and Biology* 23(4): 597-609.
57. Hsu, P. W., R. W. Prager, A. H. Gee and G. M. Treece (2008). Real-time freehand 3D ultrasound calibration. *Ultrasound Medicine and Biology* 34 (2): 239–251.
58. Lindseth, F., G. A. Tangen, T. Lango and J. Bang (2003). Probe calibration for freehand 3-D ultrasound. *Ultrasound Medicine and Biology* 29 (11): 1607–1623.
59. Leotta, D. F. (2004). An efficient calibration method for freehand 3-D ultrasound imaging systems. *Ultrasound Medicine and Biology* 30 (7): 999–1008.
60. Dandekar, S., Y. Li, J. Molloy and J. Hossack (2005). A phantom with reduced complexity for spatial 3-D ultrasound calibration. *Ultrasound Medicine and Biology* 31 (8): 1083–1093.
61. Gee, A. H., N. E. Houghton, G. M. Treece and R. W. Prager (2005). A mechanical instrument for 3D ultrasound probe calibration. *Ultrasound Medicine and Biology* 31 (4): 505–518.
62. Gooding, M. J., S. H. Kennedy and J. A. Noble (2005). Temporal calibration of freehand three-dimensional ultrasound using image alignment. *Ultrasound Medicine and Biology* 31 (7): 919–927.
63. Mercier, L., T. Lango, F. Lindseth and D. L. Collins (2005). A review of calibration techniques for freehand 3-D ultrasound systems. *Ultrasound Medicine and Biology* 31 (4): 449–471.
64. Poon, T. C. and R. N. Rohling (2005). Comparison of calibration methods for spatial tracking of a 3-D ultrasound probe. *Ultrasound Medicine and Biology* 31 (8): 1095–1108.
65. Rousseau, F., P. Hellier and C. Barillot (2005). Confhusius: A robust and fully automatic calibration method for 3D freehand ultrasound. *Medical Image Analysis* 9 (1): 25–38.
66. Shattuck, D. P., M. D. Weinshenker, S. W. Smith and O. T. von Ramm (1984). Explososcan: A parallel processing technique for high speed ultrasound imaging with linear phased arrays. *Journal Acoustic Society America* 75 (4): 1273–1282.
67. von Ramm, O. T. and S. W. Smith (1990). Real time volumetric ultrasound imaging system. *SPIE* 1231:15–22.
68. Smith, S. W., H. G. Pavy, Jr. and O. T. von Ramm (1991). High-speed ultrasound volumetric imaging system. Part I. Transducer design and beam steering. *IEEE Transactions Ultrasonics Ferroelectrics Frequency Control* 38: 100–108.
69. Turnbull, D. H. and F. S. Foster (1991). Beam steering with pulsed two-dimensional transducer arrays. *IEEE Transactions Ultrasonics Ferroelectrics Frequency Control* 38: 320–333.
70. von Ramm, O. T., S. W. Smith and H. G. Pavy, Jr. (1991). High-speed ultrasound volumetric imaging system. Part II. Parallel processing and image display. *IEEE Transactions Ultrasonics Ferroelectrics Frequency Control* 38: 109–115.
71. Smith, S. W., G. E. Trahey and O. T. von Ramm (1992). Two-dimensional arrays for medical ultrasound. *Ultrasonic Imaging* 14(3): 213–233.
72. Oralkan, O., A. S. Ergun, C. H. Cheng, J. A. Johnson, M. Karaman, T. H. Lee and B. T. Khuri-Yakub (2003). Volumetric ultrasound imaging using 2-D CMUT arrays. *IEEE Transactions Ultrasonics Ferroelectrics Frequency Control* 50 (11): 1581–1594.
73. Sklansky, M. (2004). Specialty review issue: Fetal cardiology—Introduction. *Pediatric Cardiology* 25 (3): 189–190.

74. Devore, G. R. and B. Polanko (2005). Tomographic ultrasound imaging of the fetal heart: A new technique for identifying normal and abnormal cardiac anatomy. *Journal Ultrasound Medicine* 24 (12): 1685–1696.

75. Xie, M. X., X. F. Wang, T. O. Cheng, Q. Lu, L. Yuan and X. Liu (2005). Real-time 3-dimensional echocardiography: A review of the development of the technology and its clinical application. *Progress Cardiovascular Disease* 48 (3): 209–225.

76. Prakasa, K. R., D. Dalal, J. Wang, C. Bomma, H. Tandri, J. Dong, C. James, et al. (2006). Feasibility and variability of three-dimensional echocardiography in arrhythmogenic right ventricular dysplasia/cardiomyopathy. *American Journal Cardiology* 97 (5): 703–709.

77. Nelson, T. R., D. B. Downey, D. H. Pretorius and A. Fenster (1999). *Three-dimensional ultrasound.* Philadelphia PA: Lippincott-Raven.

78. Fenster, A. and D. Downey (2000). Three-dimensional ultrasound imaging. In *Handbook of medical imaging, volume 1, physics and psychophysics. In text* (J. Beutel, H. Kundel and R. Van Metter. Bellingham, WA, SPIE Press.) 1: 433–509.

79. Fenster, A. and D. Downey (2001). Three-dimensional ultrasound imaging. *Proceedings SPIE* 4549: 1–10.

80. Pretorius, D. H. and T. R. Nelson (1995). Fetal face visualization using three-dimensional ultrasonography. *Journal Ultrasound Medicine* 14 (5): 349–356.

81. Nelson, T. R., D. H. Pretorius, M. Sklansky and S. Hagen-Ansert (1996). Three-dimensional echocardiographic evaluation of fetal heart anatomy and function: Acquisition, analysis, and display. *Journal Ultrasound Medicine* 15 (1): 1–9, quiz 11–12.

82. Deng, J. and C. H. Rodeck (2006). Current applications of fetal cardiac imaging technology. *Current Opinion Obstetrics and Gynecology* 18 (2): 177–184.

83. Levoy, M. (1990). Volume rendering, a hybrid ray tracer for rendering polygon and volume data. *IEEE Computer Graphics Applications* 10: 33–40.

84. Fruhauf, T. (1996). Raycasting vector fields. *Visualization '96. Proceedings* 115–120.

85. Sun, Y. and D. L. Parker (1999). Performance analysis of maximum intensity projection algorithm for display of MRA images. *IEEE Transactions Medical Imaging* 18 (12): 1154–1169.

86. Kniss, J., G. Kindlmann and C. Hansen (2002). Multidimensional transfer functions for interactive volume rendering. *IEEE Transactions on Visualization and Computer Graphics* 8 (3): 270–285.

87. Lusis, A. J. (2000). Atherosclerosis. *Nature* 407 (6801): 233–241.

88. Delcker, A. and H. C. Diener (1994). 3D ultrasound measurement of atherosclerotic plaque volume in carotid arteries. *Bildgebung* 61 (2): 116–121.

89. Delcker, A. and H. C. Diener (1994). Quantification of atherosclerotic plaques in carotid arteries by three-dimensional ultrasound. *British Journal Radiology* 67 (799): 672–678.

90. Delcker, A. and C. Tegeler (1998). Influence of ECG-triggered data acquisition on reliability for carotid plaque volume measurements with a magnetic sensor three-dimensional ultrasound system. *Ultrasound Medicine and Biology* 24 (4): 601–605.

91. Palombo, C., M. Kozakova, C. Morizzo, F. Andreuccetti, A. Tondini, P. Palchetti, G. Mirra, G. Parenti and N. G. Pandian (1998). Ultrafast three-dimensional ultrasound: Application to carotid artery imaging. *Stroke* 29 (8): 1631–1637.

92. Delcker, A., H. C. Diener and H. Wilhelm (1995). Influence of vascular risk factors for atherosclerotic carotid artery plaque progression. *Stroke* 26 (11): 2016–2022.

93. Schminke, U., L. Motsch, B. Griewing, M. Gaull and C. Kessler (2000). Three-dimensional power-mode ultrasound for quantification of the progression of carotid artery atherosclerosis. *Journal Neurology* 247 (2): 106–111.

94. Zhao, X. Q., C. Yuan, T. S. Hatsukami, E. H. Frechette, X. J. Kang, K. R. Maravilla and B. G. Brown (2001). Effects of prolonged intensive lipid-lowering therapy on the characteristics of carotid atherosclerotic plaques in vivo by MRI: A case-control study. *Arteriosclerosis Thrombosis Vascular Biology* 21 (10): 1623–1629.

95. O'Leary, D. H. and M. L. Bots (2010). Imaging of atherosclerosis: Carotid intima–media thickness. *European Heart Journal* 31 (14): 1682–1689.

96. Fenster, A. and D. B. Downey (2000). Three-dimensional ultrasound imaging. *Annual Review Biomedical Engineering* 2: 457–475.

97. Chiu, B., M. Egger, J. D. Spence, G. Parraga and A. Fenster (2008). Quantification of carotid vessel wall and plaque thickness change using 3D ultrasound images. *Medical Physics* 35 (8): 3691–3710.

98. Chiu, B., M. Egger, J. Spence, G. Parraga and A. Fenster (2008). Development of 3D ultrasound techniques for carotid artery disease assessment and monitoring. *International Journal Computer Assisted Radiology Surgery* 3 (1): 1–10.

99. Ding, M. and A. Fenster (2004). Projection-based needle segmentation in 3D ultrasound images. *Computer Aided Surgery* 9 (5): 193–201.

100. Hu, N., D. B. Downey, A. Fenster and H. M. Ladak (2003). Prostate boundary segmentation from 3D ultrasound images. *Medical Physics* 30 (7): 1648–1659.

101. Ladak, H. M., Y. Wang, D. B. Downey and A. Fenster (2003). Testing and optimization of a semiautomatic prostate boundary segmentation algorithm using virtual operators. *Medical Physics* 30 (7): 1637–1647.

102. Wang, Y., H. N. Cardinal, D. B. Downey and A. Fenster (2003). Semiautomatic three-dimensional segmentation of the prostate using two-dimensional ultrasound images. *Medical Physics* 30 (5): 887–897.

103. Ding, M., B. Chiu, I. Gyacskov, X. Yuan, M. Drangova, D. B. Downey and A. Fenster (2007). Fast prostate segmentation in 3D TRUS images based on continuity constraint using an autoregressive model. *Medical Physics* 34 (11): 4109–4125.

13

Optical Coherence Tomography for Imaging Biological Tissue

Michael K. K. Leung and Beau A. Standish

CONTENTS

Clinicians and medical scientists are faced with an ever increasing number of choices for the early detection of life-threatening medical conditions, such as heart disease or cancer. Several of these pathologies require invasive biopsy procedures to verify the presence and stage of disease progression. Once these factors are identified, the patient must then undergo treatment where existing modalities used in the medical industry lack the resolution for treatment monitoring such that in vivo measurements can be correlated to the gold standard of disease-free survival—namely, histology. Optical coherence tomography (OCT) is an exciting, high-resolution, noninvasive, volumetric imaging modality that may provide both structural and functional information, such as blood flow detection, to aid in the early detection and treatment monitoring of diseases. As this optically based technology continues to improve, there is great potential for OCT to become a widely accepted tool to aid in the clinical decision-making process, where emphasis is placed on the ability to provide proper patient risk stratification and subsequent appropriate therapy or therapies. In this chapter, an introduction to the working principles of OCT technologies and the extension of OCT for blood flow detection are presented with respect to the field of biological tissue imaging.

13.1 Introduction

Optical coherence tomography (OCT) has been developed as an imaging modality to visualize subsurface tissue morphology at a resolution (~10 µm in tissue) approaching histology [1]. Current state-of-the-art, ultrahigh resolution systems have achieved submicron spatial resolutions in both in vivo and ex vivo imaging scenarios [2–4], allowing for the detection of biological subcellular features. In vivo endoscopic OCT systems with 10–20 µm spatial resolution have been sufficient in resolving larger structures such as muscular layers of bulk tissue in the gastrointestinal wall [5], along with extension into intraluminal imaging to detect vessel wall structures as a way to stratify patient risk or monitor the placement of stents in coronary arteries [6].

For imaging moving targets, such as blood flow, Doppler OCT has been used to investigate fluid dynamics, interstitial blood flow, hereditary hemorrhagic telangiectasia, retinal blood flow, and the vascular response of photodynamic therapy [7–11]. Modern frequency domain (FD) OCT systems are capable of acquiring and processing three-dimensional (3D) subsurface (~3 mm in depth) images of tissue at multiple volumes per second [12,13]. This increase in system speed has been crucial for the early adoption of OCT as a clinical tool because large anatomical regions can now be imaged in seconds, such as the previously mentioned coronary artery or gastrointestinal tract [3,14].

The technique of OCT itself is considered analogous to ultrasound. However, instead of measuring backscattered pressure waves, OCT measures backscattered photons using an interferometer, avoiding the difficult task of directly measuring the time of flight of the backscattered light. The following sections present an introduction to the working principles of OCT technologies and the extension of OCT for blood flow detection for use in imaging biological tissue.

13.2 Frequency Domain OCT

Optical coherence tomography is an emerging noninvasive imaging modality that can yield real-time, three-dimensional subsurface (~3 mm in depth) images of tissue structure at a spatial resolution (~10 µm) that approaches histology. No preparation of the sample is required, and current state-of-the-art ultra-high resolution systems have achieved submicron spatial resolutions, allowing for the detection of subcellular features [15]. Optical coherence tomography images are similar in appearance to those obtained with ultrasound. Figure 13.1(a)–(c) show sample OCT images of different regions of the finger. To interrogate a sample, instead of measuring backscattered pressure waves, OCT measures backscattered photons using an interferometer, avoiding the difficult task of directly measuring the time-of-flight of the backscattered light. In turbid media and other scattering tissue, the penetration depth of imaging is limited primarily by scattering. The maximum imaging depth of OCT is approximately 1–3 mm at wavelengths between 800 and 1300 nm for a variety of tissues [16]. The axial and transverse resolutions of OCT are decoupled. The axial resolution depends on light source characteristics such as spectral bandwidth and central wavelength, whereas the transverse resolution is dependent on the focusing optics.

To date, two main embodiments of OCT exist. The first generation of systems was based on time-domain OCT (TD-OCT), and these systems can be routinely found in commercial Food and Drug Administration (FDA)-approved systems, used primarily in ophthalmology. The second-generation frequency domain OCT (FD-OCT) systems are more prevalent in research, although commercial interests are gaining momentum.

In TD-OCT, one-dimensional depth ranging is achieved through low-coherence interferometry [17]. Using broadband light, interference fringes are observed only when the reference and sample arm optical path length are matched within the coherence length of the light source. Refractive indices vary between interfaces within a sample manifest as intensity peaks in the detected interference pattern [18]. A reference arm is translated linearly in time during imaging to capture entire depth profiles (an A-scan) By acquiring multiple A-scans at different spatial locations, two- (B-mode) or three-dimensional images can be obtained similar to those of Figure 13.1(a)–(c). The imaging speed of TD-OCT is generally restricted due to the requirement to translate the reference arm mechanically. This limits its use in screening large tissue volumes, such as significant portions of a tumor or the walls of an artery [6].

In FD-OCT, depth ranging is performed by means of spectral interferometry [19]. The reference arm is kept stationary, and depth information is acquired by an inverse Fourier transform of the spectrally resolved interference fringes [20]. Two configurations of FD-OCT exist. One, called spectral domain OCT (SD-OCT), separates individual spectra components using a spectrometer and a charge-coupled device array, and generally uses a superluminescent diode as light source. The other is called swept-source OCT (SS-OCT), which uses a wavelength-swept tunable laser source and a single photodetector (together acting as a "time-resolved" spectrometer). The depth ranging principles for both techniques are the same and differ only in method in acquiring the interference signal.

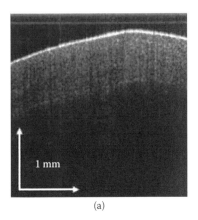

(a)

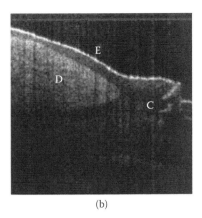

(b)

FIGURE 13.1
Structural B-mode OCT images of the different parts of the human finger: (a) the nail, (b) the nail root, and (c) the fingerprint. (d) Schematic explaining the notation used to describe the dimensions of a 3D OCT image data set. A B-mode image is located on the x–z plane. An A-scan extends in the z, or depth, direction. The x–y direction is also called the en-face plane. Labels: D, dermis; E, epidermis; C, cuticle; F, fingerprint ridges; J, epidermal–dermal junction; S, sweat ducts.

13.2.1 Signal Formation in Frequency Domain OCT

This section describes a derivation of the principle of FD-OCT, which is based on spectral interferometry. To understand depth ranging, assume that the light backscattered from the imaged object consists of reflected elementary plane waves U from different depths z:

$$U(z) = U_0 e^{-ik_0 nz} \qquad (13.1)$$

where
U_0 is the amplitude

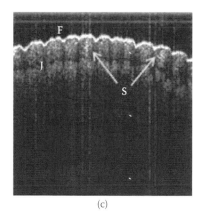

(c)

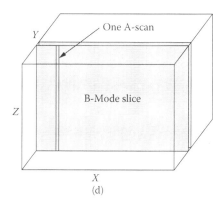

(d)

FIGURE 13.1 *(Continued)*

$k_0 - 2\pi/\lambda_0$ is the wave number
λ_0 is the wavelength
n is the refractive index (≈ 1.3 in tissue)
i is the imaginary number

For a monochromatic source with wave number k_0, a single interface reflector that is detected via interferometry is given by

$$
\begin{aligned}
I_{\Delta z}(k_0) &= \left| (U_R + U_S) \right|^2 \\
&= \left| U_0 \left(e^{-ik_0 nz} + e^{-ik_0 n(z+2\Delta z)} \right) \right|^2 \\
&= U_0^2 \left[2 + e^{ik_0 n 2\Delta z} + e^{-ik_0 n 2\Delta z} \right] \\
&= 2I_0 \left[1 + \cos(2k_0 n\Delta z) \right]
\end{aligned}
\tag{13.2}
$$

where the additional $2\Delta z$ accounts for the round-trip path length difference. The plane waves originating from the reference and sample arms are U_R and U_S, respectively. Ignoring dispersion, for a material with depth-dependent reflectivity $a(z)$, the intensity from many different depths can be summed as

$$I(k_0) = 2I_0\left[1 + \int_0^\infty a(z)\cos(2k_0 nz)dz\right] + \text{mutual inteference terms (MIT)} \quad (13.3)$$

The MIT, which describes the mutual interference of the elementary waves, has the expression

$$MIT = \int_0^\infty \int_0^\infty a(z')a(z)e^{-i2k_0 n(z-z')}dzdz' \quad (13.4)$$

This term lies in baseband frequencies (i.e., at $z = 0$) and is generally much weaker than the signal of interest. Therefore, the MIT can be removed by filter as the object signal only needs to be a small offset away from $z = 0$, which is usually the case during OCT imaging. When measurements are performed with many difference frequencies, the interference signal $I(k)$ takes on the following form:

$$I(k) = B(k)\left(1 + \int_0^\infty a(z)\cos(2knz)dz + MIT\right) \quad (13.5)$$

where $B(k)$ is spectral intensity distribution of the laser source (swept source spectrum, or bandwidth of the superluminescent diode in the case of SD-OCT). It can be seen that the depth z of scattering amplitudes is encoded in the argument (frequency, $2nz$) of the cosine function.

To achieve a suitable form with which a Fourier transform can be performed, $a(z)$ can be replaced by the symmetrical expansion $\hat{a}(z) = a(z) + a(-z)$, since $a(z)$ is zero on the opposite side of the reference plane [19]. The expression then becomes

$$I(k) = B(k)\left(1 + \int_{-\infty}^\infty \hat{a}(z)e^{-i2knz}dz + MIT\right) \quad (13.6)$$

Finally, by the definition of the Fourier transform and ignoring the MIT,

$$FT^-[I(k)] \approx FT^-[B(k)] \otimes [\delta(z) + \hat{a}(z)] \quad (13.7)$$

where FT^- is the inverse Fourier transform and $\otimes$ denotes the convolution operator. The Dirac delta function is represented by $\delta(z)$. The depth-dependent reflectivity $\hat{a}(z)$ of the sample is thereby recovered. It can also be seen that the light source spectrum $B(k)$ determines the axial resolution of the system, where the general expression for the axial resolution $\bar{z}$ of the FD-OCT system is [21]:

$$\bar{z} = \frac{2\sqrt{2\ln 2}}{\pi} \frac{\lambda_0^2}{\Delta\lambda} \tag{13.8}$$

where λ_0 represents the center wavelength of a Gaussian light source and $\Delta\lambda$ is the $1/e^2$ width of the spectrum.

As an example, given a $\Delta\lambda$ of 110 nm and λ_0 of 1310 nm, the axial resolution that can be achieved is ~12 μm in air. It has been shown that the FD-OCT system offers superior sensitivity compared to TD-OCT systems, which improves the signal-to-noise ratio (SNR) [22]. In addition, faster scanning speeds can be obtained by FD-OCT as mechanical translation of the reference mirror is no longer required. These benefits are crucial for wide field imaging of biological tissues.

13.2.2 Choice of Wavelength for OCT Imaging

This section briefly discusses the wavelength of the light source used in OCT imaging. OCT is based on detection of light that is backscattered only once (to a first-order approximation) by the imaging target. Therefore, to achieve high penetration depth and sensitivity, scattering or absorption by the sample must be minimized. Equation (13.8) states that the central wavelength λ_0 of the light source should be low to obtain good axial resolution. However, tissue scattering tends to increase with decreasing wavelengths. As well, tissue absorption is high for the wavelength range of 200–600 nm due to the inherent absorption by hemoglobin and above 1000 nm due to water [23].

For ophthalmometry (the current main application of OCT), light is required to penetrate the vitreous humor of the eye, which has a volume of 98%–99% water, to reach the retina. Based on the preceding description, a good compromise has been found by using light sources in the wavelength range of ~800 nm. Recently, there has been a shift to the 1000 nm regime for imaging of the eye. This allows ~200 nm of additional penetration depth compared to 800 nm, which suffers from high absorption and scattering from the retinal pigment epithelium [24]. Although water absorption at this wavelength is significantly higher, the International Council on Non-Ionizing Radiation Protection (ICNIRP) guidelines for maximal permissible light exposure in the eye increases with wavelength (from ~1.7 mW at 800 nm to ~5 mW at 1060 nm) [24]. Hence, loss due to absorption may be compensated by using a laser that can provide higher incident power.

For imaging biological tissue, there are advantages to imaging in the 1300 nm range for several reasons. First, due to the explosion of the telecom industry, there is widespread availability of low-cost fiber optic components to develop complete OCT systems in the 1300 nm range. Second, tissue (e.g., gastrointestinal tract, interstitial, epithelium) is not concealed under a thick layer of water, as in the eye; thus, water absorption is not a significant problem. Therefore, to enhance penetration depth and minimize scattering effects, a higher wavelength such as 1300 nm is typically chosen to image biological tissue.

13.2.3 Swept-Source System Description

A schematic of a standard polygon-based OCT system is shown in Figure 13.2 [25]. The laser is in a fiber-ring-cavity configuration, with a semiconductor optical amplifier (BOA1017, Covega, Washington, DC) as the gain medium. Wavelength tuning is accomplished by a polygon mirror [26] with typical output sweeping ranges ($\Delta\lambda$) of ~100 nm centered at 1310 nm. These system characteristics result in axial resolutions of ~10 µm in tissue and average output power of 20–40 mW. Due to the speed with which the polygon can be spun, A-scan repetition rates can reach over 50 kHz.

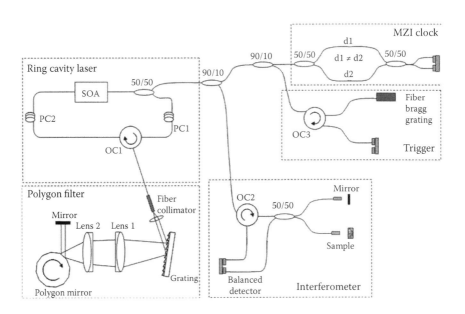

FIGURE 13.2
System schematic of a polygon-based swept source OCT imaging system used for biological tissue imaging. The system consists of multiple modules. (1) The light source is a ring cavity laser. (2) Wavelength tuning used for swept source OCT is achieved by a polygon filter. (3) Signals from the sample arm and reference arm are combined in the interferometer. (4) A-scan triggering and signal recalibration using a Mach–Zehnder interferometer clock are required for data acquisition. Labels: PC, polarization controller; OC, optical circulator; SOA, semiconductor optical amplifier. Ratios denote the routine splitting ratios of fiber optic couplers.

In the current optical filter design, a spinning polygon mirror is used to sweep a beam of light across a diffraction grating. The sweeping motion causes a change in incident angle to the grating that is linear in time. Since the data acquisition sampling rate is constant, this means that the interference signal is acquired linearly in wavelength. To recalibrate wavelength-space data to k-space (as used in the derivations) such that a standard fast Fourier transform can be used to retrieve the depth-intensity profile, a clock signal is generated using a Mach–Zehnder interferometer (MZI) clock [27]. A fiber Bragg grating (FBG) can provide the A-scan trigger. The FBG reflects a particular wavelength of light and transmits all others and it is used to provide a trigger signal that indicates the beginning of a particular wavelength sweep. For instance, given a sweeping range of ~100 nm centered at 1310 nm, the FBG would be designed to reflect wavelengths near 1260 nm.

13.2.4 Structural OCT

In the structural imaging mode, OCT signal intensity indicates the local reflectivity of a particular depth-dependent volume of tissue. For a given two-dimensional (2D) image frame, after inverse Fourier transform, the value of a given pixel S is calculated as [28]

$$S = \frac{1}{MN} \sum_{m=1}^{M} \sum_{n=1}^{N} \left[I_{m,n}^2 + Q_{m,n}^2 \right]$$

(13.9)

where I and Q are the real and imaginary components of the complex inverse Fourier transformed interference fringe signal. M and N represent the number of voxels to average spatially in the axial and lateral directions (i.e., within the same B-mode frame), respectively, to improve SNR. The number of voxels to average is hence $M \times N$.

13.3 Methods of Imaging Blood Vessels with OCT

Two functional extensions of OCT offer the ability to visualize and quantify changes in the tumor vasculature after a therapeutic treatment. Doppler OCT (DOCT), which utilizes similar principles as Doppler ultrasound, permits quantitative measures of flow velocities within vessels ~100 μm in diameter to be measured and quantified [28]. Speckle variance OCT (SVOCT) is a newly developed technique that, while discarding flow information, can identify vessels whose velocity and/or dimension are too small to be detected by DOCT (~10–15 μm diameter) [29]. The strengths and weaknesses of both techniques as applied to biological tissue are discussed next.

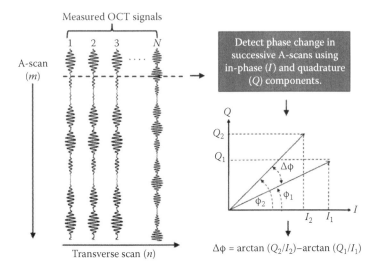

FIGURE 13.3
Doppler frequency detection from moving elements (i.e., blood) using DOCT. A change in phase between two successive A-scans can be calculated using the in-phase (I) and quadrature (Q) components to calculate the phase shift between two successive A-scans.

13.3.1 Doppler OCT

Doppler optical coherence tomography has been used in a number of clinical applications to investigate fluid dynamics in the gastrointestinal tract, interstitial blood flow, and retinal blood flow and for therapeutic monitoring [5,30–32]. The principle of DOCT is borrowed from ultrasound, where flow can be calculated by comparing the phase shifts in consecutive A-scans. A complex signal is readily available from the inverse Fourier transform. To compute Doppler information, the complex signal is separated into its in-phase (I) and quadrature (Q) components. Figure 13.3 shows a flow chart where the mean phase shift can be calculated by evaluating the phase angle of individual OCT signals, consisting of their in-phase and quadrature components, followed by the computation of the phase difference between axial scans. This value can then be related to the Kasai autocorrelation velocity estimator [33] through a trigonometric identity [34], yielding the following equation to calculate the mean Doppler frequency shift (f_D) used to display regions of blood flow. Using the Kasai autocorrelation function, the mean Doppler frequency shift can be calculated as follows [35]:

$$f_D = \frac{f_a}{2\pi} \arctan \left\{ \frac{\displaystyle\sum_{m=1}^{M}\sum_{n=1}^{N-1}(I_{m,n+1}Q_{m,n} - Q_{m,n+1}I_{m,n})}{\displaystyle\sum_{m=1}^{M}\sum_{n=1}^{N-1}(Q_{m,n+1}Q_{m,n} - I_{m,n+1}I_{m,n})} \right\} \tag{13.10}$$

where f_D is the Doppler frequency shift, f_a is the axial scan frequency, m represents the indices in the depth direction (M = total number of indices), and n represents the indices in the lateral direction (N = total number of indices), resulting in a 2D color Doppler image. The arctangent component gives the Doppler phase shift. From f_D, the velocity v of the moving target can be calculated as

$$v = \frac{\lambda_0 f_D}{2n_t \cos(\theta_D)} \quad (13.11)$$

where θ_D is the angle between the optical axis and the direction of flow, λ_0 is the center wavelength of the laser, and n_t is the index of refraction of the sample. In the case of imaging biological tissue, θ_D is assumed to be the angle between the tissue surface and scan beam, which is typically 70°–80°.

A trade-off exists in DOCT, where improved sensitivity to low blood velocities results in a reduction in the maximum detectable velocity. To achieve great sensitivity to slow-moving flow, f_a should be low to allow sufficient phase buildup to exceed the noise floor of the imaging system. However, in such a condition, aliasing may occur if the imaged blood flow is high, due to sampling rate limitations. Conversely, increasing the A-scan sampling rate increases the dynamic range of flow velocities that can be detected, but lowers the detection threshold for slow-moving flow.

This trade-off is one of the factors limiting the broad application of DOCT for acquiring accurate velocity maps in biological tissue. The range of blood flow velocities, which is inversely proportional to the vascular cross-sectional area, between arteries, veins, and capillaries is very broad (centimeters per second to submillimeters per second) [36,37]. For a given A-scan repetition rate f_a optimized for the measurement of the blood flow in the venules (which have relatively low flow compared to arteries), significant aliasing will be observed within the arterial blood vessels. For this reason, it is difficult to capture a snapshot of the complete vasculature in a 3D tissue volume, with each vessel having nonaliased velocity information. Therefore, DOCT's utility in imaging and quantifying biological tissue has been limited to several niche areas or for only acquiring architectural information of the vessels [38]. That is, the velocity information is discarded, and the Doppler signal is used as a binary metric to identify regions of blood flow or no blood flow.

Another limitation of DOCT is its relatively long acquisition time, since oversampling is required [28]. To image a useable volume of tissue (such as the dorsal skin slab in a mouse model, 5×5 mm²), the acquisition time is of the order of tens of minutes. Note that the pulsatile nature of flow requires a sufficient number of repeated acquisitions to obtain a mean value for velocity. For human imaging, heart rates are ~60 beats per minute. This means many repeated acquisitions would be required, further lengthening the acquisition time to obtain an average blood velocity map. Therefore, the benefit of quantitative DOCT in tissue may be limited to monitoring specific vessels, where repeated acquisition over a small spatial volume can be accomplished rapidly [39].

13.3.2 Speckle Variance OCT

Recently, a new OCT technique called speckle variance, which calculates interframe speckle modulation (changes in pixel intensity as a function of time), has been developed [29]. This technique is angle and flow-velocity independent and is more sensitive in detecting microvasculature compared to DOCT, at the expense of lacking quantification of blood velocity information. The intrinsic contrast of SVOCT is based on time-dependent scattering properties of fluids and solids. Speckle variance OCT is calculated from the following equation [29]:

$$SV_{ijk} = \frac{1}{N_f} \sum_{i=1}^{N} (S_{ijk} - S_{mean})^2 \qquad (13.12)$$

where
N_f is the number of frames used for variance calculation
i is the frame number
j,k are indices of corresponding pixels in the transverse and axial directions, respectively
S is the structural OCT intensity

Essentially, it is a variance calculation of a given pixel at N_f different time points, each separated by the time required to acquire a frame, or B-mode image. It has been shown that, at the imaging frame rate of the system used for typical experiments (~40 frames per second), complete decorrelation of structural intensity occurs even in stationary scattering fluids; the origin comes from intrinsic Brownian motion [40]. This property allows SVOCT to detect vasculature even if there is no flow, unlike phase-sensitive techniques.

Figure 13.4 shows fluorescence and white light pictures of a mouse, which highlight the imaged regions (box), via OCT, to demonstrate Doppler and speckle variance imaging. These regions are shown in Figure 13.5, which highlights the ability of OCT to provide functional imaging of biological tissue. The SVOCT image (Figure 13.5a) is what is referred to as a "first-generation" picture, acquired in mid-2008. The second generation is discussed in the next section. This image is a projection in the en-face direction (x–y plane). The corresponding DOCT images at the indicated slice locations (Figure 13.5d–h) are shown (x–z plane). A number of observations can be made here to compare and contrast the DOCT and SVOCT techniques.

First, the number of detected blood vessels in Figure 13.5(a), using SVOCT, is clearly much greater than that of Figure 13.5(b), acquired using DOCT. The

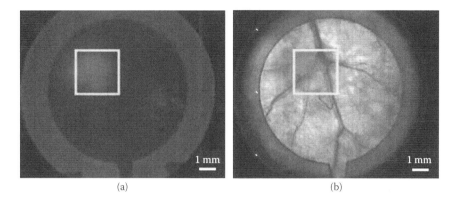

(a)   (b)

FIGURE 13.4
(See color insert.) Wide-field (a) fluorescence and (b) corresponding white light image of a tumor-bearing (ME-180) nude mouse implanted within a mouse window chamber. The square region is imaged with Doppler and speckle variance optical coherence tomography (shown in Figure 13.5).

lower sensitivity of DOCT requires vessels to have sufficient diameter and flow velocity in order for them to be detected. Second, Figure 13.5(b) and (c) show a reconstruction of many DOCT image slices into 3D, where a threshold was applied to show only the direction of flow. The angle dependence of OCT can be observed here, where the flow direction seems to reverse in approximately the middle of the image due to orientation of how the beam is used to scan the tissue. This angle dependence complicates flow measurement over a large 3D volume. Third, aliasing can be observed in Figure 13.5(d) and (e), where artery–vein pairs are present. Flow velocity may be calculated from the Doppler shift in the vein, but is obscured in the artery due to aliasing.

Although, SVOCT has the ability to image down to the capillary level, it is also very prone to motion artifacts. In DOCT, moderate bulk tissue motion may be removed by analyzing the mean phase of the image. It is assumed that, for a given A-scan, the diameters of blood vessels are much smaller than the region, which consists of bulk tissue (easily satisfied in most cases). Then, the detected mean phase, which would come mostly from the bulk tissue because of the previous assumption, can be subtracted. This is currently not possible for SVOCT, where correlation between variance and magnitude of motion has yet to be established as the speckle variance intensity is identical whether the imaged fluid is stationary or moving. Therefore, it is not possible to subtract the bulk tissue motion by methods used in phase-sensitive techniques.

13.3.3 Optimized Speckle Variance OCT

An optimized version of SVOCT imaging has been developed by Mariampillai et al. [40]. Previously, acquisition of an entire 3D volume was performed by raster scanning, as shown in Figure 13.7(a). In this scan pattern, two consecutive

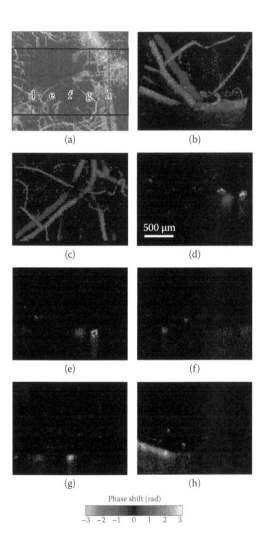

FIGURE 13.5
(See color insert.) Functional imaging of a tumor-bearing nude mouse 1 week after ME-180 cell implantation. (a) Speckle-variance OCT image (3×3 mm^2) of a tumor and surrounding blood vessels. A necrotic core is present, which manifests as a region devoid of vessels. The labels indicate the locations of DOCT image slices. (b, c) Three-dimensional reconstruction of the detected Doppler signal viewed from an angle and parallel (x–z plane) and perpendicular (x–y plane) to the imaging beam, respectively. (d–h) Corresponding DOCT image slices labeled in (a). Each image is 2.0 mm across and has a 1.7 mm depth of view.

frames, even though they are very close, are still in spatially different positions. In the improved SVOCT scheme, the scan pattern is altered such that the same region is imaged multiple times, as shown in Figure 13.6(b). This reduces the spatial decorrelation that occurred with the original method and improves the rejection of stationary and nonfluid objects [40].

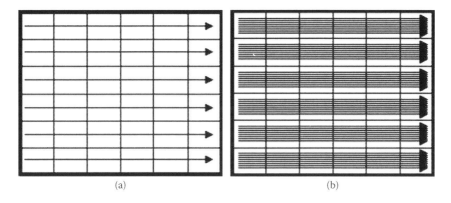

(a)   (b)

FIGURE 13.6
Speckle variance optical coherence tomography scan patterns. In the schematic, each row in the grid represents a single frame, and each cell represents a voxel. (a) First-generation, raster scan pattern. (b) Second-generation, repeated acquisitions in a given frame.

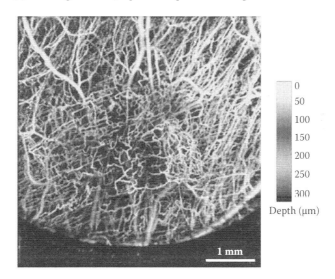

FIGURE 13.7
(See color insert.) Second-generation speckle variance optical coherence tomography image of the mouse dorsal skin. The color indicates the relative depth of the vessels. A tumor mass (ME-180) is in the center of the image. The black border at the bottom is the edge of the plastic fastener of the tissue window.

Figure 13.7 shows an exemplary second-generation SVOCT image of biological in vivo mouse tissue with an implanted tumor. Vasculature down to the capillary level may be detected. In addition, it has been color coded to indicate the relative depth of the vessels. The location of tumors may be identified by two features, and this detection technique may lend itself to the clinical environment to detect tumors or be used as a quantitative method to

TABLE 13.1

Strengths and Weaknesses of Doppler and Speckle Variance Optical Coherence Tomography

Technique	Strengths	Weaknesses
Doppler OCT	1. Can quantify flow velocities 2. Three dimensional	1. Angle dependence 2. Prone to aliasing 3. Limited sensitivity to small/low-flow vessels
Speckle variance OCT	1. High sensitivity to blood vessels regardless of flow 2. Angle independence	1. Binary metric 2. Two-dimensional projection image 3. Prone to motion artifacts

monitor therapeutic responses. The first feature includes the physical vessel architecture as tumorous vessels are different when compared to normal blood vessels. The vessels near the center of Figure 13.7 are more tortuous (tumor), compared to normal vessels, which do not change in direction or tortuosity as frequently. The second feature includes vessel density. Although there is angiogenesis within the tumor, the vessel density tends to be less where a tumor mass is present. This is observed in the center of Figure 13.7.

As stated, the Doppler and speckle variance techniques have their own advantages and disadvantages as outlined in Table 13.1. It is important for the researcher or clinician to understand their unique requirements when imaging biological tissue and to choose the appropriate method to obtain relevant and useful data.

13.4 Current Limitations, Future Solutions, and Conclusions

Optical coherence tomography is a promising noninvasive, real-time, high-resolution, volumetric imaging modality that has found initial clinical utility for imaging biological tissue such as atherosclerotic detection in the coronary artery, gastrointestinal imaging, and ophthalmic applications. Although imaging speeds and biomedical OCT research have increased drastically over the last several years, there are still substantial hurdles for the widespread clinical adoption of OCT.

Essential requirements of OCT as a realistic platform for routine biomedical and clinical imaging necessitate a system that is cost effective and yields high-resolution and/or functional imaging along with extensive scientific study to demonstrate clinical utility. As the field of OCT is rapidly expanding, there is a degree of optimism that, in the foreseeable future, OCT will become a standard clinical tool. It has already found a foothold in ophthalmic imaging and is in the early stages of clinical use for intraluminal images such as of the coronary artery. However, several hurdles exist before this technique becomes a standard imaging option for widespread biomedical or clinical environments. Although the high resolution of OCT is extremely beneficial for identifying microstructural and microvascular architecture, there are issues with the manipulation, evaluation, and storage of the acquired data. A typical pullback data set, commonly produced for gastrointestinal imaging, can approach 40 GB and consist of ~1200 individual cross-sectional images [41]. This overload of data must be simplified, as it would take an extensive amount of human capital by highly qualified personnel to analyze each of the large 3D data sets thoroughly. A potential solution to this problem includes the incorporation of smart algorithms that have the ability to identify regions of interest via pattern recognition algorithms to filter these large data sets down to a manageable set of "high-risk" images that necessitate additional clinical review.

With continued hardware and software OCT advancements, this platform technology has the potential to provide evidence-based disease detection along with an ability to track disease progression longitudinally. Therefore, these inherent system characteristics have resulted in a new cost-effective solution to understanding biological processes as a first step in ultimately providing superior health care to patients.

References

1. D. Huang, E. A. Swanson, C. P. Lin, J. S. Schuman, W. G. Stinson, W. Chang, M. R. Hee, et al. Optical coherence tomography. *Science* 254:1178–1181 (1991).
2. K. Bizheva, A. Unterhuber, B. Hermann, B. Povaûay, H. Sattmann, A. Fercher, W. Drexler, M. Preusser, H. Budka, and A. Stingl. Imaging ex vivo healthy and pathological human brain tissue with ultra-high-resolution optical coherence tomography. *Journal of Biomedical Optics* 10:011006 (2005).
3. B. J. Vakoc, M. Shishko, S. H. Yun, W. Y. Oh, M. J. Suter, A. E. Desjardins, J. A. Evans, et al. Comprehensive esophageal microscopy by using optical frequency-domain imaging (with video) (a figure is presented). *Gastrointestinal Endoscopy* 65:898–905 (2007).
4. S. Yazdanfar, M. D. Kulkarni, and J. A. Izatt. High resolution imaging of in vivo cardiac dynamics using color Doppler optical coherence tomography. *Optics Express* 1:424–431 (1997).
5. V. X. D. Yang, S. J. Tang, M. L. Gordon, B. Qi, G. Gardiner, M. Cirocco, P. Kortan, et al. Endoscopic Doppler optical coherence tomography in the human GI tract: Initial experience. *Gastrointestinal Endoscopy* 61:879 890 (2005).
6. G. J. Tearney, S. Waxman, M. Shishkov, B. J. Vakoc, M. J. Suter, M. I. Freilich, A. E. Desjardins, et al. Three-dimensional coronary artery microscopy by intracoronary optical frequency domain imaging. *JACC: Cardiovascular Imaging* 1:752–761 (2008).

7. B. A. Standish, X. Jin, J. Smolen, A. Mariampillai, N. R. Munce, B. C. Wilson, I. A. Vitkin, and V. X. D. Yang. Interstitial Doppler optical coherence tomography monitors microvascular changes during photodynamic therapy in a Dunning prostate model under varying treatment conditions. *Journal of Biomedical Optics* 12:034022 (2007).

8. J. Moger, S. Matcher, C. Winlove, and A. Shore. Measuring red blood cell flow dynamics in a glass capillary using Doppler optical coherence tomography and Doppler amplitude optical coherence tomography. *Journal of Biomedical Optics* 9:982 (2004).

9. B. White, M. Pierce, N. Nassif, B. Cense, B. Park, G. Tearney, B. Bouma, T. Chen, and J. de Boer. In vivo dynamic human retinal blood flow imaging using ultra-high-speed spectral domain optical coherence tomography. *Optics Express* 11:3490–3497 (2003).

10. S. Tang, M. Gordon, V. Yang, M. Faughnan, M. Cirocco, B. Qi, E. Yue, G. Gardiner, G. Haber, and G. Kandel. In vivo Doppler optical coherence tomography of mucocutaneous telangiectases in hereditary hemorrhagic telangiectasia. *Gastrointestinal Endoscopy* 58:591–598 (2003).

11. B. Standish, K. Lee, X. Jin, A. Mariampillai, N. Munce, M. Wood, B. Wilson, I. Vitkin, and V. Yang. Interstitial doppler optical coherence tomography as a local tumor necrosis predictor in photodynamic therapy of prostatic carcinoma: An in vivo study. *Cancer Research* 68:9987 (2008).

12. R. Huber, D. Adler, and J. Fujimoto. Buffered Fourier domain mode locking: Unidirectional swept laser sources for optical coherence tomography imaging at 370,000 lines/s. *Optics Letters* 31:2975–2977 (2006).

13. D. Adler, Y. Chen, R. Huber, J. Schmitt, J. Connolly, and J. Fujimoto. Three-dimensional endomicroscopy using optical coherence tomography. *Nature Photonics* 1:709–716 (2007).

14. G. van Soest, T. Goderie, E. Regar, S. Koljenovi, G. van Leenders, N. Gonzalo, S. van Noorden, T. Okamura, B. Bouma, and G. Tearney. Atherosclerotic tissue characterization in vivo by optical coherence tomography attenuation imaging. *Journal of Biomedical Optics* 15:011105.

15. K. Bizheva, A. Unterhuber, B. Hermann, B. Povay, H. Sattmann, A. F. Fercher, W. Drexler, et al. Imaging ex vivo healthy and pathological human brain tissue with ultra-high-resolution optical coherence tomography. *Journal of Biomedical Optics* 10:1–7 (2005).

16. M. E. Brezinski and J. G. Fujimoto. Optical coherence tomography: High-resolution imaging in nontransparent tissue. *IEEE Journal on Selected Topics in Quantum Electronics* 5:1185–1192 (1999).

17. A. F. Fercher, W. Drexler, C. K. Hitzenberger, and T. Lasser. Optical coherence tomography—Principles and applications. *Reports on Progress in Physics* 66:239–303 (2003).

18. P. H. Tomlins and R. K. Wang. Theory, developments and applications of optical coherence tomography. *Journal of Physics D: Applied Physics* 38:2519–2535 (2005).

19. M. W. Lindner, P. Andretzky, F. Kiesewetter, and G. Häusler. In *Handbook of optical coherence tomography,* ed. B. E. Bouma, and G. J. Tearney, 335–357. New York: Marcel Dekker, Inc. (2002).

20. A. F. Fercher, C. K. Hitzenberger, G. Kamp, and S. Y. El-Zaiat. Measurement of intraocular distances by backscattering spectral interferometry. *Optics Communications* 117:43–48 (1995).

21. S. H. Yun, and B. E. Bouma. Wavelength swept lasers. In *Optical coherence tomography: Technology and applications,* ed. W. Drexler, and J. G. Fujimoto, 359–377. New York: Springer (2008).

22. M. A. Choma, M. V. Sarunic, C. Yang, and J. A. Izatt. Sensitivity advantage of swept source and Fourier domain optical coherence tomography. *Optics Express* 11:2183–2189 (2003).

23. M. E. J. van Velthoven, D. J. Faber, F. D. Verbraak, T. G. van Leeuwen, and M. D. de Smet. Recent developments in optical coherence tomography for imaging the retina. *Progress in Retinal and Eye Research* 26:57–77 (2007).

24. A. Unterhuber, B. Povay, B. Hermann, H. Sattmann, A. Chavez-Pirson, and W. Drexler. In vivo retinal optical coherence tomography at 1040 nm—Enhanced penetration into the choroid. *Optics Express* 13:3252–3258 (2005).

25. G. Y. Liu, A. Mariampillai, B. A. Standish, N. R. Munce, X. Gu, and I. A. Vitkin. High power wavelength linearly swept mode locked fiber laser for OCT imaging. *Optics Express* 16:14095–14105 (2008).

26. W. Y. Oh, S. H. Yun, G. J. Tearney, and B. E. Bouma. 115 kHz tuning repetition rate ultrahigh-speed wavelength-swept semiconductor laser. *Optics Letters* 30:3159–3161 (2005).

27. R. Huber, M. Wojtkowski, J. G. Fujimoto, J. Y. Jiang, and A. E. Cable. Three-dimensional and C-mode OCT imaging with a compact, frequency swept laser source at 1300 nm. *Optics Express* 13:10523–10551 (2005).

28. V. X. D. Yang, M. L. Gordon, B. Qi, J. Pekar, S. Lo, E. Seng-Yue, A. Mok, B. C. Wilson, and I. A. Vitkin. High speed, wide velocity dynamic range Doppler optical coherence tomography (part I): System design, signal processing, and performance. *Optics Express* 11:794–809 (2003).

29. A. Mariampillai, B. A. Standish, E. H. Moriyama, M. Khurana, N. R. Munce, M. K. K. Leung, J. Jiang, et al. Speckle variance detection of microvasculature using swept-source optical coherence tomography. *Optics Letters* 33:1530–1532 (2008).

30. H. Li, B. A. Standish, A. Mariampillai, N. R. Munce, Y. Mao, S. Chiu, N. E. Marcon, B. C. Wilson, A. Vitkin, and V. X. D. Yang. Feasibility of interstitial Doppler optical coherence tomography for in vivo detection of microvascular changes during photodynamic therapy. *Lasers in Surgery and Medicine* 38:754–761 (2006).

31. Y. Wang, B. A. Bower, J. A. Izatt, O. Tan, and D. Huang. In vivo total retinal blood flow measurement by Fourier domain Doppler optical coherence tomography. *Journal of Biomedical Optics* 12:041215 (2007).

32. B. A. Standish, K. K. C. Lee, X. Jin, A. Mariampillai, N. R. Munce, M. F. G. Wood, B. C. Wilson, I. A. Vitkin, and V. X. D. Yang. Interstitial Doppler optical coherence tomography as a local tumor necrosis predictor in photodynamic therapy of prostatic carcinoma: An in vivo study. *Cancer Research* 68:9987–9995 (2008).

33. C. Kasai, and K. Namekawa. Real-time two-dimensional blood flow imaging using an autocorrelation technique. *Ultrasonics Symposium Proceedings,* pp. 953–958, (1985).

34. W. D. Barber, J. W. Eberhard, and S. G. Karr. A new time domain technique for velocity measurements using Doppler ultrasound. *IEEE Transactions on Biomedical Engineering* 32:213–229 (1985).

35. R. S. C. Cobbold. Pulsed methods for flow velocity estimation and imaging. In *Foundations of biomedical ultrasound,* ed. R. S. C. Cobbold. Oxford, England: Oxford University Press (2005).

36. C. J. Hartley, L. H. Michael, and M. L. Entman. Noninvasive measurement of ascending aortic blood velocity in mice. *American Journal of Physiology—Heart and Circulatory Physiology* 268:H499–H505 (1995).

37. A. C. Guyton, and J. E. Hall. Overview of the circulation; medical physics of pressure, flow, and resistance. In *Textbook of medical physiology,* 11th ed., ed. A. C. Guyton, and J. E. Hall, 161–170. New York: Elsevier (2006).

38. B. J. Vakoc, R. M. Lanning, J. A. Tyrrell, T. P. Padera, L. A. Bartlett, T. Stylianopoulos, L. L. Munn, et al. Three-dimensional microscopy of the tumor microenvironment in vivo using optical frequency domain imaging. *Nature Medicine* 15:1219–1223 (2009).

39. H. A. Collins, M. Khurana, E. H. Moriyama, A. Mariampillai, E. Dahlstedt, M. Balaz, M. K. Kuimova, et al. Blood-vessel closure using photosensitizers engineered for two-photon excitation. *Nature Photonics* 2:420–424 (2008).

40. A. Mariampillai, M. K. K. Leung, M. Jarvi, B. A. Standish, K. Lee, B. C. Wilson, A. Vitkin, and V. X. D. Yang. Optimized speckle variance OCT imaging of microvasculature. *Optics Letters* 35:1257–1259 (2010).

41. M. J. Suter, B. J. Vakoc, P. S. Yachimski, M. Shishkov, G. Y. Lauwers, M. Mino-Kenudson, B. E. Bouma, N. S. Nishioka, and G. J. Tearney. Comprehensive microscopy of the esophagus in human patients with optical frequency domain imaging. *Gastrointestinal Endoscopy* 68:745–753 (2008).

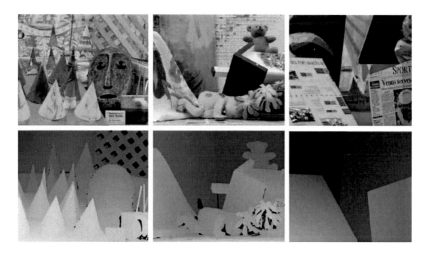

FIGURE 1.13
Stereo test images from the Middlebury database (http://vision.middlebury.edu/stereo/). Top is original images and bottom is disparity images. From left: cone, teddy, and Venus.

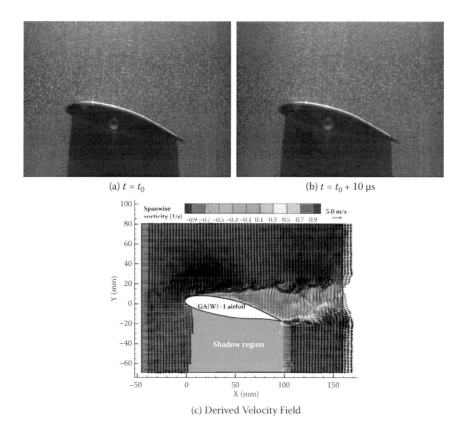

(a) $t = t_0$

(b) $t = t_0 + 10\ \mu s$

(c) Derived Velocity Field

FIGURE 4.1
A pair of PIV images and the corresponding velocity distribution. (Hu, H. and Yang, Z. 2008. *ASME Journal of Fluid Engineering* 130 (5): 051101. With permission.)

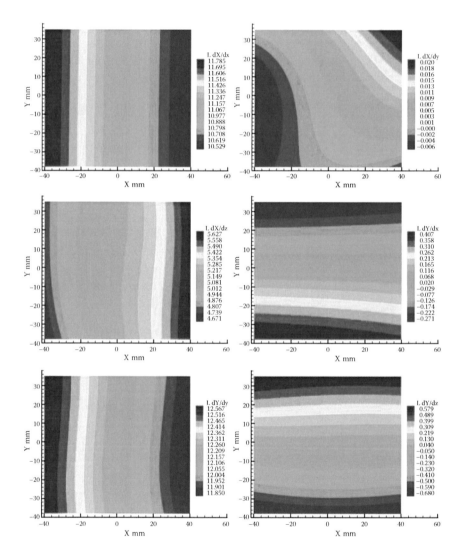

FIGURE 4.8
The gradients of the left-hand image recording camera for stereo image recording.

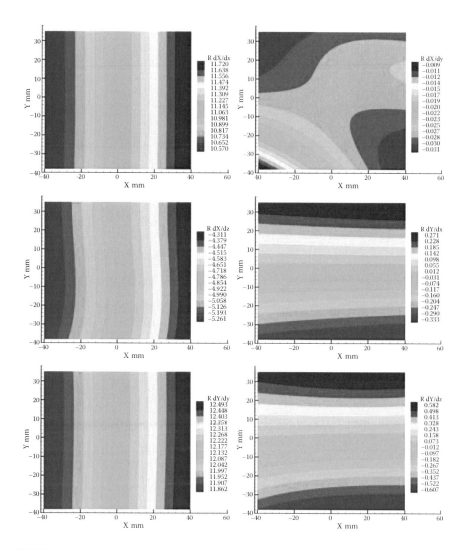

FIGURE 4.9
The gradients of the right-hand image recording camera for stereo image recording.

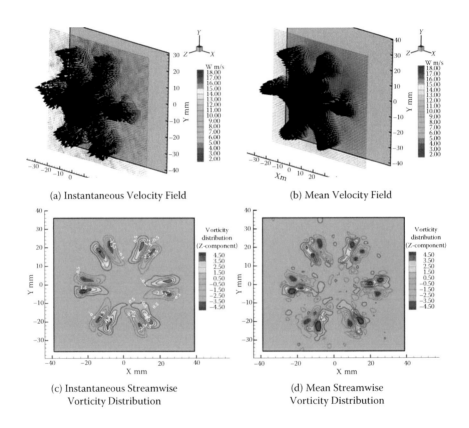

(a) Instantaneous Velocity Field

(b) Mean Velocity Field

(c) Instantaneous Streamwise
Vorticity Distribution

(d) Mean Streamwise
Vorticity Distribution

FIGURE 4.13
Stereo PIV measurement results in the $Z/D = 0.25$ ($Z/H = 0.67$) cross plane.

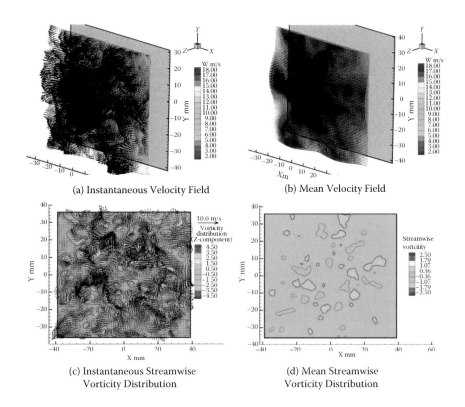

(a) Instantaneous Velocity Field

(b) Mean Velocity Field

(c) Instantaneous Streamwise
Vorticity Distribution

(d) Mean Streamwise
Vorticity Distribution

FIGURE 4.14
Stereo PIV measurement results in the Z/D = 3.0 (Z/H = 8.0) cross plane.

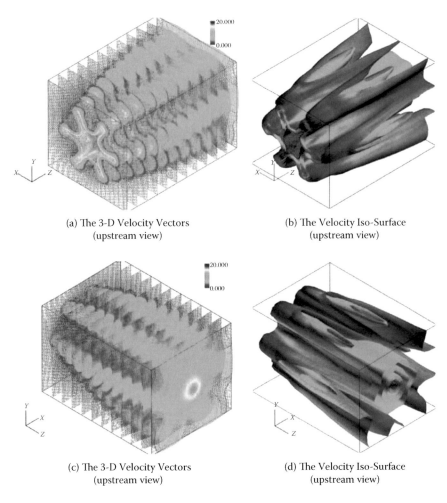

(a) The 3-D Velocity Vectors
(upstream view)

(b) The Velocity Iso-Surface
(upstream view)

(c) The 3-D Velocity Vectors
(upstream view)

(d) The Velocity Iso-Surface
(upstream view)

FIGURE 4.15
Reconstructed three-dimensional flow fields of the lobed jet mixing flow.

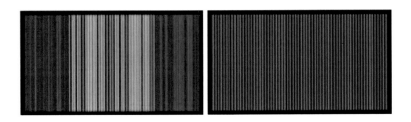

FIGURE 5.1
Pattern proposed by Pages et al. RGB pattern and luminance channel. (Pages, J. et al. *17th International Conference on Pattern Recognition, ICPR 2004* 4:284–287, 2004. With permission.)

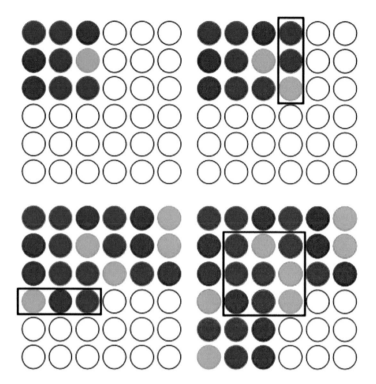

FIGURE 5.2
Code generation direction followed by Morano et al. with colored spots representation. (Morano, R. A. et al. *IEEE Transactions on Pattern Analysis and Machine Intelligence* 20 (3): 322–327, 1998. With permission.)

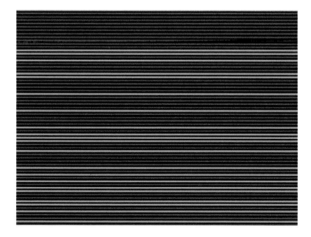

FIGURE 5.8
Pattern of the proposed method; $m = 64$ sinusoidal fringes are coded in color using a De Bruijn code generator algorithm.

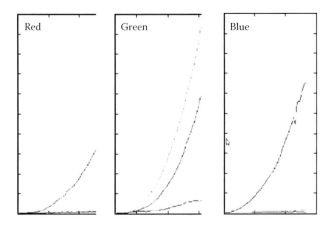

FIGURE 5.9
Received color intensities for projected increasing values of red, green, and blue, respectively.

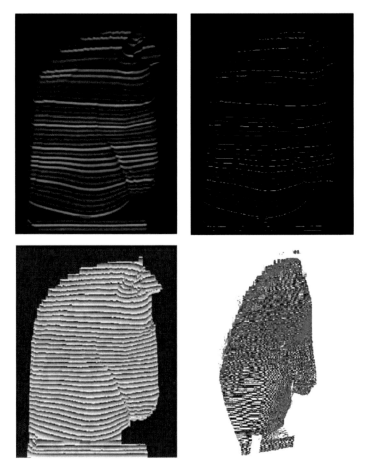

FIGURE 5.12
Proposed algorithm: input image (top left), extracted color slits (top right), combined slits and WFT fringes (bottom left), and 3D cloud of points (bottom right).

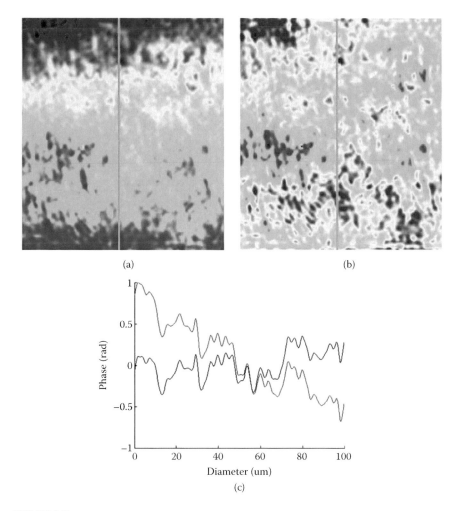

FIGURE 6.7
(a) Phase with subpixel tilt; (b) phase without subpixel tilt; (c) phase profile comparison along the dark lines in (a) and (b).

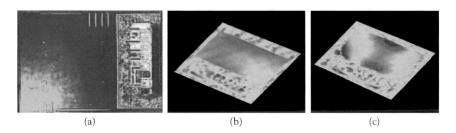

FIGURE 6.12
Profile of accelerometer: (a) bare, unmounted; (b) mounted on ceramic substrate; (c) mounted on plastic substrate.

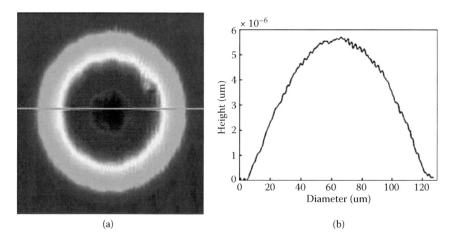

(a)

(b)

FIGURE 6.22

(a) Height map of a single microlens; (b) height profile along the solid line in (a).

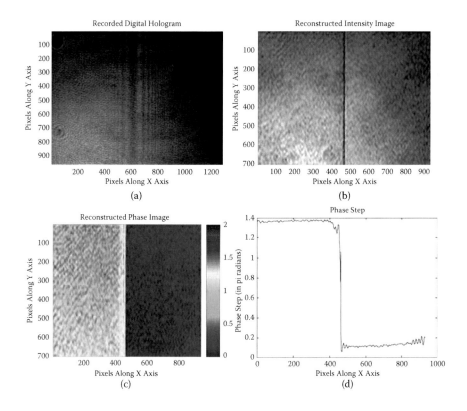

FIGURE 6.24

(a) Recorded digital hologram numerically reconstructed; (b) intensity image; (c) phase image; (d) phase step height measured from digitally recorded hologram with the TN-LCSLM addressed with 0 and 255 grayscales in two equally separated regions.

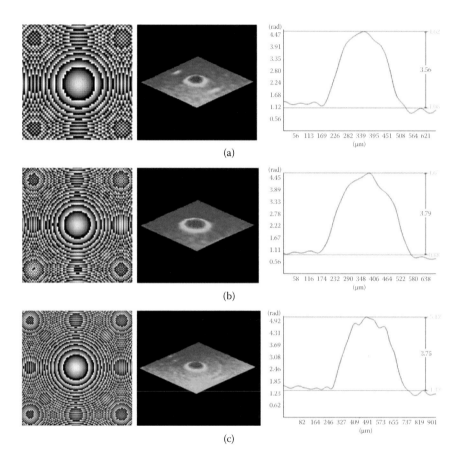

FIGURE 6.25
Diffractive optics lens with focal lengths with their numerical phase reconstruction using DH method and line profile traced at the center in respective order: (a) 80 mm; (b) 120 mm; (c) 160 mm.

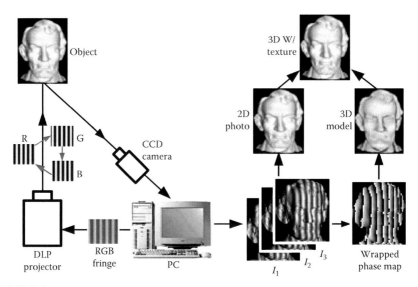

FIGURE 9.4
The layout of the real-time 3D profilometry system we developed. (Modified from Zhang, S. *Optics and Lasers in Engineering* 48:149, 2010. With permission.)

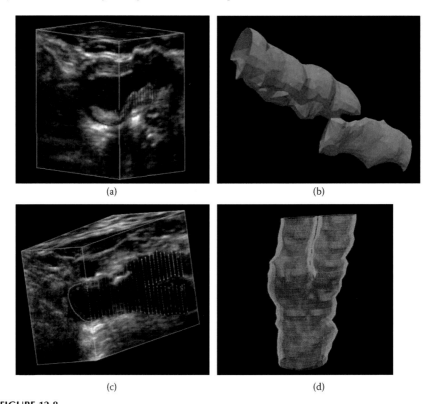

(a)

(b)

(c)

(d)

FIGURE 12.8
Manual segmentation of the CCA, ICA, and ECA lumen and outer wall boundaries from 3D US images are used to calculate the vessel wall volume (VWV). The reconstructed surfaces for the lumen and outer wall boundaries from the manual segmentations are shown.

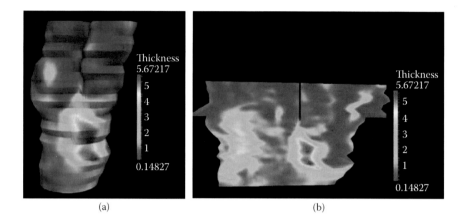

(a)   (b)

FIGURE 12.9
(a) Vessel wall thickness map for a patient with moderate stenosis. Manual segmentations of the lumen and outer wall boundaries were used to generate the thickness maps (indicated in millimeters). (b) Corresponding flattened thickness map for better visualization.

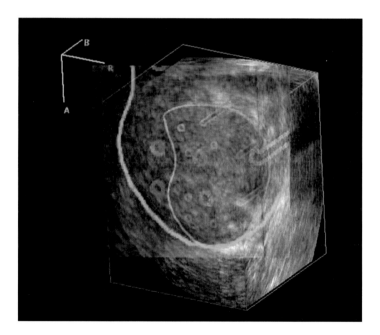

FIGURE 12.11
A 3D US image of the prostate acquired using an end-firing endocavity rotational 3D scanning approach (rotation of a TRUS transducer), which was used to guide a biopsy using the system shown in Figure 12.10. The transducer was rotated around its long axis, while 3D US images were acquired and reconstructed. The image also showed the segmented boundary of the prostate and the locations of the biopsy cores within the prostate.

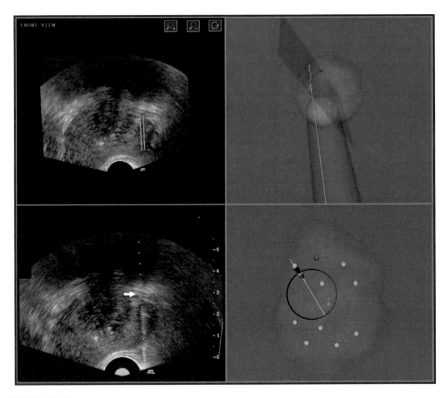

FIGURE 12.12

The 3D TRUS-guide biopsy system's interface is composed of four windows: (top left) the 3D TRUS image dynamically sliced to match the real-time TRUS transducer 3D orientation; (bottom left) the live 2D TRUS video stream; (right side) the 3D location of the biopsy core is displayed within the 3D prostate models. The targeting ring in the bottom right window shows all the possible needle paths that intersect the preplanned target by rotating the TRUS about its long axis. This allows the physician to maneuver the TRUS transducer to the target (highlighted by the red dot) in the shortest possible distance. The biopsy needle (arrow) is visible within the real-time 2D TRUS image.

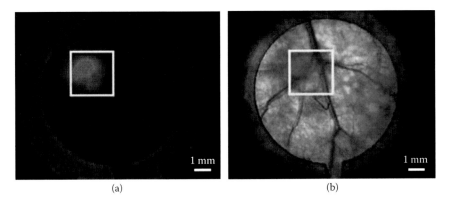

(a) (b)

FIGURE 13.4

Wide-field (a) fluorescence and (b) corresponding white light image of a tumor-bearing (ME-180) nude mouse implanted within a mouse window chamber. The square region is imaged with Doppler and speckle variance optical coherence tomography (shown in Figure 13.5).

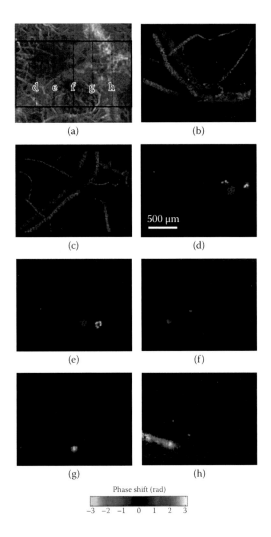

Phase shift (rad)

−3 −2 −1 0 1 2 3

FIGURE 13.5
Functional imaging of a tumor-bearing nude mouse 1 week after ME-180 cell implantation. (a)
Speckle-variance OCT image (3×3 mm^2) of a tumor and surrounding blood vessels. A necrotic
core is present, which manifests as a region devoid of vessels. The labels indicate the locations
of DOCT image slices. (b, c) Three-dimensional reconstruction of the detected Doppler signal
viewed from an angle and parallel (x–z plane) and perpendicular (x–y plane) to the imaging
beam, respectively. (d–h) Corresponding DOCT image slices labeled in (a). Each image is 2.0
mm across and has a 1.7 mm depth of view.

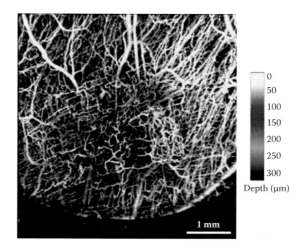

FIGURE 13.7
Second-generation speckle variance optical coherence tomography image of the mouse dorsal skin. The color indicates the relative depth of the vessels. A tumor mass (ME-180) is in the center of the image. The black border at the bottom is the edge of the plastic fastener of the tissue window.

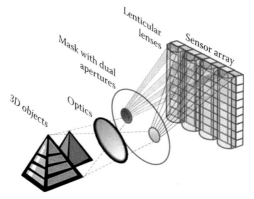

FIGURE 14.7
VisionSense stereoscopic camera: The camera has a mask with two apertures, a lenticular microlens array in front of the sensor chip. Each lenslet is 2 pixels wide. Rays from the 3D object that pass through the left aperture generate a left view on columns marked with a red color, and rays that pass through the right aperture generate a right view image on neighboring columns marked with a green color. A pair of stereoscopic images is thus generated using a single sensor chip. (Yaron, A. et al. www.visionsense.com.)

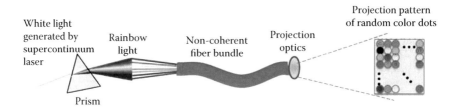

FIGURE 14.11
Spectrally encoded fiber-based structured lighting probe. (Clancy, N. T. et al. *Biomedical Optics Express* 2:3119–3128. With permission.)

14

Three-Dimensional Endoscopic Surface Imaging Techniques

Jason Geng

CONTENTS

This chapter provides an overview of state-of-the-art three-dimensional (3D) endoscopic imaging technologies. Physical objects in the world are 3D, yet traditional endoscopes can only acquire two-dimensional (2D) images that lack depth information. This fundamental restriction greatly limits our ability to perceive and to measure quantitatively the complexity of real-world objects, as well as to understand the spatial relationship among them. In both medical imaging and industrial inspection applications, 3D surface imaging capability would add one more dimension, literally and figuratively, to the existing imaging technologies. Over the past decades, tremendous new technologies and methods have emerged in the 3D surface imaging field. We provide a classification of these technologies first and then describe each category in detail, with representative designs and examples. This overview would be useful to researchers in the field since it provides a snapshot of the current state of the art, from which subsequent research in meaningful directions is encouraged. This overview also contributes to the efficiency of research by preventing unnecessary duplication of already performed research.

14.1 Introduction

The term "endoscopy" is coined from the Greek words *endo,* meaning "inside," and *skopeein,* meaning "to see." Endoscopy is a broad term used to describe any examination of the inside of the body or a physical structure with the help of an endoscope. A flexible, rigid, or semirigid endoscope consists of a camera and an illuminator or set of illuminators at the tip or at the base. Transmission through flexible endoscopes is generally through fiber optic cables or video cables, which are connected to the host computer, controller, and light-generation mechanism. In general, endoscopic imaging systems use a fiber optic illumination bundle that is disposed side by side with the imaging sensor optics at the end of a small insertion tube. The miniature diameter of the insertion tube facilitates easy insertion into cavities of the human body or physical structure for viewing, acquiring images, and certain interventions (such as taking samples, making diagnoses, delivering drugs, etc.). Though generally there is uniformity to endoscope design, manufacturers do vary the specifications of instruments in any given category of endoscopes. Design variables include insertion tube length, diameter, and stiffness characteristics; imaging sensor resolution and signal-to-noise ratio; imaging optics configurations, quality, aberration, and distortion; instrument channel size and number; and configuration of the distal end of the insertion tube [1–4].

The physical world around us is three dimensional; yet, traditional video endoscopes are only able to acquire 2D images that lack depth information. This fundamental restriction has greatly limited our ability to perceive and to measure the complexity of real-world objects.

In medical endoscopic imaging applications, most existing endoscopes used in minimally invasive surgery (MIS) for diagnosis and treatment are monocular based; therefore, they provide only 2D images for in vivo visualization. The lack of depth perception inherent in the current endoscopic imaging technology significantly affects a surgeon's ability to determine the size, shape, and precise location of anatomical structures and to maneuver safely and efficiently in a confined space, thus often impairing the efficiency and outcomes of diagnoses and operations.

In industrial inspection applications, lack of quantitative 3D measurement capabilities of existing endoscopic instruments limits the effectiveness and efficiency of nondestructive inspection tasks. Such systems are often used to inspect inaccessible locations for damage or wear that exceeds an operational limit or to check whether a manufactured part or assembly meets its specifications. It would be desirable to produce a 3D model or surface map for comparison to a reference, 3D viewing, reverse engineering, or detailed surface analysis. However, traditional endoscopic devices are not designed to perform such tasks.

14.1.1 Extant Endoscope Technologies and Limits

Medical endoscopes, originated in the early nineteenth century, are optical instruments used for viewing internal organs through the human body's natural openings (mouth, ear, throat, rectum, etc.) or through a small incision in the skin. Classical rigid endoscopes have a number of periscopic and field lenses in order to convey the image from the distal end to the eyepiece or image sensor. In some cases, as many as 40–50 lenses may be used that can cause considerable optical aberration, light loss, and ghost images. These instruments' rigid bodies greatly limit their ability to access deeper sites of body lumina [1–4].

In 1957, Hirschowitz, at the University of Michigan, invented the first flexible endoscope using a bundle of precisely aligned (i.e., coherent) flexible optical fibers to transmit images. Flexible fiber endoscopes permit visualization of normally inaccessible areas (by rigid endoscopes) within the body without discomfort for patients. Endoscopes help medical procedures to be less invasive, thereby reducing tissue trauma, risk of complications, operation costs, and recovery times. By allowing physicians to see and operate inside a human body, the invention of endoscopes forever changed the face of medical practice.

Conventional endoscopes use either bundles of coherent optical fibers to transmit a 2D image (we herein refer to these as fiber bundle endoscopes) or solid-state, charge-coupled device (CCD) or complementary metal oxide semiconductor (CMOS) sensors at the distal end for superior image quality (we herein refer to these as video endoscopes).

For fiber bundle endoscopes, existing ultrathin endoscopes contain coherent bundles with 2,000 to 30,000 fibers and a millimeter diameter. They can image internal organs via very small channels. However, achieving good image quality for fiber bundle endoscopes with millimeter diameters is very challenging, due to these drawbacks:

- *Limited room for further miniaturization:* Each optical fiber, including its cladding, has a finite diameter. Only a limited number of optical fibers (e.g., 10,000 ~ 30,000 pixels) can be packed into a very confined space with ultrasmall diameter. Each fiber has a minimum diameter of 4 μm. This means that a minimum possible diameter of a fiber bundle scope with 800 × 600 pixels is at least 3 mm.

- *Poor image quality:* The cladding itself is also a problem, as it does not transmit image data and typically results in a honeycomb pattern superimposed on the image (Figure 14.3).

- *Expensive:* The manufacturing process of high-resolution miniature fiber bundles is complex and error prone, making them very expensive devices.

- *Fragile/not highly flexible:* Bundles with a high density of fibers and clad materials are fragile and not very flexible.

- *Lack of 3D imaging capability:* More importantly, none of the existing fiber bundle endoscopes provides 3D information, which is crucial for diagnosis and is particularly useful when conducting surgical operations in confined spaces that can only be accessed by small instruments.

Compared with fiber bundle endoscopes, video endoscopes have advantages in many aspects: The image resolution and quality are much higher and video endoscopes can achieve much better flexibility, durability, and lower costs than fiber bundle endoscopes. However, for traditional video endoscopes, no real-time, full-field, high-resolution 3D measurement capability is available.

14.1.2 Traditional Methods of Measuring the Sizes of Targets Using an Endoscope

One traditional method of measuring the size of a target object under endoscope observation is to rely on rough comparisons of the object size with an object with known dimensions from the image on the video viewing. The measurement results are often subjective and error prone, depending heavily on the operator's experience and proper placement of the comparison object.

Another traditional measurement method used by endoscopists relies on providing a physical stand-off over the lens on the end of the probe insertion tube, at which point the magnification is known and the end of the probe is adjusted until it just touches the object to be viewed at the stand-off. With this known magnification, the image can be measured on the screen and the precise size determined [6].

The past several decades have marked tremendous advances in research, development, and commercialization of 3D surface imaging technologies, stimulated by application demands in a variety of market segments, advances in high-resolution and high-speed electronic imaging sensors, and ever increasing computational power. However, the unique features of endoscopic imaging make it a challenging task to apply the 3D surface imaging techniques directly to the endoscopic imaging instruments:

- The miniature size of components makes it extremely difficult and costly to fabricate optical electronic and structural components.
- A narrow baseline due to the small diameter of endoscopes often limits the accuracy of 3D surface reconstruction.

14.1.3 Organization of This Chapter

In this chapter, we provide an overview of recent advances in 3D endoscopic surface imaging technologies. The chapter is organized as follows: Section 14.2 provides a classification framework of various 3D surface imaging technologies available. Section 14.3 focuses on dual sensor stereo techniques. Section 14.4 describes a few representative single sensor stereo techniques.

Both dual sensor and single sensor stereo techniques are 3D surface imaging schemes based on a pair of stereo images of a target to obtain a 3D surface profile of the target. Section 14.5 describes several 3D surface imaging techniques based on structured light that use one sensor and a miniature structured-light projector to obtain 3D surface profiles. If the texture of the target surface is not prominent, the structured-light techniques can often obtain better 3D imaging results. The shape from video (SfV) is another group of 3D modeling techniques that can be applied to the endoscopic 3D imaging. Shape from video is an important aspect and warrants a serious discussion. However, due to space limits, we will leave this topic to a separate article.

Over the past decades, tremendous new technologies and methods have emerged in the 3D surface imaging field. This overview provides a snapshot of the current state of the art, from which subsequent research in meaningful directions is encouraged. This overview also contributes to the efficiency of research by preventing unnecessary duplication of already performed research.

14.2 Classification of 3D Endoscopic Surface Imaging Techniques

The term "3D imaging" refers to techniques that are able to acquire true 3D data (i.e., values of some property of a 3D object, such as the distribution of density) as a function of the 3D coordinates (x, y, z). Examples from the medical imaging field are computed tomography (CT) and magnetic resonance imaging (MRI), which acquire volumetric pixels (or voxels) of the measured target, including its internal structure.

By contrast, surface imaging deals with measurement of the (x,y,z) coordinates of points on the surface of an object. Since the surface is, in general, nonplanar, it is described in a 3D space, and the imaging is called 3D surface imaging. The result of the measurement may be regarded as a map of the depth (or range), z, as a function of the position (x, y) in a Cartesian coordinate system, and it may be expressed in the digital matrix form $\{z_{ij} = (x_i, y_j), i = 1, 2, ..., L, j = 1, 2, ..., M\}$. This process is also referred to as 3D surface measurement, range finding, range sensing, depth mapping, surface scanning, etc. These terms are used in different application fields and usually refer to loosely equivalent basic surface imaging functionality, differing only in details of system design, implementation, and/or data formats [7].

Numerous techniques for 3D endoscopic surface imaging are currently available. In this chapter, we first classify these techniques into four categories: dual chips at the tip, single chip–dual optical channels, structured light, and video-to-3D modeling techniques, as illustrated schematically in Figure 14.1. Once 3D images are obtained, comprehensive 3D display technology has to be developed and utilized to provide users an effective visualization tool to maximize the utilities of 3D image data. This classification

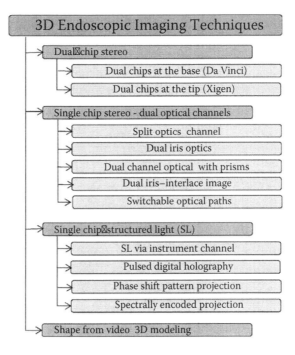

FIGURE 14.1
Classification of 3D endoscopic surface imaging techniques.

framework may serve as a road map for reviewing the 3D endoscopic surface imaging technology.

It would be an impossible task to cover all possible 3D surface imaging techniques in this chapter. Instead, we select a few representative techniques to discuss in order to gain perspective of the entire field and to understand fundamental technical principles and typical system characteristics.

14.3 3D Acquisition Using Dual Sensor Chips

This 3D image acquisition technique is based on a single pair of imaging sensors to acquire binocular stereo images of the target scene in a manner similar to human binocular vision, thus providing the ability to capture 3D information of the target surface (Figure 14.2). The geometric relationship between two image sensors and an object surface point P can be expressed by the triangulation principle as

$$R = B \frac{\sin\beta}{\sin(\alpha + \beta)}$$

where B is the baseline between the two image sensors and R is the distance between the optical center of an image sensor and the surface point P. The (x,y,z) coordinate values of the target point P can then be calculated precisely based on the R, α, β, and geometric parameters.

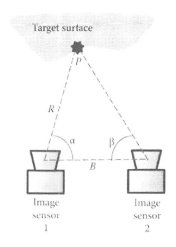

FIGURE 14.2
Concept of stereo 3D surface imaging.

The image sensor may be located at the proximal end of the probe, as with an optical rigid borescope or fiberscope, or at the distal end, as with a video borescope or endoscope. There are essentially two basic design configurations for the dual sensor chip 3D endoscopes:

1. Place two sensor chips at the tip: If the size of sensor chips is sufficiently small, they can be packaged at the tip (distal end) of the endoscope housing. This is an ideal configuration if the performance of small chips meets the 3D imaging requirements in resolution, frame rate, signal-to-noise ratio, etc. Since optics are placed at the tip, the endoscope housing can be made flexible, providing tremendous advantages in miniature flexible endoscope product design and applications.

2. Place two sensor chips at the base: Some high-performance sensor chips often have larger sizes that are not suitable to be placed at the tip, due to restriction of endoscope diameter. In these cases, chips can be placed at the base, and relay optics can be used to lead the acquired optical energy to the sensor chip. However, such system designs usually require rigid outer housings to host the optical train assembly, so this is suited for laparoscopes with rigid housing and shorter length.

We now discuss two representative designs of dual sensor chip endoscopes.

14.3.1 Dual Sensor Chips at the Base

A number of stereo endoscope products adopt the dual sensor chip at the base design configuration. One of the most prominent state-of-the-art medical devices that use stereo endoscopes is the Da Vinci surgical robot, including the one used by the Da Vinci robotic surgery system (Intuitive Surgical System, www.intuitivesurgical.com [8]). It consists of a surgeon's console containing two master manipulators, a patient side cart with up to four robotic arms—three for the slave instrument manipulators, which can be equipped with removable instruments, and a stereo endoscope camera manipulator connected to a high-performance stereo vision system. The endoscopic vision system of the Da Vinci robot delivers high-resolution video to the operator located at the surgeon console. This provides surgeons with visual sharpness that is greater than anything previously available. As the surgeon operates, the Da Vinci vision system displays high-definition video in stereo for true perception of depth. The immersive quality of the 3D vision provides a virtual extension of the surgeon's hands and eyes into the patient's body.

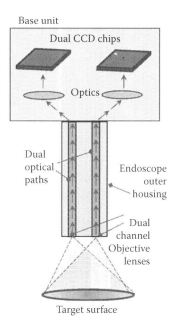

FIGURE 14.3
Stereo endoscope on Da Vinci robotic surgery system (www/intuitivesurgical.com) [8].

However, stereo cameras or endoscopes are only able to offer stereo image pairs; no quantitative 3D measurement and visualization can be performed without advanced 3D reconstruction algorithms. Existing stereo endoscopes/laparoscopes only provide in vivo stereo viewing ability to their operators. Lack of sophisticated image processing algorithms and software for 3D surface image reconstruction prevents these devices from providing in vivo quantitative 3D visualization, 3D measurement (sizing), and 3D registration capability.

Figure 14.3 illustrates the 3D image acquisition mechanism of this design. There are dual optical paths built in on the body of the endoscope, where the optical energy collected by the dual channel objective lenses is relayed by the dual optical paths toward the back end of the endoscope housing. There is a set of specially designed prisms and optical lenses that adjust the dual optical paths such that the large image sensor chips can be hosted at the base unit to receive the collected optical energy for generating a pair of stereo images.

U.S. Patent 5,860,912 [9] shows another example of the dual chips at the base design configuration. Two independent optical channels are used to acquire stereo images and relay them back to the dual image sensor chips. Figure 14.4 provides an example of optical design of a dual chip at the base

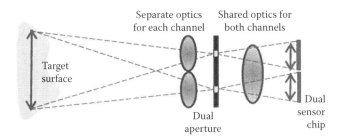

Separate optics for each channel   Shared optics for both channels

Target surface

Dual aperture

Dual sensor chip

FIGURE 14.4
Example of dual chips at the base optical design: Olympus stereo endoscope (U.S. Patent 5,743,846).

stereo endoscope, designed by Olympus (U.S. Patent 5,743,846) [11]). Note that this design employs dual irises and, in some portions, dual optical trains to facilitate the stereo image optical paths. On the rear portion of the optical train, both channels share the same set of optics. The footprints of stereo channels fall onto two sensor chips, respectively. If the size of sensor chip is large, the optical path needs to be split into two to provide sufficient space for sensor chip installation.

14.3.2 Dual Sensor Chips at the Tip

The recent advance of miniature CMOS sensor modules makes it feasible to build miniature stereo endoscopes where dual sensor modules are placed at the distal end of the endoscope while still keeping the diameter of the stereo endoscope minimal.

Xigen LLC, Gaithersburg, Maryland, has recently developed an ultraminiature flexible stereo endoscope based on the latest advances in miniature CMOS imaging sensor technology [13] [23–28]. Figure 14.5 shows a prototype of an ultraminiature stereo endoscope made by Xigen with an outer diameter of only $\phi = 2.8$ mm. It has a pair of miniature CMOS sensors, each of which is 1 mm × 1 mm × 1.5 mm in physical dimension. The entire endoscope head consists of a stereo pair of CMOS sensors, fiber illumination means, and the outer housing. To the best of our knowledge, this is the smallest stereo endoscope available to date.

14.3.2.1 Unique Features of the Ultrathin 3D Stereo Endoscope

The 3D stereo endoscope technology has several unique capabilities for medical diagnosis, intervention procedures, and minimally invasive surgeries:

- It provides real-time stereo 3D image visualization of the surgical site to surgeons, helping them gain depth sensation on manipulation of instruments in surgery.

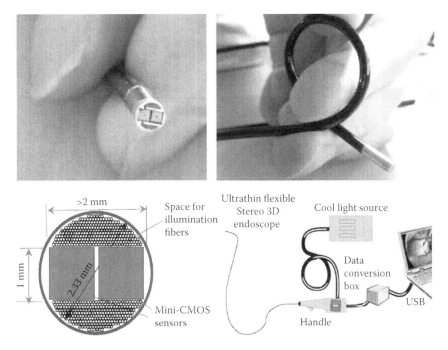

FIGURE 14.5
Xigen's ultraminiature flexible stereo endoscope (j = 2.8 mm). (Geng, J. 2010. Novel ultra-min-iature flexible videoscope for on-orbit NDE. Technical report.)

- It provides quantitative 3D measurement (sizing) of targets and surface profile.
- It can be built with a diameter of ~2.8 mm.
- Three-dimensional images provide quantitative measurement and sizing capability for surgeons during operations.
- Three-dimensional images acquired by the miniature 3D stereoscope provide 3D visual feedback for surgeons during manipulation, positioning, and operation.
- The acquired 3D images facilitate real-time true 3D display for surgery.
- The 3D surface data of a surgical site can be generated continuously in real time, or in snapshot fashion triggered by the operator. The 3D surface data enable image-guided interventions by providing self-positioning capability for surgical instruments, via real-time 3D registration of preoperative images (CT, MRI, etc.) and intraoperative (endoscopic) images.
- Flexibility of the cable allows for dexterous control of viewing direction.

14.3.2.2 Minimal Diameter for Reducing Skin Damage

Reducing the diameter could reduce the traumatic damage to the skin or tissue and eliminate surgical scars. The clinical feedback we received suggested that if the diameter of endoscopes is smaller than 2 ~ 3 mm, it would act like a needle and cause minimal damage to skin and tissues and the surgical scar can be totally eliminated. We therefore should design our stereo 3D endoscope with a diameter smaller than 3 mm. The overall diameter of the NextGen 3D design depends on the separation distance (i.e., the baseline) between two sensor modules. The minimal diameter is achieved by leaving no separation space between the two sensors, resulting in a 3D endoscope 2.33 mm in diameter.

14.3.2.3 The Ultrathin 3D Stereo Endoscope: Real-Time 3D Visual Feedback

The real-time 3D imaging capability of the ultraminiature 3D stereo addresses the clinical needs of real-time 3D video in diagnosis, treatment, and MIS for navigation, manipulation, rough sizing, etc. These uses of 3D images often do not need highly accurate 3D surface profile data. Instead, a rough estimate of distance, proximity, and/or direction would suffice for the initial decision making. One of the most important requirements in these applications is the real-time 3D video capability. Clinicians need real-time visual feedback in 3D in order to perform dexterous maneuvers in a speedy and safe fashion.

14.3.2.4 Overall System Configuration

The overall system design of the proposed ultrathin 3D stereo endoscope is shown in Figure 14.5. This novel ultrathin 3D stereo endoscope is able to

- Provide a pair of stereo images
- with a resolution of >250 × 250 pixels in video image
- at 44 frames per second acquisition rate
- with an ultrathin outer diameter of ~2.8 mm
- and integrated sensor chip and optics design, eliminating the need to add components at the tip

14.4 3D Acquisition Using a Single Chip with Dual Optical Channels

14.4.1 Single Chips with Split Channel Optics

Instead of using two sensor chips to acquire a stereo image pair, a number of designs split the sensing area of a single sense chip into two portions by using specially designed split channel optics and acquire a stereo image pair

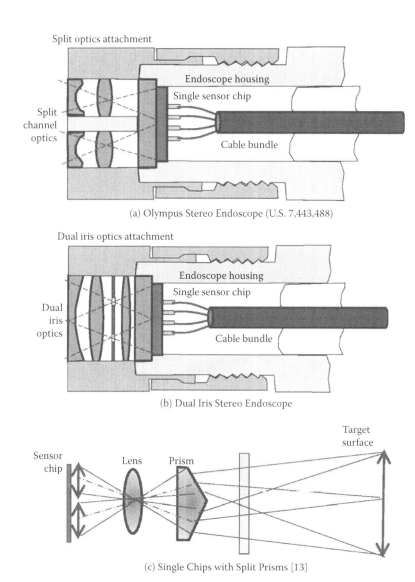

(a) Olympus Stereo Endoscope (U.S. 7,443,488)

(b) Dual Iris Stereo Endoscope

(c) Single Chips with Split Prisms [13]

FIGURE 14.6
Dual iris stereo endoscope.

with reduced image resolution (in comparison with the original resolution of the sensor chip). Figure 14.6(a) shows a split channel optics stereo image acquisition system designed by Olympus (US Patent 7,443,488) [14]. This design facilitates a set of interchangeable optical attachments, offering users multiple options to have different fields of view (FOV) and viewing directions (forward-looking or side-viewing angles). One unit of the attachment set is the split channel optics. It consists of two identical sets of optics, each of which has an effective image footprint on half the area of the single sensor chip. In other words, the entire sensing area of a single sensor chip is split into two halves, acquiring two images simultaneously of a stereo image pair.

The advantages of using split channel optics to acquire stereo images include:

1. No significant changes are made on electronics and sensors.
2. Acquisition of both images in a stereo pair is simultaneous; no time delay problem may occur as on other time-sequential acquisition methods.
3. The potential problem of multichip acquisition with potential discrepancies in image brightness, focus, contrast, etc., is eliminated.

The potential drawbacks of this type of design include:

1. Complex design
2. Difficulty in aligning the optics to have proper image footprints
3. Due to necessity of ensuring sufficient margins between two image footprints on the single chip, frequent occurrences of a black band that may render a significant portion of the sensing area useless
4. Size of the single endoscope outer housing limiting the baseline of the stereo image acquisition

With the small size of endoscopes, this type of design may result in a "weak 3D" effect, meaning that the 3D effect is not quite strong due to the small separation distance between two imaging channels.

14.4.2 Single Chips with Dual Iris Optics

A logic extension of the split channel optics design concept is to employ a dual iris on single channel optics. Figure 14.6(b) illustrates the concept. The design is very similar to a monocular endoscope design, except that there is a specially designed iris diaphragm that has two irises (instead of one) on it. In a normal optical system, replacing a single iris diaphragm with a dual iris diaphragm may result in an image blur because slightly different images coming from different irises may reach the same pixel location, reducing the sharpness of images. However, the optics of a dual iris system are designed such that the footprints of images coming from different irises located in different portions of the sensing area on the single chip, thus facilitating the simultaneous stereo image acquisition using a single chip and single optical channel.

14.4.3 Single Chips with Split Channel Optics Using Prisms

There are many different ways to design split channel optics. For example, one design uses two prisms for left and right sides of a sensing area on the single chip (U.S. Patent application 2005/0141088 [15]). The apparatus comprises three periscope prisms, so the viewing areas of the left and right images are side by side with correct orientation. The optical paths of the left and right channels are separated via the prisms.

Another straightforward way to split the optical channel using a simple prism is shown in Figure 14.6(c) [13]. The refraction of tilted prism surfaces bends optical rays into two optical paths. With careful optical design, the footprints of these two optical paths on the image sensor chip could be separated into two regions, forming a stereo image pair.

14.4.4 Single Chips with Dual Irises and Interlaced Optics

An Israeli company, VisionSense, has introduced a single chip stereo endoscope product, 6.5 mm in diameter, for performing sinus surgeries [16]. The idea of a stereoscopic camera based on a lenticular array was first proposed by the French physicist G. Lippmann. The VisionSense adaptation of this stereoscopic plenoptic camera is shown in Figure 14.7. The 3D object is imaged by a single set of optics with two apertures. This setup generates a telecentric objective in which all the rays passing the center of each aperture emerge as a parallel beam behind the lens. The sensor chip is covered by a sheet of lenticular array—an array of cylindrical microlenses with zero power in the horizontal axis. Each lenticule covers exactly two pixel columns. Rays that pass through a point at the left aperture are emitted as a parallel beam marked in red color. These rays are focused by the lenticular array on the pixels on the right side under the lenslets. Similarly, rays that pass through the

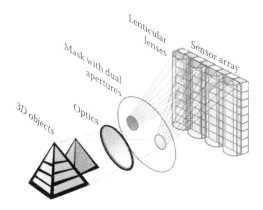

FIGURE 14.7
(See color insert.) VisionSense stereoscopic camera: The camera has a mask with two apertures, a lenticular microlens array in front of the sensor chip. Each lenslet is 2 pixels wide. Rays from the 3D object that pass through the left aperture generate a left view on columns marked with a red color, and rays that pass through the right aperture generate a right view image on neighboring columns marked with a green color. A pair of stereoscopic images is thus generated using a single sensor chip. (Yaron, A. et al. www.visionsense.com.)

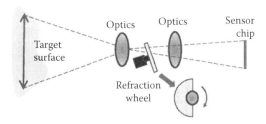

FIGURE 14.8
Single chips with switchable optical paths. (Lee, Y. H. U.S. Patent application 12162482.)

right aperture are focused by the lenslets on the left pixel columns marked in green color.

Thus, a point on the 3D object is imaged twice: once through the left aperture generating an image on the pixel in a red color, and once through the right aperture generating an image on the pixel in a green color. The pair of pixels form a stereoscopic view of the point in the scene. The left and right images can be acquired simultaneously. The distance between a pixel of the left view to that of the right view (disparity) is a function of the distance of the corresponding point from the camera, from which the 3D range can be calculated.

14.4.5 Single Chips with Switchable Optical Paths

U.S. Patent application 2009/0040606 discloses an interesting design of a single chip stereo endoscope [17]. This design (Figure 14.8) utilizes a single optical channel to collect an image from the target and a single image sensor to produce a dynamic stereo image in sequential (even/odd frame) fashion. It places a rotating, transparent half-plate at the entrance pupil position. When the rotating plate is in the position where the transparent plate is not in the optical path of the imaging system, the image sensor acquires a "left" image. When the transparent plate is in the optical path of the imaging system, the optical path is shifted by the refraction of the transparent plate, and the "right" image acquired by the image sensor has parallax disparity from the left image. The rotating angle of the transparent plate is synchronized with the timing of the acquisition frame of the image sensor such that the left and right images of the stereo image pair are acquired in sequential fashion. Using one image sensor, this system is claimed to eliminate the possible dizziness provoked by disparities in focus, zoom, and alignment between two separate images from two sensors.

14.5 3D Acquisition Using a Single Chip with Structured Light

Stereo endoscopes are able to produce stereoscopic views of the target surface for viewing and display. If quantitative 3D (x,y,z) coordinate data of surface points

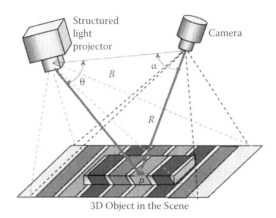

FIGURE 14.9

Illustration of structured light 3D surface imaging principle. (J. Geng, J. 2011. *Advances in Optics and Photonics* 3:128–160. With permission.)

are needed, stereo images can only provide information where two points on the image can be correlated. This can be problematic when little surface texture exists on the target. The correlation process can also require significant processing, so producing a full 3D surface map can be time consuming. It is more typical to correlate only a small number of points needed for basic measurements.

Laser scanners are a popular approach to acquiring 3D surface profile data from a large object. In a typical commercial 3D laser scanner system, a single profile line is controlled to scan across the entire target surface. The data acquired during the scanning process is used to build a 3D profile model of the target surface. Due to the use of a scanning component, it is generally not practical to adopt a similar approach in an endoscope imaging system because of limitations on the miniature dimension of the entire probe size.

One practical method of full-field 3D surface imaging for endoscopes is based on the use of "structured light" (i.e., active illumination of the scene with a specially designed 2D spatially varying intensity pattern) [7]. As illustrated in Figure 14.9, a spatially varying 2D structured illumination is generated by a special projector or a light source modulated by a spatial light modulator. The intensity of each pixel on the structured-light pattern is represented by the digital signal $\{I_{ij} = (i, j), i = 1, 2, \ldots, I, j = 1, 2, \ldots, J\}$, where (i, j) represents the (x,y) coordinate of projected pattern. The structured-light projection patterns discussed herein are 2D patterns.

An imaging sensor (a video camera, for example) is used to acquire a 2D image of the scene under the structured-light illumination. If the scene is a planar surface without any 3D surface variation, the pattern shown in the acquired image is similar to that of the projected structured-light pattern. However, when the surface in the scene is nonplanar, the geometric shape of the surface "distorts" the projected structured-light pattern as seen from the camera. The principle of structured-light 3D surface imaging techniques is to extract the 3D surface shape based on the information from the "distortion" of the projected structured-light pattern. Accurate 3D surface profiles of objects in the scene can be computed using various structured-light principles and algorithms.

As shown in Figure 14.9, the geometric relationship between an imaging sensor, a structured-light projector, and an object surface point can be expressed by the triangulation principle as

$$R = B\frac{\sin(\theta)}{\sin(\alpha+\theta)}$$

The key for triangulation-based 3D imaging is the technique used to differentiate a single projected light spot from the acquired image under a 2D projection pattern. Various schemes have been proposed for this purpose, and this chapter will provide an overview of various methods based on the structured-light illumination.

Numerous techniques for surface imaging by structured light are currently available. However, due to the miniature size and complexity of optical/structural and electronic designs, there is little published literature on using structured light on 3D endoscopic image acquisition.

14.5.1 Structured Light via Instrument Channel

A relatively easy approach to implement 3D surface endoscopic imaging by applying the structured-light technique without building a special endoscope is to insert a miniature structured-light projector via the instrument channel of a regular endoscope. Schubert and Muller [18] presented a structured-light method for bronchoscopy that can be used for measurement of hollow biological organs. For this purpose, a fiber probe projecting a ring of laser light (laser diode, 675 nm) is inserted into the instrument channel.

There is a cone-shaped right angle reflector placed at the end of the fiber such that the fiber light source generates a side-view "sheet of light" around it, forming a "ring of light" on the lumen surface. Using a position registration device, the distance between the tip of the fiber light source and the tip of the camera lens is fixed and known. The 3D profile of target surface is estimated by the deformation of a projected ring of laser light. By viewing the location of the light ring on the image, the diameter of the light ring can be calculated using simple triangulation. By moving the endoscope through the entire length of the lumen section, a complete 3D surface profile of the lumen structure can be obtained. This method enhances the 3D grasp of endoscopically examined lesions.

This method is able to generate only a "ring" of 3D data at one time. To produce 3D surface data, the endoscope has to be moved and its position must be known in order to register a stack of rings into a complete surface profile.

14.5.2 Endoscopic Pulsed Digital Holography for 3D Measurements

Saucedo et al. [19] and Kolenovic et al. [20] have examined the deformation of a 3D scene with an electronic speckle pattern interferometer. A stiff, minimally invasive endoscope is extended with an external holographic camera. Saucedo et al. [19] extended this approach and developed an endoscopic pulsed digital holography approach to endoscopic 3D measurements. A rigid endoscope and three different object illumination source positions are used in pulsed digital holography to measure the three orthogonal displacement components from hidden areas of a harmonically vibrating metallic cylinder. In order to obtain simultaneous 3D information from the optical setup, it is necessary to match the optical paths of each of the reference object beam pairs and to incoherently mismatch the three reference object beam pairs, such that three pulsed digital holograms are incoherently recorded within a single frame of the CCD sensor. The phase difference is obtained using the Fourier method and by subtracting two digital holograms captured for two different object positions.

In the experiment, the high-resolution CCD sensor (1024 × 1024, pixel elements, with an area of $\Delta x \times \Delta x = 9 \ \mu m^2$) receives the image. The depth of field of the endoscope is from 3 to 12 mm and the stand-off distance from the endoscope edge to the object surface may vary from 5 to 25 mm. Pulses from a Nd:YAG laser emitting at 532 nm are divided initially into two beams, one that serves as reference and the other as object. Each beam is further divided into three reference and object beams by means of beam splitters. Each object beam is made to converge with a lens into a multimode optical fiber, and the lens-fiber set is attached to a sliding mechanical component that is later used to adjust the optical path length, like the one introduced by the distance from the endoscope edge to the object surface. The remaining part of the fiber length is attached to the endoscope so that all three object beams illuminate the surface area from three different positions by means of a mechanical support at the end of each fiber. Finally, the three reference beams are sent to the CCD sensor using single mode optical fibers.

The target object in the experiment is a metallic cylinder of 13 mm diameter, 19 mm height, and 0.3 mm width. The cylinder is tightly fixed to a mechanical support so that the imaginary origin of the rectangular coordinate system rests always on its center. The cylinder is harmonically excited using a mechanical shaker on a point perpendicular to the optical axis. The excitation frequencies are scanned so that the resonant modes are identified and one is chosen at 2180 Hz, with the laser pulses fired at a separation of 80 μs so that two object positions are acquired during a vibration cycle. Each pulse captures three incoherent digital holograms and their individual phase difference is obtained by simply subtracting the phase information from one pulse to the other. The displacement information may now be calculated.

14.5.3 Phase Shift Structured Light

Phase shift is a well-known fringe projection method for 3D surface imaging. A set of sinusoidal patterns is projected onto the object surface. The intensities for each pixel (x, y) of the three projected fringe patterns are described as

$$I_1(x, y) = I_0(x, y) + I_{mod}(x, y)\cos\left(\phi(x, y) - \theta\right)$$

$$I_2(x, y) = I_0(x, y) + I_{mod}(x, y)\cos\left(\phi(x, y)\right)$$

$$I_3(x, y) = I_0(x, y) + I_{mod}(x, y)\cos\left(\phi(x, y) + \theta\right)$$

where
$I_1(x, y), I_2(x, y)$, and $I_3(x, y)$ are the intensities of three fringe patterns
$I_0(x, y)$ is the DC component (background)
$I_{mod}(x, y)$ is the modulation signal amplitude
$\phi(x, y)$ is the phase
θ is the constant phase shift angle

Since there are multiple lines in the acquired images, which line is which (or absolute phase) must be determined in order to calculate an accurate 3D surface profile. The absolute phase at a given point in the image is defined as the total phase difference (2π times the number of line periods) between a reference point in the projected line pattern and the given point. Phase unwrapping is the process that converts the wrapped phase to the absolute phase. The phase information can be retrieved (i.e., unwrapped) from the intensities in the three fringe patterns:

$$\phi'(x, y) = \arctan\left[\sqrt{3}\,\frac{I_1(x, y) - I_3(x, y)}{2I_2(x, y) - I_1(x, y) - I_3(x, y)}\right]$$

The discontinuity of arc tangent function at 2π can be removed by adding or subtracting multiples of 2π on the $\phi'(x, y)$ value:

$$\phi(x, y) = \phi'(x, y) + 2k\pi$$

where k is an integer representing projection period.

Note that unwrapping methods only provide a relative unwrapping and do not solve for the absolute phase. The 3D (x, y, z) coordinates can be calculated based on the difference between measured phase $\phi(x, y)$ and the phase value from a reference plane [7]. In a simple case,

$$\frac{Z}{L-Z} = \frac{d}{B}, \quad \text{or} \quad Z = \frac{L-Z}{B}d$$

Simplifying the relationship leads to

$$Z \approx \frac{L}{B}d \propto \frac{L}{B}(\phi - \phi_0)$$

Phase-shifting methods have not been practical for use in miniature imaging devices such as borescopes and endoscopes. The components required to produce suitable line pattern projections for phase-shifting methods typically comprise a projector, scanner, piezomirror, etc. Among other things, miniature moving parts are extremely difficult to fabricate and maintain reliably in long-term operation, and the size limitations of miniature probes on endoscopes make the use of these components structurally challenging.

Armbruster and Scheffler [1] developed a prototype of an endoscope that measures the 3D scene by deformation of several projected lines. The accuracy of this structured-light method is increased by a phase shift of the lines. U.S. Patent 7,821,649 B2 [21] proposed a phase shift pattern projection mechanism, which involves no moving parts, that can be built in miniature size.

The illumination device on an endoscopic probe comprises multiple independently controllable light emitters and a fringe pattern mask, as shown in Figure 14.10. When one of the emitters is on, it generates a fringe pattern on the surface of the 3D object in the scene. When another emitter is on, it also generates fringe patterns on the 3D object, but with an offset in the horizontal

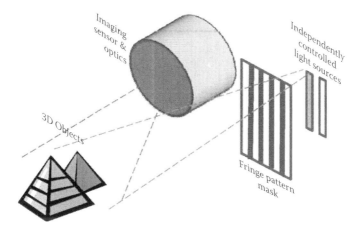

FIGURE 14.10
U.S. Patent 7,821,649 B2 proposed a phase shift pattern projection mechanism that involves no moving parts and miniature size. (Bendall, C. A. et al. U.S. Patent 7,821,649 B2. GE Inspection Technologies.)

position. This mechanism facilitates generation of sequential fringe projection patterns with controllable offset on horizontal positions and thus can be used to produce the phase shift projection patterns for structured-light-based 3D surface imaging.

Each of the fringe sets comprises a structured-light pattern that is projected when one emitter group of light emitters is emitting. The probe further comprises an image sensor for obtaining an image of the surface and a processing unit that is configured to perform phase shift analysis on the image. An imaging sensor is placed on the side of the fringe pattern generator with known geometric parameters with respect to the location of fringe pattern generator. The 3D surface image can be calculated using the phase shift principle.

14.5.4 Spectrally Encoded Structured Light

Researchers at Imperial College London, UK, developed a structured light scheme that uses a flexible fiber bundle to generate multispectral structured illumination that labels each projected point with a specific wavelength. Figure 14.11 illustrates the principle of the spectral illumination generation. A supercontinuum laser is used as a "white light" source. In the visible spectral range (400 ~ 700 nm), variation of the emission spectrum of the supercontinuum laser source is within a reasonable range and can be used as a broadband light source. The broadband laser light from the supercontinuum is dispersed by a prism. The rainbow spectrum light is then coupled into the end of a linear array of a fiber bundle, which consists of 127 cores with 50 μm in diameter. The linear array of the fiber bundle then forms a flexible noncoherent fiber bundle of the required length (up to several meters) to pass the spectral light illumination to the distal end of the probe.

At the distal end, the fibers with different spectral colors are randomly placed. The projected color pattern is a magnified image of the end face of the bundle formed by the projection lens. The identification and segmentation of each light spot is based on recovery of the peak wavelength of each spot, using knowledge of the relationship between the red–green–blue color space and the wavelength of the light.

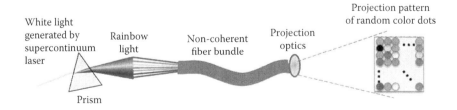

FIGURE 14.11
(See color insert.) Spectrally encoded fiber-based structured lighting probe. (Clancy, N. T. et al. *Biomedical Optics Express* 2:3119–3128. With permission.)

Using the spectrally encoded fiber bundle as the structured light and a video camera (CCD/CMOS) as imaging sensor, a 3D endoscope can be constructed to acquire real-time 3D surface images. Reconstructed 3D data for ovine kidney, porcine liver, and fatty tissue have varying physical features (convex/concave curve, "step" discontinuity, and miscellaneous "fine" structure). The reconstructed surface profiles were observed to match the observed surface profiles of the tissues well, which can be observed in the color photographs presented. These tests demonstrate that the technique may be applied on ex vivo tissue, while the validation with the test objects demonstrates the accuracy that may be obtained.

14.6 Future Directions of Endoscopic 3D Imaging

Three-dimensional endoscopic surface imaging is an exciting new frontier for 3D surface imaging technology development. Numerous methods and approaches have been proposed and tested in laboratories. However, tremendous work still has to be done in order to bridge 3D imaging technology to the practical applications of medical diagnosis and treatment and industrial inspection.

There are several challenges in the future development of 3D surface imaging endoscopes:

1. *Miniaturization of instruments:* Applications always demand smaller, faster, more accurate, and cheaper instrument tools. In terms of size (diameter), existing endoscope products have an array of options ranging from 4 to 15 mm. The endoscpes with these sizes may suffice most application needs. However, there are certain applications for which smaller endoscopes would be ideal—for accessing smaller holes in industrial inspection or for minimizing damage of skin for minimally invasive surgery.

2. *Lack of consistent and reliable surface features for performing 3D reconstruction:* Biological tissues and lumen surfaces are notoriously difficult for performing feature extraction, correlation, and 3D reconstruction, due to lack of consistent and reliable surface features.

3. *Trade-off between miniature size and required baseline for triangulation:* As we know, to achieve a certain accuracy level, 3D surface imaging techniques relying on triangulation require sufficient length of baseline separation. On the other hand, the miniature size of endoscopes places a physical limitation on the length of the baseline. One of the challenges in 3D endoscopes is the trade-off between smaller diameter and sufficient baseline.

4. *Go beyond the surface imaging:* Some applications in both industrial inspection and medical imaging demand subsurface or even volumetric 3D imaging capability. New technologies will have to be developed in order to extend the capability of current 3D surface imaging endoscopes into these new territories.

5. *Seamless integration with existing 2D endoscopes:* Most users of endoscopes prefer a 3D endoscope that can perform all functions of existing 2D endoscopes and, upon demand, perform 3D surface imaging functions. In practical applications, it is unreasonable to ask a user to use a separate 3D endoscope when he or she needs to acquire 3D surface images. The seamless integration of a 3D surface imaging capability into existing 2D endoscopes is important.

Although exciting progress has been made in terms of developing a variety of 3D imaging methods for endoscopes, we are still far away from achieving our ultimate goal, which is to develop viable hardware and software technology that can provide the unique capability of 3D surface imaging with the comparable image quality, speed, and system cost of 2D counterparts.

The field of true 3D surface technology is still quite young compared to its 2D counterpart, which has developed over several decades. It is our hope that this overview chapter provides some stimulation and attraction for more talented people to this fascinating field of research and development.

References

1. Armbruster and Scheffler. 2006. US endoscope markets. F441-54, www.frost.com.
2. Frost and Sullivan. 2004. Endoscopy marketers—Industry overview.
3. Millennium Research Group. 2006. US markets for laparoscopic devices 2006. April.
4. Millennium Research Group. 2004. US markets for arthroscopy, 2005. November.
5. C. M. Lee, C. J. Engelbrecht, T. D. Soper, F. Helmchen, and E. J. Seibel. 2010. Scanning fiber endoscopy with highly flexible, 1-mm catheterscopes for wide-field, full-color imaging. *Journal Biophotonics* 3 (5–6):385–407.
6. C. A. Bendall et al. Fringe projection system and method for a probe using a coherent fiber bundle. U.S. Patent 7812968 (GE Inspection Technologies).
7. J. Geng. 2011. Structured-light 3D surface imaging: A tutorial. *Advances Optics Photonics* 3:128–160.
8. Intuitive Surgical System, www.intuitivesurgical.com.
9. M. Chiba. Stereoscopic-vision endoscope system provided with function of electrically correcting distortion of image. U.S. Patent 5860912 (Olympus Optical Co.).

10. Japanese patent 28278/1993.
11. S. Takahashi et al. Stereoscopic endoscope objective lens system having a plurality of front lens group. U.S. Patent 5743846 (Olympus Optical Co.).
12. Everest XLG3™ VideoProbe® System operating manual by GE Inspection Technologies. www.everestvit.pL/pdf/GEST-65042.xlg3brochure.pdf.
13. J. Geng. 2010. Novel ultra-miniature flexible videoscope for on-orbit NDE. Technical report.
14. K. Ogawa. Endoscope apparatus, method of operating the endoscope apparatus. U.S. Patent 7,443,488 (Olympus Optical Co.)
15. J. A. Christian. Apparatus for the optical manipulation of a pair of landscape stereoscopic images. U.S. Patent application 2005/0141088.
16. A. Yaron et al. Blur spot limitations in distal endoscope sensors. www.visionsense.com.
17. Y. H. Lee. 3-Dimensional moving image photographing device for photographing. U.S. Patent application 12162482.
18. M. Schubert and A. Müller. 1998. Evaluation of endoscopic images for 3-dimensional measurement of hollow biological organs. *Biomedizinische Technik* (Berlin) 43:32–33.
19. A. T. Saucedo, F. Mendoza Santoyo, M. De la Torre-Ibarra, G. Pedrini, and W. Osten. 2006. Endoscopic pulsed digital holography for 3D measurements. *Optics Express* 14 (4):1468–1475.
20. E. Kolenovic, W. Osten, R. Klattenhoff, S. Lai, C. von Kopylow, and W. Jüptner. 2003. Miniaturized digital holography sensor for distal three-dimensional endoscopy. *Applied Optics* 42 (25):5167–5172.
21. Bendall, C. A. et al. Fringe projection system and method for a probe suitable for phase-shift analysis. U.S. Patent 7,821,649 B2 (GE Inspection Technologies).
22. N. T. Clancy, D. Stoyanov, L. Maier-Hein, A. Groch, G.-Z. Yang, and D. S. Elson. 2011. Spectrally encoded fiber-based structured lighting probe for intraoperative 3D imaging. *Biomedical Optics Express* 2:3119–3128.
23. J. Geng. 2009. Video-to-3D: Gastrointestinal tract 3D modeling software for capsule cameras. Technical report.
24. J. Geng. 1996. Rainbow three-dimensional camera: New concept of high-speed three-dimensional vision systems. *Optical Engineering* 35:376–383. doi:10.1117/1.601023.
25. J. Geng. 2008. 3D volumetric display for radiation therapy planning. *IEEE Journal of Display Technology,* Special Issue on Medical Display 4 (4):437–450, invited paper.
26. J. Geng. 2011. Overview of 3D surface measurement technologies and applications: Opportunities for DLP®-based structured illumination. *Emerging Digital Micromirror Device Based Systems and Applications III* (Conference 7932), SPIE Photonics West, CA, Jan., invited paper.
27. R. Y. Tsai. 1987. A versatile camera calibration technique for high-accuracy 3D machine vision metrology using off-the-shelf cameras and lenses. *IEEE Transactions on Robotics and Automation* 3 (4):323–344.
28. R. M. Soetikno, T. Kaltenbach, R. V. Rouse, W. Park, A. Maheshwari, T. Sato, S. Matsui, and S. Friedland. 2008. Prevalence of nonpolypoid (flat and depressed) colorectal neoplasms in asymptomatic and symptomatic adults. *JAMA* 299 (9):1027–1035.

15

Biometrics Using 3D Vision Techniques

Maria De Marsico, Michele Nappi, and Daniel Riccio

CONTENTS

Scientists claim that sometimes just 20 seconds are enough time in which to recognize a person. However, the human ability to recognize a person is quite limited to people who are closer or that have been known or associated with. On the contrary, an automatic identification system may require a longer time for recognition, but is able to recognize people in a larger set of potential identities. Nowadays, the most popular biometric identification system is certainly represented by fingerprints. However, present biometric techniques are numerous and include, for example, those exploiting hand shapes, iris scanning, face and ear feature extraction, handwriting recognition, and voice recognition. Early biometric systems were implemented by exploiting one-dimensional (1D) features such as voice sound, as well as two-dimensional (2D) ones such as images from fingerprints or the face. With technology advances and cost decreases, better and better devices and capture techniques have become available. These have been investigated and adopted in biometric settings too. Image vision techniques have not been excluded from this evolution-supported acceleration. The increase of computational resources has supported the development of stereo vision and multiview reconstruction. Later, three-dimensional (3D) capture devices, such as laser or structured-light scanners as well as ultrasound-based systems, were introduced. The third dimension has therefore represented a significant advancement for the implementation of more and more accurate and efficient recognition systems. However, it also presents new challenges and new limits not yet overcome, which are the main motivation for the research in this context.

15.1 2D, 3D, 2D + 3D Biometrics

Traditional automatic identification systems may be divided into two categories: *knowledge based,* which exploit information that the user must know, such as user name, login, and password, and *token based,* which exploit special objects like smart-cards, magnetic cards, keys, etc. Both approaches present weaknesses, since passwords may be forgotten or guessed by others, and objects may be lost, stolen, or duplicated. *Biometrics* allows recognizing a subject according to physical or behavioral features, and its usage potential is very high: access control for critical areas such as penitentiary structures, an investigation tool for search and identification of missing persons or criminals, subject identification during bank transactions, immigration control, authentication during computer and network use, and local as well as remote procedures. A human feature can be considered a biometric key suitable for recognition if it satisfies the following requirements:

- *Universality:* each person must own the biometric trait.
- *Uniqueness:* two persons must be sufficiently distinguishable according to the biometric trait.
- *Permanence:* the biometric trait must resist aging.
- *Collectability:* the biometric trait must be easy to capture and quantitatively measurable.

It is possible to claim that no biometric key is optimal by itself, but rather there is a wide range of possible choices. Selecting one or another depends on the system at hand and on the controlled context. Different factors play their role in the choice of the biometrics to use (face, fingerprint, iris) and of the capturing and processing modality (infrared, thermic, 2D, 3D). Among them, ambient conditions and user typology are particularly important. The operating setting may heavily influence device performance and biometric trait stability, while a user may be *cooperative* (interested in being recognized) or *noncooperative* (uninterested or unaware of the recognition process).

15.1.1 Some 2D Biometrics and Their Limits

Biometric traits can be further classified into *physiological* and *behavioral*. Biometrics in the first category are related to the way a person is and appears, and they tend to be more stable in time; examples are fingerprints, face appearance, ear morphology, and configuration of the retina's blood vessels. On the other hand, behavioral biometrics reflects an aspect of the person's attitude and therefore depends on psychology and habits. This causes such biometric traits to be more variable in time. Many biometrics have been studied over the years (see Figure 15.1).

- *DNA* (deoxyribonucleic acid) represents the most reliable identification code for a person, despite the number of similarities that can be found among relatives. Though widely exploited in forensics for identification, it does not represent a viable biometric technique since many factors limit its use (most of all, the required time, the required equipment, and its being seen as a form of intrusiveness).

- Deep medical investigations have demonstrated that the *ear* complies with the main principles of biometrics. Its advantages are the limited area, which allows faster processing; and the lack of expression variations, which limits intraclass differences. However, it undergoes strong variations when the subject is not aligned with respect to neck rotations (i.e., when the ear is not perfectly frontal with respect to the capture device).

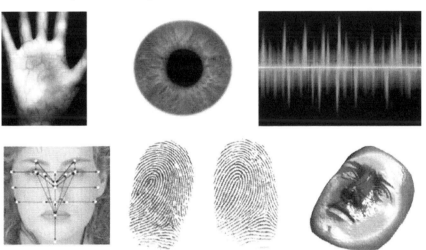

FIGURE 15.1
Some examples of existing biometric traits: vein patterns, iris, voice, 2D face, fingerprints, 3D face.

- The *face* is the most immediate feature through which we recognize a person. However, it presents a number of limitations that are difficult to overcome and limit its reliability. As a matter of fact, though it is faster and more accepted because it is less invasive, this form of identification is far from the recognition rates assured by fingerprints.

- *Fingerprints* are legally recognized as a highly reliable biometric technique and have been long exploited for civil as well as military identification and for incrimination of suspect subjects. Even the FBI has adopted such biometrics as an identification system so that it is surely the most accepted among invasive biometrics. Moreover, since fingerprints were proposed as an identification trait about 50 years ago, we have both wide and deep studies on the topic, as well as many very efficient algorithms that are the core of most present systems. Though especially reliable, fingerprints are not suited for online systems or when the user is not aware or consenting.

- *Gait* is a unique trait and represents a complex spatial biometrics. It is not so distinctive, yet provides sufficient recognition features for a low-security system. Moreover, it provides the same features of acceptability and noninvasiveness of other biometric techniques such as face recognition or thermography. Disadvantages come from the variability in time: A person's way of walking may vary due to a number of factors, such as age, weight, and alcohol use. Moreover, this technique is based on a video capture of steps, and therefore measurement and analysis of the joints' movements require a high computational cost.

- *Hand and fingers geometry* is a consolidated technique based on the capture of the image of an open hand on a guide panel. Hand features like shape, palm width, finger dimensions, etc., are relatively invariant and peculiar, though not very distinctive. Among advantages, we have a good acceptability from the user supported by a relative computational speed and compactness of extracted features. Disadvantages come from the limited distinctiveness, which limits its large-scale use and supports its use as a verification technique.

- The formation of the human *iris* is determined by morphological processes during embryonic development. The iris is part of an annular muscle that allows the amount of light that reaches the eye retina to vary. The layout of radial muscle fibers and their color represent a unique biometric feature for each subject. This feature is captured from the objective of a small color camera while the subject looks at it. This biometrics assures a very high distinctiveness for each eye, even of the same person, and therefore offers accuracy and reliability levels higher than those of other biometrics. The great disadvantage comes from its acceptability and from the necessary user cooperation during the capturing process.

- *Signature* is a quite distinctive feature that is commonly used to verify identity in different settings. It is easy to capture and highly accepted by most users. Disadvantages come from the high variability of the trait due to different factors. This requires a very robust system for effective recognition and does not assure high genuineness levels since it can be easily forged by experts.
- *Voice* recognition is highly accepted, like the signature; the voice can be easily captured and processed. Disadvantages are the great instability of the feature, which can be conditioned by many factors, and the ease of forging it.

15.1.2 The Third Dimension in Biometric Systems

Most research in the field related to biometric systems has long regarded 1D or 2D capture sources, such as voice, face, ear, or fingerprint. However, we recently experimented with a fast technological evolution and a related decrease of the costs of hardware components and devices, like 3D scanners, *motion capture* devices, or multicamera hardware and software. These factors spurred research interest toward solutions that had formerly appeared not to be viable. We can mention gait analysis and recognition, as well as 3D face and ear recognition. The amount of work devoted to 3D face recognition is surely outstanding among biometric 3D techniques. The related range of methodologies is very wide and spans from the adaptation of 2D techniques to the 3D setting to the implementation of specific approaches for this kind of information. The third dimension allows at least limiting, if not overcoming, many problems related to face recognition (e.g., pose and illumination variations). In second place we find the ear, for which the third dimension surely represents a way to address problems related to location of such a trait in an in-profile image. As a matter of fact, the upper part of the ear presents an extremely marked curvature, which is much more easily identified within a 3D model.

The counterpart of this higher richness of information and therefore of the higher achievable recognition accuracy is represented by the huge amount of data to process. This causes some complex problems, which are far easier in 2D, especially for data normalization and preprocessing. One of the main problems in 3D settings is the alignment of the (biometric) models of two objects before classification—for instance, two faces. This is because it is not possible to define a canonical pose, and there are more degrees of freedom. Biometric applications have inherited alignment algorithms commonly used in other 3D settings, most of all the iterative closest point (ICP) technique. This iterative technique requires a reference model as input and a model to align, and it modifies the pose of the latter until a distance criterion between the two is minimized. This algorithm presents two significant disadvantages that mainly derive from the fact that it does not exploit any specific knowledge about the object at hand.

Rather, it operates on three-dimensional shapes in the general sense, and therefore it is slow and does not guarantee convergence to a unique pose.

The types of data operated by a 3D classification system can be of different natures, though in most cases we can reduce them to two standard cases: *point clouds* and *polygon meshes.* Point clouds that are too dense or meshes that are too complex might require a huge amount of computation and therefore significantly slow down the system. A way to get around this problem is *subsampling,* where the number of points in the cloud (or of polygons in the mesh) is pruned to obtain a simpler representation, though as representative as possible. Therefore, such pruning is not performed at random, but is based on discarding those points with less representative results according to a predefined criterion. Another important preprocessing step for data captured through a 3D device is region smoothing, which smoothes parts of the model that are too sharp in order to facilitate the location of possible curvature zones, like in the ear.

15.1.3 3D Capture Systems

At present different technologies exist that can provide a three-dimensional reproduction of the captured object, according to working principles that can be very different. Of course, each has specific features that make it preferable in specific settings as well as unadvisable in others.

One of the earliest among the previously mentioned techniques is stereo vision, where the scene is captured by two or more cameras which are calibrated among them. In other terms, the intrinsic and extrinsic parameters of single cameras are known in advance (through the process known as calibration), and this makes it possible to compute the depth of the scene, as well as of the objects within it, through a triangulation technique. The main critical point in this approach is in searching corresponding scene points in different images. An alternative introduced in relatively recent years is represented by laser scanners. Even in this case, if the relevant object is within a quite limited distance, its three-dimensional reconstruction exploits triangulation, based on laser light. Limiting factors for the diffusion of this technology in biometric settings are elapsed times (from many seconds to some minutes) and still relatively high costs.

A further evolution is represented by structured-light scanners. Though based on a triangulation process, these scanners are different because a specific pattern is projected over the object to be captured to increase the location precision of corresponding points. The main limit of scanners exploiting structured light is just this projection of a visible pattern on the object. In the specific case of face biometrics, this may result particularly in discomfort for the user. In 1998 Raskar et al. [1], at the University of North Carolina, implemented the first imperceptible structured-light scanner. The working principle is based on the idea of projecting a pattern and its inverse in a consecutive way and at an extremely high speed. In this way the subject should perceive only the white light. Despite the proof of concept, many aspects of this technology must still be improved. An alternative solution is the projection of the pattern within the infrared spectrum.

In addition to optical systems, other 3D capturing technologies are spreading (e.g., ultrasound [2]). These present some advantages with respect to other systems. For example, they are not influenced by surface tainting factors like stains or dirt or by skin temperature; moreover, they are able to provide information about the skin surface and about the thin layer underneath, therefore allowing one to obtain a 3D volume of tissues just under the skin (about 10 mm). Such capture devices have been exploited especially for fingerprints and palm prints. Scanning time may be reduced by using scanner arrays, which are able to scan a whole line of points at a time, instead of X–Y scanners, which scan the surface point by point.

Signature recognition requires totally different devices to capture related data. In particular, classical systems exploit devices equipped with accelerometers and gyroscopes, allowing capture of speed and angle of hand movements while a document is signed. In other cases, it is not the pen but rather the signing surface that is equipped with sensors—tablets with different layers with different sensitivity—to measure pen pressure on the paper. Only recently, devices that also record the sound from the point of a ballpoint pen when it moves on the paper during a signature have been introduced. As we can see, even these devices are reaching an extremely high level of complexity, in the same way as technologies adopted for image and volume capture.

15.2 Face

Evaluations such as FERET (face recognition technology) tests and the face recognition vendor test 2002 [3] have underlined that the current state of the art in 2D face recognition is not yet sufficient for biometric applications. As a matter of fact, the performance of the 2D face recognition algorithms is still heavily affected by the pose and illumination conditions of the subject. Much effort has been spent to overcome these drawbacks, but the obtained results in terms of recognition rate confirmed that this is a very hard problem. Nowadays, the 3D capturing process is becoming cheaper and faster and recent work has attempted to solve the problem directly on a 3D model of the face (see Figure 15.2). Few databases of 3D face models are publically available at present; moreover, in most cases the number of subjects is limited and the quality is often very low.

The constant progress of 3D capturing technologies also influenced the kinds of recognition algorithms. The first algorithms directly processed clouds of points [4] after a suitable triangulation, while the more recent ones work on

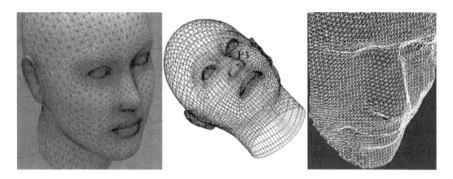

FIGURE 15.2
Examples of 3D meshes of human faces.

a mesh, considering in some cases the information provided by both the 3D shape and the texture. The 3D RMA (Royal Military Academy) [5] is an example of a database of 3D face models represented by clouds of points. It has long been the only publicly available database, even if its quality is quite low. On the other hand, 3D meshes (wrl, 3ds, etc.) are available today from the newer technologies, but in most cases they are just part of proprietary databases.

The vast majority of face recognition research and all of the main commercial face recognition systems use normal intensity images of the face. All these methods are referred to as 2D. On the other hand, 3D techniques consider the whole shape of the head. Since the early work on 3D face recognition was done over 15 years ago and the number of published papers is rapidly growing, a brief description of the most interesting algorithms in the literature follows.

Some of the first approaches to 3D face recognition worked on range data directly obtained by range sensors, due to the lower costs of this hardware compared with the laser scanners used, for example, by Gordon [6]. As a matter of fact, in Achermann, Jiang, and Bunke [7], the range images are captured by means of a structured-light approach. The most important potential disadvantage of this choice is the lack of some data due to occlusions or improperly reflected regions. This problem can be avoided by using two sensors, rather than one, and applying a merging step for integrating the obtained 3D data.

The initial step is sensor calibration so that such parameters as projection matrix, camera direction, etc., are computed. Then, merged images are computed; for every original 3D data point, the coordinates in the merged range image are computed according to the parameters of the virtual sensor. If 3D points of two different surfaces have to be mapped onto the same pixel, a sort of z-buffering is applied to disambiguate the mapping. The template images obtained from this acquisition process are then used as training and testing sets for two different approaches.

The first approach exploits eigenfaces. The dimension of the space of face templates is reduced by applying principal component analysis (PCA) for both training and testing so that, for each testing image, the nearest one in terms of Euclidean distance is searched. Another method, exploiting HMMs (hidden Markov models), is also tested on the template images. As this technique is only applicable on 1D signals, the template images are first transformed into a monodimensional signal by means of a sliding window that moves along the image from the top to the bottom and from the left to the right. The involved HMM has five states. For every person in the database, the parameters of the HMM are calculated in a training phase. When a test image is presented, the probability of producing this image is computed by means of the Viterbi algorithm.

In 2D approaches, the features used in describing faces are still often limited to eyes, nose, mouth, and face boundaries, while neglecting the additional information provided by low-contrast areas, such as jaw boundary, cheeks, and forehead. Therefore, it is clear that an approach based on range and curvature data has several advantages over intensity image approaches thanks to the higher amount of available information. Furthermore, curvature has the valuable characteristic of being *viewpoint invariant.* Gordon [6] proposed a method that defines a set of high-level regions (e.g., eyes, nose, and head), including the following features: *nose bridge* (nasion), *nose base* (base of septum), *nose ridge, eye corner cavities* (inner and outer), *convex center of the eye* (eyeball), *eye socket boundary, boundary surrounding nose,* and *opposing positions on the cheeks.* Each of these regions on the face image is described in terms of a set of relations of depth and curvature values.

Since several regions can fulfill a set of constraints, this set is designed in order to reduce the search to a single definition of the feature. The set of constraints is given by

- Sign of Gaussian and mean curvature
- Absolute extent of a region on the surface
- Distance from the symmetry plane
- Proximity to a target on the surface
- Protrusion from the surrounding surface
- Local configuration of curvature extremes

The high-level features and regions are used to compute a set of low-level features, where the most basic scalar features correspond to measurements of distances. The set of low-level descriptors is given by *left and right eye width; eye separation; total span of eyes; nose height, width, depth; head width; maximum Gaussian curvature on the nose ridge; average minimum curvature on the nose ridge;* and *Gaussian curvature at the nose bridge and base.* For each face image, this set of features is computed, placing it in the space of all possible faces, while the Euclidean distance is used as a measure in the scaled feature space.

Other approaches directly work on clouds of 3D points, like the algorithm proposed by Xu et al. [4], which applies to the face models of the 3D RMA database (models are represented by scattered point clouds). The first problem to be addressed consists of building the mesh from the clouds of points. This is done by means of an iterative algorithm. The nose tip is localized first as the most prominent point in the point cloud. Then a basic mesh is aligned with the point cloud, subdivided, and tuned step by step. Four steps are considered to be enough for the refinement process. Point clouds have different orientations, and resulting meshes preserve this orientation; an average model is computed and all the meshes are aligned with it by tuning six parameters for the rotations and six for the translations. Due to possible noise, some built mesh models cannot describe the geometric shape of the individual. These mesh models are called nonface models. Each mesh contains 545 nodes and is used as a bidimensional intensity image in which the intensity of the pixel is the Z-coordinate of the corresponding node. The eigenfaces technique is applied to these intensity images. After computing the similarity differences between test samples and the training data, the nearest neighbor (NN) classifier and the k-nearest neighbor (KNN) classifier are used for recognition.

The 3D morphable model-based approach [8] has been shown to be one of the most promising ones among all those presented in the literature. This face recognition system combines deformable 3D models with a computer graphics simulation of projection and illumination. Given a single image of a person, the algorithm automatically estimates 3D shape, texture, and all relevant 3D scene parameters. The morphable face model is based on a vector space representation of faces. This space is constructed such that any convex combination of the examples belonging to the space describes a human face. In order to assure that continuous changes on coefficients represent a transition from one face to another, avoiding artifacts, a dense point-to-point correspondence constraint has to be guaranteed. This is done by means of a generalization of the optical flow technique on gray-level images to the three-dimensional surfaces.

Two vectors, **S** and **T**, are directly extracted from the 3D model, where **S** is the concatenation of the Cartesian coordinates (x, y, z) of the 3D points and **T** is the concatenation of the corresponding texture information (R, G, B). Furthermore, the PCA is applied to the vectors S_i and T_i of the example faces $i = 1, 2, \ldots, m$, while Phong's model is used to describe the diffuse and specular reflection of the surface. In this way, an average morphable model is derived from training scans (obtained with a laser scanner). Then, by means of a cost function, the fitting algorithm optimizes a set of shape coefficients and texture coefficients along with 22 rendering parameters concatenated in a feature vector ρ (e.g., pose angles, 3D translations, focal length).

A similar approach, but working on two orthogonal images, has been proposed by Ansari and Mottaleb [9]. This method uses the 3D coordinates of a set of facial feature points, calculated from two images of a subject, in order to deform a generic 3D face model. Images are grabbed by two cameras with perpendicular optical axes. The 3D generic model is centered and aligned by means of Procrustes analysis, which models the global deformation, while local deformations are described by means of 3D spline curves. The front and profile view of a subject are used in order to locate facial features, such as eyes and mouth, by means of a probabilistic approach. This model contains 29 vertices divided into two subsets: 15 principal vertices and 14 additional vertices.

A multimodal approach combining results from both 3D and 2D recognition has been investigated by Wang, Chua, and Ho [10]. The method applies on both range data and texture. In the 3D domain, the point signature is used in order to describe the shape of the face, while the Gabor filters are applied on the texture in order to locate and characterize 10 control points (e.g., corners of the eyes, nose tip, corners of the mouth). The PCA analysis is then applied separately to the obtained 3D and 2D feature vectors, and the resulting vectors are integrated to form an augmented vector that is used to represent each facial image. For a given test facial image, the best match in the galley is identified according to a similarity function or SVM (support vector machine).

One limitation to some existing approaches to 3D face recognition involves sensitivity to size variation. Approaches that use a purely curvature-based representation, such as extended Gaussian images, are not able to distinguish between two faces of similar shape but different size. Approaches based on PCA or ICP avoid this problem, but their performance falls down when changes in expression are present between gallery and probe images. Even multimodal recognition systems require more sophisticated combination strategies. As a matter of fact, in most cases, the score results are computed separately for 2D and 3D and then combined together. It is at least potentially more powerful to exploit possible synergies between the two modalities.

15.3 Ear

The ear represents a rich and stable biometric trait. It can be easily captured at a distance even with unaware subjects, though, in this case, it might be partially occluded by hair and/or earrings. Research has been especially focused on implementing processing and matching techniques based on 2D images, which are, however, strongly influenced by subject pose and by illumination conditions during capture. Addressing such limitations is possible by working on three-dimensional models of the ear captured by range sensors, laser scanners, or structured-light scanners. These captured 3D models are far less sensitive to pose and illumination and allow a significant precision increase during both segmentation and matching. Yan and Bowyer [11] demonstrated that 3D system performance is significantly higher than that from 2D methods.

Even for the ear, the pipeline of a 3D-based system is generally not much different from that of a 2D system, but for the capture and analysis tools. The scene reconstructed from a 3D capture system undergoes a detection process to locate the ear region. The ear is then segmented and processed to extract the features used for matching with other feature vectors from different ear models. However, in some cases, it may happen that the sequence of steps is slightly different, due to a specific capture method or to a nonconventional matching method. For instance, this is the case for techniques that exploit the reconstruction of a model through stereoscopic vision or through shape-from-shading techniques starting from video frames (more details follow).

15.3.1 Ear Capture

Many 3D approaches for ear recognition are based on range data capture (see Figure 15.3). Higher robustness of such systems to pose and illumination is obtained at the cost of often too expensive devices, which are further characterized by the requirement of an almost complete immobility of the subject for a time lapse of some seconds. On the other hand, 2D image capture is quite easy and viable in many scenarios where 3D standard technology is not usable. For these reasons, research has focused on techniques able to reconstruct 3D information from 2D samples (images). As for the ear, the techniques that are most used and have undergone most progressive improvements are multiview reconstruction (MVR), structure from motion (SFM), and shape from shading (SFS).

Liu, Yan, and Zhang [12] proposed a semiautomatic method, where motion analysis and multiview epipolar geometry are the foundations of the 3D model reconstruction process. In a first attempt, the correspondence between homologous points of the ear in different images is identified automatically through Harris corner detection and the RANSAC (random-sample consensus)

FIGURE 15.3
(a) Range image, (b) visible image, and (c) rendering of the image according to range information of an ear.

algorithm. However, the limited number of obtained correspondences suggested that the authors introduce a further step of manual adjustment, based on an interactive process of ear contour division, to locate correspondences. Though this increases the number of correspondences, the obtained model still presents a relatively limited number of vertices (330–600), which provide a point cloud (or even a mesh) more sparse than the one that can be obtained through a pure 3D capture system (range scanner, structured light).

Zhou, Cadavid, and Abdel-Mottaleb [19] and Cadavid and Abdel-Mottaleb [20] focused their attention on reconstruction techniques from video, along two different lines: structure from motion and shape from shading. In SFM, ear image details are discarded through a smoothing process based on force field. The output of this process is the input for the edge detection implemented through the ridges and ravines detection algorithm. Tracking of characteristic points is performed through the Kanade–Lucas–Tomasi algorithm [21], while the reconstruction of the 3D model is produced by the algorithm by Tomasi and Kanade. Matching between two different ear models is computed according to the partial Hausdorff distance (PHD).

Along the other line, the SFS algorithm extracts a set of frames from a video and independently processes each of them. It first locates the ear region and then approximates its 3D structure through the actual shape-from-shading algorithm. The models obtained are aligned through the ICP algorithm so that recognition can be performed by cross validation. Even this approach presents some disadvantages: first of all, sensitivity to illumination variations since it derives depth information from scene reflectance features.

In order to address some of the limitations of SFM and SFS techniques, Zeng et al. [13] proposed an improvement of the SFM model where images are captured by a pair of calibrated cameras; the scale invariant features transform, together with a coarse to fine policy, is used to identify matches between corresponding points. The 3D ear model is computed through triangulation and refined through a bundle adjustment technique.

15.3.2 Recognition Process

In their first work in 2004, Chen and Bhanu [14] only addressed the ear location problem, without reporting any results regarding recognition rates. The first step of their algorithm applies a step edge detection associated with a threshold to identify the most evident contours (sharp edges) in regions surrounding the ear. This first step is followed by a dilation of contour points and by a search for connected components, whose labeling process aims at determining all candidate regions. Each such region is represented by a rectangle, which is expanded toward the four main directions to minimize the distance from a reference template that has been computed in advance. The region with the minimum distance is then considered the ear region.

In a following work [22], the same authors provided a description of a complete ear recognition system. The detection phase was far more refined than the one in the previous work and enriched with more details. Skin detection was performed according to the statistical model presented by Jones and Rehg [16]. Characteristic points are put in correspondence through a local-to-global registration procedure, instead of training a reference template. Global registration focuses on helix and antihelix regions and is therefore performed through the DARCES [17] algorithm, which solves the problem of aligning rigid structures without any prealignment. A local deformation process is performed after global registration. Matching between two models (probe/gallery) is partly based on information from the helix/antihelix alignment process, which is performed during the detection phase (information about the global rigid transformation that is initially applied), and partly on some local surface descriptors, called local surface patch (LSP), which are computed in those characteristic points that are a minimum or a maximum of shape indices. Distance between two 3D models is then computed by root mean square registration error.

In 2008, Cadavid and Mottaleb presented a system for detection [18], modeling, and recognition of the ear from video, based on a shape-from-shading technique. Successively, they presented a far more refined method together with Zhou in 2010 [19], which only detects the ear in range images. Their aim was to identify features able to characterize the peculiar 3D ear structure that was, at the same time, robust to noise and to pose variations. To address this, they started from the histograms of oriented gradients (HOGs) descriptor [23] used by Dalal and Triggs in pedestrian detection. The descriptor introduced by the authors is called histograms of categorized shapes and is used to represent regions of 3D range images. The detection window is divided into overlapping blocks, for each of which a histogram of shape indices and of curvature is computed over single pixels in the block. The histogram of the detection window is given by chaining the histograms of its blocks.

Yan and Bowyer, who are authors of many works on the topic, have also made a significant contribution to the research about ear-based recognition. Their method is composed of a detection part, based on both 2D and 3D information, and a recognition part based on multibiometrics strategies. Ear detection partly works on the 2D original image through a skin detector. Once the ear pit is identified, a contour detection algorithm exploits both color from the 2D image and depth information from the range image to separate the ear from the remaining part of the range image. Matching is based on ear surface segmentation and on curvature estimation. The recognition process was also studied as a multibiometric one [15] by experimenting with multimodal, multiexpert, and multisample approaches. From the authors' studies, it was determined that all integration methods take advantage of the presence of more samples for the same subject, while it is not possible to find a single fusion rule that overcomes all the others in all cases; on the contrary, a different fusion rule exists for different settings that is the best for the specific case.

15.4 Hand-, Palm-, and Fingerprints

Hand geometry is a biometric trait that deserves special attention and for which a number of devices are sold and commonly adopted. However, different factors, such as a relative ease of spoofing in 2D systems, a capture process that is not particularly comfortable due to the required hand positioning, and hygienic issues because the physical contact of the hand with the capture device is required, limit its spread. Passing from 2D to 3D (see Figure 15.4) solves some of these problems. But one has to face a technical problem. A 3D contactless device must handle the additional factor of hand position, since the latter is less constrained during the capture process.

At least five different biometric traits can be extracted from the hand: fingerprints, palm prints, hand geometry, vein pattern, and finger shape.

Fingerprints are the most widespread biometrics, thanks to their massive use in forensics. They have become an identification mean that is particularly familiar in the collective imagination, with a discrete acceptability level. On the other hand, they are often associated with use by security forces to find criminals. This factor, together with the hygienic problem of contact with the sensor, contributes to lowering the viability of 2D image-based fingerprint recognition.

Palm prints present many similarities with fingerprints: They are also characterized by lines, contours, and minutiae, though they are generally captured at a lower resolution (commonly about 100 dpi), with the advantage of a possible contactless capture. The true limit of this kind of biometrics is

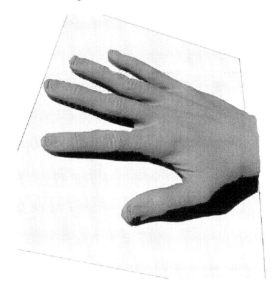

FIGURE 15.4
Three-dimensional pose-invariant hand recognition.

in the capture devices' dimensions, which make their integration in small systems, like mobile devices, difficult if not impossible. Furthermore, they are very easy to deceive and therefore prone to spoofing attacks.

These kinds of problems are common with systems based on hand geometry recognition, which are easily deceivable and attackable by impostors. However, this biometric trait, which is based on the measurement of some ratios between distances of hand elements, has conquered a large chunk of the market thanks to the speed of extraction and the matching process. However, such speed is paid for in terms of accuracy. As a matter of fact, hand geometry does not guarantee the same accuracy levels typical of fingerprints and palm prints. Therefore, it is not used in high-security applications. Finally, individual hand geometry features are not descriptive enough for identification and are not thought to be as unique as, for example, fingerprints.

Blood vessels within the hand make up an intricate reticulum, the pattern of which is certainly characteristic of the single subject. This offers a number of advantages compared with other hand characteristics, apart from its uniqueness. First of all, it is possible to capture it contactless, therefore eliminating potential problems related to sensor cleanness. Furthermore, the extracted features are particularly stable in time and not affected by particular external conditions if captured through near infrared (NIR) or thermal (IR) technology, and the obtained pattern is difficult to replicate in a spoofing attack.

The analysis of fingers' shapes and textures often joins the previous traits, both for the back and for the fingertip. In particular, lines on the knuckles seem to present a highly distinctive property.

Research on these biometrics has produced a high number of solutions based on 2D images that often present common problems such as pose and illumination variations, pattern deformation or bending, and spoofing vulnerability. In general, a 2D imaging system for capturing hand features includes a charge-coupled device (CCD) camera, an oriented light source, and a flat support surface. When the system requires hand contact with the surface, pegs may guide hand positioning; in some cases, the equipment is integrated with a mirror, making the hand side projected on the CCD so as to have a side image of the hand also. In a few cases the third dimension has been exploited and therefore the input sample is captured through a 3D scanner, producing a range image.

Woodard and Flynn [24] used a 3D scanner with laser light to capture a color image and a range image of the hand. In Malassiotis, Aifanti, and Strintzis [25], the sensor was expressly created through a color camera and a standard video projector to capture range images. With regard to hand geometry, the two methods cited differ in the way the range image is segmented to extract matching features. In the first case, a combination of skin and contour detection is exploited to separate the hand from a uniform background, while a convex hull algorithm run on the hand contour allows extracting the index, middle, and ring fingers from the range image. The discriminating features are represented by the curvature indices computed for each point in the extracted regions. Malassiotis et al. exploit the only range image for segmentation by modeling the hand in it through a mixture of Gaussian curvatures. Matching features include the 3D width and average curvature of each of the four considered fingers. This last method was tested on a relatively small archive, and therefore the evaluations of the provided performances are not truly representative for large-scale use.

Woodard and Flynn [26,27] presented the first 3D approach for finger recognition. The method analyzes the back of the hand—in particular of the index, middle, and ring fingers. For each pixel, minimum and maximum curvatures are computed in order to compute shape index. In this way a shape index image is obtained for each finger. These images then represent the input for the matching phase.

In other cases, such as in Raskar et al. [1], the capture technique is the true original element with respect to other techniques in the literature. In the specific case, 3D ultrasonic images are captured from the internal region of the palm of the hand. The capture system is composed of an ultrasound imaging machine with a high-frequency linear array (12 MHz).

Kanhangad, Kumar, and Zhang [28] deepen the aspects related to fusing information from both a 2D image and a 3D model of the hand, captured at the same time, for a hand-geometry-based recognition. The method works without hand position constraints and identifies position and orientation for the four considered fingers (excluding the thumb) based on knuckles (tips) and bendings (valleys). For each point on the fingers' surface, the average curvature and the unit normal vector are computed as features that are then used for matching according to ad hoc defined metrics. Kanhangad, Kumar, and Zhang [29] presented a further development of this strategy using a method that estimates the hand pose starting from information from range image (3D) and texture image (2D) that is aimed at normalizing texture and extracting palm print and hand geometry. Three-dimensional features include the surface code, based on curvature, and the shape index; both are evaluated in the points of the palm of the hand. Information from the 2D image and the 3D range image is fused together through a weighted sum of scores.

Tsalakanidou, Malassiotis, and Strintzis [30] experimented with fusing face biometrics with hand geometry. Samples were captured by a real-time, low-cost sensor that produced a color 2D image (texture) and a 3D model (range image). The user is asked to position the hand in front of the face with the back toward the sensor, which captures a number of samples while the user is asked for different finger positions (closed, open, slanted). The face is detected from the range image according to a priori knowledge of the searched object. An interactive procedure guides the user toward a correct face position in front of the sensor, while captured images are normalized and passed to the classifier. The latter is constituted by a probabilistic matching algorithm [31] applied to both 2D and 3D images. Assuming that the hand is not still, it is extracted by exploiting information from face positioning and segmented through a blob detector. Signature functions are extracted from finger geometry and then passed to the classifier. Fusion is performed at score level after score normalization. The authors experimented with different normalization functions (min–max, z-score, median–MAD, tanh, quadratic-line-quadratic [QLQ]) and different fusion rules (simple sum, product, max-score, weighted sum). The best performance in terms of equal error rate (EER) came from using QLQ and weighted sum.

15.5 Signature

Electronic signature from the capture of a handwritten one is designed for contract, document, receipt, and register signing. The dynamic aspect of a handwritten signature is very important, not only because it is the perfect way to authenticate a voluntary act, but also because it allows identifying the author (i.e., to associate each electronic signature to a person). Electronic signature includes static and dynamic data. Static data are revealed by the signature's two-dimensional outline and may indicate some unique traits to a graphologist. Dynamic data of an electronic signature are much more difficult to analyze but are more precise. Only dynamic data, pressure, direction, speed, and speed variations during the signature can offer high security for the identification of a signature. Anybody, after a suitable training period, can imitate the outline of the handwritten signature of another person, and it is not difficult to obtain a sample of a signature from any person. Nevertheless, the impostor cannot know, and in any case could not imitate, the signature's dynamic elements. Moreover, the acceptability level of signature recognition-based systems is high, since users usually sign and do not notice differences between the traditional and the biometric methods. System vulnerability is deemed quite low, and capture devices are reasonably cheap (from 100 to 1000 euros). The main disadvantage is the stability of the sample, since the way of signing may vary over time.

As observed before, traditional signature verification methods are subject to spoofing when they operate in a 2D setting. However, a number of works in the literature exploit the third dimension, intended as the degree of pressure during signing, in order to increase the degree of security of this biometric. In particular, Rubesh, Bajpai, and Bhaskar [32] proposed a system with a special pad, the aim of which was to measure the pressure so as to be able to use any kind of pen (see Figure 15.5). The presented method exploits further additional information, such as speed, acceleration, direction, interruption points (pen ups/downs), the total time, and the length. Further parameters are derived through curve fitting, surface fitting, and solid-angle computation methods. This approach was designed to be used in the context of financial document and transaction signing.

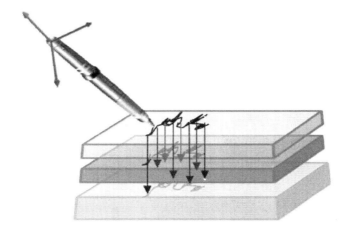

FIGURE 15.5
A nonlinearly spaced pad for the 3D acquisition of a signature.

Haskell, Hanna, and Sickle [33] characterize the signature through curvature moments, computed in a 3D space including spatial coordinates and signing speed. For each signature, the average vector and the associated covariance matrix are computed, while matching is performed through Mahalanobis distance.

15.6 Gait

In the biometrics field, the term *gait* indicates each person's particular way of walking. Therefore, gait recognition is the verification/recognition of the identity of a subject based on the particular way of walking. Gait recognition is a relatively recent biometric, though the architecture of a gait-based system is not substantially different from more traditional biometrics; as a matter of fact, such a system captures input from a moving subject, extracts unique characteristics and translates them into a biometric signature, and then exploits the signature during the matching phase. According to the claim by Gafurov [34], gait recognition systems based on 2D imaging can be classified into three main groups based on: machine vision, floor sensors, and wearable sensors. Most methods in the first group are based on silhouette extraction [35,36], though some exceptions can be found [37,38] where stride and cadence of a person, or some static parameters of the body (e.g., maximum distance between head and pelvis, distance between feet), are exploited.

An important advantage of this approach is that input samples can be captured at a distance, when other biometrics cannot be used. It is worth noting that, in such a context, sensor-based approaches could not be adopted. As a matter of fact, they require mounting a number of sensors in the layer below the floor. When a person treads upon this kind of flooring, they capture data that are input to the rest of the processing pipeline. Features typically used in these kinds of approaches are the maximum heel strike time or the maximum heel strike width. Though nonintrusive, such systems present the great disadvantage of requiring the installation of specific sensors.

As for wearable sensor-based systems, sensors are worn by the subject. Though there is no specific constraint and therefore they might be positioned at any body part, experiments in the literature put them on the pelvis [39] or on the legs [40]. Even in this case, the obtained error rates demonstrate that, at present, gait recognition can be mainly exploited to support other kinds of biometrics. Moreover, classical approaches to gait recognition are limited by internal factors related to the subject (e.g., pathologies, accidents, aging, weight variations) as well as by external factors (e.g., viewing angles, illumination conditions, type of flooring). Given the intrinsic nature of the former, it is highly unlikely that possible technological solutions, though advanced, can address them. On the contrary, since the second group is tightly related to the exploited imaging type and to the method, it seems more viable to devise enhancing solutions in terms of both usability and accuracy. The third dimension represents, in this case, a valid approach to 2D imaging.

In 3D-based gait analysis systems, the subject is typically captured by two or more view angles, which allow one to reconstruct a three-dimensional model. Static and dynamic features of the model are then analyzed.

Using more cameras and, consequently, more viewpoints allows reconstructing a 3D volumetric space of the subject; to this aim, visual hulls, introduced by Laurentini [41], are one of the most commonly used techniques. Among the first to use this gait recognition technique were Shakhnarovich, Lee, and Darrell [42], who reconstructed the visual hull starting from the silhouettes extracted from video clips captured from four cameras. This allows identification of the subject's trajectory and synthesis of a silhouette in canonical pose by positioning a virtual camera within the reconstructed volumetric space. However, matching exploits purely 2D techniques, so the approach performs 2D gait analysis within a 3D reconstructed scenario.

Dockstader and Tekalp [43] introduced a relatively structured method, based on strong and weak kinematic constraints, through which they extracted specific gait patterns to be matched. However, the work is more focused on the model construction than on actual gait analysis. In the same way, Bhanu and Han [47] exploited a kinematic model to extract static and kinematic features from monocular video sequences. This is done by performing the fitting of the 3D kinematic model to the 2D silhouette of the subject, which is extracted from the same sequences. The system implements different fusion strategies (product, sum rule, min rule, and max rule) of static and dynamic model parameters.

Urtasun and Fua [44] exploited a 3D temporal model in a similar setting. Using a motion model based on PCA and exploiting a robust human tracking algorithm, the authors reformulated the problem of people tracking in terms of minimization of a differentiable objective function, the variables of which are represented by the PCA weights. Such a model allows using deterministic optimization methods without resorting to probabilistic ones, which are computationally more expensive. In this way the system is robust to changes in viewpoint or to partial occlusions.

A further proposal along this line was presented by Guoying et al. [45], where the subject was videotaped by more video cameras and therefore from different viewpoints. In this way it is possible to create a three-dimensional model of the subject. A local optimization algorithm is used to divide the model into key segments, the length of which represents a set of model static features. Lower limb trajectories represent a dynamic feature of the subject; after being normalized with respect to time through a linear model, they are used for matching. Such an approach allows significant improvement in system performance when the surface upon which the subject moves is nonoptimal in terms of capture conditions.

The method proposed by Shakhnarovich, Lee, and Darrell [46] represents one of the first attempts to fuse face and gait in a multibiometric setting. Along this line, research was further extended by Seely et al. [48,49], who focused on fusing gait, face, and ear in a particular capture system (multibiometric tunnel) implemented at Southampton University. This tunnel facilitates the capture of biometric data for a large number of persons, so the university was able to collect a suitable biometric database. Moreover, this tunnel allowed studies addressed to the modalities of gait change when the subject carries an object.

15.7 Conclusions

Biometric systems based on three dimensions have high potential and can significantly improve, in many cases, the accuracy that can be obtained with techniques solely based on 2D imaging. Such high potential is the base for noticeable research efforts in the last years on different fronts. First of all, there is a continuous search for new technologies to overcome the limits of current, mostly diffused 3D capture systems. Such limits include, among others, the fact that the capture process with structured light may be uncomfortable for the user or that some devices require too long for capture or 3D model reconstruction, and occlusions are still an open problem.

Present research is moving along this line by studying alternative approaches such as imperceptible scanning. Graphics processing unit programming may be a potential solution to capture 3D modeling times. The field of view and the depth of field of present technologies must be further increased to allow capturing larger objects in wider settings, such as the full subject body for gait recognition. Second, research must still work on improving the accuracy of the model reconstruction and segmentation process to facilitate the tasks that follow in the pipeline of recognition systems. The third dimension significantly increases problem complexity and present segmentation techniques are not yet able to handle the huge amount of data coming from a 3D capture efficiently and effectively.

Finally, systems accuracy is not yet at optimal levels, since the used classifiers do not completely exploit the 3D potential. Most techniques used for 3D have been directly inherited from the 2D setting. In other words, 3D data have often been mapped on a new kind of 2D image (e.g., depth map images), to which standard methods such as PCA have been applied. Only in a following phase have ad hoc techniques been especially devised for 3D models—for example, shape indices and curvature histograms. Even more recently, attempts have been made to combine 3D with 2D in a specific way or the different 3D techniques through suitable protocols and fusion rules; the results seem to encourage proceeding along this direction.

References

1. Raskar, R., Welch, G., Cutts, M., Lake A., Stesin, L., and Fuchs, H. The office of the future: A unified approach to image-based modeling and spatially immersive displays. *Proceedings of the 25th Annual Conference on Computer Graphics and interactive Techniques (SIGGRAPH '98)*. ACM, New York, pp. 179–188, 1998.

2. Iula, A., Savoia, A., Longo, C., Caliano, G., Caronti, A., and Pappalardo, M. 3D ultrasonic imaging of the human hand for biometric purposes. *Ultrasonics Symposium (IUS), 2010 IEEE*, pp. 37–40, Oct. 11–14, 2010.

3. Phillips, P. J., Grother, P., Michaels, R. J., Blackburn, D. M., Tabassi, E., and Bone, J. FRVT 2002: Overview and summary. Available at www.frvt.org (March 2003).

4. Xu, C., Wang, Y., Tan, T., and Long, Q. A new attempt to face recognition using 3D eigenfaces. *6th Asian Conference on Computer Vision (ACCV)* 2:884–889, 2004.

5. http://www.sic.rma.ac.be/~beumier/DB/3d_rma.html (October 25 2011).

6. Gordon, G. G. Face recognition based on depth and curvature features. *Proceedings of IEEE Computer Society Conference on Computer Vision & Pattern Recognition* 808–810, June 1992.

7. Achermann, B., Jiang, X., and Bunke, H. Face recognition using range images. *Proceedings of the International Conference on the Virtual Systems and Multimedia (VSMM97)*, pp. 129–136, September 1997.

8. Blanz, V. and Vetter, T. Face recognition based on fitting a 3D morphable model. *IEEE Transactions on Pattern Analysis and Machine Intelligence* 25 (9):1063–1074, 2003.

9. Ansari, A. and Abdel-Mottaleb, M. 3D face modeling using two orthogonal views and a generic face model. *Proceedings of the International Conference on Multimedia and Expo (ICME '03)* 3:289–292, 2003.

10. Wang, Y., Chua, C., and Ho, Y. Facial feature detection and face recognition from 2D and 3D images. *Pattern Recognition Letters* 3(23):1191–1202, 2002.

11. Ping, Y. and Bowyer, K. W. Ear biometrics using 2D and 3D images. *IEEE Computer Society Conference on Computer Vision and Pattern Recognition* 1, 121–128, 2005.

12. Heng, L., Yan, J., and Zhang, D. 3D ear reconstruction attempts: Using multi-view. *International Conference on Intelligent Computing* 578–583, 2006.

13. Zeng, H., Mu, Z-C., Wang, K., and Sun, C. Automatic 3D ear reconstruction based on binocular stereo vision. *IEEE International Conference on Systems, Man and Cybernetics* 5205–5208, Oct. 11–14, 2009.

14. Chen, H. and Bhanu, B. Human ear detection from side face range images. *Proceedings International Conference Image Processing* 3, 574–577, 2004.

15. Yan, P. and Bowyer, K. Multi-biometrics 2D and 3D ear recognition, audio- and video-based biometric person authentication. *Lecture Notes in Computer Science* 3546:459–474, 2005.

16. Jones, M. J. and Rehg, J. M. Statistical color models with application to skin detection. *International Journal Computer Vision* 46 (1):81–96, 2002

17. Chen, C. S., Hung, Y. P., and Cheng, J. B. RANSAC-based DARCES: A new approach to fast automatic registration of partially overlapping range images. *IEEE Transactions Pattern Analysis and Machine Intelligence* 21 (11):1229–1234, Nov. 1999.

18. Cadavid, S. and Abdel-Mottaleb, M. 3D ear modeling and recognition from video sequences using shape from shading. *19th International Conference on Pattern Recognition* 1–4, Dec. 8–11, 2008.

19. Zhou, J., Cadavid, S., and Abdel-Mottaleb, M. Histograms of categorized shapes for 3D ear detection. 2010 *Fourth IEEE International Conference on Biometrics: Theory Applications and Systems* (BTAS) 1–6, Sept. 27–29, 2010.

20. Cadavid, S. and Abdel-Mottaleb, M. Human identification based on 3D ear models. *First IEEE International Conference on Biometrics: Theory, Applications, and Systems* 1–6, Sept. 2007.

21. Lucas, B. D. and Kanade, T. An iterative image registration technique with an application to stereo vision. *International Joint Conference on Artificial Intelligence* 674–679, 1981.

22. Chen, H. and Bhanu, B. Human ear recognition in 3D. *IEEE Transactions on Pattern Analysis and Machine Intelligence* 29 (4):718–737, 2007.

23. Dalal, N. and Triggs, B. Histograms of oriented gradients for human detection. *CVPR 2005* 886–893.

24. Woodard, D. L. and Flynn, P. J. Finger surface as a biometric identifier. *Computer Vision and Image Understanding* 100 (3):357–384, 2005.

25. Malassiotis, S., Aifanti, N., and Strintzis, M. G. Personal authentication using 3-D finger geometry. *IEEE Transactions on Information Forensics and Security* 1 (1):12–21, 2006.

26. Woodard, D. L. and Flynn, P. J. 3D finger biometrics. *BioAW 2004*, LNCS 3087, 238–247, 2004.

27. Woodard, D. L. and Flynn, P. J. Finger surface as a biometric identifier. *Computer Vision and Image Understanding* 100 (3):357–384, 2005.

28. Kanhangad, V., Kumar, A., and Zhang, D. Combining 2D and 3D Hand geometry features for biometric verification. *CVPR 2009.*

29. Kanhangad, V., Kumar, A., and Zhang, D. Human hand identification with 3D hand pose variations. Computer Vision and Pattern Recognition Workshop, 17–21, 2010.

30. Tsalakanidou, F., Malassiotis, S., and Strintzis, M. G. A 3D face and hand biometric system for robust user-friendly authentication. *Pattern Recognition Letters* 28:2238–2249, 2007.

31. Moghaddam, B., Wahid, W., and Pentland, A. Beyond eigenfaces: Probabilistic matching for face recognition. *Proceedings International Conference on Automatic Face and Gesture Recognition* (FGR '98) 30–35, Nara, Japan, 1998.

32. Rubesh, P. M., Bajpai, G., and Bhaskar, V. Online multi-parameter 3D signature verification through curve fitting. *IJCSNS International Journal of Computer Science and Network Security* 9 (5): 38–44, May 2009.

33. Haskell, R. E., Hanna, D. M., and Sickle, K. V. 3D signature biometrics using curvature moments. *International Conference on Artificial Intelligence* 718–721, Las Vegas, Nevada, 2006.

34. Gafurov, D. A survey of biometric gait recognition: Approaches, security and challenges. This paper was presented at the NIK-2007 conference; see http://www.nik.no/

35. Liu, Z. and Sarkar, S. Simplest representation yet for gait recognition: Averaged silhouette. *International Conference on Pattern Recognition* 211–214, 2004.

36. Liu, Z., Malave, L., and Sarkar, S. Studies on silhouette quality and gait recognition. *Computer Vision and Pattern Recognition* 704–711, 2004.

37. BenAbdelkader, C., Cutler, R., and Davis, L. Stride and cadence as a biometric in automatic person identification and verification. *Fifth IEEE International Conference on Automatic Face and Gesture Recognition* 357–362, May 2002.

38. Johnson, A. Y. and Bobick, A. F. A multi-view method for gait recognition using static body parameters. *Third International Conference on Audio- and Video-Based Biometric Person Authentication* 301–311, June 2001.

39. Gafurov, D., Snekkenes, E., and Buvarp, T. E. Robustness of biometric gait authentication against impersonation attack. *First International Workshop on Information Security (IS'06),* OnTheMove Federated Conferences (OTM'06), 479–488, Montpellier, France, Oct. 30–Nov. 1 2006. Springer LNCS 4277.

40. Gafurov, D., Helkala, K., and Sondrol, T. Gait recognition using acceleration from MEMS. *1st IEEE International Conference on Availability, Reliability and Security (ARES)* 432–437, Vienna, Austria, April 2006.

41. Laurentini, A. The visual hull concept for silhouette-based image understanding. *IEEE Transactions on Pattern Analysis and Machine Intelligence* 16 (2): 150–162, 1994.

42. Shakhnarovich, G., Lee, L., and Darrell, T. Integrated face and gait recognition from multiple views. *CVPR* 1:439–446, 2001.

43. Dockstader, S. L. and Tekalp, A. M. A kinematic model for human motion and gait analysis. *Proceedings of the Workshop on Statistical Methods in Video Processing (ECCV),* 49–54, Copenhagen, Denmark, June 2002.

44. Urtasun, R. and Fua, P. 3D tracking for gait characterization and recognition. *Proceedings 6th International Conference Automatic Face and Gesture Recognition* 17–22, 2004.

45. Guoying, Z., Guoyi, L., Hua, L., and Pietikäinen, M. 3D gait recognition using multiple cameras. *Proceedings of the 7th International Conference on Automatic Face and Gesture Recognition (FGR'06)*, 529–534, April 2006.

46. Shakhnarovich, G., Lee, L., and Darrell, T. Integrated face and gait recognition from multiple views. *CVPR* 1:439–446, 2001.

47. Bhanu, B. and J. Han. Human recognition on combining kinematic and stationary features. *Proceedings International Conference Audio, Video-Based Biometric Person Authentication* 2688:600–608, Guildford, UK, 2003.

48. Seely, R. D., Goffredo, M., Carter, J. N., and Nixon, M. S. View invariant gait recognition. *Handbook of Remote Biometrics Advances in Pattern Recognition* Part I, 61–81, 2009.

49. Seely, R., Carter, J., and Nixon, M. Spatio-temporal 3D gait recognition. In *3D video—analysis, display and applications.* London: The Royal Academy of Engineering, 2008. ePrint ID:267082, http://eprints.soton.ac.uk/id/eprint/267082

Index